POLGARA THE SORCERESS

By David Eddings

THE BELGARIAD

Book One: *Pawn of Prophecy*
Book Two: *Queen of Sorcery*
Book Three: *Magician's Gambit*
Book Four: *Castle of Wizardry*
Book Five: *Enchanters' End Game*

THE MALLOREON

Book One: *Guardians of the West*
Book Two: *Kings of the Murgos*
Book Three: *Demon Lord of Karanda*
Book Four: *Sorceress of Darshiva*
Book Five: *The Seeress of Kell*

THE ELENIUM

Book One: *The Diamond Throne*
Book Two: *The Ruby Knight*
Book Three: *The Sapphire Rose*

THE TAMULI

Book One: *Domes of Fire*
Book Two: *The Shining Ones*
Book Three: *The Hidden City*

High Hunt
The Losers

By David and Leigh Eddings

The Prequel to the Belgariad: *Belgarath the Sorcerer*

Voyager

POLGARA
THE SORCERESS

David and Leigh Eddings

HarperCollins*Publishers*

Voyager
An Imprint of HarperCollins*Publishers*
77–85 Fulham Palace Road,
Hammersmith, London W6 8JB

The *Voyager* World Wide Web site address is
http://www.harpercollins.co.uk/voyager

Published by *Voyager* 1997
1 3 5 7 9 8 6 4 2

A catalogue record for this book
is available from the British Library

ISBN 0 246 13844 0

Set in Postscript Palatino by
Rowland Phototypesetting Ltd,
Bury St Edmunds, Suffolk

Printed and bound in Great Britain by
Caledonian International Book Manufacturing Ltd, Glasgow

DEDICATION

And finally, after fifteen years, this book is dedicated to our readers. It's been a long journey, hasn't it? It's been quite a project for us, and your patience and enthusiasm have helped us more than you can imagine. Thank you for your fortitude, and we hope that what we've done pleases you.
    Warmly,
        David & Leigh Eddings

PROLOGUE

KAIL, THE RIVAN WARDER, objected strenuously when King Belgarion told him that he and his queen planned to make the journey to the northern end of the Vale of Aldur unattended, but Garion uncharacteristically put his foot down. 'It's a family gathering, Kail. Ce'Nedra and I don't need a cluster of servants underfoot. They'd just be in the way.'

'But it's dangerous, your Majesty.'

'I rather doubt that anything'll turn up that I can't handle, old friend,' Garion told him. 'We're going alone.' The Rivan Queen was a bit startled by the firmness in Garion's voice.

Then there was the argument about fur. Queen Ce'Nedra was Tolnedran by birth and Dryad by heritage. Those backgrounds were both southern, and the notion of wearing animal skins made Ce'Nedra's flesh creep. Garion, however, was at least partially Alorn, and he'd traveled extensively in the north in the winter-time. 'You're going to wear fur, Ce'Nedra,' he adamantly told his tiny wife, 'because if you don't, we aren't going anywhere until the weather warms up.' Garion seldom delivered ultimatums to her, and Ce'Nedra was shrewd enough not to argue about the matter any further. She obediently dressed herself in Alorn fur garments, spoke at some length with the nurse who would oversee the royal children during her absence, and then she and her husband left the Isle of the Winds aboard the disreputable Captain Greldik's dubious ship on the morning tide.

They purchased horses and supplies in Camaar and set out toward the east. The regularly spaced Tolnedran hostels along the highway to Muros provided adequate lodgings each night, but after Muros, they were largely on their own. The Rivan King, however, had spent a great deal of time living out in the open, and his little wife was forced to concede that he was adequate when the time came to set up camp.

The Rivan Queen was realistic enough to know just how ridiculous she looked while gathering firewood in those camps. The bulky fur garments she wore gave her a roly-poly appearance, her flaming red hair streamed down her back, and because of her size she could only carry a few sticks at a time. The unwanted image of a red-haired beaver trudging through the snow came to her quite often.

3

The snow was deep in the Sendarian mountains, and it seemed to Ce'Nedra that her feet would never be warm again. She could not give her husband the satisfaction of admitting that, however. This trek was her idea, after all, and she'd have sooner died than admit that it might have been a mistake.

Ce'Nedra was like that sometimes.

It was snowing lightly and was bitterly cold when they came down out of the mountains and rode south across the snowy plains of Algaria. Although it definitely went against the grain to confess it, even privately, Ce'Nedra was actually glad that her husband had been so insistent about fur clothing.

And then as a chill evening was settling over southern Algaria and when lowering clouds were spitting tiny pellets of snow, they topped a rise and saw the little valley on the northern edge of the Vale of Aldur where Poledra's cottage and the surrounding outbuildings lay. The cottage had been there for eons, of course, but the barns and sheds were Durnik's additions, and they gave the place the appearance of a Sendarian farmstead.

Ce'Nedra wasn't really interested in comparative architecture at that point, however. All she really wanted to do was to get in out of the cold. 'Do they know that we're coming?' she asked her husband, her breath steaming in the biting cold.

'Yes,' Garion replied. 'I told Aunt Pol that we were on the way a couple of days ago.'

'Sometimes you're a very useful fellow to have around, your Majesty,' Ce'Nedra smiled.

'Your Majesty is *too* kind.' His reply was a bit flippant.

'Oh, Garion.' They both laughed as they pushed on down the hill.

The cottage – they'd always called it that, though in actuality it was growing to be a fairly large house – nestled at the side of an ice-bound little stream, and the snow was piled up to the bottom of the windows. There was a kind of golden invitation about the way the soft lamplight spilled out across the snow, and the column of blue smoke from the central chimney rose straight up toward the threatening sky. The Rivan Queen definitely approved of that indication that warmth and comfort were no more than a quarter mile away.

And then the low door opened, and Durnik stepped out into the dooryard. 'What kept you?' he called up to them. 'We were expecting you along about noon.'

'We hit some deep snow,' Garion called back. 'It was slow going there for a while.'

'Hurry on down, Garion. Let's get Ce'Nedra in out of the cold.' What a *dear* man he was!

Ce'Nedra and her husband rode into the snowy dooryard and swung down from their saddles.

'Go inside, both of you,' Durnik instructed. 'I'll see to your horses.'

'I'll help with that,' Garion offered. 'I can unsaddle a horse almost as well as you can, and I need to stretch my legs anyway.' He took Ce'Nedra by the arm and guided her to the doorway. 'I'll be right back, Aunt Pol,' he called inside. 'I want to help Durnik with the horses.'

'As you wish, dear,' the Lady Polgara replied. Her voice was rich and filled with love. 'Come in here, Ce'Nedra. Let's get you warm.'

The Rivan Queen almost ran inside, hurled herself into the arms of Polgara the sorceress, and kissed her soundly.

'Your nose is cold, Ce'Nedra,' Polgara observed.

'You should feel my feet, Aunt Pol,' Ce'Nedra replied with a little laugh. 'How can you *stand* the winters here?'

'I grew up here, dear, remember? I'm used to the weather.'

Ce'Nedra looked around. 'Where are the twins?'

'They're down for their afternoon nap. We'll get them up for supper. Let's get you out of those furs and over to the fireplace. As soon as you warm up a little, I've got water heating, and you can have a nice hot bath.'

'Oh, *yes!*' the Rivan Queen replied fervently.

Part of the difficulty with Alorn fur garments lies in the fact that they don't have buttons, so they're customarily tied on. Undoing frozen knots can be quite a chore, particularly if one's fingers are stiff with cold. And so it was that Ce'Nedra was almost forced to simply stand in the center of the room with her arms outstretched while Polgara removed her outer garments. Then, once the furs were off, the Rivan Queen went to the fireplace and stretched her hands out to the crackling flames.

'Not too close, dear,' Polgara warned. 'Don't burn yourself. How does a nice hot cup of tea sound?'

'Heavenly!'

After Ce'Nedra had drunk her tea and soaked in a tub of steaming water for about a half-hour, she actually began to feel warm again. Then she dressed in a plain gown and returned to the kitchen to help feed the twins. Polgara's children were a year old now, and they'd begun to walk – although not very well. They also seemed to have some difficulty managing their spoons, and quite a bit of their supper ended up on the floor. The twins had flaxen, curly

5

hair, and they were absolutely adorable. Their vocabulary was very limited – at least in any language Ce'Nedra could understand. They talked to each other extensively in some strange tongue, however.

'They're speaking "twin",' Polgara explained. 'It's not uncommon. Each set of twins develops its own private language. Beldaran and I spoke to each other in "twin" until we were about five. It used to drive poor uncle Beldin wild.'

Ce'Nedra looked around. 'Where are Garion and Durnik?'

'Durnik's made some more improvements,' Polgara replied. 'I'd imagine he's showing them off. He's added several rooms at the back of the cottage, so at least you and Garion won't have to sleep in the loft.' She carefully wiped the chin of one of the twins. 'Messy person,' she chided gently. The child giggled. 'Now then, what's this all about, Ce'Nedra? Why did you make this trip in the dead of winter?'

'Have you read Belgarath's story yet?' Ce'Nedra asked.

'Yes. It was characteristically long-winded, I thought.'

'You won't get any argument from me about that. How could he *possibly* have written that much down in under a year?'

'Father has certain advantages, Ce'Nedra. If he'd actually had to *write* it, it'd probably have taken him much, much longer.'

'Maybe *that's* why he left so many things out.'

'I don't exactly follow you, dear.' Polgara gently wiped the face of the second twin and then set them both down on the floor.

'For someone who pretends to be a professional story-teller, he certainly did a third-rate job.'

'He more or less covered everything that happened, I thought.'

'There are some awfully large gaps in that story, Aunt Pol.'

'Father *is* seven thousand years old, Ce'Nedra. In that long a time there were bound to be periods when nothing was happening.'

'He didn't go into anything that happened to *you*, though. He didn't say very much about those years you spent at Vo Wacune or what you did in Gar og Nadrak or any of those other places. I want to know what *you* did.'

'What on earth for?'

'I want the *whole* story, Aunt Pol. He left so much out.'

'You're as bad as Garion was. He always used to badger my father for more details every time the Old Wolf told him a story.' Polgara broke off abruptly. 'Away from the fireplace!' she said sharply to the twins.

They giggled, but they did as they were told. Ce'Nedra gathered that it was a game of sorts. 'Anyway,' she picked up the thread of her thought, 'Belgarath sent some letters when he had those last few chapters delivered to Riva. The letter he sent to me is what gave me the idea of coming here to talk with you. First he accused us all of getting together and bullying him into writing the history. He said that he knew there were gaps in the story, but he suggested that *you* could fill them in.'

'How typical,' Polgara murmured. 'My father's an expert at starting things and then tricking others into finishing them for him. Well, this time he's out of luck. Forget it, Ce'Nedra. I don't pretend to be a storyteller, and I've got better things to do with my time.'

'But –'

'No buts, dear. Now, go call Garion and Durnik in for supper.'

Ce'Nedra was shrewd enough not to raise the issue again, but a way around Polgara's refusal had already begun to form in her devious little mind.

'Garion, dear,' she said when she and her husband were in bed later that night in the warm and comfortable darkness.

'Yes, Ce'Nedra?'

'You can reach out and talk to your grandfather, can't you?'

'I suppose so. Why?'

'Wouldn't you like to see him – and your grandmother? I mean, we're this close anyway, and it's not really very far from Belgarath's tower to the cottage here, and they'd be terribly disappointed if we let this opportunity for a visit slip by, wouldn't they?'

'What are you up to, Ce'Nedra?'

'Why must I always be "up to" something?'

'You usually are.'

'That's not very nice, Garion. Isn't it just possible that all I want is a family reunion?'

'I'm sorry. Maybe I misjudged you.'

'Well – actually, your Aunt Pol's being a little stubborn about this. I'm going to need some help convincing her to write her story.'

'Grandfather won't help you. He already told you that in his letter.'

'I'm not talking about help from him. I want to talk to Poledra. Aunt Pol will listen to her mother. Please, Garion.' She said it in her most winsome and appealing tone.

'All right. I'll talk it over with Durnik and see what he thinks.'

'Why don't you let *me* talk with Durnik? I'm sure I can persuade him that it's a good idea.' She nuzzled at her husband's neck affectionately. 'I'm nice and warm now, Garion,' she said invitingly.

'Yes, I noticed that.'

'Are you really *very* sleepy?'

'Not *that* sleepy, dear,' and he turned to embrace her.

This wouldn't be terribly difficult, Ce'Nedra decided. She was an expert at getting her own way, and she was confident that she could get Garion and Durnik to agree with her plan. Poledra, on the other hand, might take a little more work.

Garion, as he usually did, slipped quietly out of bed before it was even light. The Rivan King had grown up on a farm, and farmers habitually rise early. Ce'Nedra decided that it might not be a bad idea to keep track of him for the next couple of days. A chance conversation between her husband and Durnik might disrupt her plan – Ce'Nedra deliberately avoided the word 'scheme'. So she touched the fingertips of her right hand to Beldaran's amulet and searched with her mind for Garion.

'Oh, hush.' It was Durnik's voice, and it was peculiarly gentle. 'It's only me. Go back to sleep. I'll feed you later.'

There was a muttering, some soft, grumbling sounds – birds of some kind, Ce'Nedra judged. Then they clucked a bit and settled back down again.

'Do you always talk to them that way?' It was Garion's voice.

'It keeps them from getting excited and flying off in the dark and hurting themselves,' Durnik replied. 'They insist on roosting in that tree right here in the dooryard, and I have to pass that tree every morning. They know me now, so I can usually persuade them to settle down again. Birds pick these things up fairly quickly. The deer take a little longer, and the rabbits are timid and very flighty.'

'You feed them all, don't you, Durnik?'

'They live here, too, Garion, and this farm produces more food than Pol and I and the babies can possibly eat. Besides, that's one of the reasons we're here, isn't it? The birds and the deer and the rabbits can look out for themselves in the summer, but winter's a lean time, so I help them out a bit.'

He was such a *good* man! Ce'Nedra's eyes almost filled with tears. Polgara was the pre-eminent woman in all the world, and she could have chosen any king or emperor for a husband and lived in a palace. She'd chosen a simple country blacksmith instead and lived on this remote farmstead. Now Ce'Nedra knew why.

As it turned out, Durnik was fairly easy to manipulate. Ce'Nedra's suggestion of 'a little family re-union, since we're all here anyway', brought him over to her side almost immediately. Durnik was too innocent to suspect ulterior motives in others. It was so easy that Ce'Nedra was almost ashamed of herself.

Garion was not nearly so innocent. He *had* lived with his wilful little Dryad wife for quite a while now, after all. With both Durnik and Ce'Nedra urging the reunion, though, he didn't really have any choice. He *did* cast a few suspicious looks in Ce'Nedra's direction before he sent his thought out to his grandfather, however.

Belgarath and Poledra arrived a day or so later, and the old man's expression when he greeted the Rivan Queen clearly indicated that he knew that she was 'up to something'. That didn't really concern Ce'Nedra very much, though. What she was 'up to' didn't involve Belgarath. She concentrated on Poledra instead.

It was several days before Ce'Nedra had the chance to get her husband's grandmother off to one side for some serious talk, family reunions being what they are and all. Polgara's twins, of course, were the center of everyone's attention. The twins enjoyed that, and Ce'Nedra was patient. The right moment would come, she was sure of that, so she simply enjoyed the closeness of the peculiar family into which she had married and bided her time.

There was a strange quality about the tawny-haired Poledra that made Ce'Nedra a little hesitant about approaching her. Ce'Nedra had read Belgarath's story several times, and she was fully aware of Poledra's peculiar background. She frequently caught herself studying Belgarath's wife, looking for wolfish traits. They were probably there, but Ce'Nedra was Tolnedran, and wolves are not so common in Tolnedra that she'd have recognized the traits even if they'd been more obvious. The thing that disturbed Ce'Nedra the most was the disconcertingly direct way Poledra had of looking at people. Cyradis had called Poledra 'the Woman who Watches', and the Seeress of Kell had been right on that score. Poledra's golden eyes seemed quite capable of seeing through all of Ce'Nedra's defences and concealments into that secret place where the Rivan Queen stored her motives. The tiny queen *really* didn't want anybody snooping around in there.

Finally she screwed up her courage one morning and approached Polgara's golden-eyed mother. Garion, Belgarath, and Durnik were outside, conducting one of their endless surveys of the farmstead, and Polgara was bathing the twins. 'I need to ask a favor of you, Lady Poledra.' Ce'Nedra was not certain of the proper form of address, so she fell back on a somewhat inappropriate usage.

'I rather suspected you might,' Poledra replied quite calmly. 'You went to a great deal of trouble to arrange this gathering, and you've been watching me for the last several days. I was fairly certain that you'd eventually get to the point. What's bothering you, child?'

9

'Well – "bother" might not be the exact term,' Ce'Nedra amended, averting her eyes slightly. Those penetrating golden eyes made her nervous. 'There's something I need from Polgara, and she's being stubborn about it. You know how she can be sometimes.'

'Yes. It's a family trait.'

'I didn't say that very well, did I?' Ce'Nedra apologized. 'I love her, of course, but –'

'What do you want from her? Don't run in circles, Ce'Nedra. Get to the point.'

Ce'Nedra was not accustomed to being addressed so bluntly, but she chose not to take offence. She side-tracked slightly instead. 'Have you read the history book your husband just finished writing?' she asked.

'I don't read often,' Poledra replied. 'It's hard on the eyes. Besides, he didn't write it. He spoke it, and it just appeared on paper while he was talking. He cheats sometimes. I heard most of it while he was talking. It wasn't *too* inaccurate.'

'That's what I'm getting at. He left quite a bit out, didn't he?'

'In places, yes.'

'But your daughter could fill in those places, couldn't she?'

'Why would she want to do that?'

'To complete the story.'

'Stories aren't really that important, Ce'Nedra. I've noticed that men-folk tell stories over their ale-cups to fill in the hours between supper and bedtime.' Poledra's look was amused. 'Did you really come all this way just to get a story? Couldn't you find anything better to do – have another baby, or something?'

Ce'Nedra changed direction again. 'Oh, the story isn't for me,' she lied. 'It's for my son. Someday he'll be the Rivan King.'

'Yes, so I understand. I've been told about that custom. Peculiar customs should usually be observed, though.'

Ce'Nedra seized that advantage. 'My son Geran will be a leader someday, and he needs to know where he is and how he got there. The story will tell him that.'

Poledra shrugged. 'Why's it so important? What happened yester-day – or a thousand years ago – isn't going to change what happens tomorrow, is it?'

'It might. Belgarath's story hinted at the fact that things were going on that I didn't even know were happening. There are two worlds out there running side by side. If Geran doesn't know about both of them, he'll make mistakes. That's why I need Polgara's story – for the sake of my children – and hers.' Ce'Nedra bit off the term 'puppies' at the last instant. 'Isn't caring for our children the most important thing we do?' Then a thought came to her. '*You* could tell the story, you know.'

'Wolves don't tell stories, Ce'Nedra. We're too busy being wolves.'

'Then it's going to be up to Polgara. My son will *need* the rest of the story. The well-being of his people may depend on his knowing. I don't know what Aldur has planned for Polgara's children, but it's very likely that *they'll* need the story as well.' Ce'Nedra was quite proud of that little twist. The appeal to Poledra's innate sense of pack loyalty might very well be the one thing to turn the trick. 'Will you help me persuade Polgara?'

Poledra's golden eyes grew thoughtful. 'I'll think about it,' she said.

That wasn't exactly the firm commitment Ce'Nedra'd been hoping for, but Polgara brought out the twins at that point, so the Rivan Queen wasn't able to pursue the matter further.

When Ce'Nedra awoke the following morning, Garion was already gone, as usual. Also, as usual, he'd neglected to pile more wood on the fire, and the room was decidedly cold. Shivering, Ce'Nedra got out of bed and went looking for warmth. She reasoned that if Garion was up, Durnik would be as well, so she went directly to Polgara's bedroom and tapped lightly on the door.

'Yes, Ce'Nedra,' Aunt Pol replied from inside. She *always* seemed to know who was at her door.

'May I come in?' Ce'Nedra asked. 'Garion let the fire go out, and it's freezing in our room.'

'Of course, dear,' Aunt Pol replied.

Ce'Nedra opened the door, hurried to the bed, and crawled under the covers with Aunt Pol and the babies. 'He always does that,' she complained. 'He's so busy trying to sneak away that he doesn't even think about putting more wood on the fire.'

'He doesn't want to wake you, dear.'

'I can always go back to sleep if I want, and I *hate* waking up in a cold room.' She gathered one of the twins in her arms and cuddled the little child close. Ce'Nedra was a mother herself, so she was very good at cuddling. She realized that she really missed her own children. She began to have some second thoughts about the wisdom of a journey in the dead of winter based on nothing more than a whim.

The Rivan Queen and her husband's aunt talked about various unimportant things for a while, and then the door opened and

11

Polgara's mother came in carrying a tray with three cups of steaming tea on it. 'Good morning, mother,' Polgara said.

'Not too bad,' Poledra replied. 'A little cold, though.' Poledra was *so* literal sometimes.

'What are the men-folk up to?' Aunt Pol asked.

'Garion and Durnik are out feeding the birds and animals,' Poledra said. '*He's* still asleep.' Poledra almost never spoke her husband's name. She set her tray down on the small table near the fireplace. 'I think we need to talk,' she said. She came to the bed, took up the twins, and deposited them back in the curiously constructed double cradle that Durnik had built for his children. Then she handed Polgara and Ce'Nedra each a cup of tea, took the remaining one up herself, and sat in the chair by the fire.

'What's so important, mother?' Polgara asked.

Poledra pointed one finger at Ce'Nedra. '*She* talked with me yesterday,' she said, 'and I think she's got a point we should consider.'

'Oh?'

'She said that her son – and *his* sons – will be leading the Rivans someday, and there are things they'll need to know. The well-being of the Rivans might depend on their knowing. That's a leader's first responsibility, isn't it? – whether he's leading people or wolves.'

Ce'Nedra silently gloated. Her thrown-together arguments the previous morning had evidently brought Poledra over to her side.

'Where are we going with this, mother?' Polgara asked.

'You have a responsibility as well, Polgara – to the young,' her mother replied. 'That's our first duty. The Master set you a task, and you haven't finished it yet.'

Polgara gave Ce'Nedra a hard look.

'I didn't do anything, Aunt Pol,' Ce'Nedra said with feigned innocence. 'I just asked for your mother's advice, that's all.'

The two sets of eyes – one set tawny yellow, the other deep blue – fixed themselves on her.

Ce'Nedra actually blushed.

'She wants something, Polgara,' Poledra said. 'Give it to her. It won't hurt you, and it's still a part of the task you freely accepted. We wolves rely on our instincts; humans need instruction. You've spent most of your life caring for the young – and instructing them – so you know what's required. Just set down what really happened and be done with it.'

'Not *all* of it, certainly!' Polgara sounded shocked. 'Some of those things were too private.'

Poledra actually laughed. 'You still have a great deal to learn, my daughter. Don't you know by now that there's no such thing as privacy among wolves? We share everything. The information may be useful to the leader of the Rivans someday – and to your own children as well – so let's be sure they have what they need. Just do it, Polgara. You know better than to argue with me.'

Polgara sighed. 'Yes, mother,' she replied submissively.

Ce'Nedra underwent a kind of epiphany at that point, and she didn't entirely like it. Polgara the Sorceress was the pre-eminent woman in the world. She had titles beyond counting, and the whole world bowed to her, but in some mysterious way, she was still a wolf, and when the dominant female – her mother in this case – gave an order, she automatically obeyed. Ce'Nedra's own heritage was mixed – part Borune and part Dryad. She'd argued extensively with her father, the Emperor of Tolnedra, but when Xantha, Queen of the Dryads, spoke, Ce'Nedra might complain a bit, but she instinctively obeyed. It was built into her. She began to look at Polgara in a slightly different way, and by extension, at herself also in a new fashion.

'It's a start,' Poledra said cryptically. 'Now then, daughter,' she said to Polgara, 'it won't be all that difficult. I'll talk with *him*, and he'll show you how to do it without all that foolishness with quill-pens and ink. It's your obligation, so stop complaining.'

'It shall be as my mother wishes,' Polgara replied.

'Well, then,' Poledra said, 'now that *that's* settled, would you ladies like to have another cup of tea?'

Polgara and Ce'Nedra exchanged a quick glance. 'I suppose we might as well,' Polgara sighed.

PART ONE

Beldaran

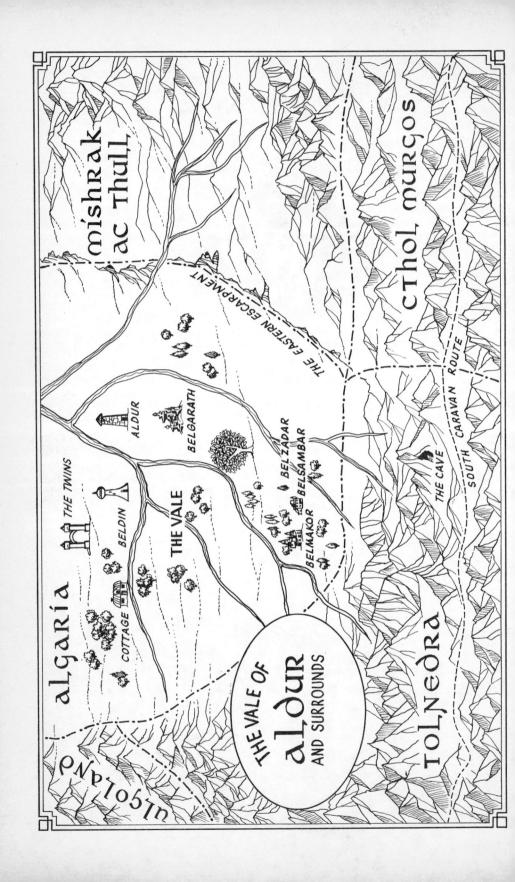

ALGARIA

MISHRAK AC THULL

CTHOL MURGOS

ULGOLAND

TOLNEDRA

THE TWINS

BELDIN

COTTAGE

THE VALE

ALDUR

BELGARATH

THE EASTERN ESCARPMENT

BEL ZADAR

BELSAMBAR

BELMAKOR

THE CAVE

SOUTH CARAVAN ROUTE

THE VALE OF
ALDUR
AND SURROUNDS

CHAPTER 1

This was not my idea. I want that clearly understood right at the outset. The notion that any one person can describe 'what really happened' is an absurdity. If ten – or a hundred – people witness an event, there will be ten – or a hundred – different versions of what took place. What we see and how we interpret it depends entirely upon our individual past experience. My mother, however, has insisted that I undertake this ridiculous chore, and I will, as always, do as she tells me to do.

The more I've thought about it, though, the more I've come to realize that when Ce'Nedra first broached the subject to me, and later to my mother, her obviously specious argument about 'the well-being of the young' actually had more merit than that devious little girl realized. One day Geran *will* be the Rivan King and the Guardian of the Orb, and over the centuries, I've found that people with at least a nodding acquaintance with true history make the best rulers. At least they don't repeat the mistakes of the past.

If all Geran and his sons really needed to rule the Rivans were to be a flat recounting of the deeds of assorted rulers of assorted kingdoms in ages past, the tiresome repetition of the 'and then, and then, and then' that so delights the stodgy members of the Tolnedran Historical Society would be more than sufficient.

As my daughter-in-law so cunningly pointed out, however, the 'and thens' of those Tolnedran scholars deal with only a part of the world. There's another world out there, and things happen in that other world that Tolnedrans are constitutionally incapable of comprehending. Ultimately it will be this unseen world that the Rivan King must know if he is to properly perform his task.

Even so, I could have devoutly maintained that my father's long-winded version of the history of our peculiar world had already filled in that obvious gap. I even went so far as to re-read father's tedious story, trying very hard to prove to myself – and to my mother – that I'd really have nothing to add. Soon father's glaring omissions began to leap off the page at me. The old fraud *hadn't* told the whole story, and mother knew it.

In father's defense, however, I'll admit that there *were* events that took place when he wasn't present and others during which he didn't fully understand what was *really* happening. Moreover, some of the omissions which so irritated me as I read had their origin in his desire to compress seven thousand years of history into something of manageable length. I'll forgive him *those* lapses, but couldn't he at least have gotten names and dates right? For the sake of keeping peace in the family, I'll gloss over his imperfect memory of just who said what in any given conversation. Human memory – and that's assuming that my father's human – is never really all *that* exact, I suppose. Why don't we just say that father and I remember things a little differently and let it go at that, shall we? Try to keep that in mind as you go along. Don't waste your time – and mine – by pointing out assorted variations.

The more I read, the more I came to realize that things *I* know and father doesn't would be essential parts of Geran's education. Moreover, a probably hereditary enthusiasm for a more complete story began to come over me. I tried to fight it, but it soon conquered me. I discovered that I actually *wanted* to tell my side of the story.

I have a few suspicions about the origins of my change of heart, but I don't think this is the place to air them.

The central fact of my early life was my sister Beldaran. We were twins, and in some respects even closer than twins. To this very day we're still not apart. Beldaran, dead these three thousand years and more, is still very much a part of me. I grieve for her every day. That might help to explain why I sometimes appear somber and withdrawn. Father's narrative makes some issue of the fact that I seldom smile. What's there to smile about, Old Wolf?

As father pointed out, I've read extensively, and I've noticed that biographies normally begin at birth. Beldaran and I, however, began

18

just a bit earlier than that. For reasons of her own, mother arranged it that way.

So now, why don't we get started?

It was warm and dark, and we floated in absolute contentment, listening to the sound of mother's heart and the rush of her blood through her veins as her body nourished us. That's my first memory – that and mother's thought gently saying to us, 'Wake up.'

We've made no secret of mother's origins. What *isn't* widely known is the fact that the Master summoned her, just as he summoned all the rest of us. She's as much Aldur's disciple as any of us are. We all serve him in our own peculiar ways. Mother, however, was not born human, and she perceived rather early in her pregnancy that Beldaran and I had none of those instincts that are inborn in wolves. I've since learned that this caused her much concern, and she consulted with the Master at some length about it, and her suggested solution was eminently practical. Since Beldaran and I had no instincts, mother proposed to the Master that she might begin our education while we were still enwombed. I think her suggestion might have startled Aldur, but he quickly saw its virtue. And so it was that mother took steps to make certain that my sister and I had certain necessary information – even before we were born.

During the course of a normal human pregnancy, the unborn lives in a world consisting entirely of physical sensation. Beldaran and I, however, were gently guided somewhat further. My father rather arrogantly states that *he* began my education after Beldaran's wedding, but that's hardly accurate. Did he *really* think that I was a vegetable before that? My education – and Beldaran's – began before we ever saw the light of day.

Father's approach to education is disputational. As first disciple, he'd been obliged to oversee the early education of my various uncles. He forced them to think and to argue as a means of guiding them along the thorny path to independent thought – although he sometimes carried it to extremes. Mother was born wolf, and her approach is more elemental. Wolves are pack-animals, and they don't think independently. Mother simply told Beldaran and me, 'This is the way it is. This is the way it always has been, and always will be.' Father teaches you to question; mother teaches you to accept. It's an interesting variation.

At first, Beldaran and I were identical twins and as close as that term implies. When mother's thought woke us, however, she rather carefully began to separate us. I received certain instruction that

19

Beldaran didn't, and she received lessons that *I* didn't. I think I felt that wrench more keenly than Beldaran did. She knew her purpose; I spent years groping for mine.

The separation was very painful for me. I seem to remember reaching out to my sister and saying to her in our own private language, 'You're so far away now.' Actually, of course, she wasn't. We were both still confined in that small, warm place beneath mother's heart, but always before our minds had been linked, and now they were inexorably moving apart. If you think about it a bit, I'm sure you'll understand.

After we awoke, mother's thought was with us continually. The sound of it was as warm and comforting as the place where we floated, but the place nourished only our bodies. Mother's thought nourished our minds – with those subtle variations I previously mentioned. I suspect that what I was and what I have become is the result of that womb-dark period in my life when Beldaran and I floated in perfect sisterhood – until mother's thought began to separate us.

And then in time there was another thought as well. Mother had prepared us for that intrusion upon what had been a very private little world. After my sister and I had become more fully aware and conscious of our separation and some of the reasons for it, Aldur's thought joined with hers to continue our education. He patiently explained to us right at the outset why certain alterations were going to be necessary. My sister and I had been identical. Aldur changed that, and most of the alterations were directed at *me*. Some of the changes were physical – the darkening of my hair, for example – and others were mental. Mother had begun that mental division, and Aldur refined it. Beldaran and I were no longer one. We were two. Beldaran's reaction to our further separation was one of gentle regret. Mine was one of anger.

I rather suspect that my anger may have been a reflection of mother's reaction when my vagrant father and a group of Alorns chose to slip away so that they could go off to Mallorea to retrieve the Orb Torak had stolen from the Master. I now fully understand why it was necessary and why father had no choice – and so does mother, I think. But at the time she was absolutely infuriated by what, in the society of wolves, was an unnatural desertion. My somewhat peculiar relationship with my father during my childhood quite probably derived from my perception of mother's fury. Beldaran was untouched by it, since mother wisely chose to shield her from that rage.

*   *   *

20

A vagrant and somewhat disturbing thought just occurred to me. As I mentioned earlier, father's educational technique involves questioning and argumentation, and I was probably his star pupil. Mother teaches acceptance, and Beldaran received the full benefit of *that* counsel. In a strange sort of way this would indicate that I'm my father's true daughter, and Beldaran was mother's.

All right, Old Wolf. Don't gloat. Wisdom eventually comes to all of us. Someday it might even be your turn.

Mother and the Master gently told my sister and me that once we were born, mother would have to leave us in the care of others so that she could pursue a necessary task. We were assured that we would be well cared for, and, moreover, that mother's thought would be with us more or less continually, even as it had been while we were still enwombed. We accepted that, though the notion of physical separation was a little frightening. The important thing in our lives from the moment that our awareness had awakened, though, had been the presence of mother's thought, and as long as that would still be with us we were sure that we'd be all right.

For a number of reasons it was necessary for me to be born first. Aldur's alterations of my mind and my personality had made me more adventurous than Beldaran anyway, so it was natural for me to take the lead, I suppose.

It was actually an easy birth, but the light hurt my eyes right at first, and the further separation from my sister was extremely painful. In time, however, she joined me, and all was well again. Mother's thought – and Aldur's – were still with us, and so we drowsed together in perfect contentment.

I'm assuming here that most of you have read my father's 'History of the World'. In that occasionally pompous monologue he frequently mentioned 'The humorous old fellow in the rickety cart'. It wasn't long after Beldaran and I were born that he paid us a call. Although his thought had been with us for months, that was the first time we actually saw the Master. He communed with us for a time, and when I looked around, a sudden panic came over me.

Mother was gone.

'It's all right, Polgara,' mother's thought came to me. 'This is necessary. The Master has summoned one who'll care for you and your sister. That one is short and twisted and ugly, but his heart's good. It'll be necessary to deceive him, I'm afraid. He *must* believe

21

that I'm no longer alive. No one – except you and Beldaran – must know that it's not true. The one who sired you will return soon, but he still has far to go. He'll travel more quickly without the distraction of my presence.'

And that's how uncle Beldin entered our lives. I can't be entirely sure what the Master told him, but he wept a great deal during those first few days. After he got his emotions under control, he made a few tentative efforts to communicate with my sister and me. To be honest about it, he was woefully inept right at first, but the Master guided him, and in time he grew more proficient.

Our lives – my sister's and mine – were growing more crowded. We slept a great deal at first. Uncle Beldin was wise enough to put us in the same cradle, and as long as we were together, everything was all right. Mother's thought was still with us – and Aldur's – and now uncle Beldin's, and we were still content.

My sister and I had no real sense of the passage of time during our first few months. Sometimes it was light and sometimes dark. Beldin was always with us, though, and we were together, so time didn't really mean very much to us.

Then, after what was probably weeks, there were two others as well, and their thought joined with the ones which were already familiar. Our other two uncles, Beltira and Belkira, had entered our lives.

I've never fully understood why people have so much difficulty telling Beltira and Belkira apart. To me, they've always been separate and distinct from each other, but I'm a twin myself, so I'm probably a little more sensitive to these variations.

Beldaran and I had been born in midwinter, and uncle Beldin had moved us to his own tower not long afterward, and it was in that tower that we spent our childhood. It was about midsummer of our first year when father finally returned to the Vale. Beldaran and I were only about six months old at the time, but we both recognized him immediately. Mother's thought had placed his image in our minds before we were ever born. The memory of mother's anger was still very strong in my mind when Beldin lifted me from my cradle and handed me to the vagabond who'd sired me. I wasn't particularly impressed with him, to be honest about it, but that prejudice may have been the result of mother's bitterness about the way he'd deserted her. Then he laid his hand on my head in some ancient ritual of benediction, and the rest of my mind suddenly came awake as *his* thought came flooding in on me. I could feel the

22

power coming from his hand, and I seized it eagerly. *This* was why I'd been separated from Beldaran! At last I realized the significance of that separation. *She* was to be the vessel of love; *I* was to be the vessel of power!

The mind is limitless in certain ways, and so my father was probably unaware of just how much I took from him in that single instant when his hand touched my head. I'm fairly sure that he *still* doesn't fully understand just exactly what passed from him to me in that instant. What I took from him in no way diminished him, but it increased me a hundred-fold.

Then he took up Beldaran, and my fury also increased a hundred-fold. How *dared* this traitor touch my sister? Father and I were not getting off to a good start.

And then came the time of his madness. I was still not familiar enough with human speech to fully understand what uncle Beldin told him that drove him to that madness, but mother's thought assured me that he'd survive it – eventually.

Looking back now, I realize that it was absolutely essential for mother and father to be separated. I didn't understand at the time, but mother's thought had taught me that acceptance is more important than understanding.

During the time of my father's insanity, my uncles frequently took my sister to visit him, and that didn't improve my opinion of him. He became in my eyes a usurper, a vile man out to steal Beldaran's affection away from me. Jealousy isn't a particularly attractive emotion, even though it's very natural in children, so I won't dwell here on exactly how I felt each time my uncles took Beldaran away from me to visit that frothing madman chained to his bed in that tower of his. I remember, though, that I protested vociferously – at the top of my lungs – whenever they took Beldaran away.

And that was when Beldin introduced me to 'the puzzle'. I've always thought of it as that. In a peculiar sort of way 'the puzzle' almost came to take on a life of its own for me. I can't be entirely certain how Beldin managed it, but 'the puzzle' was a gnarled and twisted root of some low-growing shrub – heather, perhaps – and each time I took it up to study it, it seemed to change. I could quite clearly see one end of it, but I could never find the other. I think that 'the puzzle' helped to shape my conception of the world and of life itself. We know where one end is – the beginning – but we

23

can never quite see the other. It provided me with endless hours of entertainment, though, and that gave uncle Beldin a chance to get some rest.

I was studying 'the puzzle' when father came to uncle Beldin's tower to say his goodbyes. Beldaran and I were perhaps a year and a half old – or maybe a little younger – when he came to the tower and kissed Beldaran. I felt that usual surge of jealousy, but I kept my eyes firmly fixed on 'the puzzle', hoping he'd go away.

And then he picked me up, tearing my attention away from what I was working on. I tried to get away from him, but he was stronger than I was. I was hardly more than a baby, after all, although I felt much older. 'Stop that,' he told me, and his tone seemed irritable. 'You may not care much for the idea, Pol, but I'm your father, and you're stuck with me.' And then he kissed me, which he'd never done before. For a moment – only a moment – I felt his pain, and my heart softened toward him.

'No,' mother's thought came to me, '*not yet.*' At the time, I thought it was because she was still very angry with him and that I was to be the vessel of her anger. I know now I was mistaken. Wolves simply don't waste time being angry. My father's remorse and sorrow had not yet run their course, and the Master still had many tasks for him. Until he had expiated what he felt to be his guilt, he'd be incapable of those tasks. My misunderstanding of mother's meaning led me to do something I probably shouldn't have done. I struck out at him with 'the puzzle'.

'Spirited, isn't she?' he murmured to uncle Beldin. Then he put me down, gave me a little pat on the bottom, which I scarcely felt, and told me to mind my manners.

I certainly wasn't going to give him the satisfaction of thinking that his chastisement in any way had made me change my opinion of him, so I turned, still holding 'the puzzle' like a club, and glared at him.

'Be well, Polgara,' he told me in the gentlest way imaginable. 'Now go play.'

He probably still doesn't realize it, but I almost loved him in that single instant – almost, but not quite. The love came later, and it took years.

It was not long after that that he turned and left the Vale, and I didn't see him again for quite a number of years.

24

CHAPTER 2

Nothing that ever happens is so unimportant that it doesn't change things, and father's intrusion into our lives could hardly be called unimportant. This time the change was in my sister Beldaran, and I didn't like it. Until my father returned from his excursion to Mallorea, Beldaran was almost exclusively mine. Father's return altered that. Now her thoughts, which had previously been devoted to me, became divided. She thought often of that beer-soaked old rogue, and I resented it bitterly.

Beldaran, even when we were hardly more than babies, was obsessed with tidiness, and my aggressive indifference to my appearance upset her greatly.

'Can't you at least comb your hair, Pol?' she demanded one evening, speaking in 'twin', a private language that had grown quite naturally between us almost from the time we were in the cradle.

'What for? It's just a waste of time.'

'You look awful.'

'Who cares what I look like?'

'*I* do. Sit down and I'll fix it for you.'

And so I sat in a chair and let my sister fuss with my hair. She was very serious about it, her blue eyes intent and her still-chubby little fingers very busy. Her efforts were wasted, of course, since nobody's hair stays combed for very long; but as long as it amused her, I was willing to submit to her attentions. I'll admit that I rather enjoyed what became an almost nightly ritual. At least when she was busy with my hair she was paying attention to *me* instead of brooding about our father.

In a peculiar way my resentment may have shaped my entire life. Each time Beldaran's eyes grew misty and distant, I knew that she

25

was brooding about our father, and I could not bear the separation implicit in that vague stare. That's probably why I took to wandering almost as soon as I could walk. I *had* to get away from the melancholy vacancy in my sister's eyes.

It almost drove uncle Beldin to the brink of insanity, I'm afraid. He could not devise any latch on the gate that blocked the top of the stairs in his tower that I couldn't outwit. Uncle Beldin's fingers have always been large and gnarled, and his latches were bulky and rather crude. My fingers were small and very nimble, and I could undo his devices in a matter of minutes whenever the urge to wander came over me. I was – still am, I suppose – of an independent nature, and *nobody* is ever going to tell *me* what to do.

Have you noticed that, father? I thought I noticed you noticing.

The first few times I made good my escape, uncle Beldin frantically searched for me and scolded me at some length when he finally found me. I'm a little ashamed to admit that after a while it even became a kind of game. I'd wait until he was deeply engrossed in something, quickly unhook his gate, and then scamper down his stairs. Then I'd find someplace to hide where I could watch his desperate search. In time I think he began to enjoy our little entertainment as well, because his scoldings grew progressively less vehement. I guess that after the first several times he came to realize that there was nothing he could do to stop my excursions into the outside world and that I wouldn't stray too far from the foot of his tower.

My adventuring served a number of purposes. At first it was only to escape my sister's maudlin ruminations about father. Then it became a game during which I tormented poor uncle Beldin by seeking out hiding places. Ultimately, though it's very unattractive, it was a way to get *someone* to pay attention to me.

As the game continued, I grew fonder and fonder of the ugly, gnarled dwarf who'd become my surrogate parent. Any form of emotionalism embarrasses uncle Beldin, but I think I'll say this anyway. 'I love you, you dirty, mangy little man, and no amount of foul temper or bad language will ever change that.'

If you ever read this, uncle, I'm sure that will offend you. Well, isn't that just too bad?

It's easy for me to come up with all sorts of exotic excuses for the things I did during my childhood, but to put it very bluntly I was

26

totally convinced that I was ugly. Beldaran and I were twins, and we should have been identical. The Master changed that, however. Beldaran was blonde, and my hair was dark. Our features were similar, but we were not mirror images of each other. There were some subtle variations – many of them existing only in my own imagination, I'm sure. Moreover, my excursions outside uncle Beldin's tower had exposed my skin to the sun. Beldaran and I both had very fair skin, so I didn't immediately develop that healthy, glowing tan so admired in some quarters. I burned instead, and then I peeled. I frequently resembled a snake or lizard in molt. Beldaran remained indoors, and her skin was like alabaster. The comparison was not very flattering.

Then there was the accursed white lock in my hair which father's first touch had bestowed upon me. How I hated that leprous lock of hair! Once, in a fit of irritation, I even tried to cut it short with a knife. It was a very sharp knife, but it wasn't *that* sharp. The lock resisted all my sawing and hacking. I *did* manage to dull the knife, however. No, the knife wasn't defective. It left a very nice cut on my left thumb as my efforts to excise the hideous lock grew more frantic.

So I gave up. Since I was destined to be ugly, I saw no point in paying any attention to my appearance. Bathing was a waste of time, and combing merely accentuated the contrast between the lock and the rest of my hair. I fell down frequently because I was awkward at that age, and my bony knees and elbows were usually skinned. My habit of picking at the resulting scabs left long streaks of dried blood on my lower legs and forearms, and I chewed my fingernails almost continually.

To put it rather simply, I was a mess – and I didn't really care.

I gave vent to my resentment in a number of ways. There were those tiresome periods when I refused to answer when Beldaran talked to me, and my infantile practice of waiting until she was asleep at night and then neatly rolling over in our bed to pull all the covers off her. That one was always good for at least a half-hour fight. I discarded it, however, after uncle Beldin threatened to have Beltira and Belkira build another bed so that he could make us sleep apart. I was resentful about my sister's preoccupation with our father, but not *that* resentful.

As I grew older, my field of exploration expanded. I guess uncle Beldin had grown tired of trying to find me after I'd escaped from his tower – either that or the Master had advised him to let me wander. The growth of my independence was evidently important.

I think I was about six or so when I finally discovered the Tree which stands in the middle of the Vale. My family has a peculiar attachment to that Tree. When my father first came to the Vale, it was the Tree that held him in stasis until the weather turned bad on him. Ce'Nedra, who *is* a Dryad, after all, was absolutely entranced by it, and she spent hours communing with it. Garion has never spoken of *his* reaction to the Tree, but Garion had other things on his mind the first time he saw it. When Eriond was quite young, he and Horse made a special trip just to visit with it.

It surprised me the first time I saw it. I could not believe that anything alive could be that huge. I remember the day very well. It was early spring, and a blustery wind was bending the grass in long waves atop the knolls in the Vale and scudding dirty grey clouds across the sky. I felt very good and oddly free. I was quite some distance from uncle Beldin's tower when I topped a long, grassy rise and saw the Tree standing in solitary immensity in the next valley. I'll not cast any unfounded accusations here, but it just so happened that a break in the clouds permitted a single shaft of sunlight to fall like a golden column upon the Tree.

That got my immediate attention.

The Tree's trunk was much larger than uncle Beldin's tower, its branches reached hundreds of feet into the air, and its lateral limbs shaded whole acres. I stared at it in amazement for a long time, and then I very clearly heard – or felt – it calling to me.

I somewhat hesitantly descended the hill in response. I was wary about that strange summons. The bushes didn't talk to me, and neither did the grass. My as yet unformed mind automatically suspected anything out of the ordinary.

When at last I entered the shade of those wide-spread branches, a strange sort of warm glowing peace came over me and erased my trepidation. Somehow I knew that the Tree meant me no harm. I walked quite resolutely toward that vast, gnarled trunk.

And then I put forth my hand and touched it.

And that was my second awakening. The first had come when father had laid his hand upon my head in benediction, but in some ways *this* awakening was more profound.

The Tree told me – although 'told' is not precisely accurate, since the Tree does not exactly speak – that it was – *is*, I suppose – the oldest living thing in the entire world. Ages unnumbered have nourished it, and it stands in absolute serenity in the center of the Vale, shedding years like drops of rain from its wide-spread leaves. Since it pre-dates the rest of us, and it's alive, we're all in some peculiar way its children. The first lesson it taught me – the first lesson it teaches everyone who touches it – was about the nature of time. Time, the slow, measured passage of years, is not exactly what we think it is. Humans tend to break time up into manageable pieces – night and day, the turning of the seasons, the passage of years, centuries, eons – but in actuality time is all one piece, a river flowing endlessly from the beginning toward some incomprehensible goal. The Tree gently guided my infant understanding through that extremely difficult concept.

I think that had I not encountered the Tree exactly when I did, I should never have grasped the meaning of my unusual life-span. Slowly, with my hands still on the Tree's rough bark, I came to understand that I would live for as long as necessary. The Tree was not very specific about the nature of the tasks which lay before me, but it *did* suggest that those tasks would take me a very long time.

And then I *did* hear a voice – several, actually. The meaning of what they were saying was totally clear to me, but I somehow knew that these were not human voices. It took me quite some time to identify their source, and then a rather cheeky sparrow flittered down through those huge branches, hooked his tiny claws into the rough bark of the Tree a few feet from my face, and regarded me with his glittering little eyes.

'Welcome, Polgara,' he chirped. 'What took you so long to find us?'

The mind of a child is frequently willing to accept the unusual or even the bizarre, but this went a little far. I stared at that talkative little bird in absolute astonishment.

'Why are you looking at me like that?' he demanded.

'You're *talking*!' I blurted.

'Of course I am. We all talk. You just haven't been listening. You should really pay closer attention to what's going on around you. You aren't going to hurt me, are you? I'll fly away if you try, you know.'

'N-no,' I stammered. 'I won't hurt you.'

'Good. Then we can talk. Did you happen to see any seeds on your way here?'

'I don't think so. I wasn't really looking for seeds, though.'

'You should learn to watch for them. My mate has three babies back at the nest, and I'm supposed to be out looking for seeds to feed them. What's that on your sleeve?'

I looked at the sleeve of my smock. 'It seems to be a seed of some kind – grass, probably.'

'Well, don't just stand there. Give it to me.'

I picked the seed off my sleeve and held it out to him. He hopped off the side of the Tree and perched on my finger, his head cocked and his bright little eye closely examining my offering. 'It's grass, all right,' he agreed. Then he actually seemed to sigh. 'I *hate* it when all there is to eat is immature grass-seed. It's early in the season, and those seeds are so tiny right now.' He took the seed in his beak. 'Don't go away. I'll be right back.' Then he flew off.

For a few moments I actually thought I'd been dreaming. Then my sparrow came back, and there was another one with him. 'This is my mate,' he introduced her to me.

'Hello, Polgara,' she said. 'Where did you find that seed? My babies are very hungry.'

'It must have caught on my sleeve up near the top of that hill,' I ventured.

'Why don't we go up there and have a look,' she suggested, brazenly settling on my shoulder. The first sparrow followed his mate's lead and perched on my other shoulder. All bemused by this miracle, I turned and started back up the grassy hill.

'You don't move very fast, do you?' The first sparrow noted critically.

'I don't have wings,' I replied.

'That must be awfully tedious.'

'It gets me to where I'm going.'

'As soon as we find those seeds, I'll introduce you to some of the others,' he offered. 'My mate and I'll be busy feeding the babies for a while.'

'Can you actually talk to other kinds of birds?' That was a startling idea.

'Well,' he said deprecatingly, 'sort of. The larks always try to be poetic, and the robins talk too much, and they're always trying to shoulder their way in whenever I find food. I really don't care that much for robins. They're such bullies.'

And then a meadowlark swooped in and hovered over my head. 'Whither goest thou?' he demanded of my sparrow.

'Up there,' the sparrow replied, cocking his head toward the hill-top. 'Polgara found some seeds up there, and my mate and I have babies to feed. Why don't you talk with her while we tend to business?'

'All right,' the lark agreed. 'My mate doth still sit upon our eggs, warming them with her substance, so I have ample time to guide our sister here.'

'There's a seed!' the female sparrow chirped excitedly. And she swooped down off my shoulder to seize it. Her mate soon saw another, and the two of them flew off.

'Sparrows are, methinks, somewhat overly excitable,' the lark noted. 'Whither wouldst thou go, sister?'

'I'll leave that up to you,' I replied. 'I'd sort of like to get to know more birds, though.'

And that began my education in ornithology. I met all manner of birds that morning. The helpful lark took me around and introduced me. His rather lyrical assessments of the varied species were surprisingly acute. As I've already mentioned, he told me that sparrows are excitable and talky. He characterized robins as oddly aggressive, and then added that they tended to say the same things over and over. Jays scream a lot. Swallows show off. Crows are thieves. Vultures stink. Hummingbirds aren't really very intelligent. If he's forced to think about it, the average hummingbird gets so confused that he forgets exactly how to hover in mid-air. Owls aren't really as wise as they're reputed to be, and my guide referred to them rather deprecatingly as 'flying mouse-traps'. Seagulls have a grossly exaggerated notion of their own place in the overall scheme of things. Your average seagull spends a lot of his time pretending to be an eagle. I normally wouldn't have seen any seagulls in the Vale, but the blustery wind had driven them inland. The assorted waterfowl spent almost as much time swimming as they did flying, and they were very clannish. I didn't really care that much for ducks and geese. They're pretty, I suppose, but their voices set my teeth on edge.

The aristocrats of birds are the raptors. The various hawks, depending on their size, have a complicated hierarchy, and standing at the very pinnacle of birddom is the eagle.

I communed with the various birds for the rest of the day, and by evening they had grown so accustomed to me that some of them, like my cheeky little sparrow and his mate, actually perched on me. As evening settled over the Vale I promised to return the next day, and my lyric lark accompanied me back to uncle Beldin's tower.

'What have you been doing, Pol?' Beldaran asked curiously after I'd mounted the stairs and rejoined her. As was usual when we were talking to each other privately, Beldaran spoke to me in 'twin'.

'I met some birds,' I replied.

'"Met"? How do you meet a bird?'

'You talk to them, Beldaran.'

'And do they talk back?' Her look was amused.

'Yes,' I answered in an off-hand manner, 'as a matter of fact, they do.' If she wanted to be snippy and superior, I could play that game, too.

'What do they talk about?' Her curiosity subdued her irritation at my superior reply.

'Oh, seeds and the like. Birds take a lot of interest in food. They talk about flying, too. They can't really understand why I can't fly. Then they talk about their nests. A bird doesn't really live in his nest, you know. It's just a place to lay eggs and raise babies.'

'I'd never thought of that,' my sister admitted.

'Neither had I – until they told me about it. A bird doesn't really need a home, I guess. They also have opinions.'

'Opinions?'

'One kind of bird doesn't really have much use for other kinds of birds. Sparrows don't like robins, and seagulls don't like ducks.'

'How curious,' Beldaran commented.

'What are you two babbling about now?' uncle Beldin demanded, looking up from the scroll he'd been studying.

'Birds,' I told him.

He muttered something I won't repeat here and went back to his study of that scroll.

'Why don't you take a bath and change clothes, Pol,' Beldaran suggested a bit acidly. 'You've got bird-droppings all over you.'

I shrugged. 'They'll brush off as soon as they dry.'

She rolled her eyes upward.

I left the tower early the next morning and went to the small storehouse where the twins kept their supplies. The twins are Alorns, and they *do* love their beer. One of the major ingredients in beer is wheat, and I was fairly sure they wouldn't miss a small bag or two. I opened the bin where they kept the wheat and scooped a fair amount into a couple of canvas bags I'd found hanging on a hook on the back wall of the shed. Then, carrying the fruits of my pilferage, I started back for the Tree.

'Whither goest thou, sister?' It was my poetic lark again. It occurs to me that my affinity for the studied formality of Wacite Arendish speech may very well have been born in my conversations with that lark.

'I'm going back to the Tree,' I told him.

'What are those?' he demanded, stabbing his beak at the two bags I carried.

'A gift for my new-found friends,' I said.

'What is a gift?'

'You'll see.'

Birds are sometimes as curious as cats, and my lark badgered me about what was in my bags all the way back to the Tree.

My birds were ecstatic when I opened the bags and spread the wheat around under the Tree, and they came in from miles around to feast. I watched them fondly for a time, and then I climbed up into the Tree and sprawled out on one huge limb to watch my new friends. I got the distinct impression that the Tree approved of what I had done.

I thought about that for quite a long time that morning, but I was still baffled about just exactly how I'd come by this unusual talent.

'*It's the Tree's gift to you, Polgara.*' It was mother's voice, and suddenly everything became clear to me. Of course! Why hadn't *I* thought of that?

'*Probably because you weren't paying attention,*' mother observed.

In the years that followed, the Tree became like a second home to me. I spent my days on my favorite perch with my skinny legs stretched out on the huge limb and my back against the massive trunk. I fed my birds and we talked. We came to know each other better and better, and they brought me information about the weather, forest fires, and occasional travelers passing through the Vale. My family was always carping about my shabby appearance, but my birds didn't seem to mind.

As those of you who know me can attest, I have an occasionally sharp tongue. My family was spared all sorts of affronts because of my fondness for the Tree and its feathered inhabitants.

The seasons rolled by, and Beldaran and I grew into an awkward coltishness – all legs and elbows. And then one morning we discovered that we had become women during the night. There was some fairly visible evidence of the fact on our bed-clothing.

'Are we dying?' Beldaran asked me in a trembling voice.

'*Tell her to stop that, Polgara!*' mother's voice came to me sharply. That was something I could never understand. Mother talked to me directly, but she never intruded into Beldaran's mind. I'm sure there was a reason for it, but mother never got around to explaining.

'What's happening, mother?' I demanded. To be honest about it, I was quite nearly as frightened as my sister was.

'*It's a natural process, Polgara. It happens to all women.*'

'Make it stop!'

'*No. It has to happen. Tell Beldaran that it's nothing to get excited about.*'

'Mother says that it's all right,' I told my sister.

'How can it be all right?'

'Shush. I'm trying to listen to mother.'

'Don't you shush me, Polgara!'

'Then be still.' I turned my attention inward. *'You'd better explain this, mother,'* I said. *'Beldaran's about ready to fly apart.'* I didn't really think it was necessary to admit that *my* seams were starting to come undone as well.

Then mother gave us a somewhat clinical explanation for the bloodstains on our bedding, and I passed the information on to my distraught sister.

'Is it going to go on forever now?' Beldaran asked me in a trembling voice.

'No, only for a few days. Mother says to get used to it, because it'll happen every month.'

'Every month?' Beldaran sounded outraged.

'So she says.' I raised up in bed and looked across the room toward Uncle Beldin's bed – the place where all the snoring was coming from. 'Let's get this cleaned up while he's still asleep,' I suggested.

'Oh, dear Gods, yes!' she agreed fervently. 'I'd *die* if he found out about this.'

I'm fairly sure that our misshapen uncle was aware of what was happening, but we never got around to discussing it, for some reason.

Uncle Beldin has theorized about when the members of my extended family develop what father calls 'talent', and he's concluded that it emerges with the onset of puberty. *I* may have had something to do with that conclusion. I think I was about twelve or so. It was 'that time of the month' for Beldaran and me, and my sister was feeling mopey. I, on the other hand, was irritable. It was all so inconvenient! Mother had mentioned the fact that 'something might happen' now that Beldaran and I had reached a certain level of maturity, but she was a little vague about it. Evidently, it's sort of necessary that our first venture into the exercise of our 'talent' be spontaneous. Don't ask me why, because I haven't got the faintest notion of a reasonable explanation for the custom.

As I remember the circumstances of that first incident, I was dragging a large bag of wheat down to the Tree to feed my birds. I was muttering to myself about that. Over the years my birds had come to depend on me, and they were not above taking advantage of my generosity. Given half a chance, birds, like all other creatures, can be lazy. I didn't mind feeding them, but it seemed that I was spending more and more time hauling sacks of wheat from the twins' tower to the Tree.

When I reached the Tree, they were all clamoring to be fed, and that irritated me all the more. As far as I know, not one single bird has ever learned how to say 'thank you'.

There were whole flocks of them by now, and they cleaned up my daily offering in short order. Then they started screeching for more.

I was seated on my favorite perch, and the shrill importunings of the birds made me even *more* irritable. If there were only *some* way I could have an inexhaustible supply of seed on hand to keep them quiet.

The jays were being particularly offensive. There's something about a jay's squawking that cuts directly into me. Finally, driven beyond my endurance, I burst out. 'More seeds!' I half-shouted.

And suddenly, there they were – heaps and heaps of them! I was stunned. Even the birds seemed startled. I, on the other hand, felt absolutely exhausted.

Father has always used the phrase 'the Will and the Word' to describe what we do, but I think that's a little limited. *My* experience seems to indicate that 'the *Wish* and the Word' works just as well.

Someday he and I'll have to talk about that.

As is usually the case, my first experiment in this field made a lot of noise. I hadn't even finished my self-congratulation when a blue-banded hawk and two doves came swooping in. Now, hawks and doves don't normally flock together – except when the hawk is hungry – so I immediately had some suspicions. The three of them settled on my limb, and then they blurred, changing form before my very eyes.

'Seeds, Polgara?' Beltira said mildly. *'Seeds?'*

'The birds were hungry,' I said. What a silly excuse for a miracle *that* was!

'Precocious, isn't she?' Belkira murmured to uncle Beldin.

'We should probably have expected it,' Beldin grunted. 'Pol never does *anything* in the normal way.'

'Will I be able to do that some day?' I asked the twins.

'Do what, Pol?' Belkira asked gently.

'What you just did – change myself into a bird and back?'

'Probably, yes.'

35

'Well now,' I said as a whole new world of possibilities opened before my eyes. 'Will Beldaran be able to do it too?'

Their expressions seemed to grow a bit evasive at that question. 'No more of this, Pol,' uncle Beldin said sternly, 'not until we've explained a few things to you. This is *very* dangerous.'

'Dangerous?' That startled me.

'You can do almost anything you put your mind to, Pol,' Beltira explained, 'but you *can't* uncreate things. Don't *ever* say, "Be not". If you do, the force you've unleashed will recoil back on you, and *you'll* be the one who's destroyed.'

'Why would I want to destroy anything?'

'It'll happen,' Beldin assured me in that growling voice of his. 'You're almost as bad-tempered as I am, and sooner or later something will irritate you to the point that you'll want to make it go away – to destroy it – and that'll kill you.'

'Kill?'

'And more than kill. The purpose of the universe is to create things. She won't let you come along behind her and undo her work.'

'Wouldn't that also apply to making things?'

'Whatever gave you that idea?'

'If unmaking things is forbidden, it seems logical that making them would be too.'

'Making things is all right,' Beldin assured me. 'You just made about a half-ton of bird-seed and you're still here, but don't ever try to erase what you've done. If it's not right, that's just too bad. Once it's been made, you're stuck with it.'

'That hardly seems fair,' I protested.

'Did you really expect life to be fair to you, Pol?' He replied.

'But if I make it, it's mine, isn't it? I should be able to do anything I want with it, shouldn't I?'

'That's not the way it works, Pol,' Beltira told me. 'Don't experiment with it. We love you too much to lose you.'

'What else is it that I'm not supposed to do?'

'Don't attempt the impossible,' Belkira said. 'Once you've committed your will to something, you *have* to go through with it. You can't turn the will off once you've unleashed it. It'll keep drawing more and more out of you to try to get the job done, and it'll eventually take so much out of you that your heart will stop, and then you'll die.'

'How am I supposed to know what's possible and what isn't?'

'Come to one of *us* before you start,' Beltira said. 'Talk it over with us and we'll let you know if it's all right.'

36

'*Nobody* tells me what to do!' I flared.

'Do you want to die?' Beldin demanded bluntly.

'Of course not.'

'Then do as you're told,' he growled. 'No experimenting on your own. Don't do *anything* this way without consulting with one of us first. Don't try to pick up a mountain range or stop the sun. We're trying to protect you, Pol. Don't be difficult.'

'Is there anything else?' I was a little sullen at that point.

'You're very noisy,' Belkira said bluntly.

'What do you mean, "noisy"?'

'When you do something this way, it makes a sound we can hear. When you made all that birdseed, it sounded like a thunderclap. Always remember that we're not the only ones in the world with this particular gift. There'll be times when you won't want to announce the fact that you're around. Here, I'll show you.'

There was a large rock not far from the Tree, and uncle Belkira looked at it and frowned slightly. Then the rock seemed to vanish, and it instantly reappeared about a hundred yards away.

It wasn't exactly a noise. I *felt* it more than I heard it, but it still seemed to rattle my teeth.

'Now do you see what I mean?' Belkira asked me.

'Yes. That's quite a sound, isn't it?'

'I'm glad you enjoyed it.'

They went on piling restrictions on me for quite some time. 'Is that all?' I asked finally. They were beginning to make me tired.

'There'll be more, Pol,' Beltira said. 'Those are just the things you need to know right now. Like it or not, your education's just begun. You've got to learn to control this gift. Study very hard, Pol. Your life probably depends on it.'

'*Just smile and agree with them, Polgara,*' mother's voice advised me. '*I'll take care of your education myself. Smile and nod and keep the peace when they try to instruct you, Pol. Don't upset them by doing anything unusual while they're around.*'

'Whatever you say, mother,' I agreed.

And that's how I *really* got my education. My uncles were frequently startled by just how fast I picked things up. They no sooner mentioned a particular feat than I did it – flawlessly. I'm sure they all thought they had a budding – but very dirty – genius on their hands. The truth of the matter was that mother had already taught me those rudimentary tricks. My mind and mother's mind had been linked since before I was born, and so she was in a much better position to gauge the extent of my understanding. This made her a far better teacher than my uncles. It was about then that uncle Beldin left on some mysterious errand, and so my education fell on the twins' shoulders – at least they thought it did. In actuality, mother taught me most of what I know.

I naturally told my sister about what had happened. Beldaran and I didn't really have any secrets from each other.

Her face became rather wistful. 'What was it like?' she asked me.

'I'll show you how,' I told her. 'Then you can find out for yourself.'

She sighed. 'No, Pol,' she replied. 'Mother told me not to.'

'Told? You mean she's finally talking to you?'

'Not when I'm awake,' Beldaran explained. 'Her voice comes to me when I'm dreaming.'

'That's a terribly cumbersome way to do it.'

'I know, but there's a reason for it. She told me that you're supposed to *do* things. I'm just supposed to *be*.'

'To be what?'

'She hasn't told me yet. She'll probably get around to it one of these days.'

And that sent me away muttering to myself.

Mother told me about several of the things I might be capable of doing, and I tried them all. Translocation was a lot of fun, actually, and it taught me how to muffle the noise. I spent whole days bouncing rocks here and there about the Vale.

There were many tricks mother explained to me that I wasn't able to practice, since they required the presence of other people, and aside from the twins and Beldaran, nobody else was around. Mother rather sternly told me *not* to experiment with Beldaran.

What my uncles chose to call my 'education' took me away from my Tree and my birds for extended periods of time, and I didn't like that very much. I already knew about most of what they were telling me anyway, so it was all very tedious and monotonous for me.

'*Keep your temper, Polgara,*' mother told me on one occasion when I was right on the verge of an outburst.

'But this is all so boring!' I protested.

'*Think about something else, then.*'

'What should I think about?'

'*Have the twins teach you how to cook,*' she suggested. '*Humans like to stick their food in a fire before they eat it. It's always seemed like a waste of time to me, but that's the way they are.*'

And so it was that I started to get two educations instead of one. I learned all about translocation and about spices at almost the same time. One of the peculiarities of our gift is the fact that imagination plays a very large part in it, and I soon found that I could imagine what a given spice would add to whatever dish I was preparing. In this particular regard I soon even outstripped the twins. *They* measured things rather meticulously. *I* seasoned food by instinct – a pinch, a dollop, or a handful of any spice always seemed to work out just right.

'That's too much sage, Pol,' Beltira protested when I dug my hand into one of his spice-pots.

'Wait, uncle,' I told him. 'Don't criticize my cooking until you've tasted it.'

And, as usual, the stew I was preparing came out perfect.

Beltira was a little sullen about that, as I recall.

And then there came a very important day in my life. It was the day – night actually – when mother revealed the secret of changing shape.

'*It's really quite simple, Polgara,*' she told me. '*All you really have to do is form the image of the alternative shape in your mind and then fit yourself into it.*'

Mother's idea of 'simple' and mine were miles apart, however.

'*The tail-feathers are too short,*' she said critically after my third attempt. '*Try it again.*'

It took me *hours* to get the imagined shape right. I was almost on the verge of giving up entirely. If I got the tail right, the beak was wrong – or the talons. Then the wing-feathers weren't soft enough. Then the chest wasn't strong enough. Then the eyes were too small. I was right at the edge of abandoning the whole notion when mother said, '*That looks closer. Now just let yourself flow into it.*' Mother's ability to see into my mind made her the best teacher I could possibly have had.

As I started to slip myself into the image I'd formed, I felt as if my body had turned into something almost liquid – like honey. I literally seeped into that imaginary shape.

And then it was done. I was a snowy owl. Once again, mother's intimate contact with my mind simplified things enormously. There are far too many things involved in flying for anyone to pick it up immediately, so mother quite simply instilled all those minuscule shifts and dexterity in my mind. I thrust with my soft wings, and I was immediately airborne. I circled a few times, learning with every silent sweep of my wings, and those circles grew inexorably wider.

There's an ecstasy to flying that I won't even try to describe. By the time dawn began to stain the eastern horizon, I was a competent bird, and my mind was filled with a joy I'd never known before.

'You'd better go back to the tower, Pol,' mother advised. 'Owls aren't usually flying in the daytime.'

'Do I have to?'

'Yes. Let's not give our little secret away just yet. You'll have to change to your own form as well.'

'Mother!' I protested vehemently.

'We can play again tomorrow night, Pol. Now go home and change back before anyone wakes up.'

That didn't make me *too* happy, but I did as I was told.

It was not long after that that Beldaran took me to one side. 'Uncle Beldin's bringing father back to the Vale,' she told me.

'Oh? How do you know that?'

'Mother told me – in a dream.'

'A dream?' That startled me.

'She always talks to me in my dreams. I told you about that already.'

I decided not to make an issue of it, but I reminded myself to have a talk with mother about it. She always came to *me* when I was awake, but for some reason she spoke to my sister in the hazy world of dreams. I wondered why there was such a difference. I *also* wondered why mother had told Beldaran about our vagrant father's homecoming and hadn't bothered to let *me* know about it.

It was early summer when uncle Beldin finally brought father home. Over the course of the years since father had left the Vale, uncle Beldin had kept track of him and had reported on his various escapades, so I was not just *too* excited about his return. The idea of admitting that a beer-soaked lecher was my father didn't appeal to me all that much.

He didn't *look* too bad when he came up the stairs to the top of Beldin's tower, but I knew that appearances could be deceiving.

'Father!' Beldaran exclaimed, rushing across the floor to embrace him. Forgiveness is a virtue, I suppose, but sometimes Beldaran carried it to extremes.

I did something that wasn't very nice at that point. My only excuse was that I didn't want father to get the mistaken impression that his homecoming was a cause for universal rejoicing. I didn't *quite* hate him, but I definitely didn't like him. 'Well, Old Wolf,' I said in as insulting a tone as I could manage, 'I see you've finally decided to come back to the scene of the crime.'

CHAPTER 3

Then I proceeded to give my father a piece of my mind – several pieces, actually. I told him – at length – precisely what I thought of him, since I didn't want him to mistakenly believe that Beldaran's sugary display of sweetness and light was going to be universal. I *also* wanted to assert my independence, and I'm fairly sure I got *that* point across to him. It wasn't really very attractive, but I was only thirteen at the time, so I still had a few rough edges.

All right, let's get something out in the open right here and now. I'm no saint, and I never pretended to be. I've been occasionally referred to as 'Holy Polgara', and that's an absolute absurdity. In all probability the only people who'll really understand my feelings as a child are those who are twins themselves. Beldaran was the absolute center of my life, and she had been since before we were born. Beldaran was *mine*, and my jealousy and resentment knew no bounds when father 'usurped' her affection. Beldaran and her every thought belonged to *me*, and he stole her! My snide comment about the 'scene of the crime' started something that went on for eons. I'd spend hours polishing those snippy little comments, and I treasured each and every one of them.

Many of you may have noticed that the relationship between me and my father is somewhat adversarial. I snipe at him, and he winces. That started when I was thirteen years old, and it didn't take long for it to turn into a habit that's so deeply engrained in me that I do it automatically now.

One other thing as well. Those who knew Beldaran and me when we were children have always assumed that I was the dominant twin, the one who took the lead in all twinly matters. In actuality, however, Beldaran was dominant. I lived almost entirely for her approval, and in some ways I still do. There was a serene quality about Beldaran that I could never match. Perhaps it was because mother had instilled Beldaran's purpose in her mind before we were ever born. Beldaran *knew* where she was going, but I hadn't the foggiest notion of *my* destination. She had a certainty about her I could never match.

Father endured my ill-tempered diatribe with a calm grace that irritated me all the more. I finally even lapsed into some of the more colorful aspects of uncle Beldin's vocabulary to stress my discontent – not so much because I enjoyed profanity, but more to see if I could get some kind of reaction out of father. I was just a little miffed by his calm indifference to my sharpest digs.

Then in the most off-hand way imaginable, father casually announced that my sister and I would be moving into his tower to live with him.

My language deteriorated noticeably at that point.

After father had left uncle Beldin's tower, Beldaran and I spoke at some length in 'twin'.

'If that idiot thinks for one minute that we're going to move in with him, he's in for a very nasty surprise,' I declared.

'He *is* our father, Polgara,' Beldaran pointed out.

'That's not *my* fault.'

'We must obey him.'

'Have you lost your mind?'

'No, as a matter of fact, I haven't.' She looked around uncle Beldin's tower. 'I suppose we'd better start packing.'

'I'm not going anyplace,' I told her.

'That's up to you, of course.'

I was more than a little startled. 'You'd go off and leave me alone?' I asked incredulously.

'You've been leaving *me* alone ever since you found the Tree, Pol,' she reminded me. 'Are you going to pack or not?'

It was one of the few times that Beldaran openly asserted her authority over me. She normally got what she wanted in more subtle ways.

She went to a cluttered area of uncle Beldin's tower and began rummaging around through the empty wooden boxes uncle had stacked there.

'I gather from the tone of things that you girls are having a little disagreement,' uncle said to me mildly.

'It's more like a permanent rupture,' I retorted. 'Beldaran's going to obey father, and I'm not.'

'I wouldn't make any wagers, Pol.' Uncle Beldin had raised us, after all, and he understood our little power structure.

'This is right and proper, Pol,' Beldaran said back over her shoulder. 'Respect, if not love, compels our obedience.'

'*Respect*? I haven't got any respect for that beer-soaked mendicant!'

'You should have, Pol. Suit yourself, though. I'm going to obey him. You can do as you like. You *will* visit me from time to time, won't you?'

How could I possibly answer that? Now perhaps you can see the source of Beldaran's power over me. She almost never lost her temper, and she always spoke in a sweetly reasonable tone of voice, but that was very deceptive. An ultimatum *is* an ultimatum, no matter how it's delivered.

I stared at her helplessly.

'Don't you think you should start packing, dear sister?' she asked sweetly.

I stormed out of uncle Beldin's tower and went immediately to my Tree to sulk. A few short answers persuaded even my birds to leave me alone.

I spent that entire night in the Tree, hoping the unnatural separation would bring Beldaran to her senses. My sister, however, concealed a will of iron under that sweet, sunny exterior. She moved into father's tower with him, and after a day or so of almost unbearable loneliness, I sulkily joined them.

This is not to say that I spent very much time in father's cluttered tower. I slept there and occasionally ate with my father and sister, but it was summer. My Tree was all the home I really needed, and my birds provided me with company.

As I look back, I see a peculiar dichotomy of motives behind that summer sabbatical in the branches of the Tree. Firstly, of course, I was trying to punish Beldaran for her betrayal of me. Actually, though, I stayed in the Tree because I liked it there. I loved the birds, and mother was with me almost continually as I scampered around among the branches, frequently assuming forms other than my own. I found that squirrels are very agile. Of course I could always become a bird and simply fly up to the top-most branches, but there's a certain satisfaction in actually climbing.

It was about midsummer when I discovered the dangers involved in taking the form of a rodent. Rodents of all sorts, from mice on up the scale, are looked upon as a food source by just about every other species in the world with the possible exception of goldfish. One bright summer morning I was leaping from limb to limb among the very top-most branches of the Tree when a passing hawk decided to have me for breakfast.

'Don't do that,' I told him in a disgusted tone as he came swooping in on me.

He flared off, his eyes startled. 'Polgara?' he said in amazement. 'Is that really you?'

'Of course it is, you clot.'

'I'm very sorry,' he apologized. 'I didn't recognize you.'

'You should pay closer attention. All manner of creatures get caught in baited snares when they think they're about to get some free food.'

'Who would try to trap *me*?'

'You wouldn't want to find out.'

'Would you like to fly with me?' he offered.

'How do you know I can fly?'

'Can't everybody?' he asked, sounding a bit startled. He was evidently a very young hawk.

To be absolutely honest, though, I enjoyed our flight. Each bird flies a little differently, but the effortless art of soaring, lifted by the unseen columns of warm air rising from the earth, gives one a sense of unbelievable freedom.

All right, I like to fly. So what?

Father had decided to leave me to my own devices that summer, probably because the sound of my voice grated on his nerves. Once, however, he *did* come to my Tree – probably at Beldaran's insistence – to try to persuade me to come home. *He*, however, was the one who got a strong dose of persuasion. I unleashed my birds on him, and they drove him off.

I saw my father and my sister occasionally during the following weeks. In actuality, I stopped by from time to time to see if I could detect any signs of suffering in my sister. If Beldaran was suffering, though, she managed to hide it quite well. Father sat off in one corner during my visits. He seemed to be working on something quite small, but I really wasn't curious about whatever it might have been.

It was early autumn when I finally discovered what he'd been so meticulously crafting. He came down to my Tree one morning, and Beldaran was with him. 'I've got something for you, Pol,' he told me.

44

'I don't want it,' I told him from the safety of my perch.

'Aren't you being a little ridiculous, Pol?' Beldaran suggested.

'It's a family trait,' I replied.

Then father did something he's very seldom done to me. One moment I was comfortably resting on my perch about twenty feet above the ground. At the next instant I was sprawled in the dirt at his feet. The old rascal had translocated me! 'That's better,' he said. 'Now we can talk.' He held out his hand, and there was a silver medallion on a silver chain hanging from his fingers. 'This is for you,' he told me.

Somewhat reluctantly I took it. 'What am I supposed to do with this?' I asked him.

'You're supposed to wear it.'

'Why?'

'Because the Master says so. If you want to argue with Him, go right ahead. Just put it on, Pol, and stop all this foolishness. It's time for us all to grow up.'

I looked rather closely at the amulet and saw that it bore the image of an owl. It occurred to me that this somehow very appropriate gift had come from Aldur instead of father. At that point in my life decorations of any kind seemed wildly inappropriate, but I immediately saw a use for this one. It bore the image of an owl, my favorite alternative form – and mother's as well. Part of the difficulty of the shape-change is getting the image right, and father was evidently a very talented sculptor. The owl was so lifelike that it looked almost as if it could fly. This particular ornament would be *very* useful.

When I put it on, something rather strange came over me. I'd have sooner died than have admitted it, but I suddenly felt complete, as if something had always been missing.

'And now we are three,' Beldaran said vapidly.

'Amazing,' I said a bit acidly. 'You *do* know how to count.' My unexpected reaction to father's gift had put me off-balance, and I felt the need to lash out at somebody – anybody.

'Don't be nasty,' Beldaran told me. 'I know you're more clever than I am, Pol. You don't have to hit me over the head with it. Now why don't you stop all this foolishness and come back home where you belong?'

The guiding principle of my entire life at that point had been my rather conceited belief that nobody told me what to do. Beldaran disabused me of that notion right then and there. *She* could – and occasionally did – give me orders. The implied threat that she would withhold her love from me brought me to heel immediately.

The three of us walked on back to father's tower. He seemed a little startled by my sudden change of heart, and I believe that even to this day he doesn't fully understand the power Beldaran had over me.

Perhaps it was to cover his confusion that he offered me some left-over breakfast. I discovered immediately that this most powerful sorcerer in the world was woefully inadequate in the kitchen. 'Did you do this to perfectly acceptable food on purpose, father?' I asked him. 'You *must* have. Nobody could have done something this bad by accident.'

'If you don't like it, Pol, there's the kitchen.'

'Why, I *do* believe you're right, father,' I replied in mock surprise. 'How strange that I didn't notice that. Maybe it has something to do with the fact that you've got books and scrolls piled all over the working surfaces.'

He shrugged. 'They give me something to read while I'm cooking.'

'I knew that *something* must have distracted you. You couldn't have ruined all this food if you'd been paying attention.' Then I laid my arm on the counter-top and swept all his books and scrolls off onto the floor. 'From now on, keep your toys out of my kitchen, father. Next time, I'll burn them.'

'*Your* kitchen?'

'*Somebody's* going to have to do the cooking, and you're so inept that you can't be trusted near a stove.'

He was too busy picking up his books to answer.

And *that* established my place in our peculiar little family. I love to cook anyway, so I didn't mind, but in time I came to wonder if I hadn't to some degree demeaned myself by taking on the chore of cooking. After a week or so, or three, things settled down, and our positions in the family were firmly established. I complained a bit now and then, but in reality I wasn't really unhappy about it.

There was something *else* that I didn't like, though. I soon found that I couldn't undo the latch on the amulet father had made for me, but I was something of an expert on latches and I soon worked it out. The secret had to do with time, and it was so complex that I was fairly certain father hadn't devised it all by himself. He *had* sculpted the amulet at Aldur's instruction, after all, and only a God could have conceived of a latch that existed in two different times simultaneously.

Why don't we just let it go at that? The whole concept still gives me a headache, so I don't think I'll go into it any further.

*   *   *

46

My duties in the kitchen didn't really fill my days. I soon bullied Beldaran into washing the dishes after breakfast while I prepared lunch, which was usually something cold. A cold lunch never hurt anybody, after all, and once that was done, I was free to return to my Tree and my birds. Neither father nor my sister objected to my daily excursions, since it cut down on my opportunities to direct clever remarks at father.

And so the seasons turned, as they have a habit of doing.

We were pretty well settled in after the first year or so, and father had invited his brothers over for supper. I recall that evening rather vividly, since it opened my eyes to something I wasn't fully prepared to accept. I'd always taken it as a given that my uncles had good sense, but they treated my disreputable father as if he were some sort of minor deity. I was in the midst of preparing a fairly lavish supper when I finally realized just how much they deferred to him.

I forget exactly what they were talking about – Ctuchik, maybe, or perhaps it was Zedar – but uncle Beldin rather casually asked my father, 'What do *you* think, Belgarath? You're first disciple, after all, so you know the Master's mind better than we do.'

Father grunted sourly. 'And if it turns out that I'm wrong, you'll throw it in my teeth, won't you?'

'Naturally.' Beldin grinned at him. 'That's one of the joys of being a subordinate, isn't it?'

'I hate you,' Father said.

'No you don't, Belgarath,' Beldin said, his grin growing even broader. 'You're just saying that to make me feel better.'

I can't count the number of times I've heard *that* particular exchange between those two. They always seem to think it's hilarious for some reason.

The following morning I went on down to my Tree to ponder this peculiar behavior on the part of my uncles. Evidently father had done some fairly spectacular things in the dim past. *My* feelings about him were uncomplimentary, to say the very least. In my eyes he was lazy, more than a bit silly, and highly unreliable. I dimly began to realize that my father is a very complex being. On the one hand, he's a liar, a thief, a lecher, and a drunkard. On the other, however, he's Aldur's first disciple, and he can quite possibly stop the sun in its orbit if he wants to. I'd been deliberately seeing only his foolish side because of my jealousy. Now I had to come to grips with the other side of him, and I deeply resented the shattering of my illusions about him.

I began to watch him more closely after I returned home that day, hoping that I could find some hints about his duality – and even more fervently hoping that I could not. Losing the basis for one's prejudices is always very painful. All I really saw, though, was a rather seedy-looking old man intently studying a parchment scroll.

'Don't do that, Polgara,' he said, not even bothering to look up from his scroll.

'Do what?'

'Stare at me like that.'

'How did you know I was staring?'

'I could feel it, Pol. Now stop.'

That shook my certainty about him more than I cared to admit. Evidently Beldin and the twins were right. There were a number of very unusual things about my father. I decided I'd better have a talk with mother about this.

'He's a wolf, Pol,' mother told me, 'and wolves play. You take life far too seriously, and his playing irritates you. He can be very serious when it's necessary, but when it's not, he plays. It's the way of wolves.'

'But he demeans himself so much with all that foolishness.'

'Doesn't your particular foolishness demean you? You're far too somber, Pol. Learn how to smile and to have some fun once in a while.'

'Life is serious, mother.'

'I know, but it's also supposed to be fun. Learn how to enjoy life from your father, Polgara. There'll be plenty of time to weep, but you have to laugh as well.'

Mother's tolerance troubled me a great deal, and I found her observations about *my* nature even more troubling.

I've had a great deal of experience with adolescents over the centuries, and I've discovered that as a group these awkward half-children take themselves far too seriously. Moreover, appearance is everything for the adolescent. I suppose it's a form of play-acting. The adolescent *knows* that the child is lurking just under the surface, but he'd sooner die than let it out, and I was no different. I was so intent on being 'grown-up' that I simply couldn't relax and enjoy life.

Most people go through this stage and outgrow it. Many, however, do not. The pose becomes more important than reality, and these poor creatures become hollow people, forever striving to fit themselves into an impossible mold.

Enough. I'm not going to turn this into a treatise on the ins and outs of human development. Until a person learns to laugh at himself, though, his life will be a tragedy – at least that's the way *he'll* see it.

The seasons continued their stately march, and the little lecture mother had delivered to me lessened my *interior* antagonism toward father. I *did* maintain my exterior facade, however. I certainly didn't want the old fool to start thinking I'd gone soft on him.

And then, shortly after my sister and I turned sixteen, the Master paid my father a call and gave him some rather specific instructions. One of us – either Beldaran or myself – was to become the wife of Iron-grip and hence the Rivan Queen. Father, with rather uncharacteristic wisdom, chose to keep the visit to himself. Although I certainly had no particular interest in marrying at that stage of my life, my enthusiasm for competition might have led me into all sorts of foolishness.

My father quite candidly admits that he was sorely tempted to get rid of me by the simple expedient of marrying me off to poor Riva. The Purpose – Destiny, if you wish – which guides us all prevented that, however. Beldaran had been preparing for her marriage to Iron-grip since before she was born. Quite obviously, I hadn't been.

I resented my rejection, though. Isn't that idiotic? I'd been involved in a competition for a prize I didn't want, but when I lost the competition, I felt the sting of losing quite profoundly. I didn't even speak to my father for several weeks, and I was even terribly snippy with my sister.

Then Anrak came down into the Vale to fetch us. With the exception of an occasional Ulgo and a few messengers from King Algar, Anrak was perhaps the first outsider I'd ever met and certainly the first who ever showed any interest in me. I rather liked him, actually. Of course he *did* propose marriage to me, and a girl always has a soft spot in her heart for the young man who asks her for the first time. Anrak was an Alorn, with all that implies. He was big, burly, and bearded, and there was good-humored simplicity about him that I rather liked. I *didn't* like the way he always reeked of beer, however.

I was busy sulking in my Tree when he arrived, so we didn't even have time to get acquainted before he proposed. He came swaggering down the Vale one beautiful morning in early spring. My birds alerted me to his approach, so he didn't really surprise me when he came in under the branches of my Tree.

'Hello, up there,' he called to me.

I looked down from my perch at him. 'What do you want?' It wasn't really a very gracious greeting.

'I'm Anrak – Riva's cousin – and I came here to escort your sister to the Isle so Riva can marry her.'

That immediately put him in the camp of the enemy. 'Go away,' I told him bluntly.

'There's something I need to ask you first.'

'What?'

'Well, like I said, I'm Riva's cousin, and he and I usually do things together. We got drunk together for the first time, and visited a brothel together for the first time, and even both killed our first man in the same battle, so as you can see, we're fairly close.'

'So?'

'Well, Riva's going to marry your sister, and I thought it might be sort of nice if I got married, too. What do you say?'

'Are you proposing marriage to me?'

'I thought I said that. This is the first time I've ever proposed to anybody, so I probably didn't do a very good job. What do you think?'

'I think you're insane. We don't even know each other.'

'There'll be plenty of time for us to get to know each other after the ceremony. Well, yes or no?'

You couldn't fault Anrak's directness. Here was a man who got right down to the point. I laughed at him, and he looked just a bit injured by that. 'What's so funny?' he demanded in a hurt tone of voice.

'You are. Do you actually think I'd marry a complete stranger? One who looks like a rat hiding in a clump of bushes?'

'What's that supposed to mean?'

'You've got hair growing all over your face.'

'That's my beard. All Alorns wear beards.'

'Could that possibly be because Alorns haven't invented the razor yet? Tell me, Anrak, have your people come up with the idea of the wheel yet? Have you discovered fire, by any chance?'

'You don't have to be insulting. Just say yes or no.'

'All right. *No!* Was there any part of that you didn't understand?' Then I warmed to my subject. 'The whole notion is absurd,' I told him. 'I don't know you, and I don't like you. I don't know your cousin, and I don't like him either. As a matter of fact, I don't like your entire stinking race. All the misery in my life's been caused by Alorns. Did you *really* think I'd actually marry one? You'd better

50

get away from me, Anrak, because if you don't, I'll turn you into a toad.'

'You don't have to get nasty. You're no prize yourself, you know.'

I won't repeat what I said to him then – this document might just fall into the hands of children. I spoke at some length about his parents, his extended family, his race, his ancestors and probable descendants. I drew rather heavily on uncle Beldin's vocabulary in the process, and Anrak frequently looked startled at the extent of my command of the more colorful side of language.

'Well,' he said, 'if that's the way you feel about it, there's not much point in our continuing this conversation, is there?' And then he rather huffily turned and strode back up the Vale, muttering to himself.

Poor Anrak. I was feeling a towering resentment over the fact that some unknown Alorn was going to take my sister away from me, and so he had the privilege of receiving the full weight of my displeasure. Moreover, mother'd strongly advised me to steer clear of any lasting entanglements at this stage of my life. Adolescent girls have glandular problems that sometimes lead them to make serious mistakes.

Why don't we just let it go at that?

I had absolutely no intention of going to the Isle of the Winds to witness this obscene ceremony. If Beldaran wanted to marry this Alorn butcher, she was going to have to do it without my blessing – or my presence.

When they were ready to leave, however, my sister came down to my Tree and 'persuaded' me to change my mind. Despite that sweet exterior that deceived everyone else, my sister Beldaran could be absolutely ruthless when she wanted something. She knew me better than anyone else in the world did – or could – so she knew exactly where all my soft spots were. To begin with, she spoke to me exclusively in 'twin', a language I'd almost forgotten. There were subtleties in 'twin' – mostly of Beldaran's devising -- that no linguist, even the most gifted, could ever unravel, and most of them stressed her dominant position. Beldaran was accustomed to giving me orders, and I was accustomed to obeying. Her 'persuasion' in this situation was, to put it honestly, brutal. She reminded me of every time in our lives when we'd been particularly close, and she cast those reminders in a past tense peculiar to our private tongue that would more or less translate into 'never again', or 'over and done

51

with'. She had me in tears within five minutes and in utter anguish within ten. 'Stop!' I cried out finally, unable to bear the implicit threat of a permanent severing of all contact any longer.

'You'll come with me then?' she asked, reverting to ordinary speech.

'Yes! Yes! Yes! But please stop!'

'I'm so happy about your decision, Pol,' she said, embracing me warmly. Then she actually apologized for what she'd just done to me. Why not? She'd just won, so she could afford to be graceful about the whole thing.

I was beaten, and I knew it. I wasn't even particularly surprised to discover when Beldaran and I returned to father's tower that she'd already packed for me. She'd known all along just how things would turn out.

We set out the next morning. It took us several weeks to reach Muros, since we traveled on foot.

Beldaran and I were both uneasy in Muros, since we'd never really been around that many people before. Although I've changed my position a great deal since then, at first I found Sendars to be a noisy people, and they seemed to me to have a positive obsession with buying and selling that was almost laughable.

Anrak left us at Muros to go on ahead to advise Riva that we were coming. We hired a carriage, and the four of us, father, uncle Beldin, Beldaran and I rode the rest of the way to Camaar. Frankly, I'd have rather walked. The stubby ponies drawing the carriage didn't really move very fast, and the wheels of the carriage seemed to find every single rock and rut in the road. Riding in carriages didn't really become pleasant until some clever fellow came up with a way to install springs in them.

Camaar was even more crowded with people than Muros had been. We took some rooms in a Sendarian inn and settled down to wait for Riva's arrival. I found it rather disconcerting to see buildings every time I looked out the window. Sendars appeared to have a kind of revulsion to open spaces. They always seem to want to 'civilize' everything.

The innkeeper's wife, a plump, motherly little woman, seemed bent on 'civilizing' me as well. She kept offering me the use of the bath-house, for one thing. She rather delicately suggested that I didn't smell very sweet.

I shrugged off her suggestions. 'It's a waste of time,' I told her. 'I'll only get dirty again. The next time it rains, I'll go outside. That should take the smell and the worst of the dirt off me.'

She also offered me a comb and a brush – which I also refused. I wasn't going to let the Alorn who'd stolen my sister away from me get some idea that I was taking any pains to make myself presentable for *his* sake.

The nosey innkeeper's wife then went so far as to suggest a visit to a dressmaker. *I* wasn't particularly impressed by the fact that we'd shortly be entertaining a king, but *she* was.

'What's wrong with what I'm wearing?' I asked her pugnaciously.

'Different occasions require different clothing, dear,' she replied.

'Foolishness,' I said. 'I'll get a new smock when this one wears out.'

I think she gave up at that point. I'm sure she thought I was incorrigibly 'woodsy', one of those unfortunates who've never received the benefits of civilization.

And then Anrak brought Riva to our rooms. I'll grant that he was physically impressive. I don't know that I've ever seen anyone – except the other men in his family – quite so tall. He had blue eyes and a black beard, and I hated him. He muttered a brief greeting to my father, and then he sat down to look at Beldaran.

Beldaran looked right back.

It was probably the most painful afternoon I'd spent in my entire life up until then. I'd hoped that Riva would be more like his cousin, Anrak, blurting out things that would offend my sister, but the idiot wouldn't say anything! All he could do was look at her with that adoring expression on his face, and Beldaran was almost as bad in her obvious adoration of him.

I was definitely fighting a rear-guard action here.

We all sat in absolute silence watching them adore each other, and every moment was like a knife in my heart. I'd lost my sister, there wasn't much question about that. I wasn't going to give either of them the satisfaction of seeing me bleed openly, however, so I did all of my bleeding inside. It was quite obvious that the separation of Beldaran and me which had begun before we were ever born was now complete, and I wanted to die.

Finally, when it was almost evening, my last hope died, and I felt tears burning my eyes.

Rather oddly – I hadn't been exactly polite to him – it was father who rescued me. He came over and took my hand. 'Why don't we take a little walk, Pol?' he suggested gently. Despite my suffering, his compassion startled me. He was the last one in the world I'd have expected *that* from. My father *does* surprise me now and then.

He led me from the room, and I noticed as we left that Beldaran didn't even take her eyes off Riva's face as I went away. That was the final blow, I think.

Father took me down the hallway to the little balcony at the far end, and we went outside, closing the door behind us.

I tried my very best to keep my sense of loss under control. 'Well,' I said in my most matter-of-fact way, 'I guess that settles that, doesn't it?'

Father murmured some platitudes about destiny, but I wasn't really listening to him. Destiny be hanged! I'd just lost my sister! Finally, I couldn't hold it in any longer. With a wail I threw my arms around his neck and buried my face in his chest, weeping uncontrollably.

That went on for quite some time until I'd finally wept myself out. Then I got my composure back. I decided that I wouldn't *ever* let Riva or Beldaran see me suffering, *and*, moreover, that I'd take some positive steps to show them that I really didn't care that my sister was willingly deserting me. I questioned father about some things that wouldn't have concerned me before – baths, dress-makers, combs, and the like. I'd show my sister how little I really cared. If *I* was suffering, I'd make sure that *she* suffered too.

I took particular pains with my bath. In my eyes this was a sort of funeral – mine – and it was only proper that I should look my best when they laid me out. My chewed off fingernails gave me a bit of concern at first, but then I remembered our gift. I concentrated on my nails and then said, 'Grow.'

And that took care of that.

Then I luxuriated for almost an hour in my bath. I wanted to soak off all the accumulated dirt, certainly, but I was surprised to discover that bathing *felt* good.

When I climbed out of the barrel-like wooden tub, I toweled myself down, put on a robe, and sat down to deal with my hair. It wasn't easy. My hair hadn't been washed since the last rainstorm in the Vale, and it was so tangled and snarled that I almost gave up on it. It took a lot of effort, and it was very painful, but at last I managed to get it to the point where I could pull a comb through it.

I didn't sleep very much that night, and I arose early to continue my preparations. I sat down in front of a mirror made of polished brass and looked at my reflection rather critically. I was somewhat astonished to discover that I wasn't nearly as ugly as I'd always imagined. As a matter of fact, I was quite pretty.

'Don't let it go your head, Pol,' mother's voice told me. 'You didn't actually think that I'd give birth to an ugly daughter, did you?'

54

'I've always thought I was hideous, mother,' I said.

'You were wrong. Don't overdo it with your hair. The white lock doesn't need any help to make you pretty.'

The blue dress father'd obtained for me was really quite nice. I put it on and looked at myself in the mirror. I was just a little embarrassed by what I saw. There wasn't any question that I was a woman. I'd been more or less ignoring certain evidences of my femaleness, but that was no longer really possible. The dress positively screamed the fact. There *was* a problem with the shoes, though. They had pointed toes and medium heels, and they hurt my feet. I wasn't used to shoes, but I gritted my teeth and endured them.

The more I looked in my mirror, the more I liked what I saw. The worm I'd always been had just turned into a butterfly. I still hated Riva, but my hatred softened just a bit. He hadn't intended it, but it was *his* arrival in Camaar that had revealed to me what I *really* was.

I was pretty! I was something even beyond pretty!

'What an amazing thing,' I murmured.

My victory was made complete that morning when I demurely – I'd practiced for a couple of hours – entered the room where the others were sitting. I'd more or less taken the reactions of Riva and Anrak for granted. Uneducated though I was, I knew how they'd view me in my altered condition. The face I looked at was Beldaran's.

I'd rather hoped to see just a twinge of envy there, but I should have known better. Her expression was just a little quizzical, and when she spoke, it was in 'twin'. What passed between us was intensely private. 'Well, finally,' was all she said, and then she embraced me warmly.

CHAPTER 4

I'll admit that I was a little disappointed that my sister didn't turn green with envy, but no triumph is ever total, is it?

Anrak's face grew melancholy, and he sighed. He explained to Riva how much he regretted not having pressed his suit.

Isn't that an absurd turn of phrase? It makes Anrak sound like a laundress with a hot flat-iron.

Sorry.

His rueful admission made my morning complete, and it opened whole new vistas to me. Being adored is a rather pleasant way to pass the time, wouldn't you say? Not only that, both Anrak and his cousin automatically ennobled me by calling me 'Lady Polgara', and that has a rather nice ring to it.

Then Riva's cousin came up with a number of profound misconceptions about what father calls our 'talent'. He clearly believed that my transformation had been the result of magic and even went so far as to suggest that I could be in two places – and times – simultaneously. I rather gently tweaked his beard on that score. I found myself growing fonder and fonder of Anrak. He said such nice things about me.

It was perhaps noon by the time we went down to the harbor to board Riva's ship. Beldaran and I had never seen the sea before, nor a ship, for that matter, and we both were a little apprehensive about our upcoming voyage. The weather was fine, though there were all those waves out there. I'm not sure exactly what we'd expected, but all the ponds in the Vale had absolutely flat surfaces, so we weren't prepared for waves. There was also a peculiar odor about the sea. It had a sharp tang to it that overlaid the more disgusting smells that characterize every harbor in the world. I suppose it's human nature to dispose of garbage in the simplest way possible, but it struck me as improvident to dump it into a body of water that'll return it to you on each incoming tide.

The ship seemed quite large to me, but I found the cabins below decks tiny and cramped, and everything seemed to be coated with a black, greasy substance. 'What's that smeared all over the walls?' I asked uncle Beldin.

'Tar,' he replied with an indifferent shrug. 'It helps to keep the water out.'

That sort of alarmed me. 'The boat's made of wood,' I said. 'Isn't wood supposed to float?'

'Only when it's one solid piece, Pol. The sea wants to have a level surface, and empty places under that surface offend it, so it tries to seep in and fill up those spaces. And the tar keeps the wood from rotting.'

'I don't like it.'

'I'm sure your opinion hurts its feelings.'

'You always have to try to be clever, don't you, uncle?'

'Look upon it as a character defect if you like.' He grinned.

After Beldaran and I had deposited our belongings in our tiny cabin, we went back up on deck. Riva's sailors were making the vessel ready to depart. They were burly, bearded men, many of whom were stripped to the waist. All that bare skin made me just a little jumpy for some reason.

There seemed to be ropes everywhere – an impossible snarl passing through pulleys and running upward in an incomprehensible tangle. The sailors untied the ropes that held the ship up against the wharf, and then pushed us a ways out and took their places at the oars. One ruffian with an evil face sat cross-legged in the stern and began to pound rhythmically on a hide-topped drum to set the pace for the oarsmen. The ship moved slowly out through the crowded harbor toward the open sea.

Once we were past the breakwater, the sailors pulled in their oars and began hauling on various ropes. I still don't fully understand exactly how a sailor can tell one rope from another, but Riva's men seemed to know what they were doing. Large horizontal beams with tightly rolled canvas attached to them crept up the masts as the chanting sailors pulled on the ropes in a unison set by the rhythm of the chant. The pulleys squealed as the canvas-bearing beams rose to the tops of the masts. Then aloft, other sailors, agile as monkeys, untied the canvas and let it roll down. The sails hung slack for a few moments. Then a breeze caught them and they bellied out with a booming sound.

The ship rolled slightly to one side, and then it began to move. Water foamed as the bow of the ship cut into the waves, and the breeze of our passage touched my face and tossed my hair. The waves were not high enough to be alarming, and Riva's ship mounted each one with stately pace and then majestically ran down the far side.

I absolutely loved it!

The ship and the sea became unified, and there was a music to that unification, a music of groaning timbers, creaking ropes, and booming sails. We moved out across the sun-touched waves with the music of the sea filling our ears.

I've frequently made light, disparaging remarks about Alorns and their fascination with the sea, but there's a kind of holiness in it – almost as if true sailors have a different God. They don't just love the sea; they worship it, and in my heart I know why.

'I can't see the land any more!' Beldaran exclaimed that evening, looking apprehensively sternward.

'You aren't supposed to, love,' Riva told her gently. 'We'd never get home if we tried to keep the Sendarian coast in plain sight the whole way to the Isle.'

The sunset on the sea ahead of us was glorious, and when the moon rose, she built a broad, gleaming highway across the glowing surface of the night-dark sea.

All bemused by the beauty around me, I sat down on a convenient barrel, crossed my arms on the rail, and set my chin on them to drink in the sense of the sea. I remained in that reverie all through the night, and the sea claimed me as her own. My childhood had been troubled, filled with resentments and a painful, almost mortifying sense of my own inadequacy. The sea calmed those troubled feelings with her serene immensity. Did it really matter that one little girl with skinned knees felt all pouty because the world didn't genuflect every time she walked by? The sea didn't seem to think so, and increasingly as the hours passed, neither did I.

The dawn announced her coming with a pale light just above the sternward horizon. The world seemed filled with a grey, shadowless luminescence, and the dark water became as molten silver. When the sun, made ruddy by the sea mist, mounted above the eastern

58

horizon, he filled my heart with a wonder such as I'd never known before.

But the sea wasn't done with me yet. Her face was like molten glass, and then something immense swelled up from beneath without actually breaking the surface. The resulting surge was untouched by foam or silly little splashings. It was far too profound for that kind of childish display. I felt a sudden sense of superstitious terror. The mythology of the world positively teems with sea-monsters, and Beltira and Belkira had amused Beldaran and me when we were very young by telling us stories, usually of Alorn origin. No sea-going people will ever pass up the chance to talk about sea-monsters, after all.

'What's that?' I asked a sleepy-eyed sailor who'd just come up on deck, and I pointed at the disturbance in the water.

He squinted over the rail. 'Oh,' he said in an off-hand way, 'those be whales, my Lady.'

'Whales?'

'Big fish, my Lady.' He squinted at the sea again. 'It's the time of year when they flock together. I'd guess that there be quite a few down there.'

'Is that why the water's bulging up like that – because there are so many?'

'No, my Lady. One whale all by himself can make the sea heave that way.'

I was sure he was exaggerating, but then an enormous dark form erupted from the water like a mountain aborning. I couldn't believe what I was seeing! Nothing alive could be that big!

Then he crashed with a boom back into the sea, sending great sheets of water in all directions, and he slapped his tail down against the surface with another huge noise and disappeared.

Then he jumped again, and again.

He was playing!

And then he was not alone. Other whales also came surging up out of the sea to leap and play in the morning sun like a crowd of overgrown children frolicking in a play yard.

And they laughed! Their voices were high-pitched, but they were not squeaky. There was a profound depth to them and a kind of yearning.

One of them – I think it was that first one – rolled over on his side to look at me with one huge eye. There were wrinkles around that eye as if he were very, very old, and there was a profound wisdom there.

And then he winked at me and plunged back into the depths.

No matter how long I live, I'll always remember that strange meeting. In some obscure way it's shaped my entire view of the world and of everything that's hidden beneath the surface of ordinary reality. That single event made the tedious journey from the Vale and this voyage worth while – and more.

We were another two days reaching Riva, and I spent those days filled with the wonder of the sea and of those creatures she supported as a mother supports her children.

The Isle of the Winds is a bleak, inhospitable place that rises out of a usually storm-tossed sea, and when viewed from the water the city seems as unwelcoming as the rock upon which it's built. It rises steeply from the harbor in a series of narrow terraces, and each row of houses stands at the brink of the terrace upon which it's built. The seaward walls of those houses are thick and windowless, and battlements surmount them. In effect this makes the city little more than a series of impenetrable walls rising one after another to the Citadel which broods down over the entire community. Whole races could hurl themselves at Riva with no more effect than the waves have upon the cliffs of the Isle itself. As the Master said, 'All the tides of Angarak cannot prevail against it,' and when you add the Cherek fleet patrolling the waters just off the coast, you have the potential for the extinction of any race foolish enough even to contemplate the notion of making war on the Rivans. Torak's crazy, but he's not *that* crazy.

Beldaran and I had taken some rather special pains to make ourselves presentable that morning. Beldaran was to be Queen of Riva, and she wanted to make a good impression on her future subjects. I was *not* going to be the queen, and my target was a certain specific segment of the population. I was rather carefully taking aim at all the young men, and I think I hit most of them. What a glorious thing it is to be universally adored! My father's slightly worried expression made my morning complete.

'*Don't let it go to your head, Polgara,*' mother's voice cautioned me. '*What you're seeing on all those vacant faces isn't love. Young males of all species have urges that they can't really control. In their eyes you're not a person; you're an object. You don't really want to be no more than a thing, do you?*'

The prospect of incipient thinghood put a slight damper on my enjoyment of the moment.

Traditionally, Rivans wear grey clothing. As a matter of fact, the other western races call them 'grey-cloaks'. Young people, however, tend to ignore the customs of their elders. Adolescent rebellion has been responsible for all manner of absurd costumes. The more ridiculous a certain fashion is, the more adolescents will cling to it. The young men crowding the edge of the wharf with yearning eyes put me in mind of a flower garden planted by someone with absolutely no sense of taste. There were doublets down there in hues I didn't even have names for, and some of those short jackets were varicolored, and the colors clashed hideously. Each of my worshipers, however, was absolutely convinced that his clothing was so splendid that no girl in her right mind could possibly resist him.

I felt an almost uncontrollable urge to burst out laughing. My father's concern about what he felt to be my fragile chastity was totally inappropriate. I wasn't going to surrender to some adolescent whose very appearance sent me off into gales of laughter.

After the sailors had snubbed up the mooring ropes, we disembarked and started up the stairs that lead from the harbor to Riva's Citadel. That series of stair-stepping walls that are part of the city's defenses were revealed as a part of the houses in which the Rivans lived. The houses seemed bleak on the outside, but I've since discovered that the interiors of those houses are places of beauty. In many ways they are like the Rivans themselves. All the beauty is on the inside. The streets of Riva are narrow and monotonously straight. I strongly suspect that Riva had been guided by Belar in the construction of the city. Everything about it has a defensive purpose.

There was a shallow courtyard surrounded by a massive wall at the top of the stairs. The size of the roughly squared-off stones in that wall startled me. The amount of sheer physical labor which had gone into the construction of the city was staggering. We entered the Citadel through a great iron-bound door, and I found the interior of my sister's new home depressingly bleak. It took us quite some time to reach our quarters. Beldaran and I were temporarily ensconced in a quite pleasant set of rooms. I say temporarily because Beldaran would soon be moving into the royal apartment.

'You're having fun, aren't you, Pol?' My sister asked me once we were alone. Her voice seemed just a bit wistful, and she spoke in 'twin'.

'I don't exactly follow you,' I replied.

'Now that you've decided to be pretty, you've got every young man you come across fawning all over you.'

'You've always been pretty, Beldaran,' I reminded her.

She sighed a rather sweet little sigh. 'I know,' she said, 'but I never got the chance to play with it. What's it like to have everybody around you dumbstruck with adoration?'

'I rather like it.' I laughed. 'They're all very foolish, though. If you're hungry for adoration, get yourself a puppy.'

She also laughed. 'I wonder if all young men are as silly as these Rivans are. I'd sort of hate to be the queen of the idiots.'

'Mother says that it's more or less universal,' I told her, 'and it's not just humans. Wolves are the same way, and so are rabbits. She says that all young males have what she calls "urges". The Gods arranged it that way, I guess – so that there'll always be a lot of puppies.'

'That's a depressing turn of phrase, Pol. It sort of implies that all I'm here for is to produce babies.'

'Mother says that passes after a while. I guess it's supposed to be fun, so enjoy it while you can.'

She blushed.

'Now, if you'll excuse me, I think I'll go break a few hearts.'

There was a large hall near the center of the Citadel that seemed to be where the members of Riva's court gathered for fun and games. The throne room was reserved for more formal occasions, and unlike the rowdy throne room in Val Alorn where the Chereks mixed business and pleasure, Riva's Citadel had separate places for separate activities. The door to the hall was open, and I peeked around the edge of that door to assess my competition.

Rivan girls, like all Alorns, tend to be blonde, and I saw an immediate advantage there. My dark hair would make me stand out in the middle of what appeared to be a wheat field. The young people in that large room were doing young-people things, flirting, showing off, and the like. I waited, biding my time until one of those lulls in the general babble hushed the room. Somehow I instinctively knew that the hush would eventually come. *That* was when I'd make my appearance. Entrances are *very* important in these circumstances.

I finally got a little tired of waiting. '*Make them be still, mother,*' I pleaded with the presence that had been in my mind since before I was born.

'*Oh, dear,*' mother sighed.

Then a hush fell over the brightly dressed throng.

I'd considered the notion of some kind of fanfare, but that might have been just a trifle ostentatious. Instead, I simply stepped into the precise center of the doorway and stopped, waiting for them all to notice me. My blue gown was rather nice, so I was sure I'd attract attention.

I think mother – or possibly Aldur – had fallen in with my scheme. There was a fairly large window high in the wall opposite the door and after I'd stood in the doorway for a moment, the sun broke through the clouds which almost perpetually veiled the Isle, and its light came through the window to fall full upon me.

That was even better than a fanfare. I stood regally in the middle of that sun-flooded doorway, letting all the eyes in the room feast themselves on me.

Dear Gods, that was enjoyable!

All right, it was vain and a little silly. So what? I was young.

There was a small group of musicians at the far end of the room – I'd hardly call them an orchestra – and they struck up a tune as I regally entered the hall. As I'd rather hoped they would, most of the young men began to move in my general direction, each of them mentally refining some opening remark that he hoped would get my attention. You have no idea how strained and inane some of those remarks were. After about the fourth time someone compared my eyes to a spring sky, I began to realize that unrestrained creativity was not exactly rampant among adolescents. It somehow seemed that I was adrift in a sea of platitudes. I got compared to summer days, starry nights, and dark, snow-capped peaks – a rather obvious reference to the white streak in my hair. They swarmed around me like a flock of sparrows, elbowing each other out of the way. The Rivan girls began to look a little sulky about the whole business.

A young blond fellow in a green doublet – quite handsome, actually – pushed his way to the forefront of my suitors and bowed rather floridly. 'Ah,' he said, 'Lady Polgara, I presume?' *That* was a novel approach. He gave me a rather sly smile. 'Tedious, isn't it? All this empty conversation, I mean. How much time can one *really* spend talking about the weather?'

That earned him a few dark looks as a number of my suitors hastily revised their opening remarks.

'I'm certain you and I can find something more pleasant to talk about,' he continued smoothly, 'politics, theology, or current fashion, if you'd like.' He actually seemed to have a mind.

'We might want to think about that a bit,' I countered. 'What's your name?'

He slapped his forehead in feigned chagrin. 'How *stupid* of me,'

63

he said. 'How could I possibly have been so absent-minded?' He sighed theatrically. 'It's a failing of mine, I'm afraid. Sometimes I think I need a keeper.' He gave me a sly look. 'Would *you* care to volunteer for the post?' he offered.

'You still haven't told me your name,' I reminded him, ignoring his offer.

'You really shouldn't let me get sidetracked that way, Lady Polgara,' he chided gently. 'Before I forget again, I'm Kamion, an incipient baron – just as soon as my childless uncle dies. Where were we?'

I'll confess that I liked him. His approach had some genuine originality, and his little-boy manner was appealing. I realized at that point that this whole business might just be a bit more challenging than I'd expected. Not *all* of my suitors were freshly weaned puppies. *Some* of them even had brains. That was rather refreshing. After all, if you've seen one furiously wagging tail, you've seen them all. I actually experienced a slight twinge of disappointment when the swarming suitors swept Kamion away.

The platitudes came thick and fast after that, but nobody chose to talk about the weather for some reason.

The Rivan girls grew sulkier and sulkier, and just to tweak them a little more I dispensed a number of dazzlingly regal smiles. My suitors found those smiles absolutely enchanting; the girls didn't.

The afternoon progressed in a *very* satisfactory way, and then the musicians – lutanists for the most part – struck up a new tune, and a thin, weedy young man dressed all in black and wearing a studiously melancholy expression pushed his way forward. 'Would you care to dance, Lady Polgara?' he asked me in a broken-hearted tone. He bowed. 'Permit me to introduce myself. I'm Merot the poet, and I might be able to compose a sonnet for you while we dance.'

'I'm very sorry, my lord Merot,' I replied, 'but I've lived in isolation, so I don't really know how to dance.' It wasn't true, of course. Beldaran and I had been inventing dances since we were children, but I was fairly certain that the rhythm of a meadowlark's song might be just a little difficult for this self-proclaimed poet to comprehend.

Merot was obviously a poseur, but so were most of the others. He seemed to think that his carefully manicured short black beard and tragic expression made him irresistible to all the girls. *I* didn't have too much trouble resisting him, though. Maybe it was his rancid breath that made me keep my distance.

'Ah,' he responded to my confession of terpsichorean ineptitude, 'what a pity.' Then his gloomy eyes brightened. 'I could give you private lessons, if you'd like.'

'We might discuss that sometime,' I parried, still staying back from that foul breath.

'Might I offer you a poem then?' he suggested.

'That would be nice.'

What a mistake *that* was! Merot assumed an oratorical stance and began to recite in a tediously slow manner with that gloomy voice of his. He spoke as if the fate of the universe hung on his every word. I didn't notice the sun darken, though, or feel any earthquakes.

He went on and on and *on*, and his *pose* as a poet was much, much better than his actual verse. Of course I wasn't really acquainted with poetry at that stage of my life, but it seemed to me that lingering lovingly over every single syllable is not really the best way to keep the attention of your audience. At first I found him tedious. Tedious descended rather rapidly into boring, and boring disintegrated into near despair. I rather theatrically rolled my eyes upward. Several of my suitors caught the hint immediately and moved in to rescue me.

Merot was still standing in the same place reciting as the crowd flowed away from him. He might have loved me, but he obviously loved himself more.

The other ladies in the room were growing increasingly discontented, I noticed. Despite their fairly obvious expressions of invitation, the dance floor remained deserted. My suitors evidently didn't want to be distracted. Quite a few of the ladies pled headaches and quietly left the room. It might have been my imagination, but after they left I seemed to hear a gnawing sound – a sound that was remarkably like the sound of someone eating her own liver. There was a certain musical quality about that to my ears.

Then, as evening began to descend upon the Isle of the Winds, Taygon came up to join me. Taygon did *not* have to elbow his way through the crowd. Everybody got out of his way. He was big. He was burly. He was garbed in chain mail. He had a huge blond beard. He wore a sword. 'Lady Polgara!' he said in a booming voice, 'I've been looking for you!'

That was ominous. 'I'm Taygon the Warrior. I'm sure you've heard of me. My deeds are renowned throughout the length and breadth of Aloria.'

'I'm terribly sorry, Lord Taygon,' I apologized in mock confusion. 'I grew up in almost total isolation, so I don't really know what's going on in the world – besides, I'm just a silly girl.'

65

'I'll kill any man who says so!' He glared at the others threat-eningly.

How on earth was I going to deal with this barbarian? Then I made a mistake – one of several that day. 'Ah –' I floundered, 'since I've been so out of touch, I'd be enthralled to hear of some of your exploits.'

Please be a little more forgiving. I *was* an absolute novice that day, after all.

'My pleasure, Lady Polgara.' It might have been *his* pleasure, but it certainly wasn't *mine*. Did he *have* to be so graphic? As he spoke, I suddenly found myself awash in a sea of blood and looking out at an entire mountain range of loose brains. Brightly colored entrails snarled around my feet, and disconnected extremities floated by – twitching.

It was only by a supreme act of will that I was able to keep from throwing up all over the front of his chain-mail shirt.

Then dear, dear Kamion rescued me. 'Excuse me, Sir Taygon, but Lady Polgara's sister, our future queen, requires her presence. I know that we'll all be made desolate by her absence, but a royal command cannot be disobeyed. I'm certain that a warrior of your vast experience can understand the importance of obeying orders.'

'Oh, of course, Kamion,' Taygon replied automatically. He bowed clumsily to me. 'You must hurry, Lady Polgara. We mustn't keep the Queen waiting.'

I curtsied to him, not trusting myself to answer. Then Kamion took my elbow and guided me away.

'When you come back,' Taygon called after me, 'I'll tell you about how I disemboweled an offensive Arend.'

'I can hardly wait,' I said rather weakly over my shoulder.

'Do you *really* want to hear about it, my Lady?' Kamion murmured to me.

'Frankly, my dear Kamion, I'd sooner take poison.'

He laughed. 'I rather thought you might feel that way about it. Your face was definitely taking on a slight greenish cast there toward the end.'

Oh, Kamion was smooth. I began to admire him almost in spite of myself.

'Well?' my sister asked when I rejoined her, 'how was it?'

'Just wonderful!' I replied exultantly. 'They were all smitten with me. I was the absolute center of attention.'

'You've got a cruel streak in you, Polgara.'

'What's that supposed to mean?'

'I've been cooped up in here all afternoon, and you've come back to rub my nose in all your conquests.'

'Would *I* do that?' I asked her archly.

'Of course you would. I can see you absolutely running through the halls to get back so that you could gloat.' Then she laughed. 'I'm sorry, Pol. I couldn't resist that.'

'You're above all that now, Beldaran,' I told her. 'You've already caught the man you want. I'm still fishing.'

'I'm not sure that I'm the one who really caught him. There were a lot of other people involved in that fishing trip, too: Aldur, father – mother, too, probably. The notion of an arranged marriage is just a little humiliating.'

'You *do* love Riva, don't you?'

'Of course. It's humiliating all the same. All right, tell me what happened. I want every single detail.'

I described my afternoon, and my sister and I spent a great deal of our time laughing. Even as I had, Beldaran particularly enjoyed the reaction of the Rivan girls.

That afternoon was my last unsupervised excursion into the untamed jungle of the adolescent mating ritual. From then on, father sat scowling in a spot where everybody could see him. It wasn't really necessary, of course, but there was no way that father could know that mother was already keeping an eye on me. His presence *did* set certain limits on the enthusiasm of my suitors, and I was of two minds about that. None of my suitors were likely to go *too* far with him sitting there, but I was fairly sure that I could take care of myself, and father's insistence on being present robbed me of the chance to find out if I could.

For some reason Kamion made father particularly nervous, and I couldn't understand exactly why. Kamion had exquisite manners, and he never once did anything at all offensive. Why did my aged sire dislike him so much?

Got you that time, didn't I, Old Wolf?

Then King Cherek and his sons, Dras Bull-neck and Algar Fleet-foot, arrived for the wedding, and things began to get just a bit more serious. Despite the way Beldaran and Riva felt about each other, my sister had been right. Theirs was an arranged marriage. The possibility that my father might *also* decide to arrange one for me

– just to protect me from all those fawning suitors – raised its ugly head. There was in those days – probably even still existing – the idea that women are intellectually inferior to men. Men did – and many still do – automatically assume that women are empty-headed ninnies who'll fall prey to the first glib young man who comes along with certain ideas in his mind. The result, of course, is the virtual imprisonment of almost all women of a certain rank. What my father and all those other primitives can't seem to realize is that we'll resent that imprisonment and go to almost any lengths to circumvent it. That might help to explain why so many girls become involved with inappropriate young men. In most cases the character of the young man doesn't make a jot of difference. The girl in question is driven by a desire to show them that she *can* do it, rather than by empty-headed lust.

That's frequently the reason for so many arranged marriages. The father marries his daughter off as soon as possible to 'protect' her. After she marries, any dalliances she chooses to take up to amuse herself are her husband's problem.

The possibility that father might choose to shackle me to either Dras or Algar made me distinctly uneasy for a while.

CHAPTER 5

For some reason, mother had always been a bit vague about father's now-famous trip to Mallorea, and I felt that I might need some information in order to counter any absurd notions that could come popping into his head. I went looking for uncle Beldin.

I found him high in one of the towers of the citadel. He was nursing a tankard of beer and looking out at the sullen black waves surging under a threatening sky. I broached the subject directly. 'How much can you tell me about father's expedition to Mallorea?' I demanded.

'Not much,' he replied. 'I wasn't in the Vale when Cherek and the boys came to fetch him.'

'You *do* know what happened, though, don't you?'

'The twins told me,' he said, shrugging. 'As I understand it, Cherek and the boys came slogging through the snow in the dead of winter with some kind of half-wit notion that the priests of Belar had dredged up out of what the Alorns call "the auguries". Sometimes Chereks can be awfully gullible.'

'What are auguries?' I asked him.

'Supposedly a way to foretell the future. The priests of Belar all get roaring drunk, and then they gut a sheep and fondle his entrails. The Alorns have a quaint belief that sheep-guts can tell you what's going to happen next week. I'd rather strongly suspect that the ale plays a large part in the ceremony. Alorns are enthusiastic about it. I don't imagine the sheep care much for the idea, though.'

'Who could possibly be gullible enough to believe something that absurd?'

'Your incipient brother-in-law, for one.'

'Oh dear. Poor Beldaran.'

'Why this sudden interest in quaint Alorn customs, Pol?' he asked.

'It occurred to me that father might want to get me out of his hair by marrying me off to Algar or Dras, and I don't think I'm ready for marriage just yet. I want to come up with some arguments to nip that in the bud.'

He laughed. 'Not to worry, Pol,' he told me. 'Belgarath's a little strange sometimes, but he's not *that* strange. Besides, the Master wouldn't let him get away with it. I'm fairly sure he has other plans for you.'

As it turned out, that proved to be a gross understatement. Although *I* was fairly certain that there was no Alorn husband in my immediate future, Dras and Algar hadn't heard the news as yet, so a pair of Alorn kings joined my crowd of suitors.

Dras was the more aggressive of the two, since he was the eldest. I found his attentions something of a relief. He was direct and honest, unlike the adolescent Rivans with their clumsily contrived conversational ploys. Dras already knew who he was, so he wasn't inventing it as he went along. 'Well,' he said to me a couple of days after he, his father, and his brother had arrived, 'what do you think? Should I ask my father to speak with yours?'

'About what, your Majesty?' I feigned innocence.

'Our wedding, of course. You and I could get married at the same time your sister and Riva do.'

His approach didn't leave me much maneuvering room. 'Isn't this all coming just a little fast, Dras?'

'Why waste time, Polgara? The marriage would be advantageous to both of us. You get to be a queen and I get a wife. Then we can both get all this courting nonsense over with.'

That didn't go down too well. I rather resented his off-hand dismissal of my entertainment. I was having fun, and he was trying to take all the adventure out of it. 'Let me think it over, Dras,' I suggested.

'Of course,' he said generously. 'Take all the time you want, Pol. How about this afternoon?'

Can you believe that I didn't even laugh in his face?

Algar's courtship was *very* trying for me. The niceties of the courtship ritual require the female to respond to the overtures of the male. I've seen this again and again among my birds. It's always the male bird who has the bright plumage. He's supposed to strut and shake his colorful feathers while the female admires him.

Humans are much the same. The male shows off, and the female responds – but how can you possibly respond to someone who can go for days on end without saying a word? Algar was very intelligent, but he talked almost as much as a rock does. To be honest about it, I found his silence rather intriguing – and irritating at the same time. 'Don't you *ever* talk about the weather, Algar?' I asked him once in a fit of exasperation.

'What for?' he replied. He pointed at a window. 'It's right out there. Go look for yourself.'

You see what I mean about Algar?

I was of two minds about the double-pronged courtship of this pair of kings. They were huge men, both in terms of their physical size and their exalted rank. Their very presence kept my other suitors away. On the one hand, I resented that. I'd been having fun, and then they'd come along and spoiled it. On the other hand, though, their presence spared me hours of listening to the babble of assorted young men whose brains had been shut down by the various exotic substances coursing through their veins.

Cold logic – and mother's continued presence in my mind – advised me that this sojourn on the Isle of the Winds was a period of training preparing me for things to come. The fact that I was the daughter of 'Belgarath the Sorcerer' assured me that I'd be spending periods of my life at various royal courts. I'd need to know all the tricks those periods would inevitably involve. The inane, self-aggrandizing babble of my adolescent admirers taught me how to endure 'small talk' – *nobody* can talk smaller than an adolescent male on the prowl. Dras and Algar, their minds filled with the burdens of state, taught me about the serious matters that are going on while all those young butterflies are busy admiring themselves.

It was uncle Beldin who pointed out the obvious to my father, and then father had a word with King Cherek Bear-shoulders, advising him that I was *not* a candidate for the queenly throne of either Drasnia nor Algaria. That took some of the fun out of my little game, but I still had all those strutting young peacocks around to entertain me.

Then one morning as I was passing down the corridor toward the hall where I customarily held court, mother spoke *firmly* to me. *'Haven't you had about enough of this, Pol?'*

'I'm just passing the time, mother,' I told her.

'Don't waste the effort of trying to come up with lame excuses, Pol.

71

You've managed to put aside your fascination with being dirty. Now it's time to leave this other game behind as well.'

'Spoilsport.'

'That will do, Polgara.'

I sighed. *'Oh, all right.'* I wasn't really very gracious about it.

I decided that I needed one last triumph, though. I'd been playing the empty-headed charmer – little more than a *thing* in the eyes of my suitors. As mother had pointed out earlier, thinghood's rather degrading. Since I was going to leave all that behind, I thought it might be appropriate to let the other players in the game know just exactly who I *really* was. I loitered in the corridor considering options.

The easiest thing, of course, would have been a display of my 'talent'. I toyed with the notion of levitation. I was almost positive that even the braggart Taygon would get my point if I were to come floating into the hall about ten feet off the floor and trailing clouds of glory, but I dismissed the idea almost immediately. It was just *too* juvenile. I wanted them to realize that I was above them, but *really* –

Then I remembered something. Back in the Vale I'd frequently joined in the chorus of my birds, and I'd picked up certain tricks.

I entered the hall with a feigned show of pensiveness and drifted on to the far end to speak briefly with the musicians. The middle-aged lutanist who led the little group was delighted with the notion. I guess he was tired of being ignored by this flock of peacocks. He stepped to the front of the little platform where the musicians performed their unnoticed art. 'My lords and ladies,' he announced, 'the Lady Polgara has graciously agreed to favor us with a song.'

The applause was gratifying, but hardly well-educated. They'd never heard me sing before. As vapid as my suitors were, though, they'd have applauded me even if my voice came out like the raucous squawking of a crow.

It didn't, though.

My lutanist friend took up a melody that seemed to be of Arendish origin. It was set in a minor key, at any rate, and that seemed to fit in with the Arendish proclivity to view their lives in terms of classic tragedy. I didn't know the words to the song, so I improvised on the spot.

I enjoy singing – as Durnik may have noticed – and I began in a clear, girlish soprano. When we reached the second verse, however, I added harmony in a contralto voice. Singing in two voices at the same time is rather pleasant, but my audience wasn't really ready for it. There were assorted gasps and a lot of wide-eyed looks, and, more importantly, an absolute silence.

In the third verse I added a soaring coloratura that reached high above the soprano and modified the contralto harmony to accommodate that third voice.

Then, in the fourth verse, just to nail my point home, I divided my three voices and sang in counterpoint, not only musically but also linguistically. It was rather like a round, when each singer repeats her predecessor's first phrase a measure or so later to provide a complex harmony. I sang in three different voices, and each of those voices sang different words.

There were some very wild-eyed looks out there when I concluded my song. I gravely curtsied to my admirers, and then I slowly walked toward the door. For some reason my suitors didn't crowd around me this time. Isn't that odd? They opened a path for me instead, and *some* of their expressions verged on an almost religious exaltation.

Kamion, my urbane blond suitor, stood near the door. His expression was one of yearning regret as I passed out of his life forever. With exquisite grace he bowed to me as I went out from that place, never to return.

My sister's wedding was fast approaching, and, though we didn't talk about it, we both wanted to spend as much time with each other as possible. Since Beldaran was to be queen, a fair number of young Rivan ladies had attached themselves to her. After her wedding and subsequent coronation, they would become her ladies in waiting. I've noted that a king can be a remote, even isolated person, since his power is all the company he really needs. Queens, though, like other women, need company. I *also* noted that I made my sister's companions just a bit nervous. I suppose that's not too surprising. Beldaran's disposition was sunny, and mine wasn't, for one thing. Beldaran was about to be married to a man she loved to the point of distraction, and about all that lay in *my* future was the loss of a sister who'd always been the absolute center of my life. Moreover, Beldaran's companions had heard of my farewell performance for the adolescents, and sorcerers – sorceresses in my case – always seem to make people nervous.

Our major preoccupation at that time was Beldaran's wedding gown, and that brought Arell into our lives.

I'm certain that common Rivan name's familiar to Ce'Nedra.

*   *   *

Arell was a dressmaker. Most of the ladies who follow that profession are thin, wispy girls of a retiring nature. Arell wasn't like that at all. In some ways she was like a drill sergeant, issuing commands in a crisp, businesslike tone of voice that brooked no nonsense. She was, as they say, generously proportioned. Though she was only in her mid-thirties, she had what is called a matronly bosom. She was also a somewhat earthy lady. Since her alternate profession involved midwifery, there was very little in the functions of the human body that surprised her. In many ways she was much the same kind of person Queen Layla of Sendaria came to be.

There was a great deal of blushing going on as she spoke of the physical side of marriage while her flickering needle dipped in and out of the gleaming white fabric that was to become my sister's wedding gown. 'Men worry too much about that kind of thing,' she said on one occasion, biting off the thread on the hem of Beldaran's gown. 'No matter how big and important they seem in the outside world, they all turn into little boys in the bedroom. Be gentle with them, and don't *ever* laugh. You can laugh later, when you're alone.'

My sister and I didn't really need Arell's instruction. Mother had carefully explained the entire procedure to us. But how was Arell to know that?

'Does it hurt?' one of Beldaran's blonde companions asked apprehensively. That question always seems to come up in these discussions among young women.

Arell shrugged. 'Not too much, if you relax. Just don't tense up, and everything will be all right.'

I don't really need to go into much greater detail on that subject, do I?

Although our attention to the business of dressmaking kept our fingers busy, and Arell's clinical descriptions of intimacy occupied our minds, our little frenzy of dressmaking was actually a kind of farewell for my sister and me. We spoke to each other almost exclusively in 'twin', and we were seldom very far from each other. The apartment we shared was a bright, sun-filled set of rooms that overlooked a garden. The windows of our apartment were not on the seaward side of the Citadel, so they were not the defensively narrow embrasures that pierced the thick wall on the far side. Beldaran and I were probably not going to spend our time shooting arrows at the roses in the garden below, so our windows were broad and quite tall. When the prevailing clouds permitted, the sun shone very brightly into the rooms cluttered with scraps of fabric, bolts of cloth and those necessary wooden stands upon which our various gowns were to be hung. Without those stands, each of us would have been obliged to stand for days on end during the tedious business of fitting.

The walls of the Citadel are uniformly grey, both inside and out, and grey's a depressing color. Evidently some considerate Rivan lady had noticed that fact, so those apartments customarily used by ladies were softened by stout fabric hangings in various hues. The hangings in *our* apartment were alternately deep blue and rich gold, and the rough stone floor was softened here and there with golden lambskin rugs, a real blessing for those women who tend to go about barefooted when they're not in public. Ladies' shoes may *look* very nice, but they're not made for comfort. There was a balcony outside the main room in our apartment, and it had a stone bench built out from the balustrade at its outer edge. When the weather was fine, Beldaran and I spent most of our time out there, sitting very close.

We didn't speak often, since words aren't really necessary between twins. We *did*, however, remain in almost constant physical contact with each other. That's one of the characteristics of twinhood. If you have occasion to observe a set of twins, you'll probably notice that they touch each other far more often than is the case with untwinned brothers and sisters.

There was a deep sadness in our communion. Beldaran's marriage would inevitably draw us apart, and we both knew it. We'd always been one. Now we'd be two, and I think we both hated the concept of twoness.

When Beldaran's gown was finished to Arell's satisfaction, our mentor turned her attention to the rest of us. Since I was the sister of the bride, I came next.

'Strip,' Arell commanded me.

'*What?*' I exclaimed. I didn't really think I could be shocked, but I was wrong.

'Take off your clothes, Polgara,' she said quite firmly. 'I need to see what I'm working with.'

I actually blushed, but I did as she told me to.

She studied my near naked body with pursed lips and a speculative eye. 'Not too bad,' she observed.

That was hardly complimentary.

'You're lucky, Polgara,' she told me. 'Most girls your age are quite flat-chested. I think we might want to take advantage of that to draw attention away from the fact that you're just a little hippy.'

'I'm *what*?' I exclaimed.

'You were built to bear children, Polgara. It's useful, but it makes your clothes hang all wrong.'

'Is she telling me the truth?' I asked Beldaran, speaking in 'twin' so that Arell couldn't understand me.

'You *are* sort of round down there, Pol,' Beldaran replied. Then she grinned a naughty little grin at me. 'If we cut your gown low enough in the back, we could show off the dimples on your bottom.'

'I'll get you for that, Beldaran,' I threatened.

'No you won't, Pol,' she said, stealing a favorite joke from uncle Beldin and our father. 'You're just saying that to make me feel better.'

My gown was blue, and Arell's design left my shoulders and a significant part of my upper torso bare. It was trimmed with snowy lace, and it was really a very nice gown. I almost choked when I first tried it on and looked at myself in the mirror, however. 'I can't wear this in public!' I exclaimed. 'I'm half naked!'

'Don't be such a goose, Polgara,' Arell told me. 'A well-designed gown's supposed to highlight a woman's best features. You've got a shapely bosom. I'm not going to let you hide it in a canvas bag.'

'It really looks very nice, Pol,' Beldaran assured me. 'Nobody's going to be looking at your hips if you wear that.'

'I'm getting just a little tired of all this talk about hips, Beldaran,' I said acidly. 'You're not exactly scrawny yourself, you know.'

'The whole secret to wearing a daring dress is to be proud of what it reveals,' Arell told me. 'You've got a good figure. Flaunt it.'

'This is Beldaran's party, Arell,' I protested. '*She's* the one who's supposed to attract attention, not me.'

'Don't be so coy, Polgara,' she scolded me. 'I've heard all about your little experiments in self-display in that large room down the hall, so don't play innocent with me.'

'At least I didn't take my clothes off.'

'You might as well have. Who designed those awful gowns you used to wear?'

'Well – I needed a dress in Camaar, and father had a dressmaker sew one up for me. When we got here, I had another dressmaker copy it for the rest of them.'

'I might have known,' she sniffed. 'Don't ever let a Sendar design your clothes. They're the prissiest people in the world. All right,' she said then, 'let's get to work on the dresses for these other ladies.' She squinted around at Beldaran's attendants. 'Green, I think,' she mused. 'We don't want the dresses of the rest of the wedding party to clash with those of the bride and her sister.'

I've sometimes wondered about Arell. She was just a bit too domineering to be entirely an Alorn lady. I think I'll talk with mother about that. Mother's not above tampering with people at times.

Beldaran, of course, was nervous on the night before her wedding. It may not appear so, but brides are usually almost as nervous as grooms are on that particular night. Women are better at hiding things, though.

'Don't take it so seriously, Beldaran,' Arell advised my sister. 'A wedding's a chance for others to enjoy themselves. The bride and groom aren't much more than ornaments.'

'I'm not feeling very ornamental right now, Arell,' Beldaran replied. 'Would you excuse me please? I think I'll go throw up for a while.'

The night passed, as nights are in the habit of doing, and the day dawned clear and sunny – a rarity on the Isle of the Winds. It's a nice island, but it has an almost impossible climate.

The wedding was scheduled for midday, largely because Alorn males celebrate on the night before a wedding, and they tend to feel a little delicate the following morning, so they need some time to pull themselves together.

We had plenty to keep us busy, though. Beldaran took the ritual pre-nuptial bath, and when she emerged, her attendants anointed her gleaming body with rosewater. Then there was all the business with hair, and that consumed most of the rest of the morning. Then we all sat around in our undergarments to avoid wrinkling our gowns.

At the last possible minute we all dressed, and Arell critically examined all of us. 'It'll do, I suppose,' she noted. 'Enjoy the wedding, girls. Now scoot.'

We all trooped on down to the antechamber just outside the Hall of the Rivan King, where the wedding was to take place.

I was a bit puzzled by my sister's behavior once we entered that antechamber. She seemed almost inhumanly composed. All traces of her previous nervousness had vanished, and she seemed bemused and distant. Mother explained my sister's detachment to me later.

Much of what happened during the wedding was symbolic, and Beldaran was following some very precise instructions.

I kept watch at the door, and so it was that I saw the arrival of Riva, his father, and his brothers.

They were all dressed in *chain mail*, and there were swords bolted at their hips! I knew that Alorns were a warlike people, but *really*! In a sort of gesture to the formality of the occasion, their mail shirts were all brightly burnished. I *hoped* that they'd done something about the characteristic smell of armor, though. Armor of any kind has a very distinctive fragrance about it, and I didn't think it'd be appropriate for all the ladies in Beldaran's entourage to faint dead away during the ceremony.

Then father joined us, and he didn't smell *too* strongly of beer. I often make an issue of my father's bad habits, but I'll concede that he doesn't really drink all that much. Evidently his years on the waterfront in Camaar had gotten most of that out of his system. 'Good morning, ladies,' he greeted us. 'You all look quite beautiful. Are we ready?'

'As ready as we'll ever be, I suppose,' I replied. 'Did you manage to keep Riva sober last night?'

'I didn't have to, Pol. I watched him rather closely, and he hardly drank anything at all.'

'An Alorn who doesn't try to plunge headfirst into every beer barrel he passes? Amazing!'

'Excuse me,' he said then. 'I need to talk with Beldaran. Beldin and I've made a few preparations she needs to know about.'

I found out what he meant a little while later.

My father has an exquisite sense of timing. He gave the crowd in Riva's throne room some time to settle down, and then I quite clearly heard the thought he sent out to uncle Beldin. *'All right,'* he said silently, *'we might as well get started.'*

Uncle Beldin responded with a silvery fanfare played upon hundreds of phantom trumpets. The sound was impressive enough to silence all the wedding guests. The fanfare was followed by a wedding hymn sung very softly by an ethereal non-existent choir. I'm something of a musician myself, and I was enormously impressed by my dwarfed uncle's complex harmony.

Then at a signal from father, Beldaran went out through the door of the antechamber and stepped into the center of the doorway to the Hall of the Rivan King. She stood there, allowing herself to be admired, and then the Master bestowed his benediction upon her in the form of a beam of bright white light.

When I think back on it, I realize now that the Master was blessing the entire Rivan line – the line that was to ultimately produce the Godslayer.

I removed my cloak, and father's eyes grew a little wild. 'Nice dress,' he noted from between clenched teeth. Sometimes my father's very inconsistent. He admires the attributes of *other* ladies, but he grows quite upset when I display *mine*.

We moved into place, one on either side of Beldaran, and walked with stately pace down the aisle that led past the pits where burning peat provided warmth to the front, where Riva and his family awaited us.

'*It's going quite well, don't you think?*' Mother's voice asked me.

'*It's not over yet, mother,*' I replied. '*These are Alorns, after all, so there's still an enormous potential for disaster.*'

'*Cynic,*' she accused.

Then I noticed the Master's Orb on the pommel of a massive sword hanging point down above the throne. It was a little hard to miss, since it glowed with an intensely blue fire.

It was the first time I'd ever seen the Orb. I was impressed. I've seen that glow many times since then, but the only time I've ever seen it so bright was on the day when Garion took that sword down off the wall. In its own way the Orb was *also* blessing the wedding of Beldaran and Riva.

When we reached the area just in front of the throne, my father and I surrendered custody of Beldaran over to Riva and stepped back a pace. The Rivan Deacon came forward at that point, and the ceremony began.

My sister was radiant, and Riva's worshipful eyes never left her face. Since this was a state wedding, the Rivan Deacon had expanded the ceremony extensively. Women, of course, absolutely *love* weddings. After the first hour, though, the wedding guests began to grow restless. The benches in the Hall of the Rivan King are made of stone, so they're not really very comfortable for the ladies. The gentlemen were all looking forward to the extensive carousing that plays such an important part in Alorn weddings.

Out of respect, however, we all managed to stifle our yawns.

My sister and Riva endured the droning sermon of the ecclesiast lecturing them on the duties of marriage. I idly noted in passing that all the rights fell to the groom, and the duties and obligations were the bride's domain.

After another three quarters of an hour, the Deacon's quickening cadence indicated that he was nearing his conclusion. He was a brave man; I'll give him that. Every man in the hall was wearing a sword, and he'd tested the congregation's patience to the limit.

I'd stopped paying much attention to him a long time ago, and then mother's voice inside my head made me very alert. 'Polgara,' she said, 'keep a firm grip on your nerves.'

'What?'

'Don't get excited. Something's going to happen to you at this point. It's symbolic, but it's quite important.'

A moment later her meaning became very clear. I felt a gentle kind of warmth, and then I, like the Orb, began to glow a bright blue. Mother explained later that the glow was the Master's benediction upon something which I would do at some point in the far distant future.

'Listen very carefully, Polgara,' mother's voice said then. 'This is the most important event in the history of the west. Beldaran's the center of human attention, but the Gods are watching you.'

'Me? What on earth for, mother?'

'At the exact moment that Beldaran and Riva are declared man and wife, you'll have to make a decision. The Gods have chosen you to be the instrument of their will, but you have to accept that.'

'Accept what?'

'A task, Polgara, and you must accept it or reject it right here and now.'

'What kind of task?'

'If you accept, you'll be the guardian and protector of the line which descends from Beldaran and Riva.'

'I'm not a soldier, mother.'

'You're not expected to be, Polgara. You won't need a sword for this task. Consider your decision carefully, my daughter. When the task presents itself to you, you'll recognize it immediately; and if you take it up, it'll consume the rest of your life.'

Then the Rivan Deacon finally arrived at his long-delayed climax.

Above me I heard the ghostly flutter of soft wings just over my head, and I glanced upward. Mother, all snowy white, hovered in the still air, her huge golden eyes intent. Then she curved away from me and flew on soft wings to the rear of the hall to perch on one of the rafters.

Then, as the Rivan Deacon pronounced the words that forever took my sister away from me, mother said, 'Do you accept, Polgara?'

The formality of her question demanded a formal response so I took the sides of my blue gown in my fingertips, spread the gown slightly, and curtsied my acceptance even as Riva kissed his new bride.

'Done! And Done!' A strange new voice exulted as Destiny claimed me for its own.

PART TWO

Father

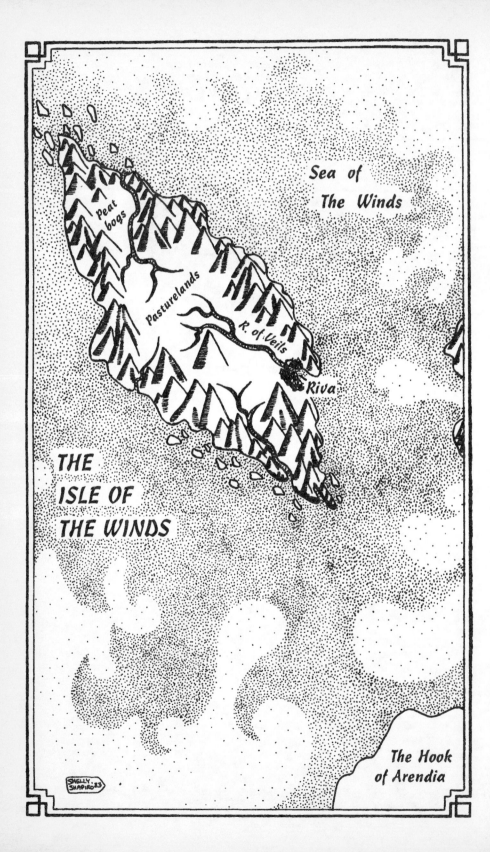

Sea of
The Winds

Peat
bogs

Pasturelands

R. of Veils

Riva

THE
ISLE OF
THE WINDS

SHELLY
SHAPIRO '83

The Hook
of Arendia

CHAPTER 6

That was the first time I'd come into contact with what father chooses to call 'Garion's friend', and I didn't fully understand the source of that 'Done! And Done!' that rang so exultantly in my mind. It's probably just as well that I didn't, since no one is ever fully prepared for that first encounter with the Purpose of the Universe, and my collapsing in a dead faint might have disrupted my sister's wedding just a bit.

Following the ceremony, the wedding party and the guests all adjourned to the large banquet hall just down the corridor for the traditional wedding feast. Once we were settled on the benches at the groaning table where meat and fowl and all manner of delicacies awaited our attention, King Cherek Bear-shoulders rose to his feet. 'My Lords and Ladies,' he said, lifting his brimming ale-tankard, 'I propose a toast to the bride and groom.'

The assembled Alorns gravely and soberly rose to their feet, raised their tankards, and intoned, 'The bride and groom!' in unison.

I thought that was rather nice.

Then Dras Bull-neck proposed a toast to his father.

Then Algar Fleet-foot proposed a toast to his brother Dras, and Bull-neck responded by toasting his brother Algar.

The gravity of that Alorn assemblage was rapidly fading, and the sobriety faded right along with it. Just about everyone at the table seemed to feel obliged to honor *somebody* with a toast, and it was a very long table. As I recall, they never did get completely around it.

'This is disgusting,' I muttered to uncle Beldin, who was sitting beside me.

Beldin, who was uncharacteristically clean – largely at Beldaran's insistence – put on a look of pious innocence. 'Surely you can't object to the desire to honor those we love and respect, Pol,' he said. 'Excuse me a moment,' he added. Then he stood up. 'Ladies and gentlemen!' he thundered, 'I give you the Lady Polgara!'

'Lady Polgara!' They roared in unison, and they all drank deeply to me.

At some point about midway through the banquet, Beldaran and Riva slipped away. The party grew progressively rowdier, and uncle Beldin was drinking everything in sight.

I endured it for as long as I could, but then a bearded Alorn at the far end of the table rose unsteadily to his feet, spilled half his ale over the lady who sat beside him, and lifted his tankard. He belched. 'Par'n me,' he said absently. 'Ladies an' Gennelmun, I give you my dog, Bowser!'

'To Bowser!' they all shouted enthusiastically, and then they drank.

That did it! I stood up.

'To whom did you want to drink, Pol?' Beldin asked, his eyes unfocused and his speech slurred.

I know I shouldn't have done it, and I apologized profusely the next morning, but I was just a little irritated at that point. 'Why to you, of course, uncle dear,' I replied sweetly. 'My Lords and Ladies,' I announced, 'I give you my dear, dear uncle Beldin.'

And then I poured a tankard of ale on his head and stormed out of the banquet hall, followed by the rest of the ladies.

Alorns have an enormous capacity for strong ale, so their celebration lasted for three days.

I chose not to attend.

On the morning of the fourth day after the wedding, father stopped by my rooms. We chatted for a while, and then Cherek Bear-shoulders was admitted. Cherek looked decidedly unwell, but he seemed to be more or less sober. 'I was talking with Dras and Algar this morning,' he said, 'and Algar thought we might want to get together to exchange some information. We don't have much chance to meet and talk very often, and there's a lot going on in the world.'

'Probably not a bad idea,' father agreed. 'Why don't you go get Riva, and I'll see if I can locate Beldin.' He squinted at me. 'Why don't you join us as well, Pol?' he suggested.

'What on earth for?'

'For my peace of mind, daughter dear,' he said somewhat pointedly.

'It shall be as my father commands,' I replied with feigned obedience.

'She has beautiful manners, doesn't she?' Cherek noted.

'Don't make such hasty judgments, Cherek,' father warned him.

And so it was that I sat in on the first sessions of what came to be known as 'the Alorn Council'. At the outset I only sat in the background and listened. The main topic of discussion was the presence of Angaraks on this side of the Sea of the East, and I didn't really know very much about Angaraks.

I'd been a bit apprehensive about being in such close proximity to Dras and Algar, fearing that one – or both – might seize this opportunity to press unwelcome suits. That was when I discovered that kings probably don't make very good husbands, since when politics rears its head, a king becomes all business. Dras and Algar had obviously stopped thinking of me as a woman. For them I was simply another council member.

My isolated childhood had not prepared me for the concept of racial differences, and I'm not talking here about purely physical differences. Alorns tend to be tall and blond, while Tolnedrans tend to be short and dark. All other differences are largely cultural. Alorns are encouraged to enjoy a good fight, while Tolnedrans are encouraged to make money. I discovered early on in the discussions that Angaraks are encouraged to be afraid of Torak – and by extension of his Grolim priesthood. Despite some superficial differences, there's a Thull lurking at the bottom of every Angarak soul.

So long as Torak's people had remained in Mallorea, they'd posed no real threat, but now that the Murgos, Nadraks, and Thulls had crossed the land bridge, the Alorns felt that it was time to stop just talking about the Angaraks and to start doing something about them.

It seemed to me, though, that everyone else in the room was missing something. They appeared to hate all Angaraks indiscriminately, paying far too little attention to the cultural differences that made Angarak society much less monolithic than it appeared on the surface. The typical Alorn's approach to any problem is to start sharpening his battle-axe, but I saw at the outset that the only thing direct confrontation would accomplish would be the solidification of the Angaraks, and that was the last thing we wanted.

I was right on the verge of triumphantly pointing that out when mother stopped me. *'That isn't the way to do it, Pol,'* her voice told me. *'Men are afraid of intelligent women, so suggest instead of announcing. Plant the seed of an idea in their minds and let it grow. They'll be much more likely to come around if they think the idea was theirs in the first place.'*

'But –' I started to protest.

'*Try it my way, Pol,*' she said. '*Just point them in the right direction and then tell them how wonderful they are when they do it right.*'

'*I think it's silly, mother, but I'll try it.*'

My first rather self-effacing suggestion had to do with establishing trade relations with the Nadraks, and much to my surprise that went down rather smoothly. I sat back and let the Alorns discuss the notion long enough to forget where it came from, and then they decided to give it a try. Then I planted the idea of making some overtures to the Tolnedrans and Arends, and Cherek and his boys accepted that as well.

In his sometimes misguided history of the world, my father notes that I enjoyed politics. He was right about that, but he missed the *real* point entirely. When father uses the word 'politics' he's talking about relations between nations. When I use the word, though, I'm talking about the various subtle ways a woman can get men to do what she wants them to do.

If you want to see an expert in this art, go watch Queen Porenn in action. The *real* genius, however, is Queen Layla of Sendaria.

We met off and on several more times that week, but our most important decisions were made in that first session. When I realized that the men were going to spend most of their time chewing old soup, I let my mind wander. I considered mother's revelation, and the more I thought about it, the more sense it made. There are differences between men and women, and the obvious physical differences are the least important. The differences in our minds are far more relevant.

Bear-shoulders offered to take father, uncle Beldin and me to the Sendarian coast in his war-boat, but the night before we were to leave, uncle Beldin changed his mind about that. 'Maybe I'd better go back to Mallorea and keep an eye on old Burnt-face instead,' he said. 'The Murgos, Nadraks, and Thulls are just an advance party, I think. They aren't going to be able to accomplish very much without reinforcements from Mallorea. Nothing's really going to happen on this side of the Sea of the East until Torak orders his armies to march north from Mal Zeth.'

'Keep me posted,' father told him.

'Naturally, you clot,' Beldin retorted. 'Did you think I was going to go to Mallorea just to renew old acquaintances with Urvon and Zedar? If Burnt-face starts to move, I'll let you know.'

It was midsummer by the time father and I reached the Vale, and the twins were eagerly awaiting our return. They'd prepared a feast for us, and we ate in that airy, pleasant tower of theirs as evening settled golden over the Vale. I've always liked their tower for some reason. Father's tower is messy and cluttered, uncle Beldin's is fanciful on the outside, but quite nearly as cluttered as father's on the inside. The twins, however, had the foresight to build closets and storerooms on the lower levels of *their* tower, so they can put things away. Father probably won't care for this comparison, but his tower's very much like a single room set on top of a pole. It's a solid stone stump with a room on the highest level, and uncle Beldin's isn't much better.

After we'd finished eating, uncle Belkira pushed back his plate. 'All right,' he said, 'now tell us about the wedding – and about this monumental change in Polgara.'

'The change in Pol is easy,' father replied. 'She just slipped around behind my back and grew up.'

'Young people have a habit of doing that,' uncle Belkira noted.

'There was a little more to it than that, father,' I said. 'Beldaran was always the pretty one.'

'Not really, Pol,' uncle Belkira disagreed. 'She's blonde, and you're brunette. That's the only real difference. You're both beautiful.'

I shrugged. 'All girls want to be blonde,' I told him. 'It may be a little silly, but we do. After I realized that I'd never be as pretty as she is, I tried to go the other way. When we reached Camaar and she and Riva finally met each other, I saw that how I looked was the farthest thing from her mind, so I cleaned myself up.' I laughed a little ruefully. 'It took me hours to comb all the snarls out of my hair. Then we reached the Isle of the Winds, and I discovered that I wasn't as ugly as I'd thought.'

'That might just be the grossest understatement in history,' father said. 'Now that she's cleaned off all the dirt, she's moderately presentable.'

'More than moderately, Belgarath,' Beltira said.

'Anyway,' father continued, 'when we reached the Isle of the Winds, she stunned a whole generation of young Rivans into near-insensibility. They absolutely adored her.'

'Was being adored nice, Pol?' Belkira teased.

'I found it quite pleasant,' I admitted, 'but it seemed to make father very nervous. I can't for the life of me understand why.'

89

'Very funny, Pol,' father said. 'Anyway, after the wedding, we had a talk with Bear-shoulders and his sons. They've had some contacts with the Angaraks, and we're all beginning to grope our way toward a greater understanding of the differences between the Murgos, Thulls, and Nadraks. We can thank Pol for that.' His sidelong glance was as sly as mine had been. 'You didn't think I noticed what you were doing, did you, Pol? You *were* very smooth about it, though.' Then he looked ruminatively at the ceiling. 'As Pol so gently pointed out, we're more likely to have some luck with the Nadraks than with the Murgos or Thulls. The Thulls are too stupid and too much afraid of the Grolims to be of much use, and Ctuchik controls the Murgos with an iron fist. The Nadraks are greedy, though, so a bit of judicious bribery might win them over – at least enough to make them a useful source of information.'

'Are there any signs that more Angaraks are coming across the land-bridge?' Beltira asked.

'Not from what Bull-neck's been able to discover. Torak's evidently biding his time, waiting for the right moment. Beldin went back over to Mallorea to keep an eye on him – at least that's what he *says* he's going to do. I still think he might want to take up that discussion about white-hot hooks with Urvon, though. Anyhow, he pointed out that the Murgos, Nadraks, and Thulls are just an advance party. The game won't really get started until Torak decides to come out of seclusion at Ashaba.'

'He doesn't have to hurry for *my* sake,' Belkira said.

We spent the next couple of weeks giving the twins greater and greater detail about our visit to the Isle and about Beldaran's wedding. From time immemorial the twins have very seldom left the Vale, largely because, as Beltira humorously notes, 'somebody has to mind the store.' We're all a part of the same family, however, so they're naturally hungry for information about our various adventures in the outside world.

I was quite melancholy during the weeks that followed, of course. I still felt the pain of my separation from my sister most keenly. Oddly, that separation brought father and me closer together. In my eyes, father and I had been competing for Beldaran's affection ever since he'd returned to the Vale after his extended bout of drunken debauchery. With Beldaran's marriage that competition had vanished. I still insulted father from time to time, but I think that was more out of habit than anything else. I certainly wouldn't admit it, but I began to develop a certain respect for him and a strange back-door affection. When he chooses to be, my father *can* be a likeable old sot, after all.

Our lives in his tower settled down into a kind of domestic routine that was easy and comfortable. I think a lot of that may have come about because I like to cook and he likes to eat. It was a tranquil time. Our evening conversations were stimulating, and I enjoyed them.

It's an article of the religion of every adolescent that he – or she – knows far more than his elders; the half-formed mind suffers fools almost ecstatically. Those evening conversations with my father rather quickly stripped me of *that* particular illusion. The depth of his mind sometimes staggered me. Dear *Gods*, that old man knows a lot!

It was not only my growing respect for this vast sink of knowledge that prompted me to offer myself up as his pupil one evening while we were doing the dishes. The Master – and mother – had a hand in that decision as well. Their frequent suggestions that I was an uneducated ninny probably had a great deal to do with my offer.

Father's initial response set off an immediate argument. 'Why do I need *that* nonsense?' I demanded. 'Can't you just *tell* me what I need to know? Why do I have to learn how to read?'

He was diplomatic enough not to laugh in my face. Then he patiently explained why I absolutely *had* to be able to read. 'The sum of human knowledge is there, Pol,' he concluded, pointing at all the books and scrolls lining the walls of the tower. 'You're going to need it.'

'What on earth for? We have "talent", father, and the primitives who wrote all that stuffy nonsense didn't. What can they have possibly scribbled down that'd be of any use to us?'

He sighed and rolled his eyes upward. 'Why me?' he demanded, and he obviously wasn't talking to me when he said it. 'All right, Pol,' he said then, 'if you're so intelligent that you don't need to know how to read, maybe you can answer a few questions that've been nagging at me for quite some time now.'

'Of course, father,' I replied. 'I'd be happy to.' Notice that I walked right into the trap he'd set for me.

'If you have two apples here and two apples over there, how many do you have altogether?' When my father's trying to teach some prospective pupil humility, he always starts there.

'Four apples, of course,' I replied quickly – too quickly, as it turned out.

'Why?'

'What do you mean, "Why?" It just *is*. Two apples and two apples are four apples. Any idiot knows that.'

'Since you're not an idiot, you shouldn't have any trouble explaining it to me, should you?'

I stared at him helplessly.

'We can come back to that one later. Now then, when a tree falls way back in the forest, it makes a noise, right?'

'Of course it does, father.'

'Very good, Pol. What *is* noise?'

'Something we hear.'

'Excellent. You're really very perceptive, my daughter.' He frowned then, a bit spuriously, I thought. 'There's a problem, though. What if there's nobody around to hear the noise? Is it really there, then?'

'Certainly it is.'

'Why?'

'Because –' I floundered to a stop at that point.

'Let's set that one aside as well and move on. Do you think the sun is going to come up tomorrow morning?'

'Well, naturally it will.'

'Why?'

I should have expected that 'why' by now, but I was exasperated by his seemingly simple-minded questions, so I hadn't even thought before I answered. 'Well,' I said lamely, 'it always has, hasn't it?'

I got a very quick and very humiliating lesson in probability theory at that point.

'Pressing right along then,' he said urbanely. 'Why does the moon change her shape during the course of a month?'

I stared at him helplessly.

'Why does water bubble when it gets hot?'

I couldn't even answer *that* one, and I did all the cooking. He went on – and on, and on.

'Why can't we see color in the dark?'

'Why do tree leaves change color in the autumn?'

'Why does water get hard when it's cold? And why does it turn to steam when it gets hot?'

'If it's noon here, why is it midnight in Mallorea?'

'Does the sun go around the world, or does the world go around the sun?'

'Where do mountains come from?'

'What makes things grow?'

'All right, father!' I exclaimed. '*Enough*! Teach me how to read!'

'Why, of course, Pol,' he said. 'If you wanted to learn so badly, why didn't you say so in the first place?'

And so we got down to work. My father's a disciple, a sorcerer, a statesman, and sometimes a general, but more than anything else he's a teacher – probably the best one in the world. He taught me how to read and write in a surprisingly short period of time – perhaps because the first thing he wrote down for me was my own name. I thought it looked rather pretty on the page. Before long I began dipping into his books and scrolls with an increasing thirst for knowledge. I've got a tendency to want to argue with books, though, and that gave father a bit of trouble, probably because I argued out loud. I couldn't seem to help it. Idiocy, whether spoken or written, offends me, and I feel obliged to correct it. This habit of mine wouldn't have caused any trouble if I'd been alone, but father was in the tower with me, and he was intent on his own studies. We talked about that at some length, as I recall.

The reading was stimulating, but even more stimulating were our evening discussions of various points that had come up in the course of my studies during the day. It all started one evening when father rather innocently asked, 'Well, Pol, what did you learn today?'

I told him. Then I told him about my objections to what I'd read – firmly, even challengingly.

Father never passes up an opportunity for a good argument, so he automatically defended the texts while I attacked them. After a few evenings so enjoyably spent, these disputes became almost ritualistic. It's a pleasant way to end the day.

Our arguments weren't *all* intellectual. Our visit to the Isle of the Winds had made me more aware of my personal appearance, so I started paying attention to it. Father chose to call it vanity, and that also started an ongoing argument.

Then, early one morning in the spring, mother's voice came to me before I'd even started making breakfast. *This is all very nice, Pol,*' she said, '*but there are other things you need to learn as well. Put your books aside for today and come to the Tree. We'll let* him *teach you how to use your mind. I'll teach you how to use your will.'*

So after breakfast I rose from the table and said, 'I think I'll walk around a bit today, father. I'm starting to feel a little cooped-up here in the tower. I need some air. I'll go look for herbs and spices for tonight's supper.'

'Probably not a bad idea,' he agreed. 'Your arguments are getting a little dusty. Maybe a good breeze will clear your head.'

'Maybe,' I replied, resisting the impulse to retort to that veiled insult. Then I descended the spiral stairs and ventured out into the morning sun.

It was a glorious day, and the Vale's one of the loveliest places in the world, so I took my time as I drifted through the bright green knee-high grass down to that sacred hollow where the Tree spreads forth his immensity. As I drew closer, my birds welcomed me with song, hovering over me in the lucid morning.

'*What took you so long, Pol?*' mother's voice asked.

'I was enjoying the morning,' I replied aloud. No one else was around, so there was no need to do it the other way. 'What shall we do today, mother?'

'*Continue your education, of course.*'

'I hope your teaching won't be as dusty as father's sometimes is.'

'*I think you might like it. It's in the same general area, though.*'

'Which area are we talking about?'

'*The mind, Pol. Up until now you've been learning to use your talent in the outside world. Now we'll go inside.*' She paused as if searching for a way to explain a very difficult concept. '*All people are different,*' she began, '*but the various races have distinguishing characteristics. You can recognize an Alorn when you see one because of his physical appearance. You can also recognize his mind when you encounter it.*'

'You're going to teach me how to hear what other people are thinking?'

'*We might get to that later. It's more difficult, so let's concentrate on this one right now. When you're trying to pinpoint a stranger's race or tribe, you're not concentrating on* what *he's thinking, but rather the* way *he's thinking.*'

'Why's this so important, mother?'

'*We have enemies out there in the world, Pol. You'll need to be able to recognize them when you come across them. The Master's taught me how to imitate the manner of the various races, so I'll be able to show you how to tell the difference between a Murgo and a Grolim or between an Arend and a Marag. There'll be times when your safety and the safety of those in your care will hinge on your ability to know just who's in your general vicinity.*'

'I suppose that stands to reason. How are we going to go about this?'

'*Just open your mind, Pol. Submerge your own personality and* feel *the nature of the various minds I'll show you.*'

'Well,' I said a bit dubiously, 'I'll try it, but it sounds awfully complicated.'

'I didn't say it was going to be easy, Pol. Shall we begin?'

None of it made much sense at first, mother threw the same thought at me over and over, changing only the way it was presented. The major break-through came when I realized that the different thought patterns seemed to have different colors attached to them. It wasn't really overt, but rather a faint tinge. In time, though, those colors grew more pronounced, and my recognition of Murgo thought or Alorn thought or Tolnedran thought became almost instantaneous.

The mind of the imitation Murgo mother conjured up for me was very dark, a kind of dull black. The Grolim mind, by contrast, is a hard, glossy black, and I could see – or feel – the difference almost immediately.

Sendars are green. Tolnedrans are red. Rivans, of course, are blue. I increasingly recognized those colors, and by midday I'd become fairly proficient at it.

'That's enough for today, Pol,' mother told me. *'Go back to the tower and spend the afternoon with your books. We don't want your father to start getting suspicious.'*

And so I returned to the tower, establishing what would become a pattern for quite a number of years – mornings belonged to mother and afternoons belonged to father. I was to receive two educations at the same time, and that was just a little challenging.

The next morning mother reviewed what I'd learned the previous day by flashing various thought-patterns at me. 'Sendar,' I said in response to a green-tinged mind. 'Murgo,' I identified the dull black thought. 'Arend.' Then, 'Tolnedran.' The more I practiced, the quicker the identifications came to me.

'Now, then,' mother said, *'Let's move on. There'll be times when you'll need to shut off the minds of your friends – put them to sleep, so to speak, except that it's not exactly sleep.'*

'What's the reason for that?'

'We aren't the only ones in the world who know how to recognize thought patterns, Pol. The Grolims can do it, too, and anybody who knows the art can follow the thought back to its source. When you're trying to hide, you don't want someone standing right beside you shouting his head off.'

'No, probably not. How do I go about putting the loud-mouthed idiot to sleep?'

'It's not really sleep, Pol,' she corrected. *'The thought-patterns you've come to recognize are still there in a sleeping person's mind. You have to learn how to shut down his brain entirely.'*

95

'Won't that kill him? Stop his heart?'

'No. *The part of the brain that makes the heart keep beating is so far beneath the surface that it doesn't have any identifying color.*'

'What if I can't wake you up again?'

'*You're not going to do it to me. Where's the closest Alorn?*'

'That'd be the twins,' I replied.

'*Don't reason it out, Pol. Reach out and find them with your mind.*'

'I'll try.' I sent my mind out in search of that characteristic turquoise that identified a non-Rivan Alorn. It didn't take me very long. I knew where they were, of course.

'Good,' mother said. '*Now, imagine a thick, wooly blanket.*'

I didn't ask why; I just did it.

'*Why white?*' mother asked curiously.

'It's their favorite color.'

'*Oh. All right, then, lay it over them.*'

I did that, and I noticed that my palms were getting sweaty. Working with your mind is almost as hard as working with your arms and back.

'*Are they asleep?*'

'I think so.'

'*You'd better go look and make sure.*'

I used the form of a common barn-swallow. The twins always throw open their windows when the weather's nice, and I'd seen swallows flying in and out of their tower many times. I flew to the towers and flitted in through the twins' window.

'Well?' mother's voice called out to me, '*are they asleep?*'

'*It didn't work, mother. Their eyes are still open.*' I didn't want to alert the twins to my presence, so I sent my thought out silently.

'*Are they moving at all?*'

'*No. Now that you mention it, they look like a pair of statues.*'

'*Try flying right at their faces. See if they flinch.*'

I did – and they didn't. '*Not a twitch,*' I reported.

'*It worked, then. Try to find their minds with yours.*'

I tried that and there was nothing around me but an empty silence. '*I'm not getting anything, mother.*'

'*You picked that up very quickly. Come back to the Tree and then we'll release them.*'

'*In a moment,*' I said. Then I located my father and turned *his* mind off, too.

'Why did you do that?' mother asked.

'*Just practicing, mother,*' I replied innocently. I knew that wasn't really very nice, but somehow I couldn't resist.

In the weeks that followed, mother taught me other ways to tamper with the human mind. There was the highly useful trick of erasing memories. I've used that many times. There've been occasions when I've been obliged to do things in out-of-the-ordinary ways, and when I didn't want the people present at the time to start telling wild stories to others. Sometimes it's much easier to just blot out the memory of the event than it is to come up with a plausible explanation.

Closely related to that trick is the trick of implanting false memories. When you use the two tricks in tandem you can significantly alter someone's perception of what really happened during the course of any given event.

Mother also taught me how to 'grow' – to expand myself into immensity. I haven't used that one very often, because it *does* tend to make one conspicuous.

Then, since every trick usually has an opposite, she taught me how to 'shrink' – to reduce myself down to the point of near invisibility. That one's been *very* useful, particularly when I wanted to listen to people talking without being seen.

These two tricks are closely related to the change of form process, so they were quite easy to learn.

I also learned how to make people ignore my presence. This is another way to achieve a kind of invisibility. Since I was still infected with adolescence at the time, the notion of fading into the background didn't appeal to me very much. All adolescents have a driving urge to be noticed, and virtually everything they do almost screams, 'Look at me! See how important I am!' Invisibility isn't the best way to satisfy that urge.

The business of 'making things' – creation, if you will – was in some ways the culmination of that stage of my education, since, if looked at in a certain way, it encroaches on the province of the Gods. I started out by making flowers. I think that might be where all of us start. Creation is closely related to beauty, so that might explain it, although flowers are easy and making them is a logical place to begin. I cheated a little at first, of course. I'd wrap twigs with grass and then convert the object thus produced into a flower. Transmutation isn't really creation, though, so I eventually moved on to making flowers out of nothing but air. There's a kind of ecstasy involved in creation, so I probably overdid it, dotting that shallow swale where the Tree lived with whole carpets of brightly colored blooms. I told myself I was only practicing, but that wasn't entirely true, I guess.

Then one morning in the late spring of my eighteenth year, mother said, '*Why don't we just talk today, Pol?*'

'Of course.' I sat down with my back against the Tree, waving off a few birds. I knew that when mother said 'talk', she actually meant for me to listen.

'*I think it might be time for you to let your father know what you're capable of doing, Polgara. He hasn't fully grasped the idea of just how fast you're maturing. You have things to do, and he's just going to get in your way until he realizes that you're not a child any more.*'

'I've mentioned that to him any number of times, mother, but I can't seem to get the idea across to him.'

'*Your father deals in absolutes, Pol. It's very hard for him to grasp the notion that things – and people – change. The easiest way to change his mind is to demonstrate your abilities to him. You'll have to do it eventually anyway, and it's probably best to do it now – before he gets his concept of you set in stone in his mind.*'

'What'd be the best way to do it, mother? Should I invite him to come outside and watch me show off?'

'*That's just a little obvious, don't you think? Wouldn't it be better just to do something during the normal course of events? An off-hand demonstration would probably impress him more than something that had clearly been carefully staged. Just do something without making a fuss about it. I know him, dear, and I know the best way to get his attention.*'

'I shall be guided by you in this, mother.'

'*Very funny, Polgara.*' Her tone wasn't very amused, though.

I suppose we all have an urge to be theatrical, so my demonstration of my ability was rather carefully staged. I deliberately let father go hungry for a couple of days while I pretended to be deeply engrossed in a book of philosophy. He raided my kitchen until he'd exhausted the supply of everything remotely edible, and my father has absolutely no idea of where I store things. Eventually, he *had* to say something about his incipient starvation.

'Oh, bother,' I replied with studied preoccupation. Then, without even looking up from the page I was reading I created a half-cooked side of beef for him. It wasn't quite as pretty as a flower, but I know it got father's attention.

CHAPTER 7

It snowed on the eve of our eighteenth birthday, one of those gentle snows that settle softly to earth without making much fuss. Blizzards are very dramatic, I suppose, but there's something restful about a quiet snow that just tucks the world in the way a mother tucks a small child into bed after a busy day.

I awoke early, and after I'd built up the fire, I stood at one of the windows brushing my hair and watching the last of the clouds move ponderously off toward the northeast. The sun mounted above those clouds to reveal a clean, white world unmarred by a single footprint. I wondered if it had snowed on the Isle of the Winds as well and what Beldaran might be doing on 'our' day.

Father was still asleep, but that wasn't really unusual, since he's never been an early riser. As luck had it, he wasn't even snoring, so my morning was filled with a blessed silence that was almost like a benediction. I made a simple breakfast of porridge, tea, and bread, ate, and hung the pot on one of the iron hooks in the fireplace to keep it warm for father. Then I put on my fur cloak and went out to face the morning.

It was not particularly cold, and the damp snow clung to every limb of the widely scattered pines in the Vale as I trudged toward the Tree and my regular morning appointment with mother. A single eagle soared high over the Vale, flying for the sheer joy of it, since no other birds or animals had ventured out yet. 'Polgara!' he screamed his greeting to me, dipping his wings to show his recognition. I waved to him. He was an old friend. Then he veered away, and I continued on down the Vale.

The eternal Tree was dormant during the winter months, but he was not really asleep. I could sense his drowsy awareness as I topped the rise and looked down into his protected little valley.

'You're late, Pol,' mother's voice noted.

'I was enjoying the scenery,' I explained, looking back at the single line of tracks I'd left in the newly fallen snow. 'What's Beldaran doing this morning?'

'She's still asleep. The Rivans held a ball in her honor last night, and she and Iron-grip were up quite late.'

'Were they celebrating her birthday?'

'Not really. Alorns don't make that much fuss about birthdays. Actually they were celebrating her condition.'

'What condition?'

'She's going to have a baby.'

'She's *what*?'

'Your sister's pregnant, Polgara.'

'Why didn't you tell me?'

'I just did.'

'I meant, why didn't you tell me earlier?'

'What for? She's mated now, and mated females produce young ones. I thought you knew all about that.'

I threw up my hands in exasperation. Sometimes mother's attitude toward life drove me absolutely wild.

'I don't know that you need to tell him about this. He'd start getting curious about how you came to find out about it. It's easier just to keep quiet about these things than it is to invent stories. I think we should concentrate on something new this morning. Humans have a very well-developed sense of the awful. The things that frighten them the most always seem to lurk at the back of their minds, and it's not very hard to tap into those thoughts. Once you know what a man's truly afraid of, he'll cooperate if you show it to him.'

'Cooperate?'

'He'll do what you tell him to do, or tell you things that you want to know. It's easier than setting fire to his feet. Shall we get started?'

I was melancholy for the rest of the winter. Beldaran's pregnancy was but one more indication of our separation, and I saw no reason to be happy about it. I sighed a great deal when I was alone, but I made some effort to keep my feelings under wraps when father and the twins were around, largely to keep mother's ongoing presence in my mind a secret.

Then in the spring Algar and Anrak came to the Vale to bring us the news and to escort us to the Isle of the Winds.

It took us the better part of a month to reach the Isle, and Riva himself was waiting for us on the stone wharf that jutted out into the harbor. I noted that Beldaran had finally persuaded him to shave off his beard, and I viewed that as an improvement. Then we mounted the stairs to the Citadel, and I was reunited with my sister. She was awkward-looking, but she seemed very happy.

After they'd proudly shown us the nursery, we had a rather lavish supper and then Beldaran and I finally got the chance to be alone. She took me along the corridor that led from the royal apartments to a polished door that opened into those rooms Beldaran and I had shared before her wedding to Iron-grip. I noted that there had been a number of modifications. The hanging drapes that covered the bleak stone walls were almost universally blue now, and the golden lambskin rugs had been replaced with white ones. The furnishings were of heavy, dark-polished wood, and all the seats were deeply cushioned. The fireplace was no longer just a sooty hole in the wall, but was framed and mantled instead. Candles provided a soft, golden light, and it all seemed very comfortable. 'Do you like it, Pol?' Beldaran asked me.

'It's absolutely lovely,' I replied.

'These are your rooms now,' she said. 'They'll always be here when you need them. I do hope you'll use them often.'

'As often as I can,' I assured her. Then I got down to business. 'What's it like?' I asked her as we seated ourselves on a well-cushioned divan.

'Awkward,' she replied. She laid one hand on her distended belly. 'You have no idea of how often this gets in the way.'

'Were you sick every morning? I've heard about that.'

'Right at first, yes. It went away after a while, though. The backache didn't come until later.'

'Backache?'

'I'm carrying quite a bit of extra weight, Pol,' she pointed out, 'and it's in a very awkward place. About the best I can manage right now is a stately waddle, and even that puts a lot of pressure on my back. Sometimes it feels as if I've been this way forever.'

'It'll pass, dear.'

'That's what Arell tells me. You remember her, don't you?'

'She was the lady who supervised all that dressmaking, wasn't she?'

Beldaran nodded. 'She's also a very good midwife. She's been telling me all about labor, and I'm not really looking forward to it.'

'Are you sorry?'

101

'About being pregnant? Of course not. I just wish it didn't take so long, is all. What have *you* been doing?'

'Getting educated. Father taught me how to read, and I'm reading my way through his library. You wouldn't *believe* how much nonsense has accumulated over the years. I sometimes think the Tolnedrans and the Melcenes were running some kind of a race with absolute idiocy as the prize. Right now I'm reading "The Book of Torak". The Master's brother seems to have some problems.'

She shuddered. 'How awful! How can you bear to read something like that?'

'It's not the sort of thing you'd choose for light entertainment. It's written in old Angarak, and even the language is ugly. The notion of an insane God's more than a little frightening.'

'Insane?'

'Totally. Mother says that he always has been.'

'Does mother visit you often?'

'Every day. Father tends to sleep late, so I go down to the Tree and spend that part of the day with mother. She's teaching me, too, so I'm getting what you might call a well-rounded education.'

Beldaran sighed. 'We're getting further and further apart, aren't we, Pol?'

'It happens, Beldaran,' I told her. 'It's called growing up.'

'I don't like it.'

'Neither do I, but there's not much we can do about it, is there?'

It was rainy and blustery the following morning, but I put on my cloak and went down into the city anyway. I wanted to have a talk with Arell. I found her dress shop in a little cul-de-sac not far from the harbor. It was a tiny, cluttered place littered with bolts of cloth, spools of lace, and twisted hanks of yarn.

The bell on the door to Arell's shop jingled as I entered, and she looked up from her needlework. 'Polgara!' she exclaimed, leaping to her feet and sweeping me up in a motherly embrace. 'You're looking well,' she said.

'So are you, Arell.'

'Do you need a new dress? Is that why you came?'

'No. Actually I'd like some information about Beldaran's condition.'

'She's pregnant. I'm sure you noticed that.'

'Very funny, Arell. What's involved in giving birth?'

'It's painful, it's messy, and it's exhausting. You don't want all the details, do you?'

'Yes, as a matter of fact I do.'

'Are you thinking of setting up in business as midwife?'

'Probably not. My interest is a little more general. Things happen to people – things that need to be fixed. I want to learn how to fix them.'

'Women don't become physicians, Pol. The men-folk don't approve.'

'That's too bad, isn't it? You can't possibly imagine just how indifferent I am about the approval or disapproval of men.'

'You'll get yourself in trouble,' she warned. 'All we're supposed to do is cook, clean house, and have babies.'

'I already know about all that. I think I'd like to expand my knowledge just a bit.'

Arell pursed her lips. 'You're serious about this, aren't you?'

'Yes, I think I am.'

'I can teach you what you'll need to know about childbirth, but –' she broke off. 'Can you keep a secret?'

'Lots of secrets, Arell. I know about things my father hasn't even dreamed of yet, and I've been keeping them from him for years now.'

'There's a herbalist here in Riva. He's grouchy, and he doesn't smell very nice, but he knows which herbs to use to cure certain ailments. And then there's a bone-setter over on the other side of town as well. He's got hands the size of hams, but he's got the right touch. He can twist and wrench a broken bone back into place with no trouble at all. Did you want to learn surgery as well?'

'What's surgery?'

'Cutting people open so that you can fix their insides. I'm fairly good at that myself, though I don't talk about it too often. There's a surgeon here on the Isle as well as the herbalist and the bone-setter. He's sort of fond of me because I taught him how to sew.'

'What's sewing got to do with cutting people open?'

She rolled her eyes upward and sighed. 'Oh, dear,' she said. 'What do you do with a tunic after your father's ripped it?'

'Sew it up, of course.'

'Exactly. You do the same thing to people, Pol. If you don't, their insides are likely to fall out.'

I choked on that a little bit.

'Let's start out with childbirth,' Arell suggested. 'If that doesn't make you sick to your stomach, we can move on to other specialties.'

I learned about 'labor pains', the 'breaking of water', and 'after-birth'. I also learned that there's bleeding involved, but that it's nothing to be alarmed about.

Then Arell took me around to introduce me to her three

colleagues, passing me off as her pupil. Argak the herbalist had a tiny shop filled to the rafters with shelf after shelf of glass jars that contained his wares. The place was none too clean, but then neither was Argak. He reminded me a great deal of uncle Beldin in that regard. He was at least as grumpy and bad-smelling as Arell had told me he was, but I was there to learn from him, not to enjoy his company. A bit of flattery was about all it took to unlock his secrets, and I learned a great deal about alleviating pain and suffering and how to control disease with various leaves, roots, and dried berries.

Salheim the bone-setter was actually a blacksmith, huge, bearded and very blunt. He was not above re-breaking an arm that had set wrong – usually by laying it across the anvil in front of his glowing forge and rapping it smartly with his hammer. Salheim fixed things that were broken – chairs, people's legs and arms, wheels, and farm implements. Usually he didn't even bother to take off his burn-spotted leather apron when he set a bone. He was, like all smiths, enormously strong. I once saw him literally pull a broken leg back into its proper position by bracing his foot against his anvil, taking hold of the offending limb and hauling on it. 'Tie that board to his leg to hold it in place, Pol,' he told me, straining to keep the twisted leg of his screaming patient in place.

'You're hurting him,' I protested.

'Not as much as having that broken bone jabbing up into his leg muscles will,' he replied. 'They always scream when I set a bone. It's not important. Learn to ignore it.'

Balten the surgeon was actually a barber, and he had slim, delicate hands and a slightly furtive look on his face. Cutting people open – except for fun – was illegal in most Alorn societies in those days, so Balten had to practice his art in secret – usually on the cutting-board in his wife's kitchen. Since he needed to know where things were located inside the human body, he also needed to open a fair number of the recently deceased so that he could make maps for reference purposes. I think he used a shovel in the local graveyard almost as often as he used his surgical knives in the kitchen. His anatomical studies were usually a bit hurried, since he had to return his subjects to their graves before the sun came up. As his student, I was frequently invited to participate in his ghoulish entertainment.

I'll admit that I didn't care much for that part of my medical studies. I rather like gardening, but the crops Balten and I dug up on those midnight excursions weren't very appealing, if you want to know the truth.

*   *   *

There's another of my 'talents', father. Did you know that your daughter's quite a proficient grave-robber? Next time you come by, I'll dig somebody up for you, just to show you how it's done.

'It's best to get them drunk before you start cutting them open, Pol,' Balten told me one evening as he filled a tankard with strong ale for our latest patient.

'Is that to avoid the pain?' I asked.

'No. It's to keep them from flopping around while you're slicing them open, and when you get your knife into a man's entrails, you want him to stay perfectly still. Otherwise, you'll cut things you shouldn't be cutting.' He took hold of my wrist rather firmly as I reached out for one of his curved knives. 'Be careful, Pol!' he warned. 'Those knives are very sharp. A sharp knife is the key to good surgery. Dull ones always make a mess of things.'

And that was my introduction to the study of medicine. Alorns are a blunt, practical people, and my four teachers – Arell, Argak, Salheim, and Balten – taught me a no-nonsense approach to healing. I think I took my cue from the brutal bone-setter. 'If it's broken, fix it. If it's not, don't.' I've studied medical texts from all corners of the world, and I've yet to find anything more to the point than that pithy instruction.

This is not to say that I spent all of my time immersed in afterbirth, broken bones, and internal organs. I spent hours with my sister, and there was the business of persuading my former suitors that I didn't want to play any more.

Merot the poet was fairly easy to deal with. He advised me with some pride that he was currently engaged in writing the greatest epic in the history of mankind.

'Oh?' I said, shying back from that foul breath of his.

'Would you like to hear a few lines, Lady Polgara?' he offered.

'I'd be delighted,' I lied with an absolutely straight face.

He drew himself up, struck a dramatic pose with one ink-stained hand on the breast of his somber doublet, and launched himself ponderously into verse. If anything, his delivery was even more tedious and drawn out than it'd been the last time. I waited with a vapid expression on my face until he was deeply immersed in the product of his own genius, and then I turned and walked away, leaving him reciting his masterpiece to a blank wall. I'm not sure if the wall was impressed. I never had occasion to ask it. Merot was impressed enough for both of them, though.

My new-found expertise in the functions of the human body

helped me to dispense with 'mighty Taygon'. I innocently asked him about the contents of the assorted digestive organs he'd been so liberally strewing about the landscape. For some reason my graphic description of a bit of half-digested mutton made Taygon's face turn green, and he fled from me, his hand tightly pressed over his mouth to keep his lunch inside where it belonged. Evidently Taygon had no problems with blood, but other body fluids disturbed him more than a little.

Then I drifted around in the large, gaily decorated room where the children played. I knew many of them from my last visit, but the whole purpose of the place was to pair off the young, and marriage had taken its toll among my former playmates. There were new ones to take their places, however, so the numbers remained more or less constant.

'Ah, there you are, my Lady.' It was the blond, super-civilized Baron Kamion. He wore a plum-colored velvet doublet, and if anything he was even more handsome than before. 'So good to see you again, Polgara,' he said with a deep, graceful bow. 'I see that you've returned to the scene of your former conquests.'

'Hardly that, my dear Baron,' I replied, smiling. 'How have you been?'

'Desolate because of your absence, my Lady.'

'Can't you ever be serious, Kamion?'

He neatly sidestepped that. 'What on earth did you do to poor Taygon?' he asked me. 'I've never *seen* him in that condition before.'

I shrugged. 'Taygon pretends to be a total savage, but I think his poor little tummy's just a bit delicate.'

Kamion laughed. Then his expression became pensively thoughtful. 'Why don't we take a bit of a stroll, my Lady?' he suggested. 'There are a few things I'd like to share with you.'

'Of course, Baron.'

We left the room arm in arm and strolled down an airy corridor that ran along the garden side of the Citadel, pausing now and then to admire the roses. 'I don't know if you've heard, Polgara,' Kamion said, 'but I'm betrothed now.'

'Congratulations, Kamion.' I'll admit that I felt a small pang. I liked Kamion, and under different circumstances it might have gone even further.

'She's a very pretty girl, and she absolutely adores me, for some reason.'

'You *are* a rather charming gentleman, you know.'

'That's mostly a pose, dear lady,' he admitted. 'Under all that

106

polish there's still a gauche, insecure adolescent. Growing up can be *so* trying – or had you noticed?'

I laughed. 'You have no idea of just how trying *I* found it, Kamion.'

He sighed, and I knew that it wasn't a theatrical sigh. 'I'm very fond of my intended bride, of course,' he told me, 'but candor compels me to admit that one word from you would put an end to my betrothal.'

I touched his hand fondly. 'You know that I'm not going to say that word, dear Kamion. I have much too far to go.'

'I rather suspected that might be the case,' he admitted. 'The entire purpose of this little chat has been my desire to have you as a friend. I realize that actual friendship between men and women is unnatural – and probably immoral – but you and I aren't ordinary people, are we?'

'No, not really.'

'Duty's a cruel master, isn't it, Polgara? We're both caught up in the coils of destiny, I suppose. You must serve your father, and Iron-grip's asked me to serve as one of his counselors. We're both involved in affairs of state, but the problem lies in the fact that we're talking about two different states. I'd still like to have you for a friend, though.'

'You *are* my friend, Kamion, like it or not. You might come to regret it in time, but you're the one who suggested it in the first place.'

'I'll never regret it, Pol.'

And then I kissed him, and a whole world of 'might-have-beens' flashed before my eyes.

We didn't talk any more after that. Kamion gravely escorted me back to my rooms, kissed my hand, and went on back the way we had come.

I didn't see any reason to mention that little interlude to Beldaran.

It was at my suggestion that father took Riva, Anrak, and Algar up into one of the towers of the Citadel for 'conferences' during the final days of Beldaran's pregnancy. That's not really a good time to have the men-folk underfoot.

Beldaran's delivery was fairly easy – or so Arell assured me. It was the first time I'd ever witnessed the procedure, though, so it seemed moderately horrendous to me, and after all, Beldaran *was* my sister.

In due time, Beldaran was delivered, and after Arell and I'd cleaned the baby boy up, I took him to Riva. Would you believe that this 'mighty king' seemed actually afraid of the baby?

Men!

The baby, Daran, had a peculiar white mark on the palm of his right hand, and that concerned Riva quite a bit. Father'd explained it to us, though, so I knew what it meant.

The ceremony of introducing Iron-grip's heir to the Master's Orb the next morning moved me more than I can say. A very strange sensation came over me when the infant crown prince in my arms laid his hand on the Orb in greeting and he and I were both suffused with that peculiar blue aura. In an obscure way the Orb was greeting me as well as Daran, and I caught a brief glimpse of its alien awareness. The Orb and its counterpart, the Sardion, had been at the very center of creation and, before they were separated by 'the accident', they were the physical receptacle of the Purpose of the Universe. I was to be a part of that Purpose, and, since mother's mind and mine were merged, she was also included.

Father and I stayed on at the Isle for another month, and then the old wolf started getting restless. There were some things he wanted to do, and my father absolutely *hates* having things hanging over his head. As he explained, the Gods of the West had departed, and we were now to receive our instructions through prophecy, and father *definitely* wanted to have a look at the two prophets who were currently holding forth – one in Darine and the other in the fens of Drasnia. The Master had advised him that the term 'The Child of Light' would be the key that'd identify the *real* prophets, as opposed to assorted gibbering madmen, and father yearned to hear that peculiar signal as a verification of authenticity.

Anrak sailed us to the Sendarian coast and dropped us off on a beach near where the city of Sendar now stands.

I found trekking through the trackless stretches of that seemingly endless primeval forest decidedly unpleasant. Had our expedition to Darine taken place a few years earlier when I was still 'woodsey' and unkempt, I might have enjoyed it, but now I missed my bathtub, and there were so many bugs. I can still survive in the woods when it's necessary, but *really*!

I knew of an alternative to our fighting our way through the dense underbrush, of course, but the problem lay in how to broach the subject without revealing my second education – and its source. I dropped a few hints about the alternative mode of travel, but father was being impossibly dense, so I finally came right out and asked him, 'Why should I walk when I can fly?'

108

He protested a bit, and I think that might have been because he didn't really want me to grow up. Parents are like that sometimes. He finally agreed, though, and he explained the procedure of changing into another form at length. Then he explained it again – and again – until I was almost ready to scream with exasperation.

Eventually we got down to business, and I automatically assumed the familiar form of the snowy owl.

I wasn't at all prepared for his reaction. Father tends to keep his emotions rather tightly controlled, but this time I think they got the better of him. Would you believe that he actually cried? A sudden wave of compassion swept over me as I finally realized just how much he had suffered when he thought that mother had died.

I chose the form of a different owl, and father 'went wolf', as he calls it. He was a very impressive wolf, I'll give him that, and he could almost keep up with me.

We reached Darine in three days, and resumed human form before we entered the city and went looking for Hatturk, the local clanchief. Along the way father gave me a brief history of the Bear-Cult. Aberrations appear in all religions from time to time, but the heresies implicit in the Bear-Cult are so absurd that no rational human could ever swallow such patent nonsense.

'Who ever said the Bear-Cultists are rational?' Father shrugged.

'Are we certain that this Hatturk fellow's a Cultist?'

'Algar thinks so, and I respect Algar's judgment. Frankly, Pol, I don't care if Hatturk worships caterpillars just as long as he's obeyed Algar's instructions and put scribes to work copying down everything this prophet says.'

We slogged down the muddy street in the smoky early-morning light. I think every city in the northern latitudes has that continual pall hanging over it. A thousand chimneys *are* going to put out a lot of smoke, and, since the early morning air is quite still, the smoke just hangs there.

Hatturk's house was a pretentious building made of logs, and it was literally crawling with overgrown, bearded Alorns dressed in bear-skins and all well armed. Frankly, the odor of the place was almost overpowering – a fragrance comprised of spilled beer, assorted open cesspools, rank bear-hides, unwashed and unhousebroken hunting dogs, and rancid armpits.

When a still-tipsy Alorn awoke his chief to announce father's arrival, Hatturk came stumbling down the stairs, fat, bleary-eyed, and unkempt.

Father rather crisply told him why we'd come to Darine, and this 'leader of men' offered to take us to the house of Bormik, the supposed Darine prophet. Hatturk was probably still about half-drunk from the previous night, and I think he said much more than he'd have said if he'd been completely sober. Beer *does* have its uses, I suppose.

The most alarming information he let slip had to do with his decision *not* to obey his king's instructions involving scribes. Bormik had been giving us instructions, and this foul-smelling cretin had arbitrarily chosen to let them slip by unrecorded!

Bormik's cottage lay on the eastern outskirts of Darine, and he lived there with his middle-aged daughter, Luana, who evidently looked after him. Luana was a spinster, and the fact that she always seemed to be staring at the tip of her nose might have had something to do with that. She kept her father's cottage neat, however, and I noted that she even had flowers on the table.

'Polgara,' mother's voice sounded in the silences of my mind, *'she will know what her father's said. She's the key to this problem. Ignore what the men are doing. Concentrate on Luana instead. Oh, you might need some money. Steal your father's purse.'*

I had to muffle a laugh when I heard that.

Once Bormik had begun oracularizing, father's attention was so completely caught up in what the prophet was saying that he wasn't even aware of the fact that I'd deftly filched the leather bag of money from his belt.

All right, stealing things from people isn't very nice, but father'd been a thief himself when he was younger, so he probably understood.

Then I joined Luana, who was sitting off to one side, darning a pair of her father's wool stockings. 'You have a nice house here, Luana,' I said to her.

'It keeps the weather off us,' she replied indifferently. Luana wore a plain grey dress, and her hair was pulled back into a severe bun at the back of her head. The fact that she was so profoundly cross-eyed must have shaped her entire life. She'd never married, and probably never would, and, though she was neat, she made no attempt to make herself attractive. It hadn't been so long ago that *I'd* been 'ugly' myself that I'd forgotten how it felt.

'Does your father have those "spells" very often?' I asked her, broaching the subject rather carefully.

'All the time,' she said. 'Sometimes he goes on like that for hours.'

110

'Does he ever repeat himself?'

'That's what makes it so tiresome, Lady Polgara. I've heard those "speeches" of his so many times that I could probably recite them myself – not that I really have to.'

'I didn't quite follow that, Luana.'

'There are certain words that set him off. If I say 'table', I'll get one speech – that I've already heard a dozen times. If I say 'window', I'll get another – that I've also heard more often than I care to remember.'

We were safe! Mother had been right! Luana could call up the entirety of the Darine Codex with a series of key words. All I needed now was a way to get her cooperation. 'Have your eyes always been that way?' I asked her. I rather suspect that mother might have had something to do with that blunt question.

Luana's face turned pale with anger. 'I don't see where that's any of your business,' she retorted hotly.

'I'm not trying to be insulting, Luana,' I assured her. 'I've had some instruction as a physician, and I think the condition can be corrected.'

She stared at me – well, at her nose, actually, but I think you get the point. 'Could you really do that?' she asked me with an almost naked longing.

'*Tell her yes,*' mother advised.

'I'm sure I can,' I said.

'I'd give anything – *anything*! Lady Polgara, I can't even bear to look in a mirror. I don't leave the house because I can't stand to listen to all the laughter.'

'You say you can make your father repeat all those speeches?'

'Why would I want to endure that?'

'So that you can look at yourself without shame, Luana. I'll give you some money so that you can hire scribes to write down what your father says. Can you read and write?'

'Yes. Reading fills empty hours, and a woman as ugly as I am has a lot of empty hours.'

'Good. I'll want you to read over what the scribes take down to make sure it's accurate.'

'I can do that, Lady Polgara. As I said before, I could probably recite most of my father's speeches from memory.'

'Let's get it right from his own mouth.'

'Why are the ramblings of that senile old fool so important, Lady Polgara?'

'Your father may or may not be senile, Luana, but that's not really

111

important. The speeches are coming from Belar – and from the other Gods. They're telling *my* father and me what we're supposed to do.'

Her off-center eyes went very wide.

'Will you help us, Luana?'

'I will, Lady Polgara – *if* you fix my eyes.'

'Why don't we take care of that right now?' I suggested.

'Here? Right in front of the men-folk?'

'They won't even notice what we're doing.'

'Will it hurt?'

'*Will it?*' I asked mother.

'*No. This is what you do, Pol.*' And she gave me some very detailed instructions.

It was not a surgical procedure. Balten's tools hadn't been quite tiny enough for that kind of precision, so I did it 'the other way'. It involved the muscles that held Luana's eyes in place and some other things that had to do with the way her eyes focused. The most time-consuming part of it was making those minute adjustments that eliminated all signs of her previous condition. 'I think that's got it,' I said.

'Pol,' father said after Bormik had broken off his extended proclamation.

'In a minute, father,' I waved him off. I looked intently at Luana's now-straight eyes. 'Done,' I told her softly.

'Can I look at them?'

'Of course. You have very pretty eyes, Luana. If they satisfy you, will you stick to your part of the bargain?'

'Even if it costs me my life,' she replied fervently. Then she went to the mirror hanging on the far wall. 'Oh, Lady Polgara!' She exclaimed, her now straight eyes streaming tears of pure joy. 'Thank you!'

'I'm glad you like it, dear,' I told her. I stood up. 'I'll check with you from time to time, Luana. Be well.' Then I followed father out through the door.

'I think I'll turn Hatturk into a toad,' father muttered.

'What on earth for?' Then I frowned. 'Can we actually do that?'

'I'm not sure. Maybe this is the time to find out, and Hatturk's the perfect subject. We've lost more than half of this prophecy because of that man's idiocy.'

'Relax, father,' I told him. 'We haven't lost a thing. Luana's going to take care of it for us. It's all arranged.'

'What did you do, Pol?' he demanded.

'I fixed her eyes. She'll pay me for that by getting scribes to write down the whole prophecy.'

'But some of it's already slipped past us.'

'Calm down, father. Luana knows how to get Bormik to repeat what he's already said. We'll have the whole prophecy.' I paused. 'The other one's in Drasnia, isn't it?'

He gaped at me.

'Close your mouth, father. It makes you look like an idiot. Well, are we going on to Drasnia or not?'

'Yes,' he replied in an exasperated tone of voice, 'we *are* going on to Drasnia.'

I smiled at him with that sweet expression that always drives him absolutely wild. 'Were you going to hire a boat?' I asked him, 'or would you rather fly?'

Some of the things he said at that point don't bear repeating.

CHAPTER 8

The Gulf of Cherek is an Alorn lake in many respects. That's largely because of the Cherek Bore, since only Alorns are brave enough – or foolish enough – to attempt a passage through that howling maelstrom. I'll admit in retrospect that the relative isolation of the Gulf served a purpose in antiquity. It gave the Alorns a place to play and kept them out of mischief in the rest of the kingdoms of the west.

The port city of Kotu at the mouth of the Mrin River was, like all Alorn cities at that time, built largely of logs. My father objects to log cities because of the danger of fire, but my objection to them is aesthetic. A log house is ugly, and when you get right down to it the chinking between the logs is really nothing more than dried mud. Kotu was built on an island, so there wasn't all that much space for it to spread out. The streets were narrow, muddy, and crooked, and the houses were all jumbled together with their upper stories beetling out like belligerent brows. The harbor, like every harbor in the world, smelled like an open cesspool.

The ship which bore us from Darine to Kotu was a Cherek merchantman, which is to say that the heavy weaponry was not *openly* displayed on deck. We reached Kotu late on the afternoon of a depressingly murky day, and King Dras Bull-neck was there waiting for us – along with a sizeable number of colorfully dressed young Drasnian noblemen who obviously hadn't made the trip from Boktor just to enjoy the scenery in the fens. I recognized several of them, since they'd attended Beldaran's wedding, and they'd evidently told their friends about me.

We spent the night in a noisy Alorn inn that reeked of spilled beer, and it was late the following morning when we started upriver for the village of Braca, where the Mrin Prophet was kenneled.

I spent most of the rest of that day on deck dazzling the young Drasnians. They'd made a special trip just to see me, after all, so I felt that I owed them *that* much at least. I wasn't very serious about it, but a young lady ought to keep in practice, I guess. I broke a few hearts – in a kindly sort of way – but what *really* interested me was the surreptitious way the Drasnians had of wriggling their fingers at each other. I was fairly certain that it wasn't just a racial trait, so I sent out a carefully probing thought and immediately realized that they were not simply exercising their fingers. What I was seeing was a highly sophisticated sign-language, the movements of which were so minute and subtle that I was frankly amazed that any thick-fingered Alorn could have devised it.

'Dras,' I said to Bull-neck that evening, 'why do your people wiggle their fingers at each other all the time?' I already knew what they were doing, of course, but it was a way to broach the subject.

'Oh,' he replied, 'that's just the secret language. The merchants invented it as a way to communicate with each other while they're cheating somebody.'

'You don't seem to have a very high opinion of merchants, Dras,' father noted.

Dras shrugged. 'I don't like swindlers.'

'Right up until the time when they pay their taxes?' I suggested.

'That's an entirely different matter, Pol.'

'Of course, Dras. Of course. Does there happen to be someone among your retainers who's more proficient at this sign-language than the others?'

He thought about it. 'From what I hear, Khadon's the most skilled. I think you met him at your sister's wedding.'

'A little fellow? Not much taller than I am? Blond curly hair and a nervous tic in his left eyelid?'

'That's him.'

'I think I'll see if I can find him tomorrow. I'd like to know a little more about this secret language.'

'Whatever for, Pol?' father asked.

'I'm curious, father. Besides, I'm supposed to be getting an education right now, so I should probably learn something new, wouldn't you say?'

I rose early the next morning and went up on deck looking for Khadon. He was standing near the bow of the boat staring out at the fens with a look of distaste. I put on my most winsome expression and approached him. 'Ah,' I said, 'there you are, Lord Khadon. I've been looking all over for you.'

'I'm honored, Lady Polgara,' he replied, bowing gracefully. 'Is there something I can do for you?'

'Yes, as a matter of fact there is. King Dras tells me that you're highly skilled in the use of the secret language.'

'The king flatters me, my Lady,' he said with a becoming show of modesty.

'Do you suppose you could teach this language to me?'

He blinked. 'It takes quite a while to learn, my Lady.'

'Did you have something else to do today?' I said it with a transparent look of exaggerated innocence.

He laughed. 'Not a single thing, Lady Polgara. I'll be happy to instruct you.'

'Let's get started then, shall we?'

'Of course. I'd much rather look at you than at this pestilential swamp.' He gestured out at the dreary fens. I don't think I've ever met a Drasnian who actually liked the fens.

Khadon and I seated ourselves on a bench in the bow of that wide-beamed river-boat, and we began. He moved the fingers of his right hand slightly. 'This means "good morning,"' he told me.

In a little while other young Drasnians came up on deck, and I noticed some rather hard looks being directed at Khadon, but that didn't particularly bother me, and I'm sure it didn't bother my teacher either.

Khadon seemed a bit startled by how quickly I picked up the sign language he was teaching me, but I don't think he entirely grasped how much I actually learned during the next couple of days. Although he was probably not fully aware of it, Khadon carried the entire lexicon of the secret language in his head, and mother had taught me ways to lift that sort of thing gently from peoples' minds.

The village of Braca lay about midway between Kotu and Boktor, and it was built on a grey mudbank that jutted up on the south side of the sluggishly flowing Mrin River. The dozen or so shanties in Braca were all built of bone-white driftwood, and most of them were on stilts, since the Mrin flooded every spring. Fishing nets hung from long racks near the water, and muddy-looking rowboats were moored to rickety docks, also constructed of driftwood. There was a crudely built temple of Belar some distance back from the river's edge, and Bull-neck advised us that the Mrin Prophet was kept there. The overall prospect of Braca was singularly uninviting. The Mrin River was a muddy brown, and the endless sea of grass and reeds that marked the fens themselves stretched unbroken from horizon to horizon. The odor of rotting fish hung over the town like a curse, and the clouds of mosquitoes were sometimes so thick that they quite nearly blotted out the sun.

Dras and the local priest of Belar led my father and me along the shaky driftwood dock where our boat was moored and then up the muddy, rutted track to the temple. 'He's the village idiot,' the priest told us rather sadly. 'His parents were drowned in a flood shortly after he was born, and nobody knows what his name is. Since I'm the priest, they turned him over to me. I make sure that he's fed, but there's not much else I can do for him.'

'Idiot?' father asked sharply. 'I thought he was a madman.'

The priest, a kindly old man, sighed. 'No, Ancient One,' he said. 'Madness is an aberration in a normal human mind. This poor fellow doesn't *have* a mind. He can't even talk.'

'But –' father started to protest.

'He never once uttered a coherent sound, Ancient One – until a few years back. Then he suddenly started to talk. Actually, it sounds more like recitation than actual talking. Every so often, I'll pick up a phrase from "The Book of Alorn". King Dras told us all to keep an eye out for assorted madmen, since they might possibly say something that'd be useful for you to know. When our local idiot started talking, I was fairly sure that it was the sign of something significant.'

'When his Reverence's word reached me, I came down here and had a look for myself,' Dras picked up the story. 'I listened to the poor brute for a while, and then I hired some scribes to come here and stand watch over him – just the way you instructed that day back on the banks of the Aldur when you divided up father's kingdom. If it turns out that he's not a real prophet, I'll send the scribes back to Boktor. My budget's a little tight this year, so I'm trimming expenses.'

'Let me hear him talk before you close up shop here, Dras,' father said. 'His Reverence is right. An idiot who suddenly starts talking's a little out of the ordinary.'

We went around behind the shabby little temple, and I saw that beast for the first time.

He was filthy, and he seemed to enjoy wallowing in the mud, much as a pig would – and probably for the same reason. A mosquito can't bite through a thick coating of muck. He didn't have what you could really call a forehead, since his hairline seemed almost to merge with his beetling brows, and his head was peculiarly deformed, sloping back from that jutting browridge. His deep-sunk eyes contained not the faintest glimmer of human intelligence. He slobbered and moaned and jerked rhythmically on the chain that kept him from running off into the fens.

I felt an almost overpowering wave of pity come over me. Even death would have been better than what this poor creature endured.

'No, Pol,' mother's voice told me. 'Life is good, even for such a one as this, and like you and me and all the rest, he has a task to perform.'

Father spoke at some length with Bull-neck's scribes and read a few pages of what they had already transcribed. Then we returned to the ship, and I went looking for Khadon again.

It was about noon on the following day when one of the scribes came down to the river to advise us that the Prophet was talking, and we trooped once more to that rustic temple to listen to the voice of God.

I was startled by the change that had come over the sub-human creature crouched in the mud beside his kennel. There was a kind of exaltation on his brutish face, and the words coming from his mouth – words he could not possibly have understood – were pronounced very precisely in a rolling sort of voice that seemed almost to have an echo built into it.

After a while he broke off and went back to moaning and rhythmically yanking on his chain.

'That should do it,' father said. 'He's authentic.'

'How were you able to tell so quickly?' Dras asked him.

'Because he spoke of the Child of Light. Bormik did the same thing back in Darine. I spent some time with the Necessity that's inspiring these Prophets and using them to tell us what we're supposed to do. I'm very familiar with the term "Child of Light". Pass that on to your father and brothers. Any time some crazy man starts talking about "the Child of Light" we'll want to station scribes nearby.' He squinted out at the dreary fens. 'Have your scribes make me a copy of everything they've set down so far and send it to me in the Vale.'

After we returned to Bull-neck's ship, father decided that he and I should go south through the fens rather than return by way of Darine. I protested vigorously, but it didn't do me very much good. Dras located an obliging fisherman, and we proceeded south through that smelly, bug-infested swamp.

Needless to say, I did *not* enjoy the journey.

We reached the southern edge of the fens somewhat to the west of where Aldurford now stands, and father and I were both happy to put our feet on solid ground again. After our helpful fisherman had poled his narrow boat back into the swamp, my father's expression grew slightly embarrassed. 'I think it's about time for us to have a little talk, Pol,' he said, avoiding my eyes rather carefully.

'Oh?'

'You're growing up, and there are some things you should know.'

I knew what he was getting at, and I suppose that the kindest thing I could have done at that point would have been to tell him right out that I already knew all about it. He'd just dragged me through the fens, though, so I wasn't feeling very charitable just then. I put on an expression of vapid stupidity and let him flounder his way through a moderately inept description of the process of human reproduction. His face grew redder and redder as he went along, and then he quite suddenly stopped. 'You already know about all of this, don't you?' he demanded.

I batted my eyelashes at him in feigned innocence and his expression was a bit sullen as we continued our journey through Algaria to the Vale.

Uncle Beldin had returned from Mallorea when we got home, and he told us that there was absolute chaos on the other side of the Sea of the East.

'Why's that, uncle?' I asked him.

'Because there's nobody in charge. Angaraks follow orders very well, but they tend to fly apart when there's nobody around to *give* those orders. Torak's still having religious experiences at Ashaba, and Zedar's camped right at his elbow taking down his every word. Ctuchik's down in Cthol Murgos, and Urvon's afraid to come out of Mal Yaska because he thinks I might be hiding behind some tree or bush waiting for the chance to gut him.'

'What about the generals at Mal Zeth?' father asked. 'I thought they'd leap at the chance to take over.'

'Not as long as Torak's still around, they won't. If he snaps out of that trance and discovers that the general staff's been stepping out of line, he'll obliterate Mal Zeth and everybody in it. Torak doesn't encourage creativity.'

'I guess that only leaves Ctuchik for us to worry about, then,' father mused.

'He's probably enough,' Beldin said. 'Oh, he's moved, by the way.'

Father nodded. 'I'd heard about it. He's supposed to be at a place called Rak Cthol now.'

Beldin grunted. 'I flew over it on my way home. Charming place. It should more than satisfy Ctuchik's burning need for ugliness. Do

119

you remember that big lake that used to lie to the west of Karnath?'

'I think so.'

'It all drained out when Burnt-face cracked the world. It's a desert now with a black sand floor. Rak Cthol's built on the top of a peak that sticks up out of the middle of it.'

'Thanks,' father said.

'What for?'

'I've been meaning to go have a talk with Ctuchik. Now I know where to find him.'

'Are you going to kill him?' my uncle asked eagerly.

'I doubt it. I don't think any of us – either on our side or theirs – should do anything permanent until all those prophecies are in place. That's what I want to talk with Ctuchik about. Let's not have any more "accidents" like the one that divided the universe in the first place.'

'I can sort of go along with that.'

'Keep an eye on Polgara for me, will you?'

'Of course.'

'I don't need a keeper, father,' I said tartly.

'You're wrong about that, Pol, ' he told me. 'You tend to want to experiment, and there are *some* areas where you shouldn't. Just humor me this time, Pol. I'll have enough on my mind while I'm on the way to Rak Cthol without having to worry about you as well.'

After father left, life in the Vale settled down into a kind of homey domesticity. The twins and I took turns with the cooking, and Beldin spent his time browsing through his extensive library. I continued to visit the Tree – and mother – during the long days, but evenings were the time for talk, and Beldin, the twins, and I gathered in this or that tower for supper and conversation after the sun had gone down each evening.

We were in uncle Beldin's fanciful tower one perfect evening, and I was standing at the window watching the stars come out. 'What sparked all this curiosity about healing, Pol?' Beldin asked me.

'Beldaran's pregnancy, most likely,' I replied, still watching the stars. 'She *is* my sister, after all, and something was happening to her that I'd never experienced myself. I wanted to know all about it, so I went to Arell's shop to get some first-hand information from an expert.'

'Who's Arell?' Belkira asked.

I turned away from the stars. 'Beldaran's midwife,' I explained.

'She has a shop for that?'

'No. She's also a dressmaker. We all got to know her when we were getting things ready for Beldaran's wedding. Arell's a very down-to-earth sort of person, and she explained the whole process to me.'

'What led you to branch out?' Beldin asked curiously.

'You gentlemen have corrupted me,' I replied, smiling at them. 'Learning just one facet of something's never quite enough, so I guess I wanted to go on until I'd exhausted the possibilities of the subject. Arell told me that certain herbs help to quiet labor pains, and that led me to Argak the herbalist. He's spent a lifetime studying the effects of various herbs. He's even got a fair-sized collection of Nyissan poisons. He's a grumpy sort of fellow, but I flattered him into giving me instruction, so I can probably deal with the more common ailments. Herbs are probably at the core of the physician's art, but some things can't be cured with herbs alone, so Arell and Argak took me to see Salheim the smith, who's also a very good bone-setter. He taught me how to fix broken bones, and from there I went to see a barber named Balten to learn surgery.'

'A barber?' Belkira asked incredulously.

I shrugged. 'You need sharp implements for surgery, uncle, and a barber keeps his razors very sharp.' I smiled slightly. 'I might have actually contributed something to the art of surgery while I was there. Balten usually got his patients roaring drunk before he started cutting, but I talked with Argak about it, and he concocted a mixture of various herbs that puts people to sleep. It's faster and much more dependable than several gallons of beer. The only part of surgery I didn't care for was grave-robbing.'

'Grave-robbing?' Beltira exclaimed, shuddering.

'It's part of the study of anatomy, uncle. You have to know where things are located before you cut somebody open, so surgeons usually dig up dead bodies to examine as a way to increase their knowledge.'

Uncle Beldin looked around at the groaning bookshelves that covered almost every open wall of his lovely tower. 'I think I've got some Melcene texts on anatomy knocking around here someplace, Pol,' he said. 'I'll see if I can dig them out for you.'

'Would you please, uncle?' I said. 'I'd much rather get that information from a text-book than carve it out of somebody who's been dead for a month.'

They all choked on that a bit.

My uncles were interested in what had happened on the Isle

of the Winds, of course, since we were all very close to Beldaran, but they were *really* curious about the two Prophets. We had entered what the Seers at Kell call 'the Age of Prophecy', and the Master had advised my father that the two Necessities would speak to us from the mouths of madmen. The problem with that, of course, lay in the whole business of deciding *which* madmen to listen to.

'Father seems to think he's found the answer to that problem,' I told them one evening when we'd gathered in the twins' tower. 'He believes that the Necessity identifies itself by putting the words "the Child of Light" into the mouths of the *real* prophets. We all know what the expression means, and ordinary people don't. At any rate, both Bormik and the idiot in Braca used the term.'

'That's convenient,' Belkira noted.

'Also economical,' I added. 'Bull-neck was a little unhappy about the expense of paying scribes to hover over every crazy man in his entire kingdom.'

It was during that time of homey domesticity that mother explained the significance of the silver amulet father had fashioned for me. '*It gives you a way to focus your power, Pol,*' she told me. '*When you're forming the idea of what you want to do – something that you're not really sure you can do – channel the thought through your amulet, and it'll intensify your will.*'

'Why does Beldaran have one, then, mother? I love her, of course, but she doesn't seem to have "talent."'

Mother laughed. '*Oh, dear, dear Polgara,*' she said to me. '*In some ways Beldaran's even more talented than you are.*'

'What are you talking about, mother? I've never seen her do *anything.*'

'*I know. You probably never will, either. You always do what she tells you to do, though, don't you?*'

'Well –' I stopped as *that* particular thought came crashing in on me. Sweet, gentle Beldaran *had* dominated me since before we were born. 'That isn't fair, mother!' I objected.

'*What isn't?*'

'First she's prettier than I am, and now you tell me that she's more powerful. Can't I be better at *something* than she is?'

'*It's not a competition, Polgara. Each of us is different, that's all, and each of us has different things we have to do. This isn't a foot-race, so there aren't any prizes for winning.*'

I felt a little silly at that point.

Then mother explained that Beldaran's power was passive. '*She makes everybody love her, Pol, and you can't get much more powerful than that. In some ways, she's like this Tree. She changes people just by being there. Oh, she can also hear with her amulet.'*

'Hear?'

'She can hear people talking – even if they're miles away. A time will come when that'll be very useful.'

Ce'Nedra discovered that quite some time later.

It was almost autumn when father returned from Rak Cthol. The sun had gone down when he came clumping up the stairs of his tower where I was preparing supper and talking with uncle Beldin. Making some noise when you enter a room where there's someone with 'talent' is only good common sense. You don't really want to startle someone who has unusual capabilities at his disposal.

'What kept you?' Uncle Beldin asked him.

'It's a long way to Rak Cthol, Beldin.' Father looked around. 'Where are the twins?'

'They're busy right now, father,' I told him. 'They'll be along later.'

'How did things go at Rak Cthol?' Beldin asked.

'Not bad.'

Then they got down to details.

My concept of my father had somehow been based on the less admirable side of his nature. No matter what had happened, he was still Garath at the core: lazy, deceitful, and highly unreliable. When the occasion demanded it, though, the Old Wolf could set 'Garath' and all his faults aside and become 'Belgarath'. Evidently, *that* was the side of him that Ctuchik saw. Father didn't come right out and say it, but Ctuchik was clearly afraid of him, and that in itself was enough to make me reconsider my opinion of the sometimes foolish old man who'd sired me.

'What now, Belgarath?' uncle Beldin asked after father'd finished.

Father pondered that for a while. 'I think we'd better call in the twins. We're running without instructions here, and I'll feel a lot more comfortable if I know that we're running in the right direction. I wasn't just blowing smoke in Ctuchik's ear when I raised the possibility of a *third* destiny taking a hand in this game of ours. If Torak succeeds in corrupting every copy of the Ashabine Oracles, everything goes up in the air again. Two

123

possibilities are bad enough. I'd really rather not have to stare a third one in the face.'

And so we called the twins to father's tower, joined our wills, and asked the Master to visit us.

And, of course, he did. His form seemed hazy and insubstantial, but, as father explained to the rest of us later on, it was the Master's counsel we needed, not the reassurance of his physical presence.

Even I was startled when the first thing the Master did was come directly to me, saying, 'My beloved daughter.' I knew he liked me, but that was the first time he'd ever expressed anything like genuine love. Now, *that's* the sort of thing that could go to a young lady's head. I think it startled my father and my uncles even more than it startled me. They were all very wise, but they were still men, and the notion that I was as much the Master's disciple as they were seemed to unsettle them, since most men can't seem to accept the fact that women have *souls*, much less minds.

Father's temporary disquiet faded when the Master assured him that Torak could not alter the Ashabine Oracles enough to send Zedar, Ctuchik, and Urvon down the wrong path. No matter how much Torak disliked his vision, he would not be permitted to tamper with it in any significant fashion. Zedar was with him at Ashaba, and Zedar was to some degree still working for us – at least insofar as he would protect the integrity of prophecy. And even if Zedar failed, the Dals would not.

Then the Master left us, and he left behind a great emptiness as well.

Things were quiet in the Vale for the next several years, and our peculiar fellowship has always enjoyed those quiet stretches, since they give us a chance to study, and study is our primary occupation, after all.

I think it was in the spring of the year 2025 – by the Alorn calendar – when Algar Fleet-foot brought us copies of the complete Darine Codex and the half-finished Mrin. Algar was in his mid-forties by now, and his dark hair was touched with grey. He'd finally begun to put some weight on that lean frame of his and he was very impressive. What was perhaps even more impressive was the fact that he'd actually learned how to talk – not a great deal, of course, but getting more than two words at a time out of Algar had always been quite an accomplishment.

My father eagerly seized the scrolls and probably would have gone off into seclusion with them at once, but when Algar casually announced the upcoming meeting of the Alorn Council, I badgered my aged sire about it until he finally gave in and agreed that a visit to the Isle might not be a bad idea.

Fleet-foot accompanied father, Beldin and me to the city of Riva for the council meetings, though the affairs of state weren't really very much on our minds. The supposed earth-shaking significance of those 'councils of state' were little more than excuses for family get-togethers in those days, and we could quite probably have taken care of the entire *official* agenda with a few letters.

In my case, I wanted to spend some time with my sister, and I'd clubbed my father into submission by suggesting that he ought to get to know his grandson.

That particular bait might have worked just a little too well. Daran was about seven that year, and father has a peculiar affinity for seven-year-old boys for some reason. But I think it goes a little deeper. I've noticed that mature men get all gushy inside when they come into contact with their grandsons, and my father was no exception. He and Daran hit it off immediately. Although it was spring and the weather on the Isle was abysmally foul, the two of them decided to go off on an extended fishing expedition, of all things. What *is* this thing with fishing? Do *all* men lose their ability to think rationally when they hear the word 'fish'?

The note my father left for us was characteristically vague about little things like destinations, equipment, and food supplies. Poor Beldaran worried herself sick about what our irresponsible father was up to, but there was nothing she could do. Father can evade the most determined searchers.

I was worried more about something else. My twin seemed very pale, and there were dark circles under her eyes. She coughed quite a bit and was at times listless almost to the point of exhaustion. I spent quite a bit of time with Arell and with our resident herbalist, who concocted several remedies for his queen. They seemed to help my sister a little, but I was still very concerned about the condition of her health.

Inevitably, Beldaran and I were growing further and further apart. When we'd been children, we'd been so close that we were almost one person, but after her marriage, our lives diverged. Beldaran was completely caught up in her husband and child, and I was involved in my studies. If we'd lived closer to each other, our separation might not have been so obvious and painful, but we were separated by all those empty leagues, so there wasn't much opportunity for us to stay in touch.

*   *   *

This is very painful for me, so I don't think I'll pursue it any further.

After a month or so, father, Beldin, and I returned to the Vale and to the waiting Darine Codex.

CHAPTER 9

It was late summer when we returned home from the Isle of the Winds. It's nice to visit loved ones, but it always feels good to come back to the Vale. There's a peace here that we find in no other place. I suppose that when you get right down to it, the Vale of Aldur is hardly more than an extension of the southern tip of Algaria, but I think that if you come here, you'll notice the difference immediately. Our grass is greener, for some reason, and our sky seems a deeper blue. The land is gently rolling and dotted here and there with dark pines and with groves of snowy-trunked birch and aspen. The mountains of Ulgoland lying to the west are crested with eternal snows that are always tinged with blue in the morning, and the starker mountains of Mishrak ac Thull that claw at the sky beyond the Eastern Escarpment are purple in the distance. My father's tower and the towers of my uncles are stately structures, and since they were in no hurry when they built them, they had plenty of time to make sure that the stones fit tightly together, which makes the towers seem more like natural outcroppings than the work of human hands. Everything here is somehow perfectly right with nothing out of place and no ugliness anywhere to be seen.

Our fawn-colored deer are so tame as to sometimes be a nuisance, and underfoot there are always long-eared rabbits with puffy white tails. The fact that the twins feed them might have something to do with that. I feed my birds, too, but that's an entirely different matter.

It's probably because our Vale lies at the juncture of two mountain ranges that there's always a gentle breeze blowing here, and it undulates the grass in long waves, almost like a sea.

When we returned home father seemed quite fully prepared to go into absolute seclusion with the Darine Codex clasped to his bosom, but my uncles would have none of that. 'Hang it all, Belgarath,' Beltira said with uncharacteristic heat one evening as the sun was touching the sky over Ulgo with fire, 'you're not the only one with a stake in this, you know. We all need copies.'

Father's expression grew sullen. 'You can read it when I'm finished. Right now I don't have time to fool around with pens and ink-pots.'

'You're selfish, Belgarath,' uncle Beldin growled at him, scratching at his shaggy beard and sprawling deeper into his chair by the fire. 'That's always been your one great failing. Well, it's not going to work this time. You aren't going to get any peace until we've all got copies.'

Father glowered at him.

'You're holding the only copy we have, Belgarath,' Belkira pointed out. 'If something happens to it, it might take us months to get a replacement.'

'I'll be careful with it.'

'You just want to keep it all to yourself,' Beltira accused him. 'You've been riding that "first disciple" donkey for years now.'

'That has nothing to do with it.'

'Oh, *really*?'

'This is ridiculous!' Beldin burst out. 'Give me that thing, Belgarath.'

'But –'

'Hand it over – or do we want to get physical about it? I'm stronger than you are, and I can *take* it from you if I have to.'

Father grudgingly handed him the scroll. 'Don't lose my place,' he told his gnarled little brother.

'Oh, shut up.' Beldin looked at the twins. 'How many copies do we need?'

'One for each of us, anyway,' Beltira replied. 'Where do you keep your ink-pots, Belgarath?'

'We won't need any of that,' Beldin told him. He looked around and then pointed at one of father's work-tables which stood not far from where I was busy preparing supper. 'Clear that off,' he ordered.

'I'm working on some of those things,' father protested.

'Not very hard, I see. The dust and cobwebs are fairly thick.'

The twins were already stacking father's books, notes, and meticulously constructed little models of obscure mechanical devices on the floor.

My father's always taken credit for what Beldin did on that perfect evening, since he can annex an idea as quickly as he can annex any

128

other piece of property, but my memory of the incident is very clear. Beldin laid the oversized scroll Luana had prepared for us on the table and untied the ribbon that kept it rolled up. 'I'm going to need some light here,' he announced.

Beltira held out his hand, palm-up, and concentrated for a moment. A blazing ball of pure energy appeared there, and then it rose to hang like a miniature sun over the table.

'Show-off,' father muttered at him.

'I told you to shut up,' Beldin reminded him. Then his ugly face contorted in thought. We all felt and heard the surge as he released his Will.

Six blank scrolls appeared on the table, three on either side of the original Darine. Then my dwarfed uncle began to unroll the Darine Codex with his eyes fixed on the script. The blank scrolls, now no longer blank, unrolled in unison as he passed his eyes down the long, seamless parchment Fleet-foot had sent to us.

'Now that's something that's never occurred to me,' Beltira said admiringly. 'When did you come up with the idea?'

'Just now,' Beldin admitted. 'Hold that light up a little higher, would you, please?'

Father's expression was growing sulkier by the minute.

'What's *your* problem?' Beldin demanded.

'You're cheating.'

'Of course I am. We all cheat. It's what we do. Are you only just now realizing that?'

Father spluttered at that point.

'Oh, dear,' I sighed.

'What's the matter, Pol?' Belkira asked me.

'I'm living with a group of white-haired little boys, uncle. When *are* you old men ever going to grow up?'

They all looked slightly injured by *that* particular suggestion. Men always do, I've noticed.

Beldin continued to unroll the original codex while the twins rapidly compared the copies to it line by line. 'Any mistakes yet?' the dwarf asked.

'Not a one,' Beltira replied.

'Maybe I've got it right then.'

'How much longer are you going to be at that?' father demanded.

'As long as it takes. Give him something to eat, Pol. Get him out of my hair.'

Father stamped away, muttering to himself.

Actually, it took Beldin no more than an hour, since he wasn't actually reading the text he was copying. He explained the process to us later that evening. All he was really doing was transferring the *image* of the original to those blank scrolls. 'Well,' he said at last, 'that's that. Now we can all snuggle up to the silly thing.'

'Which one's the original?' father demanded, looking at the seven scrolls lined upon the table.

'What difference does it make?' Beldin growled.

'I want my original copy.'

And then I laughed at them, even as I checked the ham we were having for dinner.

'It's not funny, Pol,' father reprimanded me.

'I found it fairly amusing. Now, why don't you all go wash up? Supper's almost ready.'

After we'd eaten, we each took up our own copy of Bormik's ravings and retired to various chairs scattered about father's tower to be alone with the word of the Gods – or with the word of that unseen Purpose that controlled the lives of every living thing on the face of the earth.

I took my copy to my favorite oversized chair beside the fireplace in the kitchen area and untied the ribbon that kept it rolled up. There was a brief note from Luana inside. 'Lady Polgara,' Bormik's daughter began. 'Thus I've kept my part of our bargain. I feel I must thank you once more for your gift to me. I'm living in central Algaria now, and would you believe that I actually have a suitor? He's older, of course, but he's a good, solid man who's very kind to me. I thought that I'd never marry, but Belar's seen fit to provide me a chance for happiness. I can't begin to thank you enough.'

It hadn't been Belar who'd rewarded Luana, of course. Over the years I've noticed again and again that the Purpose that created everything that is, that was, or ever will be has a sense of obligation, and it always rewards service. I don't have to look any further than the faces of my own children and my husband to see mine.

The handwriting on Luana's note was identical to the script in which our copies of the Darine Codex were cast, a clear indication that she'd meticulously copied off the document her scribes had produced. It hadn't really been necessary, of course, but Luana appeared to take her obligations very seriously.

The Darine Codex, despite its occasional soarings, is really a rather pedestrian document, since it seems almost driven by a need to keep track of time. I know why now, but when I first read through it, it was tedious going. I thought that the tediousness was no more than a reflection of Bormik's deranged mentality, but I now know that such was not the case.

Uncle Beldin ploughed his way through the Darine in about six months, and then one evening in midwinter he trudged through the snow to father's tower. 'I'm starting to get restless,' he announced. 'I think I'll go back to Mallorea and see if I can catch Urvon off guard long enough to disembowel him just a little bit.'

'How can you disembowel somebody just a little bit?' father asked with an amused expression.

'I thought I'd take him up to the top of a cliff, rip him open, wrap a loop of his guts around a tree stump and then kick him off the edge.'

'Uncle, *please*!' I objected in revulsion.

'It's something in the nature of a scientific experiment, Pol,' he explained with a hideous grin. 'I want to find out if his guts break when he comes to the end or if he bounces instead.'

'That will *do*, uncle!'

He was still laughing that wicked laugh of his as he went down the stairs.

'He's an evil man,' I told my father.

'Fun, though,' father added.

The twins had watched Beldin's mode of copying the Darine Codex very closely and had duplicated the procedure with the uncompleted Mrin. I think it was that incompleteness that made us all pay only passing attention to the Mrin – that and the fact that it was largely incomprehensible.

'It's all jumbled together,' father complained to the twins and me one snowy evening after we'd eaten supper and were sitting by the fire in his tower. 'That idiot in Braca has absolutely no concept of time. He starts out talking about things that happened before the cracking of the world and in the next breath he's rambling on about what's going to happen so far in the future that it makes my mind reel. I can't for the life of me separate one set of EVENTS from another.'

'It think that's one of the symptoms of idiocy, brother,' Beltira told him. 'There was an idiot in our village when Belkira and I were just children, and he always seemed confused and frightened when the sun went down and it started to get dark. He couldn't seem to remember that it happened every day.'

'The Mrin mentions *you* fairly often though, Belgarath,' Belkira noted.

Father grunted sourly. 'And usually not in a very complimentary way, I've noticed. It says nice things about Pol, though.'

'I'm more loveable than you are, father,' I teased him.

'Not when you talk *that* way, you aren't.'

I'd browsed into various passages in the Mrin myself on occasion. The term the Prophet used most frequently to identify father was 'ancient and beloved', and there were references to 'the daughter of the ancient and beloved' – me, I surmised, since the daughter mentioned was supposed to do things that Beldaran was clearly incapable of doing. The incoherent time-frame of the Prophecy made it almost impossible to say just exactly *when* these things were going to happen, but there was a sort of sense that they'd be widely separated in time. I'd always rather taken it for granted that my life-span was going to be abnormally long, but the Mrin brought a more disturbing reality crashing in on me. Evidently I was going to live for thousands of years, and when I looked at the three old men around me, I didn't like that idea very much. 'Venerable' is a term often applied to men of a certain age, and there's a great deal of respect attached to it. I've never heard anyone talking about a venerable woman, however. The term attached to *us* is 'crone', and that didn't set too well with me. It was a little vain, perhaps, but the notion of cronehood sent me immediately to my mirror. A very close examination of my reflection didn't reveal any wrinkles, though – at least not yet.

The four of us spent about ten years – or maybe it was only nine – concentrating our full attention on the Darine Codex, and then the Master sent father to Tolnedra to see to the business of linking the Borune family with the Dryads. Father's use of chocolate to persuade the Dryad Princess Xoria to go along with the notion has always struck me as more than a little immoral.

No, I'm *not* going to pursue that.

The twins and I remained in the Vale working on the Darine Codex, and a sort of generalized notion of what lay in store for mankind began to emerge. None of us liked what we saw ahead very much. There was a lot of turmoil, frequent wars, and incalculable human suffering yet to come.

Three more years passed, and then one night mother's voice came to me with an uncharacteristic note of urgency in it. '*Polgara!*' she said. '*Go to Beldaran – now! She's very ill! She needs you!*'

'What is it, mother?'

'I don't know. Hurry! She's dying, Polgara!'

That sent a deathly chill through me, and I ran quickly to the twins' tower. 'I have to leave,' I shouted up the stairs to them.

'What's wrong, Pol?' Beltira called to me.

'Beldaran's ill – very ill. I have to go to her. I'll keep in touch with you.' Then I dashed back outside again before they could ask me how I knew that my sister was so sick. Mother's secret absolutely *had* to be protected. I chose the form of a falcon for the journey. Speed was essential, and owls don't fly very fast.

It was the dead of winter when I left the Vale and sped north along the eastern edge of the mountains of Ulgoland. I chose that route since I knew I'd encounter storms in those mountains, and I didn't want to be delayed. I flew almost as far north as Aldurford, keeping a continual eye on the range of peaks that separated Algaria from the Sendarian plain. It was obvious that the weather was foul over those mountains. Finally, there wasn't any help for it. I had to turn west and fly directly into the teeth of that howling storm. It's sometimes possible to fly above a storm. Summer squalls and spring showers are fairly localized. Winter storms, however, involve great masses of air that tower so high that going over the top of them is virtually impossible. I pressed on with the wind tearing at my feathers and the stinging snow half blinding me. I was soon exhausted and had no choice but to swirl down into a sheltered little valley to rest and regain my strength.

The next day I tried staying down in those twisting valleys to avoid the full force of the wind, but I soon realized that I was beating my way through miles of snow-clogged air without really accomplishing anything. Grimly I went up into the full force of the wind again.

I finally passed the crest of the mountains and soared down the west slope toward the Sendarian plain. It was still snowing, but at least the wind had diminished. Then I reached the coast, and the fight started again. The gale blowing across the Sea of the Winds was every bit as savage as the wind in the mountains had been, and there was no place to rest among those towering waves.

It took me five days altogether to reach the Isle of the Winds and I was shaking with exhaustion when I settled at last on the battlements of the Citadel early on the morning of the sixth day. My body screamed for rest, but there was no time for that. I hurried through the bleak corridors to the royal apartments and went in without bothering to knock.

The main room of those living quarters was littered with discarded clothing and the table cluttered with the remains of half-eaten meals. Iron-grip, his grey clothes rumpled and his face unshaven, came out of an exhausted half-doze as I entered. 'Thank the Gods!' he exclaimed.

'Aunt Pol!' my nephew, who looked at least as haggard as his father, greeted me. Daran was about twenty now, and I was surprised at how much he had grown.

'Where is she?' I demanded.

'She's in bed, Pol,' Riva told me. 'She had a bad night, and she's exhausted. She coughs all the time, and she can't seem to get her breath.'

'I need to talk with her physicians,' I told them crisply. 'Then I'll want to look at her.'

'Ah –' Riva floundered. 'We haven't actually called in any physicians yet, Pol. I think Elthek, the Rivan Deacons', been praying over her, though. He says that hiring physicians is just a waste of time and money.'

'He tells us that mother's getting better, though,' Daran added.

'How would *he* know?'

'He's a priest, Aunt Pol. Priests are very wise.'

'I've never known a priest yet who knew his right hand from his left. Take me to your mother immediately.' I looked around at all the litter. 'Get this cleaned up,' I told them.

Daran opened the bedroom door and glanced in. 'She's asleep,' he whispered.

'Good. At least your priest isn't inflicting any more of his mumbo-jumbo on her. From now on, keep him away from her.'

'You *can* make her well, can't you, Aunt Pol?'

'That's why I'm here, Daran.' I tried to make it sound convincing.

I scarcely recognized my sister when I reached the bed. She'd lost so much weight! The circles under eyes looked like bruises, and her breathing was labored. I touched her drawn face briefly and discovered that she was burning with fever. Then I did something I'd never done before. I sent a probing thought at my sister's mind and merged my thought with hers.

'*Polgara?*' her sleeping thought came to me. '*I don't feel well.*'

'*Where is it, Beldaran?*' I asked gently.

'*My chest. It feels so tight.*' Then her half-drowsing thought was gone.

I'd more or less expected that. The accursed climate on the Isle of the Winds was killing my sister.

I probed further, deeper into her body. As I'd expected, the center of her illness was located in her lungs.

I came out of the bedroom and softly closed the door behind me. 'I have to go down into the city,' I told Riva and Daran.

'Why?' Riva asked me.

'I need some medications.'

'Elthek says that those things are a form of witchcraft, Pol,' Riva said. 'He says that only prayers to Belar can cure Beldaran.'

I said some things I probably shouldn't have said at that point. Riva looked startled, and Daran dropped the clothing he'd been picking up. 'Just as soon as my sister's on the mend, I'm going to have a long talk with your precious Rivan Deacon,' I told them from between clenched teeth. 'For right now, tell him to stay away from Beldaran. Tell him that if he goes into her room again, I'll make him wish he'd never been born. I'll be back in just a little while.'

'I'll send Brand with you,' Riva offered.

'Brand? Who's he?'

'Baron Kamion. Brand's sort of a title. He's my chief advisor, and he carries a lot of the weight of my crown for me.' Riva made a rueful face. 'I probably should have listened to him this time. He said a lot of the things you've already said – about the Deacon, I mean.'

'Why didn't you listen to him? Tell him to catch up with me.' Then I stormed out of the royal apartment and went along the grim, torchlit corridor toward the main entrance to the Citadel, muttering some of uncle Beldin's more colorful epithets along the way.

Kamion caught up with me just as I reached the massive doors that opened out into the snowy courtyard. He was older, of course, and he seemed more sober and serious than he'd been the last time I'd seen him. His blond hair was touched at the temples with grey now, but I noted with approval that he hadn't gone so completely Alorn as to grow a beard. He wore a grey woolen cloak and carried another over his arm. 'It's good to see you again, Pol,' he said. Then he held out the extra cloak. 'Here,' he said. 'Put this on. It's cold out there.'

'I'm feeling *very* warm right now, Kamion,' I told him. 'Couldn't you keep that idiot priest away from Riva?'

He sighed. 'I tried, Pol. Believe me I tried, but his Majesty likes to get along with people, and Elthek waves his religious office around like a war-banner. He's half-convinced most of the population that he speaks for Belar, and that's very difficult to counter. His Majesty's the keeper of the Orb, and that makes him a holy

135

object in the eyes of the priesthood. In a peculiar way the priests seem to think they own him. They have no real understanding of the Orb, so they seem to believe that it'll do anything Riva tells it to do. They don't comprehend the limitations. Would you believe that Elthek even went so far as to suggest that his Majesty try to cure his wife by touching her with the Orb?'

'That would have killed her!'

'Yes, I know. I managed to persuade him not to try it without some guidance from either you or your father.'

'At least he had enough sense to listen to you.'

'Can you cure my queen, Pol?' he asked as we went out into the courtyard.

I looked directly at his handsome face and knew that I could tell him a truth that I'd hidden from Riva and Daran. 'I'm not sure, Kamion,' I admitted.

He sighed. 'I was afraid it was more serious than we thought at first,' he admitted. 'What's causing the illness?'

'The filthy climate of the God-forsaken island!' I burst out. 'It's destroying my sister's lungs. She can't breathe here.'

He nodded. 'The queen's been falling ill every winter for quite a number of years now. What do we need from the city?'

'I need to talk with Arell, and then I'm going to ransack the shop of a herbalist named Argak. I think I might want to talk with a man named Balten as well.'

'I think I know him. He's a barber, isn't he?'

'That's his day-job, Kamion. At night he's a grave-robber.'

'He's *what*?'

'Actually, he's a surgeon, and he digs up dead bodies so that he can study them. You need to know what you're doing when you cut into people.'

'Surely you're not going to cut into the queen's body?' he exclaimed.

'I'll take her apart and put her back together again if that's what it takes to save her life, Kamion. I don't think Balten's going to be of much use, but he might know something about lungs that I don't. Right now I'd strike a bargain with Torak himself if he could help me save Beldaran.'

Arell was older, of course. Her hair was grey now, but her eyes were very wise. 'What kept you, Pol?' she demanded when Kamion and I entered her cluttered little dress shop.

'I only heard about Beldaran's illness recently, Arell,' I replied. 'Is Argak still in business?'

136

She nodded. 'He's as crotchety as ever, though, and he hates being awakened before noon.'

'That's just too bad, isn't it? I need some things from his shop, and if he doesn't want to wake up, I'll have Lord Brand here chop open the door with his sword.'

'My pleasure, Pol,' Kamion said, smiling.

'Oh, another thing, Arell,' I said. 'Could you send for Balten, too?'

'Balten's in the dungeon under the temple of Belar right now, Pol. A couple of priests caught him in the graveyard the other night. He had a shovel, and there was a dead body in his wheel-barrow. They're probably going to burn him at the stake for witchcraft.'

'No. They're not. Go get him out for me, would you, please, Kamion?'

'Of course, Pol. Did you want me to chop down the temple?'

'Don't try to be funny, Kamion,' I told him tartly.

'Just a bit of levity to relieve the tension, my Lady.'

'Levitate on your own time. Let's all get busy, shall we?'

Kamion went off to the temple of Belar while Arell and I went to Argak's chemistry shop. I wasn't really very gentle when I woke up my former teacher. After Arell and I had pounded on his shop door for about five minutes, I unleashed a thunderclap in the bedroom upstairs. Thunderclaps are impressive enough outdoors. Sharing a room with one is almost guaranteed to wake you up. The stone building was still shuddering when Argak's window flew open and he appeared above us. 'What was that?' he demanded. His eyes were wide, his sparse hair was sticking straight up, and he was trembling violently.

'Just a little wake-up call, dear teacher,' I told him. 'Now get down here and open the door to your shop or I'll blow it all to splinters.'

'There's no need to get violent, Pol,' he said placatingly.

'Not unless you try to go back to bed, my friend.'

It took me about an hour to locate all the medications I thought I might need, and Argak helpfully suggested others. Some of those herbs were fairly exotic, and some were actually dangerous, requiring carefully measured doses.

Then Kamion returned with Balten. Evidently even the arrogant priests of Belar knew enough not to argue with the Rivan Warder. 'What's behind all this idiotic interference from the priests?' I demanded of my teachers. 'This sort of thing wasn't going on when I was studying here.'

'It's Elthek, the new Rivan Deacon, Pol,' Arell explained. 'He's hysterical about witchcraft.'

137

'That's a pose, Arell,' Balten told her. 'Elthek tries to keep it a secret, but he's a Bear-Cultist to the bone. He receives instructions regularly from the High Priest of Belar in Val Alorn. The Cult's goal has always been absolute domination of Alorn society. All this nonsense about witchcraft isn't really anything more than an excuse to eliminate competition. Elthek wants the population here on the Isle to turn to the priesthood in any kind of emergency – including illness. The practice of medicine can effect cures that seem miraculous to ordinary Alorns. Elthek doesn't like the idea of miracles that come from some source other than the priesthood. That's what's behind all those long-winded sermons about witchcraft. He's trying to discredit those of us who practice medicine.'

'Maybe so,' Argak grumbled darkly, 'but all the laws pointed right at us come from the throne.'

'That's not entirely his Majesty's fault,' Kamion told him. 'Alorn custom dictates that all religious matters are the domain of the priesthood. If Elthek presents a proposed law to the throne as a religious issue, Iron-grip automatically signs and seals it – usually without even bothering to read it. He and I have argued about that on occasion. Elthek fills the first paragraph of a proposed "theological ordinance" with all sorts of religious nonsense, and our king's eyes glaze over before he gets to the meat of the document. Elthek keeps insisting that prayer is the only way to cure disease.'

'He'd actually sacrifice my sister for a political idea?' I exclaimed.

'Of course he would, Pol. He doesn't worship Belar, he worships his own power.'

'I think Algar had the right idea,' I muttered darkly. 'As soon as Beldaran gets well, we might want to do something about the Bear-Cult here on the Isle.'

'It'd certainly make *our* lives easier,' Arell noted. 'I'm getting a little tired of being called a witch.'

'Why don't we all go up to the Citadel?' I suggested.

'You'll get us burned at the stake, Pol,' Argak objected. 'If we openly practice medicine – particularly in the Citadel – the Deacon's priests will clap us into the dungeon and start gathering firewood.'

'Don't worry, Argak,' I said grimly. 'If anybody's going to catch on fire, it'll be Elthek himself.'

And so we all climbed the hill to the Citadel. Now that I was aware of the situation and was paying closer attention, I noticed that there seemed to be far more priests in that fortress than were really necessary.

Beldaran was awake when we all trooped into her bedroom, and after we'd examined her, we gathered in the next room for a consultation.

'The condition appears to be chronic,' Balten observed. 'This should have been looked into a long time ago.'

'Well, we can't turn around and go backward in time,' Arell said. 'What do you think, Argak?'

'I wish she weren't so weak,' Argak said. 'There are some compounds that'd be fairly efficacious if she were more robust, but they'd be too dangerous now.'

'We've got to come up with *something*, Argak,' I said.

'Give me some time, Pol. I'm working on it.' He rummaged through the case of little glass vials he'd brought from his shop. He selected one of the vials and handed it to me. 'In the meantime, dose her with this every few hours. It'll keep her condition from deteriorating further while we decide what to do.'

Arell and I went into Beldaran's room. 'Let's air out the room, clean her up, change her bedding, and comb her hair, Pol,' Arell suggested. 'That always makes people feel better.'

'Right,' I agreed. 'I'll get some more pillows, too. She might be able to breathe a little easier if we prop her up.'

Beldaran seemed to feel much better after Arell and I had attended to those little things that men can't seem to think of. She did *not* enjoy Argak's medication, however. 'That's *terrible*, Pol,' she said after I gave it to her.

'That's the whole idea, Beldaran,' I said lightly, trying to keep my concern for her out of my voice. 'Medicine's *supposed* to taste bad. If it's bad enough, you get well just so that you don't have to drink any more of it.'

She laughed wearily, and then went into an extended bout of coughing.

I sat over my sister's bed for the next day and a half while Argak, Arell, and Balten concocted other medications. Argak's first compound did little more than alleviate some of Beldaran's more obvious symptoms, and we all concluded that we were going to have to take more heroic measures.

Argak's next concoction put Beldaran into a deep sleep. 'It's a natural part of the healing process,' I lied to Riva and Daran. My colleagues and I had enough to worry about already, and we didn't need the two of them hovering over us adding to our anxiety.

This was not going the way I'd hoped. My studies had made me arrogant, and I'd been convinced that with a little help from my teachers I could cure *any* ailment. Beldaran's illness, however, stub-

139

bornly refused to respond to any measures we could devise. I frequently went for days with only brief naps, and I began to develop an irrational conviction that my sister's illness had somehow become conscious, aware of everything we were trying to do to save her and thwarting us at every turn. I finally concluded that we'd have to go beyond the limitations of the physician's art to save Beldaran. In desperation, I sent my thought out to the twins. *'Please!'* I silently shouted over the countless leagues between the Isle and the Vale. *'Please! I'm losing her! Get word to my father! I need him, and I need him in a hurry!'*

'Can you hold off the illness until he gets there?' Beltira demanded.

'I don't know, uncle. *We've tried everything we know. Beldaran doesn't respond to anything we can come up with. She's sinking, uncle. Get hold of father immediately. Get him here as quickly as you can.'*

'Try to stay calm, Polgara,' Belkira told me, his voice very crisp. *'There's a way you can support her until Belgarath gets there. Use your Will. Give her some of* your *strength. There are things we can do that others can't.'*

That possibility hadn't even occurred to me. We'd extended the procedures we were using to the very edge – almost experimenting – and some of the medications we were dosing Beldaran with were extremely dangerous – particularly in her weakened condition. If Belkira were right, I could support her with my Will and thus we could make use of even more dangerous medications.

I hurried down the corridor to the royal apartment and I found an Alorn priest who'd somehow managed to slip past the guards in the corridor. He was performing some obscene little ceremony that involved burning something that gave off a cloud of foul-smelling green smoke. *Smoke? Smoke* in the sick-room of someone whose lungs are failing? 'What are you doing, you idiot?' I almost screamed at him.

'This is a sacred ceremony,' he replied in a lofty tone of voice. 'A mere woman wouldn't understand it. Leave at once.'

'No. You're the one who's leaving. Get out of here.'

His eyes widened in shocked outrage. 'How dare you?' he demanded.

I quenched his smoldering fire and blew the stink of it away with a single thought.

'Witchcraft!' he gasped.

'If that's what you want to call it,' I told him from between clenched teeth. 'Try a little of this, you feeble-minded fool.' I clenched my Will and said, 'Rise up!' lifting him about six feet above

140

the floor. I left him hanging there for a while. Then I translocated him to a spot several hundred yards out beyond the walls of the Citadel.

I was actually going to let him fall at that point. He was hundreds of feet above the snowy city and I was sure that he'd have plenty of time to regret what he'd done while he plummeted down toward certain death.

'*Pol! No!*' It was mother's voice, and it cracked like a whip inside my head.

'*But –*'

'*I said no! Now put him down!*' Then she paused for a moment. '*Whenever it's convenient, of course,*' she added.

'*It shall be as my mother wishes,*' I said obediently. I turned to my sister and gently infused her wasted body with my Will, leaving the priest of Belar suspended, screaming and whimpering, over the city. I left him out there for a few hours – six or eight, ten at the very most – to give him time to contemplate his sins. He *did* attract quite a bit of attention as he hovered up there like a distraught vulture, but all priests adore being the center of attention, so it didn't really hurt him.

I sustained Beldaran with the sheer force of my Will for almost ten days, but despite my best efforts and every medication my teachers and I could think of, her condition continued to deteriorate. She was slipping away from me, and there was nothing I could do to prevent it. I was exhausted by now, and strange thoughts began to cloud my enfeebled mind. I have very little coherent memory of those horrible ten days, but I *do* remember Beltira's voice coming to me about midnight when a screaming gale was swirling snow around the towers of the Citadel. '*Pol! We've found Belgarath! He's on his way to the Isle right now!*'

'*Thank the Gods!*'

'*How is she?*'

'*Not good at all, uncle, and my strength's starting to fail.*'

'*Hold on for just a few more days, Pol. Your father's coming.*'

But we didn't have a few more days. I sat wearily at my sister's bedside through the interminable hours of that long, savage night, and despite the fact that I was channeling almost every bit of my Will into her wasted body, I could feel her sinking deeper and deeper into the darkness.

And then mother appeared at my side. It was not just her voice this time. She was actually there, and she was weeping openly. '*Let her go, Pol,*' she told me.

'No! I will *not* let her die!'

'Her task is complete, Polgara. You *must* let her go. If you don't, we'll lose both of you.'

'I can't go on without her, mother. If she goes, I'll go with her.'

'No, you won't. It's not permitted. Release your Will.'

'I *can't* mother. I *can't*. She's the center of my life.'

'Do it, my daughter. The Master commands it – and so does UL.'

I'd never heard of UL before. Oddly, no one in my family had ever mentioned him to me. Stubbornly, however, I continued to focus my Will on my dying sister.

And then the wall beside Beldaran's bed started to shimmer, and I could see an indistinct figure within the very stones. It was very much like looking into the shimmery depths of a forest pool to see what lay beneath the surface. The figure I saw there was robed in white, and the sense of that presence was overwhelming. I've been in the presence of Gods many times in my life, but I've never encountered a presence like that of UL.

Then the shimmering was gone, and UL himself stood across my sister's bed from me. His hair and beard were like snow, but there were no other marks of age on that eternal face. He lifted one hand and held it out over Beldaran's form, and as he did so, I felt my Will being returned to me. 'No!' I cried. 'Please! No!'

But he ignored my tearful protest. 'Come with me, beloved Beldaran,' he said gently. 'It is time to go now.'

And a light infused my sister's body. The light seemed to rise as if it were being sighed out of the wasted husk which was all that was left of her. The light had Beldaran's form and face, and it reached out to take the hand of UL.

And then the father of the Gods looked directly into my face. 'Be well, beloved Polgara,' he said to me, and then the two glowing forms shimmered back into the wall.

Mother sighed. 'And now our Beldaran is with UL.'

And I threw myself across my dead sister's body, weeping uncontrollably.

CHAPTER 10

Mother was no longer with me. I felt a terrible vacancy as I clung to my dead sister, weeping and screaming out my grief. The center of my world was gone, and all of the rest of it collapsed inward.

I have very little memory of what happened during the rest of that dreadful night. I think that people came into my sister's room, but I didn't even recognize their faces. There was weeping, I'm fairly sure of that, but I really can't be certain.

And then Arell was there, solid, dependable, a rock I could cling to. She held me in her arms, rocking me back and forth until someone – Argak, I think – handed her a cup. 'Drink this, Pol,' she instructed, holding the cup to my lips.

It was bitter, and I momentarily thought that it might be poison. What a perfect solution. All the pain would go away now. I drank eagerly, and my weeping gradually subsided as I sank down into blank oblivion in Arell's arms.

I was in my own bed when I awoke, and I can't really say how much time had passed. Arell sat at my bedside, and I vaguely noticed that the windows had been barred while I slept. 'Your father's here, Pol,' Arell told me when my eyes opened.

'How nice of him to take the trouble,' I replied bitterly. Arell had not poisoned me, and I felt somehow betrayed by that fact.

'That's about enough of that, Polgara.' Arell's tone was crisp. 'People die. It happens. This isn't the time for accusations or recriminations. The death of a loved one can either tear a family apart or it can bind the survivors closer together. Which do you want it to be, Pol?' Then she stood up, smoothing the front of her grey dress. 'Don't go looking for anything sharp, dear. I've had your room purged of everything with an edge, and stay away from the windows. Now get dressed, wash your face in cold water, and comb your hair. You're a mess.' Then she left, and I got out of bed to lock the door behind her.

It was evening again, though I couldn't tell you what day it was, and father came knocking at my door. 'It's me, Pol. Open up.'

'Go away,' I told him.

'Open the door, Pol. I need to talk to you.'

'Get away from me, father.' Even as I said it, I knew that it was more than a little silly. No lock in this world will keep my father out if he really wants in. I gave up and opened the door.

He was all business, though his face was bleak. He bluntly reminded me that our overriding responsibility now was the Rivan line. Riva himself was totally incapacitated by his grief, and somebody had to assume his duties – both as king and as the guardian of the Orb. Daran was only twenty, but he was Riva's heir and therefore the only possible choice. 'The Angaraks have eyes everywhere, Pol,' father reminded me, 'and if there's any sign of weakness here, you can expect a visit from Ctuchik – or maybe even from Torak himself.'

That brought me up short. I pushed my grief and desolation back. 'What do we do?'

'You're going to pull yourself together and take charge here. I'm putting Daran into your hands. I've talked with Brand, and he fully understands the situation. He'll help you as much as he can, but the ultimate responsibility's still yours. Don't fail me, Pol. I'll take you to Brand's quarters. He's talking with Daran there right now. They're Alorns, Pol, so keep a tight rein on them.'

'You'll be here, won't you?'

'No. I have to leave.'

'You're not even going to stay for the funeral?' That shocked me for some reason. Father's always been a bit informal, but –

'I've got the funeral in my heart, Pol, and no amount of ceremony or preaching by some tiresome priest is going to make it go away.'

It was only an off-hand remark, but it reminded me that I had a score to settle with a certain priest of Belar. If Elthek, the Rivan Deacon, hadn't pretended to be so hysterically afraid of witchcraft, my sister might have received proper medical attention soon enough to save her life. A desire for revenge isn't really very admirable, but it *does* tend to stiffen one's back in the face of sorrow. Now I had *two* reasons to get hold of myself – Elthek and Ctuchik. I had enemies on both sides of the theological fence.

Father took me to Kamion's book-lined study, and then he left us.

'There are precedents for a regency,' Kamion told my sorrowing nephew and me, 'quite a few, actually. The fact that a man's a king doesn't automatically exempt him from ordinary human incapacity.'

'Lord Brand,' Daran objected, 'the people won't accept me as their ruler. I'm too young.'

'Your father was even younger than you are when he established the kingdom, Daran,' I reminded him.

'But he had the Orb, Aunt Pol.'

'Right. And now *you* have it.'

He blinked. 'Nobody but father can touch the Orb.'

I smiled at him. I suppose it was a sad smile, but the fact that I could do it at all surprised me. 'Daran,' I said, 'your father put your hand on the Orb before you were twenty-four hours old. It knows who you are.'

'Could he take the sword down off the wall?' Kamion asked me intently.

'I'm not entirely positive. I'll look into it.'

'That *would* give his Highness' regency a visible sign of legitimacy and head off objections from any quarter.'

'I think I'm getting a glimmer of an idea here, gentlemen,' I told them. 'I'll have to speak with my Master about it – and with Riva himself – but if I'm right, there won't be any objections to Daran's regency from anyone.'

'And then I can deal with the Rivan Deacon,' Daran said, his young face hardening.

'Would you care to define "deal with", your Highness?' Kamion asked politely.

'I haven't entirely decided yet, Lord Brand. I'm torn between running a sword into his belly and twisting it or burning him at the stake. Which do you prefer, Aunt Pol?'

Alorns! 'Let's get your authority firmly established *before* the blood-bath, Daran,' I suggested. 'Let Elthek worry for a while before you run your sword into him or start using him for firewood. We have other things to take care of first.'

'I guess you're right, Aunt Pol,' he conceded. 'Do you have the authority to close the harbor, Lord Brand?'

'I suppose so, your Highness,' Kamion replied, 'but why?'

'This is an island, Lord Brand. If we close the harbor, Elthek can't get away from me.'

'Oh, dear,' I sighed.

It was much later when I was alone in my chambers that I was finally able to reach out with my mind. *'Mother, I need you.'* Then I waited, growing more apprehensive by the moment.

'Yes, Pol?' Her voice was filled with fathomless sorrow.

'Can Daran take up his father's sword?'

'Of course he can, Pol.'

'And will the sword respond to him in the same way it responds to Riva?'

'Naturally. What's this all about, Pol?'

'Alorn politics, mother. Riva can't function just now, so Daran's going to have to rule the Isle until his father recovers. I want to head off any arguments before they even get started.'

'Don't overdo things, Pol.'

'Of course not, mother.'

It's always been my opinion that funerals should be private affairs for just the immediate family, but my sister had been the queen of the Rivans, and that called for a state funeral.

'The Rivan Deacon will officiate, of course,' Kamion advised my nephew and me. 'It's unfortunate, but –'

'No. He *won't*,' Daran said firmly.

'Your Highness?'

'Elthek killed my mother. If he even comes near the funeral, I'll chop him all to pieces. There's a chaplain here in the Citadel. *He'll* officiate.'

'That's your Highness's final word on the matter?'

'It is, Lord Brand.' Then Daran stormed away.

'I'll talk to him, Kamion,' I said quietly. 'The Deacon won't officiate, but I *do* want him to be present. Something's going to happen that I want him to see.'

'Secrets, Pol?'

'Just a little surprise, old friend. I'm going to make the transfer of power *very* visible.'

Elthek was offended, naturally, but Kamion was smooth enough to unruffle his feathers, using such terms as 'personal spiritual advisor', and 'the wishes of the immediate family'.

The formal funeral was conducted in the Hall of the Rivan King, and my sister's bier was directly in front of the throne where Riva, sunk in bottomless melancholy, sat brooding over his wife's pale body.

The priest who officiated was a gentle, kindly old man who was clearly not a Cultist. He gave us what comfort he could, but I doubt that any of us heard much of what he said. Elthek, the Rivan Deacon,

146

sat near the front of the Hall, his face filled with injured pride. He was a tall, thin man with burning eyes and a grey-shot beard that reached almost to his waist. At one point during the family chaplain's sermon, I caught Elthek glaring at me, and then his face twisted into a smirk that said volumes. He seemed almost delighted that I'd failed to save my sister's life. He came very close to joining Belar out among the stars at that point.

Beldaran was interred in a hastily prepared royal mausoleum at the end of a long hallway inside the Citadel, and Riva wept openly as the heavy stone lid of the crypt slid gratingly over her. Then Kamion and I escorted him back to the Hall. I'd spoken with my distraught brother-in-law for a time just before the funeral, so he knew exactly what to do. 'My friends,' he addressed the assembled nobles and clergy, 'I will be going into seclusion for some time. The kingdom will be secure, however.' He went to his throne, reached up, and took his huge sword down from the wall. As it always did when he took it in his hand, the sword burst into blue fire, but it appeared that even the Orb grieved for my sister because the fire seemed to me to be a bit subdued. The grieving king turned to face the assemblage, holding the flaming symbol of his authority aloft.

There was an absolute, almost fearful silence among the mourners. 'My son, Prince Daran, will stand in my stead,' Riva declared in tones that clearly brooked no opposition. 'You will obey him even as you would obey me.' Then he switched the sword around in those huge hands, taking it by its fiery blade and extending the hilt to Daran. 'Thus I transfer all power to my son!' he boomed.

Somewhere a bell started to ring, a deep-toned sound that seemed to shake the very stones around us. I knew with absolute certainty that no bell on the Isle was large enough to make that sound. Daran reverently took the sword from his father and raised it above his head. The fire of the Orb burst forth, running up that massive blade and enveloping the young prince in a sort of nimbus of blue light.

'All hail Daran!' Kamion commanded in a great voice, 'Regent of the Isle of the Winds!'

'Hail Daran!' the crowd echoed.

Elthek's face was pale with fury and his hands were trembling. He obviously hadn't even considered the possibility of a regency, and certainly not a regency so supernaturally accepted. Clearly, he'd assumed that the grief-stricken Riva would try to continue to perform the duties of the throne, and a situation like that would have been almost made to order for the Rivan Deacon's gradual usurpation of power. Kamion would have been shunted off to one side, and Elthek, speaking for the distraught Riva, would have insinuated himself into a position of unassailable authority. The blazing sword of the Rivan King in the hands of Daran effectively cut off Elthek's path to power, and the Deacon was clearly unhappy about it. I managed to catch his eye, and just to rub it in a bit, I returned his smirk.

Riva, as he'd announced, went into seclusion, and Daran, Kamion and I took over the reins of government. Daran flatly – and wisely, I think – refused to sit on his father's throne, but presided instead from a plain chair placed behind a common table piled high with the documents which are the curse of every ruler in the world.

I discovered that winter and early spring just how tedious affairs of state can really be, and I marveled at the hunger some men have for a throne – any throne. Alorns are basically an informal people, and an Alorn king is usually nothing more than a glorified clan-chief who's readily accessible to any of his subjects. That's fine outside in the open, I suppose, but once the business of running a kingdom moves indoors, problems start to crop up. The formal setting of a throne room calls for formal speeches, and this unfortunately brings out the worst in some people. Oratory, however grand, is really nothing more than a way for a pompous man to stand up and in effect say, 'Look at me,' and most of the 'petitions to the throne' Daran was forced to endure were pure nonsense.

'Must they go on and on like that?' Daran complained one rainy evening after we'd closed up shop for the day.

'It's just a way of showing off, your Highness,' Kamion explained.

'I can see them, Kamion,' Daran said. 'They don't have to wave their arms and make speeches. Can't we do *something* to cut all this nonsense short?'

'You could shorten your work-day, dear,' I suggested.

'What?'

'You could hold court for an hour every morning and then pack up and go back to your office. The fact that others are waiting in line and time is limited might encourage those orators to get to the point.' Then another idea came to me. '*Or*, you could require each speaker to hold an iron rod in his hand while he's talking.'

'What good would that do?'

I smiled. 'I'll just gradually heat the rod until it's white-hot, Daran. I think the speaker might hurry right along once his hand starts to smoke.'

'I *like* that one,' Daran said.

'Unfortunately, it smacks of witchcraft,' Kamion observed, 'and

Elthek might want to make an issue of it. I think we can come up with something else.'

What Kamion devised positively reeked of genius. The next morning a portly baron was reading aloud – badly – from a prepared text presenting all sorts of reasons why he should be exempt from certain provisions of the tax-code.

'I think I've come up with the answer to our problem,' Kamion murmured to Daran and me. He strolled to the edge of the dais, stepped down and casually approached the speaker. 'May I see that, old boy?' he asked politely, holding his hand out for the sheaf of paper in the baron's hand. Then he firmly took the document from the startled noble and glanced at it. 'Very interesting,' he said. 'His Highness will consider it and let you know what his decision is in a month or so.'

'But –' the baron began to protest.

'The matter *will* receive the Prince Regent's full attention, old boy. Was there anything else?'

The baron began to splutter.

Kamion looked around. 'Ah, corporal of the guard,' he said to one of the soldiers at the door.

'Yes, my Lord Brand?'

'Could you find me a bushel basket somewhere?'

'I think so, my Lord.'

'Do be a good fellow and see what you can turn up.'

'Of course.'

Kamion returned to the dais and then faced the assemblage. 'One of the problems his Highness has been encountering lies in the fact that the finer points of many of your petitions are glossed over when you present them to the throne aloud, gentlemen, and what you have to say deserves better than that. As soon as the good corporal returns with that basket, he'll pass among you and you can deposit your petitions in the basket. That way, you'll all be able to go about your business without wasting time waiting for your turn to speak. Think of all the hours you'll save that way, and all the important things you'll be able to accomplish.'

They gaped at him. I knew for a fact that *most* of these nobles didn't *have* anything better to do. The hours spent in the throne room were their only reason for existence.

Then the corporal returned with the basket and, at Kamion's instruction, passed among the throng to receive all the laboriously prepared petitions, which were reluctantly surrendered.

'Excellent, gentlemen!' Kamion said. 'Capital! Now, why don't we all go back to work?' He glanced at the window. 'Pity it's raining,' he noted. 'If it weren't, we could all go fishing. Shall we adjourn?'

Daran rose from his chair, and Kamion and I followed him from the hall.

'You haven't really done me any favors, Kamion,' Daran complained when we reached our impromptu office. 'Now I have to *read* all that idiocy.'

'It won't take very long, your Highness,' Kamion assured him. He went to the fireplace and dumped the contents of the basket into the flames. 'Oops,' he said. 'How clumsy of me.'

Daran and I collapsed in helpless laughter.

In many respects, I think it was Kamion's urbane and civilized manner that helped me through the difficult time after Beldaran's death. He was very wise, absolutely loyal, and he had a charm about him that made everything he touched go smoothly. I knew his wife quite well – well enough to know that although she wasn't happy about the way his duties kept him away from her, she understood that his position required him to spend long hours with Daran and me. There was never anything improper about the relationship between Kamion and me, but had our situation been different –

Well, there's no need to go into that, is there?

It was early in the summer of the year 2038 that something came up that was far more serious than long-winded petitions to the throne sententiously delivered. Although the coast-line of the Isle of the Winds looks barren and hostile, the interior valleys are often lush and fertile – particularly in the southern part of the island. Rank among the Alorns was – still is, probably – based on the ownership of land suitable for agriculture, and those southern valleys are highly coveted. There was a Baron Garhein, a typical Alorn bully, who lived down there, and he had a son, Karak, who, as it turned out, was a drunken brute. Their neighbor, Baron Altor, had a daughter, Cellan, who was a beautiful, gentle, and cultured girl. After extensive haggling, Garhein and Altor arranged a marriage between their children, and the arrangements involved a dowry of land.

It was not a happy union. Karak came to the bridal chamber roaring drunk and forced his attentions on Cellan in the most brutal way imaginable. Things went downhill from there. Karak turned out to be a wife-beater, among other things, and word of this got

150

back to Altor, who mounted an expedition to rescue his daughter. There were quite a few casualties on both sides, but Altor succeeded in taking his daughter home again. Then he declared the marriage null and void and took back the dowry. Garhein went up in flames – not so much about the wrecked marriage but rather about the loss of the land. The feud between the two began to expand as cousins, uncles, nephews, and the like enlisted on one side or the other. Solitary ploughmen were butchered, and crops and houses were burned.

Word of all this eventually reached the Citadel, and Daran, Kamion and I gathered in Kamion's book-lined study to consider options.

'They're both very powerful men,' Kamion told us gravely, 'and they both have extended families. We're going to have to take steps, or we'll have another Arendia on our hands.'

'Can a marriage actually be dissolved like that?' Daran asked.

'There are arguments on both sides about that, your Highness,' Kamion replied. 'In most cases, it depends on the relative power of the two fathers. If the husband's father is the more powerful, the wife's considered to be property. If it's the other way around, she isn't.'

Daran frowned. 'Have I got a big enough army to go down there and force a settlement on those two hot-heads?'

'I'd hold that in reserve, your Highness. Let's try talking to them first. A general mobilization probably wouldn't hurt, though. It'd be a demonstration of the fact that you aren't happy about the situation.'

'What shape is the treasury in, Aunt Pol?' Daran asked me. 'Can I afford a general mobilization?'

'I suppose so – if you don't drag it out too long.' Then an idea came to me. 'Why don't we hold a tournament instead?'

'I'm sorry, Aunt Pol, but I didn't understand that.'

'It's an Arendish custom, your Highness,' Kamion explained. 'It's a sort of military contest involving archery contests, mock sword-fights, axe throwing, jousting matches – that sort of thing.'

'What's jousting?'

'Two armored men try to knock each other off the backs of their horses with twenty-foot lances.'

'What a peculiar notion.'

'We could probably skip over that part,' Kamion said. 'Alorns don't usually fight on horseback.' He looked at me. 'It's really a very good idea, Pol. It'd give Garhein and Altor an idea of just how much force

151

the throne can muster, and the nobles would have to pay their own way. We make our point without emptying out the treasury.'

'What if nobody comes?' Daran fretted.

'They'll come, dear,' I assured him. 'It's a chance to show off. The planting's all done now, so there's nothing really very pressing to keep people away. It'll be an honor to be invited, so we can be fairly sure that every nobleman on the Isle will put in an appearance.'

'Including Garhein and Altor?'

'Exactly. We can summon them to the Citadel during the festivities. They'll already be here in the city anyway, so they won't be able to refuse.'

'*And* we can make an object lesson of them,' Kamion added. 'There are other little disputes festering on various parts of the Isle. If you come down hard on Garhein and Altor, other nobles should get the point.'

'That might be just a bit optimistic, Kamion,' I suggested. 'We *are* talking about Alorns, after all.'

The invitations to the games went out, and the City of Riva was teeming with burly Alorns when Altor and Garhein arrived. The fact that almost every able-bodied man on the Isle had responded to the Prince Regent's invitation wasn't lost on them. The regency wasn't yet a year old, but Daran's authority was already well-established. We gave the two feuding barons a bit of time to absorb that, and then Daran summoned them to the Citadel. The meeting was held in the throne room where all the symbols of power were much in evidence.

I'll state candidly here that my sympathies were wholly on the side of Baron Altor and his daughter in the light of Karak's open brutality, but I'll have to admit that the differences between Garhein and Altor were very slight. Both of them were big, burly, bearded, and not very bright. They wore chain mail shirts, but no swords, since Kamion had prudently decided to have everyone who entered the throne room disarmed at the door. Garhein had rusty-colored hair that stuck out in all directions, while Altor had greased-down black hair that looked much like a wet horsetail streaming down his back. Though it was early in the day, the brutish Karak was already drunk. He was a flabby young man with a sparse beard and unkempt hair, and I could smell him from half-way across the throne room. Altor's daughter, Cellan, was the only one of the group to appear even remotely civilized. She was pretty, in a blonde, busty, Alorn sort of way, but her blue eyes were every bit as hard as her father's.

152

The feuding families had been prudently seated on opposite sides of the Hall of the Rivan King. Word of the meeting had spread, and the hall was filled with curious onlookers.

Daran, Kamion and I'd had plenty of time to lay out exactly what we were going to do, so the entire event was carefully staged. The palace guard had been turned out, of course, and armed, hulking soldiers in mail shirts lined the walls just to make sure that there wouldn't be any interruptions or surprises. We'd had Daran's chair and table removed from the dais, so when we entered the packed hall, my nephew went directly to his father's throne and sat down.

That caused quite a stir.

'All right, then,' Daran said crisply, 'let's get down to business here.' There was a no-nonsense tone in his voice indicating that he was fully in charge. 'My father's distressed by certain things that've been happening on the southern end of the Isle, and we don't want to upset him any further, do we?' He leaned forward. 'My Lord Barons Garhein and Altor, come here.' He pointed imperiously at a spot directly in front of the dais.

The two warring hot-heads approached warily.

'I'm going to put a stop to all this nonsense right here and now,' my sandy-haired nephew informed them. 'The next one of you who breaks the king's peace had better start packing, because he'll be moving immediately to the northern end of the Isle.'

'Your Highness!' Garhein protested. 'It's all rock up there! Nobody can live on the northern end of the Isle!'

'If you draw your sword one more time, Garhein, you'll get a chance to try. You could probably raise goats. Goats eat almost anything.'

Garhein's son Karak lurched to his feet. 'You can't do that!' he bellowed at Daran in a drunken voice.

'Can you sober this fool up, Aunt Pol?' Daran asked me.

'Of course,' I replied.

'Would you, please?'

We'd been fairly certain that the beer-soaked Karak would interrupt at some point in the proceedings, so I was fully prepared.

Daran had already demonstrated *his* power. Now it was my turn. The fact that Elthek, the Rivan Deacon, was in attendance made my performance a bit excessive, I'll admit. Daran, Kamion and I were spreading object lessons in all directions that day. 'Bring that drunkard here,' I instructed the huge Master of the Guard.

'At once, Lady Polgara,' the vastly bearded soldier replied. He bulled his way through the startled crowd, grasped Karak by the scruff of the neck and dragged him to the front of the Hall.

I held out my hand, snapped my fingers and willed a tankard to be there. Then I took a glass vial from my sleeve and poured the contents into the tankard. I raised the oversized cup and said, 'Beer.' There was an absolute silence in the Hall, so the sound of the stream of foamy, amber beer pouring out of empty air above the tankard was clearly audible. I glanced at Elthek and noted with some satisfaction that his eyes were bulging and his mouth gaped open. People who pretend to perform magic are always very startled when they encounter the real thing. Then I advanced on the cringing, smelly Karak. 'Now be a good boy and drink this,' I instructed.

He looked at the tankard as if it were a snake and put both his hands behind his back.

'Make him drink it, Sergeant,' Daran instructed the Master of the Guard.

'My pleasure, your Highness,' the big soldier replied. He roughly seized one of the drunkard's hands and interlaced his fingers with Karak's. 'Drink it!' he thundered.

Karak struggled weakly.

Then the soldier began to squeeze – slowly. The sergeant had shoulders like an ox and hands the size of hams. He probably could have made a rock bleed just by squeezing it.

Karak rose up on his tiptoes, squealing like a pig.

'Drink it!' the Sergeant repeated.

'Your Highness!' Garhein protested.

'Shut up!' Daran snapped. 'You people *will* learn to do as I tell you!'

The sergeant continued to squeeze Karak's hand in that overpowering grip of his, and the drunkard finally snatched the tankard from my hand and noisily drank it.

'Ah, Sergeant,' I said to the soldier, 'I expect that our young friend here might start feeling unwell in a few moments. Why don't you take him over near the wall so he doesn't splash all over everybody?'

The sergeant grinned broadly and dragged Karak off to one side where the sodden young man became noisily ill.

'Lady Cellan,' Daran said then, 'would you be so good as to approach the throne for a moment?'

Cellan obediently, though a little hesitantly, came to the dais.

'Do you wish to return to your husband?' Daran asked.

'Never!' she burst out. 'I'll kill myself first! He beats me, your

154

Highness. Every time he gets drunk – which is every day – he takes his fists to me.'

'I see.' Daran's face hardened. 'No decent man ever hits a woman,' he declared, 'so, by order of the throne, the marriage of Karak and Cellan is hereby dissolved.'

'You can't do that!' Garhein roared. 'It's a woman's duty to submit to her husband's chastisement when she misbehaves.'

'It's also a nobleman's duty to submit to chastisement from the throne when *he* misbehaves,' Kamion advised him. 'You're pressing your luck, Baron Garhein.'

'Now we come to the question of the ownership of that parcel of land,' Daran said.

'The land is *mine!*' Garhein bellowed.

'It's *mine!*' Altor countered. 'It reverted to me entirely when his Highness dissolved the marriage.'

'Actually, dear chaps,' Kamion said smoothly, 'the land belongs to the crown. The entire island does. You hold *all* your land in trust – at the crown's pleasure.'

'We could probably argue the fine points of the law for weeks,' Daran said, 'but legal arguments are very boring, so, in order to save time – and bloodshed – we'll simply divide that disputed parcel of land right down the middle. Half goes to Baron Garhein, and Half to Baron Altor.'

'Unthinkable!' Garhein protested.

'Start thinking about goats then, Garhein, or landless vagabond-age. You *will* do as I tell you to do.' Then my nephew's eyes narrowed. 'Now, just to keep you two and your assorted partisans and kinsmen out of mischief, you're going to build a fifteen-foot wall right down the middle of that parcel of land. It'll give you something to do, and it'll keep you away from each other. I want to see a lot of progress on that wall, gentlemen, and I want to see both of you out there carrying rocks, too. You're not going to just pass this off to your underlings.'

'That's twenty miles, your Highness!' Altor gasped.

'Is that all? You should be able to finish up in a decade or two, then. I want you to go to opposite ends and start building. I'll have the sergeant here mark the exact center and you can think of it as a race. I might even let the winner keep his head as a prize. Lord Brand knows the name of every one of your partisans, and they'll be joining you in your great work – either willingly or in chains. Have I made myself clear?'

They glowered at him, but wisely chose not to say anything.

'I'd suspect that you gentlemen aren't going to be popular among your kinsmen,' Kamion noted. 'I suggest that you wear mail shirts during the construction – just as a precaution.'

'Now we come to that sick fellow over in the corner,' Daran said, rising from his father's throne rather grimly.

By now Karak had pretty much emptied his stomach of everything he'd eaten or drunk for the past several weeks. He was pale and trembling violently when the hulking sergeant dragged him back to the dais.

'Decent men don't beat their wives, Karak,' Daran said, 'so I'm going to teach you decency right here and now.' He reached behind the throne and picked up a long, limber whip.

'You *can't*!' Garhein almost screamed. 'My son's a nobleman!'

'You and I seem to have conflicting definitions of nobility, Garhein,' Daran told him. 'Since this sodden beast is your son, though, I'll defer to you in the matter. I'm either going to flog him or chop off both his hands. Take your pick.'

'Behanding him *would* keep him from hitting women, your Highness,' Kamion noted clinically, 'and it might cut down on his drinking, too – unless he'd like to lap his beer out of a bowl like a dog.'

'Good point, Lord Brand,' Daran noted. He reached up and took down his father's sword, which leaped joyously into bright blue flame. 'Well, Garhein?' he said, 'which is it going to be?' He held out the flaming sword in one hand and the whip in the other.

Garhein gaped at him.

'*Answer me*!' Daran roared.

'Th-the whip, your Highness,' Garhein stammered.

'Wise choice,' Kamion murmured. 'Having a son and heir without any hands could be *so* demeaning.'

Then the Master of the Guard, who'd obviously already been instructed upon what to do, ripped off Karak's doublet, kicked his feet out from under him and seized him by one ankle. 'Just to keep him from crawling under the furniture, your Highness,' he explained, firmly planting his foot on Karak's other ankle.

'Thank you, Sergeant,' Daran said. Then he hung the sword back up, let his cloak fall to the floor, removed his doublet, and rolled up his sleeves. 'Pushing right along then,' he said and proceeded to flog the screaming, squirming drunkard to within an inch of his life. Cellan, I noticed, loved every minute of it. Alorns are such a simple, uncomplicated people at times.

After Daran had finished, he tossed his whip down and picked up his clothes again. 'I think that concludes our business here for the day, my friends,' he announced to the shocked assemblage. 'If I remember correctly, the archery contest begins this afternoon. I might even shoot off a quiver of arrows myself. I'll see you all there, then.'

After the three of us had returned to Kamion's study, I put it to the two of them directly. 'You had that flogging all planned in advance, didn't you?'

'Of course, Aunt Pol,' Daran grinned at me.

'Without consulting me?'

'We didn't want to upset you, Pol,' Kamion said smoothly. 'Did you really find it too offensive?'

I pretended to consider it. 'Not really,' I conceded. 'Considering Karak's behavior, it was more or less appropriate.'

'We talked about some alternatives,' Kamion said. 'I thought it might be sort of nice if I called that beer-soaked bully out, gave him a sword and then chopped him to pieces, but his Highness decided that might upset you, so we settled for the flogging instead – less messy, you understand.'

'And the threat to chop off his hands?'

'I just made that up on the spur of the moment, Aunt Pol,' Daran admitted. 'I think it might have gotten my point about wife-beating across, though.' Then he snapped his fingers. 'Why don't we enter that in the criminal code, Kamion?'

'You're a barbarian, Daran,' I accused him.

'No, Aunt Pol, I'm an Alorn. I know my people, and I know what frightens them. I don't want to rule by terror, but I *do* want other Rivans to understand that things can get very nasty if they do something that I don't like, and I *really* don't like wife-beating.' He leaned back in his chair and looked speculatively out the window at the bright sunny day. 'That's really at the center of all power, Aunt Pol,' he mused. 'We can try to act civilized and polite, but at the bottom of it all, the power of any ruler is based on a threat. Fortunately, we don't have to carry that threat out too often. If I'd known I was going to have to be a savage to sit in my father's place, I wouldn't be here at all. I'd still be running, and neither you nor grandfather would ever have been able to find me.'

I was so proud of him at that point that I almost exploded.

News of Daran's handling of the feud between Garhein and Altor spread far and wide throughout the Isle, and the Rivans began to look at their youthful Prince Regent with a new respect. Daran was working out just fine.

CHAPTER 11

Anrak sailed into the harbor late the following summer. Over the years I'd noted that Anrak moved around a lot. Most men settle down eventually, but Anrak was born to wander. The cousin of Iron-grip, Bull-neck, and Fleet-foot had grey hair by now, but there was still an irrepressible quality of youth about him. He visited with Riva for quite some time and then joined Kamion, Daran, and me in a blue-draped conference chamber high in one of the towers of the Citadel. As Kamion's seemingly endless succession of children had begun to spill over into his study, it had become necessary for us to find another place to work. 'My cousin's not going to get over his wife's death, is he, Pol?' Anrak asked as we all sat at a long conference table. 'He talks about old times, but he doesn't seem to even mention anything that's happened recently. It's almost as if his life ended when your sister died.'

'In many ways it did, Anrak,' I told him, 'and mine very nearly did, too.'

He sighed. 'I've seen it happen before, Pol. It's too bad.' He sighed again and then looked at Daran. 'How's he doing?' he asked as if Daran weren't sitting right there.

'We have some hopes for him,' Kamion replied. Then he recounted the story of the flogging.

'Good for you, Daran,' Anrak said approvingly. 'Oh, before I forget, my uncle Bear-shoulders asked me to pass something along to you.'

'How is he?' Daran asked.

Anrak shrugged. 'Old,' he said. 'You still wouldn't want to cross him, though. He's having trouble with the Bear-Cult, and he wanted me to warn you about it.' He leaned back in his chair, a thoughtful expression on his face. 'Back in the old days, the Cult didn't really have any kind of coherent system of beliefs. All they were really doing was trying to find some theological justification for pillaging the southern kingdoms. That all changed after Belgarath and the others took the Orb back from Torak, though. Now they want Riva – or his successor – to lead them south with that flaming sword. Right now, Riva's at the very center of what the Cultists choose to call their religion.'

'We've had some problems here, too,' Kamion noted. 'Elthek, the Rivan Deacon, leads the Cult here on the Isle. Since he's the high priest of Belar, we have to step around him rather carefully. Iron-grip didn't want any direct confrontations with the Church, so he didn't step on the Deacon's neck the way he probably should have.'

'I'm not nearly as accommodating as my father is,' Daran noted. 'The time's not far off when I'm going to kill Elthek.'

'Isn't that illegal?' Anrak asked.

'I'll change the law,' Daran replied.

I looked at him rather closely and saw that it was almost time to pull him up short. My nephew, emboldened by his success with Garhein and Altor, hovered right on the verge of becoming a tyrant.

'Is Bull-neck having the same problems in Drasnia?' Kamion asked Anrak.

'It's even worse there,' Anrak replied moodily. 'After Fleet-foot trampled all over the Cult in Algaria, the survivors fled into the fens and then into the border country off toward Gar og Nadrak. The Cult controls virtually everything east of Boktor.'

'I'd say that the core of the problem's here, then,' Kamion observed. 'This is where the Orb is, and if the Cult can gain control of the Orb's Guardian, we'll all be marching south before long.'

'You could solve that by making every priest of Belar here on the Isle swim back to Val Alorn,' Anrak said with an evil grin.

'In full armor,' Daran added.

'No.' I said it firmly. 'Some of those priests are innocent, and people need the comforts of religion. I *do* think that Kamion's right, though. We *don't* want the Cult so close to the Orb.'

'What's the alternative to extermination, Aunt Pol?' Daran asked.

'Exile?' Kamion suggested.

'You aren't going to be popular in Val Alorn and Boktor if you send them a fresh wave of fanatics,' Anrak said.

'I wasn't thinking of that,' Kamion told him. 'I want these home-grown Cultists someplace where we can keep an eye on them.'

'Dungeons are good for that,' Anrak said.

159

'It costs too much money to keep people locked up,' Daran objected. Why is it that every ruler in the world spends all his time worrying about money? Then my nephew's eyes brightened. 'Lord Brand,' he said, 'do you remember what I threatened Garhein and Altor with last summer?'

'Sending them to the northern end of the Isle, you mean?'

'Exactly.'

'The Cultists would just shed their vestments and sneak back, your Highness.'

'It's a little hard to sneak across open water, Kamion,' Daran laughed. 'There are some little islets strung out above the main Isle. If we send all the cultists up there, we won't have to worry about them any more.'

'They're Alorns, your Highness,' Kamion reminded him. 'Boat-building's in their blood.'

'What are they going to build boats out of, my Lord?'

'Trees, I'd imagine.'

'There won't *be* any trees on those islets, Kamion. I'll have all the trees cut down before we exile the Cult.'

'You're still going to have to feed them, Daran,' Anrak said.

'They can feed themselves. We'll give them seed, animals, and farm tools, and they can either take up farming or starve.'

Anrak's grin grew broader. 'It's got some possibilities,' he agreed. 'You'll have to patrol the coast of their private little prison to keep their adherents from rowing boats across the water to rescue them, though.'

'I think I can persuade my grandfather Cherek to handle that for me. He doesn't want any more Cult priests in Val Alorn, so I'm sure he'll want to keep *our* Cultists here. He's got ships out there to hold off the Angaraks anyway, so it won't really cost him anything extra.'

'The only thing left is to find an excuse for it,' Kamion told them.

'Any cooked-up story would work, wouldn't it?' Anrak asked.

Kamion winced. 'Let's try for a little authenticity, Anrak. Lies get out of hand sometimes. You have to keep expanding them.'

'Maybe we could catch them during one of their secret ceremonies,' Anrak suggested. 'They're fairly offensive to decent people.'

'Oh?' Daran said. 'What's involved?'

Anrak shrugged. 'They all put on bear-skins and get roaring drunk. Their wives and daughters don't wear anything at all, and there's a lot of indiscriminate –' He hesitated, looked at me, and then he actually blushed. 'Anyway,' he rushed on, 'the priests perform what they call magic, which isn't really anything but fairly clumsy carnival trickery, and –'

'Perfect!' I exclaimed.

'I didn't follow that, Aunt Pol,' Daran said.

'Didn't Elthek persuade your father to outlaw witchcraft?'

'Well – yes, I suppose so. It was really just a way to keep the physicians from curing illnesses, though – getting rid of the competition.'

'A strict interpretation of those laws would make those secret Cult ceremonies with all that imitation magic a form of witchcraft, wouldn't it?'

'Oh, that's beautiful, Pol!' Kamion said admiringly.

'If we can find out where and when one of those ceremonies is taking place, we can swoop in during the entertainment and round them up,' Anrak said. 'We'll have enough to indict the whole Cult.' He thought for a moment. 'If you can hold off until the autumn equinox, you'll probably get every Cult-member on the Isle. That's a big day for the Cult.'

'Oh?' Daran said. 'Why's that?'

'There's a tradition that Torak cracked the world on the autumnal equinox. I'm not sure why, but the Cult always celebrates the event. Every district in Cherek, Drasnia, and Algaria has its own Cult party on that night.'

'I've got informants among the general population,' Kamion mused. 'It shouldn't be too hard to find out where those ceremonies take place. I'll put out the word, and we should have what we need in a week or so.'

Daran sighed disconsolately. 'Another perfectly good idea just went down a rat-hole,' he mourned.

'Which idea was that, dear?' I asked him.

'I was hoping that I could make Elthek himself take up farming, but if we exile the whole lot of them, the ordinary people in the Cult are probably going to feed the priests.'

'Oh, I wouldn't worry too much about that, Daran,' Anrak said. 'I've sailed along the north coast of the Isle. There are *lots* of islets up there, but none of them is really big enough to support more than a half-dozen people. If he wants to eat, Elthek's going to have to get his hands dirty.'

'Marvelous,' Daran beamed.

Kamion's spies advised us that, unlike the Cult practice in the other Alorn kingdoms, the Cultists here *all* gathered in a narrow gorge in the mountains rearing above the Citadel. Evidently our Deacon believed in keeping a firm grip on his adherents.

Kamion and I had a small argument about a week before the autumnal equinox. He was *very* upset when I told him that I was going with him to that gorge. 'Out of the question,' he told me. 'It'll be too dangerous.'

'And what are you going to do if it turns out that the Deacon can *really* perform magic, Kamion? You won't be able to help Daran very much if Elthek turns you into a toad, you know.'

'That's absurd, Pol. Nobody can do that.'

'Don't be too sure, Kamion. *I* probably could – if I set my mind to it. If Elthek *does* have talent in that area, I'm the only one on the Isle who can counter it. I'm coming along, Kamion, so don't argue with me about it.'

The soldiers who were to take the Cult into custody were all carefully selected, and for reasons of security they were *not* told what their mission was going to be. Kamion dispatched them into the mountains in squads with instructions to stay out of sight. The Cultists started drifting into the city in the waning days of summer, and then began drifting out again after a few days as Elthek sent them up the gorge to make preparations for the celebration. The whole affair took on an almost comic aspect with groups of armed men creeping around in the forests assiduously avoiding each other. I spent a great deal of *my* time in feathers during those two weeks, flying from tree to tree as I kept an eye on the Cultists to make certain that there weren't any last-minute changes of plan.

Our plan was really quite simple. We decided to secrete a fair number of highly respected nobles and commons in the woods on the steep sides of the gorge to observe Elthek's ceremony, and then, when we had enough damning evidence – and when the Cultists were too drunk to stand – we'd send in the soldiers to round them all up. It wasn't until the day preceding the autumnal equinox that Kamion and I quite firmly told Daran that he wouldn't be going along. 'You'll be sitting in judgment, your Highness,' Kamion told him. 'You'll lose all appearance of impartiality if you lead the attack.'

'But –' Daran started to protest.

'No buts, dear,' I said. 'If you were actually the king, it might be different, but you're only your father's regent, so you have to be a little careful. It's your father's throne you're defending, not your own.'

'It *will* be.'

'There's a lot of difference between "will be" and "is", Daran.

You have to give the appearance of impartiality in this situation. You can spend tomorrow evening sitting in front of a mirror practicing expressions of shock and outrage. Then, when Anrak, Kamion and I drag the Cultists before you and present the case against them, no one can accuse you of having been in on our scheme from the very start. Appearances are *very* important in situations like this.'

'Your Highness might want to keep in mind the fact that witch-craft's a capital offense,' Kamion pointed out. 'In actuality, you could burn the lot of them at the stake.'

'Could I really do that, Aunt Pol?' Daran asked me.

'Don't get carried away, dear. Sentencing them to exile's really an act of mercy, you realize.'

'Part of the idea here is to build your reputation, your Highness,' Kamion explained.

'I don't think it's very fair,' Daran sulked.

'No, your Highness, it's not. It's politics, and politics aren't meant to be fair. Oh, incidentally, after the trial, it might not be a bad idea for you to agonize over your final judgment for a week or so.'

Daran stared at him blankly.

'It'll give me some time to spread word of the charges and our proof all over the Isle – public relations, you understand.'

'I know what I'm going to do to them, Brand.'

'Of course you do, dear,' I told him. 'Just don't do it so quickly. Give Elthek and his cohorts some time to worry before you pass judgment on them.'

'Where am I going to keep them while I pretend to be making up my mind?'

'Elthek's got a fairly extensive dungeon under the temple of Belar, your Highness,' Kamion suggested without even cracking a smile. 'As long as it's there anyway –'

Daran burst out laughing at that point.

And then the day arrived, dawning murky with the threat of incipient rain. 'Wonderful,' Anrak said sourly, looking out the window of our blue-draped conference room as morning stained the sky over the Isle. 'I *hate* crawling around in the woods when it's raining.'

'You won't melt,' I assured him. 'If you'd like, you could bring a cake of soap along tonight. I think it's almost time for your annual bath.'

'I think you did me a big favor that day back in the Vale when you turned down my marriage proposal, Pol,' he replied.

'What's this?' Daran asked.

'I was young and foolish at the time, Daran,' Anrak explained. 'Some men just aren't meant to get married.'

That gave me something to think about. Daran would be twenty-three years old on his next birthday, and I didn't really want him to grow *too* accustomed to bachelorhood.

It rained off and on all that day, a filmy, misty kind of rain that wreathed the towers of the Citadel and obscured the city and the harbor. The sky cleared in the late afternoon, though, and we were treated to one of those glorious sunsets that almost make living in rainy country worthwhile.

No, I didn't have anything to do with it. You know how my father feels about tampering with the weather.

The nobles and commons who joined us that evening to serve as witnesses were all men of impeccable character and good reputation. They were not, despite Anrak's objections, coached or prompted in any way. Indeed, they were not even advised in advance that they were going to spend an entertaining evening out in the still-dripping forest. Kamion, acting in his official capacity as Rivan Warder, simply sent men out to round them all up as the sun went down. Most of them were at supper when they were summoned to the Citadel, and there was a bit of grumbling about that.

'What's this all about, Kamion?' a white-bearded old earl demanded when we all gathered in the stables. The earl's name was Jarok, a fairly common Alorn name.

'I want you all to see something, my Lord Jarok,' Kamion replied.

'What are we supposed to look at?' Jarok was obviously not happy. He was an old man with a young wife, and he'd had other plans for the evening, I guess.

'I'm not at liberty to discuss it, my Lord,' Kamion told him. 'All you and the others need to know is that you're going to witness a crime being committed this evening. The criminals will be taken into custody and they'll be tried later for their crime. You gentlemen will perform your civic duty and testify at that trial.'

'Belar's teeth, Kamion!' the grouchy old Jarok swore, 'just hang the rogues and have done with it.'

'We aren't talking about a simple burglary or an incidental murder, my Lord. This is a wide-ranging conspiracy that threatens the security of the throne and the entire kingdom. We want to stamp it out, so we'll need an iron-clad case to take before the Prince Regent.'

'That bad?' Jarok blinked. 'It's really bad enough to take before Daran himself instead of a magistrate?'

'Probably even worse, my Lord. If possible, I'd take the matter to Riva himself.'

'What are we waiting for, then? Let's go!'

I *love* the way Alorns can change direction in the blink of an eye, don't you?

The ride up the gorge which adjoined the one where the Cult was meeting wasn't very pleasant. The moon and stars were out, but the woods were absolutely soaked by the day's rain, and we were all wet to the skin by the time we reached the narrow pass that connected the two deep valleys. Things got worse at that point. We all dismounted and started wading up the hill through the sodden undergrowth.

The Cultists' bonfire down at the bottom of the gorge was clearly visible when we reached the crest, but it became less so as we crept down through the trees.

'I haven't had this much fun in years, Pol,' Anrak whispered to me as we struggled down the steep hill.

'Did you plan to ever grow up, Anrak?' I asked him rather tartly as I tried to unsnag the hem of my dress from a thorny bush.

'Not if I can help it, dear Lady.' His grin was infectious, and I had to stifle a laugh.

The clearing which surrounded the Cult's bonfire was quite large. 'Spread out, gentlemen,' Kamion's instructions were passed around in whispers. 'Let's try to see everything that happens out there.' The nobles and merchants and craftsmen comprising our group of witnesses obediently fanned out, moving as silently as possible and all crouched low to avoid being seen. Then we all sank down onto the wet ground to watch.

Elthek had not yet put in an appearance, and the Cultists, all dressed in bearskins, were gathered about the fire drinking strong ale and singing – badly – old Alorn folk-songs. One of the soldiers Kamion had out in the woods came crawling up to join us. He was a stocky man with a no-nonsense kind of face. 'What are your orders, Lord Brand?' he whispered.

'Tell your men to stay out of sight, Sergeant,' Kamion instructed. 'Did those people around the fire leave any sentries out there in the forest?'

'No, my Lord Warder. As soon as the first ale-barrel was broached, they all came in out of the woods.' The soldier coughed in a slightly embarrassed way. 'Ah – Lord Brand?'

'Yes, Sergeant?'

'I know it isn't proper for me to take any kind of action without orders, but something came up, and I had to deal with it on my own.'

'Oh?'

'When those people around the fire started coming up the gorge, it was fairly obvious that they were members of the Bear-Cult. Some of my men have sympathies in that direction, so I had to take steps. Nobody got hurt,' he added hastily, 'at least not too badly. I've got those men chained to trees a couple of miles up the gorge, and their mouths are stuffed full of old boot socks to keep them from shouting out warnings. Is it all right that I did that, my Lord?'

'Perfectly all right, Captain.'

'Ah – I'm only a sergeant, my Lord.'

'Not any more, you aren't. What's your name, Captain?'

'Torgun, my Lord.'

'All right then, Captain Torgun. Go back to your men and spread them out so that you've got every possible escape route covered.' Kamion lifted a curved hunting horn. 'When you hear me blow on this, order your men to charge. I want everyone wearing a bear-skin clapped in chains.'

'They'll probably try to fight, my Lord. Do I have permission to use force?'

'Do whatever it takes, Captain Torgun.'

The newly promoted soldier's answering grin was one of the most evil I've ever seen. 'Try not to kill *too* many of them, Captain,' I added – just as a precaution, you understand.

The look of innocence he gave me was so transparent that I almost burst out laughing. 'Of course not, Lady Polgara. I wouldn't dream of it.' Then he slithered away.

'Good move there, Kamion,' Earl Jarok whispered hoarsely. 'Field promotions are one of the best ways to get good officers. That fellow would follow you into fire right now.'

'Let's hope it doesn't come to that, my Lord. Being wet's bad enough.'

The party around the bonfire was getting rowdier as the ale flowed freely. The Cultists were all shuffling around the fire, tankards in hand, trying to imitate the shambling walk of their totem. Then Elthek came up the gorge and trailing along behind him were most of the priests of Belar on the Isle of the Winds.

'We're going to decimate the priesthood, I'm afraid,' Kamion whispered to Anrak and me.

'It won't be hard to find replacements, Kamion,' Anrak assured him. 'The priestly life's fairly comfortable, and it doesn't involve much sweating.'

Then Elthek addressed the shaggy congregation for an hour or so, punctuating his oration with simple tricks of 'magic'. The flames in the bonfire changed colors several times as the Deacon's underlings surreptitiously tossed assorted powders into the coals. A 'ghost', which was no more than a gauzy veil suspended on a black string, appeared, billowing in the heat of the fire. A second moon, actually a large glass globe filled with fireflies, rose over the gorge. Rocks started to bleed, and a 'dead' sheep was resurrected. It was all fairly transparent, but Elthek ladled on high drama and the drunken Cultists were all suitably impressed.

'What do you think, Pol?' Kamion asked me. 'Is that witchcrafty enough for our purposes?'

'Witchcrafty?' I asked in some amusement.

'I've always had this way with words,' he said modestly.

'You're the expert in this area, Pol,' Anrak said. 'Is Elthek *really* performing magic out there?'

'No. It's all pure fakery. It should be enough to convict him, though.'

'My feelings exactly,' Kamion said. He reached for his hunting horn.

'Aren't you going to wait for the naked girls?' Anrak sounded disappointed.

'Ah – no, Anrak. I don't think so. Let's not complicate the trial by adding women to the list of the accused.' He lifted his horn and blew a long, brazen note, calling in Captain Torgun and his men.

The soldiers were well trained, and the Cultists were far gone in drink, so it wasn't even a very interesting fight, and the casualties were minimal. Elthek kept screaming, 'How dare you?' but I noticed that he didn't reach for his sword. Finally, Captain Torgun grew tired of the screaming and stilled the Deacon's objections with his fist.

It was dawn by the time the line of chained Cultists were dragged into Riva's city. We threw them into the dungeon under the temple of Belar and then Kamion spoke briefly with Captain Torgun before he, Anrak and I escorted our group of witnesses back up the hill to the Citadel to advise Daran that our little excursion had been successful.

The 'trial' took place the following day in the public square in front of the temple. I noticed that Captain Torgun's soldiers had

167

passed the time erecting a fair number of posts in the square and piling firewood around them – just in case.

'Why are we doing this here instead of in the throne room?' I asked Daran before the proceedings began.

'I want everyone here in the city to hear the testimony, Aunt Pol,' he explained. 'Let's fix it so that the Bear-Cult doesn't reappear just as soon as my back's turned.'

Daran sat on a large, ornate chair – Elthek's, actually – which Torgun's soldiers had dragged out of the temple and placed where everyone could see it. Then the Bear-Cultists, still in chains and seriously disheveled, were dragged up out of the temple dungeon and forced to sit in a huddled group at the foot of the broad stair that led up to the temple door. The square was full of people as the proceedings began.

Kamion, Warder of Riva, rose to his feet to address the assembled citizens. 'A crime has been committed here on our island, my friends,' he began, 'and we are gathered here to sit in judgment.'

'What crime are we talking about, Lord Brand?' a well-coached townsman demanded in a booming voice that could be heard all over the square. The Rivan Warder, I noted, was not the sort to leave anything to chance.

'The crime of witchcraft,' Kamion replied.

Elthek, battered and bruised by Captain Torgun's fists, tried to leap to his feet, but that's a little hard to do when you're chained to other people.

The proceedings went smoothly, I thought. Kamion's questioning was masterly, and the witnesses all confirmed the fact that Elthek had performed 'magic' at the gathering in the gorge.

Then Captain Torgun dragged the Rivan Deacon to his feet.

'What say you to the charges?' Kamion demanded of the prisoner.

'Lies! All lies!' Elthek almost screamed. 'And that law doesn't apply to me!'

'The law applies to everybody,' Daran told him firmly.

'I'm a priest! I'm a Deacon of the Church of Belar!'

'All the more reason for you to obey the law.'

'It wasn't really magic!'

'Oh?' Daran said mildly. '*I* can't call up ghosts or create another moon or make rocks bleed. Can you, Lord Brand?'

'I wouldn't even want to try, your Highness,' Kamion replied.

'Let's get on with this,' Earl Jarok boomed.

'How say the people?' Daran asked in a loud, formal voice. 'Are these men guilty of the charge of witchcraft?'

'*YES!*' the crowd roared. I wouldn't be at all surprised to find that deer on the other side of the Isle were startled by the sound.

'Return the prisoners to the dungeon,' Daran instructed. 'I will consider this matter and devise a suitable punishment for this foul crime.'

I'll be the first to admit that the entire business was crudely staged, but we're talking about Alorns here, and subtlety's never been an Alorn strong point.

The extended period during which Daran 'considered' his final judgment gave the prisoners plenty of time to look out through the tiny, barred, ground-level windows at the grim stakes out in the square.

It was cloudy on the day when Daran announced his judgment, one of those cool, dry days when the clouds obscuring the sky gave no hint of rain, but when the light casts no shadows. We all trooped down to the temple square again, and the convicted felons were dragged up out of the dungeon to learn their fate. The artfully prepared stakes surrounding the square hinted strongly at what that fate was going to be, and the captives all seemed moderately terror-stricken.

Daran took his place in the seat of judgment, and an anticipatory silence fell over the crowd. Although it was cloudy, it wasn't really dark, but there were still quite a few burning torches in the hands of the gathering.

'I've considered this matter, my friends,' Daran announced, 'and I've come to my decision after much thought. The crime of witchcraft is abhorrent to decent men, and every effort should be made to stamp it out. This particular outbreak, however, is the result of stubborn stupidity rather than a deliberate courting of the powers of darkness. The Bear-cult is misguided rather than intrinsically evil. We're not going to need those torches, friends, so put them out.'

There were some murmurs of disappointment about that.

'I've spoken with my father, the king, about this,' Daran continued, 'and he agrees with me that our main goal in this situation should be to separate the Cultists from the rest of the population. We *could* separate them by building fires with them, but father agrees with me that such a course might be a bit extreme in this case. It is therefore our decision that these criminals be sentenced to perpetual internal exile instead. They will be taken immediately to the archipelago standing at the northern end of the Isle and remain on those islets for the rest of their lives. Our decision is final, and this matter is now closed.'

169

There were shouts of protest from the crowd, but Captain Torgun somewhat ostentatiously moved his troops into position.

Elthek, the former Rivan Deacon, smiled faintly.

'Don't be *too* happy, Elthek,' Kamion told him. 'His Highness has sent word to his grandfather, and the Cherek fleet will make sure that none of the Cultists who evaded capture will be able to rescue you. You *will* stay there for the rest of your life, old boy. Oh, incidentally, winter's coming on, so you'd better get to work as soon as you arrive building some sort of shelter. Winter comes early up there, so you haven't got much time.'

'What are we going to eat?' one of the prisoners demanded.

'That's entirely up to you. We'll give you some fishhooks, and there are wild goats up there. That should get you through the winter. When spring gets here, we'll drop off some farm tools, chickens, and seeds for planting.'

'That's all right for peasants,' Elthek objected, 'but what about us? You surely don't expect the priesthood to grub in the dirt for food, do you?'

'You're not a priest any more, dear boy,' Kamion informed him. 'You're a convicted felon, and the throne has no obligations to you whatsoever. Dig or die, Elthek. It's entirely up to you. There are seabirds up there, and I'm told that bird-droppings make excellent fertilizer. You're a very creative fellow, so I'm sure you'll do just fine.' Then he smiled faintly as Elthek's expression showed that he was gradually beginning to realize just exactly what Daran's seeming leniency really meant. 'I'd just love to stay and chat with you some more, dear boy,' the Warder said, 'but his Highness and I have pressing business at the Citadel. Affairs of state, you understand.' He raised his voice slightly. 'I think the prisoners are ready now, Captain Torgun,' he said. 'Would you be so kind as to escort them to their ships? They have a great deal of work ahead of them, and I'm sure they're all eager to get started.'

'At once, Lord Brand!' Torgun replied, saluting smartly.

'Ah, Elthek,' I said sweetly to the crestfallen clergyman.

'What?' his response was surly.

'Have a nice voyage, and I *do* hope you'll enjoy your new home and your new occupation.'

And that was the last time that the Bear-Cult reared its head on the Isle of the Winds. It's been some three thousand years and more since Elthek and his cohorts took up subsistence farming on those rocky little islets, and even though they're Alorns, the Rivans took Daran's lesson very much to heart. The notion of spading bird manure into rocky soil in order to eke out a miserable existence doesn't appeal to very many people, and those wind-swept islets will always be there – waiting.

The following spring came late, and I began to grow more and more restless. Then, late one night when a wind-driven rainstorm tore at the towers of the Citadel and I tossed restlessly in my bed, mother's thought came to me. *'Polgara,'* she said, *'don't you think it's about time for Daran to get married?'*

To be quite honest about it, my mother's question startled me, since I still – irrationally, I suppose – thought of my nephew as a child. To concede that he was growing up would have further separated me from Beldaran, I guess. Everybody has these little lapses.

The next day, however, when Daran, Kamion and I met for our usual discussion of the state of the kingdom, I rather closely examined my nephew and was forced to admit that mother was probably right. Daran had sandy blond hair, and fair-haired people always seem to look younger than brunettes do. He was a muscular young man, though, and wrestling with the chores of his regency had given him a maturity far beyond his years.

'Why are you looking at me that way, Aunt Pol?' he asked curiously.

'Oh, no particular reason. I think you missed a spot under your chin while you were shaving this morning, is all.'

He ran his fingers up and down his neck. 'Yes,' he agreed, 'it is a little furry down there, isn't it? Do you think I should grow a beard?'

'No,' I told him, 'definitely not. There are enough shaggy people around here already. Now, then, what are we going to do about this shortage of priests? Most of them are up north with Elthek.'

'We can get along without priests, Aunt Pol. The priests of Belar always seem to get Bear-Cult ideas, for some reason, and I don't want to go through that again.'

'We need priests, Daran.'

'What for?'

'To perform weddings and funerals,' I told him rather bluntly. 'Young people here on the Isle are beginning to find alternatives to marriage, and that should probably be discouraged, wouldn't you say? I'm sure it's all very entertaining, but it *does* tend to erode the morals of your people, don't you agree?'

He actually blushed about that.

'Why don't you let me take care of the problem, your Highness?'

171

Kamion suggested. 'We *could* recruit priests of Belar in Cherek and Drasnia, but that might just reintroduce the Bear-Cult here on the Isle. I'll talk with the palace chaplain about it, and we can probably set up a theological seminary in the temple. *I'll* lay out the curriculum, though, so we can be fairly sure that unorthodoxy doesn't creep in.'

'You're the scholar, Kamion,' Daran shrugged. 'Do whatever you think best.' He looked at the window where midmorning light streamed into the room. 'What hour would you say it is?' he asked me. 'I've got an appointment with my tailor this morning.'

'It's the fourth hour past dawn, dear,' I told him.

'It seems later for some reason.'

'Trust me, Daran.'

'Of course, Aunt Pol.' He rose to his feet. 'I'll be back after lunch.' He flexed his arms. 'This doublet's getting a little tight across the shoulders. Maybe my tailor can let it out a bit.' Then he crossed to the door and left the room.

'Kamion,' I said.

'Yes, Pol?'

'Let's find him a wife. Bachelorhood's habit-forming, I've noticed.'

Kamion burst out laughing.

'What's so funny?'

'I've never heard it put that way before, Pol. Why don't I draw up a list of all the eligible – and unattached – young noblewomen here?'

'Not just the noblewomen, Kamion,' I told him quite firmly.

'Is the prince allowed to marry a commoner?' Kamion seemed startled.

'He's allowed to marry anyone I tell him to marry, Kamion,' I said. 'We're dealing with a very unusual family here, so normal rules don't apply. *We* won't be choosing Daran's wife. That decision's going to come from someone else.'

'Oh? Who?'

'I'm not at liberty to discuss it – and you wouldn't believe me if I told you.'

'One of *those* things?' he asked with some distaste.

'Exactly. Get started on your list while I get some instructions.'

He sighed.

'What's wrong?'

'I *hate* this, Pol. I like for things to be rational.'

Then it was my turn to laugh. 'Do you actually believe that the process of love and marriage is rational, Kamion? We humans aren't

172

exactly like birds attracted to a display of bright feathers, but we come very close. Trust me in this, my friend.'

'You're using that phrase quite a lot this morning, Pol.'

'If you and Daran would just listen to me, I wouldn't have to repeat myself so often. Run along now, Kamion, I've got work to do.'

I returned to my rooms and went looking for mother with my mind.

'Yes, Polgara?' her thought came to me.

'Kamion's seeking out all of the eligible young women on the Isle, mother. How do we determine which of them to choose?'

'You'll know – and so will Daran.'

'We aren't going to let him make the decision, are we? He's a nice boy, but this is important.'

She actually laughed. 'Just bring them into the Hall of the Rivan King one by one, Pol,' she told me. 'You'll know immediately – and so will Daran.'

And so we did it that way. Our approach wasn't really very subtle. Kamion let it be generally known that Daran was looking for a wife – although that was probably the furthest thing from the Prince Regent's mind. The young women on the Isle were paraded, one by one, before the throne in the Hall of the Rivan King. They all wore their finest clothing, and each of them was given about five minutes to try to snare our increasingly nervous – even frightened – young man.

It went on for days, and poor Daran was engulfed by treacle-laden smiles as the girls of Isle of the Winds each tried to enchant him.

'If this goes on much longer, Aunt Pol, I'm going to run away,' he threatened one evening.

'Don't do that, dear,' I said. 'I'd just have to chase you down and bring you back. You *have* to get married, Daran, because you *have* to produce an heir to your father's throne. That obligation takes precedence over all others. Now go get some sleep. You're starting to look just a bit haggard.'

'So would you if people kept looking at you like a side of beef.'

It was the next day, I think, when *she* came into the hall. She was quite small, and her hair was almost as dark as mine. Her large luminous eyes, however, were so dark as to be almost black. Her father was a very minor nobleman, hardly more than a peasant, who had a small holding back in the mountains. Her name was Larana, she wore a plain dress, and she entered the Hall rather hesitantly. Her eyes were downcast, and there was a faint flush on her alabaster cheeks.

I heard Daran's breath catch in his throat, and I turned sharply to look at him. His face had gone very pale, and his hands were trembling. More importantly, though, was the fact that the Master's Orb on the pommel of his father's sword was glowing a soft pink, a blush almost exactly matching the one on Larana's cheeks.

I stepped over to where the Rivan Warder stood. 'Send the rest of them away, Kamion,' I advised him. 'We've found the one we want.'

Kamion was staring incredulously at the rosy Orb. 'Was that supposed to happen, Pol?' he asked, his voice a little strangled.

'Of course,' I replied in an off-hand sort of way. 'You didn't think we were just going to have all those girls draw straws, did you?' Then I stepped down from the dais and approached the bride-to-be. 'Good morning, Larana,' I greeted her.

'Lady Polgara,' she responded with a graceful curtsey.

'Why don't you come with me, dear?' I said.

'But –' she looked at Daran with an almost naked longing.

'You'll have time to talk with him later, dear,' I assured her. 'Lots of time, I'd imagine. There are some things you'll need to know, so let's get them out of the way right at the outset.' I firmly took our bride-to-be by the arm and led her toward the door.

'Aunt Pol.' Daran's voice almost had a note of panic in it.

'Later, dear,' I told him. 'Why don't you and Lord Brand go to our meeting room? Larana and I'll be along in a little while.'

I took Larana to my rooms, sat her down, and gave her a cup of tea to settle her nerves. Then I told her in rather general terms something about the peculiar family she'd soon be joining.

'I thought all those stories were just that, Lady Polgara – stories. Are you saying that they're all really true?'

'They've probably been exaggerated a bit, dear,' I said, 'but they're still more or less true.'

'Does the prince know? That I've been selected, I mean?'

'Oh, dear, dear Larana,' I laughed. 'Didn't you see his face? Right now he'd walk through fire just to get to you.'

'But I'm so ordinary.'

'No, dear,' I said firmly. 'You've never been ordinary, and you never will be. Drink your tea now, and then we'll join the menfolk.'

She set down her cup. 'Shouldn't we hurry, Lady Polgara?' she asked. 'I wouldn't want him to get away.'

'Not to worry, dear. He's not going to get away from you. Let him wait just a bit. It'll be good for him.'

When the two of us joined Kamion and Daran in the blue-draped tower room, I was treated to a repetition of that day in the inn at Camaar when my sister and Riva first met.

'Aren't they going to say anything to each other, Pol?' Kamion whispered to me after about half an hour of absolute silence.

'They *are* saying things to each other, Kamion. Listen with your eyes, not your ears.'

He looked at the happy couple and saw the absolute adoration on their faces. 'I think I see what you mean, Pol. It's almost embarrassing to be in the same room with them.'

'Yes,' I agreed. Then I looked speculatively at Larana. 'You'd better give me about ten days before you schedule the wedding, Kamion. I have to have a long talk with Arell about Larana's wedding dress and a few other details.'

'It's all settled then? That quick? *My* courtship went on for half a year or more.'

I patted his cheek. 'This is more efficient, dear boy,' I told him. '*You'll* probably have to make most of the decisions here on the Isle for the next couple of months. Daran's not going to be very rational for a while. Oh, you'd better talk with Riva and let him know what's afoot. He'll have to be present, of course, and we'll want to give him time to prepare himself to appear in public again.'

'That might be a little tricky, Pol. He's become very reclusive in the past year. If I didn't know better, I'd almost say that he's afraid of people.'

'Let him know what's happening, Kamion, and then I'll talk with him.'

Kamion looked at the children again. 'The next problem is how we're going to get those two apart. Besides, it's starting to get dark outside, and we should probably feed them.'

'They aren't hungry, Kamion. Give them another couple of hours, and then I'll take Larana to my quarters for the night.'

'Be sure to lock your door. Keeping Daran and Larana away from each other might be just a bit difficult.'

'I'll take care of it, Brand. Send for Arell, would you, please? Tell her that I'll need her first thing in the morning.' Then I went over to where the children were still gazing into each others' eyes. 'Did you ask her yet, Daran?' I said, shaking his shoulder to get his attention.

'Ask her what, Aunt Pol?'

175

I gave him a long, steady look.

He flushed slightly. 'Oh,' he said, 'that. It's not really necessary, Aunt Pol.'

'Why don't you do it anyway, Daran? These little formalities are the very soul of civilized behavior.'

'Well, if you think I should. It's already been decided, though.' He looked at the young woman who'd fill the rest of his life. 'You will, won't you, Larana?' he asked.

'Will what, my Lord?' she replied.

'Marry me, naturally.'

'Oh,' she said, 'that. Of course I will, my Lord.'

'See?' I said. 'Now that wasn't so difficult, was it?'

There had been cries of outraged anguish from those girls who'd been waiting to meet the Crown Prince and then had been summarily dismissed, and Kamion and I were besieged by equally outraged fathers vehemently protesting – not so much the disappointment of their daughters as the evaporation of their own opportunities for social prestige and access to the throne. But Kamion and I were able to smooth all the ruffled feathers with mysterious references to 'fate', 'destiny', and 'preordination'. Our arguments were a bit specious, I'll admit, but convincing lies are the very soul of diplomatic discourse.

Arell quite nearly outdid herself with Larana's wedding gown, a lacy fantasy in palest blue. Larana and I really hit it off when she confided to me that blue was her favorite color. I wholeheartedly approved of the girl's good taste.

The wedding took place about noon on a sunny spring day, and the Hall of the Rivan King, suitably decorated for the happy occasion, was flooded with bright sunlight.

I'm not entirely sure who arranged that. I know that *I* didn't.

There was the usual banquet after the wedding, but I'd visited the brewery before dawn and made some modifications in the favorite beverage of every Alorn who's ever lived. The beer *tasted* like beer, and it looked and smelled exactly like beer, but it didn't produce the usual results. The wedding guests, as wedding guests always do, drank to excess, but nothing happened. There were no arguments, no fights, no falling down, no snoring in corners, and no throwing up. There *were* some monumental headaches the following morning, however. I was certainly not cruel enough to take *all* the fun out of drinking too much.

After the ceremony had taken place, I spent most of the rest of the day with my brother-in-law. Riva Iron-grip's hair was almost snow-white by now, and he seemed to be in failing health. 'It's almost all finished now, isn't it, Pol?' he said a bit sadly.

'I didn't exactly follow that, Riva.'

'My work's almost all done, and I'm very tired. As soon as Larana produces an heir, I'll be able to rest. Would you do me a favor?'

'Of course.'

'Have some workmen build a new crypt for Beldaran and me. I think we should sleep beside each other.'

The natural response to such a request would be to scoff with such idiocies as, 'You aren't going to need a burial place for a long time,' and the like, but I loved and respected Iron-grip too much to insult him that way. 'I'll see to it,' I promised.

'Thank you, Pol,' he said. 'Now, if you don't mind, I think I'll go to bed. It's been a hectic day, and I'm very, very tired.' Then he rose and with stooped shoulders, he quietly left the banquet hall.

Things went along smoothly on the Isle for several years after the wedding. There was a certain concern about the fact that Larana didn't immediately blossom into motherhood, but I calmed everyone as best I could. 'These things take time,' I said.

I said it so often that I got sick of hearing it myself.

Then, in 2044 by the Alorn calendar, Cherek Bear-shoulders died, plunging all of Aloria into mourning. Cherek had been a titan, and his death left a huge vacancy.

That winter, Larana quietly advised us that she was with child, and we were all moderately thrilled by the news. Her son was born the following summer, and Daran named him Cherek, in honor of his deceased paternal grandfather. After the ceremony when the infant's hand was placed on the Orb and it responded in the usual way, we took him to Riva's quarters to allow the king to see his grandson.

'It's all right, isn't it, father?' Daran asked, 'naming him after *your* father, I mean?'

'Father would be pleased,' Riva said, his voice sounding very weary. He reached out, and I handed his grandson to him. He held the baby for quite some time with a gentle smile on his aged face. Then he drifted off to sleep.

He never woke up.

The funeral was solemn, but not really marred by excessive grief. Riva's seclusion had removed him from public view, and many on the Isle were probably a bit surprised to discover that he'd still been alive.

After the funeral, I did some thinking. Daran and Kamion had things well in hand, and there was no real reason for me to remain.

And so, in the spring of 2046, I packed up all my things in preparation for my return to the Vale.

PART THREE

Vo Wacune

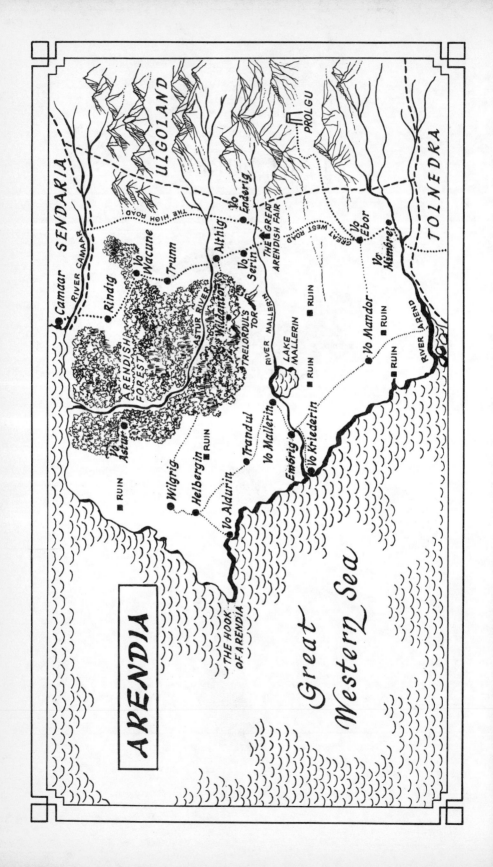

CHAPTER 12

As luck had it – although luck probably had nothing to do with it – Anrak stopped by the Isle on one of those pointless voyages of his just as I was making my preparations to leave, and he volunteered to take me as far as Camaar. I'd never really understood Anrak. About half the time he didn't even have a cargo when he put out to sea. His arrival gave me a perfect excuse to cut short the tedious business of farewells. Why *do* people always drag that out so much? After you've said 'goodbye' a couple of times, you've said it, haven't you?

The weather was partially cloudy when Anrak's sailors slipped the hawsers and raised the sails, and I stood on the aft deck watching the Isle of the Winds slowly receding behind us. I'd matured on the Isle. There'd been happy times and times filled with almost unbearable grief and pain, but that's the nature of life, isn't it?

The rocky island was still low on the horizon astern when a peculiar certainty came over me. I'd not only said farewell to friends and relatives when I'd boarded Anrak's ship, but I'd also said good-bye to what most people would call a normal life. I was forty-six years old now, and if the lives of my father and my uncles were any indication of what lay ahead of me, I was entering unexplored country. I would come to know and love people and then watch them drop away one by one while I went on. There was a dreadful kind of loneliness implicit in that realization. Others would leave, but I would continue on down through all the uncertain, endless years stretching out before me.

'Why so sad, Pol?' Anrak, who was standing at the tiller not far away, asked me.

'No particular reason.'

'We'll hit open water soon,' he assured me. 'That should make you feel better.' He looked out at shafts of sunlight moving majestically across the water.

'I didn't exactly follow that, Anrak.'

'She'll wash off your melancholy. She's very good at that.'

'She? She who?'

'The sea, Pol. No matter how bad things get, she always takes the sorrow away and clears your head. Landsmen don't understand that, but we do.'

'You love the sea, don't you, Anrak?'

'Of course. She surprises me sometimes, and she's occasionally bad-tempered, but most of the time she and I get along fairly well. I love her, Pol. She's all the wife I've ever needed.'

I always remind myself of that conversation when I'm obliged to have dealings with that rogue, Captain Greldik. Greldik and Anrak, though separated by three thousand years, are cut from the same bolt of cloth, viewing the sea as a living thing with a personality all her own.

I bought a horse named Baron in Camaar. Baron was a good, sensible bay who was old enough to have outgrown that silliness so characteristic of younger horses, and he and I got along well. I wasn't really in any hurry, so I didn't push him, and Baron seemed to approve of that. We more or less strolled across the neat fields of southern Sendaria toward Muros. We stayed at village inns along the way, and when no inn was available, we slept outdoors. With the exception of that peculiarly cosmopolitan port at Camaar, southern Sendaria was in the domain of the Wacite Arends in those days, and I found the lilting brogue of the Wacite peasants rather charming. I *didn't* find the repeated warnings of innkeepers and stablemen about robbers and outlaws on the road very entertaining, though. 'But, me Lady,' one officious village innkeeper warned when I told him that I was traveling alone, ''tis fearful dangerous for a woman alone out there. Robbers be wicked men who'll most likely want t' take advantage of th' fact that y' have no protection, don't y' know.'

'I can deal with them, good master innkeeper,' I told him quite firmly. These continual warnings were starting to make me tired.

The River Camaar branched about half-way to Muros, and the land beyond that fork in the river was as thickly forested as northern Arendia now is. For most people in the modern era the term 'primeval forest' has a poetic sound to it, calling up images of park-like

182

surroundings inhabited by fairies, elves, and occasional trolls. The reality was far more gloomy. If you leave a tree to its own devices for fifteen hundred or so years, it just keeps growing. I've seen trees eighteen to twenty feet thick at the base, trees that go up a hundred and fifty feet before they sprout a limb. The limbs of that tree and its neighboring trees interlock to form a roof high overhead that blocks out the sun and sky and creates a permanent damp green twilight on the forest floor. The undergrowth is dense in most places, and wild creatures abound in the dim light – and wild men as well.

The Wacite Arends had brought the melancholy institution of serfdom with them when they'd migrated north of the Camaar River, and a serf who lives near a forest always has an option available to him if serfdom becomes too tedious. Once he's taken up residence in the woods, however, the only occupation available to him is banditry in most cases, and travelers are his natural prey.

The two that I met on the muddy forest road to Muros late one afternoon were shabby, unshaven, and about half-drunk. They stepped out of the bushes bordering the road brandishing rusty butcher-knives. 'I'll be after takin' th' horse, Ferdish,' one rogue said to the other.

'Fair enough, Selt,' Ferdish replied, scratching vigorously at one armpit and leering at me, 'an' I'll be after takin' th' woman herself, don't y' know.'

'Y' always do, Ferdish,' Selt noted. 'Y've got quite an eye fer th' ladies, I've noted.'

There were any number of things I could have done, of course, but I didn't really care for their proprietary attitude, and I thought a bit of education might be in order here. Besides, there was something I wanted to try out – just to see if it'd actually work. 'It's all settled, then, gentlemen?' I asked them rather casually.

'All settled, me darlin',' Ferdish smirked at me. 'Now, would y' be so good as t' get down so that Selt here kin try out his new mount whilst me an' you have a bit of a frolic?'

'You're *sure* this is what you really want?' I pressed.

'It's what we're goin' t' *have*, Lady-o,' Selt laughed coarsely.

'Oh, good,' I said. 'My beast and I are hungry, and we've been wondering who we were going to have for supper.'

The ragged pair stared at me uncomprehendingly.

'I *do* want to thank you two for coming along just when my stomach was starting to rumble.' I looked at them critically. 'A bit scrawny, perhaps,' I noted, 'but travelers have to get used to short rations, I guess.'

Then I released my Will slowly to give them every opportunity to enjoy the transformation taking place before their very eyes. Baron, who'd been idly cropping at a clump of grass by the side of the road, raised his head, and his neck began to elongate even as scales, claws, wings, and other dragonish appurtenances started to appear. My own transformation was every bit as slow. My shoulders expanded, my arms grew longer, fangs started to protrude from between my lips, and my face took on an Eldrakish overcast. When the alteration was completed, my pair of shabby outlaws stood frozen in terror, gaping at a monstrous ogress with blazing eyes and clawed hands sitting astride a huge, smoking dragon. 'Feeding time, Baron,' I rasped in a harsh, guttural voice. 'What do you think? Should we kill them first, or should we eat them alive?'

Ferdish and Selt, still frozen stock-still in horror, clung to each other, screaming.

Then Baron belched, and a great cloud of sooty fire came billowing out of his mouth.

'Now, why didn't I think of that?' I growled. 'What a wonderful idea, Baron. Go ahead and cook them a little before we eat them. It's evening, after all, and we'll both sleep better with a hot meal in our bellies.'

Ferdish and Selt must have suddenly remembered a pressing engagement elsewhere, because they left without even saying good-bye. As I remember, there was a lot of screaming, stumbling, crashing in the brush, and the like, in their departure.

'Shall we press on then, Baron?' I suggested, and he and I continued our ambling stroll through the damp, gloomy forest.

Oh, don't be so gullible. Of *course* I didn't actually convert Baron and myself into those monsters. Ferdish and Selt weren't worth that kind of effort, and illusion is just as effective as reality most of the time. Besides, to be perfectly honest about it, I hadn't the faintest notion in those days of what an ogress or a dragon really looked like, so I just improvised.

We reached Muros the following day, and I purchased supplies. Then, the next morning at daybreak Baron and I struck out for the Sendarian mountains. If you absolutely must be alone in the wilderness, I strongly recommend the mountains. A kind of peace comes over me in high country that I feel in no other surroundings. To be perfectly honest, I loitered, frequently making my night's encampment long before it was really necessary. I swam in icy mountain lakes, startling the local trout, I'm sure, and I browsed through thickets of berry-bushes when they presented themselves. It was with some regret that I came down out of the mountains and rode out onto that endless sea of grass that is the Algarian plain.

The weather held fair, and we arrived in the Vale a few days later. Father and the twins greeted me warmly, but uncle Beldin, as usual, was off in Mallorea keeping an eye on the enemy and trying to come up with a way to lure Urvon out of Mal Yaska.

It felt odd to be back in the Vale after the years I'd spent on the Isle of the Winds. I'd been at the center of things in the Citadel, and there was always something going on that needed my immediate attention. To be honest about it, I missed those affairs of state, and the remoteness of the Vale made it impossible for me to even know about them, much less take a hand. My father, who's much more observant than he sometimes appears to be, noticed the signs of my discontent. 'Are you busy, Pol?' he asked me one autumn evening after supper.

'Not really,' I replied, setting aside the medical text I'd been reading.

'You're having problems, aren't you?' he asked me, his white hair and beard ruddy in the firelight.

'I can't seem to get settled back down,' I admitted.

He shrugged. 'It happens. It usually takes me a year or so to get my feet back on the ground after I've been out in the world for a while. Study's something you have to do every day. If you put it aside, you have to learn how all over again. Just be patient, Pol. It comes back after a while.' He leaned back, looking reflectively into the fire. 'We're not like other people, Pol, and there's no point in pretending that we are. We're not here to get involved in running the world. That's what kings are for, and for all of me they're welcome to it. *Our* business is here, and what's going on out there doesn't really mean anything to us – at least it shouldn't.'

'We live in the world too, father.'

'No, Pol, we don't – at least not in the same world as the people out there live in. *Our* world's a world of first causes and that inevitable string of EVENTS that's been growing out of those causes from the moment the Purpose of the Universe was divided. Our only task is to identify – and influence – certain incidents that are so minute and unremarkable that ordinary people don't even notice them.' He paused. 'What are you studying right now?'

'Medical texts.'

'Why? People are going to die anyway, no matter how much you try to prevent it. If one thing doesn't carry them off, something else will.'

'We're talking about friends and family here, father.'

He sighed. 'Yes, I know. That doesn't alter the facts, though. They're mortal; we aren't – at least not yet. Set your hobby aside, Polgara, and get down to business. Here.' He handed me a thick, heavy scroll. 'This is your copy of the Mrin Codex. You'd better get started on it. There'll probably be tests later on.'

'Oh, father,' I said, 'be serious.'

'I am. The tests that'll grow out of *this* course of study are likely to have far-reaching consequences.'

'Such as?'

'Oh, I don't know – the end of the world, possibly – or the coming of the one who'll save it.' He gave me an inscrutable look. 'Be happy in your work, Pol,' he told me as he returned to his own copy of the ravings of that idiot on the banks of the Mrin.

The next morning I put on my grey Rivan cloak, saddled Baron, and rode out into the blustery autumn day. The Tree, standing deep in eternity, had begun to deck himself out in his autumn finery, and he was absolutely glorious. The birds, probable descendants of my cheeky sparrow and lyric lark, swooped down to greet me as I approached. I'm not sure why, but I've never encountered a bird who didn't call me by name when he first caught sight of me.

Mother didn't respond when I sent my thought out to her, but I don't think I'd really expected her to reply. Mother was still mourning the death of my sister.

I didn't press the issue, since it was the Tree I'd come to visit. We didn't speak, but then we never do. Our communion couldn't have been put into words. I immersed myself in his sense of timelessness, absorbing his eternal presence, and in a somewhat gentler manner he confirmed father's blunt assessment of the previous night. Father, Beldin, the twins, and I were *not* like other people, and our purpose was not like theirs.

After a time, I simply reached out my hand, laid it on the rough bark of the Tree, sighed, and returned to father's tower and the waiting Mrin Codex.

Father and I made periodic visits to the Isle of the Winds during the next half-century or so – usually for meetings of the Alorn Council. There were new kings in Cherek, Drasnia, and Algaria, but father and I weren't as close to them as we'd been to Bear-shoulders, Bull-neck, and Fleet-foot. Because fairly extended periods of time passed between our visits, I was keenly aware of the fact that Daran and Kamion were visibly older each time we went to the Isle.

My father's hinted at this, but one of us had probably better come right out with it. Our situation is most peculiar, and it requires certain adjustments. As those we've come to know and love grow older, it's absolutely necessary for us to distance ourselves from them. The alternative is quite probably madness. Endless grief will eventually destroy the human mind. We're not heartless, but we *do* have duties, and those duties oblige us to protect our ability to function. As I watched Daran and Kamion become crotchety, querulous old men, I knew they'd eventually leave us and that there was nothing I could do about it.

The Vale serves us as a kind of sanctuary – a place where we can absorb our grief and come to terms with it – and the presence of the Tree there is an absolute necessity.

If you think about it for a while, I'm sure you'll understand.

In time, word inevitably reached us that both Daran and Kamion had gone on. 'They were very tired anyway, Pol,' was all my father said before he went back to his studies.

My first century was drawing to a close when uncle Beldin returned from Mallorea. 'Burnt-face is still at Ashaba,' he reported, 'and nothing's going to happen over there until he comes out of seclusion.'

'Is Zedar still with him?' father asked.

'Oh, yes. Zedar's stuck to Torak like a leech. Proximity to a God seems to expand Zedar's opinion of himself.'

'Some things never change, do they?'

'Not where Zedar's concerned, they don't. Is Ctuchik doing anything interesting?'

'Nothing momentous enough to make waves. Is Urvon still hiding at Mal Yaska?'

Beldin's chuckle was hideous. 'Oh, indeed he is, Belgarath. Every now and then I drift on up to his neighborhood and butcher a few Grolims. I always leave a survivor or two – just to be sure that Urvon gets word that I'm still out there waiting for the pleasure of his company. I'm told that he usually retires to the dungeon on those occasions. He seems to think that thick stone walls might keep me from getting at him.' He squinted thoughtfully. 'Maybe when I go back, I'll slip into his temple and litter the place with dead Grolims – just to let him know that there isn't really anyplace where he can hide from me. Keeping Urvon nervous is one of my favorite pastimes. What kind of celebration do we have planned?'

'Celebration? What celebration?'

'Polgara's hundredth birthday, you clot. You didn't really think I came all the way back here just for the pleasure of *your* company, did you?'

The celebration of my birthday was lavish – even grotesquely overdone. Ours was a small, highly unique society, and since father, Beldin and I traveled extensively and were away for long periods of time, we seldom had the opportunity to join the twins in the Vale to draw our shared uniqueness about us. We're sometimes wildly different from each other – except for the twins, of course – but we're all members of a tiny closed society that shares experiences and concepts the rest of the world cannot begin to comprehend. Along toward the end of the festivities when my elders were all more than slightly tipsy and I was tidying up, mother's voice rang gently in the vaults of my mind. *'Happy birthday, Pol,'* was all she said, but it was nice to know that the last member of our little group was also in attendance.

The uneasy truce between Drasnia and Gar og Nadrak fell apart a few years later when the Nadraks – probably at Ctuchik's prodding – began raiding across their common border. Ctuchik *definitely* didn't approve of any kind of peaceful contacts between Angaraks and other races, and trade was exactly the sort of thing he most abhorred, since ideas have a way of being exchanged along with goods, and new ideas weren't welcome in Angarak society.

In the south, the merchant princes of Tol Honeth were growing increasingly desperate because of the stubborn refusal of the Marags to even consider commercial contacts of any kind. The Marags didn't use money and had no idea whatsoever of what it meant. They *did*, however, have access to almost unlimited amounts of free gold, since the stream-beds of Maragor are littered with it. Gold is pretty, I guess, but when you get right down to it, it has little actual value. You can't even make cooking pots out of it, because it melts. I think the Marags were actually amused when they discovered that a Tolnedran would give them almost anything in exchange for what they considered to be no more than another form of dirt. The problem, I think, lay in the fact that the merchants of Tolnedra didn't really have anything the Marags wanted badly enough to take the trouble to bend over to pick up the gold littering the bed of every stream in Maragor.

The thought of all that gold just lying there with no way to get at it – except to possibly give fair value – sent the Tolnedrans to the verge of desperation. A few of the children of Nedra decided to just skip over the tedious business of swindling the Marags and to go right to the source. Those expeditions into Maragor were a mistake, of course, largely because of the Marag religious practice of ritual cannibalism. The Tolnedrans who sneaked across the border looking for gold encountered Marags – who were looking for lunch.

After no more than a few wealthy – but still greedy – Tolnedran merchants had gone into Marag cooking pots, their heirs and assigns began to pressure the imperial throne to do something – anything – to prevent honest thieves from ending up on a Marag supper-table. Unfortunately, Emperor Ran Vordue was new to his throne, and he eventually succumbed to the importunings of the merchant class. Thus, in 2115, the Tolnedran legions swept across the border into Maragor intent on nothing less than the extermination of the entire Marag race.

My father had always been fond of the Marags, and he was preparing to rush south to 'take steps' when the Master uncharacteristically paid him a call and bluntly told him to keep his nose out of things that didn't concern him. Father's protests were long and loud, but Aldur was adamant. 'This *must* take place, my son,' he told father. 'It is a necessary part of the PURPOSE which doth guide us all.'

'But –' father started to protest.

'I will hear no more of this!' the Master thundered. 'Stay home, Belgarath!'

Father muttered something under his breath.

'What was that?' the Master demanded.

'Nothing, Master.'

I'd have given a great deal to have witnessed *that* exchange.

And so Maragor perished – except for those few captives who were sold to the Nyissan slavers. But that's another story.

The invasion of Maragor and the massacre of the inhabitants brought the Gods into the whole sorry business. Nedra chastised those of his children most involved, and Mara's grief-stricken response closed haunted Maragor off from further Tolnedran incursions. That in itself would have been punishment enough, but then Belar took a hand in the chastisement of the avaricious Tolnedrans by encouraging his Chereks to start raiding up and down the Tolnedran coast. The Chereks didn't really need *too* much encouragement, since if you scratch the surface of any normal Cherek, you'll find a pirate lurking underneath. This gave the Tolnedrans other things to keep them busy instead of all that brooding about the gold in

Maragor or worrying about being sent to the monastery at Mar Terrin, so I don't think I need to belabor this sorry sequence of events any further.

I *am*, however, convinced that father exaggerated the contention between the Gods that supposedly erupted following the destruction of the Marags. Nedra was clearly unhappy with his people for their atrocious behavior, and I wouldn't be at all surprised to find that Belar sent his Chereks to the Tolnedran coast at the invitation of his brother. When you want to punish a Tolnedran, all you have to do is take the fruits of his thievery away from him.

The raids continued for several centuries until, in the mid-twenty-sixth century, Ran Borune I drove his fat, lazy legions out of their garrisons and ordered them to start earning their pay.

My father, my uncles, and I really didn't pay too much attention to the bickering between the Tonedrans and the Chereks, but continued our ongoing struggle with the Mrin Codex. We *did* pay attention when Ctuchik began sending more and more Murgos down the Eastern Escarpment into Algaria in probing raids that had two basic purposes. Ctuchik wanted to check the defenses of the Algars, certainly, but he also wanted to mount his warrior class on better horses. Murgo ponies were about the size of large dogs, and Algar horses were vastly superior. My father spent a great deal of time in Algaria during the twenty-second and twenty-third centuries devising cavalry tactics which the Algars use even to this day. When Ctuchik's losses became unacceptable, those raids were largely discontinued. Part of the charm of Torak's personality was derived from the fact that he viewed his Angaraks as little more than breeding stock, a view that Ctuchik shared. Torak's third disciple wanted to increase his herd, not diminish it.

The endless civil war in Arendia continued – and continued, and continued – as the three warring duchies maneuvered, connived, and formed tentative alliances – often dissolved in the middle of a battle. It was ultimately the turmoil in Arendia that took me out of the seclusion of the Vale and back into the world again.

My three hundredth birthday had passed more or less unnoticed. Father maintains that I went to Vo Wacune in the twenty-fifth century, which isn't *too* far off the mark. He only missed by a hundred years, and old people are always a little vague about dates.

My, that was fun, wasn't it, father?

*   *   *

Actually, my excursion into Arendia started in the year 2312. I was asleep one night – despite father's snoring – and I awoke with that restless feeling that there were eyes on me. I rolled over and saw the ghostly form of the white snowy owl glowing in the moonlight in my window. It was mother. *'Polgara,'* she said crisply, *'you'd better pack a few things. You're going to Vo Wacune.'*

'Whatever for?' I demanded.

'Ctuchik's stirring up trouble in Arendia.'

'The Arends don't need any help, mother. They can stir up trouble enough by themselves without any outside assistance.'

'Things are a little more serious this time, Pol. Ctuchik has underlings posing as Tolnedran merchants in each of the duchies. They're using various stories to persuade the three dukes that Ran Vordue is offering an alliance, but Ran Vordue doesn't know anything about it. If Ctuchik's plan works, there'll be a war between Arendia and Tolnedra. The Wacite duke's the most intelligent of the three, so go to Vo Wacune, find out what's going on, and put a stop to it. The Master's depending on you, Pol.'

'I'll leave at once, mother,' I promised.

The next morning I began to pack.

'Moving, Pol?' father asked mildly. 'Was it something I said?'

'I've got something to attend to in Arendia, father.'

'Oh? What's that?'

'That's none of your business, Old Man,' I told him. 'I'm going to need a horse. Get me one.'

'Now look here, Pol –'

'Never mind, father. I'll do it myself.'

'I want to know what you think you're going to do in Arendia, Pol.'

'Wanting and getting are two different things, father. The Master's told me to go to Arendia to fix something. I know the way, so you won't have to come along. Now, will you go to the Algars and get me a horse, or am I going to have to take care of it myself?'

He spluttered a bit, but by midmorning there was a saddled chestnut mare named Lady waiting for me at the foot of the tower. Lady was not quite as large as Baron had been, but she and I got along well.

It was late afternoon before I caught the familiar sense of father's presence coming from a few miles behind. Actually, I'd been wondering what'd been keeping him.

I rode north along the eastern fringes of Ulgoland and then crossed the Sendarian mountains into Wacite territory with father tailing along behind me, changing his form every hour or so.

191

I crossed the upper reaches of the Camaar River and entered the vast forest of northern Arendia, and it wasn't too long before I encountered a Wacite patrol under the command of an obviously inexperienced young nobleman with an attitude problem. 'Hold, wench!' he commanded haughtily as he and his men came crashing out of the bushes. *Wench*? The young man and I weren't getting off to a good start here. 'Wither goest thou?' he demanded arrogantly.

'Vo Wacune, my Lord,' I replied politely.

I want you all to appreciate – and admire – my inhuman self-control during that incident. I didn't even once consider turning him into a toad – well, not very seriously anyway.

'What is thy business in our fair city?' he demanded.

'It is just that, my Lord – *my* business.'

'Rise not above thyself, wench. The commons do not speak thus to their betters. Methinks 'twere best that I take thee into custody, for thy speech doth proclaim thee alien, and aliens are not welcome in this realm.'

'That might explain thy lack of manners and good breeding, surly boy,' I said bluntly. 'Contact with civilized people would possibly have improved thee, though that is much to hope for.' I sighed. 'This is burdensome, but it doth appear that the thankless task of educating thee in civil usage falleth to me. Attend to my words most acutely, uncouth knave, for thou shalt discover me to be a most exacting instructor.' I gathered in my Will.

He gaped at me. Evidently no one had ever chided him about his bad manners before. Then he half-turned, obviously intending to speak sharply to his snickering troops.

'At the outset I must tell thee that thou must give me thine undivided attention whilst I am instructing thee,' I told him coldly. I was a dozen feet away from him, and there was nothing visible to account for the ringing blow that took him full in the face. It wasn't just a little slap either, and he rocked back in his saddle, his eyes slightly glazed.

'Moreover,' I continued relentlessly, 'thou shalt henceforth address me as "my Lady". Shouldst the term "wench" cross thy lips once more, I will make certain that thou shalt regret it unto thy dying day.' *This* blow took him straight in the mouth, and it knocked him out of his saddle. He came up spitting blood and teeth.

'Have I perchance gained thine attention, knave?' I asked him pleasantly. Then I murmured 'sleep' under my breath, and his eyes and the eyes of his sniggering men all went absolutely blank. I rode on with a faint smile, leaving the little group staring at the empty place where I'd just been. I left them in stasis for an hour or so, and by then Lady and I were several miles away. Then I sent my thought back to the place where they were. 'Wake up,' I told them.

They'd not been aware of the fact that they'd been napping, of course, so it appeared to them that I'd simply vanished. I learned somewhat later that the rude young noble had entered a monastery not long after our encounter, and that his men had all deserted and were nowhere to be found. At least one source of bad manners had been dried up in the Duchy of Wacune.

The city of Vo Wacune reared its loveliness out of the surrounding forest, and it absolutely took my breath away. I've never seen a city so beautiful. Vo Astur was almost as grey as Val Alorn, and Vo Mimbre is yellow. The Mimbrates call it 'golden', but that doesn't hide the fact that it's just plain old yellow. Vo Wacune was sheathed all in marble, even as Tol Honeth is. Tol Honeth, however, strives for grandeur, while Vo Wacune tried for – and achieved – beauty. Its slender towers soared white and gleaming toward a sky that smiled benevolently down on the most beautiful city in the world.

I paused in the forest to change clothes before I followed the gently winding road leading to the gates. I put on the blue velvet gown and cape I'd worn on ceremonial occasions on the Isle of the Winds, and as an after-thought I added a silver circlet – just to make the point that the term 'wench' wasn't really appropriate.

The guards at the city gates were civil, and I entered Vo Wacune with father trailing along behind me trying to look inconspicuous.

My years on the Isle had taught me how to assume a commanding presence, and I was soon escorted to a large hall where the duke sat in semi-regal splendor. 'Your Grace,' I greeted him with a curtsey, 'it is imperative that we speak privately. I must disclose my mind unto thee out of the hearing of others.' I just *adore* archaic speech, don't you?

'That is not customary, Lady – ?' he replied, fishing for my name. The duke was a handsome fellow with flowing brown hair, and he wore a regal purple velvet doublet and a circlet that stopped just short of being a crown.

'I will identify myself unto thee when we are alone, your Grace,' I advised him and went on to suggest the possibility of spies lurking in the background. Arends absolutely adore intrigue, so the duke walked right into that one. He rose, offered me his arm, and led me to a private chamber where we could talk. Father, in the form of a somewhat flea-bitten hound, trailed along behind us.

The duke escorted me to a pleasant room where filmy curtains billowed in the breeze coming in through the open windows. He shooed my father out, closed the door, and then turned to me. 'And now, dear Lady,' he said, 'prithee disclose thy name unto me.'

'My name's Polgara, your Grace,' I replied. 'You may have heard of me.' I deliberately dropped the archaic speech. Archaism, though quite lovely, has a tendency to lull the mind, and I wanted his Grace to be very alert.

'The daughter of Ancient Belgarath?' He said it in a startled tone.

'Exactly, your Grace.' I was a little surprised to find that he knew of me. I probably shouldn't have been. What some in the west refer to as 'the brotherhood of sorcerers' is the stuff of myth and legends, and Arends have a natural affinity for that sort of thing.

'My poor house is overwhelmed that thou hast so graciously honored it with thy presence.'

I smiled at him. 'Please, your Grace,' I said in a slightly whimsical tone, 'let's not get carried away here. Your house is the most beautiful I've ever seen, and I'm the one who's honored to be received here.'

'That *was* a little extravagant, wasn't it?' he admitted with a rueful unArendish candor. 'Thy statement, however, startled me, and I fell back on extravagance to cover my confusion. To what do we owe the pleasure of thy divine company?'

'Hardly divine, your Grace. You've been receiving some bad advice lately. There's a Tolnedran merchant here in Vo Wacune who's been telling you that he speaks for Ran Vordue, but he's lying. Ran Vordue probably doesn't even know him. The house of Vordue is *not* offering you an alliance.'

'I had thought my discussions with the merchant Haldon were most private, Lady Polgara.'

'I have certain advantages, your Grace. Things here in Arendia have a habit of changing almost hourly, so perhaps you could tell me with whom you're currently at war.'

'The Asturians – this week,' he replied wryly. 'Should that war chance to grow boring, we can always find some excuse to declare war on Mimbre, I suppose. We haven't had a good war with the Mimbrates for nearly two years now.' I was *almost* certain that he was joking.

'Are there any alliances?' I asked.

'We have a rather tentative agreement with the Mimbrates,' he replied. 'The Mimbrates have no more reason to be fond of Asturians than do we. If truth be known, however, my alliance with Corrolin of Mimbre is little more than an agreement that he will not attack my southern border whilst I deal with that wretched little drunkard, Oldoran of Asturia. I had hopes of an alliance with Tolnedra, but if thine information should prove true, those hopes are dashed.' He slammed his fist down on the table. 'What doth Haldon hope to achieve by this deception?' he blurted out. 'Why would he bring this spurious offer from his emperor?'

'Ran Vordue isn't Haldon's master, your Grace. Haldon speaks for Ctuchik.'

'The Murgo?'

'Ctuchik's lineage is a little more complicated than that, but let it pass for now.'

'Of what concern are Arendish internal affairs to the Murgos?'

'Arendish internal affairs concern *everyone*, your Grace. Your poor Arendia's an ongoing disaster, and disasters have a way of spreading. In this case, though, Ctuchik *wants* the strife to spread. He wants confusion here in the west to open the door for his Master.'

'His Master?'

'Ctuchik's one of Torak's disciples, and the time's not too far off when the Dragon-God's going to invade the western kingdoms. This Haldon's only one of the people Ctuchik's insinuated into Arendia. There are others who are stirring up similar mischief in Asturia and Mimbre. If each duchy can be persuaded that it has an alliance with the Tolnedrans, and the legions don't appear when and where you expect them to, you, Corrolin, and Oldoran will probably attack Tolnedra – either individually or in some hastily-formed alliance. That's Ctuchik's ultimate goal – war between Arendia and Tolnedra.'

'What a ghastly thought!' he exclaimed. 'No alliance between Corrolin, Oldoran, and me could ever be firm enough for us to withstand the imperial legions! We'd be swarmed under!'

'Precisely. And if Tolnedra crushes and then annexes Arendia, the Alorns will be drawn in to protect *their* interests. All the kingdoms of the west could go up in flames.' A thought came to me at that point. 'I think I'd better suggest to my father that he go have a look at Aloria. If Ctuchik's stirring things up here in the south, he could very well be doing the same in the north. We don't need another outbreak of clan wars in the Alorn kingdoms. If everybody here in the west is fighting everybody else, the door'll be wide open for an invasion from Mallorea.'

'I would not insult thee for all this world, Lady Polgara, but

195

Haldon hath documents bearing the seal and signature of Ran Vordue.'

'The imperial seal isn't that difficult to duplicate, your Grace. I can make one for you right here and now, if you'd like.'

'Thou art most skilled in the devious world of statecraft, Lady Polgara.'

'I've had some practice, your Grace.' I thought for a moment. 'If we do this right, we might be able to turn Ctuchik's scheme to our own advantage. I'm not trying to be offensive here, but it's a part of the Arendish nature to need an enemy. Let's see if we can re-direct that enmity. Wouldn't it be nicer to hate Murgos rather than each other?'

'Far nicer, my Lady. I've met a few Murgos, and I've never encountered one that I liked. They are a most unlovable race, it seemeth to me.'

'Indeed they are, your Grace, and their God is even worse.'

'Doth Torak plan immediate action against the west?'

'I don't think even Torak himself knows what he plans, your Grace.'

'Prithee, Lady Polgara, my friends do call me Kathandrion, and this vital information which thou hath brought unto me hath surely made thee my friend.'

'As it pleaseth thee, Lord Kathandrion,' I said with a polite little curtsey.

He bowed in reply, and then he laughed. 'We *are* getting along well, aren't we, Polgara?' he suggested.

'I rather thought so myself,' I agreed, a little startled by the duke's lapse into what I considered to be normal speech. As we came to know each other better, Kathandrion stepped down from 'high style' more and more frequently, and I took that to be an indication of a fair level of intelligence. Kathandrion could – and frequently did – stun his listeners into near-insensibility with flowery language, but there was a real mind hiding behind all those 'thees,' 'thous,' and 'forasmuches'. When he chose to speak normally, his tone was often humorously self-deprecatory, and his ability to laugh at himself was most unArendish. 'We'd probably better get used to each other, Kathandrion,' I told him. 'I have a suspicion that you and I have a long way to go together.'

'I could not wish for more pleasant company, dear Lady.' He reverted to 'high style', and the sudden contrast also contained a hidden chuckle. This was a *very* complicated man. Then he sighed just a bit theatrically.

'Why so great a sigh, friend Kathandrion?'

'If the truth be known, thou hast given me reason to consider abdication, Polgara,' he lamented. 'The peace and quiet of a monastery do beckon unto me most invitingly. Are international politics always so murky?'

'Usually. Sometimes they're worse.'

'I wonder if they'll make me shave my head,' he mused, tugging a long, brown strand of hair around so that he could look at it.

'I beg your pardon?'

'When I enter the monastery.'

'Oh, come now, Kathandrion. We're having fun, aren't we?'

'Thou has a peculiar definition of that word, Polgara. I was quite content with hating Asturians and Mimbrates. Life was so simple then. Now hast thou loaded my poor brain top-full of other strife to consider – and it is not that capacious a brain.'

I put my hand affectionately on his arm. 'You'll do just fine, Kathandrion. I'll see to it that you don't make too many mistakes. Just how stringent are the rules of evidence here in Vo Wacune?'

'Rules of evidence?'

'How far will you have to go to prove that the Tolnedran's a knave?'

He laughed. 'Thou art unschooled in Arendish customs, I see,' he said. 'We are Arends, Polgara. Evidence and proof are quite beyond our capabilities. I rule here by decree. If *I* say that a man's a villain, then he's a villain, and he takes up immediate residence in my dungeon. Our nature is such that we must keep things simple.'

'How terribly convenient. I need further information, however. Have him picked up, if you would, please. There are some questions I'd like to ask him before he takes up residence down in the cellar. I want to know just exactly how widespread this plot is before I go on to Vo Astur and Vo Mimbre.'

'Wilt thou require the services of a professional interrogator?'

'A torturer, you mean? No, Kathandrion. There are other ways to get the truth out of people. Once I know the full extent of Ctuchik's scheme, I should be able to spoke his wheel.'

'Hast thou ever met this miscreant Ctuchik?'

'Not yet, your Grace,' I said bleakly. 'I expect it's coming, though, and I'm rather looking forward to it. Shall we go now?'

I paused momentarily at the door to look critically at the hound sprawled just outside in the hallway. 'All right, father,' I said. 'You can go home now. I can manage here quite well without you.'

He even managed to look a little guilty.

197

CHAPTER 13

The more I came to know the Arendish people, the more I appreciated Kathandrion. Whole volumes have been devoted to a misconception about the nature of Arends. The ongoing disaster men call Arendia is not so much the result of congenital stupidity as it is a combination of blind impulsiveness, an irresistible urge toward high drama, and an inability to back away from a course of action once it's been embarked upon. At least Kathandrion was willing to listen for a moment before he plunged into something. His first impulse in this case, naturally, was to have Ctuchik's underling seized and dragged in chains through the streets of Vo Wacune – probably at high noon. He was right on the verge of issuing orders to that effect as we proceeded down the corridor to his throne room.

'Kathandrion,' I suggested gently, 'we're dealing with a conspiracy here. Do we really want to alert all the other conspirators with a public display?'

He looked quickly at me. 'Not too bright an idea, right?' he suggested.

'I've heard better.'

'One of these days I'll have to learn to think my way through a notion before I start issuing commands,' he said.

'I would, if I were you.'

'I'll work on it. How would *you* approach this matter?'

'Lie a little bit. Send a note to Haldon asking him to stop by at his convenience for a bit of private conversation.'

'What if he doesn't find it convenient until some time next week?'

'He'll be here almost immediately, Kathandrion. Trust me. I've done this sort of thing before. He'll take that "at your convenience" to mean just as soon as he gets his clothes on. There are many ways to use power, Kathandrion. A light touch is far better than a sledge-hammer.'

'What a novel thing to suggest. This is Arendia, Polgara. Commands here must be delivered in short, easy-to-understand language, preferably in words of one syllable or less.'

I found myself growing fonder of Duke Kathandrion by the moment. The invitation he dictated to a scribe when we returned to the throne room was artfully innocuous, and, as I'd predicted, Haldon arrived within the hour.

Evening was settling over the fairy-tale city of Vo Wacune as Kathandrion escorted our guest to a room conveniently located near the head of the stairs leading down to the dungeon. There was but a single lamp in the room, and I sat in a chair with a high back and facing the window. Thus, I was to all intents and purposes invisible.

I carefully sent out my thought as the two of them entered, and the color I encountered didn't have that characteristic red overtone that would have identified the merchant as Tolnedran, but was dull black instead. The man known as Haldon was a Murgo. I could see his reflection in the glass of the window, and his features had none of the characteristics of the Angarak race. That explained quite a bit.

'It was good of thee to come by on such short notice, worthy Haldon,' Kathandrion was saying.

'I am ever at your Grace's call,' the green-mantled fellow replied, bowing.

'Prithee, sit, my friend. We are alone, so there is no need for ceremony.' Kathandrion paused artfully. 'It hath recently been proposed to me that some commercial advantage might accrue to the Duchy of Wacune were I to command some port facilities constructed on the southern bank of the Camaar River within the boundaries of my realm, and it seeméd me that thou wert best qualified to evaluate the notion. Would such facilities indeed enhance trade between Wacune and the empire?'

'Indeed they would, your Grace!' the imitation Tolnedran replied enthusiastically. 'The emperor himself has frequently expressed interest in just such a project.'

'Splendid!' Kathandrion said. 'Capital! In view of our forthcoming alliance, might I prevail upon thee to suggest to thine emperor a sharing of the cost of construction of those facilities?'

'I'm certain that the emperor would look most favorably upon such a proposal.'

A Tolnedran of any rank willing to spend money? That idea in itself would have been enough to expose the so-called Haldon as a fraud.

I'd suggested to the duke that he engage our suspect in some frivolous discussion of a spurious topic 'to put him off his guard'. In reality, I needed but a moment or two to touch Haldon's mind to confirm his racial background. The 'port facility' myth was of Kathandrion's own devising, and it confirmed my earlier evaluation of his intelligence.

I let them ramble on for a while, and then I rose from my chair and stepped into the lamplight. 'I hate to interrupt such pleasant discourse, gentlemen,' I told them, 'but we have far to go before dawn, so perhaps we'd better move right along.' Neither Arends nor Murgos are accustomed to having women intrude in state matters, so I think my crisp interruption startled them both.

The Murgo looked sharply at me, and his face went deathly pale. '*You!*' he gasped.

That was the first time my presence had ever gotten *that* reaction.

I was looking at him curiously. 'How *ever* did you manage to alter your features, Haldon?' I asked him. 'You don't look the least bit like an Angarak. Did Ctuchik do that to you? It must have been extremely painful.'

His eyes went wary. 'I'm sorry, madame,' he said, recovering quickly. 'I haven't the faintest idea of what you're talking about.'

'Are we actually going to play that tiresome game all the way out to its inevitable conclusion?' I asked him. 'How tedious.' Even as I spoke, I gently probed into the darkest corners of the imitation Tolnedran's mind, and I was somewhat surprised to discover that the thing he feared most in all the world was my father! I hadn't expected that, but I realized that it might make the rest of this business quite a bit easier than I'd expected.

'It seemeth me that much is transpiring here that I do not understand,' Kathandrion admitted, looking baffled.

'It's really quite simple, your Grace,' I told him. 'This gentleman who's been calling himself "Haldon" is actually a Murgo, whose real name is quite probably unpronounceable. Does that help to clarify things?'

'But he doth not *look* like a Murgo, my Lady.'

'Yes, I noticed that. We'll have to ask him how he managed it.'

'She lies!' our Murgo snarled.

'That is most unlikely,' Kathandrion replied in a chill tone. Then he looked at me. 'It doth appear that he knows of thee, my Lady.'

'Yes,' I agreed. 'Evidently Ctuchik warned him about me.' I looked sternly at our guest. 'Now we come to the more unpleasant part of the evening, I'm afraid,' I said with feigned regret. 'Would you prefer to tell us everything you know about your master's scheme right here and now? Or am I going to have to persuade you? You *are* going to tell me what I want to know – eventually. We can do it either way; it's up to you.'

His eyes went flat and were suddenly filled with hatred. 'Do your worst, witch-woman,' he said defiantly. 'I am a Dagashi, and I can withstand any torment you can devise.'

'I'm so happy that you've dropped that tiresome masquerade,' I said. 'Oh, by the way, let me relieve you of that knife you've got hidden down the back of your mantle. We'd be *so* disappointed if you decided to murder yourself – not to mention the terrible mess it'd make on the carpet.' I translocated the triangular dagger he'd had concealed under his clothes into my own hands and looked at it curiously. 'What a peculiar implement,' I noted frowning slightly. 'Ah, I see. It's a throwing knife. Very efficient-looking. Shall we press on, then?' I stared intently into his eyes as I gathered in my Will. I'll admit that I had a certain advantage in this situation. I was going to show him the image of something he was afraid of, but if it didn't work, the real thing wasn't too far away. I made a small gesture with my right hand as I released my Will.

Yes, I know. Father's been chiding me about those gestures for thirty or so centuries now, and I've been ignoring him for just as long. It's a question of style, actually, and since I'm the one who's doing it, I'll do it any way I like.

So there.

Those of you who know my father know that above all else, he's a performer. This is not say that he can't turn mountains inside out if he chooses to, but he always does things with a certain panache, a grand and flamboyant style that's *very* impressive. His face is really no more than a tool, and his expressions speak whole volumes. Believe me, I've seen all of those expressions at close range over the centuries, and so the illusion I created for the Murgo's entertainment was *very* lifelike. Initially, father's face was stern, accusatory, and the Murgo flinched back from it, his face going pale and his eyes bulging from their sockets.

Then father frowned, and the Murgo gave vent to a pathetic little squeal and tried to cover his head with his arms.

Then my father's illusory face twisted into an expression which

201

I'd seen him practicing in a mirror when he thought I wasn't watching. His eyes narrowed with his lower eyelids sliding upward, and he tilted his head slightly back so that it almost appeared that he was glaring over the top of those ominous lids. To be honest about it, the expression made him look like a madman right on the verge of tearing someone apart with his teeth.

Then I hardened the image, giving it that momentary flicker of decision that comes just prior to the releasing of the Will.

The Murgo screamed and tried to scramble from his chair in sheer panic. '*No!*' he wailed. '*Don't!*'

I froze him in place while he howled and whimpered in absolute terror. '*Please!*' he shrieked. 'Please make it go away, Polgara! I'll do anything! Anything! Just make it go away!'

There are all sorts of wild stories which have been circulated about me over the years, but I don't think Kathandrion had actually believed them before. He did now, though, and he drew himself back, looking just a little bit afraid.

'Why don't you begin by telling me your name, Murgo?' I suggested, 'and then you can tell me what a Dagashi is. We'll go on from there. Always keep in mind the fact that I can bring my father back any time you decide not to cooperate.'

'I'm known as Krachack,' the Murgo replied in a trembling voice, 'and the Dagashi are members of a secret order in Cthol Murgos. We gather information and eliminate people who are inconvenient for those who employ us.'

'Spies and hired assassins?'

'If you choose to call us so.'

'How is it that you don't have Murgo features?'

'Breeding,' he replied. 'Our mothers and grandmothers are slave-women from other races. They're killed after we're born. I'm about one quarter Murgo.'

'Peculiar,' I noted, 'particularly in view of Ctuchik's obsession with racial purity. Let's set that aside for now, though. Exactly what's the purpose of your mission here in Arendia?'

'I've been instructed to persuade Duke Kathandrion that Ran Vordue will come to his aid when he attacks Vo Astur. With the help of the legions, Kathandrion would be able to obliterate Asturia. Then I'm to hint that the combined force of Wacite Arends and Tolnedran legions would be able to turn south and do the same thing to Mimbre.'

'That's absurd,' I told him. 'What's Ran Vordue supposed to get out of this?'

'Southern Mimbre,' Krachack replied with a shrug, 'the part where most of the cities are.'

I looked at Kathandrion. 'Would it have worked?' I asked bluntly. 'Would this offer have tempted you?'

My friend looked slightly guilty. 'I do fear me that it might well have, Polgara. In my mind's eye, I would have become king of most of Arendia, and the civil wars that tear at our beloved homeland would have come to an end.'

'I doubt it,' I told him. 'A peace founded on such conniving could not have lasted.' I turned back to Krachack. 'I assume that similar schemes are afoot in Vo Astur and Vo Mimbre?' I suggested.

Krachack nodded. 'There are variations, of course – all depending on the strategic positions of the three duchies. I'm told that there are some real Tolnedrans at Vo Mimbre who've been bribed to further our plan, but that's none of my concern. The end result of our maneuvering is to be the same. The three dukes will attack each other, each expecting aid from the legions. Then, when that aid doesn't materialize, the dukes will feel that they've been betrayed. Other Dagashi, posing as Arendish patriots, will urge each one of the dukes to ally himself with the other two and to march on the empire. That's Ctuchik's goal, an ongoing war between Tolnedra and Arendia.'

'Tolnedra would crush us!' Kathandrion exclaimed.

Krachack shrugged. 'So? Ctuchik doesn't care about Arendia, and he doesn't really care about what happens to her. If Tolnedra annexes her, though, the Alorns will be dragged into it, and that's what Ctuchik *really* wants – a war between Tolnedra and Aloria. Once that starts, Ctuchik can go to Ashaba and hand Torak a divided west on a platter. Ctuchik will be Torak's most favored disciple, standing above Zedar and Urvon, and the Malloreans will come across the Sea of the East. All of Angarak will fall on the divided kingdoms of the west and annihilate them. Torak will become the God of all humanity.'

I'm sure that Lelldorin will recognize the general pattern of the scheme. A Murgo named Nachak tried something very similar in Arendia a few years back. Ctuchik *did* tend to repeat himself.

Kathandrion and I questioned Krachack the Murgo until almost dawn, and then we had him quietly taken down to the lowest level of the dungeon. The Wacite Duke was more than a little startled by the complexity of Ctuchik's plot. 'It astounds me that any man can be so devious, Polgara,' he admitted. 'Are all Murgo minds thus?'

'I rather doubt it, my friend,' I replied. 'Ctuchik studied at the feet of Torak himself, and then he had centuries to practice his art on his fellow-disciples, Urvon and Zedar. There's no love lost between those three, and Torak prefers it that way. The Dragon God brings out and exploits the worst in human nature.' I considered the situation. 'I think I'd better go on to Vo Astur directly,' I mused. 'I'm fairly sure that events there are moving to a head as rapidly as they are here – and in Vo Mimbre as well. These assorted plots almost have to be coordinated to reach their culmination at roughly the same time, and what's been happening here is rapidly coming to a climax.'

'I shall provide thee with an escort, Polgara.'

'Kathandrion,' I reminded him gently, 'you're technically at war with Asturia, remember? If I go to Vo Astur with a Wacite escort, aren't people likely to talk?'

'Oh,' he said. 'I did it again, didn't I?' He looked a bit embarrassed.

'I'm afraid so, my friend. We're going to have to work on that. Don't be concerned, Kathandrion. The Asturians won't even see me – until I'm ready for them to.'

I left later that same day, and after Lady and I had traveled for about an hour, I probed the surrounding forest with my thought. There weren't any Arends in the vicinity, but there *was* someone else. 'Well, father,' I said aloud, 'are you coming along or not?'

His silence was just ever so slightly guilty. 'Keep your nose out of this, Old Man,' I told him. 'I think this is one of those "tests" you're so fond of talking about. Watch, but don't get involved. You can grade me after it's all over. Oh, I'm going on ahead. Since you insist on trailing along after me, why don't you bring Lady with you.'

I *love* to do that to him.

Events were moving at a quickening pace, so speed was very important. I'd decided earlier to forego my favorite alternative form and to use a falcon instead.

Vo Astur was constructed of granite, and its grey walls were thick and high and surmounted by grim battlements. It was a depressing city that crouched on the southern bank of the Astur River. There were centuries-old feuds going on in Asturia, and every nobleman of any consequence lived inside a fort. The seat of the Asturian government was no exception. Asturia was filled to the brim with

204

intrigue, plots, ambushes, poisonings, and surprise attacks, so caution was the course of prudence, I guess.

There was no real point in going through the inevitable interrogation at the city gate, so I spiraled down toward the ducal palace instead as evening drew over the fortified city. I settled unobserved in a secluded corner of the courtyard and resumed my real form. Then I slipped around the outer edge of the flagstoned yard, approached the ornate door of the palace, 'encouraged' the guards to take a brief nap, and went on inside.

My father had frequently impressed upon me the idea that there are times when it's necessary for us to be unremarkable in the presence of others, and he's devised many ways to achieve that. My own favorite is to exude a sense of familiarity. It's a subtle sort of thing. People can look at me without actually seeing me. They're sure that they know me, but they can't quite remember my name. In social situations, this can be very useful. In effect, I just become a part of the background.

Kathandrion had advised me that the Asturians spoke an 'outlandish dialect', so I loitered in a long, dim corridor until a group of gaily-dressed courtiers, both men and women, came by, and I joined them and listened carefully as they spoke. I noted that the Asturians had discarded 'high style' and spoke to each other in a more commonplace fashion. Asturia was bounded on one side by the Sea of the West, and she had far more contact with outsiders than did either Wacune or Mimbre. The people here yearned to be 'modern', and so they rather slavishly imitated the speech of those outsiders with whom they came in contact. Unfortunately, many of those outsiders just happened to be sailors, and sailors probably aren't the best source of linguistic elegance. I devoutly hoped that the giddy young ladies in the group I'd joined didn't fully understand the meaning of some of the words and phrases that tumbled from their lips.

Since all three of the Arendish dukes had royal pretensions, each of their palaces had a 'throne-room', and Astur was no exception. The cluster of nobles I'd joined entered the central hall that served that purpose here, and I drifted away from them and worked my way through the slightly tipsy throng toward the front of the hall.

Over the years I've had occasion to observe drunkenness in its assorted forms, and I've noticed some variations. A man who's over-indulged in beer or ale is rowdier than one soaked in wine, and those who prefer distilled spirits tend toward open belligerence.

The Asturians preferred wine, and wine-tipplers either giggle or weep when in their cups. The Arendish fondness for high tragedy made them lean in the direction of melancholy. A drinking party in Asturia is a gloomy sort of affair, rather on the order of a funeral on a rainy night.

Oldoran, the Asturian Duke, was a small ratty little man, and he was obviously far gone in drink. He sprawled morosely on his throne with a look of profound suffering on his pouchy little face. A man in a Tolnedran mantle of an unappetizing yellow color stood just at his right elbow, frequently leaning over to whisper in the duke's ear. I carefully sent out a probing thought, and the color that came back from the supposed Tolnedran was *not* red. It appeared that I had another Murgo on my hands.

I spent the next couple of hours drifting around the hall and listening to snatches of conversation. I soon gathered that Duke Oldoran was not held in very high regard. 'Drunken little weasel' was probably the kindest thing I heard said of him. I further gathered that Oldoran was almost completely in the grasp of the counterfeit Tolnedran at his side. Though I was fairly sure that I could sever that particular connection, I couldn't for the life of me see any advantage to be had from it. I could probably change Oldoran's opinions, but I couldn't change Oldoran himself. He was a petty, self-pitying drunkard with very little intelligence and with that sublime belief so common among the truly stupid that he was the most clever man in all the world. I had a problem here.

The sodden little Oldoran kept calling for more wine, and he eventually lapsed into unconsciousness.

'It would appear that our beloved duke is a trifle indisposed,' an elderly courtier with snowy hair, but surprisingly youthful eyes, noted in a dryly ironic tone. 'How do you think we should deal with this, my lords and ladies? Should we put him to bed? Should we dunk him in that fishpond in the garden until he regains his senses? Or, should we perhaps adjourn to some other place where our revelry won't interrupt his snoring?' He bowed to the laughing throng ironically. 'I shall be guided by the collective wisdom of the court in this matter. How say you, nobles all?'

'I like the fishpond myself,' one matronly lady suggested.

'Oh, dear, no, Baroness!' a pretty young lady with dark hair and mischievous eyes objected. 'Think of what that would do to the poor carp who live there.'

'If we're going to dump Oldoran in his bed, we'd better wring him out a little first, my Lord Mangaran,' one half-drunk courtier bellowed to the ironical old nobleman. 'The little sot's soaked up so much wine that he's almost afloat.'

'Yes,' the Lord Mangaran murmured. 'I noticed that myself. His Grace has an amazing capacity for one so dwarfed.'

Then the pretty lady with the mischievous eyes struck an overly dramatic pose. 'My lords and ladies,' she declaimed, 'I suggest a moment of silence out of respect for our poor little Oldoran. Then perhaps we'd better leave him in the capable hands of Earl Mangaran, who's performed this office so often that he doesn't really need our advice. Then, after his Grace has been wrung out and poured into bed, we can toast the good fortune that's removed him from our midst.'

They all bowed their heads, but the 'moment of silence' was marred by a certain amount of muffled laughter.

I'm sure that Lelldorin, and indeed all Asturians, will be offended by what I've just set down, but it *is* the truth. It took centuries of suffering to grind the rough edges off the crude, unscrupulous Asturians. That was my first encounter with them, and in many ways they almost seemed like southern Alorns.

The young lady who'd just proposed that moment of silence laid the back of her wrist theatrically to her forehead. 'Would someone please bring me another cup of wine,' she asked in a tragic voice. 'Speaking in public absolutely exhausts me.'

The Murgo who'd been at Oldoran's elbow had faded back into the crowd, and so he was nowhere to be seen when a pair of burly footmen hoisted the snoring duke from his throne and bore him from the hall.

I withdrew to a little alcove to consider the situation. My original plan when I'd left Vo Wacune had been to expose the resident Murgo here to the duke and then let *him* deal with it, but Oldoran wasn't in the same class with Kathandrion, and I've observed over the years that stupid people rarely change their minds. I fell back on logic at that point. If Oldoran wouldn't suit my purposes, the simplest course would be to replace him with someone who would.

The more I thought about that, the better I liked the idea. The Murgo wouldn't be expecting it, for one thing. My father and uncle Beldin had described the Angarak character to me on many occasions, and Angaraks are constitutionally incapable of questioning authority of any kind. The word 'revolution' is simply not in their vocabulary.

The course of action I was considering was certainly not new. Arendish history is full of accounts of what are called 'palace coups', little disturbances that had usually resulted in the death of an incumbent. I didn't want it to go *that* far here, but I *did* want Oldoran off that throne. What I'd seen that evening strongly suggested that most of the nobles here at court shared that desire. My only problem now was the selection of Oldoran's replacement – *and* a means of getting to him on fairly short notice.

I napped briefly in an unoccupied sitting-room and went back to the central hall early the next morning to ask some questions about the clever, dark-haired young lady who'd humorously proposed that moment of silence. I described her to the servants who were cleaning up the debris of the previous evening's festivities.

'That would be the Countess Asrana, my Lady,' a sober-faced cleaning man told me. 'She's a notorious flirt and very witty.'

'That's the one,' I said. 'I think she and I were introduced some years back, and I thought I'd look her up. Where do you suppose I might find her?'

'Her apartment's in the west tower, my Lady, on the ground floor.'

'Thank you,' I murmured, gave him a small coin, and went looking for the west tower.

The countess was just a trifle indisposed when her maid escorted me into the room where she lay on a divan with bleary eyes and a cold, wet cloth on her forehead. 'I don't believe I know you,' she told me in a tragic voice.

'Are you unwell?' I asked her.

'I'm feeling just a little delicate this morning,' she confessed. 'I wish it were winter. If it were, I'd go out into the courtyard and stick my head in a snowbank for an hour or so.' Then she looked at me more closely. 'You look awfully familiar, for some reason.'

'I don't think we've ever met, countess.'

'It's not that we've met, I don't think. It's something I've heard about.' She put her fingertips to her temples. 'Oh, dear,' she groaned.

'We need to talk, Asrana,' I told her, 'but I'd better do something about your condition first.' I opened the small reticule I carried and took out a glass vial. I poured the contents into the bottom of a cup that was standing on a sideboard and then filled the cup with water. 'This won't taste very good,' I warned.

'Will it make me feel better?'

'It should.'

'Then I really don't care what it tastes like.' She drank it and then shuddered. 'That's dreadful,' she said. 'You're a physician?' she asked.

'I've had some training along those lines,' I admitted.

'What a peculiar occupation for a lady of rank,' she said. She touched her forehead. 'I believe it's actually getting better.'

'That was the whole idea, countess. As soon as the potion I just gave you takes hold a little more, there's something I'd like to talk with you about.'

'I owe you my life, dear Lady,' she said extravagantly. 'But I still seem to know you for some reason.' Then she made a little face. 'Of course, on mornings like this one all sorts of strange ideas come to me.' She shook her head slightly. 'Amazing!' she said. 'My head didn't fall off. You could make a fortune with that potion here in Vo Astur, you know. Everybody in the palace probably feels as awful as I did a while ago. Whatever it was you gave me is miraculous. I think I'll actually live now. It's almost like magic.' She stopped suddenly and looked at me as if really seeing me for the first time. Then she started to tremble. 'It *was* magic, wasn't it?'

'No, dear. Not really.'

'Oh, yes it was! You've got that white lock in your hair, and you're a physician. You're Polgara the Sorceress, aren't you? You're Belgarath's daughter!'

'My terrible secret's out, I see,' I sighed with mock regret.

'You're a million years old!'

I touched my cheek. 'Does it really show that much, Asrana?'

'Of course not, Lady Polgara,' she replied. 'You don't look a day over a hundred thousand.' Then we both laughed, and she winced. 'Rushing things a bit there,' she noted, touching her forehead slightly. 'Please don't make me laugh for a little while yet. Your spell hasn't really had time to get to the bottom of this headache yet.'

'It wasn't really a spell, Asrana – just a mixture of some fairly common herbs.' I decided not to make an issue of the fact that her mornings would be much more enjoyable if she didn't drink so much wine every evening. 'Is there something you could send your maid to fetch for you?' I asked her. 'I'd like to talk to you without anyone around.'

'Breakfast, I think. I'm suddenly ravenous. Would you join me?'

'I'd be delighted, dear.'

After the girl had left, Asrana and I got down to business. 'I'm not trying to be offensive, Countess, but I'm not very much impressed by your duke.'

'Who is? We all have to be careful not to step on him when he's in the throne room. Do you happen to have a cure for minsculism? Oldaran should probably take a double dose if you do. He's a bug, Polgara, so stepping on him's a natural reaction. Life around here would be much simpler if somebody'd just squish him and have done with it. Would you care for some wine?'

'Ah – not just now, Asrana, and you'd probably better drink water this morning, too. Mixing wine with the potion I just gave you would make you terribly ill.'

'I *knew* there had to be a drawback. Where were we?'

'We were discussing Duke Oldoran's shortcomings.'

'And shortgoings as well, as I recall.' The Countess Asrana had a quick tongue, and I rather liked her.

'If the occasion arose, which of the men here at court would be best to replace him?'

'The Earl Mangaran, of course. Have you met him?'

'I saw him last night. He doesn't seem to have a very high opinion of your duke.'

'He's not alone there. Who could possibly love his Bugship?'

'Who's that Tolnedran who seems to have taken up residence in the duke's pocket?'

'You mean Gadon? He's a merchant of some kind, and I think he's made Oldoran some sort of offer – probably dishonorable and certainly disgusting. Gadon's been knocking around the palace here for the past half-year buying up court functionaries by the gross. Nobody likes him, but he's got the duke's ear, so we have to be civil.'

'Are you in the mood for some serious plotting this morning, Asrana?'

'Now that my headache's gone away, I'm in the mood for almost anything. What should we plot about?'

'How about a revolution, Countess?'

'Oh, what fun!' she exclaimed, clapping her hands together. 'I'd just *love* to be a party to the downfall of the Bug. Are you going to kill him, Polgara? If you are, can I watch?'

'You're a bad girl, Asrana.'

'I know, and it's *so* much fun. Are we going to sneak around in the middle of the night holding whispered conversations and secretly smuggling weapons into the palace?'

'You've been reading too many bad epics, Asrana. A good plot doesn't work that way. I think we ought to have a talk with Earl Mangaran before we elevate him to the throne, don't you? He's of

210

advanced years, and that sort of surprise might be hard on his veins.'

'Spoilsport. I thought we could give him the throne for his birthday.'

'Are we likely to encounter much resistance if we move against the duke? Are there any here at court who'd back him? Relatives or officials with something to lose if we deposed him?'

'Let me deal with them, Lady Polgara. I can wrap just about any man here at court around my little finger if I really want to.'

I've broken a few hearts myself on occasion, and I've known some of the most outrageous flirts in history, but Countess Asrana was in a class by herself, and I'm certain that her towering self-confidence was fully justified.

After breakfast, the countess sent word to Earl Mangaran, asking him to meet us in the rose garden. Just to be on the safe side, I sent out a searching thought when Asrana and I went into the garden. This wasn't going to be a conversation we'd care to have overheard.

The Earl Mangaran looked weary as he joined us, but there was a tinge of impishness in his eyes nonetheless.

'Should I tell him?' Asrana asked me.

'You might as well,' I replied. 'We won't get very far with this if he doesn't know.'

'I've a bit of a surprise fer y', yer Earlship,' Asrana said in a fair imitation of the brogue of the Wacite peasants. 'This dear lass with th' unspeakable beauty is after bein' th' Lady Polgara, don't y' know. Aren't y' honored enough t' just fall down in a swoon t' make her acquaintance.'

'Please, Countess,' Mangaran said, passing a weary hand across his eyes, 'I've had a very trying morning. His Grace is absolutely impossible just now. He isn't out of bed yet, and he's already drunk. Don't start off with fairy-tales.'

'But she is, my Lord. This is really Polgara the Sorceress.' Asrana gave me a look of wide-eyed innocence. 'Sorcerize him, Lady Polgara,' she urged. 'Turn him into a toad or something.'

'Do you mind, Asrana?' I said.

'He's a skeptic, Polly. Make all his hair fall out.'

Nobody had ever called me 'Polly' before – and nobody had better ever do it again.

'Please forgive our Countess, my Lady,' Mangaran said. 'Sometimes she breaks out in this rash of cleverness. We've tried to break her of the habit, but you can see for yourself how fruitless it's been.'

'I've noticed that, my Lord,' I said. 'This time what she says is true, though.' I absently plucked a deep red rose from a nearby bush. 'Just to save some time here –' I held out my hand with the rose lying on my palm. 'Watch closely,' I instructed.

I did it slowly, in part to make it more impressive and in part to keep from alerting the Murgo who was somewhere in the palace. The rose on my palm shriveled down to almost nothing, and then it sprouted a tiny, spiraling shoot that grew quite rapidly, branching out as it reached up toward the sun. Leaves appeared first, and then the tips of the twigs swelled into buds. When the buds opened, each new rose was of a different color.

'Now *that's* something you don't see every day, isn't it, Mangaran?' Asrana suggested mildly.

The earl appeared more than a little startled. Then he quickly regained his composure. 'Well, now,' he said. 'Welcome to Vo Astur, Lady Polgara.' He bowed with exquisite grace.

I translocated my rainbow rosebush into a corner of the nearby flower bed and responded to the earl's bow with a curtsey. 'Now that we've covered that, we need to talk, my Lord.'

'You've managed to capture my undivided attention, Lady Polgara. I'm at your immediate disposal.'

'Oh, please don't dispose of him, Polly,' Asrana said, her eyes sparkling. 'If *you* don't want him, let *me* have him.'

'That will do, Asrana,' I told her. Then I looked at Mangaran. 'Are you in the mood for a touch of treason this morning, my Lord?' I asked him.

'I'm an Arend, Lady Polgara,' he said with a faint smile. 'I'm always in the mood for mischief.'

'Polly's going to kill our duke,' Asrana said breathlessly, 'and I get to watch while she does it.'

'Me too?' Mangaran said in a tone every bit as childish as Asrana's.

'Oh, dear,' I sighed. 'What have I let myself in for?'

'We'll be good, Polly,' Asrana promised. 'How are we going to exterminate the Bug?'

'We probably aren't going to,' I told them. 'He might know some things I'll need. He's being led down the garden path by a Murgo who's trying to start a war between Arendia and the Tolnedran empire.'

'Great Chaldan!' Mangaran exclaimed. 'Our duke's an idiot, but –'

'He's not the only one who's being deceived, my Lord,' I told him. 'I've just come from Vo Wacune, and the same thing's been going on there – and probably in Vo Mimbre as well. The Angaraks are trying to stir up dissent and wars here in the west in preparation for an invasion out of Mallorea. My father sent me here to Arendia to put a stop to it. I gather that your duke's too thick-witted to listen to reason, so I don't think we've got any choice but to depose him and put you in his place.'

'*Me*? Why me?'

Why does *everybody* keep saying that?

I told him why him in the bluntest way imaginable, and even the unflappable Asrana seemed just a little flapped.

'The duke has a lot of guards, Lady Polgara,' Earl Mangaran said dubiously, 'and *they* get paid even when the rest of the army doesn't. They'll defend him with their very lives.'

'We could bribe them,' Asrana suggested.

'A man who can be bribed usually isn't honorable enough to stay bribed,' Mangaran disagreed.

Asrana shrugged. 'Poison the lot of them, Polly. I'm sure you've got something in that little bag of yours that'll turn the trick.'

'That's not a very good idea, dear,' I told her. 'This is Arendia, and the bodyguards have families. If we kill them, you'll both spend the rest of your lives looking back over your shoulders for somebody with a knife to come sneaking up behind you. I'll take care of the bodyguards.'

'When are we going to do this?' Earl Mangaran asked.

'Did you have anything planned for this evening, my Lord?'

'Nothing that can't be postponed. Aren't we moving a little fast, though?'

'I think we must, my Lord. This *is* Arendia, after all, and *no* plot here is secure for more than a few hours.'

'True,' he sighed. 'Sad, but true.'

'Be of good cheer, my Lord Duke,' Asrana said roguishly. 'I'll comfort you while Polly does the dirty work.'

CHAPTER 14

History tends to gloss over revolutions, since they're an indication of that disunity and internal strife that academics find distressingly messy. They *do* happen, however, and Arendia's the perfect place for them. I take a certain pride in the one I pulled off in Asturia that summer, because it might just be the only one that's ever gone from inception to conclusion in a single day. That's no mean trick in Arendia, where the people just *love* to drag things out. Arends are addicted to high drama, and that always takes time. If it hadn't been for the presence of Krachack's counterpart here in Vo Astur, we might have been able to move at a more leisurely pace, but all it would have taken to make the whole thing crumble in my hands would have been a chance word in the wrong place at the wrong time.

Asrana looked around furtively, and when she spoke to me it was in a conspiratorial whisper. 'How do we proceed, Polly?' she asked me.

A word of advice to my family here. If *anyone* among you *ever* calls me 'Polly', you'll all get boiled hay for supper every night for a week. I let Asrana get away with it for a very specific reason.

'In the first place, Asrana, you're going to stop doing that. No crouching, no tip-toeing down dark corridors, and no whispers. Talk in a normal voice and don't keep looking around like a burglar with a sack-full of loot over his shoulder. When you do that, you might as well wave a flag, blow a trumpet, and hang a sign reading ''conspirator'' around your neck.'

'You're taking all the fun out of this, Polly,' she pouted.

'How much fun do you think spending forty years in the dungeon's going to be?'

'Not much, I suppose,' she conceded.

'Think about it, dear. Keep the idea of sleeping on moldy straw with rats for company firmly in mind all the rest of the day.' I looked at Earl Mangaran. 'I gather that Oldoran doesn't really have much support here in Vo Astur, right?'

'Almost none, Lady Polgara,' he replied. 'The members of his own family support him, of course, and there are a few nobles who've been profiting from his misrule. That's about all – except for those bodyguards I mentioned before.'

'I'll take care of the bodyguards,' I assured him. I thought about it for a moment. 'Is there someone you can depend on who has a house here in Vo Astur – a house some distance from the palace?'

He thought about it. 'Baron Torandin sort of fits that description, my Lady.'

'Does he know how to keep things to himself? And will he do as you ask without needing too many details?'

'I think so, yes.'

'Good. Ask him to have a party at his house this evening. Draw up a guest list that includes everybody with blood ties to the duke and those who have a financial stake in his remaining on the throne. Sprinkle the crowd with some neutrals just so that nothing's too obvious. I don't want any of the duke's partisans around tonight.'

He grinned at me. 'Torandin's the perfect choice, then. His parties are famous all over Asturia. Everyone he invites will be there.'

'Good. Now let's move on to *our* party. Let's keep it small and exclusive. The more people who know about our scheme, the more chance there is for word of what we're up to to reach the wrong ears. I don't want more than a dozen people to know what we're doing.'

'You can't overthrow a government with only a dozen people, my Lady!'

'You can if you do it right, my Lord. We're not going to run around waving swords and shouting slogans. Our scheme's far more subtle.'

'That's a very nasty word, Polly,' Asrana complained.

'Which word was that, dear?'

'"Scheme." Couldn't we find something more uplifting to call it?'

'Let's see. How about "plot"? "Conspiracy", maybe? "Treason"? "Betrayal of trust"? "Violation of a sacred oath"?'

'None of those sound very nice either,' she objected.

'What we're doing *isn't* nice, Asrana. Oldoran's the legal authority here in Asturia, and we're plotting his overthrow. That makes us criminals – or patriots.'

'That's a nicer word. I like that one.'

'Very well, then, Patriot Asrana. You told me that you could wrap any man in Vo Astur around your little finger. Get to wrapping.'

'I beg your pardon?'

'Go out there and start breaking hearts. Flutter your eyelashes, spread around those long, low, suggestive looks, sigh a lot and heave your bosom. Let your eyes fill with luminous tears.'

'Oh, what fun!' she exclaimed, clapping her hands in glee. 'Are you going to break hearts too, Polly?'

I shook my head. 'I'm not known here, so the people we'll be trying to recruit wouldn't be inclined to listen to me. Besides, I've got some other things to take care of. That means that you two will have to make all the necessary contacts. I want a dozen or so cohorts in the proper places at the proper time tonight. See to it.'

'Have you by any chance ever commanded troops, Lady Polgara?' Earl Mangaran asked curiously.

'Not as yet, my Lord. I can usually get things done without bloodshed. Oh, that reminds me. I *am* going to need an archer – the best you can find. I'm going to need one arrow in a very specific place at a very specific time.'

'I *knew* she was going to kill the duke!' Asrana exclaimed delightedly.

'No, dear,' I told her. 'I want the duke to come out of this alive. If we kill him, all the people at Baron Torandin's party will be up in arms tomorrow morning. The arrow's intended for somebody else. Let's get started. This day won't last forever, and we all have a lot to do. And don't sneak or look guilty. Keep that word "patriot" right in front of your eyes.'

That set things in motion, but the limitations I'd imposed kept our plot from stirring too many ripples. Regardless of their other faults, Arends are among the world's great plotters. Asrana and Mangaran moved quietly through the courtiers, sounding out the crucial ones and keeping the rest in the dark. Naturally, they extracted oaths of silence and embedded some ridiculous passwords and recognition signals in the minds of our co-conspirators. I guess the only objections they encountered had had to with the haste at which we were moving. A one-day coup didn't really fit into the Arendish conception of how things ought to be done.

By noon, our conspiracy was fairly well established. Mangaran subverted a few older, more substantial members of the court, and Asrana skimmed off the cream of the young hot-heads. My own contributions that morning were chemical in nature. The wine our co-conspirators drank for the rest of the day wouldn't have knocked a fly off the wall. Those most likely to remain loyal to Oldoran drank wine that would not only have gotten the fly, but probably the wall he perched on as well.

It was about an hour or so past noon when Mangaran's friend, the Marquis Torandin, issued his selective invitations to 'an intimate little soiree at my residence this evening'. Then Mangaran and Asrana had to go back through the ranks of their cohorts to tell them *not* to protest their exclusion from the festivities. At that particular time in Vo Astur just about everything was suspended when a good party was in the offing, and several plotters seemed torn between the conflicting delights of a good party or a good revolution.

In the second hour past noon, I had to come up with a way to keep the duke at home. I solved that by fortifying the wine he was drinking as he sprawled on his throne. By the third hour, he was comatose.

The 'Tolnedran' at his elbow began to have a few suspicions at that point, I think, but we were moving too rapidly for him by now.

Our scheme was ridiculously simple. When you're dealing with Arends, you should always try to avoid complexity. Every courtier in the palace had a number of 'valets', 'grooms', 'butlers', and the like in his entourage. Since this was Arendia, these 'servants' all had assorted weapons concealed about their persons, and they'd respond immediately to commands even though they didn't know what was going on. We had plenty of manpower should we need it, but once those who might oppose us had trooped across town to Marquis Torandin's party, our only opposition might come from the duke's own bodyguards, and tampering with the wine served to them with their evening meal would neatly get them out from underfoot. The imitation Tolnedran quite probably had a few bully-boys at his disposal, but our superior numbers made us confident that they wouldn't pose much of a problem. Our excuse for deposing Oldoran would be 'his Grace's sudden illness'. There was nothing really 'sudden' about it. Oldoran had spent years head-down in a wine barrel to achieve his current condition.

Not long before supper, I took Asrana and Mangaran back out into the rose garden to hammer down some last-minute details. 'Don't kill him,' I instructed them very firmly. 'Everything will fly apart if you do. I want everybody to pull a long face when we do this. Pretend to be concerned about Oldoran's health.' I looked at Mangaran. 'Did you speak with the abbot?' I asked.

He nodded. 'He's got everything ready. Oldoran will have pleasant quarters in the monastery and all the wine he can possibly drink. The abbot will issue periodic statements about his Grace's condition – which will probably deteriorate as time goes by.'

'Don't do anything to help that along,' I cautioned. 'Let Oldoran's liver take him off.'

'How long's that likely to take, Polly?' Asrana asked me.

'I'd give him about another six months,' I replied. 'The whites of his eyes are already yellow. His liver's turning to stone. He'll start raving before long, and *that's* when you'll want to start taking his supporters to see him. Let them observe his condition for themselves.'

'Are you the one who's making his liver go bad, Polly?' Asrana asked.

'No. He's done that all by himself.'

'Does wine really do that to people?'

'Oh, yes, dear. You might want to think about that.'

'Maybe I'd better cut back just a little bit,' she said with a slightly worried frown.

'*I* would. It's your liver, though. Now, then, I want you two to circulate among our "patriots". Impress upon them the fact that we're doing this regretfully. We don't *want* to do it, but we have no choice. Our revolution grows out of our love for Asturia.'

'That's not entirely true, Lady Polgara,' Mangaran told me candidly.

'Lie about it, then. Good politics are always based on lies. When you make these speeches, always be sure there are people in the crowd to lead the cheering. Don't leave anything to chance.'

'You're a terrible cynic, Polly,' Asrana accused.

'Possibly, but I can live with it. Pressing right along, then. *After* the duke's safely tucked away in that monastery, talk with some of the local barons. I want lots of armed men in the streets of Vo Astur by morning. Caution the barons that I want their troops to be polite. No looting, no murders, no fires, no incidental rapes. They'll be out there to maintain order and nothing else. *I'll* decide what's disorderly. Let's not give the opposition any excuses for counter-revolution. Oh, one other thing. Tomorrow morning, an old man with white hair and wearing a white robe is going to come here to the palace. He's going to make a speech, and I want everybody here at court – drunk or sober – to hear that speech. He's going to tell everybody that what we've done has been done at *his* specific orders. I don't think we'll have any trouble after that.'

'Who in all this world has that much authority?' Mangaran asked, looking slightly startled.

'My father, naturally.'

'Holy Belgarath himself?' Asrana gasped.

'I wouldn't tack "holy" onto him until after you've met him, dear,' I advised. 'And I wouldn't turn my back on him, if I were you. He has an eye for the ladies and a little difficulty in keeping his hands to himself.'

'*Really?*' she said archly. 'What an interesting idea.' Asrana, it appeared, was worse than I thought.

'Did you find my archer, Mangaran?' I asked the earl.

'Yes, Lady Polgara,' he replied. 'His name's Lammer, and he can thread a needle with an arrow at a hundred paces.'

'Good. I'll want to speak with him before we set things in motion.'

'Ah –' Mangaran said a bit tentatively, 'just exactly when's that going to be, Lady Polgara?' he asked.

'When I come into the throne room this evening, my Lord. That'll be your signal to start.'

'I'll watch for you,' he promised.

'Do that. Now, let's get to work.'

I lingered in the rose garden until they'd left. 'All right, father,' I said, speaking to a decorative lemon tree, 'you can come down now.'

He looked just a bit foolish after he'd flown down and resumed his real form. 'How did you know I was around?' he asked.

'Don't be tiresome, father. You know perfectly well that you can't hide from me. I *always* know when you're around.' I paused. 'Well? What do you think?'

'I think you're taking a lot of chances, and you're moving too fast.'

'I have to move fast, father. I can't be certain just who's in that Murgo's pocket.'

'That's exactly my point. You're hanging your whole scheme on the two who just left, and you only met them this morning. Are you sure they can be trusted?'

I treated him to one of those long-suffering sighs. 'Yes, father,' I replied, 'I'm sure. Mangaran has a lot to gain, and he *does* have a few faint tinges of patriotism lurking around his edges.'

'What about the girl? Isn't she awfully giddy?'

'That's a pose, father. Asrana's very clever, and she's got at least as much to gain as Mangaran has.'

'I didn't exactly follow that, Pol.'

'A part of the Arendish problem is the fact that women are little more than domestic animals here. Asrana's going to help take over the government, and when Mangaran's elevated to the throne, she'll be right next to the seat of power. She'll be someone to reckon with here in Asturia after tonight. This is her only opportunity to seize any kind of power, and she won't do *anything* to spoil that chance.'

He squinted. 'Maybe,' he conceded dubiously.

'Trust me, father. Will you do it?'

'Do what?'

'Make that speech tomorrow morning?'

'Why don't you do it?'

'You remember what I just said about domestic animals? This is Arendia, father. No Arendish man's going to listen to anybody wearing a skirt. I've got to move on to Vo Mimbre, so I don't have time to convince a crowd of half-drunk Asturian males that I'm not a poodle or a common house-cat. Look at it this way, father. If you make the speech, you get all the credit for what I've done – and you didn't have to do any of the dirty work.'

'I'll think about it. Why do you let that silly girl call you "Polly"? If *I* tried that, you'd set fire to my beard.'

'Yes, I would, so don't even think about it. Actually, I wasn't entirely sure of Asrana's commitment until she called me "Polly". Once she did that, I knew I had her in my pocket.'

'Could you trot that past me again?'

'She's pushing, father. Asrana *always* pushes. I let her get away with it in order to keep her right where I want her.'

'I will *never* understand women.'

'Probably not, no. Oh, before you start composing your speech for tomorrow, would you do me a favor?'

'More than likely. What did you need?'

'Oldoran's bodyguards are at supper right now. Do something to their wine. I want them all to be falling-down drunk before they go on duty.'

'I thought you didn't approve of drinking.'

'This is a special occasion, father, and special occasions allow us to bend the rules just a little bit. I want to hold down the bloodshed as much as possible this evening. It's important that Oldoran's removal from his throne appear to be administrative rather than military.'

'You're very good at this, Pol.'

'Thank you, father. Now, go to the guardroom and incapacitate the duke's bodyguards. Then start working on your speech while I get on with overthrowing the government.'

Just after supper, a sturdy peasant with a diffident air about him approached me. 'Lord Mangaran asked me to speak with you, my Lady,' he said politely. 'He said you wanted to send somebody a message. I'm supposed to deliver it for you. My name's Lammer.'

It was a bit obscure – this *was* a conspiracy, after all – but I got his point. 'Are you a good messenger?' I asked him.

'There's none better in all Asturia, my Lady. Did you want a demonstration?'

'I'll take your word for it, Lammer. I want my message to reach his brain at a specific moment.'

'I can manage that, my Lady.' He squinted. 'I'll be up in the gallery on the right side of the throne-room,' he advised me. 'I'll send the message on its way and be halfway back down the stairs that lead up to the gallery before it even arrives in his brain.'

'Excellent fellow. I'm going to go change clothes now, and then I'll go to the throne-room. Deliver my message as soon as I enter the room.'

'Yes, my Lady.' He paused. 'Um –' he said, 'who? Who's supposed to get the message, I mean?'

I told him and a flicker of a smile touched his lips. Then I went to Asrana's set of rooms to change. I used the gown I'd worn at Beldaran's wedding. It was striking enough to get everyone's attention, certainly, and I was very familiar with it, since I'd watched Arell put in every stitch.

No, of *course* I hadn't carried it to Arendia with me. It was still hanging in my wardrobe back in father's tower. I *do* have certain advantages, after all.

Asrana came in just as I was touching up my hair. 'My goodness, Polly!' she said. 'What a stupendous gown! But isn't it just a trifle daring?'

'It's intended to be, Asrana,' I told her. 'All manner of things are going to happen when I walk into the throne-room, and I want to be certain that everybody notices me.'

'Oh, you can be sure that they will, Polly. It might disrupt the plan, though. Everybody'll be so busy looking at you that they'll forget to overthrow the government.'

'Something's going to happen that'll remind them, dear,' I assured her. 'Now go get Mangaran for me. Send him here and then go to the throne-room. Circulate around and tell our people to get ready. Things are going to happen rather quickly once I enter the room.'

'Could you be a little more specific?'

'No, I don't think so. I want to surprise everybody. Don't you like surprises?'

'Not when I'm in the middle of a plot, I don't.' She looked at the sideboard where several decanters stood.

'No!' I told her quite firmly. 'Don't even think about it! I want your head on straight tonight.'

'My nerves are strung a little tight, Polly.'

'Good. I want them to be. Don't dull your edge, Asrana. Now scoot.'

She left, and Mangaran rapped on the door a few moments later. 'You wanted to see me, my Lady?'

'Yes. Come in and close the door.'

He did that.

'Go directly to the throne-room from here, my Lord,' I instructed. 'Ease your way through the crowd until you're about five feet from the throne. Oldoran *is* there, isn't he?'

He nodded. 'He sort of regained consciousness after supper, and his servants helped him to the throne. His eyes are open, but I doubt that very much is registering on his brain.'

'Good. As soon as I enter the throne-room, something rather startling is going to happen. I'll shout some instructions, and you'll follow them. We'll hustle the duke out of the throne-room. It'll *look* as if it's for his protection, but it's really an excuse to get him on his way to that monastery. I'll come into the room where you take him and give him a quick medical examination, and then we'll come out to make the announcement that he's going into seclusion "for reasons of health". You'll be taking over the government at that point. Try to sound regretful about it.'

'Exactly *what* is going to happen, Lady Polgara?'

'You don't need to know that, my Lord. I want your reactions to be very genuine. If I surprise you, they will be. I'll be giving you instructions, so just follow them. Under the circumstances, they'll be completely rational, so nobody's going to question you. Now go to the throne-room. I'll be along in just a few moments, and that's when things will start.'

*   *   *

222

I want you all to notice that I was very carefully keeping a great many details to myself. Arends have a tendency to want to be helpful, and I didn't want anybody stepping in to lend a hand at exactly the wrong moment.

I paused for a long moment before leaving Asrana's apartment, gathering a kind of calmness about me. There were a number of things I had to do in almost the same instant that Lammer's message reached its mark. Very few in the throne-room were actually privy to our little scheme, and I was going to have to channel everyone else's thinking in a specific direction. I wasn't going to leave any openings for speculation. I wanted them all to interpret the event that was about to take place in one specific way.

Then I drew in a deep breath and went out into the corridor that led to the throne-room.

I paused in the shadowy doorway to the great hall to make certain that everyone was in place. Mangaran was near the left side of the throne. Oldoran, his eyes unfocused, sat in his accustomed place. The Murgo in the yellow Tolnedran mantle stood at the befuddled duke's right elbow with a slightly bored expression on his face. His eyes, however, were moving constantly. I couldn't see Lammer up in that shadowy gallery, but I wasn't really supposed to. I sent out a quick, searching thought, and then I relaxed. Lammer was where he was supposed to be. The giddy Asrana was not far from the throne, and she absolutely sparkled. The tension of the moment had made her even more vivacious than usual.

Everything was in its proper place. We were ready.

I stepped into the doorway and paused, looking directly at the fellow in the Tolnedran mantle at the duke's side. Krachack had known me the instant he'd laid eyes on me, and I was hoping that *this* Murgo would as well.

Then, while his eyes were still starting out of their sockets, I went on into the plain view of everybody in the room. My gown had been designed to attract attention, and it still worked. Heads swivelled. People broke off what they were saying in mid-sentence to stare at me. Lammer's bow-string twanged.

The steel-tipped arrow made a crunching sound as it drove directly into the Murgo's forehead. The distance wasn't really that great, and Lammer's bow had strong limbs. The arrow plunged through the Murgo's brain, and it protruded a foot or more out behind his head. He *did* look just a bit peculiar with the feathered fletching of the arrow decorating his forehead. His body stiffened as he jerked into an erect position.

'*Assassin!*' I shouted, augmenting my voice so that the sentries on the city wall probably heard me. 'Get the duke to safety!'

And *that's* how I overthrew the government of Asturia. One arrow, one shout, and it was done. The good ones are always simple.

Even as that pseudo Tolnedran slowly toppled backward, Mangaran was moving. 'To the duke!' he bellowed. 'Shield him with your bodies!'

At first the startled courtiers hung back. There was always the possibility of more arrows, and very few in the room were *that* fond of Oldoran. But Mangaran had already hurled his own body on that of the confused duke, and others rushed forward to join him. Other courtiers were drawing their swords and looking around for somebody to stab.

Asrana was screaming in a masterful imitation of hysteria.

I moved quickly around the outskirts of the crowd to the door behind the throne. 'This way, my Lord Mangaran!' I shouted. 'Bring the duke! The rest of you, guard this door! There's treason afoot!' I wanted to nail that down.

Then I cast a hideous illusion directly in front of the stupefied Oldoran's bleary eyes, and *he* was the only one who could see it. He began to scream and gibber in absolute terror, even as several courtiers picked him up bodily and followed Earl Mangaran to the doorway where I stood. I intensified the illusion before the duke's eyes, and his screaming grew even louder as he struggled to free himself. I definitely wanted that screaming to continue.

'Should I make the announcement?' Mangaran muttered to me as he led the little cluster of men carrying the duke through the door.

'Not yet,' I replied quietly. 'Let him scream for a while. I'll be along in a few moments to examine him.' I let them on through the doorway and then firmly shut the door and set my back against it. 'Find that assassin!' I commanded. 'Hunt him down!'

That gave everyone who wasn't busy guarding the door something to do. A quick search with my mind had revealed the fact that Lammer had already left the palace grounds and was sitting in a tavern several streets away. The searchers *did* find his bow and a quiver of arrows up in the gallery, however. Lammer, I noted, was a thoroughgoing professional.

Not *everyone* in the throne-room joined in that disorganized search for the mysterious bowman, though. About a half-dozen distraught-looking Asturian nobles were gathered around the dead Murgo's body. Some of them were even wringing their hands, and one was openly weeping. I caught Asrana's eye and crooked one finger at her.

She came to me immediately. 'Yes, Polly?' she said.

'*Wipe that silly grin off your face, Asrana,*' I told her, and I *didn't* say it out loud.

'How are you – ? ' she started.

'*Hush! Listen, don't talk. Fix the names of those men around the body by the throne firmly in your mind. Those are the ones we'll have to watch out for.*' Then I spoke aloud to her – just loud enough to be heard by the courtiers guarding the door. 'Calm yourself, dear,' I told her. 'The duke's safe, and the Earl Mangaran's with him.'

'Did he get hurt?' she asked, wincing as Oldoran gave vent to a particularly piercing shriek.

'He's distraught, Asrana. The shock of this attempt on his life has unsettled him just a bit, I think. Here. Take my place. If anyone tries to rush this door, give up your life to hold them off.'

She lifted her chin and assumed a heroic pose. '*I will!*' she declared. 'They'll have to rip me to pieces and spill out all my blood. They *will* not pass!'

'Brave girl,' I murmured. Then I opened the door and went into the small antechamber where the duke was busy having hysterics. I drew Mangaran off to one side. 'All right, my Lord,' I murmured softly to him. 'Part one is over. Now it's time to move on to part two.'

'Do you have any other surprises up your sleeve, Polgara?' he murmured in reply. 'I almost lost my grip when that Murgo's forehead sprouted feathers.'

'I rather thought you might like it. I'm going to examine the duke, and my diagnosis is going to be that he's temporarily lost control of his senses.'

'Temporarily?'

'That's an interim diagnosis, Mangaran. It'll serve as an excuse for us to transport him to the monastery. We'll pull long faces and talk about lingering after effects later. You're going to have to identify me when you make your announcement, my Lord. Introduce me, and I'll advise the courtiers of my findings. My name's known well enough that nobody's going to argue with me. I'll tell them that the duke needs a safe place for his recovery, and then *you* suggest the monastery. It's a logical place – peace, quiet, security, and lots of monks around to see to his needs. We'd better get on with this, Earl Mangaran. I want him inside that monastery before

225

the Marquis Torandin's party breaks up. I don't want any unrestrained creativity about alternatives cropping up. Once the duke's safely tucked in that monastery, we can protest that it's unsafe to move him.'

'You've covered just about everything, haven't you, Polgara?'

'I've certainly tried. Look worried while I examine his Grace.'

'Why should I worry? You've tied up all the loose ends.'

'*Simulate* worry, Mangaran. Let's move right along here.'

Oldoran was still gaping at the illusion I'd set before his eyes and gibbering in terror as I leaned over to examine him. His breath was acrid, and his entire body exuded the foul reek of the confirmed drunkard. Getting that close to him wasn't pleasant. Given his current condition, I didn't have to be too subtle when I probed at his mind. There wasn't very much of it left, as I recall. Then I continued to probe, moving systematically through his major organs. His liver, naturally, was almost in ruins, and his kidneys were right on the verge of shutting down completely. His arteries were almost clogged shut, and his heart was faltering. My original estimate that he had no more than six months to live might have been just a little optimistic.

'Very well, my Lord Mangaran,' I said in a professional tone of voice for the benefit of the others in the room. 'I've finished my examination. His Grace is in serious condition – quite possibly even critical. He needs complete rest and quiet. Someone else will have to assume his duties until he recovers.'

'I shall so advise the court, my Lady,' he assured me, also speaking for the others in the rooms. 'I am not a physician, however. Might I prevail upon you to describe his Grace's condition to the court?'

'Of course, my Lord.' Then we went back out into the hub-bub of the throne room, leaving the door slightly ajar so that the courtiers could hear Oldoran's screaming.

Mangaran went to the throne, glanced briefly at the sprawled body of the Murgo in the Tolnedran mantle, and raised his voice to address the crowd. 'My Lords and Ladies,' he said in a tone filled with feigned concern, 'his Grace's condition is, I'm afraid, far more serious than we'd imagined. The shock of this foul attempt upon his life has aggravated an illness which none of us has suspected.' He made a rueful face. 'I'm not well-versed in the functions of the human body,' he confessed. 'I'm not even exactly sure how my blood gets from one place to another. Fortunately, a visitor to Vo Astur is among the finest physicians in all the world. She has examined his Grace and has reached certain conclusions, which she has agreed to share with us. The lady in question has a towering repu-

226

tation, and I'm certain that most of you have heard of her. My Lords and Ladies, may I present the Lady Polgara, daughter of Ancient Belgarath.'

There were all the usual gasps of astonishment – and disbelief – and they were followed by some dubious applause.

I stepped to Mangaran's side. 'My Lords and Ladies,' I began. 'I'd not intended to make my presence here in Vo Astur public, but the current crisis requires me to come forward to make certain things known to you. Your duke is gravely ill, and this heartless attempt on his life has exacerbated his condition.' I paused – just a bit theatrically, I suppose. 'As you can hear, your duke is a bit distraught just now.' I glanced back toward the door to the room where the duke was still screaming. 'His grace is suffering from a rare condition known as interstitial conjunctive morbialis, which afflicts not only the body, but the mind as well. In short, his Grace hovers on the verge of total physical and mental collapse.'

Don't bother tearing medical texts apart looking for 'interstitial conjunctive morbialis'. You won't find it, since it's pure gibberish that I made up right there on the spot.

It sounds absolutely awful, though, doesn't it?

'Can it be cured, Lady Polgara?' Asrana asked me.

'I can't be certain,' I replied. 'The malady is so rare that there probably haven't been more than a half-dozen cases since the disease was first identified over a century ago.'

'What course of treatment would you advise, Lady Polgara?' Mangaran asked me.

'The duke must have total rest and quiet,' I replied. 'I'd advise removing him from the palace here to some secure place where he'll be safe from further attempts on his life and where he can have absolute rest. If he remains here in the palace, the affairs of state will inevitably begin to intrude upon him, and he'll die.'

'*Die?*' Asrana gasped. 'Is it *that* serious?'

'Probably even more so,' I replied. 'His life hangs by a thread.' I turned to Earl Mangaran. 'Is there some nearby place where his Grace might be taken to begin his recovery?' I asked. 'A place such as I've just described?'

'Well, –' He said it just a bit dubiously. 'There's a monastery about an hour's ride from here, Lady Polgara. It has high walls, and the monks there spend most of their lives in silent meditation. It's secure, certainly, and it *is* quiet.'

I pretended to think about it. 'It *might* serve our purposes.' I didn't want to sound *too* enthusiastic.

'And who will assume his Grace's duties during his recovery?' one of our 'patriots' demanded.

Asrana stepped forward. 'I'm just a silly woman,' she said, 'but it seems to me that someone already *has*. Earl Mangaran seems to have everything under control. Since he's volunteered, why don't we let *him* take care of things during the duke's temporary incapacity?'

'Yes,' an elderly noble, also one of our cohorts, agreed. 'Mangaran will do nicely, I think. The Privy Council may want to discuss the matter, but in the interim, I'd suggest that the earl should continue to make decisions. We *do* have the Wacites on our eastern frontier, after all, so we don't want any signs of division or weakness to encourage them to attack.'

Mangaran sighed. 'If it is the will of the court –' He even managed to sound reluctant.

The still gibbering duke was hustled into a carriage for his trip to the monastery an hour or so before the party at the Marquis Torandin's house broke up. We left the Murgo's body where it had fallen to help persuade the returning party-goers that there really had been an assassination attempt, and with only a few exceptions the courtiers all agreed that Mangaran should continue to stand in Oldoran's stead.

It was almost dawn by the time I fell into bed to snatch a couple of hours sleep.

'*Interstitial conjunctive morbialis?*' father's voice asked mildly. '*What's that, Pol?*'

'*It's very rare, father.*'

'*It must be. I don't think I've ever heard of it before.*'

'*Probably not. This is the first case I've ever seen. Go away, Old Man. Let me get some sleep. I'll call you when it's time for you to make your speech.*'

Our coup had gone off quite smoothly. Such opposition as there was had been thrown into total disarray by the speed at which we had moved, and the sudden appearance in the throne-room of the legendary Belgarath the Sorcerer about mid-morning of the day following our little coup more or less set our arrangements in stone. Father, always a performer, strode into the throne room garbed in an almost incandescent white robe. He carried a staff, which the gullible Asturians assumed could be used to fell vast forests, blow the tops off mountains, and turn whole generations into regiments of toads. Father, quite naturally, took all the credit, and then he strongly suggested that it was *his* decision that Earl Mangaran assume the reins of the government.

The dead Murgo who'd subverted Duke Oldoran was buried with Lammer's arrow still stuck through his head, and since most of his underlings were Angaraks incapable of making decisions on their own, they had to wait for new instructions from Rak Cthol. Ctuchik had been getting all sorts of bad news lately, and I had every intention of going on to Vo Mimbre to send him some more.

Father, Mangaran, Asrana and I gathered in Asrana's apartments after everything had been nailed down to discuss our options at this point. 'My father might not agree with me,' I told them, 'but I think our next step should be some peace overtures to Kathandrion of Vo Wacune. Let's shut down this silly war.' I looked at father. 'Any objections?' I asked him.

'This is your party, Pol,' he said, shrugging. 'Do it any way you like.'

'I'd more or less intended to, father.' I cocked an eyebrow at Asrana and Mangaran. 'I'm going on to Vo Mimbre,' I advised them. 'Try not to get creative while I'm gone. Watch Oldoran's relatives and those half-dozen or so courtiers who were so upset by the sudden passing of the fellow in the Tolnedran mantle. There are probably other Murgos lurking about, though, and I think they'll *also* pose as Tolnedrans when they start showing up at court. I think the best way to deal with them would be to lean heavily on that ''interim'' business. Theoretically, you're just filling in for Oldoran until he regains his health, my Lord Mangaran. Pretend that you don't have the authority to sign treaties or agree to more informal arrangements. Tell them that they'll have to wait until the duke recovers. That should stall anything new for about half a year. Ctuchik's plan has a definite time-table, I think, and an enforced six-month delay should seriously disrupt it. The Dagashi will have to just mark time, but I won't. I'll be able to stop things at Vo Mimbre, and they won't be able to do a thing about it.'

'Did *you* teach her how to be so devious, Holy Belgarath?' Mangaran asked my father.

'No,' father replied. 'It seems to be a natural talent. I'm terribly proud of her, though.'

'An actual compliment, father?' I said. 'I think I'll faint.'

Asrana had been eyeing my father with a speculative look.

'That's a terrible mistake, dear,' I told her. 'You don't really want to get involved with him.'

'I can take care of myself, Polly,' she said, her eyes still on my father.

'Oh dear,' I said. Then I threw up my hands and left for Vo Mimbre.

CHAPTER 15

My father suggested that I stop at Vo Mandor to talk with the current baron on my way south, so Lady and I went down across the vast, deforested plain of the Mimbrate duchy. Even then that landscape was depressingly dotted with the ruins of towns, villages, and isolated castles. I'm sure that Asturia and Wacune were littered with the souvenirs of idiocies past as well, but those old wounds moldered discreetly in the forests which covered the two northern duchies. In Mimbre the grey stone ghosts of castles and the like were always painfully visible and were thus a constant reminder of the sorry history of Arendia. There are those who pass through the plains of Mimbre who find the ruins picturesque and romantic, but that's usually long after the smoke and stench have been blown away and the seasons have washed off the blood.

There wasn't much danger that Mandorallen's ancestral home would ever be part of the nameless ruins of the tides of civil war. Vo Mandor was probably what they had in mind when they coined the word 'unassailable'. It stood atop a rocky knoll, and in the process of construction the builders had hacked away the sides of that knoll to obtain the necessary building stones. The end result was a fortress situated atop a jutting peak with sheer sides hundreds of feet high that defied assault – not that it hadn't been tried a few times, Arends being what they are and all.

As I thought about it, I reached the conclusion that the site of their place of origin may have played a significant role in the formation of the character of that long, unbroken line of the Barons of Vo Mandor. If you grow up with the conviction that no one can possibly hurt you, it tends to make you just a bit rash.

The town of Vo Mandor surrounded the baron's walled keep, and the town itself was also walled. It was approached by a long, steep causeway that was frequently interrupted by drawbridges designed to impede access. All in all, Vo Mandor was one of the bleaker places on earth.

The view from the top was magnificent, though.

Mandorin, the then-current baron, was a blocky widower in his mid-forties. He had massive shoulders, silver-shot dark hair, and a beautifully manicured beard. His manners were exquisite. When he bowed, the act was a work of art, and his speech was so sprinkled with interjected compliments that it often took him about a quarter of an hour to wend his way through a sentence.

I liked him, though. Isn't that odd? Perhaps it's a character defect. Good manners are such a rarity that I'll endure excessive language and all sorts of bowing and scraping just to avoid the casual incivility so common in most of the rest of the world.

'My Lady Polgara,' the maroon-clad baron greeted me in the courtyard of his grim fortress, 'the walls of my poor house do tremble as the very leaves at the presence of the paramount lady in all this world within their confines – e'en as the mountains themselves must be seized by convulsive ague as the sense of thy passage doth strike them into their very vitals.'

'Nicely put, my Lord,' I congratulated him. 'Gladly would I linger in this happy place to hear more of thine exquisite speech, but necessity, that cruelest of masters, doth compel me to unseemly – even discourteous – haste.' I've read my share of Arendish epics, and if Baron Mandorin thought he could outtalk me, he was greatly mistaken. I've learned over the years that the best way to deal with Arends is to talk them into insensibility. The only problem with that is that they're as patient as stones, so it takes a while.

Eventually Baron Mandorin escorted me to his private study, a book-lined room carpeted and draped in blue high in the east tower of his castle, and we got down to business – *after* he'd fetched me a cushion to support my back in the already padded chair he offered me, set a plate of sweetmeats close at hand on the polished, dark wood table, sent for a pot of tea, and placed a footstool close by – just on the off chance that my feet might be tired.

'Knowest thou my father, my Lord?' I asked.

'Holy Belgarath?' he replied. 'Intimately, my Lady – which doth raise the question whether any person in all this world could possibly know so towering an individual.'

'*I* do, my Lord, and father doesn't always tower. Sometimes he

232

stoops, but we digress. It hath come to mine attention – and to my father's – that there is discord in Arendia.'

Mandorin made a rueful face. 'That, dear Lady, is the most cursory description of several eons of Arendish history it hath ever been my sad pleasure to hear. For 'certes, discord lieth at the very soul of Arendish existence.'

'Yes, I've noticed that. In this particular situation, however, the discord hath its origins outside the boundaries of this most unhappy of realms. Wacune was rent by dissention, and Asturia hath but recently enjoyed the overturn of its government.'

'Thou speakest as if these events had already passed into the pages of history, my Lady.'

'Yes, my Lord, they did.'

'I do surmise that it was *thy* hand which stilled the waves of contention in the northern duchies.'

'I had some part in it, yes,' I admitted modestly. 'I exposed the identity of an outside agitator to Duke Kathandrion of Wacune and then proceeded on to Vo Astur and overthrew the government of the incompetent Duke Oldoran. Now I've come to Mimbre.'

'I do sense a certain ominous tone in that particular pronouncement, my Lady.'

'Set thy fears to rest, Baron Mandorin. Thine heart is pure, and thou hast nothing to fear from me. I doubt that I shall have occasion to turn thee into a toad nor stand thee on empty air some miles above us.'

He smiled and inclined his head slightly. 'Prithee, my Lady,' he said, 'when we have leisure, might I beg instruction in the fine art of extravagant speech from thee?'

'You're doing fine already, Mandorin,' I told him in ordinary language. 'You don't need any lessons. To work, then. In both Wacune and Asturia, there were men who *seemed* to be Tolnedran, but were not. They proposed to Kathandrion and separately to Oldoran an alliance with Ran Vordue, dangling the undisputed crown of Arendia before their eyes as a prize for acceptance. Doth this perchance resonate in any way within thy recent memory?'

I didn't really need to ask, since his face had gone pale and his eyes were very wide.

'It has a familiar ring to it, I gather?'

'Indeed, my Lady. A similar proposal hath been broached to our own Duke Corrolin.'

'I'd rather thought it might have been. Art thou, perchance, within the circle of Duke Corrolin's immediate advisors?'

'I do sit on the Privy Council,' he admitted, 'and I must confess that I was sore-tempted by this fortuitous offer of alliance with the mighty Tolnedran empire.'

'I think I'll need some details, Baron Mandorin. Before I can unseat an opponent, I need to know which horse he's riding.'

He pondered that, evidently reassessing certain events which had recently taken place in Vo Mimbre. 'Some months ago a Tolnedran diplomat did, in fact, arrive in the golden city with a proposal, which he assured Duke Corrolin did come directly from the Imperial throne. His credentials did appear immaculate.'

'Did the Tolnedran ambassador to the court at Vo Mimbre recognize him, my Lord?'

'The current ambassador from Tol Honeth had fallen ill a month perhaps 'ere Kadon, the emissary in question, did enter the gates of Vo Mimbre. The illness is obscure, and it doth baffle the finest physicians in all of Mimbre. I do fear me that his Excellency's days are numbered.'

'Most convenient, my Lord. Coincidence, though rampant in this troubled world, doth sometimes require some small nudge from human agency to flower.'

'Poison?' he gasped, catching my meaning.

'Quite possibly, my lord. I fear me that certain Nyissan compounds are entering the politics of the other western kingdoms. Prithee, expound unto me the details of the proposal carried to Vo Mimbre by the emissary Kadon.'

'It doth bear a characteristic Tolnedran stamp, my Lady Polgara, for 'certes, as all the world doth know, the Tolnedran mind is a masterpiece of complexity and devious motivation. In short, though it doth wound me sorely to offend thy delicate sensibilities by such brutal brevity, I shall speak unto thee in unadorned terms.'

'I'd appreciate that, Lord Mandorin.'

Aren't you proud of me? I didn't once scream at him while he was exploring the outer limits of his vocabulary.

'As thou art well aware, having but recently come from the northern duchies, great antagonism did exist between Duke Kathandrion of Wacune and the now deposed Duke Oldoran of Asturia, and the Wacites do poise themselves on the Asturian border, bent on nothing less than the obliteration of their cousins to the west. Kadon suggested to our beloved Duke Corrolin that this contention in the north might prove to be an opportunity too golden to be permitted to escape, and he offered the aid of the legions in grasping this prize.'

'How, my Lord? What exactly were the legions supposed to do?'

'Granted safe passage by his Grace Corrolin, forty legions are to march north and poise themselves in northern-most Mimbre. When Duke Kathandrion's forces do march into Asturia and encircle Vo Astur, the legions will move to fortify the border between Wacune and Asturia. E'en as the legions march, the forces of Duke Corrolin will cross over into the foothills of Ulgoland, move north, and take up positions along Wacune's eastern frontier. When Kathandrion's forces begin their assault on Vo Astur, the Mimbrate army will invade Wacune from the east. By virtue of the legions lining the border between the two northern duchies, Kathandrion will be unable to rush home to defend his homeland. Vo Wacune will fall, and Kathandrion and Oldoran are to be permitted to fight a war of mutual extinction in the forests of Asturia. Then, when but few tattered remnants of the armies of Wacune and Asturia do remain, Duke Corrolin, with the aid of the legions, is to sweep both Kathandrion and Oldoran into the dust-bin of history, and all of Arendia will swear fealty to Corrolin, and he will become our undisputed king.' Mandorin, caught up in spite of himself, delivered this last in ringing tones of exaltation.

'And you and your duke actually *believed* this absurdity?' I asked, hoping to dash some cold water into the face of this enthusiast.

'I am well-versed in the arts of war, Lady Polgara,' he said in slightly injured tones. 'I found no fault nor flaw in this strategy.'

I sighed. 'Oh dear,' I murmured, covering my eyes theatrically with one hand. 'Lord Mandorin,' I said to him, 'think for a moment. Northern Arendia is one vast forest. Kathandrion and Oldoran would *not* meet Corrolin – or the legions – in pitched battle. They would simply melt into the trees. Northern Arends are born with longbows in their hands. The armored knights of Mimbre and the stately ranks of the Tolnedran legions would melt like snow in the spring in sudden rain-squalls of yard-long arrows. There's a man named Lammer in Vo Astur who can thread a needle with an arrow at two hundred paces. Neither the Mimbrates nor the legions would ever have seen the men who killed them. Armor is decorative, but it won't stop an arrow.'

'A most unseemly way to make war,' he complained.

'There's nothing seemly nor polite about war, Baron,' I told him. 'Is it polite to pour boiling pitch on visitors? Is it seemly to bash people's heads in with maces? Is it courteous to run a twenty-foot lance through the body of someone who disagrees with you? But we can discuss courtesy in all its divine intricacies later. Ran Vordue is a Tolnedran. He will not do *anything* without getting paid for it. To put it in its bluntest terms, what's in it for him?'

The baron's face grew troubled. 'I would die ere offending thee, my Lady,' he said, 'but the attachment of thy father to the Alorns is widely known, and thine own sojourn on the Isle of the Winds is legendary. The alliance which Ran Vordue hath proposed is but an initial step in his grand design, the intent of which is the destruction of the Alorns.'

'And *that* idea seemed like a good one to Corrolin?' I asked incredulously. 'Doth his Grace perchance have an extra hole in his head? It seemeth me that his brains are leaking out. The Alorns, as all the world doth know, have their faults, but no sane man chooses to make war upon them. Hath this supposed Tolnedran, Kadon, seen fit to advise the Privy Council in Vo Mimbre of a grand strategy whereby Arendia and Tolnedra can hope to survive a confrontation with those howling savages of the far north?'

His face went a trifle stiff. 'We are Arends, my Lady,' he told me a bit coldly, 'and are not without our own skills – and our own bravery. Moreover, the Tolnedran legions are the most highly-trained soldiers in all the world.'

'I am not disparaging thy bravery nor thy skill at arms, my Lord, but an average Alorn doth stand some seven feet tall and is given a sword to play with whilst still in his cradle. Moreover, by ties of blood and religion, the Alorns think and move as one. Though Tolnedra might wish it otherwise, Aloria doth still exist, stretching from Gar og Nadrak to the Isle of the Winds. An attack upon Aloria is, it seemeth me, tantamount to suicide.' I probably went a little too far there. Arends *do* have their pride, after all. 'I'm sorry, Mandorin,' I apologized. 'The rashness of the proposal startled me, that's all.' I considered the situation. 'Prithee, my Lord,' I said, 'did his Grace actually contemplate this action with nothing more than the unsupported declarations of Kadon to guide him?'

'Nay, my Lady. Simple observation lent weight to Kadon's proposal. I do assure thee that Tolnedran legions are even now massing on the southern bank of the River Arend, doubtless preparing for the long march to the point at which the boundaries of the three duchies do converge. Moreover, a Tolnedran general hath also come to Vo Mimbre to confer with the commanders of our forces.'

That truly troubled me. If Ctuchik were also subverting Tolnedra, I had a *real* problem on my hands. 'We can discuss this further as we travel the road to Vo Mimbre, my Lord,' I told Mandorin. 'It doth appear that what transpires in the golden city hath far greater complexity than what I encountered to the north.' I paused again. 'I think that it might not be wise for my name to start echoing through the halls of the ducal palace upon our arrival. I suppose you'd better adopt me, Mandorin.'

He blinked.

'Thou art a Mimbrate Arend, my Lord,' I reminded him. 'Though it is entirely possible that thou couldst singlehandedly assail a fortress, an outright lie is quite beyond thy capabilities. Let us therefore seek out a priest of Chaldan to perform the necessary ceremonies. I will become thy niece, Countess Polina, the flower of an obscure branch of thy family. Thus may I, all unnoticed, seek out the truth in this matter.'

His expression grew slightly pained. 'That is a flimsy basis for deliberate falsehood, my Lady,' he objected.

'Common purpose doth unite us, my Lord, and thine intimate acquaintanceship with mine agéd father doth make us e'en as brother and sister. Let us formalize our happy kinship, then, so that we may in joyous union proceed toward the accomplishment of our goal.'

'Have thy studies perchance taken thee into the murky realms of law and jurisprudence, Lady Polgara?' he asked me with a faint smile, 'for thy speech doth have a legalistic flavor to it.'

'Why, uncle Mandorin,' I said, 'what a thing to suggest.'

The ceremony was a charade, of course, but it satisfied Mandorin's need for a semblance, at least, of veracity at such time as he'd be obliged to announce our kinship. We went down to the ornate chapel in the baron's castle as soon as we had changed clothes. Mandorin wore black velvet, and, on an impish sort of whim, I conjured myself up a white satin gown. On the surface, at least, this 'adoption' very closely resembled a wedding.

I've never understood the Arendish religion, and believe me, I've spent a lot of time in Arendia. Chaldan, Bull-God of the Arends, seems to have a fixation on some obscure concept of honor that requires his adherents to slaughter each other on the slightest pretext. The only love an Arend seems really capable of displaying is directed toward his own sense of self-esteem, which he cuddles to his bosom like a beloved puppy. The priest of Chaldan who formalized my kinship with Baron Mandorin was a stern-faced man in an ornate red robe that managed to convey a sense of being somehow armored, but maybe that was only my imagination. He preached a war-like little sermon, urging Mandorin to carve up anybody offering me the slightest impertinence. Then he ordered me to live out my life in total, unreasoning obedience to my guardian and protector.

The fellow obviously didn't know me.

And when the ceremony was over, I was a full-fledged member of the House of Mandor.

You didn't know that we were related, did you, Mandorallen?

Given the response of the Dagashi I'd encountered in Wacune and Asturia, I knew that I was going to have to 'do something' about the white lock in my hair if I wanted to maintain any kind of anonymity in Vo Mimbre. I knew that dye, the simplest solution, wouldn't work. I'd tried that in the past and found that dye simply wouldn't adhere to the lock. After a bit of thought, I simply designed a coiffure that involved white satin ribbons artfully included in an elaborately braided arrangement that swept back from my face to stream freely down my back. The more I looked at the results in my mirror, the more I liked it. I've used it on several occasions since then, and it's never failed to attract attention – and compliments. Isn't it odd how an act born out of necessity often produces unexpected benefits? The style was so inherently attractive that I won't demean it by calling it a disguise. Then, once that identifying lock had been concealed, Baron Mandorin and I, ostentatiously accompanied by twenty or so armored knights, went to Vo Mimbre.

A great deal of nonsense has been written about Vo Mimbre, but say what you will, it *is* impressive. The terrain upon which that fortress city stands is not spectacularly defensible. It's no Rak Cthol or Riva by any stretch of the imagination, but then, neither is Mal Zeth in Mallorea. The builders of Vo Mimbre and Mal Zeth had obviously reached a similar conclusion that, put in its simplest terms, goes something like this: 'If you don't have a mountain handy, build one.'

Mandorin and I – and our clanking escort – entered Vo Mimbre and rode directly to the ducal palace. We were immediately admitted and escorted directly to Duke Corrolin's throne-room. I cannot for the life of me remember exactly why, but I once again wore that white satin gown, and I entered that great hall that was decorated with old banners and antique weapons with a faintly bridal aura hovering about me. It was probably a bad idea, since I wanted to

238

be as unobtrusive as possible, but I'm constitutionally incapable of blending in with the wallpaper or furniture.

Baron Mandorin introduced me, and, since he was Mimbrate to the core, rather incidentally noted that he would do vast violence to any man offering me the slightest impertinence. After I'd curtsied to Duke Corrolin, delivered myself of an appropriately girlish and empty-headed greeting, I was gathered up by the ladies of the court and whisked away while the menfolk got down to business. I *did* have time to note the presence of a dozen or so men wearing Tolnedran mantles in the crowd before I left, however, and when I sent out a probing thought from the middle of that gaily-dressed throng of young Mimbrate noblewomen who were rushing me away, I caught the now familiar dull black tinge that identified Murgos – or Dagashi – and I also sensed some red auras. Evidently, Kadon had raided Ctuchik's treasury for enough gold to buy up several real Tolnedrans. What troubled me the most, however, was a momentary flicker of glossy black. There was Grolim somewhere in the crowd, and that in itself was an indication that what had happened in Vo Wacune and Vo Astur had been peripheral. The core of Ctuchik's plot was here in Vo Mimbre.

It pains me to say it about my own gender, but young women, particularly young noblewomen, are a silly lot, and their conversation is top-full of empty-headed frivolity – mostly having to do with decorating themselves in such ways as to attract attention. I take a certain amount of comfort in the fact that young men aren't much better. From a clinical point of view, the condition has a chemical basis, but I don't know that discussing it at length right here would serve any useful purpose.

The white satin ribbons braided in my hair drew many compliments – and not a few imitations later – and the style made me appear younger, so the gaggle of giggling girls assumed that I shared their views on life, and they'd graciously 'rescued' me from tiresome discussions of such boring topics as the onset of general war and the mass extermination of virtually everyone on the western side of the Eastern Escarpment. I was thus treated to a fascinating afternoon of intense speculation about the impact of hemlines and hair-styles on the world situation.

Although Baron Mandorin – dare I say, uncle Mandy? – had been alerted to what was really happening and could report the details of discussions from which my gender and apparent age excluded me, there would be things happening of which he would not be aware. I needed to be present at those discussions, and, now that

239

I'd been brought up to date on current fashions, I felt that it was time to move on. I 'just happened' to come down with a very bad case of sick headache the next morning and shooed my playmates out of my rooms. Then I went to the window and 'went sparrow', to use my father's rather succinct characterization of the process.

It was still summer, so the windows of Corrolin's palace were all open, and that gave me all the opportunity I needed to eavesdrop on the discussions of the Privy Council. I settled on the window-sill, chirped a couple of times to let everyone know that I was only a bird, and then cocked my head to listen.

Duke Corrolin was speaking to a squinty-eyed, swarthy fellow in a pale blue Tolnedran mantle. 'I must advise thee, worthy Kador, that word hath but recently arrived from the northern duchies which doth advise us that Duke Oldoran hath fallen gravely ill by reason of some obscure malady. The governance of Asturia hath been placed in the hands of an aged earl yclept Mangaran.'

'Yes,' Kador replied, 'my own sources have confirmed this as well, your Grace. The initiative in the north, however, lies in the hands of Duke Kathandrion, and I've heard nothing to indicate that he's changed his mind about invading Asturia. It doesn't really matter who holds power in Vo Astur, since our plan hinges almost entirely on what's taking place in Vo Wacune.'

The thought I sent out was so light as to be virtually unnoticed, and the color which responded to it was dull black. Kador was *not* the Grolim. That startled me more than a little, and it troubled me even more. If I started probing every mind in that room, the Grolim, whoever he was, would eventually sense that *someone* was looking for him.

Then a rather ordinary-looking Tolnedran – a servant, judging by his clothing – came forward and murmured something to Kador. 'Ah,' Kador said. 'Thank you.' Then he turned back to the duke – but not before a momentary flicker of hard, glossy black ever so briefly touched my awareness. I'd found my Grolim, but I couldn't quite fathom out exactly why he'd chosen to remain in the background. From what father and my uncles had told me about the Angaraks, it was decidedly unGrolimish for a priest of the Dragon-God to assume the guise of a servant.

'My Lord,' Kador was saying to Corrolin, 'all is proceeding according to our plan. the remainder of the legions will be in place before the week is out. If I might be so bold as to suggest it, might this not be a good time for your knights to begin their journey toward the Ulgo frontier? The general in command of the legions will order his troops north as soon as his force is fully assembled. Your mounted men will move more rapidly, of course, but they have much farther to travel, and the terrain in the foothills of the Ulgo Mountains will make for slow going. Timing will be all-important when we move against Wacune.'

'It may well be as thou sayest, worthy Kador,' Corrolin admitted. 'I shall dispatch an advance party to the east on the morrow. When the legions of His Imperial Majesty do interject themselves into northern Arendia, my knights will be in place.'

In that single phrase 'the legions of His Imperial Majesty' Kador had summed up the core of my problem. Bribing an individual Tolnedran posed no particular difficulty, but bribing forty legion commanders? That might be a bit more challenging.

Then a rather horrid suspicion began to intrude itself upon me, and I did something I haven't done very often. Baron Mandorin, resplendent in his armor, sat at the long table with the other members of the Privy Council, and I sent my thought – and my silent voice – out to him. *'Uncle,'* I said to him, *'don't look around, and don't let your face show any sign that I'm talking to you. I'm going to ask you a few questions, and I want you to think the answers. Don't say anything out loud.'*

'This is a wondrous thing, Lady Polgara,' his thought responded. *'Canst thou truly hear my thought?'*

'You're doing just fine, Uncle. Now, then, has anyone other than Kador and his henchmen actually seen the legions that are supposedly encamped a few miles to the south?'

'Their watch-fires are clearly visible from the south wall of the city, my Lady.'

'Anybody can light a fire, Mandorin. Has any Mimbrate at all bothered to go down into Tolnedra to actually count the soldiers who are supposed to be camped there?'

'The Tolnedrans do not welcome incursions into their territory, my Lady, and in the light of our current delicate negotiations it would be discourteous in the extreme for us to intrude upon the ancestral home of our ally to the south.'

I said something I probably shouldn't have at that point.

'Polgara!' Mandorin gasped in shock at my choice of words.

'Sorry, Uncle,' I apologized. *'It just slipped out. Will you be in your chambers after this meeting breaks up?'*

'An it please thee, yes.'

'It will please me, uncle. I'll be gone for the rest of the day, and when I come back, we'll need to talk, I think.'

I fluttered away from my listening post on the window-sill of the council chamber, found another window that faced out from an empty chamber, and transformed myself into the falcon that was always the alternative to my preferred form. Owls *are* conspicuous in the daytime, after all.

It didn't take me long to confirm my suspicions. Although there were mounted patrols of men in legion uniforms near the south bank of the River Arend that marks the boundary between Arendia and Tolnedra, when I flew on, I saw no more men. There were several standard legion encampments in the forest with all the usual appurtenances of legion camps – log palisades, neatly pitched tents along what could only be called streets, and legion banners fluttering above the gates – but those camps were empty. My suspicions had just been confirmed. There were perhaps fifty men in legion uniforms patrolling near the border, but that was the entire extent of the supposed invasion force.

I flew back toward the border and swooped down to settle on a tree limb for a bit of constructive eavesdropping.

'This is the most tedious job I've ever had, Ralas,' I heard one unshaven fellow complain to his companion as they rode under my tree.

'Oh, it's not so bad, Geller,' Ralas replied. 'We could all be back at the lumber-camp chopping down oak-trees, you know. All we have to do here is ride up and down the river and tend a few fires at night.'

'I don't see any point to it, Ralas.'

'We're getting paid for it, Geller. That's the only point that matters to me. If Count Oldon wants us to patrol the northern boundary of his estate, I'll be happy to oblige him for as long as he wants. The horse does all the work, and that suits me right down to the ground.'

'We could get in trouble for wearing these uniforms, you know,' Geller told him, rapping on his breastplate.

'Not a chance. If you look very closely at your cloak, you'll find the count's crest embroidered on it instead of the imperial one. Nobody but an idiot's going to mistake us for *real* legionnaires.'

'Nedra's teeth!' Geller swore, slapping at a mosquito. 'Why do we have to stay so close to that accursed river?'

Ralas shrugged. 'The Count wants us to be seen from the Arendish side, I guess. I don't ask him questions – except for maybe, "When do I get paid?" That's all *I* care about.'

'I want to know *why*!' Geller burst out. 'What's the point of this silly business?'

242

I probably could have told him, but, since curiosity is the ultimate mother of wisdom, I decided to let him continue his journey along the beaten path to knowledge without any interference from me.

CHAPTER 16

Baron Mandorin was in the throne-room when I returned to the palace in Vo Mimbre, and I crossed the ornate chamber with a purposeful expression. I didn't have time for pleasantries. 'We need to talk, uncle,' I told him, '*now.*'

He looked a little startled at my abrupt approach, but that was just too bad. Our departure from that ceremonial hall might have seemed somewhat leisurely, but we went directly across to the door and on out into the corridor.

'The matter, I do perceive, hath a certain urgency?' he suggested.

'Not here, uncle,' I told him. 'Wait until we're sure we're alone.'

He got my point. We went to his chambers and he closed and locked the door behind us.

'And now – ?' he began, his face curious.

'I've just spent a rather tedious afternoon over across the river, uncle. I searched all over for those Tolnedran legions everyone's talking about, but guess what? I didn't find them.'

'But they are quite clearly visible from the city walls, Lady Polgara.'

'Oh no they're not, Baron Mandorin. What you've been seeing from the walls are common workmen dressed up in legion uniforms. There are several standard-looking legion encampments back under the trees as well, but those encampments are empty. There are probably no more than fifty men over there. They patrol the riverbank in the day-time and tend the watch fires at night. It's all for show, Mandorin. There's no military presence over there. Who's Count Oldon?'

'He is a member of Kadon's party, my Lady, and if I have heard aright, his estates do stand opposite our city here.'

'That would explain it then. He's pressed woodcutters and other laborers into his private little army, and that army has just one mission – to convince Duke Corrolin that there are genuine legions camped across the river. It's all a sham. Corrolin and his staff have been duped. What's going on here in Vo Mimbre is just more of the same sort of thing I encountered in Vo Wacune and Vo Astur.'

'I shall denounce the villain Kador publicly,' Mandorin declared hotly, 'and prove the truth of my words upon his body.'

'All that would prove is that you're a better swordsman than he is. We're going to have to come up with something better.' I considered it for a moment. 'I think it's time for Corrolin to have a talk with Ran Vordue in person. That's probably the only thing that's going to convince him.'

'Would His Imperial Majesty consent to such a meeting?'

'He will if we send the right messenger. My father's lurking about somewhere nearby – keeping an eye on me, I think. I'll suggest that he take a little trip to Tol Honeth – for reasons of his health.'

'Is he unwell?'

'He *will* be if he doesn't make that trip when I tell him to.' I considered it. 'I don't think the meeting should take place here in Vo Mimbre,' I said. 'Let's not alert the opposition. Tol Vordue would be better, I think. I'll talk with father about it and see what he says. This plot we're up against has been months in the making, Mandorin, and it'd take us more months to unravel it. A meeting between Corrolin and Ran Vordue would cut across all that tiresome business. Corrolin will come back to Vo Mimbre with the keys to his dungeon already in his hand.'

'I had not thought that affairs of state could move so rapidly, my Lady,' he marveled. 'Things here have a more leisurely pace.'

'We don't *have* much leisure, Baron. Corrolin's advance parties will be leaving Vo Mimbre tomorrow morning, and the rest of his force won't be far behind. If we don't move fast, there'll be too much momentum for us to turn things around. Oh, one more thing. Please keep this entirely to yourself. We don't need anybody else involved. Anytime more than two people know a secret, it's not a secret any more. Now, if you'll excuse me, I'll go give my father his marching orders.'

I left Baron Mandorin with a troubled expression on his face and went directly to my own quarters. I closed the door behind me and took a few precautions. Kador *did* have that Grolim in his party, after all. '*Father,*' I sent out my thought then, '*I need you.*'

'For someone who's pretending to be so independent, you're calling me out of the bushes fairly often, Pol,' he complained.

'Stop trying to be funny. I want you to go to Tol Honeth and tell Ran Vordue about what's going on here in Arendia. It'll probably get his attention. I want him to go to Tol Vordue to meet with Duke Corrolin and explain – very patiently – that he hasn't got the faintest idea about what's behind all these pseudo alliances. Have him send an official messenger to Mandorin, and the baron will get him in to meet with Corrolin. I want the duke to meet with Ran Vordue personally in Tol Vordue before the week's out, and I **don't** want anybody here in Vo Mimbre to know about that meeting.'

'I'll carry the message myself, if you'd like.' That was a surprise. 'Is there anything else I can do for you?'

'You might see if you can think up a way for me to get Corrolin out of Vo Mimbre and on downriver to Tol Vordue without having about half of his court trailing along behind,' I suggested. 'It's got me a little baffled.'

'I'll think of something. I've probably said this before, Pol, but you're very good at the sneaky side of politics.'

'Why, thank you, kind sir. You're not a so bad yourself, you know.'

'Yes, but I've had more practice. Are things coming to a head here?'

'They're getting close, so don't dawdle, father. Let's step right along here.'

The next morning we all watched fifty or so Mimbrate knights, mounted and steel clad, go clanking out of the court yard with banners flying. It was probably only on an off-chance that I heard the words, 'Bear-Cult' come from somewhere in the crowd. I circulated a bit, and I didn't actually have to go far in search of a repetition. It seemed that everybody in the palace was talking about that peculiar Alorn aberration. It was obvious that Ctuchik's underlings had been busily spreading wild stories. The goals of the Cult were absurd enough already, but the rumors that were circulating that morning left absurdity far behind. The purpose, obviously, was to stir hatred, fear, and distrust. It had been the unity of Torak's brothers that had defeated the Dragon-God during the War of the Gods, and Ctuchik was doing everything in his power to dismember that unity.

I suppose I might have tried to squelch all those rumors, but I'd long since discovered that there's no real way to stop a rumor once it's gained a foothold.

It was late afternoon of the following day when father's thought resounded in my head. 'Rejoice, my beloved daughter,' he announced,

246

'for I, with all my unspeakable skill, have accomplished the task you dropped in my lap.'

'Will you please be serious, father? Did Ran Vordue agree to meet the duke?'

'Of course he did. Have I ever disappointed you?'

'Frequently, as a matter of fact. Have you got his message?'

'It's somewhere in one of my pockets, I think. Oh, incidentally, when I give the letter to Corrolin, I'm going to suggest that he make a religious pilgrimage.

'A what?'

'I'll ask him to put on some humble-looking clothes and ride on downriver to that monastery at the mouth of the River Arend that's just across from Tol Vordue. The duke's right on the verge of going to war, and Arends always make some show of praying for victory before they go out to do violence upon their neighbors. It's a quaint custom of the race. A pilgrimage is sort of private, so Corrolin won't be taking much of an escort with him – just you and Mandorin, if I can arrange it. It shouldn't be too difficult to slip him across the river to Tol Vordue once we reach the coast. Was that sort of what you had in mind?'

'It should work out just fine, father. When will you be arriving here in Vo Mimbre?'

'Tomorrow morning. I'm going to have to stop and get something to eat. I guess I startled Ran Vordue so much that he forgot his manners. He didn't offer me any supper, and I'm absolutely famished. I'll see you tomorrow, then. Sleep well, Pol.'

And I did that. I'd probably deny it were someone to suggest it, but I always feel more secure when father takes a hand in something I'm working on. He has his faults, but once he gets down to business, he's as inexorable as the tides.

The next morning I suggested to Baron Mandorin that we might want to 'go out for a little ride, just to stir up our blood', and once we were some distance to the north of the city, we entered a fairly extensive grove of trees and found my father dozing beside a merry little stream that burbled busily over stones back in amongst the trees. He opened one eye as we dismounted. 'What kept you?' he asked us, and when he stood up, I saw that he was wearing a coarse brown monk's robe made of burlap.

'What's this?' I asked him.

'It's just my uniform, Pol,' he replied. 'I'm going to be duke's escort as we ride on downriver.' Then he looked at Mandorin. 'Amazing,' he said. 'Your hair hasn't turned white yet.'

Mandorin gave him a puzzled look.

'You've been associating with my daughter, haven't you?'

247

'Will you *please* drop all the joking around, father?' I demanded with some exasperation.

'Probably not, but we can talk about that later. How've you been, Mandorin?'

'Well, Ancient One, well.'

'I'm glad to hear it. If I remember correctly, there's a small room back behind the duke's throne. It's where he usually hangs his robe. Go on back to Vo Mimbre and ask him to step in there for a moment. Pol and I'll be waiting for the two of you there. I'll talk with Corrolin for a bit, and then we'll set out for the monastery.'

'What if –' I started.

He sighed that long-suffering sigh that always irritates me. 'Please, Pol,' he said. 'I've already covered all the "what-ifs". Go ahead, Mandorin. Pol and I'll be waiting in that cloak-room.'

Mandorin remounted, took Lady's reins, and rode off, and then father and I fell back on our alternative mode of transportation and were safely ensconced in that half-hidden little attiring-room about a quarter of an hour before the Baron of Vo Mandor even got back inside the palace.

'Ah, there you are, your Grace,' father said when Mandorin and Corrolin entered the room. 'We've been waiting for you.' He didn't even bother to rise.

Father had draped his monk's robe across the back of an unoccupied chair, and the duke saw only a seedy-looking vagabond with bad manners sitting in a room where he had no apparent business. 'What doth this mean, Baron Mandorin?' he demanded sharply of our friend.

'My Lord,' Mandorin replied, 'I have the distinct honor to present Holy Belgarath, Disciple of the God Aldur, who hath but recently arrived from Tol Honeth with an urgent communication from His Imperial Majesty, Ran Vordue of Tolnedra.'

'I do confess that I am overwhelmed,' Corrolin replied, bowing deeply to my vagrant father.

'Hail, Corrolin,' father said, still not bothering to get up. 'I knew your father quite well.' Then he fished around inside his tunic and drew out a folded sheet of parchment with a beribboned wax seal on it. 'His Imperial Majesty asked me to stop by and give this to you. Please forgive all our subterfuge in this matter, but the contents of Ran Vordue's note should probably be kept secret.'

The word 'secret' always seems to light fires in the eyes of Arends, and Corrolin was no exception. He took the letter and then looked dubiously at me.

'My niece is privy to the contents of the message, my Lord,' Mandorin advised him. 'Indeed, she was instrumental in its delivery.'

'We can get into that later,' father smoothly glossed over the fact that in Mimbrate eyes my primary concerns should have been gossip, hairstyles and hosiery.

Corrolin read the imperial message, and his eyes widened a bit. 'Have I perchance misunderstood the import of this document?' he asked. 'Should I have misread it, prithee correct me, but it doth seem that I have been invited to meet His Imperial Majesty.'

'It'd *better* say that, your Grace,' father grunted, 'because that's the way I dictated it. The meeting is to take place in Tol Vordue in about three days, and the emperor asked me to impress upon you the vital necessity for absolute secrecy in this matter. There are unfriendly eyes – and ears as well – knocking about both here in Mimbre and down there in Tolnedra as well. I think we'll all want to keep this entire affair tightly under wraps.'

'A wise precaution, Ancient One,' Corrolin agreed, 'but how am I to explain this sudden journey into Tolnedra?'

'I've taken the liberty of making some arrangements, your Grace,' father told him, reaching over to pick up the monk's robe. 'I'll wear this and act sort of holy. You're right on the verge of embarking on a war. Now, war's a serious business, and no truly devout man undertakes one without a bit of divine guidance. That's why you sent for me, wasn't it?'

Corrolin blinked. 'Forgive me, Holy One, but I have no recollection of summoning thee.'

'It must have slipped your mind. Anyway, I'm to escort you downriver to that monastery on the coast so that you can consult with the abbot there. That sort of smells religious, wouldn't you say? On the way, we'll take a little side trip to Tol Vordue so that you can meet with Ran Vordue. Then we'll go on to the monastery. You can have your spiritual consultation with the abbot, and then we'll come home.' He squinted at the elaborately-garbed duke. 'Put on something suitably devout, my Lord. When we go back into the throne room, pray a lot and let me do most of the talking. I'll make a big issue of the fact that any kind of escort would be an act of impiety and that Chaldan might be offended.'

'I had not heard of such restrictions,' Corrolin confessed.

'I'd be surprised if you had, your Grace, since I made them up just now. Baron Mandorin and his niece will go on ahead of us, you and I will leave Vo Mimbre alone, and we'll all join up again some miles on down the road. Mandorin and Polina have some information that might help you and Ran Vordue in your deliberations at Tol Vordue.'

Since all Arends just adore intrigue, Corrolin fell in with our scheme immediately, and just as immediately developed that furtive, conspiratorial air that half the population of Arendia habitually wears. Mandorin and I left the pair of them polishing the edges of their scheme and went back to the stables for our horses.

Our two pilgrims, actually singing hymns as they rode along, joined us about five miles out from Vo Mimbre, and we all rode on down the river road toward the coast.

We were followed, of course, but that was to be expected. Father took care of it, though, so it didn't give us any serious problems.

We camped out that night, and rode on through the next day and well into the evening. My father's not one to leave things to chance, so he'd hidden a boat in the bushes about a mile upriver from the monastery. We picketed our horses and pushed our boat out into the stream.

We reached the far shore about midnight and walked on along the dark, deserted road toward the city of Tol Vordue rising behind the impressive east gate. We were met there by a platoon of legionnaires and immediately escorted through the deserted streets to the ancestral house of the Vordue family. The emperor was waiting for us in the courtyard. He was of middle years and tall for a Tolnedran. He also, I noted, had a distinctly military bearing. 'All went well, I gather?' he asked my father.

Father shrugged. 'No problems,' he said.

'Good. I've had a place for our meeting prepared. I can guarantee that nobody's going to get close enough to that room to hear our discussions.' He looked at Corrolin and Mandorin. 'Which of these gentlemen is Duke Corrolin?' he asked.

Father introduced our two Mimbrates, but deliberately glossed over my presence. Then we all trooped inside and climbed an interminable flight of marble stairs to a room at the very top of a tower. It was a stark, business-like sort of room with a conference table in the center and maps littering its walls.

'I'll be brief, your Grace,' the emperor said to Corrolin after we'd seated ourselves at the table. 'I'm a plain man with no great skill at diplomatic language. Ancient Belgarath here advises me that you've been approached by a man going by the name Kador who's told you that he speaks for me. He's lying to you. I've never even heard of the man, and it's entirely possible that he's not even Tolnedran.'

Corrolin gaped at him in stunned surprise. 'But there are legions encamped almost within view of Vo Mimbre!' he protested.

'You'd better tell him, Pol,' father suggested.

'Forgive me, Ancient One,' Corrolin floundered, 'but how would Lady Polina have information concerning Tolnedran legions?'

'Is there any need to keep playing this game, Pol?' father asked me.

'No,' I replied, 'I suppose not.'

'Good. Let's clear the air, then. Duke Corrolin, I have the honor to present my daughter Polgara.'

Corrolin's quick glance at Mandorin was slightly accusatory.

'Baron Mandorin did not lie to you, your Grace,' I jumped to my friend's defense. 'By church law, he *is*, in fact, my uncle. He adopted me in front of a priest of Chaldan before we came to Vo Mimbre. I needed a disguise, so I forced him to do it. It was necessary, so let's not make an issue of it.' Then I paused. 'I'll put this in very blunt terms, your Grace. There are *not*, in fact, any legions stationed across the river from Vo Mimbre. I went down there and had a look for myself. Count Oldon, who appears to be in Kador's pocket, has decked out some of his workmen in legion uniforms just for show.'

'She's telling you the truth, your Grace,' Ran Vordue assured him. 'I have *not* offered an alliance with any faction in Arendia, and I most definitely haven't stationed any of my legions on your southern frontier. This Kador has duped you.' Then the emperor looked at me appraisingly. 'Ancient Belgarath strongly hinted that his daughter here has been running around Arendia putting out fires for the past several weeks now. Maybe we can prevail upon her to give us some details.'

And so I recounted the stories of what had happened in Vo Wacune and Vo Astur for them and revealed what I'd picked up so far in Vo Mimbre. 'It's all been a hoax, gentlemen,' I concluded. 'Ctuchik's been trying to foment a war between Arendia and Tolnedra, hoping that His Imperial Majesty would annex Arendia – which would bring the Alorns into the picture. That's what Ctuchik *really* wants – a war between the Empire and the Alorns. Arendia would have been no more than a pawn in the larger game.'

'I shall obliterate the villain Kador!' Corrolin burst out.

'I'd really rather you didn't, old boy,' Ran Vordue told him. 'Deport him back to Tolnedra instead – along with all his underlings. Let *me* deal with them.' He smiled faintly. 'My birthday's not far off,' he said. 'Why don't you give the lot of them to me as a present?'

'It shall be my excruciating pleasure to do as thou hast requested, your Imperial Majesty,' Corrolin agreed. 'I shall devote mine own attentions to such Mimbrate knights as have fallen in with this Murgo plot. They shall feel my displeasure most keenly.'

'Stout fellow,' Ran Vordue murmured. Then he looked at me. 'How did you find out about all this, Lady Polgara? My sources tell me that you've been ensconced in the Vale for the past several centuries.'

'Our Master brought it to my attention, your Majesty. Evidently he feels that I should spend some more time in the field of practical politics to broaden my horizons.'

'That brings up an interesting point,' father said, looking directly at me. 'The Master put this in *your* hands, Pol, so you're the one who's running things this time. What do we do now?'

'I'll get you for that, father,' I threatened him.

'You mean you'll *try*. Why don't you throw something on the table? Then the rest of us can take it apart and tell you why it won't work.'

'Well,' I said, 'let me see.' I fished around for something logical. 'If we look at it in a certain way, Ctuchik's done us a favor here. There's been a certain ecumenicism in his plotting. He duped all three dukes with exactly the same ploy, offering each one an alliance with Ran Vordue. Since Asturia, Wacune, and Mimbre were all deceived in the same way, couldn't we build on that shared experience? Why don't we just skip the war this time and go directly to the peace-conference? I've got a certain influence with Kathandrion and Mangaran. If Duke Corrolin invites them to a conference at – oh, let's say the Arendish Fair – I think I'll be able to persuade them to attend.'

'She makes sense, Belgarath,' Ran Vordue sided with me. 'Have you got any idea of how much it's costing me to keep fifteen legions in the garrison here in Tol Vordue, just in case the hostilities in Arendia happen to spill over into Tolnedra? I can find better uses for those troops, *and* for the money I'm wasting on them.'

'I, too, find merit in Lady Polgara's proposal,' Mandorin agreed. 'Endless war doth in time grow tiring. Mayhap, for the sake of novelty, we might try endless peace for a few months.'

'Cynic,' my father accused him. Then he stood up. 'Why don't we just let my daughter bully all concerned to the peace table at the Great Fair?' he proposed.

'Bully?' I protested.

'Isn't that what you're going to do?'

252

'If I have to, yes, but that's such an ugly word. Couldn't we call it something a little nicer?'

'Which word would you prefer?'

'I'm not sure. I'll work on it and let you know what I decide.'

'I hope you'll forgive me if I don't hold my breath.'

Father rowed us back across the estuary at the mouth of the River Arend shortly before dawn. I've noticed any number of times that he'll do things like that when he decides that he's the best one available for what would otherwise be a menial task. Both Mandorin and Corrolin were knights, far more at home on horseback than at the oars of a small boat. My father's not one to take chances. I could probably have done it at least as well as he did, but he evidently didn't think of that – and I certainly wasn't going to suggest it.

Dawn was in full flower when we beached our boat, re-saddled our horses, and rode on to the monastery. Corrolin dutifully conferred with the abbot for about a quarter of an hour – although I couldn't for the life of me understand what they might have talked about. Corrolin was *not* going to war. Maybe that was it. Maybe he was asking the abbot to convey his apologies to Chaldan for not slaughtering his neighbors. When he came out of the monastery, we took the high road that led back to Vo Mimbre. We stopped after a mile or so, though, and I cooked breakfast for us over a roadside campfire – quite a good breakfast, as I recall. My friends all ate too much, naturally, and father, now that he had a full stomach, decided that a little rest might be in order. 'We *did* stay up all night,' he reminded us. 'I can sleep in my saddle, if I really have to, but somebody's going to have to stay alert enough to steer the horses. Why don't we catch some sleep and then move on?'

We rode back a ways from the road under the leafy green canopy of the trees, unrolled our blankets, and committed ourselves to sleep. I was just on the verge of dozing off when mother's voice murmured in my drowsy brain. *'Very nicely done, Polgara,'* she complimented me.

'I rather thought so myself,' I agreed modestly.

'You sound tired.'

'I am, rather.'

'Why don't you sleep then?'

And I did, dropping off right between one thought and the next.

We all awoke about mid-afternoon and rode on to a rather shabby little inn, where we spent the night. We arose early the following morning, and we then rode straight on to Vo Mimbre.

Duke Corrolin had been mightily provoked by what his meeting with Ran Vordue had revealed, and he moved quickly, issuing orders, but no explanations. Then he invited the entire court into the throne-room where armored knights stood guard along the walls. To everyone's surprise – even mine – the duke entered the throne-room in full armor and carrying a huge two-handed broadsword. He did *not* sit down on his throne. 'My Lords and Ladies,' he began, speaking with unusual crispness for a Mimbrate Arend. 'I have but recently returned from Tol Vordue, where the emperor of Tolnedra and I did confer at some length. The outcome of that conference was a happy one. Rejoice, my loyal subjects. There will be no war.'

That got a mixed reaction, Arends being what they are and all.

Corrolin, his face bleak, smashed his mailed fist down on the back of his throne. 'Be not dismayed, my Lords and Ladies,' he boomed. 'There will be other entertainments. An extensive conspiracy hath of late befouled the air – not only here in Mimbre, but in Asturia and Wacune as well. It is my firm intention to cleanse the air here. Seize them!' This last command was issued to Mandorin and the two-score knights under his command, and Mandorin was quick to carry it out – so quick in fact that there were hardly any casualties. A dozen or so Tolnedrans, both genuine and spurious, were clapped in irons, and several Mimbrate nobles were treated in the same way.

The Grolim who'd been posing as a servant in Kador's entourage ducked under the arm of the knight who was in the middle of enfolding him in a steely embrace and darted for the door, gathering his Will as he ran. My father, however, was ready for him. Still garbed in that burlap monk's robe, the Old Wolf delivered a crashing blow to the side of the Grolim's head with his fist, and the priest of the Dragon-God fell senseless to the floor. Father, I noticed, had judiciously enveloped his right fist in lead, and his blow would have felled an ox. 'Holy Belgarath' has a colorful background, and I've noticed over the years that he'll resort to the tactics of tavern brawling almost as quickly as he'll fall back on sorcery.

The prisoners were all dragged from the room, and then Duke Corrolin described in somewhat tedious detail the Murgo plot which had come to within inches of succeeding. Then, while all the court was still in shock, he told them of the peace-conference that was already in the works. *That* caused a certain amount of grumbling, but the Duke of Mimbre ran roughshod over the protests. When you put an Arend in full armor, you can't really expect a velvet touch.

I decided to let father take the credit for my little counter-coup in Vo Mimbre. I'm more interested in results than I am in credit, but my father absolutely adores being the center of attention, so I let him bask – or wallow – in public adulation while I went on back to the northern duchies to hammer down the loose ends of my peace-conference.

Duke Kathandrion of Wacune and Earl Mangaran of Asturia had already met a few times, and Countess Asrana, her wicked eyes sparkling, assured me that they seemed to be getting along fairly well. 'They're as thick as thieves, Polly,' she said with a little smirk. 'That Kathandrion's absolutely gorgeous, isn't he?'

'Never mind, Asrana,' I told her. 'Try to keep your predatory instincts under control. What condition's Oldoran in?'

'I don't know about his liver, but his mind's definitely gone. He's seeing things that aren't really there, and he's raving most of the time. His family's very upset about that. He's got some nephews that were eyeing his throne with a great deal of interest, but I don't think the title's going to stay in the family. Mangaran's been demonstrating his capabilities at every turn, and I don't think any of Oldoran's nephews are really qualified to replace him. When are we going to convene the peace-conference?'

'Which peace-conference was that, dear?'

'The one you've been working on ever since you came to Arendia. Don't be coy, Polly. I know what you're up to – and I approve of it. Wars are all very stirring for the men, I suppose, but the lives of the ladies here and in Vo Wacune and Vo Mimbre are very tedious when all the pretty young men are out playing in the woods. Now then, what can I do to help?'

Our impromptu peace-conference was to be held, as I'd suggested, at the Great Arendish Fair, which is technically in Mimbrate territory. This automatically made Corrolin the host. To be quite honest about it, I'd have been happier with Kathandrion at the head of the table, but you can't always have things the way you'd like them. I'd have Baron Mandorin sitting at Corrolin's elbow anyway, and I was sure he could keep his duke from making *too* many mistakes. I left Vo Astur and went on across the border into Wacune. I wanted to talk with Kathandrion before our conference convened.

'We're going to have to be careful, my Lord,' I told my Wacite friend when I finally got him alone. 'There are hot-heads in all three duchies, and a chance remark at the wrong time could make this all fly apart on us without any warning. I'll be talking to the assembled notables from time to time, and I'm going to keep hammering on the fact that as long as any one of the Arendish dukes has regal ambitions, Arendia's going to be vulnerable to Murgo plotting. There might be an undisputed crown of all Arendia some day, but not right now. I think that the best we can hope for at this particular time is an agreement between you, Mangaran, and Corrolin that there *isn't* an Arendish crown, and there's no point to killing half the population in order to cram a fiction on somebody's head.'

'It seemeth me that some unspoken rebuke doth hover over that last remark, my Lady,' my handsome friend noted.

'Look upon it as a cautionary word, your Grace. I shall not rebuke thee until thine opinion of thyself doth grow *too* exalted. Look with profound distrust upon any man who pretends to offer thee a pathway to a non-existent crown. Now, then, I don't think that lasting peace is going to grow out of one meeting, so I'm going to suggest that we follow an Alorn example here in Arendia. The Alorn kings meet periodically on the Isle of the Winds for discussions of matters of mutual concern. I think we might want to give *that* notion some consideration here as well. If the three Arendish dukes meet every summer, they'll be able to deal with any frictions that might have arisen during the past year. Let's not give any imagined insults time to fester.'

'I shall strive to mine utmost to make this come to pass, my Lady.'

Then I flew on back to Vo Astur to wheedle a similar agreement out of Mangaran and Asrana. In point of fact, I spent several months on the wing in the skies over Arendia. It's not a bad idea when you're dealing with Arends to get agreements on everything *before* you gather them around the conference table. I kept my agenda simple for this first little get-together, limiting our discussions to two or three crucial points. If I could make this gathering an annual event, there'd be plenty of time at later meetings to expand peaceful contacts.

It was mid-autumn by the time we all gathered in the garishly striped royal pavilion Corrolin had ordered to be set up on the outskirts of the fair, and each ruler rose in turn to address an assembly comprised of assorted state functionaries *and* by observers from Tolnedra and from the Alorn kingdoms. Corrolin, as host, spoke first. He formally greeted the other two rulers and the emissaries from foreign lands, noting in passing that Salmissra had declined the opportunity to send an observer. He then spent about a half-hour saying nice things about me. I found *that* part of his speech fairly interesting.

After Corrolin had exhausted *his* vocabulary, Kathandrion rose and *also* waxed extravagant in his praise of me. I liked that speech too. Then Mangaran stood up and demonstrated the fact that the Asturians had not totally forgotten how to thee, thou, and what-not.

256

The shrewd old earl concluded his remarks with a little surprise, however. 'Nobles all,' he said with a faint smile. 'This gathering here on the plain of our mournful Arendia hath as its ultimate goal a lasting peace. For many, this will seem unnatural, and for others, perhaps even impious. Peace is an alien concept in Arendia, and the fact that our meeting hath lasted for quite nearly an entire afternoon with not a single drop of blood spilled may cause outrage in some quarters. Since we are flying into the very teeth of convention, let us further shock that stuffy old grand dame with yet another violation of her conception of how things ought to be done. Ladies, as all the world doth know, are creatures of delight, more beauteous, more genteel, more tender than are we, and it is the sworn duty of every right-thinking nobleman in all the world to protect and serve them. It is also known, however, that their minds are not the equal of ours. Our fulsome and most deservéd praise of Lady Polgara this day hath encouraged me to investigate a shocking possibility. Could it be that great Chaldan *hath*, in fact, given women brains? Is this possible? Then, emboldened by the fact that a divine thunderbolt had not as yet incinerated me, I pushed this heretical concept even further out into unexplored territory. It is well known, I think, that Duke Oldoran hath recently been removed from his throne and ensconced in a monastery to rave and scream out the remainder of his life. It is *also* widely bruited about that *I* was responsible for his removal. I will openly confess that this is true, but it would not have happened had it not been for the assistance of two – not one, but two – ladies. The one, of course, was Lady Polgara. I'm sure that surprises no one here. What is *not* so widely known, however, is the fact that a high-born lady in Vo Astur was *also* involved – all the way up to her pretty eyebrows. Moreover, she has advised me in most matters since I seized control of the government of the duchy of Asturia. The need for total openness at this conference impels me to reveal this and to introduce the lady who rules at my side. Nobles all, may I present the Countess Asrana, a conspiratoress without peer.'

There was some faint applause, which gradually grew less faint, swelling finally into an ovation.

'I'll get you for this, Mangaran,' Asrana said, rising to her feet.

'Promise?' he asked slyly.

Asrana struck a tragic pose. 'And now is my dreadful secret revealéd,' she declared. 'How can anyone possibly forgive me? Truly, gentlemen, it was not my fault. Polgara made me do it. It's all *her* fault.' She sighed a long, quivering theatrical sigh. 'I am exposéd now, so I guess we might as well get on with this. This unnatural gathering has been convened to explore the possibility of peace. – Isn't that *awful*? How can we live without enemies? We *have* to hate someone!' She paused, then snapped her fingers. 'I have it, my Lords! I have the solution! Let's hate Murgos instead of each other! Murgos are hideous, and Arends are the most beautiful people in the world. Murgos are dishonorable, and Arends are all nauseatingly saturated with honor. Murgos are unmannerly, and Arendish courtesy is the despair of the known world. Let us join hands, nobles all, and pledge upon our sacred honor to hate the eyebrows off every Murgo we meet.'

They were all laughing by now, and pounding on the table with delight. The Countess Asrana had neatly rolled them all up into a little ball and put them in her pocket.

'I do confess that I *like* this charming young lady, your Grace!' I heard Mandorin say to his duke. 'She is utterly delightful.'

I just happened to be watching Asrana's face when he said that about her, and her look became just a trifle smug. Then, without so much as changing expression, she winked at me. She'd obviously overheard Mandorin's remark, and it was also obvious that she felt that she'd just won something.

There was a banquet that evening, and Baron Mandorin managed to find a seat next to Asrana's where she promptly did war upon him. Her cavalry charges were outrageously winsome remarks and observations. Her siege engine of choice was a low-cut gown that went just a bit beyond the bounds of propriety. Baron Mandorin didn't *quite* sue for peace that evening, but he came very close.

The Countess shared my quarters, and I waited up for her. 'Why Mandorin?' I asked her bluntly when she came in.

'I didn't quite follow that, Polly.'

'Why are you setting your cap for Baron Mandorin? There are others here who are prettier, and he's quite a bit older than you are.'

'So much the better,' she replied, letting her hair down and shaking it out. 'With Mandorin, I won't have to endure all those calf-eyed looks and the reams of misspelled bad poetry. Mandorin's very close to the center of power in Mimbre, and I've got a similar position in Asturia. You'll be managing things in Wacune, so among the three of us, we ought to be able to keep everybody in line – long enough for peace to become a habit, at least.' Then she gave me a wicked sidelong glance. 'I hate to say it, Polly, but I'm going to have more fun than you are.'

'Are you doing this out of patriotism, Asrana?' I asked incredulously.

'You can call it that if you wish, but down at the bottom, power excites me – and the three of us are going to have almost all the power there is in poor old Arendia. You can't ask for much more than that.'

'What about love, Asrana?'

She shrugged. 'What about it? Love's for children, Polgara. It's a plaything I've outgrown. I *like* Mandorin. He's handsome and unspeakably noble. The years will erode his handsomeness, and *I'll* erode his nobility. We'll do some fairly unpopular things, I'm afraid, but Arendia's going to be better for it. If that makes me a patriot, so be it. Watch me very closely, Polly. I might even be able to teach *you* some tricks.'

By mid-morning of the next day, even the densest Arend in Duke Corrolin's pavilion was aware of the fact that something was 'going on' between our unscrupulous countess and Baron Mandorin, and I think that was *also* included in Asrana's plan. I don't think that even Ce'Nedra could ever be as duplicitous as Asrana was. By the end of that day, poor Baron Mandorin was completely in her thrall. He watched her every move and hung on her every word – since Asrana spoke frequently at our deliberations. Here was a young lady who could play two games at the same time – and both of them very well.

On the fourth day, the leaders of Mimbre, Asturia, and Wacune signed the 'instrument of peace', and immediately thereafter Duke Corrolin rose and invited everybody to stay for the wedding. Countess Asrana could move *very* fast when it suited her.

Once again I found myself pressed into service as a bridesmaid, and all went smoothly. Asrana and Mandorin were married with not so much as an earthquake or tidal wave to alert poor Arendia to a dangerous new force that had come into being right at her very heart.

PART FOUR

Ontrose

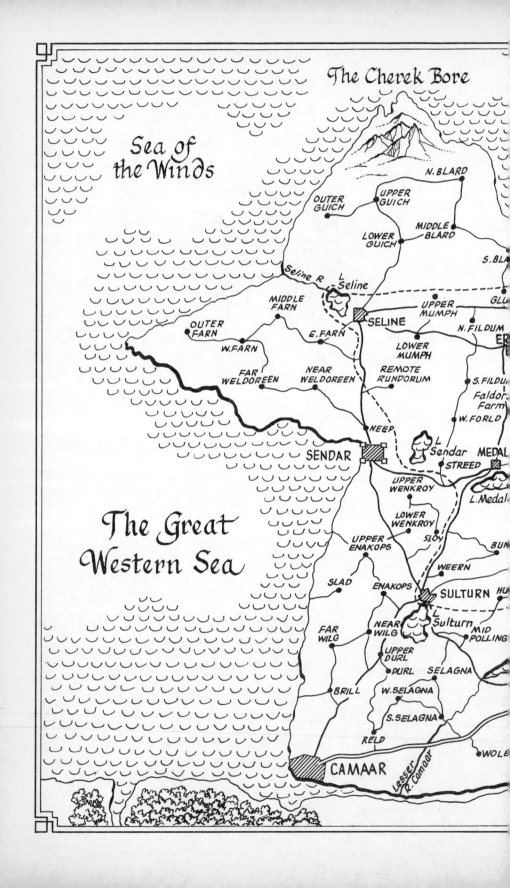

Gulf of
Cherek

ARD

DARINE

RAT
Erat

UPPER
GRALT

R. Gralt

WURG in the
MOUNTAINS

OLD

LOWER
GRALT

Darine River

DE

The Great North Road

NETHER
WLDE

OLEA

MUROS

Greater River Camaar

The
Duchy of
ERAT

CHAPTER 17

I hate to admit this, but when you get right down to the core of things, my father and I are very much alike. We both know that our primary business will always be study and the slow accumulation of knowledge. Interruptions crop up from time to time, though, and we'll both assume surly expressions when someone comes rushing into the Vale begging us to go out and save the world. Would you be at all surprised if I told you that our apparent grouchiness is only a sham? To be completely honest about it, we enjoy putting out these little brush-fires almost as much as we'd enjoy discovering just exactly why two and two makes four.

When I'd spent those years on the Isle of the Winds, I'd been at the very center of things, and I'd found that to be engrossing. Then, when I'd been called away again to deal with Ctuchik's scheme in Arendia, I'd enjoyed that just as much. Like my father, I'll always be happy to lay my book aside when the fire-bell rings.

Given the tentative nature of the peace father and I had crammed down the throats of assorted Arends, it was fairly obvious that I was going to have to stay in Arendia to make sure that it stayed crammed. And so it was that in the spring of the year 2313 I returned briefly to father's tower to pick up a few things I might need. I suppose I could have just willed what I needed into existence, but they wouldn't have been the same, for some reason.

Father had returned to the Vale during the previous winter, and when I reached his tower, he called the twins over, and the four of us got down to cases. 'I'd rather hoped to see uncle Beldin,' I said.

'He's still off in Mallorea, Pol,' Belkira said. 'What's happening in Arendia?'

'What's *always* happening in Arendia?' Beltira snorted.

'Pol took steps,' father told them. 'There's this unnatural silence hovering over Arendia right now. I think it's referred to as peace.'

'I don't know that I'd go quite *that* far, father,' I disagreed, getting up to check the ham I was baking for supper. 'Ctuchik had things fairly well stirred up, and the Arends were having a lot of fun with his little fires. Now that we've doused them with cold water, the Arends are at a loss for excuses to slaughter each other. I wouldn't really call it peace yet, though. They're sitting around waiting for somebody to come up with new reasons to go to war.'

'I'm sure they'll find something,' he said sourly.

'That's why I'm going back,' I told them. 'I want to make it very obvious to the Arends that if they don't behave themselves, I'll spank them.'

'They aren't actually children, Pol,' Belkira objected.

'Oh, *really*? You haven't been there lately, uncle. Arends are a very charming people, but a lot of that charm lies in the fact that they've never grown up.'

'Are you going to settle in one place, Pol?' Beltira asked, 'or were you planning to be a traveling fire-brigade?'

'I've had invitations from all three of the rulers in Arendia, uncle, but I think I'll set up operations in Vo Wacune. It's far more attractive than Vo Astur or Vo Mimbre, and Duke Kathandrion shows a few flickers of intelligence. At least he can see beyond his own borders. I don't think Mangaran or Corrolin can yet. I'll probably have to rush about quite a bit until peace gets to be a habit, but it's always nice to have a place to call home.' Then I thought of something the twins ought to know about. 'Ctuchik's come up with a way to disguise his agents,' I told them. 'There's a quasi-religious order headquartered in the Great Desert of Araga off to the southeast of Nyissa. They're called the Dagashi, and they're half-breed Murgos. Their mothers – and probably grandmothers as well – are slave women from other races. The Dagashi are bred down to the point that they don't have Angarak features, and they're trained as spies and assassins. Don't automatically assume that just because some-body doesn't *look* like an Angarak, it means that he isn't one.'

'That could be fairly troublesome,' Beltira said, frowning.

'It already has been several times,' I said. 'I thought we all ought to know about that. Oh, there's something else as well. Evidently the Murgos have discovered gold in their mountains. They're very free with their bribes now. I think there are iron deposits near their mines, because Murgo gold always has a reddish tinge to it. That might help us to identify somebody who's been bribed.' I leaned

266

back in my chair. 'Ctuchik's getting very much involved in things here in the west,' I mused. 'That *might* just mean that Torak's getting ready to come out of seclusion at Ashaba, or it might mean something else. I'll try to keep a lid on things in Arendia, but you gentlemen are going to have to stand watch over the other kingdoms.'

'Thanks,' father said sourly.

'Don't mention it.' I smiled sweetly at him.

Then the following morning, I packed up the things I wanted and left for Vo Wacune.

It was late spring or early summer of that year when I returned to the fairy-tale city in the Arendish forest. Kathandrion insisted that I live in the palace, and now that I had some leisure, I was able to take a bit of time to get to know a wider circle of people in the Wacite court. Kathandrion's wife was named Elisera, and she was an ethereal lady with reddish blonde hair who spent most of her time reading interminably long Arendish epics and overwrought love poetry. Her reading habits may have distorted her view of reality just a bit. She took me around to the various lords and ladies of the court, and even in the face of my protests, she insisted on introducing me as 'Polgara the Sorceress'. Despite her shortcomings, I liked her. I also liked Crown Prince Alleran, her son. Alleran was a sturdy little boy of about ten who had a very unArendish streak of good sense in him. Unfortunately, his parents were doing their very best to educate that trait out of him before he reached maturity.

I hadn't really wanted to take up residence in the ducal palace, but Kathandrion wouldn't hear of my lodging anywhere else, and so I had to put up with certain inconveniences which were made all the worse by Elisera's quaint introductions that stressed something I'd rather she'd glossed over. There's a great deal of nonsense abroad that concerns words like 'magic', 'sorcery', 'witchcraft', and the like, and most people simply lump all those designations together and assume that those of us who are talented in the field can perform any feat that's grown out of the fevered imaginations of various poets bent on outdoing the competition. All the young – and not so young – ladies-in-waiting at Kathandrion's court were fascinated by the idea of love potions, as I recall. No matter how patiently I explained the impossibility of such a concoction, I was still approached by teary-eyed hopefuls who were absolutely positive that there was a simple chemical answer to their most pressing problem. Most of them seemed very unhappy with my answer, but I'd no sooner sent one supplicant away with a pout on her face when another approached me, usually in private, with the teary assertion that she'd absolutely *die* if Baron so-and-so didn't immediately fall madly in love with her.

There was another problem as well, although I rather doubt that Ce'Nedra would see it as a problem. Duke Kathandrion casually advised me that he, Mangaran, and Corrolin had agreed that I should receive an annual stipend 'for services rendered', and they each dutifully set aside an absurd amount of gold for my use. No matter how much I protested that I didn't *need* money, I couldn't seem to get my point across. I thought that I might raise the issue when we all gathered for our annual meeting that summer at the Great Arendish Fair, but when I got there and talked with Asrana, the Baroness of Vo Mandor, she pointed a few things out to me. 'Just take the money, Polly,' she advised. 'You'll hurt their feelings if you don't, and what's more important, you'll lower your status if you start giving your services away free. If they don't pay for those services, they won't value them. In time, they'll start treating you as if you were a servant, and I don't think you'd like that. Smile and take the money.'

'What am I going to do with it?' I demanded. 'They're giving me far too much, and all it's going to do is pile up until it starts to become a nuisance.'

'Buy something with it – an estate somewhere, or a house in town.'

Now there was an idea that hadn't even occurred to me. At least if I had my own house, I could get away from the weepy-eyed girls seeking love potions to entrap vacant-eyed young men who hadn't yet realized that boys and girls are different from each other. The more I thought about it, the more I liked the idea, and so I broached the subject to Kathandrion as we rode on back to Vo Wacune after the meeting.

'Art thou discontented with the lodgings I have provided thee, my Lady?' he asked, sounding a bit hurt.

'The quarters, I do assure thee, my Lord, are exquisite. It is their location which doth stand at the core of my dissatisfaction. So long as I am within the confines of thy palace, I am at the mercy of those who yearn to achieve certain goals without exerting themselves.' I told him about that steady procession of young ladies who hungered and thirsted for unearned love and about others, no less parched and starved, who longed for mystic assistance in business dealings, intercession with the dice-cup, interference in the outcome of jousting matches, and other absurdities.

'I shall forbid them entry into the wing of my palace wherein thou art housed,' he suggested.

'Kathandrion,' I said to him patiently, 'you can forbid to your heart's content, and all they'll do is ignore you. We're dealing with obsessions here. These people all believe that they *deserve* the things they're yearning for and that I've been commanded by the Gods to come to Vo Wacune for no other reason than to arrange matters so that they get them. Nothing short of physical violence will keep them away from my door as long as I'm in the palace. That's why I'm going to need a house of my own – with a fence and a locked gate. It's the only way I'll get any sleep. I'm sure there are houses for sale in Vo Wacune. Could I prevail upon you to ask around for me and see if you can find something suitable? Don't evict anybody or anything like that, but find me a place where I can hide. If I hear any more about love potions, I think I'll scream.'

'I had not realized that the nobles at court had been so cruelly imposing upon thee, my Lady Polgara. I shall let it be known discreetly that thou art in search of a more permanent habitation.'

'I'd appreciate that, my Lord.'

'Would it really work?' he asked curiously, slipping out of 'high style'.

'Which was that, my Lord?'

'A love potion. Can you actually mix something up that would make somebody fall in love?'

'Oh, dear,' I sighed. 'Not you, too. No, Kathandrion. There's absolutely nothing that'd have that effect. There are some herbs out of Nyissa that'll arouse lust, but nothing in all the world that'll awaken love. I know that love potions play a large part in Arendish epics, but in real life, there's no such thing. It's a literary device and nothing more.'

'Ah,' he sighed. 'How painful it is to have one's illusions shattered.'

'I think that one missed me,' I confessed.

'My favorite epic tragedy doth hinge upon this literary convention thou hast described. I fear me that I will never again be able to read its stately lines with any degree of satisfaction. I will sorely lament its loss.'

'It looks as if I've got further to go than I thought,' I half-muttered.

'What sayest thou, my Lady?'

'Nothing, Kathandrion.' I laughed and laid a fond hand on his wrist.

The house I ultimately purchased was not far from the palace. It was quite large, but very reasonably priced – largely because a generation or so of neglect had caused it to fall into such disrepair as to make it almost uninhabitable. I could have taken care of that myself, I suppose, but to do it that way would have merely spread the infection which was driving me out of the palace. My first step in the renovation of my house, therefore, involved the hiring of workmen to patch the roof, shore up the foundations, replace the broken glass, chase out the birds and squirrels who'd taken up residence inside, and to dismantle the brewery an enterprising tavern-owner had set up in the basement without bothering to take out a lease on the premises. I soon discovered that day-laborers in Vo Wacune came in three grades: bad, worse, and awful.

I stopped by one morning to see how things were progressing, and I found that they weren't. My workmen were nowhere in sight, and nothing had been done since my last visit. There were still holes in the roof you could throw a cat through, none of the rotting floor-boards had been replaced, and not even one pane of glass had been set into the window-frames. I stalked through the echoing ruin testing the outer limits of uncle Beldin's vocabulary.

''Tis a rare thing t' find a lady so gifted with th' language,' someone behind me said in a thick Wacite brogue.

I spun around and saw a sturdy fellow with his face framed by a fringe of red beard leaning against my doorframe casually paring his fingernails with an evil-looking dirk. 'Who are you?' I demanded, 'and what are you doing here?'

'Th' name's Killane, Lady-O, an' yer unspeakable eloquence has drawn me here as bees are drawn t' honey, don't y' know. What seems t' be th' problem?'

'*This* is the problem!' I burst out, waving my arms at the shambles around me. 'Last week I hired some men to clean up this mess. They took my money quickly enough, but they seem to have forgotten where the house is.'

'Y' paid them in *advance*?' he asked incredulously. 'Wherever were yer brains, Lady-O? Y' *never* want t' do that. Th' pay comes *after* th' work's done, not before.'

'I didn't know that,' I confessed.

'Oh, dearie, dearie me!' he sighed. ''Tis a poor lost lamb y' are, darlin' girl. Did y' happen to'git th' names of these lazy boy-os?'

'I think the one who did all the talking was named Skelt,' I replied in a half-ashamed voice. How *could* I have been so gullible?

'Ah, *that* one,' Killane said. 'He's *almost* as dependable as th' spring weather. I'll run him down fer y', Lady-O. There's little hope that he or his lazy relatives have any of yer money left, but I'll make 'em come back here an' work off what they owe.'

'Why?' I swung immediately from extreme gullibility to extreme suspicion.

'Because y' need a keeper, lass,' he told me bluntly. 'Now, this is th' way we're goin' to' do it. I'll round up Skelt an' his worthless crew, an' I'll beat th' work they owe y' out of 'em. If, after a week, things ain't t' yer satisfaction, we kin part friends, an' no regrets. But if y' like me way o' doin' things, we kin discuss somethin' more permanent.'

I probably should have been offended by the way he just walked into my life and took charge, but I wasn't. Quite obviously, he was right. In this particular sphere of human activity, I was indeed a 'poor lost lamb'. We talked for a bit longer, and Killane modestly confessed to being 'th' best builder in all Arendia, don't y' know'. Then we went through the house and I told him what I wanted. He agreed with most of my ideas, and pointed out the flaws in the notions with which he disagreed. Then, once our survey had been completed, he passed judgement. He rather fondly patted one of the walls. 'She's still a sound old dear, though she's been sorely neglected. We kin have her back in shape in jig time.' Then he looked at me rather sternly. 'Let me tell y' right at th' outset, Lady-O, I'll not be after cuttin' no corners, so this is goin' t' bite yer purse a wee bit. But y'll be after livin' here fer a long time, an' I'll not be puttin' meself t' shame by havin' th' old dear fallin' down about yer ears a few years hence. Y'll be havin' notions that just won't work, an' I'll be after tellin' y' right t' yer face that yer bein' silly. Yer a spirited lady, I've noticed, so we'll scream at each other from time t' time, but when it's all done, y'll have a house y' kin be proud t' live in.'

'That's all I really want, Killane,' I told him.

'Then it's settled. Y' kin go back t' yer embroidery now, Lady-O. Just leave th' old dear t' me. I'll fix her.'

I've known very few men who've had such straightforward honesty, and I liked Killane right from the outset. As a matter of fact, I was so impressed by him that I ultimately married a man who could have been his brother.

I stopped by my house a few times while it was being renovated. Skelt and his assorted cousins, brothers, and what-not were a sullen group now, but most of the cuts and bruises had healed. Killane drove them unmercifully, and the work was progressing, though

271

far too slowly to suit me. I *really* wanted to get out of that palace. It was more to get away – and to avoid nagging Killane – that I rode on down to Vo Mandor that autumn to pay a call on Asrana and Mandorin. That odd marriage seemed to be working far better than any of us could possibly have had reason to believe that it might. Mandorin was absolutely enthralled by the mischievous Asrana, and his expression of vapid adoration had the peculiar effect of curbing some of her more outrageous pranks. Their marital bliss, however, failed to dull their political acumen, and they were generally successful in keeping the Mimbrates and Asturians from each other's throats.

It began to get a bit cloying after a while, so I went on down to Vo Mimbre to look in on Duke Corrolin. There were Tolnedran merchants in Vo Mimbre, naturally, since Tolnedra lay just across the river, but a bit of careful probing verified the fact that they really *were* Tolnedrans instead of Dagashi. Evidently the nose-bleed I'd given Ctuchik had persuaded him to pull in his horns.

Then, just to avoid any seeming favoritism, I rode on north to visit Mangaran in Vo Astur. There were some problems there, but I saw no evidence that they were of Murgo origin. The removal of Oldoran from the seat of power had mightily offended his family, who for some generations had looked upon all of Asturia as a private estate. For the most part, Oldoran's relatives were incompetents who satisfied their urges toward belligerence by denouncing Mangaran in highly unflattering terms. One nephew, however, a scruffy, uncouth young man named Nerasin, had actually gone beyond denunciation and was busily forming alliances in preparation for the day when the elderly Mangaran should die and the Asturian throne would fall into the hands of whoever was nimble enough to seize it. I had the strong feeling that Nerasin would have to be dealt with eventually, but for right now, Mangaran's grip on power was firm enough to keep the young trouble-maker in line.

I visited with Mangaran for a week or so, and then I went on back to Vo Wacune to see how Killane was coming with the renovations. It was autumn by now, and, though the Arendish forest consisted largely of evergreens, there were enough groves of maple, birch, and aspen to add vivid reds, yellows, and pale oranges to the vast wood, and there was that faintly dusty smell of autumn in the air. I found that to be absolutely lovely, and I didn't really hurry as I rode east. I reached the city of Vo Wacune about mid-afternoon on a lovely autumn day, passed through the ornate city gates, and rode directly to the quiet, tree-lined street where my house stood.

I noted with some satisfaction that Killane and his work-gang had repaired the marble wall which surrounded the house and that the rust-riddled old iron gate had been replaced with a new one, far more imposing and ornate.

One of the attractions of my house was the fairly extensive grounds surrounding it. At one time there had been gardens there, but when I'd bought the property, those gardens had long since been taken over by weeds. I was a bit startled when I rode through the gate. The weeds were gone, and the ancient hedges were are neatly trimmed. Killane himself was over near the side of the house spading up one of the flower-beds. He looked up as I dismounted. 'Well, now, there y' are, lass,' he greeted me. 'I was about t' send out search parties t' find y', don't y' know.'

'Gardening, Killane?' I said. 'You're a man of many talents, aren't you? How's the house coming?'

'She's all finished, Lady-O,' he replied rather proudly, 'an' she came out better than we might have expected. I've been just passin' th' time until yer return by gettin' yer flower-beds in order fer th' plantin' next spring. I took th' liberty o' bringin' in a crew o' cleanin' ladies t' polish things up inside. Would y' be after wantin' t' have a bit of a look-see?'

'I thought you'd never ask.'

'I'm hopin' that what we've done t' th' old girl satisfies y' enough t' smooth over th' jolt yer goin' t' get when I hand over all th' bills. I haggled 'em down as best I was able, but th' total's just a wee bit alarmin'.'

'I think I can manage it, Killane,' I assured him. 'Let's go look at my house.'

The newly renovated house far exceeded all my expectations. The rooms – even in the servants' quarters – were spacious, and the bathrooms were large and well-appointed. The walls, which had looked more than a little scabby, had been freshly plastered. The floors, both wood and marble, gleamed. There was a solid, comfortable quality about it, and the high marble wall surrounding it and the trees and hedges in the garden muffled any noises coming in from the street to give the entire place an air of seclusion and peace.

'It's perfect!' I exclaimed to my Wacite friend.

'Well, I don't know that I'd go *that* far, Lady-O,' Killane replied modestly. 'I did what I could w' th' old dear, but there are some nooks an' crannies that I'd have designed differently, don't y' know.'

I'd more or less decided on something during my travels, but I wasn't certain how to broach the subject to Killane. Finally, I just blurted it out. 'We get along with each other fairly well, don't we, Killane?' I asked him directly.

'Yer a reasonable sort of employer – fer a woman – an' y' seldom ask th' impossible. I kin more or less stand bein' around y'.'

'Don't strain yourself trying to flatter me, Killane.'

He laughed. 'Come t' th' point, Lady-O,' he told me. 'Don't beat around th' bush.'

'How would you like to work for me?' I put it to him.

'I thought I was.'

'I don't mean just fixing up the house. I mean permanently. This is quite a large house. I can take care of it myself, if I have to, but there'll be times when I'll have to be away for extended periods, and I'd rather not have the house fall back into the condition she was in when I first saw her. To get right to the point, I need somebody to manage the place for me. Would you be interested?'

'I'm no servant, Lady-O. Me manners ain't always too polished, don't y' know.'

'You haven't managed to offend *me* yet.'

'Give me some time, Lady-O. We've only hardly just met.'

'Would you consider it?'

'I guess we kin try it fer a year or so, me Lady.'

'Why so formal, Killane?'

'It ain't hardly proper fer me t' be callin' me employer "Lady-O",' he replied.

'I don't mind in the slightest, Killane.' I looked around. Now that all the clutter and debris had been removed, the house was almost alarmingly large. 'We're probably going to need servants, aren't we?' I suggested a bit tentatively.

'That we are, Lady-O,' he said, grinning. 'I ain't exactly th' world's greatest w' a mop or a broom, an' me cookin' leaves worlds to be desired.'

I laughed, fondly laying one hand on his wrist. 'You're the one who'll be in charge of them, Killane, so hire some people you can get along with.'

He bowed with a surprising grace. 'As y' wish, Lady-O. I'll be after bringin' in a wagon first thing in th' mornin'.'

'What for?'

'Did y' plan to' sleep on th' floor? A bit o' furniture might be in order, wouldn't y' say?' Then he pulled a bundle of paper out of his tunic pocket. 'Now, then, shall we git down t' th' unpleasant business o' all these bills?' he suggested.

It took Killane and me a couple of weeks to shop around and buy furniture, drapes, carpeting, and assorted decorations to break up the starkness of those bare white walls. And then the servants – mostly Killane's relatives – began to arrive. Nepotism offends some people, but my own peculiar situation made it seem the most natural thing in the world. It took us all a while to get used to each other, and it took me even longer to get used to being waited upon hand and foot. About the only really serious problem I had was with my cook, one of Killane's numerous cousins, who *really* didn't like the way I frequently invaded her kitchen to either lend a hand or make suggestions. In time we worked that out, and all in all, I was happy and content.

The summer after I'd taken up residence in my house, Duke Kathandrion and I went on down to the Great Fair for the annual meeting of what was coming to be known as 'the Arendish Council'. That name wasn't particularly original, but it was modeled, after all, on the 'Alorn Council' held at Riva, and Arends are fond of traditions – even those that aren't their own. There were some frictions that needed to be smoothed over, but nothing major.

What interested me far more than politics that summer was the fact that Baroness Asrana was with child.

'Is it always this awkward and cumbersome, Polly?' she asked me one evening after the day's business meeting was over.

'Usually,' I replied. 'When are you due?'

'Early this coming winter – about forever and six days.'

'I'll come down to Vo Mandor and lend you a hand.'

'Oh, you don't have to do that, Polly.'

'Yes, as a matter of fact I do. Strange as it may seem, I'm very fond of you, Asrana, and I'm not going to leave you in the hands of strangers.'

'But –'

'Hush, Asrana. It's settled.'

'Yes, ma'am.' It sounded submissive, but I knew Asrana well enough to know that submission and humility were not part of her nature.

After the council meetings were over, Kathandrion and I rode on back to Vo Wacune. 'Somehow this all seems very strange,' Kathandrion mused on the last day of our journey.

'What does?'

'Meeting and sitting down with hereditary enemies.'

'You might as well get used to it, Kathandrion. So long as I'm

275

around – and I'll be around for a long, long time – this annual get-together's going to be a fixture in Arendia. Talking with people is far better than fighting with them.'

'What an unnatural thing to suggest.'

I rolled my eyes upward with a theatrical look of long-suffering resignation. 'Arends,' I sighed.

Kathandrion laughed. 'I just *love* it when you do that, Polgara,' he said. 'It makes everything we do seem so childish.'

'It is, Kathandrion. Believe me, it is.'

The rest of the summer passed without incident, but the autumn was filled with social events. Evidently that's an Arendish custom: 'Rest all summer, and then have parties until the snow flies.'

Killane accompanied me on down to Vo Mandor when I calculated that Asrana's time was approaching. He didn't ask; he didn't suggest; he just did it. 'I'll not be after lettin' y' travel alone, Lady-O,' he told me when I protested. 'Settin aside th' dangers, yer social standin' would suffer were it t' become known that y' can't afford a proper escort, don't y' know.'

I didn't make an issue of it, since I rather enjoyed his company, and I was amused at the way servants frequently bully their employers. Killane took what he believed to be his duties quite seriously.

It was snowing when we reached Vo Mandor, a thick, swirling snow that blotted out everything more than a few yards away with a seething cloud of white. Mandorin greeted me very warmly, and he had that worried expression on his face that seems to mark the visage of every expectant father.

I turned the Baron of Vo Mandor over to Killane with instructions to keep him out of my hair and proceeded to tend the grossly expectant baroness. There were narcotic compounds I knew of to moderate her labor pains, and if it came right down to it, I could put her to sleep with a single thought. It didn't get down to that, though, because Asrana's delivery of her son was a fairly easy one. Mandorin was so proud that he nearly burst. New fathers are like that, I've noticed.

There was nothing really pressing to draw me immediately back to Vo Wacune. My house was in the care of Killane's capable relatives, and traveling in the winter isn't very pleasant, so I gave in to the urgings of Mandorin and Asrana to stay over until the bad weather was past.

It was pleasant to spend time with old friends, and then too, I got to play with the baby quite a bit. But spring inevitably arrived, and Killane and I started making preparations for our return to Vo Wacune.

As it turned out, however, another old friend came by on the afternoon of the day before we'd planned to depart. Earl Mangaran, the de facto Duke of Asturia, had been conferring with Corrolin in Vo Mimbre, and, accompanied by his heavily armed troop of bodyguards, he came riding up the long causeway to Vo Mandor.

Mangaran hadn't noticeably aged since the coup that had elevated him to the throne, but his eyes looked very tired. After all the greetings in the courtyard, Mandorin led us to a secure room high in one of the towers to discuss certain state matters. Given the nature of Vo Mandor, I didn't really think those precautions were necessary, but this *was* still Arendia, after all.

'Well, Mangaran,' Asrana asked after we'd all seated ourselves, 'did some emergency send you off to Vo Mimbre, or did you just yearn for Duke Corrolin's company?'

Mangaran passed a weary hand across his face. 'I sometimes think I might have been wiser to have left town when you ladies were plotting our little revolution,' he said. 'Now I think I know why Oldoran spent all his time up to his eyebrows in drink. There are *so* many details.' He sighed mournfully. 'I went on down to Vo Mimbre to advise Duke Corrolin that there's serious trouble in Vo Astur. Now I'm on my way to Vo Wacune to talk with Duke Kathandrion about the same matter. I'm advising the both of them that they'd better form a strong alliance. Asturia's right on the verge of going up in flames.'

'There's nothing new about that, Mangaran,' Asrana noted. 'Asturia's been smouldering since I was a little girl. Which particular embers are glowing this time?'

'I rather suspect that history's going to call this "the nephew war",' Mangaran replied with a gloomy face. 'I have no living sons, and my claim to the ducal throne is fairly specious. We *did* depose Oldoran on the flimsiest of legal grounds that day, and the one who should *legally* have taken his place was his eldest nephew, Nerasin.'

Asrana made a retching sound.

'My sentiments exactly, Baroness,' Mangaran said smoothly. Then he went on. 'Unfortunately, *my* eldest nephew isn't much better than Nerasin. He's a foolish wastrel who's up to his ears in gambling debts. To put it bluntly, I wouldn't put him in charge of a pig-pen.'

'I've met him, Polly,' Asrana told me. 'His name's Olburton, and he's at least as bad as Nerasin is. If either of those two succeeds Mangaran here, Asturia's going to simply disintegrate into little

277

clusters of warring estates.' She looked rather coolly at her husband. 'And there are those in Mimbre who might just decide to take advantage of that, aren't there, love?'

Mandorin sighed. 'I do fear me that thou hast spoken truly,' he admitted.

'And there are border nobles in Wacune who'll feel the same way,' I added. 'What *is* it about proximity to a border that brings out the worst in people?'

'Oh, that's easy, Polly,' Asrana said with a cynical laugh. 'All the world knows that the people on the other side of any border aren't really human, so whatever they happen to own rightfully belongs to *real* humans on our side of the line.'

'That's a brutal view of life, Asrana,' I scolded her.

'True, though,' she replied with a saucy toss of her head.

'I cannot believe this is truly happening,' Mandorin protested. 'The hard-won peace which we all struggled so valiantly to wrest from the jaws of unending war is now at the mercy of a pair of Asturian popinjays.'

'And to make matters worse, there's not much we can do about it,' Mangaran mourned. 'Fortunately, I won't be around when it happens.'

'What an odd thing,' Asrana noted thoughtfully. 'Peace requires rulers every bit as strong as war does. Mangaran, dear, why don't you leave a parting gift to poor old Asturia? Put a clause in your will that'll send both of these incompetent nephews to the headsman's block. A man with no head doesn't have much use for a crown, does he?'

'*Asrana!*' Mandorin gasped.

'I was only joking, love,' she assured him. Then she frowned slightly. 'It *is* a solution, though,' she mused, 'but why don't we do it *before* Mangaran's been gathered to the bosom of Chaldan? A little bit of poison in the right places would solve the whole problem, wouldn't it? Then we could poison our way through the ranks of Asturian nobility until we finally found someone competent enough to rule.'

'A bit simplistic, Asrana,' Mangaran chided.

'The simple ones are the best, old friend,' she told him. 'We're all Arends, after all, and complications confuse us.'

'I'll admit that I'm tempted,' Mangaran said with a wicked grin.

'I'd strongly advise against it,' I told them. 'The introduction of poison into politics always seems to spur imitation, I've noticed, and *everybody* has to eat now and then.'

'Poisons are very rare though,' Asrana said, 'and very expensive, aren't they?'

'Good heavens no, Asrana,' I told her. 'I could find deadly poisons growing in flower beds right here in Vo Mandor, if I really needed some. They're so common that I'm sometimes surprised that half the population doesn't die off from accidental exposure to them. There are even some ordinary plants that are a part of everybody's diet that have poisonous leaves on them. If you eat the roots, you're fine; if you eat the leaves, you're dead. If you want to kill somebody, use an axe or a knife. Don't open that door marked "poison". I'll keep an eye on things in Asturia, so please don't all of you rush into exotic solutions.'

'Spoilsport,' Asrana pouted.

Since Mangaran was going on to Vo Wacune anyway, Killane and I accompanied him, though my seneschal – if that's the proper term – was quite uncomfortable in the presence of so many Asturians. Hereditary animosities die hard, I've noticed, and peace was still something of a novelty in Arendia.

Mangaran's 'Nephew War' wasn't too hard to defuse, since the people attracted to either camp were the sort who *talked* a good fight but tended to fade back into the woodwork when trouble broke out. I had Mangaran track down the more vocal adherents of both Nerasin and Olburton, and after I'd had a few pointed interviews with the more prominent partisans on either side, the whole business cooled down noticeably. One *does* have a certain reputation, after all, and I was fairly free with some threats that I probably wouldn't have carried out even if I'd been sure just exactly how to pull them off.

The rulers of the three duchies took that to be some sort of sign from on high, and whether I really wanted the position or not, I became the semi-official presiding officer at the meetings of the Arendish Council each summer.

Things went on in this fashion for some years, and by dint of a mixture of persuasion, threats, and sheer force of will I was able to maintain the shaky peace in Arendia.

Young Alleran grew up during those years, and he was married shortly after his eighteenth birthday. I'd stayed rather close to Alleran during his formative years and had gently led him astray. His parents, Kathandrion and Elisera, had done their very best to raise him as full-bore Arend – all nobility and no brains – but I tampered just enough to keep his strain of common sense intact. Asrana's observation during the meeting at Vo Mandor was still very apt. A ruler during peacetime must be at least as strong as one who's presiding over a war, and nothing helps to make a ruler strong quite as much as common sense.

I had an unlikely assistant in my campaign to contaminate Alleran's pure Arendish understanding. Though Alleran was ostensibly visiting his 'Aunt Pol' – that particular title's been following me around for centuries – I found that more often than not, he spent his time with Killane, and who better to give instruction in practicality than a master builder? Between us, Killane and I turned out a young man eminently qualified to rule. He could 'thee' and 'thou' with the best of them, but his mind didn't stop functioning as soon as the first archaic syllable crossed his lips.

No matter what you might choose to believe, I had nothing whatsoever to do with his choice of a bride. *That* decision was dictated almost entirely by politics. Alliances between equals are almost always cemented by marriages. The bride's name was Mayasarell – one of those concocted names usually arrived at by mashing the names of several dead relatives together – and she was a lovely, dark-haired girl. She and Alleran were not exactly desperately in love with each other, but they got along fairly well, and that's a reasonable basis for a good marriage, I suppose.

The years continued their stately, ordered pace, and the annual meetings of 'the Arendish Council' at the Great Fair gave me plenty of opportunity to head off assorted idiocies before they got completely out of hand.

I think it was after the council meeting in 2324 that I made one of my periodic surveys of the land of the Arends. It was not so much that I distrusted the information I was receiving, but it's always a good idea to have a look for yourself in these matters, so Killane and I joined the party of Duke Corrolin of Mimbre and rode on down to the golden city on the banks of the River Arend.

I found nothing particularly alarming in Vo Mimbre, so after a week or so, Killane and I left to go on to Vo Mandor to look in on Mandorin and Asrana.

It was on the morning of our second day out when Killane and I had a conversation that was becoming increasingly necessary.

It wasn't long after sunrise, and my seneschal and I had ridden up a fairly steep hill, and we stopped at the top to rest our horses in the golden morning sunlight.

'Meanin' no offense, Lady-O,' Killane said a bit hesitantly, 'but could we be after havin' a bit of a chat?'

'Of course. You look troubled, Killane. What's bothering you?'

'I'm not th' cleverest man in all th' world, me Lady,' he said, 'but a man would have t' be an absolute dunce not t' see that y' ain't exactly ordinary.'

'Why, thank you, Killane.' I smiled. 'Go ahead and say it, my friend. I won't be the least bit offended.'

'They call y' Polgara th' Sorceress,' he blurted. 'Is that a true fact?'

'The "Sorceress" part of it's been blown all out of proportion,' I replied, 'but, yes, my name *is* Polgara, and I *do* have certain abilities that aren't very common.'

'An' yer father's name is Belgarath?'

I sighed. 'I'm afraid so, yes.'

'An' yer quite a bit older than y' look?'

'I certainly hope that the years aren't showing.'

'Yer a thousand years old, aren't y'?' He blurted that out almost accusingly.

'No, dear heart,' I said patiently. 'Three hundred and twenty-four, actually.'

He swallowed very hard, and his eyes got sort of wild.

'Does it really matter so much, Killane?' I asked him. 'Longevity's really nothing more than a family trait. Some people live longer than others, that's all. You've seen that yourself, I'm sure.'

'Well, yes, I suppose so, but *three hundred years!*'

'I'll say it again. Does it really matter? Our friendship's what matters, isn't it? You're my true and faithful friend. That's all that matters to me, and that's all that should really matter to you. Don't let something as silly as numbers destroy our friendship.'

'I'd sooner cut off me right hand,' he declared.

'Well, stop worrying about it, then.'

'Kin y' really an' truly perform magic?' His tone was almost boyish, and his expression seemed filled with anticipation.

'If that's what you want to call it, yes.'

'Do somethin' magical,' he urged me, his eyes alight.

'Oh, dear,' I sighed. 'All right, Killane, but if I do a few tricks for you, can we drop this silly conversation?'

He nodded eagerly.

I translocated myself to a spot some distance behind him, and he sat his horse, gaping at my suddenly empty saddle.

'I'm over here, Killane,' I advised him calmly.

He turned, his expression almost frightened.

I gestured at a nearby boulder, focusing my Will. Then I released it, and the boulder rose to hover about ten feet in the air.

Killane started visibly when I dropped it with a thud.

281

'This has always been my favorite,' I told him, and I rather slowly blurred into the form of the snowy white owl. I circled about him for a few moments, gently brushing his face with my soft wing-feathers. Then I resumed my own form and climbed back up onto my horse. 'Satisfied?' I asked my trembling friend.

'More than satisfied, me Lady,' he assured me. ' 'Twas a wondrous thing t' behold.'

'I'm glad you liked it. Now, shall we go on to Vo Mandor? If we hurry right along, we should make it by suppertime.'

CHAPTER 18

Earl Mangaran died the following spring, and I rushed to Vo Astur to examine his newly entombed body. I wanted to be certain that Asrana's simple solution to the problem of inconvenient people hadn't also occurred to others. My examination of my friend's body, however, revealed that he had died of natural causes.

Olburton, the wastrel who was Mangaran's heir, had assumed authority in Vo Astur, but most of the rest of Asturia was under the control of Nerasin, Duke Oldoran's nephew. The legalities of the situation were extremely murky. Oldoran had never actually been stripped of his crown, and Mangaran's tenure in Vo Astur had been, from a strictly legal point of view, no more than a regency. The choice between Nerasin and Olburton wasn't really much of a choice, so I kept my nose out of it. My job was to keep the three duchies at peace, and if the Asturians chose to embroil themselves in a generation or so of internal strife, that was their business, not mine.

I took some precautions, though. At my suggestion, Kathandrion and Corrolin met quietly at Vo Mandor to cement an alliance designed to keep the Asturian conflagration from spreading.

'What is thine advice here, Lady Polgara?' Kathandrion asked me once we'd all gathered in Mandorin's blue-carpeted study. 'Duke Corrolin and I could quite easily move into Asturia, dispose of both nephews and put someone to our liking on the throne in Vo Astur.'

'That's a very bad idea, Kathandrion. If the Asturians want to hate each other, that's *their* affair. If you and Corrolin take a hand in things, all you'll succeed in doing is uniting the Asturians, and they'll come crashing out of their forest to re-ignite the civil war Ctuchik was trying so hard to keep burning. Just close the borders of Asturia and let them fight it out among themselves. Eventually, someone who's strong enough is going to come along and re-unite them, and then I'll go to Vo Astur and persuade that fellow that it's in his best interests to go along with the idea that peace is better than war.'

'Persuade?' Asrana asked mildly.

'That's just a polite way of saying "bully", Asrana,' I told her. 'I'm very good at bullying people. Over the years I've noticed that rulers who're on shaky ground at home almost always start a war with some neighbor on the theory that an outside war will redirect all those pent-up hatreds. I'll strongly urge the eventual ruler of Asturia not to do that – and I can be *very* persuasive when I set my mind to it. I've devoted a great deal of time and effort to the establishment of peace in Arendia, and I'm not going to let some Asturian who thinks he's come up with an entirely new idea disrupt that peace just to consolidate his position at home. We can all hope that the ultimate winner in Asturia will be reasonable. If he's not, I'll grind his face in reasonableness until he gets my point.' I looked around sternly. 'Have I made myself clear?'

'Yes, mother,' Kathandrion replied with feigned meekness.

Corrolin burst out laughing at that, and the conference moved on to its conclusion with a good-humored tone. I'd probably overstated things, but these *were* Arends, after all. The alliance between Kathandrion and Corrolin was firmly in place when we separated. That was the important thing. Now, no amount of Asturian conniving was likely to disrupt it.

Kathandrion and I returned to Vo Wacune, and he moved his forces up to the eastern border of Asturia, while Corrolin blockaded the southern edge of that troubled duchy. Asturia was sealed off now, and 'the nephew war' was strictly confined. Emissaries from both Nerasin and Olburton scurried around making ridiculous offers in both Vo Wacune and Vo Mimbre, but Kathandrion and Corrolin steadfastly refused to even see them.

I had a few concerns about Asrana and what *she* might do. She still had many contacts in Asturia, and she *could*, if she chose to do so, greatly influence the course of events there. I knew that she held Olburton in contempt, but she absolutely despised Nerasin. Given a choice between them, she'd probably – with reluctance – come down on Olburton's side. I wanted a continuing stalemate in Asturia, so I strongly urged my enthusiastic friend to keep her nose out of things there.

All this scheming and intrigue was beginning to make me tired.

A good juggler can keep a dozen brightly colored balls in the air all at the same time – as long as the balls aren't slippery. My problem was that some knave had greased all the balls I was trying to juggle.

The year 2325 wound on down toward the annual feast-day called Erastide that marked the end of one year and the beginning of the next. There was the usual party at the ducal palace in Vo Wacune, and the highlight of the whole affair was the announcement by Crown Prince Alleran that his wife, Mayaserell, was with child. All in all, I approved of that. At least there wasn't going to be a messy argument about succession in the Duchy of Wacune.

The following spring the messiness in Asturia was climaxed by a phenomenal bow-shot of at least two hundred paces. Since the arrow involved ended up protruding from the center of Olburton's chest, things in Asturia suddenly got very noisy. Olburton had controlled the cities, while Nerasin had held sway out in the more conservative countryside. In effect, Olburton had owned the people and Nerasin the land. There'd been a kind of balance, which I'd striven to maintain, but with Olburton's death that stalemate went out the window. Nerasin did not immediately attack Vo Astur, but concentrated instead on capturing the smaller cities and towns. By the early summer of 2326, Vo Astur was an island in the middle of a hostile sea, and its situation was made all the more precarious by the petty squabbling of Olburton's relatives. The ultimate outcome was fairly predictable. By early autumn, Nerasin had reclaimed his drunken uncle's throne in Vo Astur.

And that was when Asrana stepped in, muddying the waters for all she was worth. I'm not sure exactly where she found the phrase, but the idea of 'destabilizing the government of Asturia' absolutely fascinated her, and she had plenty of contacts back home to assist her.

It was several months before word of Asrana's activities reached me in Vo Wacune, and as soon as I heard of them, I sent Killane out to shop around town for a large mirror – 'the largest you can find'. I wasn't really all that curious about my own reflection. I knew what I looked like, after all. Killane's shopping expedition was a ruse designed to get him out of the house long enough for me to slip away from him. I did *not* want an escort this time. I gave him a quarter of an hour to immerse himself in the cabinet shops in the commercial district of Vo Wacune, and then I retired to my rose-garden, stepped out of sight behind a hedge, and went falcon. I wanted to reach Vo Mandor before Asrana could come up with any more mischief.

Evening was settling on the battlements of Mandorin's castle when I arrived, winging my way out of the northeast. I settled on the parapet, sent out a quick, searching thought to locate Asrana, and then changed back. I was irritated, but not really in that state melodramatically called 'high dudgeon'. I suppose that 'medium dudgeon' would have been more apt. Fortunately, Asrana was alone, dreamily brushing her hair, when I burst in on her.

'Polly!' she exclaimed, dropping her hair brush. 'You startled me.'

'I'm going to do worse than that in a minute, Asrana. What on earth do you think you're doing in Asturia?'

Her eyes hardened. 'I'm keeping Nerasin off balance, that's all. Believe me, Polly, I know exactly what I'm doing. Right now, Nerasin's afraid to turn his back on anybody in his court, and I have it on the best authority that he never sleeps in the same bed for two nights in a row. I've spun imaginary plots in his palace like cobwebs. He's afraid to close his eyes.'

'I want you to stop it at once.'

'No, Polly,' she replied coolly. 'I don't think so. I'm Asturian myself, and I know the Asturian mind far better than you do. Nerasin's only interested in his own precious skin, so he'll ignore the alliance between Wacune and Mimbre if he thinks a war will cement his grip on power. He won't care a jot if that war kills half the men in Asturia. All I'm doing is keeping him so busy protecting his own life that he doesn't have time to start that war.'

'Asrana, he'll eventually realize that all these imaginary plots are just a ruse, and then he'll ignore them.'

'I certainly *hope* so,' she said, 'because that's when the plots will stop being imaginary. I *am* going to kill him, Polly. Look upon it as my gift to you.'

'To me?' That startled me.

'Of course. You're the one who shoved peace down all our throats, aren't you? As long as Nerasin's in power in Vo Astur, this peace of yours is in danger. I'm going to see to it that he doesn't stay in power for much longer. Once he's gone, we'll all be able to breathe much more easily.'

'Whoever replaces him will probably be just as bad, Asrana.' I had regressed to 'low dudgeon' by now.

'Well, if he is, the same thing that's going to happen to Nerasin will happen to him. I'll sift my way through the whole body of Asturian nobility until I find somebody we can live with, and if I can't find a reasonable noble, I'll promote a townsman – or even a serf, if I have to.'

'You're very serious about this, aren't you, Asrana?' When I'd first heard about her games, I'd thought she was just playing.

'Dead serious, Polly.' She lifted her chin. 'Before you came to Vo Astur, I was just a silly little ornament in Oldoran's court. You changed all that. You should always be careful when you start throwing words like "patriotism" around in the presence of Arends, you know. We tend to take things too seriously. These past few years of peace have been better for Arendia than anything that's happened to us for the last six or eight centuries. People here are actually dying of old age now. I'll depopulate Asturia if that's what it takes to keep what's coming to be known as "Polgara's Peace" from disintegrating.'

'Polgara's Peace?' That really startled me.

'Well, it certainly wasn't any of *our* doing. It's all your fault, Polly. If you hadn't waved peace in front of our faces, none of us would have known what it looks like.'

When I calmed down and looked at things from her perspective, I could see that she had a point, and, moreover, that her extensive contacts in Vo Astur made her the best qualified of all of us to keep Nerasin so thoroughly off balance that he'd never have time to cause trouble in the rest of Arendia. I chided her for not keeping me advised, extracted a promise from her that she wouldn't do anything major without consulting me first, and then I went back to Vo Wacune, coming down inside the grounds of the palace instead of my own rose-garden. I spoke with Kathandrion at some length about Asrana's activities and asked him to keep Corrolin advised. Then I went on home to give Killane the chance to scold me.

It was in the autumn of 2326 that I helped Alleran's wife, Mayaser-ell, through a difficult labor and finally delivered her of a son, who was named after his grandfather – a fairly common practice. Kathandrion was so proud of it, though, that he nearly exploded.

The borders of Asturia, both to the east and to the south, remained sealed – which is to say that no one could conveniently march an army across the lines, but nobody can totally seal a border that runs through a thick forest. Asrana's messengers and fellow-plotters had little trouble crossing that line, and I'm sure that Nerasin's people could also slip across. Vo Astur continued to bubble like a teapot that's been left over the fire too long.

It was on a blustery day in the early spring of 2327 that something happened which I have very good reason to remember. There'd been a certain parity of heavy weaponry among the three Arendish duchies, which is to say that the siege engines of an attacking force couldn't throw boulders, burning pitch, or baskets full of javelins any farther than the engines of a defending force could. The defenders of a city or fort had walls to hide behind, however, while the attackers did not, and this put the attacking force at a definite disadvantage. Large amounts of money and a great deal of engineering talent were devoted to the improvement of those engines of war, since the extension of the range of a catapult by a mere fifty paces could determine the outcome of a battle.

Kathandrion's engineers had designed a very large catapult that was based on some highly questionable theories involving pulleys, counterweights, and reciprocal tensions. Frankly, that monstrosity looked like the frame of a large house enveloped in cobwebs to me. Kathandrion was very enthusiastic about it, however, and he hovered over the shop where it was being constructed like a mother hen, and he spent his evenings deeply immersed in the engineers' drawings. I glanced at them a few times myself, and it seemed that there was something wrong with the concept, though I couldn't quite put my finger on it.

In time, the monstrosity was completed, and the engineers rolled it out into a nearby meadow to find out if it could really work. Kathandrion himself pulled off his doublet to lend a hand – or in this case, a shoulder – to the task of moving the huge thing into position. Then he bent his back to the cranking of one of the many windlasses that tightened the tangle of ropes to bowstring tautness. The entire court gathered some distance off to one side to watch the Duke of Wacune pull the lanyard that was designed to release all that pent-up force.

I was there as well, and just as all was in readiness, I had a sudden premonition. There was something wrong! 'Kathandrion!' I shouted. 'No!'

But it was too late. The boyishly grinning Duke Kathandrion jerked the lanyard.

And the entire framework exploded into a jumbled mass of snarled rope and splintered timbers! The computations of the engineers had been perfect. Unfortunately, they had *not* computed the strength of the wooden timbers that formed the frame. The sudden release of all that pent-up energy shattered those heavy beams, spraying the crew surrounding the engine with yard-long splinters that spun out faster than any arrow shot from a bow.

Duke Kathandrion of Wacune, my dear, dear friend, died instantly when a sharp-pointed chunk of wood thicker than his arm drove completely through his head.

All of Wacune went into deep mourning, but after about a week I put aside my own grief and went to the palace to speak with Alleran. His eyes were puffy from weeping as he stood at the table in his father's study staring at those fatal drawings. 'It should have worked, Aunt Pol!' he said in an anguished voice. 'What went wrong? Everything was put together exactly according to these plans.'

'It was the plans that were at the heart of the problem, your Grace,' I told him.

'Your Grace?'

'You're the Duke of Wacune now, my Lord, so you'd better pull yourself together. Even in time of grief, events move on. With your permission, I'll make the necessary arrangements for your coronation. Pull yourself together, Alleran. Wacune needs you now.'

'I'm not ready for this, Aunt Pol,' he protested.

'It's either you or your son, Alleran, and he's a lot less ready than you are. That festering sore called Asturia is on your western border, and Nerasin will jump on any perceived weakness. It's your duty, your Grace. Don't let us down.'

'If I could just figure out why this cursed thing flew all apart the way it did!' he burst out, slamming his fist down on the drawings. 'I've gone over all the arithmetic myself. It *should* have worked.'

'It did, Alleran. It did exactly what that design called for it to do. The only problem with the arithmetic was that the computations concerning the strength of the structural beams were left out. The catapult didn't work because it was too powerful. The frame should have been made of steel instead of wooden beams. The pressures were too great to be contained by a wooden frame. That's why it tore itself apart.'

'That much steel would have been very expensive, Aunt Pol.'

'I think the wood was even more expensive, your Grace. Fold those drawings up and put them away. We have a great deal to do.'

Alleran's coronation was subdued, but Corrolin traveled up from Vo Mimbre to attend, so that put a bit of iron in the back of the new Duke of Wacune. I sat in on their private discussions, but it probably wasn't really necessary. Kathandrion had been wise enough not to raise his heir in a political vacuum, and the Mimbrate emissary to the court at Vo Wacune had given Alleran instruction in the somewhat overly-involved courtesies of the Mimbrates. Their first meetings were a bit stiff, but as they came to know each other better, they started to relax. Their major concern was still Asturia, and that naturally drew them closer together.

It was in the autumn of that same year that Nerasin did something that pushed me very close to the line my father had repeatedly warned me not to cross.

Asrana and Mandorin were riding down to Vo Mimbre for what was probably only a social visit, and when they reached that band of trees that lines the River Arend and started upstream toward Vo Mimbre, a number of Asturian archers, who'd somehow managed to sneak down across the plains of Mimbre to the southern border, quite literally riddled my two dear friends with arrows. Nerasin had obviously discovered that Asrana'd been behind all the troubles he'd been having in Vo Astur, and so he'd taken some fairly typical Arendish steps.

When I heard about the deaths of my friends, I was very nearly overcome with grief. I wept for days and then steeled myself for revenge. I was quite certain that I could devise some things to do to Nerasin that would make strong men shudder in horror for several thousand years. Killane and his family wisely stayed clear of me when I came storming out of my room. My first stop was the kitchen. I was going to need some sharp implements to carry out my plans for Nerasin. My training as a cook gave me some interesting terms to work with. 'Filleting' had a nice sound to it, I thought, and so did 'de-boning'. The idea of cutting out Nerasin's bones one by one very slowly had an enormous appeal for some reason. My eyes brightened when I came across a cheese-grater.

'All right, Polgara, put the tools back where you got them. You're not going anywhere.' It was mother's voice.

'He murdered my friends, mother!' I burst out. 'I'm not going to let him get away with that!'

'I see that you're becoming very adept at following local customs,' she noted, and there was a faint touch of rebuke in her voice.

'What's that supposed to mean?'

'Why did the Master send you to Arendia?'

'To put a stop to all their foolishness.'

'Oh, now I understand. You're going to wallow in that same foolishness so that you can see what it's like. Interesting idea. Did you take the same approach in your study of medicine? Did you catch a disease so that you'd understand it better before you tried to cure it?'

'That's absurd.'

'Yes, I know. That's what I've been trying to explain to you, Polgara. All this brooding about knives and meat-hooks and cheese-graters is exactly

290

what you were sent to Arendia to put a stop to. Nerasin murdered your friends, so now you're going to murder him. Then one of his relatives will murder you. Then your father will murder somebody else in Nerasin's family. Then somebody will murder your father. Then Beldin will murder somebody else. And it will go on and on and on until nobody's even able to remember who Asrana and Mandorin were. That's what blood feuds are all about, Pol. Congratulations. You're an Arend to your fingertips, now.'

'But I loved them, mother!'

'It's a noble emotion, but wading in blood isn't the best way to express it.'

That's when I started to weep again.

'I'm glad we had a chance to have this little chat, Pol,' she said pleasantly. *'Oh, incidentally, you're going to need Nerasin a little later, so killing him and chopping him up for stew-meat wouldn't really be appropriate. Be well, Polgara.'* And then she was gone.

I sighed and put all the kitchen implements back where I'd found them.

The funeral of Asrana and Mandorin was held at Vo Mandor in the autumn of 2327, and Alleran and I, quite naturally, attended. The Arendish religion isn't good at funerals. Chaldan's a warrior God, and his priests are far more interested in vengeance than in comforting survivors. Perhaps I'm being a little picky, but it seems to me that a funeral sermon based on the theme, 'I'll get even with you for that, you dirty rascal' lacks a dignified, elegiac tone.

The blood-thirsty ranting of the priest of Chaldan who conducted the funeral seemed to move Alleran and Corrolin, though, because after the funeral and the entombment of Mandorin and Asrana, they got down to some serious plotting about appropriate responses to Nerasin's atrocious behavior. I chose to forego participation in this little exercise of pure Arendishness. I'd put my own Arendish impulses away along with the cheese-grater.

I wandered instead about the grim, gloomy halls of Mandorin's fortress, and I ultimately ended up in Asrana's dressing-room, where her fragrance still faintly lingered. Asrana had never really been what you'd call tidy, and she'd left things scattered all over her dressing table. Without even thinking, I started to straighten up, setting jars and bottles in a neat row along the bottom of her mirror, brushing away the faint dusting of face powder, and placing her combs and brushes at an aesthetically pleasing angle. I was in the act of setting down her favorite ivory comb when I changed my mind. I kept it instead, and I've carried it with me for all these years.

It lies right now on my own dressing table, not fifteen feet from where I sit at this very moment.

Of course, I was not the only one who'd been totally incensed by the murders. As I mentioned, both Corrolin and Alleran took them very personally, and the simple blockade of the borders of Asturia tightened, becoming almost like a noose, and large raiding parties swept out of both Mimbre and Wacune, savaging Asturia with a kind of studied brutality.

Despite my best efforts, the Arendish civil wars had taken up almost exactly where they'd left off when I'd first gone there. The thing they called 'Polgara's Peace' had fallen apart.

The situation in Asturia was growing more desperate as the months dragged by. Corrolin's Mimbrate knights rode almost at will through the agricultural south and west of the Asturian duchy, and Wacite archers, who were at least as proficient as their Asturian counterparts, quite literally killed everything that moved along Asturia's eastern frontier. At first this random violence seemed senseless, but when I berated Alleran for renewing the war, he gave me that innocent look that Arends are so good at and said, 'We aren't making war on the Asturians, Aunt Pol. We're making war on their food. Eventually, they'll get hungry enough to take care of Nerasin all by themselves.'

It was a brutal, ugly way to make war, but nobody's ever said that wars are pretty.

Nerasin grew increasingly desperate as food grew scarcer and scarcer on the tables in Vo Astur. His solution to his problem should have been obvious, but unfortunately, I completely missed it.

It all happened on a blustery night when I'd decided to stay home rather than go to the palace. The palace was the nerve-center of the 'food-fight', and the noise of messengers running through the halls waving dispatches announcing that ten Asturians cows and fourteen of their pigs had been killed that day was starting to get on my nerves. To my way of looking at things, the assassination of cattle hardly constituted a major victory, so I decided that I'd earned a quiet evening at home. I took a long, leisurely bath, ate a light supper, and retired early with a good book.

It was sometime after midnight when I was somewhat rudely awakened by Killane's shouting. My personal maid – Killane's youngest sister Rana, incidentally – was trying valiantly to keep him out of my bedroom, and he was just as valiantly trying to get in.

I muttered something that I won't repeat here, climbed out of bed, and pulled on my robe. 'What's going on out here?' I demanded crossly, jerking open my bedroom door.

'It's me oafish brother, me Lady,' the slender little Rana said in disgust. 'I wouldn't be surprised at all t' find that he's been drinkin'.'

'Go along w' y' now, Rana,' Killane told her. 'There be trouble at th' palace, Lady Polgara,' he said to me. 'Y'd better be after puttin' on some clothes. His Grace's messenger's waitin' fer y' out in th' sittin' room.'

'What's happened, Killane?'

'His Grace's son's bin spirited away by th' cursed Asturians, me Lady, an' th' Duke wants y' to come t' th' palace immediately.'

'Tell the messenger I'll be right with him,' I said. Then I closed the door and pulled on my clothes hurriedly, muttering curses under my breath. We'd had plenty of evidence to prove just how unprincipled Nerasin was. Why hadn't I anticipated his next move?

Abduction has long played a significant role in international politics – as Garion and Ce'Nedra can testify – but the removal of Duke Alleran's two-year-old son from the palace in Vo Wacune was the first time I'd ever encountered the practice. Some abductions are perpetrated purely for the ransom, and those are rather easily dealt with. A political abduction, however, doesn't involve money, but behavior. A message had been found on the young Kathandrion's bed, and it was fairly blunt. It told Aleran that if he didn't pull back from Asturia's eastern frontier, he'd never see his son alive again. Mayaserell was in hysterics, and Alleran wasn't much better, so there wasn't really much point in talking with them. I provided the court physicians with a compound of certain herbs that was strong enough to fell a horse, and then I spoke at some length with the young duke's advisors. 'We don't have much choice,' I told them finally. 'Do as that message demands. Then send a dispatch to Duke Corrolin in Vo Mimbre. Tell him what's happened here, and also tell him that I'm taking care of it. I want everybody to keep his nose out of this. I'll deal with it, and I don't want any enthusiasts running around cluttering things up for me.' Then I went home to think my way through the situation.

The short-range solution would have been quite simple. Clearly, I wouldn't be dealing with 'talented' people here, and locating the place where little Kathandrion was being held wouldn't have been difficult, but then we'd have all had to sit around holding our breath while we waited for Nerasin's next move. Clearly, I'd have to come up with something that would permanently keep the nominal Duke of Asturia out of mischief. Killing him would be permanent, of course, but then we'd have to deal with his successor. After what Nerasin had done to Asrana and Mandorin, I wasn't too enthusiastic about keeping him alive, but the politics of the situation – and mother's cryptic statement that someday I'd *need* Nerasin – strongly suggested that the best hope for restoring peace to Arendia lay in compelling Nerasin to do exactly what I told him to do for the rest of his life and then insuring as best I could that he lived well into his eighties. The more I thought about it, the more I became convinced that the rescue of Alleran's son and the 'civilizing' of Nerasin should not be two separate acts, but should rather be combined.

Nerasin's hired abductors could be holding the boy anywhere, but, in reality, that didn't matter. I could get exactly what I wanted in Vo Astur itself. I didn't have to tear the woods apart in a desperate search. Once I had Nerasin under my thumb, I could arrange for the boy's return without endangering him or savaging vast tracts of Asturian real estate.

My next problem was standing just outside the door to my library when I prepared to leave the next morning. His red fringe of a beard was bristling, his arms were crossed defiantly, and his expression was adamantine. 'I'll not be after lettin' y' go off by yerself, Lady-O,' he told me flatly.

'Oh, Killane,' I said, 'be serious. I won't be in any danger.'

'Yer *not* goin' off alone!'

'How are you going to stop me?' I asked mildly.

'I'll burn yer house down if y' even so much as try!'

'You *wouldn't*!'

'Try me!'

Now *that* was something I hadn't anticipated. Killane had found my soft spot. I *loved* my house, and he knew it. His threat made me go cold all over. Still, I *had* to get to Vo Astur as quickly as possible, and that meant that I almost had to use the form of a falcon. No falcon alive could carry a Wacite Arend weighing just over twelve stone, however.

The answer, of course, was fairly simple, and it would almost certainly teach my belligerent friend *not* to deliver ultimatums to me any more. I'd never done it before, but there's a first time for everything, I guess. I knew what was involved, and I was confident that I could improvise should the occasion demand it.

'All right, Killane,' I said in feigned surrender, 'if you're going to insist –'

'I am,' he said flatly. 'I'll be after saddlin' our horses, then.'

'No,' I said. 'We won't be traveling on horseback. Let's go out into the garden.'

'Whatever for?'

'You'll see.'

I'll admit that it was just a bit tricky. I knew what Killane *looked* like, but I didn't have a complete grasp of exactly how he *felt* – his own sense of his being, I suppose you could call it. Our gender differences complicated things just a bit, but I set that part aside. Killane's gender wasn't going to be particularly important for a while. He stood near a bed of winter-dormant rose-bushes with a slightly apprehensive look on his face, realizing, I suspect, that he might have pushed me just a trifle too far.

Then he started slightly, seeing something that wasn't really there near his left foot. He raised the foot, obviously intending to tramp on what he thought he was seeing.

'Leave it alone, Killane,' I said sharply to him. 'I need it just now. Look at it very closely, however.'

He stared intently at the illusion.

I had to filter the release of my will through *his* consciousness, and that was no mean trick. So far as I can recall, it was the first time I'd ever actually funneled my will through the mind of someone else. When I had everything firmly in place, I almost absently picked up a rock that weighed perhaps two pounds, and then I let my built-up Will go in the direction I had it pointed, and even as the transfer was taking place I prudently set the rock down on the tail of the small field-mouse into which the entirety of Killane's awareness and body were being transferred. There was a fair chance that the transformation might make him a bit hysterical, and I didn't really have the time to hunt him down.

The squeaking he made was pathetic, and the poor little creature's beady eyes were almost starting out of its head. I pushed back my instinctive sympathy, however. Killane *had* insisted, after all.

Then I went falcon, and that *definitely* increased the level of squeaking. I more or less ignored those shrill cries of absolute terror and strutted – that's the only word for it – over to one of the fruit-trees, selected a winter-shriveled apple on a lower limb, and pecked at the stem until it came free and fell onto the half frozen grass. I practiced with the apple for a few moments until I could hold it firmly without sinking my talons into its flesh. Then I went back to the squealing field-mouse. I took him firmly in my talons, shouldered the rock off his tail, and left for Vo Astur.

The trip wasn't bad – for me – and after we were several hundred

295

feet up in the air, Killane stopped squealing. He *did* tremble a lot, though.

It was mid-afternoon when we reached Vo Astur, and I noted as we settled onto the battlements of the palace that the parapet was largely deserted, a clear indication that discipline was lax. I disapproved of that, even though it was definitely to our advantage. Asturia was on a war footing, after all, and the lack of sentries on the parapet was an indication of unforgivable slovenliness. Still holding the trembling mouse in one claw, I hopped into a deserted sentry-box at the southwest corner of the battlements and changed Killane and myself back into our natural forms. He was staring at me in absolute horror when his real form blurred into place, and he continued that squeaking.

'Stop that!' I told him sharply. 'You're a man again. Talk. Don't squeak.'

'Don't you *ever* do that t' me again!' he gasped.

'It was your idea, Killane.'

'I never said no such thing.'

'You told me that you were going to come along. All right, you *did* come along. Now quit complaining.'

'What a *dreadful* thing that was t' do!'

'So was threatening to burn my house down. Snap out of it, Killane. We've got work to do.'

We kept watch from the tiny sentry-box until the soldiers who were scattered along the parapet gathered over on the far side in response to the inviting sound of a pair of rattling dice. Then, with no ostentatious display of furtiveness, Killane and I went down a flight of stairs into the upper floors of Nerasin's palace. I still knew my way around the ducal residence, and Killane and I slipped unobtrusively into a dusty, neglected library. In all probability, it was the safest place to hide, since study was not held in very high regard in Vo Astur just then.

The sun went down and darkness settled over Vo Astur. The noise from the throne-room seemed to suggest that the Asturians were celebrating something. Nerasin had evidently done some boasting, and his cohorts – his immediate family, for the most part – appeared to be convinced that his clever ploy would improve things in Vo Astur. I assumed that they were eating as well as drinking. That's the basic flaw in any attempt to starve a people into submission. The ones you're really after are the last ones to go hungry.

Killane kept watch at the door while I carefully reviewed the details of a dissection my teacher Balten and I had performed back on the Isle of the Winds. I wanted to make absolutely certain that a fairly common ailment would convince Nerasin to be cooperative.

I think it was almost midnight when a group of rowdy Asturian nobles came staggering up the stairs from the throne-room, turned the semi-comatose Nerasin over to the guards at the door to the royal apartment, and reeled off down the corridor singing a bawdy drinking song.

Killane and I waited. 'I'll be after doin' th' killin', Lady-O,' my friend whispered to me. 'I'd not be wantin' y' t' soil yer pretty hands on th' likes o' no Asturian.'

'We aren't going to kill anybody, Killane,' I told him firmly. 'I'm going to give Nerasin some instructions, that's all.'

'Surely y' don't think he'll be after followin' them, do y'?'

'He'll follow them, Killane. Believe me, he'll follow them.'

'I'll be absolutely fascinated t' see how y' plan t' manage that, Lady-O.' He picked up a heavy chair and very slowly twisted it apart, making only a very small amount of noise. When it was all in pieces, he selected one of the legs and swished it through the air a couple of times. 'Twill do nicely, don't y' know,' he noted, brandishing his makeshift club.

'What did you do that for?' I asked him.

'I'll be after needin' something' t' put th' guards t' sleep.'

'Why don't you check with me before you dismantle any more furniture?' I suggested. 'The guards won't be any problem.'

'I'll not be after doubtin' yer unspeakable gifts, Lady-O,' he said, 'but I think I'll be after keepin' me cudgel here – just in case.'

'Whatever makes you comfortable, I suppose.' I listened at the door for a few moments. Silence was settling over the castle. Here and there a door slammed, and the occasional bursts of laughter and rowdy song were quite some distance off. I opened the door slightly and looked at the two bored-looking guards at Nerasin's door. 'Sleep,' I murmured to them under my breath, and a moment or so later they were sprawled, snoring, one on either side of the door. 'Let's get on with this, then,' I said to Killane, and the two of us stepped out into the corridor.

The door was not locked, since it was supposed to be guarded, so Killane and I were inside Nerasin's apartment in no more than a minute.

I cast my thought about the series of connected rooms and found that nobody was awake, and then my friend and I went on into the bedroom where Nerasin sprawled snoring and only partially undressed across the canopied bed. I noticed that his bare feet were very dirty.

Killane quietly closed the door. 'Would y' be after wantin' me t' wake him?' he whispered.

'Not yet,' I murmured. 'I'd better sober him up first. Then he'll wake up all by himself, I think.' I rather carefully examined the man who called himself 'the Duke of Astur'. He was of a medium build, he had a big, bulbous nose and small, deep-set eyes. He had a weak chin and sparse, dark hair. He was none too clean, and his breath was like the odor from a freshly reopened grave.

Leeching the residue of strong drink from a man's body isn't particularly difficult, but I wanted something in place within Nerasin's body before I did that. I probed rather carefully with my thought, located his stomach, and carefully etched away the lining of the stomach wall near its bottom. Then I abraded the stomach wall itself until there was an open sore there. Nerasin's digestive juices should do the rest. Then, being careful not to move too quickly, I drained away what he'd drunk that evening. When I judged that he was just on the verge of noticing the fire I'd just built in his belly, I relaxed the muscles in his voice-box to the point that he wouldn't be able to scream – not audibly, at any rate.

The putative Duke of Asturia awoke rather suddenly.

Judging from the slightly disappointed look on his face, soundless screaming isn't very satisfying. His writhing was inspired, however.

'Good evening, your Grace,' I said pleasantly. 'Isn't the weather mild for so early in the season?'

Nerasin scrunched himself up into a tight ball, clutching at his stomach and trying with every ounce of his strength to push out at least a small squeak.

'Is something the matter, dear boy?' I asked, feigning some slight concern. 'Something you ate or drank no doubt.' I laid my hand on his profusely sweating forehead. 'No,' I said, 'it doesn't seem to be connected to any kind of food. Let me think for a moment.'

I drew a look of studious concentration over my face while my 'patient' thrashed about on his bed.

Then I snapped my fingers as if a thought had suddenly come to me. 'Of course!' I exclaimed. 'How did I miss it? It's so obvious. You've been a naughty boy, your Grace. You've done something lately that you're very ashamed of. There's nothing really wrong with your poor little tummy. You've got a guilty conscience, that's all.' Then I triggered a fresh flow of digestive juices into his stomach.

This time he was actually able to make a slight squeaking noise

– I think he did anyway. I couldn't be completely sure because he'd rolled off the bed and was crawling around under it. The squeaking might have been the sound of his toe-nails scraping on the floor-boards.

'Help his Grace back into bed, Killane,' I suggested to my grinning henchman. 'I want to see what I can do to ease his suffering.'

Killane reached under the bed, caught Nerasin by one ankle, and dragged him out into the open again. Then he bodily picked up the squirming Asturian and casually dumped him back on the bed.

'Allow me to introduce myself, your Grace. My name's Polgara. You may have heard of me.'

He even stopped wiggling. His eyes bulged out. 'Polgara the Sorceress?' he whispered, looking slightly terrified.

'The physician,' I corrected. 'You have a very serious condition, Duke Nerasin, and if you don't do just exactly what I advise you to do, I can't hold out much hope for your recovery. First of all, you're going to send word to the people you have holding Duke Alleran's son. Tell them to bring the little boy here immediately.' Then, just to make sure he got my point, I released a fresh flow of gastric juices into his inflamed stomach.

He immediately tied himself into an intricately complex knot and became very cooperative. There was a bell-pull at the head of his bed and he quite nearly tore it from its mounting when he summoned assorted servants. He gave orders in a hoarse whisper and then fell back on his bed, sweating profusely.

'There, now,' I said in a motherly sort of way, 'see how much better you feel already? I'm very pleased with how well your treatment is progressing. We'll have you back on your feet in no time. Now then, while we're waiting for your people to bring little Kathandrion here, we'd probably better go over the things you're going to have to do to prevent a relapse of this dreadful condition. You *really* don't want this to happen again, do you?'

He shook his head violently.

'The Arendish Council will be meeting at the Great Fair again this summer – as it usually does – and I really think you should make plans to attend – for reasons of your health, if you take my meaning. Then, just to be sure that this distressing condition doesn't recur, you'd probably better call all your spies, assassins, and assorted other troublemakers back here to Vo Astur. All this scheming and plotting is *very* hard on your stomach, and that delicate conscience of yours could cause all this to flare up again the moment you do anything the least bit dishonorable. It may take a bit of getting used to, Nerasin, but you might very well go down in history as the most honorable man to ever be born in the Duchy of Asturia. Doesn't that make you proud?'

He gave me a sickly little smile. 'Honor' is a nice word, but the concept was totally alien to Duke Nerasin.

'I think perhaps you should rest now,' I told him, 'but first, you'd better pass along orders that no one in Asturia should in any way interfere when my friend and I take little Kathandrion home to his parents. I know that the thought of the child's happiness just fills your heart with joy, and you wouldn't even think of hindering me, would you?

He shook his head so hard this time that it almost flew off.

Some scruffy-looking ruffians brought Alleran's young son to Nerasin's apartments shortly after dawn. 'Aunt Pol!' The little boy cried delightedly, running to me on his sturdy little legs. I swept him up into my arms and held him very close for a while.

Nerasin provided horses for Killane and me and a fairly sizeable escort to take us as far as the Wacite frontier.

'Will th' belly-ache be after goin' away in time, me Lady?' Killane asked as we rode out of the bleak granite pile known as Vo Astur.

'It'll *seem* to, Killane,' I replied. 'I'll probably have to turn it on a few more times before Nerasin falls into line, though. He'll try something sneaky in a few months, and I'll set fire to his belly again. He'll wait a little longer before he tries something else, and I'll stir the fire again. Nerasin's a thoroughgoing scoundrel, so I'll probably have to remind him about "his condition" a half-dozen or so times before he finally decides to behave himself. In the end, Arendia should be fairly quiet – for a generation or so, anyway. After that, who knows?'

CHAPTER 19

It was about noon when Killane and I returned little Kathandrion to Vo Wacune and his distraught parents. They fell all over themselves with gratitude and listened entranced to Killane's somewhat exaggerated account of just how we'd obtained the boy's release.

'I think you can pull your archers out of Asturia now, your Grace,' I told Alleran then. 'The war's over, so you can stop ambushing cows and pigs. Duke Nerasin's seen the light and he's going to behave himself from now on.'

'You can't trust that man, Aunt Pol!' Alleran protested.

'Beggin' yer pardon, yer Grace,' Killane said, 'but th' rascally Nerasin'll do just exactly as Lady Polgara tells him t' do – be it, "quit makin' war" or "sit up an' beg". She's got her fist wrapped around his tripes, don't y' know, an' he squeals like a pig every time she squeezes.'

'Do you really, Aunt Pol?' Alleran asked me incredulously.

'Killane's language is a little colorful, Alleran, but you've known him long enough to realize that. The term "tripes" isn't entirely accurate, but otherwise his description comes fairly close. From here on until the end of his life, Nerasin will fall down in a heap every time he does something that I don't like. Oh, you'd better let Corrolin know that the war's over as well, and then you two'd better start brushing up on your manners. Nerasin's coming to the council meeting this summer.'

'*What?*' Alleran exploded. 'After all the crimes he's committed?'

'Alleran, dear, that's what those council meetings are for, remember? We settle disputes over the council table now instead of on the battlefield. Whether we like him or not, Nerasin rules Asturia, so he *has* to attend those meetings, and so do you and Corrolin.'

'I'd be listening t' her, yer Grace,' Killane suggested warningly. 'She knows exactly how t' find a man's tripes now, so I wouldn't be after makin' her cross, if I was you.' He shrugged. 'It's yer own personal belly, though, so do as y' see fit.'

What a treasure that man was!

Things were a bit stiff at the meeting of the Arendish Council that summer, but Nerasin, casting frequent nervous glances in my direction, was disgustingly obsequious. Alleran and Corrolin were curtly civil to him, but the pair of them obviously had something else up their sleeves. That made me a little nervous, so I watched them very closely. An Arend with a secret under his vest might be able to keep the secret itself in hiding, but concealing the fact that he's *got* one is quite beyond his capabilities. Alleran and Corrolin were obviously 'up to something'.

The actual business meeting didn't last long, and it consisted mostly of the Dukes of Wacune and Mimbre dictating peace terms to Nerasin.

Then, when that was out of the way, Alleran rose to his feet. 'My Lords,' he announced quite formally, 'methinks the time hath come for us to express our undying gratitude to she who guides us through the alien byways of peace.' Then he looked directly at me. 'We will brook no opposition in this, my Lady Polgara, for will ye, nil ye, this is our unalterable decision. There have ever been three duchies in Arendia, but from this day forward, that will no longer be true. Duke Corrolin rules Mimbre; Duke Nerasin leads Asturia; and I try as best I can to guide Wacune; but henceforth there will be a fourth duchy in our poor Arendia, and that duchy is thine. I bid thee welcome, your Grace.' Then he looked around the pavilion. 'All hail her Grace, the Lady Polgara, Duchess of Erat!'

'Hail Polgara!' everyone in the ornate tent responded, rising to their feet and then falling to their knees in an excessive genuflection.

Now *that* took me completely by surprise. I could immediately think of a dozen reasons why it wasn't appropriate, but Alleran's assertion that they were going to do this to me whether I liked it or not silenced my objections. Since they'd seen fit to tack that 'your Grace' on to me, I decided to be gracious. I curtsied my acceptance, and they all cheered wildly. 'My Lords,' I spoke then, 'this honor quite o'erwhelms me, and I shall strive to mine utmost to be worthy of it.' Then, since they were all obviously *dying* for a speech, I saddled up my vocabulary and galloped it at full tilt around, through, and over the top of them for an hour or so. Then, when their eyes had started to glaze over, I wound down to a stirring conclusion and received the customary standing ovation.

They presented me with the elaborately decorated proclamation – signed by all three of them – that declared my duchesshood, and appended thereunto was a description of the boundaries of my realm in profoundly tedious detail.

I didn't really have time to read it because of the party that broke out at that point, but as best as I could gather from one brief glance, my duchy lay somewhere in what is now Sendaria. I gave the documents to Killane for safekeeping and then I was caught up in the giddy whirl of celebration of the founding of the fourth Arendish duchy.

It was fairly late that evening when I returned to my own pavilion to find Killane sitting at a small table illuminated by a pair of candles. He had a map of Sendaria and the scroll defining my boundaries in front of him, and his eyes were a little wild. 'Have y' looked at this, yer Grace?' he asked me.

'They didn't really give me much time, Killane,' I replied.

'I wouldn't be after tryin' t' ride around yer entire duchy in a single day, if I was you,' he said, 'nor in a week, fer that matter. Y' go on *forever* up there!' He laid his hand on the map. 'I bin tryin' t' mark yer boundaries out on this map, an' as close as I kin tell, either th' dukes took leave o' their senses, or some drunken scribe garbled some descriptions on this scroll. Look fer yerself, me Lady. I've inked in yer borders in red.' He handed me the map.

I stared at it. 'This is ridiculous!' I exclaimed. 'Let's go see Alleran. I want some clarification of this.'

Alleran was very calm about it. He looked at Killane's map with no apparent surprise. 'This looks about right to me, Aunt Pol,' he said. 'Is there some problem? You can have more land, if you'd like.'

'Alleran,' I said pointedly, trying to hold down my exasperation, 'this is well over half of central Sendaria.'

'So?'

'What do you mean, "so?" You've got me stretched from Seline to Lake Camaar!'

'Yes, I know. I notice that we didn't give you an outlet to the sea, though. Would you like to have that coast between Sendar and Camaar? It's awfully marshy there, but your serfs could probably drain those marshes for you. Did you want that island off the west coast?'

'Serfs?' I cut in.

'Of course. They're part of the land, Aunt Pol. When we get back to Wacune, I'll send word to your vassals up there and have them all come on down and swear fealty to you.'

'Vassals?'

'Naturally. You didn't think we were saddling you with open wilderness, did you?' He coughed a slightly embarrassed little cough. 'Actually, Aunt Pol, *I* provided the land for your duchy. I'm not sure which of my ancestors annexed all that ground up there, but it's more than I can handle, to be honest about it. It's not much of a present, is it? I gave you something I wanted to get rid of anyway.'

'That *does* take some of the shine off my new title,' I agreed.

'I know, and I'm sorry. The people up there are strange. Sendaria's been sort of ill-defined for so long that all kinds of people have migrated there. The races are all mixed together, and the population's definitely not pure Arendish. I don't know how to deal with them, but you're far wiser than I am, so I'm sure you'll manage better than I have. Your vassals – who used to be mine – are all pure Wacite Arends, however, so they're more or less manageable.' His expression grew slightly guilty then. 'You'll notice that I kept Darine, Muros and Camaar. I hate to appear parsimonious, but I really need the revenues from those three towns. My budget's been very tight lately.' Then he smiled slyly. 'I'll bet you thought that we were just handing you an empty title, didn't you, Aunt Pol? You'd probably better get rid of that notion right away. You've got a real duchy up north of the River Camaar, and you can do anything with it you wish.' Then his smile became a smirk. 'Now you're going to find out what the rest of us have to go through every day, so I wouldn't be too quick with any thanks, if I were you. Wait a little while first. Land and everything that goes with it is a responsibility, Aunt Pol, and sometimes it grows very heavy.'

I noticed that he glossed over the strategic location of the Duchy of Erat. Asturia had been the source of much of the trouble in Arendia for the past few centuries, and now Alleran, Corrolin, and I had that troublesome duchy hemmed in on the north, east, and south to pose a perpetual threat to Nerasin or anybody who might succeed him.

After we returned to Vo Wacune, Killane and I went on north to have a look at my new domain. I firmly declined Alleran's offer of an armed escort. I wanted to see what was *really* going on up there, and I didn't want knights, pikemen, and fanfares to announce my coming. We rode on up through Muros, took the road leading to Sulturn, and once we forded the north fork of the River Camaar, we were in 'Erat'.

'Tis fertile ground y've got here, me Lady,' Killane observed on the second day after we'd crossed the river, 'an' ample water. With a bit o' careful management, y' could git ridiculously wealthy, don't y' know.'

I was looking at a shabby collection of mud and wattle huts huddled a couple of hundred paces back from the road, however, so I wasn't really paying attention to my friend's predictions. 'Serfs?' I asked, pointing at the miserable hovels.

'It has th' look of a serfs' village,' he agreed.

'Let's ride into that clump of trees just ahead,' I said. 'I want to go have a closer look.'

'After y've seen one serfs' village, y've seen 'em all, me Lady,' he said with a shrug.

'That's the whole point, Killane. I've never seen one up close.'

We rode back in among the trees, I dismounted, and then I 'went sparrow'. I flew on back to the huts to look around. There was no furniture inside those hovels, nor anything even remotely resembling a fireplace. Each of them had a pit filled with ashes and charred sticks instead, and each also had a heap of rags in one corner that evidently served as a communal bed. There were a few scrawny dogs wandering about and some equally scrawny children. I flew on out to the nearby fields and saw wretched, dirty people hacking at the earth with the crudest possible tools under the watchful eye of a hard-faced man on horseback.

The mounted man had a whip in his hand.

I flew on back to where Killane waited and resumed my own form. 'That has to go,' I told him very firmly.

'Th' village? Tis unsightly t' be sure, me Lady, but th' serfs've got t' live someplace.'

'I'm not talking about the village, Killane. I'm talking about serfdom itself.'

He blinked. 'But th' whole o' society's based on it, me Lady.'

'Then I'll just have to rebuild the society, won't I? We'll get to that in a little while, but keep it in mind. I will *not* live my life on the backs of slaves.'

'A serf ain't no slave, me Lady,' he objected.

'Oh, really? Maybe someday you can explain the difference to me. Let's move along, Killane. There's a lot more to see here than I'd imagined.'

We stopped in secluded places rather frequently, and I spent a great deal of time wearing feathers as I snooped out the reality that lay just under the surface of my seemingly placid realm. The lives of the serfs were miserable beyond imagining, and the nobility lived in idle luxury, spending – wasting actually – money that grew out of the sweat and misery of their serfs. I found my nobles to be stupid, cruel, lazy, and arrogant. I didn't like them very much. That was also going to change.

We reached Sulturn and then turned north and rode on to Medalia, stopping frequently so that I could look into things. The land was fair, I found, but the society definitely wasn't.

After we passed Medalia, we rode on up to Seline, then turned east toward Erat. I tried as best I could to keep my equanimity. This wasn't Killane's fault, but he was the only person handy, so I don't imagine that he enjoyed the trip very much.

'If y' don't mind me sayin' it, yer Grace,' he said one afternoon when we were about half-way between Seline and Erat, 'y' seem t' be a bit waspish. Is it somethin' I've done?'

'It's not you, Killane,' I said. 'There are a lot of things wrong here – terribly wrong.'

'Well, fix em, Lady-O.'

'That's sort of what I had in mind, me boy-o.'

'If I kin be persuadin' y' t' set aside yer peevishness, y' might want t' give some thought t' where y' want t' build yer capital, yer Grace. Yer title suggests Erat, but I've been there a time or two, and it ain't th' prettiest town in all th' world, don't y' know, an' th' name "Vo Erat" ain't all that pleasin' t' th' ear.'

'Let me think my way through this before we make any quick decisions, Killane,' I suggested. 'I'm not entirely sure that I *want* a capital city.'

''Tis a cruel woman y' are, Lady-O,' he accused.

'I didn't exactly follow that.'

'This'd be me one chance t' design and build an entire city, don't y' know, an' now y've gone an' dashed me hopes. I could build y' a palace that'd make th' emperor of Tolnedra turn green w' envy.'

'What on earth do I need with a palace? I know who I am, and I don't need some grand display to remind me. But that's beside the point. My main concerns are still down in Arendia proper. Those clever little boys who put me here might prefer to have me get so involved in things up here that I'll lose track of what they're doing, but that isn't going to happen. I'm definitely going to keep my house in Vo Wacune. I want them all to realize that they're *not* going to get out from under my thumb this easily. Let's move on, Killane. I want to have a look at Erat before I decide just where to set up shop.'

Erat, as it turned out, was totally unsuitable for a seat of government. North central Sendaria had changed hands so many times over the centuries that the place was a hodge-podge of run-down and conflicting architecture. The whole thing would have had to be leveled and rebuilt to make it at all acceptable. The problem with that, however, lay in the fact that it was situated on the marshy north shore of the lake, and no matter what was ultimately erected there, it was still going to look like some town in the Drasnian fens.

Once again I took wing and scouted things from the air. The spot that ultimately caught my eye was located on the south side of the lake where a fair-sized river fed that body of water. It was a long, lushly green meadow that sloped down to the lake-shore with the river bordering it to the south. The river bank was lined with ancient white birch trees, and steep, wooded, dark green hills embraced the meadow on the other two sides. The snow-capped Sendarian mountains rose above those wooded hills to the east. There were no villages nor roads in the vicinity, and so everything was fresh and new, awaiting only my hand to make it perfect. I could view the sunrise over the mountains and the sunset over the lake. I immediately fell in love with it.

The spot was perhaps six leagues northwest of the village of Upper Gralt, and about ten leagues northeast of where the farm of a good-hearted man named Faldor is now located.

Garion should be quite familiar with the region, since he grew up there.

Killane studied the location I'd chosen, trying to find something wrong with it, I think, but he finally gave in. 'Tis adequate,' he grudgingly conceded. 'An' as luck would have it, 'tis on one of yer own estates, so there'll be no hagglin' about buyin' th' place.'

'Adequate?' I protested.

'Well – perhaps a trifle more than adequate, I suppose. I'll be after makin' a few sketches, if we've got th' time. I see about three locations where y' might want me t' build yer manor house. If we've got good sketches, we kin spend th' winter arguin' about 'em when we git back t' Vo Wacune.'

I'd already more or less decided where I wanted my house, but I didn't want to seem arbitrary, so I let Killane amuse himself with his sketch-pad while I explored the surrounding meadow and forests.

It was late autumn by the time we returned to Vo Wacune, and by then my vassals had all responded to Alleran's summons and had been impatiently waiting for me in the palace for over a month.

'They aren't happy, Aunt Pol,' Alleran warned me. 'Their families have been sworn to mine for generations now, and I'm giving them away like so many old saddles or suits of clothes. You might want to ease into this gradually.'

'Maybe,' I replied, 'but there *are* going to be changes up there, Alleran – fairly major changes – so I'm not really going to be very popular anyway. My vassals are Arends, so I'm sure that they're all mortally offended by the fact that their new ruler's a woman. There isn't much point to pretending to be all sweetness and light, is there?'

'It's your duchy, Aunt Pol. You can run it any way that suits you. When should we have the ceremony?'

'Which ceremony was that?'

'Each of them has to swear an oath of fealty to you after I've released them from their oaths to me.'

'A transfer of ownership, you mean?'

'That's a very harsh way to put it, Aunt Pol.' He considered it. 'Fairly accurate, though,' he added. 'We'll do it in my throne-room – if that's all right with you. After the ceremony, I'll nose about a bit to see if you're going to need an army to put down any rebellions.'

'You're just full of cheer today, aren't you, Alleran?' I said acidly.

The ceremony in the throne-room was a formality, of course, but Arends adore formality, so that part went off quite well. I sat imposingly on Alleran's throne, crowned, ermine-robed, and absolutely dripping regality. After my vassals had all pledged to protect, serve, and defend me with their lives, their fortunes, and their sacred honor, I gave them a little speech just to brighten up their day. I discarded all the archaisms and got right to the point. 'Now that we're all one big happy family, my Lords,' I began, 'we've got a few new rules to put in place. You've customarily paid Duke Alleran a certain tithe for the honor of serving him and administering the estates he's bestowed upon you. Now, Duke Alleran's far from being a spendthrift, but it seems to me that those tithes might be just a bit excessive. I don't think I'll really need all that much money, so why don't we just cut those tithes in half for a few years and see how that works out, shall we?'

My vassals cheered me for about a quarter of an hour for that bit of generosity. Some of them actually wept. They were Arends, after all.

When silence returned, I continued. 'Now then, since you won't be needing so much money to pay your rent, why don't we improve the lot of your serfs as well? I've cut your tithes in half, so you'll show your gratitude by cutting the amount of goods – and services – you've been extracting from your serfs by the same amount. You compel your serfs to work your land, and then you turn around and take at least half of what their own fields produce. From now on, you'll limit yourselves to one quarter of their labor, and you'll leave what they grow to feed their families alone.'

'*What?*' a stout, red-faced baron – Lageron, I think his name was – almost screamed.

'Are you having trouble with your hearing, my Lord?' I asked him. 'I said one quarter of his labor and none of his own food. A starving man can't work very well, you know.'

One of the other barons nudged Lageron and muttered in his ear. Lageron's expression of outrage softened, and his look grew sly. I was fairly certain that my barons planned to ignore the new restrictions.

'Just so that we all understand each other here, gentlemen,' I told them, 'I'm sure you've all heard wild stories about me.' I smiled. 'Nobody really believes all those fairy-tales, do they?'

They laughed at that. Then I let the smile slide off my face and put on a fair imitation of one of those expressions my father uses to intimidate people. 'You'd all better *start* believing, my Lords,' I warned them. 'No matter how wild the stories you've heard may be, you'll find that the reality is far, far worse. Don't think for a minute that you can ignore the limitations I've just placed on what you can bleed out of your serfs. I have ways to know just exactly what you're doing, and if any one of you exceeds the limitations by so much as one turnip, I'll look upon that as a violation of the oath you've just sworn, and I'll turn him out of his manor house with nothing but the clothes on his back, and his estate shall revert to me. My eyes are everywhere, my Lords, and you *will* obey me – or take up a life of landless vagabondage.'

I let that sink in for a moment, and then I once again returned to a tone of sweet reasonableness. 'A change of administration always causes a certain amount of disruption and upheaval, my Lords. Things will go more smoothly once you've grown accustomed to my little quirks. If, however, anyone here finds what I'm doing *too* inconvenient, I won't hold him to the oath he's just sworn. He's free to leave the duchy of Erat at any time, and if he can devise a way to carry his lands and his house on his back, he can take them along with him. I should advise you, though, that I don't think that even my father could do that, so the lands and houses will probably stay right where they are. Let me put it to you in the simplest possible terms. "My realm; my rules." Are there any questions?'

There was a sullen silence and no questions.

Duke Alleran, however, immediately mobilized a large force and marched it to the south bank of the River Camaar.

'That isn't really necessary, Alleran,' I told him a week later when I found out what he'd done. 'I can take care of myself, you know.'

'Just a precaution, Aunt Pol,' he told me. 'The fact that the army's there might help to keep a lid on people like Lageron. I know all those barons up there, so I know what it takes to keep them in line.'

I shrugged. 'It's up to you, Alleran,' I told him, 'but *you're* the one who's paying all those soldiers. Don't send *me* any bills.'

'Nerasin and Corrolin have agreed to help defray the costs, Aunt Pol, and to provide more troops if we happen to need them. We all want your duchy to be stable, so you might look on those friendly troops lining your southern frontier as our communal investment in peace.'

'Whatever makes you happy, dear,' I said, patting him fondly on the cheek.

In addition to the tithes I received from my vassals, there were extensive estates which I owned outright, and Killane advised me that about a quarter of the entire duchy was exclusively mine. I was still determined to abolish serfdom, so it goes without saying that I planned to emancipate my own serfs almost immediately. One of the peculiarities of that repugnant institution was the tradition that a serf who ran away and evaded capture for a year and a day was automatically a free man. If serfdom were abolished on my estates, they would in time come to be viewed as havens of refuge for runaway serfs from one end of the duchy to the other, and a strictly enforced 'no trespassing' policy would keep my vassals from amusing themselves by hunting down their departing property. It wouldn't be long until every able-bodied worker in the duchy resided on *my* land, and there'd be nobody to work the estates of my vassals.

'They'll all have t' be comin' t' yer grace – hat in hand – t' git th' manpower fer ploughin', plantin', an' harvestin',' Killane said.

'That's more or less what I had in mind, Killane,' I told him

310

smugly. 'Now, then, let's get back to the location of my manor house. I want it to face the lake and to be bordered on one side by the river, but set it on a hill to avoid any spring floods.'

When spring arrived, I opened the little vault I had hidden under the hearth in my bed-chamber, quite nearly emptied it of all my surplus money, and sent Killane north to buy materials, hire workers, and begin the construction. 'Don't butcher my forests building roads,' I told him quite firmly.

'An how am I supposed t' git all that marble t' th' buildin' site, Lady-O?' he demanded in some exasperation.

'Killane, dear boy,' I explained patiently, 'the building site is right beside that river. Build some barges and float the marble to where you'll need it.'

He blinked. 'I hadn't thought o' that,' he admitted. ''Tis a wonderful clever person y' are, me Lady.'

'Thank you.'

'I'll be after sendin' y' reports on me progress from time t' time, but I'd take it as a kindness if y'd stay away until it's all finished. I won't be after needin' y' lookin' over me shoulder every step o' th' way, don't y' know.'

'I'll be good,' I promised a bit meekly.

I lied about that, of course. I flew north at least once a week to see how things were coming along, but I didn't really see any need to let him know about those visits.

Actually, I was far too busy that summer to stand around watching the construction of my manor house. I issued the proclamation emancipating my serfs, and the priests of Chaldan immediately went up in flames. The Arendish clergy was deeply involved in the feudal system, and they recognized the dangers posed by the existence of vast tracts of unserfed real estate adjoining church lands. I was denounced from pulpits from Seline to Sulturn as an 'abolitionist'. The term didn't really take hold, though, since the sermons were delivered – for obvious reasons – to increasingly empty churches. The high priest of Chaldan, who owned vast estates down in Mimbre, made a special trip to Vo Wacune to advise me that if I didn't rescind the emancipation of my serfs, he'd have no choice but to excommunicate me.

'That doesn't really concern me, your worship,' I told him. 'I don't serve Chaldan, you know. My Master's his older brother, Aldur. Why don't we just let the two of them hammer this out? The next

311

time you talk with Chaldan, tell him what I've done and have him take it up with my Master.'

He stormed away, spluttering to himself.

My major concern that summer revolved around the fact that there wasn't really anything remotely resembling a legal system in Arendia. The dukes ruled by decree in each of those duchies, and their decrees were largely based on whims. In addition to being profoundly unjust, that approach to law was decidedly inefficient. I was certainly not going to spend all my time settling disputes and passing judgement on wrong-doers. I needed a body of written laws and fair judges who at the very least could read those laws. What passed for laws in Arendia at that time – and to some extent still does in that troubled land – were little more than a set of arbitrary rules protecting the privileges of the nobility. If there happened to be a dispute between a baron and an ordinary freeman, the baron always won. I'd encountered some of the same kind of thing on the Isle of the Winds during my stay there, and one of Kamion's major chores had been the codification of the laws. I had certain advantages Kamion hadn't had, though, so I sent my thought out to the twins and asked them to plunder my father's – and uncle Beldin's – libraries for me. I wanted every law-book available.

Then I sent a pair of Killane's nephews – and a sizeable herd of packmules – to the Vale to pick them up for me.

The Arendish Council met at the Great Fair about mid-summer that year, and I noted a number of searching looks thrown in my direction as we settled down to business. Quite obviously Aleran, Corrolin, and Nerasin had expected me to be too busy – and too frantic – to even attend the annual get-together.

'Any problems, Aunt Pol?' Alleran asked almost hopefully.

'Nothing particularly significant,' I replied with a slight shrug. 'My vassals are beginning to realize that when I say something, I really mean it.'

'Rumor hath reached me that thou hast emancipated all the serfs on thine own estates,' Corrolin noted. 'Was this truly the course of wisdom? Dost thou propose to farm those extensive lands by magic?'

'Good grief, no, Corrolin,' I told him. 'I'll hire my former serfs to do that for me.'

His eyes bulged and his mouth dropped open in sheer astonishment. 'Thou wouldst actually give a serf *money*?' he exclaimed.

'Unless he wants something else,' I replied. 'A good ox, maybe, or a new suit of clothes.' I frowned. 'The only problem I see with money lies in the fact that serfs can't count past ten – nine if they happen to have lost a finger. That's going to make payday very tedious. I may have to build some school-houses on my estates to give my former serfs the rudiments of arithmetic and a nodding acquaintance with reading.'

'Monstrous!' Nerasin exclaimed. 'You *can't* teach serfs how to read!'

'Why not? Educated workers would probably be more efficient than untutored ones, wouldn't you say?'

'Lady Polgara, there are hot-heads out there who've been writing all sorts of inflammatory nonsense. If the serfs can read, they might get their hands on documents that could start a revolution!'

'Revolutions are healthy, Nerasin. They clear the air. You probably wouldn't be where you are today if Earl Mangaran, Baroness Asrana and I hadn't removed your uncle from the throne in Vo Astur, would you? Happy workers don't revolt. It's when you start mistreating them that they come after you with pitchforks. That's not going to happen in my realm.'

'I'd sooner bite out my tongue than to try to tell you what to do, Aunt Pol,' Alleran said, 'but don't you think you're moving a little fast?'

'I'm cleaning house, Alleran,' I told him, 'and it's a *very* messy house. I'm not going to leave patches of dust in the corners just for old times sake.'

I could see from all the blank looks that what I was saying was going completely over – or through – their heads. 'Oh, dear,' I sighed. 'All right then, let me put it this way. Last summer, the three of you saw fit to elevate me to a status of equality with you. Isn't that what you had in mind?'

'Well –' Alleran said dubiously, 'I guess so.'

'Correct me if I'm wrong, but doesn't that mean that the duchy of Erat is mine – totally?'

'That was our intent, your Grace,' Corrolin conceded.

'Isn't he a nice boy?' I said to the other two. 'Now, then, since the Duchy of Erat belongs to me – absolutely – I can do anything I want to do up there, can't I? And none of you – either singly or all together – can do anything at all to interfere with me, can you?'

'There *are* rules and customs, Aunt Pol,' Alleran protested.

'Yes, I know – bad rules and bad customs. That's part of the dust and debris I'm scrubbing out of the corners.' I looked sternly at the Duke of Astur. 'Tell them what happened when you abducted little Kathandrion, Nerasin,' I said. 'Describe it in great detail – and if you've forgotten, I can always do it again – just to refresh your memory.' Then I included them all in my warning. 'If you gentlemen don't like what I'm doing inside my own borders, that's just too bad. And if it *really* upsets you, feel free to declare war on me at any time. I'll tell you this, however, the first one of you who invades my realm is going to get very, *very* sick. I won't maim your knights, or slaughter your foot-soldiers, or ride across your borders to burn the villages of your serfs. I'll take your actions personally, and my retaliation will be directed at you – personally. If you choose to attack me, I'll build fires in your own personal bellies. What I do on my own lands is *my* business. Now then, I'm very busy this summer, so what have we got on this year's agenda? Let's get to work here.'

Does that leave any doubts in anyone's mind about just who was running things in Arendia in those days?

Killane returned to Vo Wacune in mid-autumn. 'Th' weather's goin' t' pot up there, Lady-O,' he reported. 'I paid off th' buildin' crew an' told 'em all t' come back in th' spring. If we tromp around durin' th' rainy season, about all we'll manage t' do is t' turn yer beautiful meadow into a mud-bog, don't y' know, an' I'm after thinkin' y' wouldn't like that too much. I left a couple o' min t' guard th' place.'

'Very efficient, Killane,' I agreed. I knew exactly how much progress he'd made – I *had* looked things over, after all – but I let him give me glowing, though slightly exaggerated, descriptions of what had been accomplished so far.

Then he looked around at the heaps of law books piled in my library. 'An' what's all this?' he asked curiously.

'I'm setting up laws, Killane,' I replied wearily. 'It's very tedious.'

'Yer whims an' wishes are th' law, yer Grace.'

'Not when I finish with this, they won't be. I'm trying to reconcile the best of the major legal systems in the world here – mostly Tolnedran and Melcene, but with just a sprinkling of Alorn, Nyissan, and even Marag statutes thrown in to season it all. I even found a couple of ideas in Angarak legal practices that might be useful.'

'What's th' point o' strainin' yer pretty head w' all that dusty nonsense, me Lady?'

'The point is justice, Killane. That's the ultimate point of any system of law.' I gestured at the stacks of books. 'There are a lot of weeds in this garden, but I'll get them all pulled out so that the beds are ready for the roses.'

Killane completed the work on my manor house in the late summer of 2330, not too long after Duke Corrolin of Mimbre died, and, properly escorted this time, he and I journeyed north so that I could have a look at my seat of power. I'd seen it from the air on several occasions, of course, but an overhead survey doesn't really convey the impact of a building when you see it from ground level. The house stood on a rise near the north bank of the river that fed the lake, so water was accessible; and a graveled path led from my back door down to a stone wharf jutting out into the river, so deliveries would be convenient. The meadow which had first attracted my attention ran on down about a quarter mile to the lake-front to the west, and as I'd envisioned, the encircling wooded hills with the snow-capped mountains lying to the east made it all just perfect.

Am I going on too much about my house? Well, that's just too bad, isn't it? I love that house, and if I want to talk about it, I will.

The house itself was a dream in snowy marble. Killane had quite obviously taken quite a few liberties with the dimensions indicated on the detailed plans we'd agreed upon. I'd assumed that there were some finite limits implicit in the amount of money I'd given him for the construction, but Killane's skills at bargaining had given him plenty of elbow-room. His introduction of the concept of competitive bidding had definitely had an impact on costs, so he more than gave me my money's worth. The central building was several stories tall, and it was fronted by a columned portico that had a Tolnedran sort of effect. Curved wings extended out from either side of the main hall to embrace a formal garden with incipient hedges and unplanted flower-beds awaiting my attention.

The interior of the house was even more pleasing, if that's possible. The rooms were large and well-lighted by tall windows. The kitchens were extensive, and the baths at the rear of the house could only be called luxurious. Since the place was totally devoid of furnishings or drapes, though, it echoed like the inside of an empty cave. It definitely needed carpeting and drapes.

'I've taken th' liberty o' engagin' a number o' furniture-makers, yer Grace,' Killane advised me. 'I've set 'em up in a shop adjoinin' th' stables out back. Y' might want t' give some consideration t' decidin' on one particular style o' furniture fer th' place. A house with a dozen different kinds o' chairs an' tables always looks sort o' slap-dash, don't y' know.'

I definitely knew about slap-dash. Father's tower was a perfect example of it. The sheer size of the house was intimidating, and I hoped that Killane's family would be large enough to staff it. Killane and I made some decisions about furniture, draperies, carpets and other niceties, and then I returned to Vo Wacune to keep an eye on things.

By the summer of 2331, the lake-shore house was complete, and I began to divide my time between my town house in Vo Wacune and my country house on Lake Erat. Traveling back and forth between them was not as tedious for me as it would have been had I not had certain advantages.

There were still tensions in Arendia, of course, but I managed to smooth them over, so things stayed quiet.

Then in the late summer of 2333 father came by Vo Wacune for a visit. He seemed quite startled by what he perceived to be the opulence of my town house. 'What's all this?' he asked me after Killane's sister Rana had shown him into my library. I'm not entirely sure how he'd gotten past Rana. Father's always been a little careless about his appearance, and Rana had opinions about things like that.

'I'm moving up in the world, father,' I told him.

'So I see.' He flopped down in a chair beside my library table. 'Have you found a gold-mine somewhere? This place looks moderately luxurious, and I don't think you had all that much money in your pocket when you came here about twenty years ago.'

'The Dukes of Arendia saw fit to reward me for dismantling Ctuchik's schemes back then. They put me on a yearly pension – maybe in hopes that I'd retire from politics. I tried to turn it down, but they insisted. The money kept piling up until Asrana – you remember her, don't you?'

'Oh, yes,' he replied, 'the devious little Asturian lady.'

'That was Asrana, all right. Anyway, she suggested that I might spend some of the money on my own house, and this is the one I chose. Do you like it?'

He shrugged. 'It's liveable, I suppose. You were following the Master's orders, though, Pol. Taking that money was just a bit on the tacky side.'

'The Master told me to keep peace in Arendia, father, and that means getting along with the dukes. I took their money to avoid offending them. The stipend's been discontinued, though.'

'Good. But how are you maintaining this palace?'

'My estates are quite extensive, Old Wolf. They earn enough to get me by.'

'Your estates?' That seemed to startle him.

316

'They lie to the north of the River Camaar. If you think *this* house is opulent, you should see my manor house. I hope you're not too disappointed in me, father. I haven't ascended the throne of a unified Arendia – yet – but you *do* have the distinct honor to be addressing her Grace, the Duchess of Erat.'

'How did you manage that?'

I told him about the abduction and subsequent rescue of little Kathandrion and about my elevation to my current rank.

'You didn't do anything permanent to the Asturian duke, did you, Pol?' he asked, looking quite concerned. Father's rather casually killed a lot of people in his time, but for some reason he's forbidden me to follow his example. Consistency's never been one of his strong points.

I told him about Nerasin's stomach problems, and he burst out laughing. 'Brilliant, Pol!' he congratulated me. 'You ended the Arendish civil wars with a bellyache!'

'For the time being, anyway. Go get cleaned up, father. We have a party to go to this evening.'

'A party?'

'A grand ball, actually. Duke Alleran loves music and dancing, but I rather expect that you'll be the absolute center of attention.'

'Foolishness!' he snorted.

'No, father – politics. I've got Arendia in the palm of my hand right now, but just to be on the safe side, I'd like for everybody to know that I've got you in a sheath strapped to my hip if I really need you. Be regal, father, and intimidating. Make them believe that you can uproot mountains if you want to. I want them all to see just how sharp your edge is and how much damage I can do with you if I decide to whip you out of the sheath and start flailing around with you.'

'Are you trying to say that I'm your champion?' he demanded.

'You'll always be my champion, father. Now, go take a bath, trim your beard and put on a white robe. Don't embarrass me in public.'

My father's a performer. I think I've said that before. Give him a little bit of stage-direction and a fairly detailed characterization to work with and he'll turn in a truly masterful performance. He grumbled a bit at first – just as he had before that speech he'd given at Vo Astur – but the lure of sheer melodrama began to exert its pull on him, and by the time we left for Alleran's palace, he'd completely immersed himself in the role of 'Belgarath the Destroyer'. Candor compels me to point out the fact that he overplayed his role outrageously that evening, but he *was* performing for Arends, after all.

317

Arends aren't the world's greatest drama critics, so overacting doesn't seem to bother them.

Got you again, didn't I, Old Wolf?

The years plodded sedately along after father's visit. Little disputes flared up from time to time, but we were able to smooth them over during the annual meetings of the Arendish Council. My periodic excursions as a roving fire-brigade became less and less frequent as the Arends gradually became accustomed to the idea of peace. My vassals began to grudgingly admit that they were actually doing better now than they had back during 'the good old days' of serfdom, and money began to replace the barter economy which had previously prevailed. I had a few difficulties with Tolnedran merchants in some of the towns in my realm, but they largely evaporated after I standardized weights and measures and amended the criminal code to include fairly stiff fines for unrestrained creativity in the definition of pounds and inches. At first the local Tolnedrans didn't think I was serious, so for a few years my revenue from the fines actually exceeded that which my estates brought in. The money was surplus anyway, so I put it to use building schools from one end of my duchy to the other. I didn't *quite* manage universal literacy, but I was moving up on it. Then, in furtherance of a long-standing hobby of mine, I established a college of practical medicine in Sulturn. My goal was a healthy, prosperous, well-educated population, and I was purposefully marching in that direction, dragging everybody in my realm behind me.

Duke Borrolane, the successor to old Duke Corrolin, seemed a little puzzled by what I was doing and by my obvious success during our meeting in the summer of 2340.

'It's really nothing, your Grace,' I told him. 'Odd though it may seem to you, women are far more practical than men – perhaps because we're the ones who do the cooking. Men are dreamers, but no matter how exalted a dream is, it won't bake a loaf of bread. When you get right down to it, anyone who can run a kitchen can probably rule a domain – large or small.'

The actual business of the day-to-day ruling of the Duchy of Erat fell largely on Killane's shoulders. He was in his mid-fifties by now and he was a substantial-looking fellow with a no-nonsense air about him. Technically, he was my reeve, the administrator of my personal estates, but my vassals, assorted counts and barons, soon realized that his opinions carried great weight with me, and so they

318

all tried to stay on the good side of him. He didn't abuse his position or put on airs that might have offended the nobility. His standard response to petitions, complaints, disputes, and the like was fairly simple: 'I'll be after sendin' word of yer proposal t' her Grace, me Lord. We'll see what she has t' say.' Then he'd wait for a couple of weeks and deliver my 'decision' about matters I wasn't even aware of. His function in my realm was much the same as Kamion's had been on the Isle of the Winds. He served as a buffer – a filter, if you will – that kept petty details out of my hair. In effect, I gave him a general idea of what I wanted, and then he made sure that I got it without offending *too* many people. In many ways, though he probably didn't realize it, my humorous friend was an administrative genius. To put it succinctly, he ran Erat while I ran the rest of Arendia.

By 2350, however, age was beginning to creep up on him. His hair was a kind of sandy grey now, and his hearing was failing him. He took to using a staff to aid his faltering steps and an ear-trumpet to hear with. Increasingly, my visits to my lakeside estate became medical house-calls. I restricted his diet to some degree and stirred up compounds of some fairly exotic herbs to control an increasing number of infirmities. 'You're falling apart, Killane,' I shouted into his ear-trumpet on one such visit in the autumn of 2352. 'Why didn't you take better care of yourself?'

'Who'd a thought I was gonna live s' long, Lady-O?' he said with a rueful expression. 'Nobody in me family's ever lived past fifty, an' here I am at sixty-eight. I should o' bin in me grave twenty years ago, don't y' know.' Then he squinted at the ceiling. 'When y' git right down t' it, though, in th' rest o' me family, gettin' killed in a tavern brawl is what y' might call dyin' of natural causes, but I ain't been in a good brawl since th' day I first laid eyes on yer Grace. Y've gone an' spoilt me entire life, Lady Polgara. Aren't y' after bein' ashamed o' yerself?'

'Not very much, Killane,' I told him. 'I think you'd better start dropping some of your duties in the laps of whichever of your relatives seems competent. You're not getting enough rest, and you're spending too much time worrying about petty little things. Let somebody else take care of the little ones. You save yourself for the big ones.'

'I ain't dead yet, Lady-O,' he insisted. 'I kin still carry me own end.'

And he did – for another two years. Then a number of things which had been creeping up on him pounced all at once, and I

319

hovered over his sick-bed for several months. I sent word to Alleran asking him to make my apologies to the other dukes that summer. I was not going to leave my friend even for the annual meeting of the Arendish Council.

It was about midnight on a blustery autumn night when Rana shook me awake. 'Himself wants t' see y', yer Grace,' she said, 'an' I'm after thinkin' y'd better hurry right along, don't y' know.'

I hastily pulled on my robe and followed her through the empty halls to the sick-room.

'Ah, there y' are, Lady-O,' the dying man said in a weak voice. 'Go along w' y' now, Rana. There's somethin' I'll be after wantin' t' tell our Lady that y' don't need t' hear.'

His youngest sister kissed him gently and then sadly left the room.

'Now, don't y' be buttin' in on me, Lady-O,' Killane admonished me. 'There's somethin' I'm after wantin' t' get off me chest, an' I want t' spit it out before I pull th' dirt over me fer th' long sleep. You an' me, we've come a long way t'gether, an' we ain't never beaten about th' bush when we had somethin' t' say, so I'll come right out wi' it. It might not seem proper, but I'm goin' t' say this anyway. I love y', Polgara, an' I've loved y' since th' first time I set eyes on' y'. There. I've said it, an' now I can sleep.'

I kissed the dear man gently on the forehead. 'And I love you too, Killane,' I said, and he somehow seemed to hear me.

'Ah, an' aren't y' th' darlin' girl t' say so?' he murmured.

I sat at the bedside of my dear friend holding his hand, and I continued to hold it for quite some time after he'd died. Then, with tears of gentle regret streaming down my cheeks I folded his hands on his chest and pulled the sheet up over his peaceful face.

We buried him in a small grove of trees near the top of the meadow the next day, and the wind, seeming almost to share our sorrow, sighed in the evergreen trees on the hillside above us.

CHAPTER 20

Killane was gone, but he'd left me a rich legacy. We hadn't really planned it that way, but his extended family, almost without my knowing it, had become my hereditary retainers as generation followed generation in my service. There was a comfortable continuity about that. They all knew me, since I'd personally delivered most of them when their mothers had gone into labor. Mine had been the first hands that had ever touched them, and that automatically brought us closer. They knew me, and they'd been raised and trained from childhood to enter my service.

The benefits of the arrangement worked both ways, since continuity's very important to someone in my peculiar situation. As Killane himself might have put it, 'If yer after plannin' t' live ferever, yer bound t' git lonesome once in a while, don't y' know.' My hereditary retainers, both in my house in Vo Wacune and in my country estate on Lake Erat, filled in that enormous gap that the mortality of loved ones always brings into our lives.

Most of my original vassals had also died by the time that the century wound down toward the year 2400, and their successors had somehow learned better manners. The threat of what was wryly called 'Nerasin's complaint' in most of Arendia hovered over their heads, and even though they might disagree with some of my social innovations, they were prudent enough to keep their objections to themselves. The fact that their former serfs were no longer bound to the land in de facto slavery encouraged them to be polite to their workers as well – particularly after a fair number of cruel, arrogant landholders discovered that they had no workers when harvest time rolled around and they were obliged to stand helplessly watching while their crops rotted in the fields. I like to think that I might have played some small part in establishing that polite civility which is so characteristic of the archetypal Sendar. Experimenting with societies is a very engrossing pastime, wouldn't you say?

What I did in my duchy was quite deliberate, but what happened in Vo Wacune was almost an accident. I spent a great deal of my time there at the palace, since my position almost demanded that I immerse myself in politics. Politics, however, is a male preoccupation, and there were days when I wanted to be with women. Occasionally, I'd invite certain selected young ladies to my town house so that we could discuss matters that men simply wouldn't understand. As I'd observed earlier, Arendish ladies were – on the surface at least – a giddy, seemingly brainless group, interested only in fashions, gossip, and snagging suitable husbands. There *were*, however, Arendish ladies who had something between their ears besides fluff. Asrana had been a perfect example of that peculiarity. I winnowed my way through the court of the Duke of Wacune and skimmed off the best and brightest young ladies and, by carefully manipulating the seemingly random conversations in my library or my rose garden, I began to educate them. It's always a delight to watch the awakening of a mind, and after a while the random discussions at my house turned away from current fashions and empty gossip to more serious matters. My informal 'ladies academy' produced quite a few women who had a significant impact on Wacite political and social life. Women instinctively know how to gently guide and direct their husbands, and my little school subtly modified some things I heartily disapproved of.

We'd gather in my rose garden or on the terrace in the evenings as the stars came out. We'd eat chilled fruit my kitchen boy brought us, and we'd listen as the nightingales sang as if their hearts were breaking. And, since I'd gathered most of the more beautiful and interesting young women at court, the young men would come to the street outside my house and serenade us from just beyond the walls in clear tenor voices that dripped with longing. There are worse ways to spend an evening.

The twenty-fifth century was a time of relative peace in Arendia. There were occasional little brush-fires, of course, usually involving long-standing feuds between neighboring barons, but the Arendish dukes, applying sweet reason and the threat of overwhelming force, were able to smother the flames with only minimal help from me. I *did* make one suggestion, though, that seemed to be very effective. A vassal is obliged to provide his lord with warriors whenever the lord calls for them. The dukes found that peace would break out almost immediately when feuding barons were neatly stripped of all able-bodied men by the calling in of that obligation.

The world was moving on beyond the borders of Arendia. The raids along the Tolnedran coast by Cherek pirates continued through the twenty-fifth century, long after the reason behind them had been forgotten. No one even remembered Maragor, but the Chereks, those most elemental Alorns, continued to sack and burn Tolnedran coastal cities while piously explaining their barbarism by saying that they were simply following Belar's orders. All that ended rather abruptly with the ascension of the first Borune dynasty to the imperial throne in Tol Honeth in the year 2537. Ran Borune I was far more competent than had been his predecessors of the second Vorduvian dynasty. He rousted his slothful legions out of their comfortable garrison in Tol Honeth and put them to work building the highway that runs from the mouth of the Nedrane River north to Tol Vordue. The construction put legion encampments all along the coast within easy reach of the traditional Cherek targets, and the Cherek freebooters began to encounter much stiffer resistance when they came ashore. It was about that point that the Chereks decided that they'd fulfilled their religious obligations and that it was time to go find someplace else to play.

Since Ran Borune was the first of his family to occupy the imperial throne, his palace still crawled with left-over Vorduvians whose characters covered the spectrum from the near side of rascalism to the far boundaries of outright criminality. The Vorduvians had been much impressed with Ctuchik's elaborate scheme early in the twenty-fourth century. The ongoing Arendish civil wars had given the Vorduvians all sorts of opportunities to make obscene profits – largely in the arms trade. What was known in Arendia as 'Polgara's Peace' dried up their markets, and my name was routinely cursed from Tol Vordue to Tol Horb and Tol Honeth. The Borunes were a southern family, so they were not in a geographical position to be much involved in the arms trade in Arendia, so Ran Borune saw no real reason to fall in with some of the more exotic solutions to the problem suggested by the Vorduvians, the Horbites, and the Honethites.

It must have been in about 2560, after the Chereks had decided that raiding the Tolnedran coast wasn't fun anymore, that a cabal of those three families decided to stir things up in Arendia. They approached the then current duke of Mimbre, a young fellow named Salereon, and opened that box which I'd assumed had been permanently nailed shut. They began by addressing Salereon as 'your

Majesty' and explained that by saying that since Mimbre was the largest of the four duchies, the Duke of Mimbre was in reality the king of all Arendia – just as soon as he got around to annexing the rest of us. Fortunately, my careful training of the Arendish dukes took over at that point. Salereon, accompanied by only a few retainers, rode north and arrived at my manor house in the late spring to discuss the business.

'Methought I should consult with thee ere I embarked upon this venture, your Grace,' he said earnestly when the two of us were alone in my library. Salereon was a nice boy, but fearfully dense. In a way, he was actually asking my permission to declare war on me. I wasn't sure whether to explode in rage or to laugh in his face. Instead, I carefully – and slowly – explained what his Tolnedran 'friends' were trying to accomplish.

'I do confess that I had not considered that, your Grace,' he admitted. 'I had thought that, since the reasoning of the Tolnedran emissaries seemed so sound, it might have been the course of wisdom to present the matter to the Arendish Council at our meeting this very summer. It was my thought that once I had clarified the matter for thee and my dear brothers of Wacune and Asturia, I might be declared King of Arendia by general consent, thereby avoiding any disruption of our cordial relations.' He was actually sincere!

'Oh, dear,' I said.

'I do perceive that thou hast found some flaw in this most excellent proposal,' he said, looking slightly surprised.

'Dear, dear Salereon,' I said as gently as I could, 'what would you say if Nanteron of Wacune or Lendrin of Asturia came to the meeting this summer, each declaring that *he* was the natural born King of Arendia?'

'I should immediately surmise that they had taken leave of their senses, Lady Polgara. Such declarations would be absurd.' Then the sunrise of understanding began to dawn – faintly – in his eyes. He looked a bit sheepish. 'Bad decision there, wot?' he suggested.

I impulsively embraced the startled young duke. 'Your decision to bring this to me before you dropped the matter on the council table verged on sheer genius, however, Salereon,' I complimented him.

'That characterization hath not been applied to me previously, my lady,' he admitted. 'It seemeth to me that mine understanding might be somewhat deficient. Such being the case, mayhap I should be guided by thee in this.'

'That's another good decision, your Grace. You're getting better at this.' I considered it. 'I think I'll call in Nanteron and Lendrin,' I mused. 'Maybe this year we should hold the meeting of the Arendish Council here, instead of at the fair. I'll take steps to keep Tolnedrans away while the four of us talk this out. Let's keep the Arendish Council meeting in the family this time.'

Within the week, Nanteron of Wacune and Lendrin of Asturia arrived. I took them individually aside and threatened them with all sorts of horrors if they so much as cracked a smile when I announced the full extent of Salereon's mental deficiencies. I'm sure they got my point.

After we'd discussed the matter at some length, I decided that the best way to keep the Vorduvians, the Honeths, and the Horbites from meddling in Arendish internal affairs would be to place the whole business before Ran Borune I himself, and I volunteered to go to Tol Honeth and have a little chat with his Imperial Majesty in person.

I decided to skip over all the tedious formalities that would normally precede such a meeting and flew south to Tol Honeth. It took me a day or so of fluttering around the extensive grounds of the imperial compound until I found an opportunity simply too good to pass up. As it turned out, Ran Borune and I shared a hobby. The first of the Borunes was as passionate as I was about roses, and he spent several hours each day in his garden. I settled on a tree limb there and resumed my own form while he was carefully examining a somewhat sickly rose-bush.

'I think it needs more fertilizer, your Majesty,' I suggested quite calmly.

He spun around with a startled oath. He was a small man, even for a Tolnedran, and his gold mantle, the badge of his rank, seemed just a bit showy for the task in which he was engaged.

'Help me down, if you would please, your Majesty, and I'll have a look at the poor thing,' I said pleasantly.

'Who are you?' he demanded, 'and how did you get past the guards?'

'You probably know my father, Ran Borune,' I replied. 'He's a seedy-looking old fellow with white whiskers and a tendency to tell people what to do. He's been acquainted with your family for about five centuries now.'

'You mean Belgarath?'

'That's him.'

'That would mean that you're Polgara, the Duchess of Erat.'

'Exactly. I thought it might be best if we spoke privately. Would you give me a hand, please. A tree limb's not the most dignified place to perch while one's discussing matters of state.'

He helped me down, and his eyes were a little wild.

I looked at his sickly rose-bush. 'Bury a dead fish in amongst its roots, Ran Borune,' I advised. 'You planted it a little too close to that overhanging roof. The rain water's been leaching all the nutrients out of the soil. You might give some thought to moving it next winter after it's gone dormant. Now then, there's something going on that you ought to know about. The Vorduvians, Honeths, and Horbites are meddling in Arendish affairs, and we'd like to have them stop it.'

His look became exasperated. 'What are they up to *now*?' he demanded.

'They approached Duke Salereon of Mimbre and filled his head with royal ambitions. The poor boy was completely taken in by their flattery, and he was right on the verge of declaring himself the king of all Arendia. That would have re-started the Arendish civil wars almost immediately. I've spent a great deal of time and effort imposing peace on Arendia, and I'd really like to keep things up there quiet.'

'Those *idiots*!' he exploded.

'My sentiments exactly, your Majesty. Your northern nobles are a greedy lot, and they're involved in the arms trade. Peace in Arendia's cutting into their profits, so they're trying to stir things up. I'm going to do something rather radical about it, and I thought I ought to let you know why I need to take those steps.'

'You're going to invade northern Tolnedra?' He said it with a certain enthusiasm.

'No, Ran Borune,' I replied. 'I won't violate your borders. I'm going to close mine instead. The dukes of Arendia will do exactly as I tell them to do, so I'm going to close all our borders to Tolnedrans for a while.'

His face went dead white at that.

'Only for a year or so, your Majesty,' I assured him – 'just long enough to get my point across to the Honeths, Horbites, and Vorduvians. It won't *quite* bankrupt them, but it'll come close. It won't have much effect on the Borunes, the Anadiles, or the Ranites, since you're all in southern Tolnedra, but it'll definitely have an impact on the northern Tolnedrans. I'm going to keep them from tampering with the peace agreements in Arendia, and this is the best way I can think of to get their attention. I want them to bang their heads against those closed borders for a while and to try living without the profits they're bleeding out of Arendia. I think they'll come around after a while, don't you?'

His answering grin was almost vicious. 'I owe you, Polgara,' he said.

'I didn't exactly follow that.'

'My family has certain interests in the commerce with Arendia. If we sell out now, we'll make a very handsome profit, and if you close the Arendish borders to all Tolnedrans, those holdings are going to be worthless. We'll make vast amounts of money, and the northern families – who aren't among my dearest friends anyway – will take a sound drubbing.'

'What a shame,' I murmured.

'Isn't it, though? And, since I command the legions, I think my army's going to be far too busy with other matters to have time to run north to force the Arendish frontier.'

'Isn't that tragic?' Ran Borune and I were getting along very well.

'One favor, Polgara – in return for my withholding the legions from the northern families.'

'Feel free to ask, dear boy.'

'You *will* let me know when you're going to re-open those borders, won't you? Perhaps a week in advance? Long enough for me to buy up most of the assets of the Vorduvians, Honeths, and Horbites, at any rate. I should be able to buy them out at well below cost. Then, when normal commerce with Arendia resumes, I'll make millions.'

'I always like to help a friend get ahead in the world,' I said.

'Polgara, I love you!' he exclaimed exultantly.

'Ran *Borune!*' I said in feigned shock, 'we've only just met!'

He laughed, and then he danced a little jig of pure delight. 'I'll skin them, Polgara!' he crowed. 'I'll skin them alive! I'll put those arrogant northerners in debt for generations!'

'After you've stripped off their hides, you don't necessarily have to keep my part in our little arrangement a secret. I think it'd be sort of nice to have all of northern Tolnedra shudder every time someone so much as whispers my name.'

'I'll see to it,' he promised. Then he pointed at his ailing rose-bush. 'What kind of fish?' he asked.

'Carp, I think,' I replied. 'They're bigger – and fatter.'

'I'll get right at it. Would you like to go fishing with me?'

'Some other time, perhaps. I'd better get on back to Arendia. I'll close the borders in two weeks. That should give you time enough to swindle the northerners.'

'Come by any time, Polgara. My doors are always open to you.'

I changed form at that point. Ran Borune and I were getting along famously, but I *did* want him to remember exactly who I was. I circled him, brushing his startled face with my wing-tips, and then I flew off.

There are many ways to head off a war, but I'm particularly proud of that one. Not only did I virtually ruin the people who were most offending me, but I also gained a friend.

Arendia remained peaceful after that, and I even began to arrange a few intermarriages to help blur the distinctions which had always been so helpful in starting new wars.

It was early in the twenty-eighth century – about 2710, I believe – when the dukes, Gonerian of Wacune, Kanallan of Asturia, and Enasian of Mimbre made a suggestion that I thought was just a bit on the ridiculous side, but they were so enthusiastic about the whole idea that I somewhat reluctantly went along with them. I think the notion probably originated with Enasian, since the Mimbrates have always been addicted to epic poetry and its overblown conventions. What they proposed was nothing less than a grand tournament involving nobles from all four duchies, with the winner of that tournament – assuming that anyone survived a week or so of formalized mayhem – to be designated my champion.

What did *I* need with a champion?

They were all so terribly sincere, though. 'Dear Lady,' Enasian said, with actual tears standing in his eyes, 'thou *must* have a knight-protector to shield thee from insult and affront. Rude scoundrels, perceiving thine unprotected state, might exceed the bounds of courteous behavior and offer thee incivilities. My brother dukes and I, of course, would leap to thy defense, but it seemeth to me – and Gonerian and Kanallan do heartily agree – that thou shouldst have an invincible knight at arms at thine immediate disposal to chastise knavery whensoever it doth rear its ugly head.'

He was so sincere that I hadn't the heart to point out the obvious to him. I needed someone to protect and defend me almost as much as I needed a third foot. The more I thought about it, though, the more I came to realize that a 'sporting event' – particularly one involving formalized violence – could be a fairly good substitute for war, just in case someone hungered for the 'good old days'.

Because of its centralized location, we decided to hold the tournament on a field adjoining the Great Arendish Fair. Stands were erected to provide seating for the spectators, lists for jousting with lances and war-horses were laid out, and, sensing a probable need for them, I brought the entire faculty of the College of Practical

Medicine in Sulturn along with me to tend to the casualties.

Since the festivities were held in my honor, I was able to ban the more potentially lethal events. I firmly banned the grand melee, for example. There was some pouting about that, but I felt that a generalized tavern-brawl involving men in full armor might tax the capacity of our field-hospital. I also forbade the use of battle-axes and chain maces, and insisted on blunted lances. Quite naturally, the core of the tournament was the exquisitely formal jousting matches – colorful events where knights in shining armor and wearing red or gold or deep blue surcoats charged each other across the bright green turf attempting to unhorse each other with twenty-foot lances. Since even the winner of such an event is likely to hear bells ringing in his head for several hours after his victory, we interspersed other events so that the knights might recover. There were archery contests for the yeomen, catapult matches judged on distance and accuracy for the engineers, and weight lifting, pole-tossing and rock throwing contests for the serfs and freemen. There were other entertainments as well – juggling, singing, and dancing.

It was all very festive, but it went on for *weeks*, and quite naturally I had to sit through all of it wondering just what the prize might be for inhuman patience.

Eventually, as was fairly obvious he would be from the first round of jousting matches, the ultimate winner was the then-current Baron of Mandor, a massively muscular Mimbrate knight named Mandorathan. I knew him quite well, since my father had urged me to keep an eye on his family. Father quite obviously had plans for the Mandors.

I liked Mandorathan – once I persuaded him to stop falling on his knees every time I entered the room. A man in full armor is so *noisy* when he does that. I *did* notice that the level of civility at my 'court' improved enormously when my fully armored champion stood just behind my chair looking ominous. My vassals by now had fairly good manners, but Mandorathan's presence encouraged them to polish those manners until they positively gleamed.

The twenty-eighth century was a time of peace and prosperity in Arendia, and my duchy flourished, in no small part I think because my vassals followed my lead in the business of enriching the soil. There are many lakes in what is now Sendaria, and most of them have peat bogs surrounding them. I'd discovered on the Isle of the Winds that peat does wonders when plowed into the soil, and if the weather cooperated only slightly, every year in my realm was better than the previous one. I introduced new crops and brought in new strains of cattle from Algaria. I pillaged uncle Beldin's library for treatises on agriculture – largely written by scholars at the University of Melcene – and I applied the most advanced techniques in my domain. I built roads from farm to market, and to some degree I controlled prices to insure that the farmers in the duchy were not swindled by the merchants who bought their crops. I was denounced in some circles as a busybody, but I didn't really care about that. I mothered the Duchy of Erat outrageously, and as time went on, my subjects came to realize that 'Mumsy would take care of everything.'

There were a couple of things that 'Mumsy' did that they didn't like, however. I absolutely insisted that they keep their villages tidy, for one thing, and laborers eager to get to the nearest tavern after work didn't much enjoy picking up their tools before they went off to celebrate. I also put a stop to wife-beating, a favorite pastime of a surprising number of men. My methods were very direct. A man who's stupid enough to beat his wife isn't likely to listen to reason, so I instructed the constable of each village to 'persuade' wife-beaters to find another hobby. I *did* urge the constables not break *too* many bones in the process, however. A man with two broken legs can't really put in a full day's work, after all. There was, I remember, one *very* thick-headed fellow in the village of Mid Tolling who was so stubborn about it that he wound up with both arms and both legs broken before he got the point. After that, he was the politest husband you've ever seen.

The tournament at the Great Arendish Fair became a fixture, an addendum, if you will, to the annual meeting of the Arendish Council, and I think that made the chore of keeping the peace even easier. Toward the end of the century, however, the Oriman family came into power in Asturia, and the relations between the four duchies became strained. The Orimans were greedy, ambitious and devoid of anything remotely resembling scruples. The first of the Oriman dukes was a rat-like little fellow who thought he was clever. His name was Garteon, and he began find excuses not to attend the meetings of the Arendish Council. After the third year marked by his absence, I decided to go have a talk with him. My champion at that particular time was one of my own barons, a huge man of Alorn background named Torgun. We rode on down to Vo Astur, and Baron Torgun let it be known that he'd dismantle large numbers of people if I were not immediately escorted into Duke Garteon's presence. Alorns *can* be useful at times.

The unctuous little Garteon greeted me with a oily smile and fell all over himself apologizing for his repeated absences.

'Have you by chance heard of "Nerasin's complaint", your Grace?' I cut him off. 'You show all the symptoms of an onset of the disease to me, and I *am* a trained physician, so I recognize all kinds of illnesses. I'd strongly advise you to make a special point of attending the council meeting next summer. Duke Nerasin found squirming around on the floor while he squealed and vomited up blood to be terribly inconvenient.'

Garteon's face went very pale. 'I'll be there, Lady Polgara,' he promised. Evidently Nerasin's tummy-ache had entered the body of Asturian folk-lore.

'We'll be expecting you then,' I said quite firmly. Then Baron Torgun and I left Vo Astur.

'You should have let me split him down the middle, my Lady,' Torgun growled as we rode away.

'We're supposed to be civilized, Baron,' I replied. 'Civilized people don't hack up their neighbors. I think Garteon got my message. If he doesn't show up at the meeting next summer, I might have to be a bit more firm the next time he and I have one of these little chats.'

'Can you really do that?' Torgun asked curiously. 'I mean, can you actually make a man start throwing up blood?'

'If I need to, yes.'

'What do you need *me* for, then?'

'For the pleasure of your companionship, my dear Torgun. Let's move right along, shall we? It's almost harvest time, so there are all kinds of things that need my attention.'

Garteon of Asturia was defenestrated by his barons a few years later. That's one of the disadvantages of living in a palace with high towers. There's always the possibility of 'accidentally' falling out of a window about seven stories above a flagstoned courtyard.

His son, also named Garteon, was probably an even greater scoundrel than his father. Asturia was getting to be a problem.

We entered the thirtieth century, and I realized that I'd been manipulating Arendish affairs for almost six hundred years. I rather enjoyed it, actually. The Arends were much like children in many ways, and they'd come to look upon me as a wise parent to whom they brought most of their problems. More importantly, maybe, was the fact that they checked with me before they put anything major in motion. I was able to head off all sorts of potential disasters because of that.

It was in the spring of 2937 that I advised my co-rulers that Torgun's successor as my champion, a Mimbrate knight named

331

Anclasin, was getting along in years and that his hearing was beginning to fail. Moreover, he had a number of grandchildren down in Mimbre, and he really wanted to spend more time with them. Parenthood is nice, but grandparenthood is golden.

This, of course, added a certain excitement to the annual tourney at the Great Fair that summer. The winner, always referred to as 'the mightiest knight of life,' would be rewarded with the dubious pleasure of living under my thumb for the next several decades.

I arrived at the fair a few days early that summer, and my seneschal, one of Killane's descendants, nosed about and brought me some rather disturbing news. It seemed that an enterprising Drasnian merchant was accepting wagers on the outcome of the tournaments. Now, if someone wants to waste his money on gambling, that's none of my concern. What I *didn't* want was for someone to start tampering with the various events in order to determine the winner in advance. I spoke rather pointedly with the Drasnian, laying down a few rules for him to follow in his venture. The rules were fairly simple. No bribes. No tampering with equipment. No introduction of exotic herbs into the diets of contestants or of their horses. The Drasnian entrepreneur's expression was a little pained when he left my pavilion. Quite obviously, he'd had some plans that I'd just disrupted.

A formal tournament can be viewed as a kind of refinery where the slag is boiled away and only the true gold is left behind. That's probably a very offensive metaphor to those who end up on the slag-heap, but life is hard sometimes, I guess. The winnowing-down process went on for several weeks, and eventually there were only two contenders left, a pair of Wacite noblemen, Lathan and Ontrose, who'd been boyhood friends of Duke Andrion. Baron Lathan was a big, boisterous fellow with dark blond hair, and Count Ontrose was a more studious and polished man with black hair and deep blue eyes. I'd known the both of them since they were children, and I was really quite fond of them. Frankly, I was a bit surprised that the cultured Count Ontrose had advanced so far in a competition that was largely based on brute strength.

The final jousting match took place on a breezy summer morning when white puffy clouds were skipping like lambs across their blue pasture. The spectators were all gathered around the lists and were beginning to grow restive until an extended trumpet fanfare announced that the 'entertainment' was about to begin. I was seated on a regal throne flanked by Andrion of Wacune, Garteon of Asturia, and the aged Moratham of Mimbre when the pair of friends, all

332

clad in gleaming armor and with pennons snapping from the tips of their lances, rode forth to receive my blessing and instruction. They reined in side by side and dipped their lances to me in salute.

That sort of thing can go to a girl's head if she doesn't keep a firm grip on herself.

My 'instruction' was suitably flowery, but my conclusion had some *un*-flowery practicality to it. 'Don't hurt each other,' I commanded them.

Their expressions at that point were a study in contrasts. Count Ontrose, far and away the more handsome of the two, wore a look of civilized adoration. Baron Lathan, on the other hand, seemed so caught up with emotion that his features were almost distorted. There were tears in his eyes as he looked at me.

Then, with a final flourish, the armored pair posted formally to opposite ends of the lists to do battle upon each other. The 'list' in a formal joust consists of a stout waist-high rail designed, I think, to keep the horses from being injured during the festivities. A joust is a simple game, really. Each knight attempts to knock his opponent off his horse with a blunted twenty-foot lance. Draws are not infrequent, and in the event that both knights are sent crashing to the ground, they both get up, get back on their horses, and try it again. It's a very noisy affair that usually provides many business opportunities for the local bone-setter.

At the traditional signaling horn call, they both clapped down their visors, lowered their lances and charged, thundering down the lists toward each other. Their lances both struck true against those stout shields, and as usual, both lances shattered, filling the air with splinters. The jousts at a formal tourney can seriously deplete the supply of trees in a nearby forest.

They both wheeled and rode back to their original starting point.

Ontrose was laughing gaily but Lathan was glaring at his friend with a look of competitive belligerence. Baron Lathan seemed to be missing the point here. A jousting match is supposed to be a sporting event, not a duel to the death. In previous tourneys, I'd been moderately indifferent about the outcome, but *this* time was somehow different. My 'knights protectors' in the past had not really loomed very large in my life. They'd been no more than appurtenances to my station. I had an uneasy feeling this time that should Baron Lathan be the victor, he'd cause difficulties later on. Arendish literature positively swarms with improprieties involving high-born ladies and their bodyguards and Lathan seemed to be well-read. Should he happen to win, he'd clearly cause some problems. My impartiality started to slip just a bit.

The second pass with lances proved to be no more decisive than the first, and when the contestants rode back to take their places for the third, Lathan's look of open belligerence had become even more pronounced.

This was going too far, and I decided at that point to 'take steps'.

'No, Pol,' mother's voice murmured. 'Stay out of it.'

'But –'

'Do as I say!' Mother almost *never* took that tone, and it got my immediate attention. I relaxed my gathering Will.

'That's better,' she said.

As it turned out, Ontrose didn't really need any help from me. Baron Lathan appeared to be so wrought up that his skill deserted him on the third pass. He seemed to be so intent on destroying his opponent that he forgot to brace his shield properly, and Count Ontrose neatly picked him out of his saddle with that long lance of his and hurled him to the ground with a resounding crash.

'No!' The fallen knight howled, and his voice was a wail of regret and unspeakable loss.

Count Ontrose reined in sharply, swung down from his saddle, and rushed to his friend. 'Art thou injured?' he demanded, kneeling at Lathan's side. 'Have I harmed thee?'

I didn't exactly disobey mother, but I *did* send a quick, probing thought at the fallen baron. He was gasping, but that would have been quite normal. Being unhorsed in a jousting match almost always knocks the wind out of a man.

Then the physicians reached the pair, and they seemed greatly concerned. Baron Lathan had taken a very nasty fall, and the steel armor in which he was encased was so dented in on the left side of his chest that he could scarcely breathe. Once the physicians had pried him out of his armor, however, his breathing became normal, and he even congratulated Ontrose on his victory. Then the physicians carted him off to the dispensary.

Count Ontrose remounted his war-horse and rode over to claim his prize – me, in this case. He lowered his lance to me, and, in keeping with tradition, I tied a flimsy blue scarf about its tip as a visible sign of my 'favor'. 'Now art thou my true knight,' I declaimed in formal tones.

'I thank thee, your Grace,' he replied in a musical baritone, 'and I do hereby pledge unto thee my life and undying devotion.'

I thought that was terribly nice of him.

Ontrose, now 'the mightiest knight of life,' was one of those rare people who excelled at everything he put his hand to. He was a philosopher, a rose fancier, a poet, and a lutanist of the first magnitude. His manners were exquisite, but he was a complete terror in the jousting lists. Not only that, he was absolutely *gorgeous*! He was tall, slimly muscular, and his features might have served as a model for a statue. His skin was very fair, but, as I mentioned before, his long hair was lustrous blue-black. His large expressive eyes were a deep sapphire blue, and a whole generation of young Arendish ladies cried themselves to sleep over him every night for a goodly number of years.

And now he was mine.

There was a formal investiture after the tourney, of course. Arends love ceremonies. The three dukes, dressed in semi-regal finery, escorted the hero into my presence and formally asked me if this beautiful young man was acceptable to me. What an absurd question *that* was. I recited the formulaic little speech that enrolled Count Ontrose as my champion, and then he knelt to swear undying allegiance to me, offering up the 'might of his hands' in my defense. It wasn't really his hands that interested me, though.

Baron Lathan was in attendance with his left arm in a sling. His unhorsing had severely sprained his shoulder. His face was very pale, and there were even tears of disappointment in his eyes during the ceremony. Some competitors simply cannot *bear* to lose. He once again formally congratulated Ontrose, which I thought was very civilized of him. There have been times in Arendia when the loser of a jousting match has declared war on the winner. Lathan and Ontrose had been friends, and that evidently hadn't changed.

We lingered for a time at the fair, and then returned to Vo Wacune, where Ontrose took up residence in my town house.

As autumn touched the leaves, my champion and I rode north so that I could familiarize him with the peculiarities of the duchy of Erat.

'I have been advised, your Grace, that serfdom doth no longer prevail within thy boundaries, and I do confess that I have been much intrigued by that fact. The emancipation of they who stand – or grovel – at the lowest level of society is an act of sublime humanity, but I am hard put to understand how it is that the economy of this duchy hath not collapsed. Prithee, enlighten me concerning this wonder.'

I wasn't entirely certain if his education had descended into the labyrinthine sphere of economics, but I tried to explain just how it was that my duchy prospered without serfdom. I was startled – and pleased – by how quickly he grasped certain concepts that had taken me whole generations to pound into the thick heads of my vassals.

'In fine then, my Lady, it seemeth to me that thy realm doth still rest upon the backs of the former serfs – not in this case upon their unrequited labor, but rather upon their wages. For certes, now can they purchase such goods as previously were beyond them quite. The merchant class prospers, and their share of the tax burden doth lighten the load borne by the land-owners, thy vassals. The prosperity of the former serf is the base upon which the economy of the entire realm doth stand.'

'Ontrose,' I told him, 'you're a treasure. You grasped in moments what's eluded some of my vassals for six hundred years.'

He shrugged. 'It is no more than simple mathematics, your Grace,' he replied. 'An ounce apiece from the many doth far exceed a pound apiece from the few.'

'Nicely put, Ontrose.'

'I rather liked it,' he agreed modestly.

We talked of many things on our journey north, and I found my young – well, relatively young – champion to have a quick and agile mind. He also had an uncharacteristic urbanity that reminded me a great deal of my dear friend Kamion back on the Isle of the Winds.

He was suitably impressed by my manor house, and he had the uncommon good sense to make friends with my Killane-descended retainers. Moreover, his enthusiasm for roses at least equaled my own. His conversation was a delight, his impromptu concerts on his lute – often accompanied by his rich baritone – brought tears to my eyes, and his ability to grasp – and question – obscure philosophical issues sometimes astounded me.

I found myself beginning to have thoughts I probably shouldn't have had. In my mind, Ontrose was becoming more than a friend. That's when mother stepped in. *'Polgara,'* her voice came to me one night, *'this isn't really appropriate, you know.'*

'What isn't?' My response wasn't really very gracious.

'This growing infatuation of yours. This isn't the man for you. That part of your life is still a long way in the future.'

'No, mother, it's not. What you choose to call "that part of my life" will come whenever I decide it's going to come, and there's nothing that you or anybody else can do to change my mind. I'm tired of being pulled around on a string. It's my life, and I'll live it any way I choose.'

'I'm trying to spare you a great deal of heartache, Pol.'

'Don't bother, mother. Now, if you don't mind, I'd like to get some sleep.'

'As you wish, Pol.' And then the sense of her presence was gone.

Well, of course it was rude. I realized that even as I was saying it. That particular confrontation crops up in just about everyone's life. It usually comes a bit earlier, however.

By morning, I was more than a little ashamed of myself, and as time went on I regretted my childish reaction more and more. Mother's presence had always been the central fact of my life, and my little outburst had erected a wall between us that took years to tear down.

I won't demean what I felt for Ontrose by calling it an infatuation. I *will* admit that what was happening in my personal life distracted my attention from something I was supposed to be watching more closely, however. The second Garteon had been succeeded by yet a third in Asturia. Garteon III was an even bigger scoundrel than his father or grandfather had been, and most of his animosity seemed to be directed at Wacune. It was fairly obvious that there were close ties between Wacune and Erat, and the Oriman family had apparently concluded that my duchy could not survive without Wacite support. The Asturian animosity toward me personally wasn't really too hard to understand, and it probably dated back to the time of Duke Nerasin. I *had* made examples of a fair number of Asturian dukes over the centuries, after all. What the Asturians chose to overlook was the fact that I'd also jerked a goodly number of Wacites and Mimbrates up short as well. The Asturians seemed to want to look upon me as an hereditary enemy who hovered in the shadows waiting for the chance to thwart all their schemes.

What ultimately happened in northern Arendia came about largely because Duke Moratham of Mimbre was in his mid-eighties, and was quite obviously senile. His so-called 'advisors' were untroubled by scruples, and, since the doddering old Moratham automatically approved everything they put before him, they were the actual rulers of Mimbre. Garteon III of Asturia saw his chance, and, to put it crudely, he began buying up Mimbrate nobles by the score.

I should have been paying more attention. A great deal of the suffering I've endured about what happened to Wacune derives in no small measure from the fact that it was at least partially my fault.

The meeting of the Arendish Council in 2940 was placid, even tedious. Duke Moratham slept through most of it, and there wasn't really anything exciting enough going on to wake him. I'd have probably suggested a regency, but Moratham's only surviving son was quite obviously unfit to rule. He took his privileges very seriously, but gave little thought to his responsibilities.

It was after Ontrose and I had returned to Vo Wacune that my father stopped by to see how I was doing.

I was in my rose-garden when my maid escorted him out to see me. Knowing my father as I do, I'm fairly sure that he'd snooped about a few times in the two centuries or so since I'd last actually seen him, but he'd evidently not found anything to complain about, so he'd left me alone. 'Well, Old Wolf,' I greeted him, 'what have you been up to?'

'Not too much, Pol,' he replied.

'Is the world still all in one piece?'

He shrugged. 'More or less. I had to patch it a few times, but there haven't been any major disasters.'

I carefully cut one of my favorite roses and held it up for him to see. 'Would you look at this?' I said.

He hardly even glanced at it. 'Very nice,' he said indifferently. Father doesn't really have much of an eye for beauty.

'Very nice? That's all you can say? It's absolutely gorgeous, father. Ontrose developed it just for me.'

'Who's Ontrose?'

'He's my champion, father. He rights wrongs for me, and he chastises anybody who insults me. You'd be amazed at how polite people are to me when he's around.' Then I decided to stop beating about the bush. 'Oh, incidentally, he's *also* the man I'm going to marry – just as soon as he gets up the nerve to ask me.'

Father's face grew wary at that point. He knew me well enough not to come down on the wrong side of me. 'Interesting idea, Pol,' he said blandly. 'Why don't you send him around so that he and I can get to know each other?'

'You don't approve,' I accused.

'I didn't say that, Pol. I just said that I don't know him. If you're serious about this, he and I ought to have at least a nodding acquaintance with each other. Have you thought your way completely through this, though? There could be some fairly serious drawbacks, you know.'

'Such as what?'

'I'd imagine that there's quite a difference in your ages, for one thing. How old would you say he is?'

'He's grown up, father. He's over thirty.'

'That's nice, but you're about nine hundred and fifty, aren't you?'

'Nine hundred and forty, actually. So what?'

He sighed. 'You'll outlive him, Pol. He'll be old before you've turned around twice.'

'But I'll be happy, father – or aren't I supposed to have any happiness?'

'I was just pointing it out, that's all. Were you planning to have any children?'

'Of course.'

'That's not really a very good idea, you know. Your children will grow up, get old, and die. You won't. You'll go through the same thing you went through when Beldaran died, and that very nearly killed you, as I recall.'

'Maybe when I get married, my life will become normal. Maybe I'll grow old, too.'

'I wouldn't count on it, Pol. The Mrin Codex has a lot to say about you and what you'll be doing on down the road.'

'I'm not going to base my life on the ravings of an idiot, father. Besides, you got married, didn't you? If it was all right for you, it's certainly all right for me.' I deliberately glossed over mother's peculiarities. 'Besides, if Ontrose marries me, his lifespan might be extended as well.'

'Why should it? He's ordinary, and you're not. His life might *seem* longer, though. You're not the easiest person in the world to get along with. Unless this Ontrose fellow's a saint, he's probably going to have more than his share of bad days.'

'Why don't you just keep your nose out of my affairs, Old Man?'

'Please, Pol. Don't throw the word "affair" around like that. In this particular case it makes me very nervous.'

'You know where the gate is, father. Use it – now.'

And that more or less ended the conversation.

CHAPTER 21

The Privy Council of Duke Andrion of Wacune met in an airy room high in one of the towers of the palace one glowing afternoon. Our conference-room was carpeted and draped in a deep maroon, which contrasted nicely with the marble walls, and the massive furniture added that touch of permanence. 'Our alternatives, it seemeth to me, do grow more scant with the passage of time,' Duke Andrion said glumly to the rest of us. Duke Andrion was a dark-haired man in his mid-thirties, and he'd only recently ascended to the seat of power in Wacune. *My* presence at a Privy Council meeting in Vo Wacune might seem a bit odd, but I'd seen to it years ago that I was a member of all four Privy Councils in Arendia. I wanted to make sure that no Arendish duke did anything significant without my permission.

'Truly, your Grace,' Ontrose agreed with his duke. 'The Oriman family hath been bent on our destruction for years. I do fear me that war is inevitable.'

'There *are* alternatives, my Lords,' I told them quite firmly. 'Nerasin was at least as great a scoundrel as this endless succession of Garteons, and we managed to bring *him* to his senses.'

'The Oriman family hath no more sense than honor, Lady Polgara,' Baron Lathan asserted. Lathan appeared to have recovered from his defeat at the hands of Ontrose during the tournament, and they were friends again. 'It seemeth to me that Asturia must once again be subdued if the peace is to be kept.'

'Let's avoid that if possible, my Lord Lathan,' I suggested. 'Let me go talk with Garteon before we start mobilizing armies. Wars are *very* hard on the budget.'

'Oh, yes!' Andrion agreed fervently.

Then I looked quickly at Ontrose. 'No,' I said firmly.

'I fail to grasp thy meaning, your Grace,' he confessed.

'You can't go along, Ontrose. I'm going to say some things to Garteon in language I'd rather you didn't hear.'

'I cannot permit thee to go unescorted, my Lady.'

'Permit?' I asked him ominously.

'Poor choice of words there, perhaps,' he admitted.

'Very poor, Ontrose. You're a poet, so you shouldn't stumble over language that way.' I laid a fond hand on his. 'I'm only teasing, Ontrose.' Then I looked at Duke Andrion. 'Let me talk with Garteon before you start mobilizing, your Grace. His grandfather came around after I spoke with him. Perhaps that tiny bit of good sense runs in the family.'

Baron Lathan looked as if he were about to protest.

'We can always mobilize the army if I fail, Baron,' I told him. 'When we get right down to the bottom of it, the Oriman family's animosity is directed at *me*, not Wacune. I've been disrupting Asturian scheming for a long time, and I intend to continue. Wacune and Erat are like brother and sister, so Garteon knows that if he attacks Wacune, I'll attack him. Luring me into war is probably his main goal. Since this is really a squabble between Garteon and me, it's best if he and I settle it with a private little chat.'

'We shall be guided by thee, your Grace,' Andrion said.

'Excellent decision, your Grace,' I complimented him.

I went to Asturia in the usual way and snooped around Vo Astur for almost a week, but I couldn't find so much as a trace of Garteon. I loitered unobserved in the grey hallways, hoping to catch some hints about his location, but the Asturian nobility seemed totally uninformed as to his whereabouts. I flew on to look around at the estates of the members of the Oriman family, but he wasn't at any of them. I even went so far as to snoop around in several outlaw encampments back in the forest. Still no Garteon. Quite clearly, the Duke of Asturia had gone down a hole somewhere. Surely there was *someone* in Asturia who knew where he was, but whoever that someone was, he wasn't talking about it. Since Arends are constitutionally incapable of keeping a secret for more than a few hours I began to catch a strong odor of Grolim in the whole business.

I wasn't in a very good humor when I finally threw up my hands in defeat and flew back to Vo Wacune to report my failure to my friends in the palace. After some discussion, I glumly agreed that mobilization for war was the only course of action open to us at this point. 'I'll keep trying, though, gentlemen,' I assured the little gathering. 'Sooner or later, Garteon's going to have to come out of hiding. He's made me a bit peevish, and I'd like to talk with him about that – at length.'

Then Ontrose escorted me back to my town house, and we had a quiet supper. About the only good thing about my failure in Vo Astur was the fact that it persuaded my handsome champion that I was *not* omnipotent.

After supper, we adjourned to my rose-garden. I needed the peace of that lovely spot to calm my nerves.

'I do sense thy discontent, my Lady,' Ontrose sympathized.

'It's a bit more than discontent, dear friend,' I said wryly. 'Evidently, I've had too many years of easy successes, and failure upsets my opinion of myself.'

He smiled faintly, but then he sighed. 'On the morrow I fear me that, with thy permission, I must go north into thy domain. If Wacune doth mobilize, then Erat must needs follow. Given two armies, I have a few fears as to the outcome of the current unpleasantness.'

I nodded. 'I'll draw up a warrant for you to take to Malon Killaneson, my seneschal up in Erat. He'll open my treasury for you. Please treat my people kindly, dear Ontrose. Feed them well and train them to defend themselves.'

'Thou art ever the mother, dear Lady.'

I shrugged. 'It seems that way,' I agreed. 'It must have something to do with my own mother's side of the family – but we don't really need to go into that.'

Then I saw something familiar in the night sky. 'You're late,' I said.

'I?' Ontrose said in puzzlement.

'No, Ontrose, not you. I was talking to my old friend up there.' I pointed out the smeary light of the comet pasted against the stars on the velvet throat of night. 'He usually appears in the late winter, but it's almost summer now.'

'Thou hast seen this marvel before?' he asked.

'Many times, Ontrose, many times.' I made a quick mental computation. 'Thirteen times actually. I was fourteen the first time I saw him. He comes by for a visit every seventy-one years.'

Ontrose also made some calculations, and his eyes went very wide.

'Don't let it upset you, dear Ontrose,' I told him. 'People in my family tend to live for a long time, that's all. It's just a trait – like dark hair or a long nose.'

'It seemeth to me that the casual dismissal of nine centuries of life as a mere family peculiarity doth stretch the boundaries of the meaning of that term, Lady Polgara.'

'The secret to longevity lies in keeping busy, Ontrose – and avoiding fights with people who're bigger than you are, of course.' I thought back. 'I think my fourteenth summer came in one of those years I spent in my Tree,' I reminisced. 'My sister and I were having an argument about my father, and I was feeling sulky. I lived in my Tree for a couple of years to punish her.' I laughed. 'Children can be so ridiculous at times.'

'Thou hast a sister? I had not heard of that.'

'She died – many, many years ago. Her name was Beldaran, and we were twins. She was much prettier than I am.'

'Say not so, my dear Lady,' he protested. 'Thou art the paramount beauty in all this world, and I shall prove the fact upon the body of any foolish enough to gainsay my words.'

'Flatterer,' I said, touching his cheek fondly.

'To speak the truth is not flattery, my Lady.'

'To exaggerate *is*, though. I certainly wasn't all that pretty the first time my friend up there paid me a visit. My sister was so beautiful that I just gave up and let myself go to seed, so to speak. I was awkward and gangly and not really very clean – unless a passing rain-storm had just washed off most of the dirt. After my sister's betrothal, I cleaned myself up. We were sixteen then, so after I scrubbed off the dirt and combed my hair, I was moderately presentable. My sister was betrothed to Riva Iron-grip, King of the Isle of the Winds, and after we sailed to his realm, I entertained myself by breaking hearts for a while.'

'I must admit that I do not follow thee, dear Lady,' he confessed.

'Oh, dear,' I laughed. 'You *are* an innocent, aren't you, Ontrose? That's what young girls do, didn't you know that? We wear our prettiest dresses and ribbons, put on our most winsome expressions, and then go forth to do war. Our enemies are all the other pretty girls in the vicinity, and our battleground is the collective hearts of all the young men within reach.' I gave him an arch look. 'Be very careful around me, dear boy,' I warned him. 'I could break your heart with a single flutter of my eyelashes.'

'Why wouldst thou wish to shatter that which is already wholly thine, dear Lady?' he asked, and I sensed a certain subterfuge in his carefully phrased question. Ontrose was obviously not *quite* as innocent as he seemed to be. This was moving along even better than I'd hoped. Ontrose obviously no longer looked at me as an institution. We were definitely making progress now.

'Be warned, my champion,' I bantered. 'Methinks I shall unlimber mine entire arsenal upon thine unprotected heart. Defend thyself as best thou canst.'

I think my lapse into formality startled him just a bit. 'Thou wouldst take so unfair an advantage of me, Lady Polgara?' he chided lightly. 'Fie! For shame! Must I now defend thy realm 'gainst the Asturians and mine own heart 'gainst thine unspeakable charm simultaneous? I have no fears concerning the Asturians. Mine heart's fortress, however, doth already crumble before thine onslaughts, and I do fear me that I must inevitably capitulate and submit to this gentle enslavement which thou dost propose.'

I laid my hand on his arm. 'Well put, my Lord,' I complimented him. 'Very well put indeed. We shall talk about this more anon.' And then he took my hand and gently kissed it.

It was a bit flowery, but it was a start. The ladies who read this will understand, of course, but I don't think the men will. That's all right, though – as long as *somebody* understands.

The peace I'd imposed on Arendia had been based on the brutal fact that as soon as one of the duchies began to show signs of restiveness, the other three would lock into an alliance to counter its waywardness. The core of the problem *this* time was the senility of Duke Moratham of Mimbre. By now, he'd been placed in the care of a nurse who babied him like the child he'd become. The governance of the duchy was in the hands of a cluster of nobles who were far more interested in out-maneuvering each other than they were in the good of Arendia as a whole. I made several attempts to explain the realities of Arendish politics and the benefits to all of the ongoing peace to them, but they were too short-sighted and too caught up in their own chicanery to understand. I think that if their capital had been located in central Mimbre, they might have come around, but, since Vo Mimbre stands on the extreme southern border of Arendia, events in the three northern duchies might as well have been happening on the far side of the moon. Despite my best efforts, Mimbre distanced itself from the rest of us and took up a stance of strict neutrality.

I had some suspicions about the source of this Mimbrate policy. Over the centuries, many in the kingdoms of the west have viewed my family's conviction that the Angaraks were behind most of the

344

disruptions on our side of the Eastern Escarpment as an obsession. Perhaps we *are* a bit too quick to lay blame at Angarak doors, but when we're talking about Arendia, our suspicions are fully justified. Arendia has always been the key to the Angarak design to disrupt the west. Ctuchik was absolutely convinced that if he set fire to Arendia, the entire west would soon go up in flames. Unfortunately, Arendia's always been a tinder-box that'll take fire if you so much as look at it.

Ontrose went north into my realm to oversee the mobilization of my people. Though I certainly realized the necessity for that, I sorely missed him. I dreamt about him every night and thought about him just about every moment while I was awake. I made frequent trips to my duchy – more than were necessary, actually – but I *was* the Duchess of Erat, after all. Wasn't it my duty to keep an eye on things?

The armies of Wacune and Erat were not really separate, since the two duchies were so closely linked. Baron Lathan commanded Andrion's forces, and Ontrose commanded mine, but all our major strategic decisions grew out of extended conferences in either Andrion's palace or my manor house on Lake Erat. We were all very close anyway, so we moved as a unit.

By the summer of 2942, everything was in place. Our combined armies significantly outnumbered anything Garteon III could muster, and if he so much as stepped across either of our borders, we could easily crush him like an irritating bug.

'All is now in readiness,' Ontrose reported to Andrion and me when he made one of his all too infrequent journeys to Vo Wacune in the late summer of that year. 'The army of Erat doth stand poised on the north bank of the River Camaar within striking distance of Vo Astur itself. Should Garteon move his forces across the Wacite border, I will surely smash his capital. Barring the unforeseen, events have reached a stalemate. Methinks we and the Asturians will glare at each other across the various borders for some several seasons, and then we may confidently expect peace overtures from Vo Astur. The Oriman family is not well-liked by the other noble houses of Asturia, and I should not be at all surprised should Garteon III e'en as his grandfather, find his way to some high window in his palace and take flight from that vantage-point to the courtyard beneath.'

'Nicely put, my Lord Ontrose,' Andrion complimented him.

'I *am* a poet after all, your Grace,' Ontrose replied modestly. 'Facility with language hath ever been a part of my nature.'

Following our conference with Andrion, my champion and I

returned to my town house. At supper we discussed some rather obscure and difficult points of philosophy, and I was once again struck by the depth of this remarkable man's understanding. I'd have very much liked to have introduced him to uncle Beldin and then sat back to watch the sparks fly. I knew that if my plans worked out, that day would eventually come, and the prospect of introducing this paragon to my family was pleasing. My father and my uncles all lack a certain polish, and Ontrose, poet, philosopher, courtly gentleman, and the mightiest knight alive, was so polished that he almost glowed in the dark. Of all our Master's original disciples, only Belmakor could have matched his urbane civility – or so my father tells me.

After supper, we adjourned to my rose-garden as twilight descended over the glowing city of Vo Wacune. Ontrose played his lute and sang to me, and the cares of the day seemed to slip away. It was one of those perfect evenings that come all too infrequently. We talked of roses and only intermittently of the mobilization as the gentle evening slowly grew darker and the stars came out.

Then, when it was time for bed, my champion tenderly kissed me and bade me good night.

I didn't sleep very much that night, but I *did* dream.

The following morning, my Ontrose left Vo Wacune to return to the north.

Autumn that year had a dusty, almost regretful quality about it that seemed to suit my mood perfectly. I'd devoted over six centuries to beating the Arends over the head with peace, hoping to so completely ingrain it in their nature that thoughts of war would never occur to them again. That dream, however, was beginning to crumble.

Winter came early that year, announced by endless fog, the curse that bedevils northern Arendia in the off season. Fog's one of the more depressing weather conditions. It obliterates the sun and sky and lays a misty blanket of gloom over everything. We endured a kind of damp twilight for weeks on end, listening to the mournful dripping of water from the limbs of every tree while the stone faces of the buildings of Vo Wacune seemed to weep long strings of tears.

The spring that followed wasn't really much better than the winter had been. One expects a certain amount of rain in the spring, but there are also supposed to be sunny days now and then. *This* spring seemed to have forgotten about sunshine, however. Dirty clouds hung over us for weeks on end, and somber gloom stalked the streets.

Baron Lathan had been away for several months, and Andrion and I hadn't really paid all that much attention to his absence. Lathan, as commander of the Wacite army, was obliged to frequently visit military outposts, so his absence hadn't really been that unusual. When the miserable weather broke, however, he returned to Vo Wacune with some alarming news. Duke Andrion immediately summoned me to the palace to hear his friend's report. Lathan was still wearing his mud-spattered traveling clothes, and he looked positively exhausted. There were dark circles under his red-rimmed eyes, and he'd quite clearly gone without sleep for several days.

'You need hot food and rest, Lathan,' I delivered my professional opinion.

'There hath been scant time for that of late, your Grace,' he replied in an oddly dead tone of voice. Then he sighed deeply, a strangely melancholy sigh. 'I have but recently returned from Vo Astur –'

'You *what*?' I exclaimed.

'The reports of our agents in Asturia were conflicting, your Grace,' he explained. 'It seeméd to me essential that I see for myself what doth transpire in that hostile duchy. I have some facility with the uncouth speech of Asturia, and I thus experience no difficulty in passing myself off as a native. I shall not burden thee with tiresome details of my various subterfuges there. Suffice it to say that I was present when diverse members of the Asturian government and military did concoct a scheme which must needs concern thee greatly. In short, the intent of Duke Garteon is to attack thine own duchy, your Grace. Full well doth he realize that Wacune and Erat do stand poised on his eastern and northern frontiers, and at his first hostile gesture shall we move in concert to crush him.'

'Like a rotten egg,' Andrion added grimly.

Lathan smiled briefly. 'Truly,' he agreed. 'Garteon doth realize that an assault upon the borders of Wacune would be disastrous for him, and thus hath he resolved to assault not Wacune, but Erat.'

'Let him come,' I said. 'I'm as ready for him as Andrion is.'

'That doth lie at the core of his plan, your Grace,' Lathan explained in a dead-sounding voice. 'Garteon doth *not* propose a crossing of the River Camaar. Rather hath he assembled a fleet of diverse vessels at Vo Astur. I myself did personally witness the embarkation of his army aboard those ships, and I did also obtain by various means the ultimate destination of that fleet. In fine, your Grace, Garteon doth intend to sail down the Astur River and, well out of sight of land, doth he plan to sail northward, rounding the promontory which doth protrude from the northwestern coast of thy realm and

347

to ultimately make landfall at the mouth of the Seline River. His initial goal, I do fear me, is the poorly-defended city of Seline, and with that base firmly in hand, doth he intend to ravage all of northern Erat and from thence to strike deep into the heart of thy duchy. The alliance of Wacune and Erat hath ever blocked his evil design, and he clearly doth intend to destroy Erat first and *then* to move 'gainst Wacune.'

'Have they sailed yet?' I asked crisply.

'Yea, your Grace. Garteon's fleet did depart from Vo Astur some three days ago.'

'I need a map,' I told Andrion.

Wordlessly, he reached inside his doublet and produced a folded sheet of parchment.

I opened to the map and began measuring off distances. 'A fleet can only move as fast as its slowest ship,' I mused. 'If you're planning an invasion, you want all your troops in the same place at the same time. It's about two hundred and seventy leagues from Vo Astur to the mouth of the Seline River. Let's say that the best time that fleet can make will be about twenty-five leagues a day. That means eleven days – eight days from now.' Then I measured off some more distances and did some more quick arithmetic. 'We can make it!' I said with some relief.

'I do not follow thy meaning, Polgara,' Andrion confessed.

'My army's poised on the north bank of the River Camaar – right at the juncture of the north and south forks. It's seventy leagues from there to Seline. At a forced march, my army should reach Seline in seven days. It'll take the Asturians a day or so to march to Seline from the coast and my army will be in place before they get there.'

'Thou art remarkably well versed in military strategy, Polgara,' Andrion noted.

'For a woman, you mean? I've been in Arendia for six hundred years, Andrion, so I've had *lots* of experience with military matters.'

'I will send mine own army to thine assistance,' he said.

'You've got your own borders to defend, Andrion.'

''Gainst whom, dear lady?' he said with a smile. 'Garteon hath committed his entire army to the assault upon the northern reaches of thy realm. He hath no force to hurl at me.' Then he gave me a boyish kind of grin. 'Besides,' he said in plain speech, 'why should you have all the fun?'

'Oh, dear,' I sighed.

'I do perceive some flaw in these computations of thine, my Lady

Polgara,' Lathan objected. 'Thine army is encamped two day's hard ride from here, and Ontrose himself is at thy manor house on the shore of Lake Erat. There will, methinks, be some delay ere thy force can begin the march to Seline.'

'I have certain advantages, Lathan,' I reminded him. 'General Halbren's my champion's second in command, and he's a solid, practical man who can surely march troops a scant seventy leagues. I'll be talking with him before the day's out, and with Ontrose not too much later.' I squinted at the map again. 'Halbren can handle the march,' I decided. 'I think I'll have Ontrose go straight on to Seline to start reinforcing the city walls. Your army will arrive three days after mine, and I want to be sure that we're still holding the city when you get there.'

'And then will I fall upon Garteon's unprotected rear and grind him into dog-meat 'gainst the unyielding walls of thy city,' Lathan promised in a bleak voice.

'I'm sure the dogs will appreciate that,' I said lightly. '*You*, however, are going directly from here to bed. His Grace here can order your army to start the march. You can catch up with them in a day or so.'

'I command the army, your Grace,' he objected. 'It is my duty to lead them.'

'They know which way north is, Baron. They don't need you out in front to point the way. Get some sleep. You're right on the verge of falling apart.'

'But –'

'No buts, Lathan! Go to your room! Now!'

'Yes, ma'am,' he surrendered.

I had a strange, nagging feeling that something was seriously wrong with Baron Lathan. I knew that he was exhausted, but his behavior seemed somehow to be more dead than just tired. I didn't have time to investigate that, however. I went out onto the balcony of the room where we'd just held our meeting and changed my form to that of the now-familiar falcon.

General Halbren was a blocky man who'd come up through the ranks rather than having had his rank bestowed upon him as an addendum to a noble title. He was a thorough-going professional, and I had a great deal of respect for him. He carefully considered the information Baron Lathan had dredged out of Asturia and politely suggested some slight modifications to my planned response to the impending invasion of the Asturians. 'There's always the possibility that Duke Garteon may send an advance force to take Seline before the bulk of his army arrives, your Grace,' he pointed out. 'Ten leagues a day is probably the most we can expect from our foot-soldiers, but our cavalry units can cover more ground. If it's all right with you, I'll detach the cavalry and send them on ahead – just to be on the safe side.' He smiled briefly. 'Count Ontrose is very good, but defending Seline all by himself might stretch him just a bit.'

'We wouldn't want that, would we, Halbren?' I agreed. 'I'll be going on to my house now, and I'll tell him to expect reinforcements in –' I hesitated. 'How many days?'

'Four, your Grace. Five at the most. It'll be a little hard on the horses, but they won't be involved in the defense of Seline, so they'll be able to rest after they get there.'

'As it seemeth best to thee, esteemed General,' I said with an extravagant curtsey.

'*Must* you, my Lady?' he sighed.

I laughed and then went a ways outside the orderly encampment and put my feathers back on.

All in all, I was somewhat pleased at the way this was turning out. Baron Lathan's courage and enterprise had given us just enough warning of Garteon's planned invasion that we'd be ready for him when he arrived. I had enough time to evacuate all the civilians in the area, so my casualties would be minimal, and once Duke Gart-eon's army had been decimated, he'd have no choice but to capitu-late. The Battle of Seline would most probably insure another generation of peace in Arendia.

It was evening when I settled in the garden of my manor house at Lake Erat. Then I resumed my own form and went looking for Ontrose. I found him in my library studying a map. It was childish, I know, but I hadn't seen him for several weeks, so I slipped silently up behind him, reached around, and put my hands over his eyes. 'Guess who,' I murmured softly in his ear.

'Lady Polgara?' he replied, sounding startled.

'You peeked,' I accused. 'That's not fair.' Then I kissed him – several times, actually.

And then he kissed me. It was only one kiss, but it lasted for quite some time. My senses were reeling and I was breathing hard at its conclusion. I began to have some improper thoughts about then, but I decided that it might be a good idea to advise him of the current situation – little things such as marching armies across the land, defending cities, and wiping out the Asturians – before we got down to the more serious matters.

My champion was startled by the news. 'Art thou certain of this,

Polgara?' he asked. This was the first time he'd ever addressed me by my name, and that fitted in rather neatly with the plans I had for later in the evening.

'The information comes from Baron Lathan, dear heart,' I assured him. 'He slipped away and went to Asturia without telling Duke Andrion and me what he was up to. He personally heard Garteon and his underlings discussing their scheme, and he watched the embarkation of the Asturian army with his own eyes.'

'I would trust Lathan with my life, Polgara,' he said, 'and his word is not open to question. I must to horse.'

'Whatever for?'

'I must ride to the south to rouse our forces to rush to the defense of Seline.'

'Put your saddle away, dear,' I told him. 'I stopped by our army encampment on my way north. General Halbren will begin the march to Seline at dawn. He suggests that you go straight from here to Seline to prepare the city walls for the Asturian assault. He's sending the cavalry units on ahead to give you enough manpower to resist any advance attacks by crack units of Garteon's army.'

'Halbren is most practical,' Ontrose agreed. 'We are most fortunate to have him.'

'There's a bit more, Ontrose,' I told him. 'Baron Lathan's going to march the Wacite army north. He should arrive at Seline a day or so after the initial Asturian assault.'

'Dear, dear Lathan!' Ontrose almost chortled. ''Tween us both, we shall surely obliterate Garteon's army, and gentle peace shall re-emerge in poor Arendia.'

I loved Ontrose almost to the point of distraction, but the conjunction of 'obliteration' and 'gentle peace' seemed to clash just a bit. Ontrose was a poet, so he should have been a bit more careful with language than that.

'Hast thou perchance assigned numbers to those sundry events, Pol?' he asked.

'Numbers of what?'

'Of days, your Grace. When did Garteon's fleet sail?'

'Oh, now I understand. Garteon's force left Vo Astur three days ago. My computations suggest that his fleet will be at sea for eleven days – that's eight days from now. Halbren should arrive at Seline in seven days. Assuming that it'll take a day for the Asturians to march to Seline, we'll see him outside the city walls on the twelfth day. Lathan should arrive on the thirteenth day.'

'And by the fifteenth day, Garteon's army shall be no more,' my champion added grimly. 'Thy strategy is masterly, beloved.'

'Better even than that, it appears,' I said with a warm glow surging through my veins.

'I do fear me that I do not take thy meaning, Pol,' he confessed.

'I'm not talking about this incidental war, my dear,' I said rather smugly. 'That "beloved" that just escaped you had some strong overtones of surrender to it. Why don't we adjourn to some more suitable place and discuss that at greater length?'

You can't get much more obvious than that, I suppose.

He kissed me gently at that point, and I'll confess that I very nearly swooned right there in his arms. Then, with a look of towering nobility, he tenderly disengaged my arms from about his neck. 'The current crisis hath, it seemeth to me, excited us both beyond that which is seemly and proper, dearest Polgara,' he said with a certain regret. 'Let us not fall prey to heightened emotions engendered by the prospect of war. I will to horse now to remove myself from this dangerous proximity unto thee. I must to Seline to prepare our defense, and the cool night air might serve to moderate the unseemly heat which doth inflame my blood. Farewell, beloved. Let us address this matter further anon.'

And then he turned and left the room.

'Ontrose!' I screamed after him. 'You come back here!'

And would you believe that he ignored me?

The room in which I stood was my own library, and many of the things there were precious to me. I left the room rather quickly and marched down the hall to the kitchen, where I began hurling things at the wall.

Malon Killaneson, my seneschal, came running. 'Yer Grace!' he exclaimed, 'Whatever are y' doin'?'

'I'm breaking dishes, Malon!' I shouted back at him. 'You'd better get out of here, because I'm just about ready to start on people!'

He fled.

The following morning, after a sleepless night, I went falcon again. I strongly resisted my impulse to chase Ontrose down and drag him off his horse. I flew south instead. I definitely needed some exercise about then, and Duke Andrion really should be kept advised, I supposed.

I found Andrion on the city walls, and he was dressed in full armor. I flared my wings, swooped over to a concealed spot behind a jutting buttress, and resumed my own form. Unless it's absolutely necessary, I try not to do that in the presence of others. I hadn't examined Andrion recently, so I wasn't entirely sure that his heart was still sound. Then I came out from behind the buttress. 'Good morning, Andrion,' I greeted him.

He looked startled. 'I had thought that it had been thine intention to go north, Polgara. What hath delayed thee?'

'I've already been north, Andrion,' I told him. 'General Halbren's on the march, and Count Ontrose is going on ahead to Seline. Everything's moving according to schedule. When Garteon reaches Seline, we'll be ready for him. What are you doing in that silly armor?'

'It seemeth to me that thou art out of sorts this morning, Polgara.'

'Probably something I ate. What *are* you doing?'

'Posing, Pol, just posing. With both Lathan and Ontrose elsewhere occupied, the command of the local garrison hath winnowed down to me. I have garbed myself in armor, and I do posture and gesticulate here atop the battlements to reassure the citizens of Vo Wacune that they have little to fear with so mighty a warrior standing 'twixt them and the foul Asturians.'

'And it's fun, too, isn't it?'

'Well –' He said it a bit deprecatingly, and we both laughed.

'Let us return to the palace, Pol,' he suggested. 'Surely I have displayed myself enough for one morning, and I do not much care for the fragrance emanating from this suit of steel.'

'We might do that,' I agreed, '*if* you promise to walk on the downwind side.'

After we'd returned to the palace and Andrion had shed his steel, we went to his study to discuss the situation.

'I know this may sound like a personal obsession rearing its head again, Andrion,' I said, 'but I *do* rather expect that if we were to start turning over rocks in Asturia, we'd eventually find a Grolim lurking under one of them. The Asturian mind is the perfect target for Grolim chicanery. I've never yet encountered one of these Asturian schemes that didn't have a Grolim source. Ctuchik's been obsessed with the idea of starting a general war among the kingdoms of the west since the Murgos crossed the land-bridge some nine hundred years ago. He desperately wants to build a fire, and he always goes to Asturia to find kindling.'

'The War of the Gods ended two thousand years ago, Pol,' Andrion disagreed.

'No, dear one, it didn't. It's still going on, and at the moment, we're all engaged in it. I think that after the Battle of Seline's finished, I'll drift on over into Asturia and start uprooting trees until I find

353

Garteon's tame Grolim. Then I'll take him – piece by piece – on down to Rak Cthol and drop him on Ctuchik's head.' It came out from between clenched teeth.

'Thou art *truly* out of sorts today, Polgara,' he observed. 'Didst thou and thy champion perchance have a falling-out?'

'I wouldn't exactly call it that, Andrion,' I replied. 'It was more in the nature of a disagreement.'

'On a military matter?'

'No. It was more important than that. Ontrose *will* come around to my way of thinking, however. I promise you that.'

'It doth pain me to see thou and thy champion at odds,' he said. 'Might I offer my services as conciliator?'

The notion of Duke Andrion's intervention in this situation struck me as enormously funny, for some reason, and I burst out laughing. 'No, dear Andrion,' I said. 'This is one of those things Ontrose and I are going to have to work out for ourselves. Thanks for the offer, though.'

CHAPTER 22

I spent the rest of the day at my town house in Vo Wacune. My champion's remark about cooling one's blood made a lot of sense just then. We *did* have this incidental little war to get out of the way before we got down to serious business.

The temperature of my blood didn't noticeably go down, however, and by the next morning, I was about to start climbing the walls. I gave up at that point and flew on north to check the positions of our two armies.

Lathan's Wacite army was crossing the River Camaar, and he and I spoke briefly on the north bank while we watched small boats and rafts ferrying his troops across. 'All doth proceed as we have planned, your Grace,' he assured me in that strangely empty voice I'd noticed when he'd first told Andrion and me of the Asturian plan.

'What's the matter, Lathan?' I asked him very directly. 'You seem somehow sad.'

He sighed. 'It is of no moment, your Grace,' he said. 'All will be made right again soon. The end of my discontent is now clearly in sight. I will be most glad when it is behind me.'

'I certainly hope so, dear Lathan,' I told him. 'You're as gloomy as a rainy day. Well, if you'll excuse me, I'd better go see where General Halbren is.'

General Halbren had reached the northern end of Lake Sulturn by now. He advised me that he'd received word that an incoming Tolnedran merchantman had seen the Asturian fleet about eight miles off-shore near Camaar about three days ago, and that was a sure indication that everything was proceeding according to schedule. I rode along beside my solid general for the rest of that day, putting off my next meeting with Ontrose. I still wasn't entirely positive that I wouldn't do something wildly inappropriate the moment I laid eyes on him. Just the thought of my beautiful champion made my heart start to flutter.

It could very well have been that fluttering that decided my course of action the next morning. Clearly, I wasn't ready to meet Ontrose just yet, so I decided to fly out over the Great Western Sea to pinpoint the location of the Asturian fleet. If there'd been a favoring wind from the south, we might have to re-think our schedule.

I crossed the coastline at about the site of the present-day city of Sendar and then spiraled upward until I'd reached a height of several thousand feet. From up there, I could see for ten leagues in any direction. If General Halbren's information had been correct, the enemy fleet should be somewhere near where I'd flown out over open water. They weren't anywhere in sight, though, and that made me *very* nervous. Perhaps I'd underestimated their speed, so I veered off and flew north along the coast, watching the seaward side. Still nothing. By mid-afternoon I'd rounded the tip of that out-thrust peninsula, and I knew that it was impossible for them to have come this far in six days, but Garteon probably *did* have access to a Grolim and all that implies. I grimly pressed on, and just as evening was turning the sky above me a deep purple, I reached the mouth of the Seline River. There weren't any ships of any kind there. I was nearing exhaustion, so I spiraled down and roosted in an oak tree near the beach. Maybe Garteon's ships were *slower* than I'd estimated instead of faster. That meant that I'd have to back-track and cover the sea-lanes to the south instead of up this way. I *was* going to find that fleet.

I roused myself just as dawn was tinging the eastern sky and flew south, darting my eyes in every direction as I went.

It was an hour or so past noon when I finally found them. They were no more than ten leagues north of Camaar, and would you believe that they were at *anchor*? What was going on here? I veered off, crossed the coastline and came to rest on a dead snag in the marshes that lie to the north of Camaar.

This didn't make any sense! If you're planning an invasion, you don't stop to take a vacation along the way. Something very peculiar was happening. One thing was absolutely certain, though. I had to get this information to Ontrose. This turn of events had cured my fluttering, at least, so I launched myself into the air and flew north over the marshes until I reached solid ground. Then I settled to earth, resumed my own form, and used translocation instead of feathers. In effect, I hopped from hilltop to hilltop. It may sound a bit like a jerky way to travel, but if the hilltops are three or four leagues apart, it *does* enable you to cover a lot of ground in a hurry.

It was almost sunset when I reached Seline, and then I went looking for Ontrose.

I found that he was quartered in the house of the chief magistrate of Seline, an old friend of mine, actually, and I had little trouble getting in to see my beloved.

He rose to his feet and bowed as I entered. 'Your Grace,' he greeted me formally. 'Art thou still vexed with me?'

I winced, remembering the shriek I'd hurled after him when he'd left my manor house. 'No, dear Ontrose,' I assured him. 'I broke a few dishes after you left, and that made *me* feel better.'

He gave me a baffled look.

'It's a womanly sort of thing, Ontrose. You wouldn't understand. Now then, I've come across a mystery, and I think I'm going to need your help in finding a solution.'

'If it is within my power,' he said modestly.

'I certainly *hope* it is, because it has *me* baffled. After you ran away from me, I went on down to Vo Wacune to advise Andrion of our progress, and then I came back north again. Baron Lathan was ferrying his army across the River Camaar, and General Halbren had just marched north out of Sulturn, so everything's going according to our plans.'

'That is most comforting,' he said.

'Enjoy it while you can, Ontrose, because the next part has worms crawling out of it.'

'Oh?'

'I flew on out over the Great Western Sea to find out just exactly where Garteon's ships were located. It took me quite a while, but I finally found them. They're standing at anchor ten leagues to the north of Camaar.'

'What?'

'Garteon's fleet's not moving, Ontrose. The mystery I mentioned has to do with "why?" I can't even begin to imagine what he's up to.'

'Art thou certain?'

'Oh, yes, Ontrose, absolutely certain. I didn't think it'd be a good idea to fly down and ask them, so I came here instead. Is there any reason at all for a seaborne army to just stop like that?'

'None that I can fathom, your Grace.'

'Polgara,' I corrected him. 'We got past the "your Grace" business some days back, as I recall.'

'I would not insult thee by incivil informality,' he explained.

'It's the *formality* I find incivil at this point, love,' I said bluntly. 'We can discuss that later, though. Right now we have this problem that's just screaming for a solution.'

'There *is* one possible answer, Polgara,' he mused.

'Prithee enlighten me – or point me in the direction of the dishes.'

He laughed. 'In truth, I see no *other* possible solution. Clearly, the fleet stands at anchor awaiting something. Are they out of sight of land?'

'Yes.'

'Then I would venture to say that it is no signal they do await.'

'Probably not, no.'

'Then must it be a specific date. Evidently, they made better progress than they had anticipated, so now must they pause to allow the calendar to catch up with them.'

'That *does* stand to reason, Ontrose. They're waiting, not just loafing.'

'It doth give birth to yet another mystery, however,' he said, frowning. 'Setting a specific date for a military action is not uncommon, but to do so clearly implies a necessity for coordination – one force to attack here while another doth simultaneous attack there. This procedure doth lie at the core of nearly all military campaigns.'

'It makes sense, yes.'

'But with *whom* is this coordination? Lathan hath assured us that the entirety of Garteon's army did take ship at the wharves of Vo Astur. Such being the case, whom is there left in all Asturia to coordinate *with*?'

'Some outside force, perhaps?' I suggested dubiously, 'but neither the Alorns nor the Tolnedrans would become involved in Arendish squabbles. I took care of *that* centuries ago.'

My champion's eyes suddenly widened. 'Impossible!' he burst out.

'But I *did*, love,' I assured him. 'Ran Borune I and I skinned the Vorduvians, the Honeths, and the Horbites alive over a hundred years ago to keep them from meddling in Arendish politics, and my father has a firm grip on the Alorns.'

'I did not speak of that, dear Polgara,' he assured me. 'It hath just burst in upon mine awareness that Baron Lathan is not unknown in Arendia, for indeed all Arendia did witness our jousting match at the Arendish Council when I did win the coveted office as thy champion. Might it not have been that Garteon or one of his henchmen did observe – and recognize – our dear friend in Vo Astur, and then did make some show of the embarkation of the Asturian force to deceive him and thus to contaminate his report?'

'I hadn't considered that, Ontrose,' I conceded. 'Once Lathan had seen all those troops boarding those ships at the wharves of Vo Astur, the ships could easily have sailed ten miles downriver and then unloaded the soldiers on some empty riverbank where Lathan wasn't around to watch. What it boils down to, dear heart, is that we *know* that Garteon has an army, but we can't be positive exactly where it is.'

'I must to horse!' he exclaimed.

'Ontrose, dear, dear Ontrose, I *do* wish you'd stop saying that. Where are you going now? Don't tell me that you're *still* afraid of what I might do to you.'

'I must needs confer with Lathan. If we have been duped, all is lost.'

'Not lost, exactly, but we *would* be badly out of position. Let your horse sleep. *I'll* take you to Lathan.'

'But –' he started to protest.

'Trust me, dear one,' I told him, laying one finger gently against his lips. Then, as long as they were so handy, I went ahead and kissed those soft lips – just to be sure they still tasted as good as before, you understand.

'Lady Polgara?' he said uneasily.

'It's not polite to interrupt me when I'm busy, love,' I said firmly. Then I kissed him again. 'Well,' I sighed a bit regretfully, 'that's enough of that for the moment, I guess.' A thought had just come to me that might not have come to my champion. Ontrose, despite his urbanity, was really an innocent when it came to politics. His lifelong friendship with Lathan made him incapable of distrusting the baron. I'd seen enough betrayals in my time, however, to always have a few suspicions up my sleeve. 'In just a few minutes we're going to go see Baron Lathan,' I told him. 'When you talk with him, I'd rather that you didn't mention any of our random speculations about the location of Garteon's army.'

'I must confess that I do not follow thee, beloved.'

'Let's not clutter his mind with *our* speculations, Ontrose. Let him arrive at his own. I don't want to blot out *his* thinking with ours. *His* answer might just come closer to the truth than ours does. Let's not close the door on that possibility. Just tell him that Garteon's fleet is anchored and then suggest the possibility of some significant date. Let him take it from there, and let's see where *he* ends up. Lathan has a good mind, and we'd be fools to hobble it.'

'Thou art wise beyond belief, my beloved,' he said admiringly.

'You are the *nicest* boy, Ontrose,' I said, laying a fond hand on his cheek.

'How dost thou propose to transport us unto the camp of Lathan?' he asked.

'It's probably better if you don't know too many of the details, love,' I told him. 'They aren't really important, and they might upset you. Put yourself in my hands and trust me.'

'With my life, beloved.'

I decided *not* to convert him into a field-mouse as I'd done with poor Killane that time. I didn't want to demean him, and I wanted him to have a clear head when he spoke with Lathan – just in case. At my suggestion, my champion and I went outside the city to a little grove of trees. It was shortly before midnight, but a full moon made the night almost as bright as day. I touched my hand to my beloved's pale forehead and murmured, 'Sleep.' And he did that. Then I gathered my Will and shrunk him.

That's a clumsy way to put it, I know, but it *is* fairly precise.

When the process was complete, my champion resembled a small figurine about six inches tall, and he weighed no more than a few ounces. I held him in my hand for a moment, and then I shrugged, wrapped him in my handkerchief, and tucked him in my bodice to keep him safe.

Don't even *think* about saying something clever! And I mean it!

I used translocation again, and that's a little tricky at night – even with a full moon.

Baron Lathan's army was just north of Sulturn by now, and the watch-fires made his camp easy to find. I made my last jump to an open hilltop about a half-mile from his picket-lines. Then I looked around carefully, reached into my bodice, and retrieved my champion. I carefully set him down on the grass, reversed the process that'd reduced him, and then said, 'Wake up, dearest one.'

His eyes opened, and he wiped at his brow. 'It seemeth to me that I have been in some place that was quite warm,' he noted.

'Yes,' I agreed. I didn't think it was necessary to tell him exactly

360

where he'd spent the last half-hour. Now that I think about it, it probably had been quite warm there.

He looked around. 'Precisely where are we, my beloved?' he asked.

'Just north of Sulturn, dearest,' I replied. 'That's Lathan's camp down there in the valley.'

'I have slept long, it would appear.'

'About a half-hour,' I said. 'Don't start counting miles and minutes, dear heart. It'll only give you a headache. Let's just say it was one of "those things" and let it go at that.'

'I shall be guided by thee in this, beloved.'

'Good. You'll have to identify yourself at the picket-line. Throw your rank around if you have to. We must speak with Lathan just as soon as possible.'

He squared his shoulders, offered me his arm, and we went on down the hill. It only took us about ten minutes to bull our way through the Wacite encampment to Baron Lathan's tent. His orderly recognized Ontrose and immediately awakened our sleeping friend. 'Ontrose?' Lathan said, rubbing at his eyes. 'I had thought that thou wert in Seline.'

'I was there no more than an hour ago, my friend,' Ontrose told him. 'I am the most fortunate of men, for I have at my disposal a miraculous means of transport.' He smiled fondly at me.

'Your Grace,' Lathan said, scrambling out of his cot.

'Let's just set aside formalities, Baron,' I suggested. 'We have a problem which we must immediately address. Tell him, Ontrose.'

'Of a certainty, your Grace.' Then my champion looked at his friend. 'Our problem is simple to describe, Lathan,' he said. 'The solution may prove more difficult. In short, our revered Lady Polgara here hath applied her incomprehensible talent to the sometimes tedious process of gathering information. She but recently went forth to ascertain the precise location of the Asturian fleet.'

Lathan's face grew wary at that point.

'Needless to say,' Ontrose continued, 'she did succeed. The location of that fleet, however, doth baffle me. Her Grace doth assure me that Garteon's ships do stand at anchor no more than ten leagues to the north of Camaar.'

I was watching Lathan closely, and he didn't really seem all that surprised to me. I was right on the verge of sending out a probing thought.

'No, Pol,' mother's voice interrupted me. '*Let Ontrose do it. He has to find this out for himself.*'

'*Find what out for himself?*' I demanded silently.

'*You'll see.*' Then she was gone.

'Her Grace and I have struggled with this at some length,' Ontrose was saying, 'and, recalling that *thou* wert in Asturia and that it wast *thou* who didst uncover this scheme, did we conclude that thou might be best qualified to unravel this peculiar turn of events. Mine own reasoning is somewhat pedestrian, I fear me. My best surmise gropingly suggested that this pause can only be explained by some grander plan. It seemeth to me that some date must have significance in Garteon's overall scheme.'

'I cannot fault thy reasoning, Ontrose,' Lathan conceded, 'and indeed I, whilst I was in Vo Astur, did catch some hint of just such a fascination with the calendar. I had not the time, however, to pursue it.'

'Let us reason together, old friend,' Ontrose suggested. 'If a given date doth have such significance that a pause is dictated, doth that not imply that someone *else* is reading that self-same calendar?'

'It doth indeed, Ontrose!' Lathan exclaimed. I seemed to detect a slightly false note in his enthusiasm, however.

Then Ontrose, caught up in the momentum of his own reasoning, pursued it one step further. 'But to *whom* would that calendar be of such interest, Lathan? If Garteon's army is *truly* on board those ships, who is there left in Asturia to read calendars with such interest?'

Lathan's change of expression was so slight that I very nearly missed it. It was no more than a slight tightening around his eyes. 'Look out, Ontrose!' I shouted.

Clearly, Baron Lathan was about two steps ahead of my champion, and he knew exactly where his friend's line of thought would take him. He spun quickly and seized his sword from off the bench at the foot of his cot. Then he whirled, raising his sword to strike down my beloved.

I think, however, that Ontrose had not been quite so far behind Lathan as he might have appeared, for even as Lathan's sword began its fatal descent, the sword of Ontrose came whispering out of its sheath and caught Lathan's in mid-stroke.

'And now is all made clear, Lathan,' Ontrose said sadly. 'All except why.'

Lathan swung his sword again, and Ontrose easily parried the stroke. Quite obviously, my champion didn't need any help from me. I stepped back out of the way.

I'd hardly call what happened a fair fight. Lathan's only chance had been that desperate first attack. After that failed, he didn't really have any chance at all. Moreover, his expression quite clearly said that he *knew* he was going to lose. I got the uneasy feeling that he really preferred it that way.

It was noisy. A fight involving broadswords always is. The noise, naturally, attracted attention. My only contribution to the affair involved the tent where it was taking place. It still *looked* like a canvas tent, but steel is quite a bit softer than that tent was after I 'modified' it. I saw to it that there wouldn't be any interruptions.

The end of the sword fight was announced by a gush of bright blood bursting forth from Baron Lathan's mouth as my champion's sword slid smoothly through his right lung. Lathan stiffened, dropped his sword, and then collapsed.

Ontrose was weeping when he knelt at his friend's side. 'Why, Lathan, why hast thou done this?'

Lathan coughed up more blood, and I knew from that visible sign that his wound was mortal and that there was nothing I could do to save his life. 'It was to end my suffering, Ontrose,' he said in a barely audible voice.

'Suffering?'

'Agony, Ontrose. I confess freely, now that I am nearly free, that I did love – and still do love – our Lady Polgara. Thou didst wrest her from me at that accursed tourney, and my heart hath been dead within me since that day. Now do I gladly go to endless sleep, but I shall not sleep alone. Wacune shall die with me, and all else that I love.'

'What hast thou *done*, Lathan?' Ontrose demanded in a horrified voice.

Lathan coughed up more blood. 'I have betrayed thee – and all of Wacune.' His voice was growing weaker. 'All unobserved did I go into Asturia and did speak with Garteon and a foreign advisor of his whose name I did not ask.'

'Foreign?' I asked sharply.

'A Nadrak, methinks – or perchance a Murgo. He it was who devised our deception. The fleet which did depart from Vo Astur eight days ago was no more than a sham – a ploy to deceive Wacune and Erat. There *are* no troops on board those ships. Garteon's army doth wait in the forest not two leagues from Wacune's western frontier.' He coughed weakly again.

'When?' Ontrose pressed. 'When will they invade Wacune?'

'Two days hence, Ontrose.' Weak though he was, Baron Lathan's voice had a note of triumph in it. 'That tenth day from the departure of the sham fleet doth loom large upon Garteon's calendar, for upon that day shall his force march into Wacune, and, all unobstructed, shall they march to the alabaster city, which doth stand, helpless and unprotected, in their path. Vo Wacune is doomed, Ontrose, my beloved – and hated – friend. Though I am mortally wounded by thy welcome sword-thrust, I have set mine answering stroke already in motion. Four days hence shall the Asturians mount their attack upon the undefended walls of Vo Wacune, and no force at thy command can reach the city in time to prevent its fall.' He began coughing up large amounts of blood. 'I die, Ontrose,' he said in no more than a whisper, 'but I do not die alone. My life hath been a burden unto me from that day when thou didst unkindly wrench beloved Polgara from my grasp. Now may I lay down that burden and go gladly into my grave, knowing that I will not go alone. All that I have loved shall go with me, and only Lady Polgara, immortal and unassailable, shall be left behind to echo her howls of grief 'gainst the walls of heaven. It is done, and I am content.'

Then he firmly shut his lips and fixed his eyes upon my face with a look of unspeakable longing.

And then he died, and Ontrose wept.

I silently cursed myself for my inattention. There had been a hundred clues that I had completely missed. I should have *known*!

I went quickly to the door of the tent. 'Gather the officers!' I commanded the Wacites who'd been vainly trying to bull their way into the tent. 'We have been betrayed! Treason hath left Vo Wacune helpless and undefended!' Then I remembered that these men were Wacite peasants. 'Pull yerselves t'gether, me boy-os! We've got us work t' do, don't y' know.'

Then I turned back to look at my weeping champion. 'That's enough, Ontrose!' I snapped. 'Get up on your feet!'

'He was my friend, Polgara!' he wept, 'and I killed him!'

'He deserved killing. You should have killed him during the tournament. On your feet! *Now*!'

He looked startled, but he obeyed.

'That's better. Turn this army around and start it moving south immediately. I'll go tell Halbren what's happened and start him south as well. Move, Ontrose! Move! We've got a long way to go and not much time.'

He gestured toward Lathan's body. 'What of my friend here?' he asked me.

'Drop him in a ditch somewhere – or leave him where he lays. He's nothing but garbage, Ontrose. Dispose of him as you would any other garbage. I'll be back in about an hour, and then you and

I are going to Vo Wacune. We've got a war to fight down there.' Then I left the tent.

Once I was out of earshot of the encampment, I allowed myself a few moments to speak – colorfully – about the situation. Lathan's treason had quite nearly succeeded. There was no possible way I could get reinforcements to Vo Wacune in time to defend the city. Quite obviously, I was going to have to do it 'the other way'. Right at that moment, I rather liked that idea. The image of a cheese-grater came to mind, and this time, I *would* use it, whether mother liked it or not.

I translocated myself north, hop-scotching my way from hilltop to hilltop to General Halbren's camp on the shore of Lake Sendar. Halbren, as always, showed no particular surprise when I told him of Lathan's treason. I honestly believe that Halbren could have watched the sky falling with no overt expression of surprise. 'Their plan is flawed, your Grace,' he told me calmly.

'It sounds fairly devastating to me, Halbren.'

'The capture of a city is but the first step, your Grace,' he explained. 'The Asturians may indeed *take* Vo Wacune, but the combined armies of Wacune and Erat shall arrive there only a few days later, and we have overwhelming force. Believe me, your Grace, we can re-take the city any time we choose, and after we've finished, Garteon won't have enough men left to patrol the streets of Vo Astur.'

'You're just going to give up Vo Wacune?' I demanded incredulously.

'It's only a city, your Grace – a collection of pretty buildings. The important thing about a war is winning it, and we *will* win this one. After it's over, we can rebuild Vo Wacune. It'll give us a chance to straighten the streets, at least.'

'You're impossible, Halbren,' I accused. 'Start your men south. I'm going to take Ontrose on down to Vo Wacune. Don't start drawing city maps just yet, though. I think I know of a way to hold off the Asturians until our forces get there.'

Then I went on back to Lake Sulturn, found Ontrose, and took him out a ways from the already moving Wacite army. I repeated the procedure I'd used before, and I deposited my champion in the same secure place. I rather liked having him there, to be honest about it.

The dawn of the ninth day on that Asturian calendar was dawning when we arrived in Vo Wacune. I took my slumbering hero out of his convenient resting place and returned him to his normal size.

Then I woke him up, and we entered the city. We went directly to Andrion's palace told him of Lathan's treason.

'We are doomed!' he exclaimed.

'Not quite, Andrion,' I assured him. 'I'm going to have to call in reinforcements, though, I think.'

'What force is close enough to come to our aid, Polgara?'

'My father, Andrion, and he doesn't have to be close to get here in a hurry.'

'Thou dost propose to defend the walls of Vo Wacune with sorcery?'

'It isn't really illegal, Andrion. I think that between us, father and I can hold off the Asturians until our armies arrive. Father can be *very* nasty when he sets his mind to it, and I can be even worse. By the time we're done, the very mention of Vo Wacune will give every Asturian for the next thousand years screaming nightmares. You and Ontrose had better alert the city garrison and make some preparations. I'll go home and summon my father, and then I'm going to bed. I haven't slept for three days, and I'm positively exhausted.'

I reached my town house and went into my library, firmly closing the door behind me. The Killaneson family knew by now what that meant and they didn't disturb me. Before I could go searching for father, however, mother came searching for me. *'Polgara!'* she said sharply. *'The Mimbrates are going to invade southern Wacune at first light tomorrow morning.'*

'What?' I exclaimed.

'The northern Mimbrate barons have allied themselves with Garteon, and they'll come north to join the Asturian army in the siege of Vo Wacune.'

'So that's what it's been all about,' I said as it came crashing in on me. 'The Asturians pulled us out of position so that they could attack Vo Wacune with Mimbrate allies to help them.'

'Don't repeat the obvious, Pol,' mother said. *'You'd better get word of this to your father. The way things stand, Vo Wacune hasn't a chance of surviving. He's the only one who can help you right now. He's in his tower in the Vale. Hurry, Pol!'*

'Father!' I sent my thought out to him, casting it out my library window at a sky which had been obscured by an incoming storm. *'I need you!'*

'What's the matter?' his thought came back almost immediately. I took that to be a good sign. For once, he'd been home when I called. *'The Asturians are right on the verge of breaking the peace here in Arendia.*

Duke Garteon of Asturia has formed an alliance with the barons of northern Mimbre. The barons are invading Wacune from the South.'

'Where's your army?'

'Most of it's in Central Sendaria in response to an Asturian ruse. We've been lured out of position, father, and Vo Wacune's in grave danger. I need help here. We're right on the verge of losing everything I've worked for.'

'I'll get there as quickly as quickly as I can, Pol,' he promised.

That made me feel quite a bit better, and I closed my window as the storm broke over Vo Wacune.

There's no question that our situation was grave. Our armies were on the march, but there was no way they could reach Vo Wacune in time to stave off the Asturian assault on the city, and by the time our forces *did* arrive, the Mimbrates would already be here to reinforce Garteon's army. As is so often the case, everything hinged on time.

I spent the remainder of that blustery night in my library considering the situation. The Arendish mind was locked in stone on certain issues. The soul of any domain lies in its capital. Mimbre would not exist without that golden fortress on the River Arend; Asturia would be meaningless without Vo Astur; and the Wacite duchy derived almost entirely from the delicate, soaring towers of Vo Wacune. It was that peculiarity which had persuaded me *not* to establish a capital city in my own duchy. My domain *had* no center. The destruction of the city of Erat would have angered me, but it would not have devastated me. I realized clearly that if Vo Wacune were to fall, Wacune would no longer exist. Within a few generations, it would only be a fading memory. Saving the city was an absolute imperative.

The summer storm which had descended upon us, unlike most storms of that season, did not blow off with the dawn, but continued to blow and rain and make life generally miserable.

This was that fatal tenth day, however, so I pulled on my cloak and went to the palace to see how things were progressing. I found Andrion and Ontrose deep in discussion. 'Father's on his way, gentlemen,' I advised them. 'This weather's probably going to slow him down, though.'

'It will also, it seemeth to me, delay the march of our own forces from thy duchy,' Andrion added.

'Then, as matters now stand, must we defend our city with such force as is available to us here,' Ontrose concluded. 'The task, methinks, will be formidable, but not impossible.' They were worried enough already, so I decided to keep the information about the Mimbrates to myself for the time being.

The wind and rain continued for the next two days, and that somewhat slowed Garteon's advance on Vo Wacune. At least he wasn't right outside our walls at daybreak when the bad weather finally passed on through and the sun came out again. Father reached the city about noon, and he found Ontrose and me arguing in my still-damp rose-garden. My beloved mail-shirted champion was doing his level best to persuade me to leave Vo Wacune before it was too late. 'It must be, Polgara,' he urged me. 'Thou must go from Vo Wacune to a place of safety. The Asturians are almost at the city gates.' In spite of everything I'd told him about my planned reception of Garteon's forces, he was *still* worried about my safety.

'Oh, Ontrose,' I said to him, 'stop that. You know perfectly well that I can take care of myself. I'm not in any personal danger.'

That was when father, who'd gone falcon, settled into my favorite cherry tree, changed back into his own form, and climbed on down. 'He's right, Pol,' he told me bleakly. 'There's nothing you can do here.'

'Where have you been?' I demanded.

'Fighting with the weather. You'd better get your things together. We've got to get you out of here immediately.'

I couldn't believe my ears! 'Have you lost your mind? I'm not going anyplace. Now that you're here, we can drive off the Asturians.'

'No, as a matter of fact, we can't. This is one of the things that *has* to happen, and you and I aren't permitted to interfere in any way. I'm sorry, Pol, but the Mrin's very specific about that. If we tamper with this, it'll change the whole course of the future.'

'Ctuchik's probably behind this,' I said groping for some new argument to win him over. 'You're not going to let him win, are you?'

'He's not going to win, Pol. His seeming success here will come back and defeat – and destroy – him later. Certain Arends are going to be involved in his destruction, and I'm not going to do anything to disrupt that, and neither are you. The "Archer" and the "Knight Protector" are going to grow out of what happens here, so we absolutely can't interfere.'

'The fall of Vo Wacune is certain, then, Ancient One?' Ontrose asked him.

'I'm afraid so, Ontrose. Has Polgara told you about the prophecies?'

'In some measure, Holy Belgarath,' Ontrose replied. 'I cannot pretend to understand all of what she told me, though.'

'To put it very briefly, there's a war going on that's been in progress since the very beginning of time,' father explained. 'Whether we like it or not, we're all involved in that war. Vo Wacune must be sacrificed if we're to win. You're a soldier, so you understand things like that.'

Ontrose sighed and then nodded gravely. How could I possibly fight the both of them?

'You might want to talk with Duke Andrion,' father continued. 'If you hurry, you may be able to get the women and children to safety, but Vo Wacune itself won't be here in a few days. I saw the Asturians as I was coming in. They're throwing everything they've got at you.'

'They will be much diminished when they return to Vo Astur,' my beloved champion assured him bleakly.

'If it's any comfort to you, Vo Astur's going to suffer the same fate some years from now.'

'I shall hold that thought, Ancient One.'

How *could* they so casually accept a defeat which hadn't occurred yet? 'What are you two thinking of?' I demanded in a shrill voice. 'Are you both going to just lie down and play dead for Garteon? We *can* win! And if you won't help, father, I'll do it myself!'

'I can't let you do that, Pol,' he said.

'You can't *stop* me. You'll have to kill me, and what'll *that* do to your precious Mrin Codex?' I turned to my beloved with my heart shriveling within me. 'Thou art my champion, Ontrose, and more – much much more. Wilt thou defy me? Wilt thou send me packing like some thieving chambermaid? My place is at thy side.'

'Be reasonable, Pol,' father said. 'You know that I can force you to go if I have to. Don't make me do that.'

Then I became irrational. 'I *hate* you, father!' I screamed at him. 'Get out of my life!' Tears were streaming down my face. 'I'll tell the both of you right now that I *will* not go!'

'Thou art in error, dearest Polgara,' Ontrose told me in unyielding tones. 'Thou wilt accompany thy father and go from this place.'

'No! I won't leave you!' My heart was breaking. I could not defy him. I loved him too much to do that.

'His Grace, Duke Andrion, hath placed me in command of the defense of the city, Lady Polgara,' he said, falling back on a stern formality. 'It is my responsibility to deploy our forces. There is no

369

place in that deployment for thee. I therefore instruct thee to depart. Go.'

'No!' I almost screamed it. He was killing me!

'Thou art the Duchess of Erat, dear Lady Polgara, but long ere that, thou wert of the Wacite nobility, and thou hast sworn an oath of fealty unto the house of Duke Andrion. I will hold thee to that oath. Do not dishonor thy station by this stubborn refusal. Make ready, my beloved Polgara. Thou shalt depart within the hour.'

His words struck me almost like a blow. 'That was unkindly said, my Lord Ontrose,' I said stiffly. He'd thrown duty right in my face.

'The truth oft times *is* unkind, my Lady. We both have responsibilities. I will not fail mine. Do not thee fail thine. Now go!'

My eyes filled with tears, and I clung to him for a moment. 'I love you, Ontrose,' I told him.

'And I love thee as well, my dearest one,' he murmured. 'Think of me in times yet to come.'

'Forever, Ontrose.' Then I kissed him fiercely and fled back into my house to make ready for my departure.

And so my father and I left Vo Wacune, and I surely left my heart behind as I went.

PART FIVE

Geran

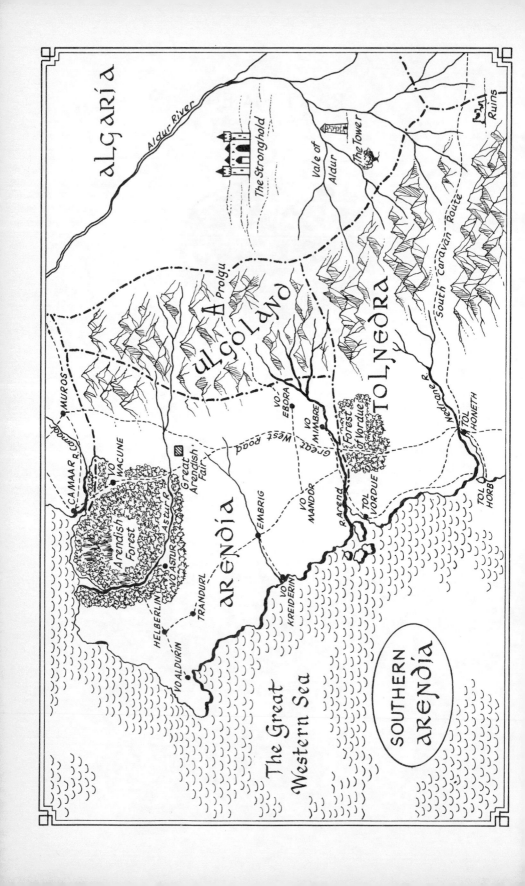

ALGARIA

Aldur River

The Stronghold

Vale of Aldur

The Tower

Ruins

ULGOLAND

Prolgu

TOLNEDRA

South Caravan Route

MUROS

VO-EBORA

VO-MIMBRE

Forest of Vordue

Nedrane R.

TOL HONETH

CAMAAR

R. Camaar

VO WACUNE

Astur R.

Great Arendish Fair

Great West Road

VO MANDOR

Arend R.

TOL VORDUE

TOL HORB

ARENDIA

Arendish Forest

EMBRIG

VO ASTUR

HELBERLIN

TRANDURL

VO ALDURIN

VO KREIDERIN

The Great Western Sea

SOUTHERN ARENDIA

CHAPTER 23

Even to this day I don't think my father fully understands exactly what Ontrose was telling me during that last conversation. When my beloved had spoken of duty, his use of that term had been all-inclusive. As a member of the court at Vo Wacune, I was duty-bound to obey the commands of Duke Andrion, but my paramount duty was to my own duchy, and that crushing responsibility over-rode everything else. Garteon of Asturia had destroyed Wacune. His next logical step would be to invade and attempt to destroy Erat as well. I'd failed to save Wacune, but I swore that I wouldn't fail to save Erat. Even though it cost me my life, I *would* obey that last command of the man I loved. It was my duty, and duty was all I had left.

I didn't bother to explain this to father. As a matter of fact, I didn't speak to him at all as the two of us rode on up out of the forests of Wacune toward the more open lands of Sendaria. Trying to explain would have been a waste of time, since as closely as I've been able to determine, father's never actually ruled even so much as a small barony, so he hasn't the faintest idea of what's involved in wearing a crown. He assumed that my sullen-seeming silence was nothing more than sulking, but in actuality it was the result of my preoccu-pation with the defense of my southern border against the inevitable Asturian invasion. Of one thing I was absolutely certain. My first step in defending my duchy would be to get this meddlesome old man out of my hair.

When we reached Muros, the city was in chaos. The merchants were desperately trying to find somebody – anybody – willing to buy up their assets at any price, the Algars had driven their herds back across the mountains to safety, and the general population was on the verge of flight. It didn't take a genius to realize that the Asturians would be at the city gates very soon. The more I thought about it, the more I became convinced that Muros would be the key to the defense of my southern frontier. The city was technically a part of the Wacite duchy, but the collapse of Wacune had left it hanging on a branch all by itself, a prize for the first passerby willing to take the trouble to pick it. Even as father and I rode out of town, I decided that I was going to annex Muros and the surrounding territory all the way down to the banks of the River Camaar. That river bank would obviously be a more defensible boundary than some imaginary line running down the middle of a wandering country lane.

First, however, I had to get clear of my father so that I could get to work. The important thing was to avoid going all the way back to the Vale with him. Once we arrived there, I'd never be able to get out from under his thumb. I maintained my pretense of sullen, suffering silence as we rode on up into the summer-touched Sendarian mountains, and when we came down onto the rolling grassland of Algaria, I was ready.

It was about noon on a glorious mid-summer day when we reached the roofless remains of mother's cottage, and that was when I reined in and dismounted. 'This is as far as I'm going,' I announced.

'What?'

'You heard me, father. I'm going to stay here.' I said it flatly and with a note of finality. I didn't want any misunderstanding.

'You have work to do, Pol.' *This?* Coming from a man who avoided work as he'd avoid the plague?

'That's too bad, father,' I told him. *'You'll* have to take care of it. Go back to your tower and snuggle up to your prophecies, but leave me out of it. We're through, father. This is the end of it. Now go away and don't bother me any more.'

That was wishful thinking, of course. I knew that father would give things a day or two to cool down before he came sneaking back to keep an eye on me, so I gave him about an hour to get out of earshot, and then I went falcon and flew back across the mountains to Erat, arriving at my manor house just at twilight. Then I went looking for my Seneschal, Malon Killaneson. Malon was a lineal descendant of one of Killane's younger brothers, and he closely resembled his many times over great uncle. He was efficient and practical, and his easy-going mannerisms made people want to cooperate with him in much the same way they had with Killane himself. I *did* rather approve of Malon's decision not to grow that

374

silly-looking fringe of a beard that had so marred Killane's appearance, though.

I found him poring over a map in my library, and he started visibly when I entered. 'Praise be!' he exclaimed. 'I thought y'd perished at Vo Wacune. How ever did y' manage t' escape, yer Grace?'

'My father decided to rescue me, Malon,' I told him. 'What's happening here?'

'I fear all is lost, me Lady,' he replied in despairing tones. 'Everybody in yer domain knows fer sure that th' Asturians kin march in an' take th' whole duchy any time they want to, so there's hopelessness drippin' off every tree an' bush. When I thought y'd been lost at Vo Wacune, me heart went down into me boots, an' I bin plannin' t' make me own escape across th' mountains into Algaria.'

'You'd desert me, Malon?' I accused.

'I thought y' was dead, yer Grace, so there wasn't nothin' left here fer me.'

'Is everything falling apart, then?'

'Pretty much so, yer Grace. Yer army's runnin' around in circles, not knowin' which way t' turn. Th' Asturians are comin', an' everybody w' the slightest touch o' good sense is lookin' fer a place t' hide, don't y' know.'

'Well, Laddy-buck,' I said in a fair imitation of his own Wacite brogue, 'do yer despairin' on yer own time. You an me, we got work t' do, so hitch up yer britches an' let's get at it. The Asturians might have taken Wacune, but s' long as I have breath, they'll not be after takin' Erat, don't y' know.'

'Now yer after soundin' like me very own dear mother, Lady Polgara,' he said, laughing. 'Is there any way at all we kin keep th' murderin' Asturians out o' our front parlor?'

'I think we can come up with something, Malon.' I thought for a moment. 'The core of our problem lies in the close ties Erat has always had with Wacune. The two duchies have never really been separate, so we aren't used to doing our own thinking.' I made a rueful face. 'It's probably my fault. I was concentrating about half of my attention on keeping the peace in all Arendia, so I've divided my time between this house and the one in Vo Wacune. I suppose I should have stayed closer to home to mind the store. More to the point, though, our army's always been little more than an extension of the Wacite force, so my generals haven't had much experience with independent thinking.' I gave him a sidelong glance. 'What say y', Laddy-buck? Would y' be after wantin' t' join me in educatin' some soldiers in th' fine art o' thinkin' fer themselves?'

'When y' talk like that, Lady-O, I'd be after wantin' t' join y' in almost anythin'.'

'Good. Go to General Halbren, the Chief of Staff. He's a good, solid man we can count on. Tell him that I'm back and that *I'll* be issuing the commands now. He'll know what to do when he passes my orders on to his subordinates. They'll need lots of details right at first, but after they realize that the commands are coming from *here* rather than Vo Wacune, we'll be able to start loosening the reins a bit. The first order I want you to pass on to Halbren is that we're going to move in and annex Muros, Camaar, and Darine – along with all the territory around our fringes. From now on, everything north of the River Camaar is mine.'

'There might be some argument about that, yer Grace. Them Wacite Barons in th' border areas be fearful independent, don't y' know.'

'They'll get over it, Malon. I'm bigger, older, and nastier than they are. I can't afford to have territory just off my left shoulder-blade that I can't control. For the time being, though, tell Halbren to concentrate on Muros. It's a rich town, so Duke Garteon of Asturia's certainly drooling in anticipation of the day when all that wealth gets transferred into his own treasury. I'm going to give him a very pointed lesson in good manners. Just as soon as he comes across the River Camaar, I'm going to trample on his face until it looks as if he's just been run over by a plow.'

'*Whoo!*' Malon said in mock surprise. 'Aren't y' th' fierce one, Lady-O?'

'I'm just getting started, Malon. If you want to see fierce, wait until I've built up some momentum. Now then, you and I have about a day and a half to get a week's work done, so let's get down to cases.' I sat down beside him, and we both started laying out our defenses on his map.

By morning, we had our troop deployment roughed in. I knew General Halbren well enough to know that I could leave the refinements up to him, so we moved on from there. 'I'm sure that at least *some* units of the Wacite army managed to escape the bonfire at Vo Wacune,' I said. 'Tell Halbren to give making contact with those people the highest priority.'

'T' swell our own ranks, me Lady?' Malon suggested.

'No. If we do things right, we won't need more men. What we *do* need is information about Asturian troop movements. My generals have to know exactly where the Asturians are massing to come across the River Camaar so that we can be ready to meet them. The Wacites hiding out in the woods down there will be our eyes. Have General Halbren impress the idea on those survivors that passing information on to us is far more important than randomly murdering any Asturians they come across.'

'Spyin' ain't considered t' be th' most honorable o' professions, me lady,' Malon reminded me.

'We'll *make* it honorable, Malon. Tell Halbren to wave the word "patriot" in front of the surviving Wacites. We have to make them understand the notion that it's a Wacite's patriotic duty *not* to get killed with even the tiniest bit of useful information still locked up in his mind.'

'That's always assumin' that there be any Wacites left down there,' Malon said. 'There's bin a steady stream o' people comin' across the River Camaar, don't y' know.'

'We'll have to make arrangements for them, I think. After we take Muros, we'll set up camps for them and provide food.'

''Tis a kindly, charitable person y' are, me Lady.'

'Kindness has nothing to do with it, Malon. I want the Wacites who choose to remain down there to know that their wives and children are safe and well cared for up here. That should encourage them to spy for us just as hard as they possibly can. Now, then, let's have a look at the defenses of our coasts.'

By evening, we'd sketched out the preparations for the inevitable war lurking just over the horizon, and then I turned to something that definitely needed attention. 'Now then, Malon, you and I are going to have to be able to communicate, and we won't have time to wait around for messengers on horseback to run back and forth between here and where I'm currently living.'

'An' where might that be, yer Grace?'

'My father and I aren't speaking right now. He was taking me back to his tower in the Vale of Aldur, but I took up residence in my mother's old house at the northern end of the Vale instead. He's the nosey type, so I'm sure he'll try to keep an eye on me. I don't want to give him any excuses to come here to start snooping around, so I'll have to stay fairly close to mother's cottage. You're going to have to pass my orders on to General Halbren.' I gave him a direct look. 'You know who I am, don't you, Malon?'

'Of course, yer Grace. Yer th' Duchess o' Erat.'

'Let's go back beyond that. Who was I before I became the Duchess?'

'I'm told y' was Polgara th' Sorceress.'

'I still am, Malon. It's not something you can get rid of. I can do things that other people can't. You know that little room at the top of the northwest tower?'

'Y' mean th' little place where th' upstairs maids bin keepin' their brooms an' mops?'

'Is *that* what they're doing with it now? That wasn't what your great uncle and I had in mind for it when we built the house. Anyway, I've cast a spell on that room. Killane and I used to use it when we needed to talk with each other when I was away. He'd go up there when he needed to tell me something, and I could hear him when he said something to me – no matter where I really was.'

'What a marvel!'

'It's fairly commonplace in my family. Why don't you go up there right now? Let's find out if it still works.'

'If that's what y'll after be wantin', yer Grace.' He rose to his feet and left, his expression dubious.

Notice that I'd hurried through the explanation and decorated it with a few out and out lies. There wasn't anything special about that room, but I wanted Malon to *believe* that there was.

I think my father explained to Garion one time that what we call ''talent'' in our family is latent in all humans, and as long as someone has reason to *believe* that something's going to happen, it probably will. If Malon was convinced that the broom closet at the top of the tower was a magic place, my plan would work.

I gave him several minutes to get up there, and then I sent my thought out to him. *'Malon Killaneson, can you hear me?'*

'As clear as if y' were standin' right beside me, yer Grace,' he exclaimed, his voice distorted.

'Don't talk, Malon. Put what you want to say in your thoughts instead. Form the words in your mind, not your mouth.'

'What a wonder!' His thought was much clearer than his voice had been.

'Give me a moment to brush the cobwebs off the spell, Malon,' I said. *'I haven't used the place in centuries.'* I've noticed that little touches of housekeeping tend to reinforce belief. *'There,'* I said after a minute or so, *'is that better?'*

'Much better, me Lady.' Actually, there was no real difference.

We tried for some distance after that, and we continued the little game until well after midnight, and by then the whole thing was firmly locked in Malon's mind. Then we returned to the library. 'I'd probably be getting back now,' I told him. 'Father's almost certain to come nosing about soon. He's got me pinned down, so you're going to have to convey my orders to General Halbren. I'll give you a written authorization to speak for me, and that should head off any arguments. You and I are going to have to stay in close contact, so I want you to go up to that tower room every day at sunset so that we can talk. You'll have to let me know what's going on and advise me about things that need my attention. I'll tell you how to deal with anything that comes up.'

'Isn't it th' clever one y' are, me Lady? Y've come up w' a way t' be in two places at once.'

'Well, not quite. It's a cumbersome way to do business, but we haven't got much choice. Once we're firmly in control of Muros, we'll have Halbren set up headquarters in some building there and I'll cast a spell on one of the rooms so that you and I'll be able to communicate there as well as here. That way you won't have to spend all your time on horseback carrying messages. Warn Halbren that when he occupies Muros there's to be no looting and no atrocities. The people in Muros aren't our enemies.'

'I'll see t' it, me Lady. Y' kin count on me.'

I wrote him an official-sounding authorization, and then I went out into the garden and put on feathers again. As it turned out, I got back to mother's cottage just in time. Even as I flew in, I saw father crawling through the tall grass toward the ruin. There was barely time to resume my own form, but just at the last instant, I veered off. An idea had just come to me, an idea that might prove useful later on. I settled into a solitary tree several hundred yards from the cottage and blurred from a falcon to a snowy owl. I knew that the form upset my father in the first place, but I also knew that his seeing me in that form might explain occasional absences. He'd assume that I was out hunting or something. I gave him about a quarter of an hour to start getting nervous, and then I flew in, resumed my own form, and made some show of moping about for the rest of the day.

My invasion of Muros was a quiet one. My army, dressed in nondescript clothing, slipped into town in twos and threes, mingling with the steady stream of refugees out of Wacune. We didn't want to announce their presence to the Asturians until the city was completely in our control. The brisk commands Malon had carried to my generals had given them a sense of purpose, and that raised the spirits of the army as a whole. Moreover, the improved morale of the army seemed to be contagious. The ordinary citizens began to realize that the world hadn't come to an end with the fall of Vo

Wacune, and that just maybe the Asturians weren't invincible. I concentrated on Muros because it would be Garteon's obvious first target, but more because I *had* to have a victory in the first major battle to put some steel back into my dispirited subjects.

The next part of my plan was more difficult to get across to my soldiers. My southern army was largely of Wacite descent, and a vast rumbling of discontent – verging on open mutiny – went through my southern forces when Malon passed the word to Halbren and the other generals that any patrol encountering Asturians was to run away. Running away isn't a part of the Arendish vocabulary, I guess. *'We're trying to lure the Asturians into a major battle, Malon,'* I explained patiently to my friend when he passed along the objections of Halbren and my other generals. *'I want Garteon's army to believe that we're completely demoralized and afraid of our own shadows up here in Erat. Then, when they come across the River Camaar, they won't expect any real resistance. That's when we'll fall on them like hungry tigers. I want their screams to reach all the way down to the bottom of whatever rat-hole Garteon's hiding in.'*

'Yer after hatin' that Garteon, ain't y', me Lady?'

'Hatred just begins to describe what I feel for him. I could cheerfully roast him alive over a slow fire for several weeks.'

'I'll start carryin' some kindlin' wood in me pocket, yer Grace.'

'What a dear fellow you are, Malon.'

'I'll be after steppin' on th' toes o' yer generals down in Muros, me Lady,' he promised. *'I'll make 'em pull in their horns an' bide their time until th' cursed Asturian come traipsin' across th' river. Then we'll have 'em fer breakfast. I'll have t' go down there in person t' git their attention, so I won't be talking' t' y' fer a week or so. Don't be after worryin' yer head about it, me Lady. I'll be busy layin' a trap fer Garteon's army, don't y' know.'*

'I understand perfectly, Malon.' The fact that he so closely resembled Killane, not only in appearance but in his manner of speech and in his thinking, made our relationship grow very close in a surprisingly short time. In a sense, I was just taking up where I'd left off several centuries earlier, so there wasn't that awkward period of what's called 'getting to know each other'.

There wasn't anything particularly original about the strategy I set in place around Muros, but the Asturians of that era weren't addicted to reading, and history books tend to be dry and dusty, so I was fairly sure they wouldn't be familiar with my tired old ploy. Halbren and my other generals finally got my point, but the common soldiers seemed to have a lot of trouble with it.

The Asturians grew steadily bolder as a result of our deception, and by early autumn Garteon's army was massing along the south bank of the River Camaar. Father's continued snooping made it totally impossible for me to personally direct the counterattack I'd been planning, so General Halbren would be on his own. Halbren was certainly up to the task, but that didn't keep me from going back to my childhood habit of biting my fingernails. A thousand 'what if's' kept me from sleeping very soundly.

There was one thing I *could* take care of, however. I instructed Malon to gather as many leaders of the Wacite resistance as he could find among the trees in the ruins of a village about half-way between Vo Wacune and the River Camaar on a certain night so that I could talk with them.

I evaded my father that evening, went falcon and flew on down to the appointed meeting place. The Asturians had burned the village, so about all that was left of it were heaps of charred timbers and tumbled stone walls. It was a moonless night, and the surrounding forest pressed in on the ruins ominously. I could sense the presence of a fair number of men, but they cautiously evaded me as I walked through the ruins toward what had been the village square where Malon was in the middle of a ragged-looking group of armed men. 'Ah, there y' are, yer Grace,' he greeted me.

He introduced me to a motley collection of Wacite patriots. Some were noblemen, several of whom I recognized from happier days. Others were serfs or village tradesmen, and I'm fairly sure that there was also a sprinkling of bandit chiefs in the group as well. As I understood it, each of these men commanded a band of what the Asturians called 'outlaws', men who entertained themselves by ambushing Asturian patrols.

'Gentlemen,' I addressed them, 'I'm a bit pressed for time here, so I'll have to be brief. The Asturians are going to invade my duchy before long. They'll probably strike across the River Camaar to lay siege to Muros. They won't expect any trouble because they think my army's made up of cowards.'

'We've heard about that, yer ladyship,' a burly serf named Beln interjected. 'We found it very hard t' believe, don't y' know. We've all got kinsmen up around Muros, an' they've never bin noted fer timidity.'

This was why I'd arranged this meeting. These Wacite leaders had to know that the seeming cowardice of my army was strategic. 'I *ordered* 'em t' be chicken-hearted, me Boy-o,' I replied in his own dialect. 'I was after settin' a trap fer th' Asturians, don't y' know.

Y' kin take it from me, Laddy-buck, me army'll shed its feathers when th' time comes.'

No, my use of his dialect was *not* a way of making fun of it. I was quite deliberately breaking down certain barriers that existed between the social classes. I wanted the Wacite resistance to be a cohesive fighting force, and that necessitated the abandonment of some ancient bad habits.

Beln looked around at his friends with a broad smirk on his shaggy, bearded face. 'Ain't she th' darlin' girl, though?' he said to them.

'It jist fills me heart w' joy t' hear y' say so, Beln,' I said. 'Now, then, after the battle on the plains of Muros – which I *am* going to win, by the way – the Asturians are going to be totally demoralized, and they'll come fleeing back across the River Camaar in total disarray. That's where *you* gentlemen come in. Don't interfere with them when they go north across the river, but when they try to come back, feel free to settle old scores. To put it bluntly, there are going to be *two* battles that day. I'll beat the Asturians out on the plains, and you'll beat them again down here in the forest when they try to run away from me.'

They cheered at that.

'Oh, one other thing,' I added. 'After their double drubbing, the Asturians are going to be so totally demoralized that they won't be paying much attention to any ordinary groups of people moving around down here. I'm sure you all have loved ones you'd like to get to safety, and there are others as well who'd rather not live under the Asturian yoke. Let it be known that they'll all be welcome in Muros. I'll see to it that they have places to live and food to eat.'

'Will that not strain thy resources, your Grace?' the blond young Baron Athan, whom I'd met several times in Vo Wacune, asked me.

'I'll manage, my Lord,' I assured him. 'I've been making preparations for the care of Wacite refugees since the fall of Vo Wacune.' I spoke to them all again. 'I know that most of you would rather stay here and fight, but get your women, children, and old people to safety. Don't leave innocents here to be taken hostage by the Asturians.'

'Thy point is well-taken, your Grace,' Athan approved. Then he said, 'In passing, my Lady, I must needs have a word with thee at the conclusion of our meeting here.'

'Of course, Baron.' Then I looked around at the other patriots. 'I'd advise moving the refugees up to the river in small groups, gentlemen. Establish safe routes through the forest and send a dozen or

382

so people up those trails each time. I'll make sure there are boats waiting to ferry them across to safety.'

We discussed the details of my proposed mass emigration for about a half hour or so, and then most of the patriots faded back into the woods. Baron Athan remained behind. 'I have a most sorrowful duty to perform, your Grace,' he told me. 'I must regretfully advise thee that Baron Ontrose, thy champion, died during the siege of Vo Wacune.'

My heart froze within me. In spite of everything, I'd still clung to some small vestiges of hope that my beloved had survived.

'I was with him when he died, your Grace,' Athan continued. 'It had been mine intent to sponge the stain of Baron Lathan's treason from off our family honor by giving mine own life in the defense of Vo Wacune, for indeed, the scoundrel Lathan was a distant cousin of mine. Count Ontrose, however, did command me to escape. He did order me to depart that I might carry the word of his death unto thee, fearing that doubt and uncertainty might distract thee from thy sworn duty. I would not cause thee pain, dear Lady, but he did utter thy name with his dying breath.'

I drew a cold iron wall around my heart. 'Thou hast performed thy mournful task most excellently, my Lord,' I thanked him. 'And now must we part. Strive to thine utmost to avenge our revered friend, Baron Athan, e'en as will I. Should the opportunity arise, we shall speak more of this tragedy anon.'

Then I left the village and went back into the dark trees. I wept for a time, but simple weeping seemed too light and innocuous for the overwhelming grief that tore at my heart. My despair needed a greater outlet. I went falcon and thrust myself blindly into the air. Birds of prey do not often scream at night, but I had more than enough reason to scream on that particular occasion. And so my screams of grief and despair trailed behind me across the dark forest of northern Wacune and on up among the peaks of the Sendarian mountains, where my desolate cries echoed back from the eternal rocks and seared the surface of every glacier inching down every mountain.

The Wacite resistance had extensive contacts across the border in Asturia, and such information obtained in this roundabout fashion eventually reached Malon, and one evening not long after the meeting in that ruined village he advised me that Duke Garteon and 'an Angarak advisor' had come out of hiding and had returned to the palace in Vo Astur. Malon's message confirmed what I'd suspected from the very start. Ctuchik *was* meddling in Arendish politics again.

My bereavement at the confirmed death of my beloved Ontrose led me into some very dark corners of my mind as I considered all sorts of things that might partially satisfy my desperate hunger for vengeance. My skill as a physician suggested any number of things that would linger for weeks – if not months. The thought of Ctuchik writhing in agony for a few seasons was very comforting.

The Asturians crossed the River Camaar to invade my domain in late autumn, and they began their march on Muros expecting little resistance. General Halbren was wise enough not to respond immediately, but waited until the Asturian army was a day's march north of the river before he counterattacked. As he put it to me later, 'I didn't think it'd be a good idea to waste a perfectly well-baited trap until the mice were all the way inside it, your Grace. I didn't want them yearning back toward the riverbank instead of concentrating on getting wiped out. All in all, it worked out fairly well, I'd say.' Halbren could be a master of understatement when he set his mind to it.

My army had been chafing at the restrictions I'd imposed on them, and when Halbren relaxed those restrictions, they came howling out of Muros like a pack of hungry wolves.

The battle of Muros was a short, ugly one. The Asturian generals had been sublimely overconfident as a result of the supposed cowardice of my army, and all they expected was a leisurely stroll from the River Camaar to the city with little if any resistance. So It was that they marched blithely into the fire I'd set to greet them. To make matters even worse for them, their soldiers weren't accustomed to fighting on open ground. Asturia's one large forest, and Muros stands on an unforested plain. *My* generals had been trained by Ontrose, so they not only knew how to fight in the woods, but also how to fight in the open. The Asturians didn't realize that they'd been encircled until they were suddenly assaulted from all sides at once. It was not so much a battle as it was a slaughter. What few Asturians escaped fled back across the River Camaar – where the bands of Wacite patriots were waiting for them.

I took some satisfaction in the knowledge that the army that had destroyed Vo Wacune and killed my beloved Ontrose was annihilated on that frosty autumn afternoon. That was the first part of my revenge.

The second part came somewhat later.

After our victory at Muros, Wacite refugees began streaming across the border, and I was a bit hard-pressed to find places to lodge them and supplies enough to feed them. Malon served as my eyes and ears – and hands – so he was a very busy man throughout that winter. We built new villages – mostly on my own estates – and my storehouses provided food. The conditions and diet were hardly luxurious, but my new subjects got through the winter. Malon had predicted that Wacite refugees of a suitable age would be eager to join my army, and he wasn't far off the mark on that score. I instructed Halbren to enlist them in new battalions led by former officers in the Wacite army. Those officers took on the chore of training the new recruits, and that left Halbren and my other generals free to defend the southern border.

Though I was still more or less confined to mother's cottage by my father's continued surveillance, Malon and I were growing more and more adept at our peculiar form of communication. When we'd set up the southern army headquarters in Muros, I actually had done a few things to our 'enchanted room' to make it possible for a selected few to also use it to communicate directly with me – just in case. I'm certain that father or one of the twins hiding nearby to watch me were convinced that I'd been rendered insensible by what had happened at Vo Wacune, but actually the blank look on my face was usually an indication that I was deep in conversation with Malon or one of my generals.

The Wacite patriots across the River Camaar continued to ambush and murder Asturians, of course, but far more importantly, they also passed word to us of Asturian troop movements and military buildups. I probably knew more about the location and condition of Garteon's army than he did. My real advantage, though, was strategic. I chose *not* to follow up my victory in the battle of Muros by invading Asturia or the former Wacune. There was no real need for me to do that, since I was getting everything I wanted without raising a finger. The mass migration of Wacite refugees across the river was effectively depopulating northern Wacune, and without serfs to work the land, Garteon's conquest hadn't gained him a single thing. All he had to show for his enormous expenditure were empty forests and weed-choked, unplowed fields. My Wacite spies kept me informed about Asturian troop concentrations, so every time Garteon tried to make another river crossing, I was ready for him. It wasn't long until Asturian soldiers – and eventually Garteon's generals – began muttering about 'witchcraft' and other absurdities, and that worked to my advantage as well. After my forces had easily repulsed a few tentative attempts to cross the river, the Asturians became convinced that 'the witch-woman of Muros' knew their inmost thoughts, and a sudden epidemic of timidity broke out in the Asturian ranks. I'm fairly certain that Garteon's tame Grolim knew better, but for some reason he wasn't able to convince the Asturian army that I couldn't turn them all into toads with a wave of my hand. The legend of 'Polgara the Sorceress' was too deeply ingrained in the Arendish consciousness to be dispelled by simple scoffing.

Then we had a stroke of luck. Had Garteon and his Grolim remained in Vo Astur, there'd have been no way for us to get at them, but finally Garteon absolutely *had* to go have a look at what his army had done to Vo Wacune. Gloating about a triumph is probably very natural, but it can be terribly dangerous sometimes. It was about a year after the battle of Muros, in the autumn of 2944, that the Duke of Asturia and his Angarak friend left Vo Astur – *alone*, if you can believe that – and traveled to the ruins of my beloved city.

Malon Killaneson had always religiously passed all information on to me just as soon as it fell into his hands, but this time he didn't. He disappeared instead. I was more than a little startled – frantic would be a better word – when General Halbren's voice broke in on my harvesting of my garden to advise me that Malon was nowhere to be found.

Horrid visions of Asturian assassins flooded my mind even as I went falcon and almost tore off my wings getting to Muros. Malon was the one indispensable man in my entire duchy.

The first thing I did upon my arrival was to order General Halbren to have his soldiers turn Muros upside down and shake it until everything fell out. All manner of interesting – and illegal – things came to light, but there was no sign of Malon.

As I mentioned before, General Halbren was a blocky professional soldier who'd been second in command of my army. His overall attitude was far more Sendarian than it was Wacite. He was solid, dependable, and almost totally unflappable. His very presence calmed me, and I was in great need of calming just then. 'Malon's simply not here, your Grace,' he reported to me on the morning after his soldiers had torn Muros apart. 'No one's seen him since the day before yesterday. He had a meeting in that office of his with a group of Wacite patriots. After they left, he stayed in his office until almost midnight, and then he left the building. I'm certain of the time, because I questioned the man who was on guard at the main entrance personally. Malon's lodgings are at an inn two streets over, and his rooms showed some evidence of a hasty departure.'

'I think we can rule out an assassination then, General,' I said.

'Assassins rarely take the trouble to carry off the body after they've finished.'

'True, your Grace.'

'The fact that Malon had time to stuff a few things into a bag sort of eliminates abduction, too, wouldn't you say?'

'It's probably safe to say that, my Lady.'

'That would seem to indicate that he left voluntarily – *without* bothering to let me know where he was going.'

'That isn't at all like him, your Grace,' Halbren noted. 'Malon *always* consults with you before he takes any action.'

'It's possible that those Wacites brought him some news about a family emergency of some kind, but I still think he'd have spoken with me before he left.'

'I'm sure of it, your Grace.'

'Did anyone else go into his office after the Wacites left?'

'No, your Grace. The guard at the door and the officer in charge of the night staff would have seen anyone, I'm sure.'

'When did the Wacites leave?'

'Three hours after sunset, your Grace.'

'And Malon left about two hours later?'

'Approximately, your Grace.'

'Let's go have a look at his office, General. We might find some kind of clue there.'

Halbren made a rueful face.

'Something wrong, Halbren?' I asked him.

'I was just wondering where my brains had gone, your Grace. The notion of searching his office never occurred to me. I tend to respect other people's privacy.'

'A commendable trait, General, but a little misplaced this time. Let's go see what Malon left on his desk.'

As it turned out, there wasn't anything on Malon's desk. He was a compulsively neat man, so he put things away when he was done with them. I knew him very well, however, and I knew that he'd have a hiding place – for his jug, if nothing else. Finding that hiding place wasn't very hard for me, since I've got certain advantages when it comes to finding things. There was a hidden drawer in his desk that *did* have the usual half-full jug of spirits. It *also* had a map of Wacune in it as well, and when I opened the map, Halbren and I immediately saw the inked-in line that traced a course from the northern border of Vo Wacune to the site of the former capital – a course that obviously avoided all the main roads and quite probably followed trails known only to forest bandits.

'Could he have gone down there, your Grace?' Halbren asked.

'I'm almost certain he did, General, and I'm going to speak to him at some length about that. He knows better than to run off on his own. You can have your men ask around, but I'm positive that Malon's across the River Camaar into Wacune by now.'

'Some emergency, perhaps?'

I shook my head. 'No, Halbren. I've trained him not to deal with emergencies personally. He's here to pass along my orders, not to run off to try to take care of things himself.' My eyes narrowed. 'When we *do* find him, he'd better have some very good excuses for this little excursion.'

General Halbren and I got to know each other even better during the two weeks that Malon spent in Wacune. I liked Halbren. In some ways he represented a transition between Arendish impulsiveness and Sendarian sensibility. Moreover, we were both angry with Malon for his unexplained disappearance. Halbren sent word to his own contacts down in Wacune, asking them to scour the forests in an all-out search for my wandering seneschal.

That took, as I've said, two full weeks, and when the Wacites finally *did* locate Malon, he was already on his way back to Muros.

I spent the better part of a day polishing the grand remonstrance I fully intended to shower down on my friend, but I never got the chance to use it. Malon looked tired, but at the same time jubilant, when General Halbren delivered him into my clutches. He had one of those irrepressible grins on his face that reminded me of Killane himself.

'Now, don't y' be after scoldin' me until y've heard me story, yer Grace,' he said as he entered. Clearly, he'd seen the storm brewing in my face.

'You're in trouble, Malon,' Halbren told him.

'I'm terrible sorry t' have caused y' both so much concern,' Malon apologized, 'but I was perfectly all right, don't y' know. A distant cousin o' mine who lives down in Wacune brought me some information a couple o' weeks ago, an' I saw right away that here was me chance t' surprise her Grace here w' a bit o' an early birthday present, don't y' know. Don't y' just love surprises, me Lady?'

'Not really, Malon. They usually involve bad news.'

'Not this time, Lady-O,' he said gaily. 'As it turns out, some o' me Wacite relatives dropped by t' tell me that Duke Garteon an' his Murgo friend had been seen in th' vicinity o' the ruins o' Vo Wacune, an' I thought it might be a golden opportunity t' settle some old accounts as has been naggin' at y'. I put almost th' entire

Killaneson family t' work on it, but it still took th' better part o' a week t' track down yer enemy. Him an' that Murgo was bein' very careful, don't y' know. Anyway, th' short of it is that we found th' two o' them, an' I set up a little ambush t' welcome 'em t' Wacune.'

'You idiot!' I stormed at him. 'That Murgo is a Grolim!'

'He might o' bin, yer Grace, but he didn't do no Grolimin' after we stuck a dozen or so arrows in 'im, don't y' know. As I remember it, he *did* start t' shout somethin' just before all them arrows swept him out o' his saddle. Anyhow, Duke Garteon drove his spurs all th' way into his horse an' tried t' make a run fer it, but we'd had th' foresight t' stretch a rope across the trail about chest high, an' it picked 'im right outta his saddle as he tried t' ride through it.'

'You captured him?' I exclaimed.

'That we did, me Lady. That we did.'

'Where is he?'

'That would sort o' depend on how well he's bin keepin' up w' his religious obligations, me Lady,' my seneschal replied a little evasively.

'What did you do with him, Malon?' I bored in.

'Well, me Lady. We all talked it over while he was layin' on th' ground tryin' t' git his breath back – th' fall off his horse havin' knocked th' wind outta 'im, don't y' know. When we first went after 'im, it'd bin our intent t' capture 'im an' deliver 'im up t' yer Grace fer disposal as y' might see fit, but now that we had 'im an' got th' chance t' look 'im over, we seen what a disgustin', weasely little rascal he was, an' I jist couldn't bear th' thought o' insultin' y' by bringin' such a mangy dog into yer presence. Th' more we talked it over, th' more it was that we couldn't bring ourselves t' dignify 'im w' no formal proceedin's, don't y' know. As we saw it, he jist didn't deserve that kind o' consideration.'

'What did you do to him? Get to the point, Malon.'

'Well, me Lady, we had this here miscreant as we didn't think was really worth th' effort o' feedin' an' guardin' all th' way back t' Muros, an' we had this here rope as had just jerked 'im out o' his saddle, an' there was all them lovely trees handy. Since everythin' was there anyway, we took it as a sign from th' Gods, so we hung 'im right there on th' spot.'

General Halbren bust out with a roar of laughter at that point.

'I should probably tell yer Grace that he didn't take it none too well,' Malon continued. 'He kept screamin' that he was th' Duke o' Asturia, an' that we couldn't do this t' him – but as it turned out, we could. If y'd like t' see 'im fer yerself, I could draw y' a map,

389

me Lady. Unless somebody's happened across 'im an' cut him down, he's probably still decoratin' that tree down there, don't y' know.'

Halbren laughed even harder.

CHAPTER 24

I've never really approved of informal justice, since there's a huge potential for mistakes implicit in the business, and it's very hard to un-hang somebody if you start having second thoughts. This case was an exception, however, since I saw several immediate advantages in Malon's rough and ready approach to the sometimes complex business of criminal justice. For one thing, it would lift the spirits of the Wacite refugees crowding the southern reaches of my domain, and by extension would also cheer up the native inhabitants. More importantly, however, the event was likely to distract the Asturians. As long as Garteon had been around, Asturia had concentrated on the annexation of my domain to the exclusion of all else. Now, at least part of their attention would be diverted by the fascinating business of choosing the departed duke's successor.

I looked at my grinning seneschal. 'All right, Malon,' I said to him, 'I don't entirely approve, but what's done is done, so let's take advantage of it. I want everybody in the entire duchy to hear about your little adventure. Feel free to boast, my friend. Then I want you to draw a map of the approximate location of Duke Garteon's remains and give it to General Halbren here.'

'Did your Grace want me to retrieve the carcass?' Halbren asked.

'No, General, we'll let the Asturians do that. Give the map to the talkiest priest of Chaldan you can find. Tell him what happened and then ask him to deliver the map to Vo Astur. I want everybody in Asturia to hear the happy news, and no Arend will ever try to make a priest keep his mouth shut about anything.'

General Halbren stifled his laughter and bowed his acknowledgment.

'I wouldn't be after expectin' much work t' git done around here fer a couple o' weeks, yer Grace,' Malon cautioned. 'Th' celebration's likely t' go on an' on an' be very noisy, don't y' know.'

'That's all right, Malon,' I shrugged. 'The harvest's over now anyway, and the people can catch up on their work later.' Then I laughed. 'Oh, Malon,' I said, 'what am I going to do with you? *Please* don't run off like that again.'

'I'll try t' remember that, yer Grace,' he promised. 'Now, if y'll excuse me, I'd better git t' drawin'.' He looked at General Halbren. 'Me map ain't goin' t' be too exact, General,' he apologized. 'I won't be able t' give y' th' tree's first name, don't y' know.'

'Oh, that's all right, Malon,' Halbren forgave him. 'The Asturians are woodsmen, so they enjoy wandering around among the trees looking for things.'

'I'm after thinkin' that Duke Garteon might not o' bin th' most popular man in all Asturia,' Malon mused. 'If he irritated his own people as much as he irritated us, our little celebration on this side o' th' river might just spread, don't y' know.'

'All right, gentlemen,' I told them, 'quit gloating and get back to work. I've got to go back to mother's cottage before my father starts dismantling the Sendarian Mountains searching for me.'

The celebration of Duke Garteon's endanglement lasted for about six weeks, I'm told. Laughter and good cheer ran from Muros all the way down the River Camaar to its mouth, and the rest of the duchy took it up from there. I'm almost sure that Malon had been right and that there were some subdued celebrations in Asturia as well.

Duke Garteon had no heir, and so his death put an end to the domination of Asturia by the Oriman family. The inevitable squabbles among assorted Asturian nobles about possession of the throne in Vo Astur so completely occupied their minds that hostilities more or less came to an end along my southern frontier. There was no overt peace-treaty, of course, but there never is in Arendia. Arends can draw up a declaration of war that's an absolute jewel of elegance, but the wording of a peace-treaty somehow escapes them.

Father and the twins were still watching me, so I began to renovate mother's cottage that winter, largely to persuade them that I was taking my supposed career as a hermitess very seriously. I re-thatched the roof, replaced the doors and broken windows, and re-mortared several tiers of stone blocks along the tops of the walls. I'm sure that Durnik wouldn't have approved of the means I used to accomplish those renovations, but after I'd hit myself on the

392

thumb with a hammer a couple of times, I neatly stacked all my tools in a corner and did it the other way.

In the spring I put in a vegetable garden. Radishes and beans aren't as pretty as roses, but they taste better, and if you can grow roses, you can certainly grow vegetables. Father evidently took my work at the cottage to mean that I'd shaken off any suicidal impulses, because he began to relax his surveillance.

As things settled down in my duchy, I heard less and less frequently from Malon. Now that the crisis had passed, he and General Halbren no longer needed much supervision. They knew what needed to be done, so they had no real reason to pester me.

Though I appeared to be tending to my vegetable garden that following summer, I was actually doing a great deal of thinking. The steps I'd taken to make my duchy efficient and humane were producing an effect I hadn't fully anticipated when I'd put them in place. A feudal system requires more or less constant supervision. My emancipation of the serfs and the establishment of a coherent legal system had prepared the way for self-government. I was rather ruefully obliged to admit that what I'd really done was quite neatly put myself out of a job. The people of my duchy didn't actually need me any more. I hoped that they still had some affection for me, but by and large, they could take care of themselves. To put it succinctly, my children had all grown up, packed, and left home.

To further facilitate the maturing of my people, I gave Malon some instructions concerning the management of my own estates, and I knew that those practices would spread to the estates of my vassals. I told him that we were going to let the practice of day-labor with a set wage-scale fall into disuse and replace it with the renting out of farmsteads. This was the next logical step toward independence and responsibility. My rents were not exorbitant, nor were they a fixed amount. They were a percentage of the income derived from the crops instead. As time went on, we'd gradually decrease that percentage until it was no more than a token. I wasn't actually *giving* them the land, but it came fairly close to that. The token rent encouraged industriousness, and the entire procedure helped to induce *that* sterling virtue into the fundamental character of the Sendars.

It may come as a surprise to dear old Faldor that his family's been paying me rent for the use of his farm for generations now.

*　　*　　*

In time, of course, Malon and Halbren grew old and passed on. I went to my manor house for Malon's funeral, and then I had a long talk with his son, a surprisingly well-educated man who, for reasons I could never understand, had chosen to use only his surname, Killaneson. Even though I didn't understand his decision, it gave me a rather warm feeling of continuity. Killaneson rarely broke into the Wacite brogue except when he was excited, but spoke instead in polite language which has come to be quite standard in my former domain.

'Do you understand what I'm trying to do, Killaneson?' I asked him when I'd finished explaining the system of rents.

'It looks to me as if your Grace is trying very hard to evade her responsibilities,' he replied with a faint smile.

'You might put it that way, my friend, but I'm actually doing this out of fondness for these people. I want to gently herd them in the direction of independence. Grownups don't really need to have mother tell them when it's time to change their clothes. Oh, one other thing, too. Why don't we let that "Erat" business fall into disuse. This land was called "Sendaria" even before anybody lived here. Let's go back to that name. The designation of the people here as "Eratians" has always set my teeth on edge, for some reason. Encourage them to start thinking of themselves as "Sendarians".'

'Why not do that with a proclamation, your Grace?'

'I'd rather not make it that formal, Killaneson. My goal here is to just quietly fade out of sight. If we do this right, a few generations from now, nobody will even remember the Duchess of Erat.'

Killaneson's voice had an almost childish note when he said, 'Please don't run off and leave us alone, Mommy.'

'Stop that,' I chided him.

Then we both laughed.

It was at the end of the thirty-first century that the debacle in the harbor at Riva took place. The Tolnedrans, convinced that there was vast hidden wealth on the Isle of the Winds, sent a fleet north to try to persuade the Rivans to open their gates to do business. The Rivans weren't really interested, so they methodically sank the Tolnedran fleet instead. Things were very tense for a while, but after the Cherek Ambassador at Tol Honeth advised Ran Borune XXIV that the Alorn kingdoms would demolish Tolnedra in response to any hostilities directed at the Isle, things settled back down to normal.

The Honethites succeeded the Borunes in the imperial palace at Tol Honeth. Say what you will about the Honeths, they *are* probably the best administrators of all the great families of the empire, so things quieted down.

As we moved into the early years of the thirty-second century, I began to reduce the staff of my manor house on Lake Erat until there were finally only a few caretakers there. I made arrangements for the rest of the Killaneson family, and I gradually began to fade from the memories of the people who had formerly been subject to me. They called themselves Sendarians now, and I had largely receded into history books and folk-lore.

I *did* have to come out of my seclusion at mother's cottage a few times, though. In the mid-thirty-second century, the Bear-Cult in Cherek persuaded King Alreg that Sendaria was a natural extension of his kingdom, and that Belar, the Alorn God, would be angry if Cherek failed its religious obligation to annex my former duchy. Once again I was going to have to try to talk some sense into some thick-headed Alorns. After one particularly offensive earl named Elbrik had stormed ashore and looted Darine, I went falcon and flew on up to Val Alorn to have a few words with the King of Cherek. I settled onto the battlements of Alreg's rambling palace and went on down several flights of stairs to his smokey throne-room.

King Alreg was an enormous man with a great, bushy blond beard. Despite the fact that there was no real need for it, he wore a steel helmet and a chain-mail shirt as he lounged, beer tankard in hand, on his oversized throne. Quite clearly, Alreg considered himself to be a warrior king.

One of the mailed guards at the door seized my arm as I entered. 'You're not supposed to be in here, woman!' he said roughly to me. 'Men only in Alreg's throne-room!'

'Did you want to keep that hand?' I asked, pointedly staring at the offending member.

'Now, see here, woman –' He *did* let go of my arm, though.

Then he went rolling across the rush-strewn floor as the force of my Will struck him full in the chest. I enhanced my voice to make myself audible over all the drunken babble. 'Alreg of Cherek!' I thundered, and the very walls shook to that overwhelming sound.

The King of Cherek, obviously about half drunk, reeled to his feet. 'Who let that woman in here?' he demanded.

'I let myself in, Alreg,' I told him. 'You and I are going to have a talk.'

'I'm busy.'

'Get un-busy – right now!' I strode on down past the smoky

fire-pit in the center of his barn-like throne-room, bowling over any Cherek warriors who tried to get in my way. Even in his slightly befuddled state, Alreg realized that something unusual was going on. I reached the foot of the dais upon which his throne stood and fixed him with a very unfriendly stare. 'I see that the seat of Bear-shoulders has descended to a drunken fool,' I noted scathingly. 'How sad. I know he'd be disappointed.'

'You can't talk to me that way!' he blustered.

'You're wrong, Alreg. I can talk to you any way I choose. Get that barbarian Elbrik out of Darine immediately!'

'You can't order me around! Who do you think you are?'

But one of the more sober men standing just behind him had gone very pale. 'Your Majesty!' he said to his king in strangled tones, 'that's Polgara the Sorceress!'

'Don't be ridiculous!' Alreg snapped. 'There's no such person!'

'Look at her, your Majesty! Look at that white streak in her hair! That's Polgara, daughter of Holy Belgarath! She can turn you into a toad if she feels like it!'

'I don't believe in any of that nonsense,' Alreg scoffed.

'I think you're about to have a religious conversion, Alreg,' I told him.

That 'turn him into a toad' business had been floating around for eons, you know, and most of the time it's been nothing more than a tired old joke. What would be the point of doing something like that? This time, however, the notion had been planted at just the right moment. I was going to have to do *something* to Alreg to get his attention, and, although the sober Cherek noble who'd recognized me had probably just thrown the expression out at random, it *had* planted the idea, and the more I thought about it, the more the notion appealed to me. For once, an absolute absurdity would serve my purpose as well or better than anything else.

I wanted to make the entire process visible, so this time I did it in a slightly different way. Rather than simply injecting Alreg into the image of a toad, I altered his features one by one. It occurred to me that I didn't really need the whole toad – just its head and feet. I could leave the rest of Alreg intact.

Alreg's head slowly began to change shape, flattening out until it had a reptilian cast. His eyes were now at the top of his head, and they began to bulge upward. Since his eyes were already bulging anyway, that part wasn't too hard. Then I dissolved his beard and extended the corners of his mouth.

'*No!*' It came out of that lipless mouth in kind of a squeaky croak.

396

I'd decided that it might be useful if he could still talk. Then I altered his hands and feet into the flipper-like appendages of the amphibian. I slightly modified his hips, shoulders, knees, and elbows, and with shrill, pathetic croaks, the King of Cherek sank down into that frog-like crouch on the seat of his throne. Then I added the warts.

I hadn't altered Alreg's size, nor tampered in any way with his clothing, so there was a man-sized toad in a mail-shirt and with a sword belted at its thick waist crouched bug-eyed on the royal throne, croaking in a shrill kind of panic.

The entire process had taken several minutes, and since Alreg's throne stood upon a dais, it had been visible to every Cherek, drunk or sober, in the entire hall.

I sensed one of the bearded Chereks behind me reaching for his sword. When he grasped what he thought was his sword-hilt, though, he wrapped his hand firmly about the head and neck of a large, angry snake instead. 'Don't do that any more,' I told him, without bothering to look around. 'You'd better tell your retainers here to behave themselves, Alreg,' I suggested to the enthroned toad. 'That's unless you have replacements handy. My father doesn't want me to kill people, but I think I can get around that. I'll just bury them without bothering to kill them first. They'll probably die of natural causes – after a while – so father won't have any cause for complaint, now will he?'

'All right!' the warty creature on the throne of Cherek squealed. 'I'll do anything you say! Please, Polgara! Please! Change me back!'

'Are you sure, Alreg?' I asked pleasantly. 'You look rather imposing this way. Think of how proud it'll make all your warriors to tell the entire world that they're ruled by a toad. Besides, you've got all these lazy, bearded louts lounging around drinking beer. You could put them all to work catching flies for you to eat. Wouldn't a nice fat fly taste delicious about now?'

I think his mind started to slip about then, because the squalling intensified and he bounded off his throne and began to hop around in circles.

I changed him back to his own form with a single thought, but he was evidently not aware of it because he continued to hop and squeal. His warriors all shrank back from him with looks of panic and revulsion on their faces.

'Oh, *do* get up, Alreg!' I told him. 'You look positively ridiculous doing that.'

He stood up, trembling violently, and stumbled back to his throne. He fell into it, staring at me in sheer terror.

'Now, then,' I said sternly, 'Sendaria's under my protection, so get your people out of there and bring them back here where they belong.'

'We're following Belar's commands, Polgara,' he protested.

'No, Alreg, you're not. Actually, you're following the orders of the Bear-Cult. If you want to jump to the tune of a group of feeble-minded religious fanatics, that's up to you, but get out of Sendaria. You can't even *begin* to imagine just how nasty things are going to get if you don't.'

'I don't know about the rest of you,' a thin, bearded Cherek, his eyes aflame with the burning light of religion, declared fervently, 'but I'm not going to take orders from a mere woman!'

'In point of fact, old boy, I'm not a mere *anything*.'

'I am an armed Cherek!' he almost screamed. 'I fear nothing!'

I made a small gesture, and his gleaming mail-shirt and his half-drawn sword rather quickly stopped gleaming and became dull red instead. Then they began to crumble, showering down onto the floor in a cascade of powdery rust. 'Don't you find that sort of disarming?' I suggested. 'Now that you're no longer an armed Cherek, aren't you just the teensiest bit afraid?' Then I grew tired of all their foolishness. 'ENOUGH!' I thundered. 'Get out of Sendaria, Alreg, or I'll tow the Cherek peninsula out to sea and sink it. Then you can try being the king of the fish for a while. Now call your people home!'

It wasn't the most diplomatic way to bring the Chereks into line, but the smug chauvinism of Alreg's court had irritated me. 'Mere Woman' indeed! Just the sound of it still makes my blood boil!

There was one beneficial side effect to my little visit to Val Alorn, incidentally. After enduring a few months of hysterical protests from discontented Bear-Cultists, Alreg moved decisively to suppress the cult once again. I've noticed that the Bear-Cult has to be put down every fifty years or so in the Alorn kingdoms.

In the century or so that followed, I receded further and further back into the pages of dusty old history books, and I seldom had occasion to visit my manor house on Lake Erat. The last of my caretakers there died, and I saw no reason to replace him. I still loved the house, though, and the notion of having it casually looted and burned didn't sit well with me, so early one spring I crossed the Sendarian Mountains to take steps to protect it. I wandered through the dusty rooms immersed in nostalgic melancholy. So much had happened here that had been central to my life. The ghosts of Killane and Ontrose seemed to accompany me down every dusty corridor, and the echoes of long ago conversations seemed to still reverberate through almost every room I entered. Erat had gone back to being Sendaria, and my duchy had shrunk down to this single lonely house.

I considered several options, but the solution was really quite simple, and it came to me one glorious spring evening as I stood on the terrace of the south wing looking out at the lake and at the veritable jungle of my untended rose-garden. What better way to conceal and protect my house than to bury it in roses?

I set to work the following morning 'encouraging' my rose-bushes to expand and encroach on the fair meadow that stretched on down to the lake. When I was done, they were no longer bushes, but trees, and they were so tightly interlaced that they'd become a thorny, impenetrable barrier that would keep my beloved house forever inviolate.

It was with a great deal of self-satisfaction that I returned to mother's cottage and my continuing studies. Now that I'd preserved the past, I could turn my attention to the future.

It's an article of my family's faith that the future lies hidden in the Darine and Mrin Codices, and studying the collected ravings of a senile old Alorn warrior and a profoundly retarded idiot who'd had to be chained up for his own protection can be very frustrating. I kept coming across veiled references to my father and me, and that was probably what kept me from throwing my hands up in disgust and taking up ornithology or horticulture instead. I gradually came to grasp the idea that there was another world superimposed on our mundane, day to day reality, and in that other world tiny events had enormous significance. A chance meeting between two tradesmen on the streets of Tol Honeth or an encounter between a pair of gold-hunters in the mountains of Gar og Nadrak could be far more important than a clash of armies. Increasingly, I came to understand that those 'incidents' were EVENTS – those very brief confrontations between the two entirely different prophecies, only one of which would ultimately determine the fate of not merely *this* world, but of the entire universe as well.

The study of something of that magnitude so totally engrossed me that I began to ignore time, and more often than not I couldn't have told you what century it was, much less what year.

I *do* know – largely because I checked some Tolnedran history books later – that in the year 3761 the last emperor of the second Borune Dynasty *chose* his successor rather than leaving the choice up to the infinitely corruptible Council of Advisors. That childless

Borune emperor, Ran Borune XII, was obviously a man of great foresight, because his decision brought the Horbite family to the imperial throne, and the Horbites – at least at that particular time – proved to be extrodinarily gifted. In many respects, the Horbites had largely been an appendage of the Honeths, in much the same way that the Anadiles are an extension of the Borunes. The first of that line, Ran Horb I, immersed himself in the Borune hobby of building highways to link Tolnedran commerce to the rest of the world. It was his son, Ran Horb II, however, who took that hobby to the point of obsession. Almost overnight, you couldn't look anywhere in the west without seeing Tolnedran construction crews carving out new highways. The Tolnedran diplomatic corps dropped everything else and concentrated on 'treaties of mutual cooperation for the good of all', thus creating the fiction that Tolnedra was just being neighborly, when in fact the highways were quite nearly for the sole use of Tolnedran merchants.

When word of all the road construction taking place in my former domain reached me at mother's cottage, I decided that I'd better set my studies aside and go to Tol Honeth to have a word with Ran Horb II to find out just exactly what his intentions were.

For once, I decided not to just pop in on the emperor, but chose instead to rely on the good offices of the Drasnian ambassador. Despite their faults – and they *do* have faults – the avaricious Drasnians are well respected by the Tolnedrans. I had to introduce myself to Prince Khanar, the nephew of King Rhalan of Drasnia, since I'd been more or less in seclusion for the past eight centuries. Khanar was no Dras Bull-neck by any stretch of the imagination. He was a small, wiry man with a quick mind and a perverted sense of humor. I was fully prepared to give him a quick demonstration of my 'talent', but oddly, that wasn't necessary. He accepted me at my word and took me across town to the palace compound. After we'd waited for an hour or so, we were escorted into the large, cluttered office of his Imperial Majesty, Ran Horb II. The emperor was a stout, businesslike fellow with receding hair and a preoccupied expression. 'Ah, Prince Khanar,' he said to my small companion, 'so good to see you again. What's afoot in Boktor?'

'All the usual chicanery, your Majesty,' Khanar shrugged. 'Lying, cheating, stealing – nothing remarkable or out of the ordinary.'

'Does your uncle know how you speak of his kingdom when you're in the presence of strangers, Khanar?'

'Probably, your Majesty. He has spies everywhere, you know.'

'Aren't you going to introduce me to the lady?'

'I was getting to that, your Majesty. I have the distinct honor to present the Lady Polgara, Duchess of Erat and the daughter of Holy Belgarath.'

Ran Horb looked at me skeptically. 'All right,' he said, 'just for the sake of argument, I'll accept that – tentatively, of course. I'll hold off on asking for proof until later. To what do I owe the honor of this visit, your Grace?'

'You're a very civilized man, your Majesty,' I noted. 'Most of the time I have to perform a few little tricks before people will listen to me.'

'I'm sure you could startle me out of my shoes, if you chose to,' he replied. 'What can I do for you?'

'I'm just seeking information, your Majesty,' I assured him. 'You're building highways in Sendaria.'

'I'm building highways almost everywhere, Lady Polgara.'

'Yes, I know. I have a certain interest in Sendaria, though. Is this construction a prelude to annexation?'

He laughed. 'Why on earth would I want to annex Sendaria?' he said. 'I'm sure it's a nice enough country, but I don't really want to own it. Those highways I'm building up there are just a way to keep the Chereks out of my purse. They'll provide a route to Boktor that bypasses the need to transport goods through that whirlpool in the Cherek Bore. Those bearded pirates in the north charge out-rageous fees to carry Tolnedran cargoes from Kotu through the Bore, and that's cutting into my tax revenues.'

'It's all strictly commercial, then?'

'Of course. If I want farm produce, I can buy it right here in Tolnedra. I don't have to go all the way to Sendaria for beans and turnips. The only thing that interests me about that place is its location.'

The glimmer of an idea flickered through my mind. 'Then stability in Sendaria would be to your advantage, wouldn't it, your Majesty?'

'Naturally, but that's what the legions are for.'

'But legions are expensive, aren't they, Ran Horb?'

He shuddered. 'You wouldn't *believe* how expensive.'

'I might.' I squinted at the ornate ceiling. 'Sendaria hasn't really had a central government since I ruled there around the turn of the millennium,' I mused. 'That lack of a government has invited all sorts of incursions from the outside. If there were a king and a government – *and* an army – the people would be secure from outside adventurers, and you wouldn't have to keep ten or so legions stationed there to maintain order.'

'Ah,' he said, *'that's* what the "Polgara" business was all about. You want to be the Queen of Sendaria.'

'Most definitely not, your Majesty. I'm far too busy for any more of that nonsense – nothing personal intended there, of course.'

'No offense taken, your Grace.' Then he leaned back in his chair. 'You know,' he said, 'that's the one thing that's always made me skeptical when I hear stories about you and your father. If Belgarath's as powerful as they say he is, he could rule the world, couldn't he?'

'He wouldn't be very good at it, your Majesty. My father absolutely hates responsibility. It interferes with his entertainments.'

'Now you've got me baffled, my Lady. If *you* don't want to rule Sendaria, who *do* you want me to put on the throne? – some lover, perhaps?'

I gave him an icy look.

'Sorry,' he apologized. 'I'll agree that a formal government in Sendaria would be to everyone's advantage, but which Sendarian do we saddle with the throne?'

'We're talking about a nation of turnip-farmers, your Majesty,' Khanar noted. 'Some of them may have titles, but they're still out in their fields at the crack of dawn just like their neighbors.'

'I think you're underestimating them, Prince Khanar,' I told him. 'A successful farmer has many more administrative skills than you might imagine, and he's probably far more practical than some spoiled noble brat who's been raised on Arendish epics where nobody ever eats or takes a bath. At least a farmer knows how to pay attention to details.'

'Now, *that's* deflating, isn't it, your Majesty?' Khanar said to the emperor. 'I absolutely *devoured* Arendish epics when I was a boy, and to be shrugged off as a "spoiled noble brat" bites sort of close to the bone.'

'This would be in the nature of an experiment, then, wouldn't it?' Ran Horb suggested. 'Do I appoint a king?'

'I wouldn't do it that way, your Majesty,' I replied. 'Appointing a ruler would just be another form of outside intervention, and it'd immediately spawn a fervent opposition. You'd have a revolution up there within a decade, and then you'd have to send fifty legions instead of ten.'

He winced at that. 'How *do* we select a king, then?'

'I could devise a test, your Majesty,' Khanar offered, 'and we could confer the crown on whichever Sendar scores the highest grade.'

'But if *you* grade the test, Prince Khanar, you'd still start a revolution,' I told him. 'The selection of the King of Sendaria can't be made by either Tolnedra *or* by Drasnia. It's going to have to come from within.'

'A tournament, perhaps?' Ran Horb said dubiously.

'These are farmers, your Majesty,' Khanar reminded him. 'A battle royal with farm implements could get *very* messy. I suppose we could give the crown to the man who raises the biggest turnip.'

'Why not hold an election?' I asked them.

'I've never had that much faith in elections,' Ran Horb said dubiously. 'An election's nothing more than a popularity contest, and popularity's hardly a measure of any kind of administrative ability.'

'Ah – your Majesty,' Khanar said, 'we're not talking about a major power here. Sendaria's a nice enough place, I suppose, but the world's not going to tremble very hard if the King of the Sendars makes a few mistakes.' He laughed then, a cynical Drasnian sort of laugh. 'Why not just turn the whole thing over to the priesthood instead? We just pick somebody who doesn't stumble over his own feet too often and then instruct the priests to advise the Sendars that this man's been chosen to rule by the Sendarian God – which God *do* the Sendars worship, by the way?'

'All seven of them,' I replied. 'They don't know about UL as yet, but they'll probably include him in their religion as well, just as soon as they find out about his existence.'

'UL?' Ran Horb said, sounding puzzled.

'The God of the Ulgos,' I told him.

'You mean that place where all the dragons are?'

'There's only one dragon, your Majesty, and she doesn't live in Ulgoland. I don't think religion would be a good basis for a Sendarian monarchy, though. It'd put the priests in command of the nation, and priests don't make very good rulers. Cthol Murgos is a fairly good example of that. I *know* the Sendars, believe me, and I think an election might be the best answer – just as long as *everybody* gets to vote.'

'Even people who don't own land?' Ran Horb asked incredulously.

'It's the best way to avoid rebellion later on,' I reminded him. 'If domestic tranquility's what we want, we don't need some large group of landless non-voters coming up with the idea of redistributing the wealth of the kingdom after a few years.'

'We can give it a try, I suppose,' the emperor said dubiously. 'If it doesn't work, maybe I *will* have to annex Sendaria. I wouldn't really want the idea of elections to spread, since I'd probably be the first one voted out of office, but Sendaria's a special case, I guess. Nobody *really* cares who gets the Sendarian throne as long as he keeps things quiet up there. We definitely don't need another Arendia on our hands.' He made a sour face. 'The Arends are starting to make me very tired. I think it's time for me to come up with a way to put an end to their perpetual civil war. It's bad for business.' Then his eyes brightened. 'All right,' he said, 'now that we've solved all the world's problems, why don't you go ahead and prove to me that you really *are* Polgara the Sorceress, your Grace.'

'Oh, dear,' I sighed.

'We've both been very, very good, my Lady,' Khanar agreed eagerly, 'and since we both behaved ourselves so well, don't we deserve some kind of little treat?'

'Why am I always surrounded by children?' I demanded, casting my eyes toward heaven.

'Probably because you bring out the little boy lurking in every one of us, Polgara.' Ran Horb was grinning openly now.

'All right,' I sighed, 'but only one. I'm not going to wear myself out just to entertain a pair of naughty little boys who managed to stay out of mischief for half an hour.'

Then I went owl – in part because it was easier – and in part because no carnival charlatan could ever hope to duplicate the feat.

I flew around the room on soft white wings for a few moments, then settled onto my chair and resumed my own form. 'Satisfied?' I asked them.

'How *ever* did you manage to do that?' Ran Horb demanded.

'It's fairly simple, your Majesty,' I replied. 'All you have to do is think very hard about the form you want and then command your being to take that form. Would you like to see something different? How about a cobra?'

'Ah – no, thank you, Lady Polgara,' he answered very quickly. 'That won't really be necessary. I'm completely convinced – aren't you, Khanar?'

'Oh, absolutely, your Imperial Majesty,' Khanar replied fervently. 'I wouldn't *think* of asking you to turn yourself into a cobra, Lady Polgara.'

'I rather thought you might both feel that way about it,' I murmured.

It may have been that conversation in the early autumn of 3817 that had moved Ran Horb to put an end to the civil war in Arendia.

In 3821 he concluded a secret treaty with the Mimbrates, and in 3822, the Mimbrates sacked and burned Vo Astur and chased the surviving Asturians into the forest. I know it's not really very nice, but I *did* take a great deal of satisfaction in the destruction of Vo Astur, since it repaid them for destroying Vo Wacune.

No, I don't think I'll pursue that. Gloating isn't really attractive, so it should be done in private.

Then, in 3827, Ran Horb II set up the election that ultimately produced the first Sendarian King. He made one mistake when he laid down the rules, however. He said that the new king had to receive a *majority* of the votes. That turned the whole business into a six-year holiday in Sendaria. There were seven hundred and forty-three candidates on the first ballot, and the winnowing-out process took a long time. Soon, Sendarians were dividing their time almost equally – mornings devoted to tending the fields and afternoons devoted to electioneering. They had so much fun that they ignored the fact that the rest of the world was laughing at them.

I *love* those people! When they're having fun, they don't care *what* the rest of the world thinks.

The ultimate winner, Fundor the Magnificent, had long since forgotten that he was still a candidate, and his elevation to the throne came as a complete surprise to him – and quite an inconvenience as well. Fundor was an agricultural experimenter who hated the taste of turnips and had been trying for years to replace that vegetable as a staple in the Sendarian diet with the rutabaga. Since nobody in his right mind willingly eats rutabagas, Fundor's obsession had virtually bankrupted him.

During the course of the six-year-long election, the Sendars had decided to establish the capital of their incipient kingdom at the city of Sendar. Their decision was based on the price of land in that part of Sendaria, and it raised screams of protest from the largely Tolnedran land-speculators in and around Darine, Camaar, and Muros.

Following Fundor's elevation to the throne, all manner of fortune-hunters flocked to the city of Sendar in the hopes of wheedling noble titles out of their new king. Fundor put them to work instead, holding back titles until he saw how well they performed various tasks. The alien concept of actually working to earn – and keep – a title offended most of the opportunists drawn to his court, but it ultimately produced a noble class with that most rare of aristocratic characteristics, a sense of responsibility.

I drifted around the new kingdom for several years, more or less unobserved, and as time passed I grew more and more certain that our experiment was working out quite well. Sendaria prospered, and the peasants were fairly content. I felt that I'd performed my final duty as the Duchess of Erat satisfactorily and had thus fulfilled my pledge to Ontrose.

Since that was out of the way now, I returned to mother's cottage and to my studies.

Ran Horb's system of highways – particularly in Sendaria – mightily offended the Chereks, of course, since it rendered their unique ability to navigate the hazards of the Cherek Bore largely irrelevant. There were rumblings of discontent coming out of Val Alorn, but since you can't really sink a highway, there wasn't very much the Chereks could do about the new state of affairs.

The Tolnedran highway system extended far beyond Sendaria, however, and its real impact was felt more in the southern kingdoms. The first contacts between various Tolnedran entrepreneurs and the Murgos were tentative and very wary, but before long the goods of the Angarak kingdoms began to appear in the marketplaces of Tol Honeth, Tol Borune, Tol Horb, and Tol Vordue. Murgo hostility began to soften, and the trade between east and west changed from a trickle to a flood.

Now nothing happens in Cthol Murgos without Ctuchik's open consent, so it was obvious to my family that Torak's disciple, crouched atop that gloomy peak in the middle of the Wasteland of Murgos, was 'up to something'. In all probability, Ctuchik wasn't really 'up to' anything more serious than spying and subverting a few Tolnedrans, but as my father and uncle Beldin were to discover after the war with Nyissa, their former brother, Zedar the apostate, had been more creative. His offer of immortality had enlisted the aid of the aging Queen Salmissra in Sthiss Tor, and that significantly altered history.

But that came a bit later. Following the establishment of the Kingdom of Sendaria, I devoted myself almost exclusively to the study of that pair of prophecies, the Mrin and the Darine, and I began to catch brief, tantalizing glimpses of 'the Godslayer'. Clearly, I was going to be intimately involved with this titan, but as time went on and I probed more deeply, I began to get the strong impression that he *wasn't* going to come riding out of nowhere garbed in shining armor, trailing clouds of glory, and announced by earthquakes and thunderclaps.

The turn of the millennium occasioned some serious celebration in the kingdoms of the west, but aside from noting that the year marked my two thousandth birthday, I paid very little attention to it.

In the early spring of 4002 I once again remembered that if I planned to eat the following winter, I'd probably better get to gardening. I set my studies aside for several weeks to concentrate on playing in the dirt.

I was spading up my vegetable garden when father swooped in. I knew immediately that something serious was afoot, since my father only flies – usually as a falcon – in emergencies. He blurred back into his natural form, and his expression was agitated. 'I need you, Pol!' he said urgently.

'I needed you once, remember?' I said it without even thinking. 'You didn't seem very interested. Now I get to return the favor. Go away, father.'

'We don't have time for this, Polgara. We have to go to the Isle of the Winds immediately. Gorek's in danger.'

'Who's Gorek?'

'Don't you have any idea at all about what's happening in the world beyond the edge of your garden? Has your brain shut down? You can't evade your responsibilities, Pol. You're still who you are, and you're coming with me to the Isle of the Winds even if I have to pick you up in my talons and *take* you there.'

'Don't threaten me, Old Man. Who's this Gorek you're so worried about?'

'He's the Rivan King, Pol, the Guardian of the Orb.'

'The Chereks patrol the Sea of the Winds, father. No fleet in the world can get past their war boats.'

'The danger's not coming from a fleet, Pol. There's a commercial enclave just outside the walls of the city of Riva. *That's* the source of the danger.'

'Are you insane, father? Why did you permit strangers on the Isle?'

'It's a long story, and we don't have time to go into it right now.'

'How did you find out about this supposed danger?'

'I just dredged the meaning out of a passage in the Mrin Codex.'

That brushed away all my scepticism. 'Who's behind it?' I demanded.

'Salmissra, as closely as I can determine. She has agents in that enclave who've been ordered to kill the Rivan King and his entire family. If she manages to pull it off, Torak wins.'

'Not as long as *I'm* still breathing, he doesn't. Is this more of Ctuchik's games?'

'It's possible, but it's little subtle for Ctuchik. It might be Urvon or Zedar.'

'We can sort that out later. We're wasting time, father. Let's go to the Isle and put a stop to this.'

CHAPTER 25

The shortest route to the Isle of the Winds involved crossing Ulgoland. Most sensible people avoid that whenever possible, but this
was an emergency, and father and I would be several thousand feet
above the hunting grounds of the Algroths, Hrulgin, and Eldrakyn.
Our brief encounter with Harpies just before we flew over Prolgu,
however, was highly suspicious. So far as I'm able to determine,
that was the only time anyone has ever seen them. Their semi-human
form makes them appear far more dangerous than they really are.
A human face does not automatically indicate human intelligence,
and their lack of a beak makes them a second-rate bird of prey.
Father and I evaded them rather easily and flew on.

Dawn was touching the eastern horizon when we flew over
Camaar. We were both on the verge of exhaustion, but we grimly
flew on out over the lead-grey waves of the Sea of the Winds. My
wings seemed almost on fire, but I drove myself to keep going. I'm
not really sure how father managed, since he doesn't really fly all
that well. Father surprises me sometimes.

We were crossing the harbor at Riva, and my eyes were fixed on
the grim battlements of the Hall of the Rivan King when mother's
voice cracked sharply in my mind. *'Pol! Down there – in the harbor!'*

I looked down and saw something splashing quite a ways out
from the gravel beach.

'It's a little boy, Pol. Don't let him drown!'

I didn't even think. Changing form in midair isn't really a good
idea. For a moment as you blur from one form to the other you're
totally disoriented, but as luck had it I was still looking at the water
after I'd shed my feathers. I arched forward and plunged down,
tensing my body for the shock of impact with the surface of the

harbor. The jolt would have been much worse had I been higher, but it still quite nearly knocked the wind out of me.

My dive took me deep down into the bone-chilling water, but I arched myself and shot toward the surface, coming up into the light and air only a few feet from the floundering little boy whose eyes were filled with terror and whose flailing arms were barely keeping him afloat.

A few strokes brought me to his side, and then I had him. 'Relax!' I told him sharply. 'I've got you now.'

'I'm drowning!' he spluttered, his voice shrill.

'No, you're not. You're safe, so stop waving your arms around. Just lay back and let me do the swimming.'

It took a little persuading to unlock the death grip of his arms around my neck, but I eventually got him calmed down and lying on his back while I towed him toward the end of one of the wharves jutting out into the bay. 'See how much easier it is when you don't fight the water?' I asked him.

'I almost had the knack of it,' he assured me. 'That's the first time I've ever tried to swim. It's not too hard, is it?'

'You should probably practice in shallower water,' I suggested.

'I really couldn't, ma'am. There was this man with a knife after me.'

'*Polgara!*' father's voice came to me. '*Is the boy all right?*'

'Yes, father,' I replied out loud, not even realizing that my voice was audible to the little boy. 'I've got him.'

'*Stay out of sight! Don't let anybody see you!*'

'*All right.*'

'Who were you talking to?' the boy asked.

'It's not important.'

'Where are we going?'

'To the end of that wharf. We'll hide there and keep very quiet until the men with the knives have been driven off.'

'All right. Is the water always this cold?'

'It was the last time I was here.'

'I don't think I've ever seen you before, ma'am.'

'No. We only just met.'

'That would explain it then.' He was such a matter of fact little fellow. I liked him immediately.

'It's probably best not to talk quite so much,' I told him. 'Gulping in a gallon or so of water right now wouldn't be good for you.'

'If you say so.'

410

We reached the end of the stone wharf, and both of us grabbed hold of a rusty iron ring to which ships were usually tied.

'What happened back there?' I asked him.

'My grandfather took us all down to the shops on the beach,' the little boy replied. 'Somebody there wanted to give us some presents. When we got to their shop, though, they all pulled out their knives. I'll bet they'll be sorry they did that. My grandfather's the king here, and he'll be very angry with them about that. I'm really cold, ma'am. Can't we get out of the water?'

'Not yet, I'm afraid. We want to be sure it's safe before we do that.'

'Do you come here to the Isle very often?' His calm way of talking reassured me just a bit. Evidently the assassination attempt had failed.

'What happened back there on the beach?' I asked him.

'I'm not really sure, ma'am,' he replied. 'Mother told me to run just as soon as the fellow with all his hair shaved off pulled out his knife. He was between me and the city gate, so the only place left to go was out here in the water. Swimming's a little harder than it looks, isn't it?'

'It takes some practice, that's all.'

'I didn't have much time for practice. Would it be polite for me to ask what your name is?'

'I'm known as Polgara,' I told him.

'I've heard of you. Aren't you related to me?'

'Distantly, yes. You might say that I'm your aunt. And what's your name?'

'I'm Geran. They call me "Prince Geran", but I don't think that means very much. My oldest brother's the one who's going to get to wear the crown when he grows up. I've been thinking about being a pirate when I grow up. That'd be pretty exciting, don't you think so, Aunt Pol?'

There it was again. I sometimes think that every little boy in the world automatically calls me 'Aunt Pol'. I smiled at him. 'I'd have a talk with my parents – and my grandfather – before I decided on piracy as a career, Geran,' I suggested. 'They might have a few objections.'

He sighed. 'I suppose you're right, Aunt Pol, but it *would* be exciting, wouldn't it.'

'I think it's over-rated.'

We clung to that rusty iron ring at the end of the wharf, shivering in the cold. I did what I could to warm the water in which we were

411

immersed, but nobody could heat the entire Sea of the Winds, so about all I could do was to take the edge off the chill.

After an hour or so – which seemed like an eternity – father's voice came to me again. *'Polgara, where are you?'*

'We're at the end of the wharf, father. Is it safe to come out yet?'

'No. Stay where you are, and keep out of sight.'

'What are you up to, Old Wolf?'

'I'm hiding the Rivan King. Get used to it, Pol, because we'll be doing it for quite a long time.'

The significance of his reference to the shivering little boy at my side was not lost on me. Clearly, Salmissra's assassins had succeeded in butchering King Gorek and almost all the members of the royal family. Geran's flight from the scene had spared him the horror of witnessing the disaster, and so he didn't seem to know that he was now an orphan. He'd have to be told, of course, and I knew exactly upon whose shoulders *that* unpleasant task would fall.

It was well after dark when father and Brand, the Rivan Warder, finally came down to the harbor. The four of us, father, Brand, Prince Geran and I, boarded an unoccupied ship and sailed out into the harbor with father manning the sails, without even bothering to rise from the bench upon which he sat. I took the shivering little prince below-decks, dried him off and created some dry clothes for him.

Then I went back up on deck to have a word with father. 'There were no other survivors, I gather?' I asked him.

'Not a one. The Nyissans were using poisoned daggers.'

'The boy doesn't know. He ran away before the killing started.'

'Good. Those Nyissans were very efficient.'

'Then it *was* Salmissra who was behind it.'

'Yes, but somebody else put her up to it.'

'Who?'

'I'm not sure. The next time I see her, I'll ask her.'

'How do you plan to get into Sthiss Tor?'

'I'm going to depopulate the Alorn kingdoms to provide myself with an escort. Then I'm going to march through Nyissa like some kind of natural disaster. I'll chase the Snake People so far back into the trees that they'll have to import daylight. You'd better tell the boy that he's an orphan.'

'Thank you.' I said it in a flat, unfriendly tone of voice.

'You're better at that sort of thing than I am, Pol. It might make him feel better if he knows that I'm going to destroy Nyissa in retaliation.'

'He's only a little boy, father, and his mother was just killed. I don't think the idea of retaliation's going to comfort him very much.'

'That's about the only thing we've got to offer him right now. You're going to have to fill in for his mother, I'm afraid.'

'What do I know about raising little boys, father?'

'You didn't do too badly with Daran after your sister died, Pol. I'm sorry to saddle you with this, but there's no one else available, and the boy absolutely *must* be protected. You're going to have to hide him. This assassination has "Angarak" printed all over it, and Ctuchik's got prophecies of his own that'll advise him that there's a survivor. The West's going to be awash with Grolims before the year's out. The protection of that little boy is the most important thing any of us are going to do right now.'

'I'll take care of it, father.' Then I went back below decks to break the news to the little prince.

He wept, of course, and I tried my best to comfort him.

A peculiar thought came to me as I held the sobbing little boy in my arms. I don't think I'd ever actually come to grips with a certain stark reality. Mother was not born a human, and that quite clearly meant that I was part wolf. Though I didn't have paws, a shaggy tail, or sharp teeth, I *did* have certain wolfish traits. Wolves are pack animals, and they all share in the responsibility of caring for the puppies, regardless of which particular female gave birth to them. My comforting of this grieving, sandy-haired little boy was instinctive, growing out of the need to protect the pack.

Once I'd come face to face with that fact, several decisions followed automatically. I needed a safe, well-hidden den first of all. Mother's cottage would *not* serve that purpose. It was too exposed and too many people knew where it was. Next, I needed a reliable source of food. The answer, of course, was obvious. My rose-choked manor house on Lake Erat had long since been forgotten, and it was virtually invisible. Moreover, the grounds around it were fertile, and I could easily grow vegetables among the rose bushes and periodically drift out on silent wings at night to poach rabbits and an occasional sheep. The manor house would provide safety and food. Prince Geran might be a little wild and uncivilized when he grew up, but at least he'd still be alive.

I also discovered that thinking wolfishly gave me a tremendous amount of insight into mother's character. Everything she'd done – even including her seeming desertion of my sister and me – had been done to defend the pack.

413

'Naturally, Pol,' her voice came to me out of nowhere. *'Are you only just now coming to realize that? You really ought to pay more attention, you know.'*

Geran was so overcome with grief that we didn't really talk very much during the two days we were at sea on our way to the coast of Sendaria, but when we reached a cove some five miles north of Camaar and went ashore, he pulled himself together enough to be able to speak coherently with Brand. He asked the Rivan Warder to take care of his people and to guard the Orb. Geran's family has always taken those two responsibilities very seriously, and despite the fact that the boy had been far down the line of succession before his entire family had been murdered, he'd clearly received instruction in the important things.

After Brand left for Camaar to commandeer a crew for his return voyage to the Isle, I spoke briefly with father, advising him of my plan to hide my new charge at my manor house on Lake Erat. He had objections, of course. Father always has objections when I tell him that I'm going to do something. He should have saved his breath, because, as always, I overrode his quibbles. You'd think that after two thousand years he'd have learned not to try to tell me what to do, but some people never learn, I guess.

Geran, his small face very serious, asked his ultimate grandfather to chastise the Serpent Queen for murdering his family.

Then father left for Val Alorn to begin gathering forces for his intended invasion of the land of the Snake People.

'Where are we going, Aunt Pol?' Geran asked me.

'I have a house here in Sendaria, Geran,' I told him. 'We should be safe there.'

'Have you got lots of soldiers there?'

'No, Geran. I don't need soldiers in that particular place.'

'Won't that be sort of dangerous? What I mean is that the snake lady probably still wants to kill me, and she's got those people with poisoned knives working for her. I'm not very big yet, so I couldn't really protect you from them.'

He was such a dear, serious little boy. I took him in my arms and held him very close for a while, and I think we both rather liked that. 'Everything's going to be all right, Geran,' I assured him. 'Nobody knows that the house is there, and it's very hard to get to it.'

'Did you put a spell on it?' he asked eagerly. Then he flushed slightly. 'That wasn't very polite was it, Aunt Pol? I've heard all kinds of stories about how you can do magic things – like casting spells and turning people into frogs and like that – but you haven't given me permission to talk about those things, so I shouldn't have just come right out and said it that way, should I?'

'It's all right, Geran,' I said. 'We're part of the same family, so we don't really have to stand on ceremony, do we? Let's go back in among the trees. This beach is right out in the open, and we *do* have enemies out there looking for us.'

'Whatever you say, Aunt Pol.'

We struck out from the beach in the general direction of Lake Sulturn, staying on the back roads and country lanes. I bought food at an isolated farm house, and the young prince and I camped out that first night. After the boy had fallen asleep in my arms, I started to think about logistics. We hadn't really covered very much ground that day, and I definitely wanted to get further inland. That open beach was just too close for my peace of mind.

I immediately dismissed the notion of 'tampering'. Father's warning about Grolims was probably quite close to the mark, and 'tampering' makes a characteristic noise that would draw every Grolim in Sendaria right to me. Geran was a sturdy little boy, but his legs weren't very long yet, so walking wasn't getting us away from the beach fast enough for my comfort. Obviously, we were going to need a horse. I checked the purse I always keep tucked under my clothing and found that I had adequate funds with me, so I sent out a probing thought, searching for a farm of some size along the road ahead. Fortunately, I found what I was looking for only a few miles away.

I dozed from time to time during that long night. Under the circumstances, a deep sleep might not have been a good idea. Then, when dawn began to touch the eastern sky, I stirred up our small fire and began cooking breakfast.

'Good morning, Aunt Pol,' Geran said when the smells of hot food woke him. 'I'm really hungry, you know?'

'Little boys are always hungry, Geran.'

'How far is it to your house?'

'About ninety leagues – almost three hundred miles.'

'My feet are really sore, Aunt Pol. I'm not used to walking all day.'

'It'll get easier in just a bit, Geran,' I assured him. 'There's another farm just ahead. I'll buy a horse there, and then we can ride.'

'That's a *very* good idea, Aunt Pol.' He seemed quite enthusiastic.

There *was* one brief problem about that when we reached the farm and I'd chosen the horse I wanted.

'Ah – these are very old coins, ma'am,' the farmer said dubiously. 'I don't think I've ever seen any quite so old.'

'They're part of my inheritance, good farmer,' I lied quickly. 'My family's a bit on the tight-fisted side, and once they get their hands on a coin, they tend to keep it.'

'That's a commendable trait, but I don't really know what these are worth in today's money.'

'Silver's silver, good farmer. It's the weight that's important, not whose picture's stamped on the front of the coin.'

'Well – I suppose you're right about that. Only –'

'I'm really in a bit of a hurry, friend. My nephew and I absolutely *must* get to Sulturn before the week's out. Why don't I just add three of these coins to cover any possible difference in value?'

'I wouldn't want to cheat you, ma'am.' In a very real sense, I'd created the Sendarian character, and now it was coming back to haunt me.

In the end, the honest farmer and I settled for two extra coins, and I became the owner of a mottled grey horse named Squire. The good farmer threw in an almost worn-out saddle, and Geran and I prepared to leave. First, however, I had a talk with Squire, who hadn't been ridden all winter and who was feeling frisky. I took him – firmly – by the chin and looked straight into his large eyes. 'Behave yourself, Squire,' I advised him. 'Do your prancing and cavorting around on your own time. You *really* don't want to make me cross, now do you?'

He seemed to get my point, and after a mile or so of getting used to each other, we settled into a rolling canter that literally ate up the miles.

'This is *much* better than walking, Aunt Pol,' Geran said enthusiastically after a little while. 'I'll bet my feet won't be sore tonight.'

'No, probably not, but some other part might be.'

Geran and Squire hit it off well almost immediately, and I felt that to be a good thing. The young prince was carrying a heavy load of grief, and his friendship with our horse helped to take his mind off that.

We reached Sulturn in two days, but I bypassed the city and took a room in a village inn rather than one of the more opulent lodging houses in Sulturn itself. I felt that it was safer that way.

We continued on toward the northeast for the next several days, and I spent a fair amount of that time giving Geran instructions in the fine art of being unobtrusive. To further that end, I dyed his characteristic sandy-colored hair black. It was just possible that

Ctuchik's Grolims might know that virtually everybody in the line of Iron-grip and my sister had the same color hair and they'd be looking for blond little boys. I also concealed the tell-tale lock in my own hair with some intricate braiding. If some Grolim happened to be searching for 'a lady with a white streak in her hair and a sandy-haired little boy', he'd look right past us.

As we approached Medalia in central Sendaria, the probing thought I kept more or less continually sweeping on ahead of us bore fruit. I caught a flash of that dull black color that identified an Angarak. It wasn't the glossy black of a Grolim, but at this particular time, I didn't want to encounter *any* Angarak, be he Murgo, Nadrak, or Thull.

I nudged Squire into a side road, and Geran and I bypassed Medalia and continued on toward the northeast along the back roads, avoiding Ran Horb's highways entirely.

All in all, it took us about two weeks to reach Lake Erat. I concealed Geran and Squire in a thicket on the south shore of the lake along about evening, went off a ways, and donned white feathers. I wasn't going to blunder into anything without looking it over very carefully, and owls have very good eyes in the dark.

The east side of Lake Erat was very sparsely populated in those days, and I soon located all my neighbors. As it turned out, there weren't any foreigners in the area at that time, so I judged that it'd be safe for us to go through the barrier I'd erected and get inside the protective walls of my house. I flew directly there and advised my rose-bushes that I'd returned and that I'd be very happy if they opened a path for me. Then I went back to fetch my nephew and his horse.

It was almost midnight when Squire waded across the river just to the south of my house, and we rode on up to the edge of the thicket and on along the narrow path the roses had opened for us.

'It's a very big house, isn't it?' Geran observed a little nervously, 'but isn't it awfully dark?'

'Nobody lives there, Geran,' I replied.

'Nobody at all?'

'Not a soul.'

'I've never lived in a place where there weren't any other people around, Aunt Pol.'

'We don't *want* other people around, Geran. That was the whole idea.'

'Well –' He said it a bit dubiously. 'The house isn't haunted, is it, Aunt Pol? I don't think I'd like to live in a haunted house.'

I didn't even smile. 'No, Geran,' I assured him. 'The house isn't haunted. It's just empty.'

He sighed. 'I think I'm going to have to learn how to do some things I'm not used to doing,' he said.

'Oh? Such as what?'

'Well, we *will* need firewood and things like that, won't we? I'm not good with tools, Aunt Pol,' he confessed. 'There were all kinds of servants in grandfather's citadel, so I never really learned how to use an axe or a shovel or things like that.'

'Look upon it as a chance to learn, Geran. Let's put Squire in the stable, and then we'll go inside. I'll fix us some supper and then we'll see about some beds.'

'Anything you say, Aunt Pol.'

We had supper, and then I set up a pair of cots in the kitchen. We could explore the house and choose more suitable quarters in the morning.

The house had been untended for quite a long time, so there were cobwebs in the corners and a thick layer of dust over everything. That was intolerable, of course. Over the years I'd paid occasional visits to my former seat of power and I'd customarily tidied up with a wave of my hand. I decided that this time I'd do it a little differently. My youthful charge had just emerged from a crushing tragedy, and I didn't want him brooding about it. He needed something to keep his mind – and his hands – busy. Cleaning the house from top to bottom and from one end to the other would probably keep us both out of mischief for quite some time. It would *also* avoid alerting any stray Grolims to our presence. At that particular time I wasn't familiar enough with Grolims to know just exactly how skilled they were in the exercise of their talents, so it was better to be a little on the safe side.

I arose just before dawn and started preparing breakfast. My kitchen had been built to feed quite a number of people, so the stoves and ovens were very large. It seemed just a little ridiculous to heat up a stove bigger than a farm wagon just to feed two people, but it was the only stove available, so I laid in the kindling and piled on firewood that had lain in the wood-box for generations. Geran had been right about one thing, it appeared. He *was* going to be spending a lot of time chopping wood.

Geran woke up when the smell of breakfast began to reach him. I've known a lot of little boys over the years, and that's one characteristic they all have in common. As a group, I've noticed that they're always hungry.

'What are we going to do today, Aunt Pol?' he asked me after he'd spooned down his second bowl of porridge.

I ran one finger across the back of an unused chair and held it out for his inspection. 'What do you see, Geran?' I asked him.

'It looks sort of dusty to me.'

'Exactly. Maybe we ought to do something about that.'

He looked around the kitchen. 'It shouldn't take us too long,' he said confidently. 'What shall we do when we're finished?'

'There's more than one room in the house, Geran,' I pointed out.

He sighed mournfully. 'I was sort of afraid you might feel that way about it, Aunt Pol.'

'You're a prince, Geran,' I reminded him. 'I wouldn't want to offend you by making you live in a dirty house.'

'It takes a lot to offend me, Aunt Pol.' He said it hopefully.

'It just wouldn't do for us to live in all this filth, Geran. We'll have the house all bright and shiny in no time at all.'

'It's a very big house, Aunt Pol.'

'Yes, it is rather, isn't it? It'll give you something to do, and you can't go outside to play.'

'Couldn't we just close off the parts where we won't be living? Then we could clean the three or four rooms we'll be staying in and let the rest go.'

'It wouldn't be right, Geran. It just wouldn't do.'

He sighed with a kind of mournful resignation.

And so the Rivan King and I started cleaning house. He wasn't *happy* about it, but he didn't sulk *too* much. The one thing I *didn't* tell him had to do with the fact that dust keeps right on settling and web-spinning spiders are the busiest creatures in the world. Just because you cleaned a room yesterday is no guarantee that it's not going to need cleaning again tomorrow.

We did other things, of course. There was a farm cart in one of the stables, and I periodically hitched Squire to the cart and went out to buy provisions from nearby farms. Geran didn't go with me on those occasions. I left him in my library the first time, and when I returned, I found him sprawled in a chair looking disconsolately out the window. 'I thought you'd be reading,' I said.

'I don't know how to read, Aunt Pol,' he admitted.

That gave us something else to do when we grew tired of cleaning house. Geran had a quick mind, and he was reading in a surprisingly short length of time.

We settled into a kind of routine, cleaning in the morning and lessons in the afternoons. It was a fairly comfortable way to live, and we were both quite content.

The twins kept me advised of the progress of father's punitive expedition into Nyissa, and I passed the news on to Geran. He seemed to take a certain amount of satisfaction in his grandfather's rampant destruction of the land of the Snake People.

Spring came, and my youthful charge and I took up gardening as a hobby. I suppose I could have continued to buy food from neighboring farms, but I didn't really like to leave Geran alone, and if my face became *too* familiar in the area, a chance word dropped in some local tavern might alert a passing Murgo.

I think it was early summer when father and uncle Beldin come by to pay us a call. I still remember Geran coming down the stairs with a sword in his hand. He was very young, but he knew that it was a man's duty to protect his women-folk. I didn't really *need* protection, but his little gesture touched me all the same. He greeted my father enthusiastically and immediately asked if the Old Wolf had kept his promise to kill the Serpent Queen.

'She was dead the last time I looked,' father replied. He was a little evasive about it, I thought.

'Did you hit her for me the way I asked you to?' Geran pressed.

'That he did, Laddy buck,' uncle Beldin said. 'That he did.'

Uncle Beldin's distorted appearance seemed to make Geran just a little apprehensive, so I introduced them.

'You aren't very tall, are you?' Geran blurted.

'It has its advantages sometimes, Laddy Buck,' uncle Beldin replied. 'I'm almost never after hittin' me head on a low-hangin' branch, don't y' know.'

'I *like* him, Aunt Pol,' Geran said, laughing.

Then father went into some of the details of the little get-together he'd planned. He pointed out the fact that the assassination of Gorek had been a major EVENT and that we'd probably better all gather in the Vale to consider our various options. He advised us that he'd go on to the Isle of the Winds to fetch Brand while uncle Beldin escorted Geran and me to the Vale.

Before we'd even finished crossing the Sendarian mountains, Geran and uncle Beldin were fast friends. I've never completely understood why old men and little boys always seem to automatically take to each other, and I'm always a little offended when the white-haired member of that little group shrugs it off by saying, 'It's a man sort of thing, Pol. You wouldn't understand.' They can talk about 'man things' until they're blue in the face, but my own suspicions strongly lean in the direction of approaching senility and its accompanying reversion to childhood, if not outright infantilism, on the part of one of them. It was *that* journey that persuaded me that no woman in her right mind should *ever* allow an old man and a little boy anywhere within five miles of any patch of water. Their hands will automatically sprout fishing poles, and nothing at all will get done for the rest of the day.

When the three of us finally reached the Vale, Geran met the twins, and they fussed over him as much as uncle Beldin had. I began to feel definitely left out.

They *did* let me do the cooking, though – and the cleaning up afterward. Wasn't that nice of them?

Father and Brand arrived after a few weeks, and we all got down to business. Geran sat quietly on a chair in a corner while we discussed the state of the world and what we were going to do about it.

Evidently my little charge had been greatly impressed with that tired old saw, 'children should be seen and not heard'. It kept him from asking a lot of questions, though.

Uncle Beltira advised us that according to the calendar of the Dals, the Third Age had ended. All of the prophecies were now in place, and now that we had our instructions, all we had to do was carry them out.

Then uncle Beldin told us that an Angarak general named Kallath was busy unifying all of Mallorea and bringing it under Torak's domination.

Prince Geran *did* bend the rules once during that discussion. 'Excuse me,' he said. 'What's supposed to happen in Arendia? Isn't that the place that scroll you've got was talking about when it said something about "the lands of the Bull-God"?'

'Very good, Geran,' father complimented the boy's perceptiveness in identifying the reference contained in the obscure language of the Mrin.

'There's going to be an EVENT, your Highness,' uncle Beltira told him.

'What kind of event?' Geran hadn't quite caught on to the peculiar emphasis my family gave that word.

'The prophecy we call the Mrin Codex uses the term when it's talking about a meeting between the Child of Light and the Child of Dark,' Belkira explained.

'Who are they?'

'Nobody, specifically,' Beldin said. 'They're sort of like titles. They get passed around quite a bit. Anyway, everything's moving in the direction of one of those EVENTS. If we're reading these things right, the Child of Light and the Child of Dark are going to meet in Arendia some time in the future, and the meeting's probably not going to be a friendly one. I don't think they'll be talking about the weather.'

'A battle?' Geran asked enthusiastically. He *was* fairly young after all.

I was in the kitchen area fixing supper. 'The arrival of this Kallath right at this particular time isn't a coincidence, is it?' I suggested.

'Probably not, Pol,' father agreed.

'Excuse me again,' Geran said. 'If Torak's got prophecies of his own, then he knows that something important's going to happen in Arendia the same as we do, doesn't he?'

'I'm sure he does,' Beldin replied.

'Do you know what I think?' the boy said, his brow knitted in concentration. 'I don't think that what happened to my family really had anything to do with somebody trying to steal the Orb. I think that Torak was just trying to keep us so busy that we wouldn't pay any attention to what this Kallath person was doing in Mallorea. If the Nyissans hadn't murdered my family when they did, one of you would have gone to Mallorea to keep Kallath from taking over the whole place. But you all got so busy punishing the Nyissans that you didn't pay any attention to what was going on in Mallorea.' He stopped, suddenly aware of the fact that we were all paying very close attention to what he was saying. 'Well,' he added apologetically, 'that's what I think anyway, and this Zedar person you all know was probably the best one to fool you, since he knows you all so well.'

'What have you done to this boy, Pol?' Beldin growled at me. 'He isn't supposed to be thinking this clearly yet.'

'I taught him to read, uncle,' I replied. 'He took it from there.'

'What a waste!' the dwarf muttered.

'I don't think I followed that, uncle.'

'The boy and I could have been arguing philosophy instead of molesting fish while we came across the mountains.'

'You absolutely *have* to tamper with things, don't you, Pol?' father said accusingly.

'Tamper? It's called "education", father. Didn't you tamper with *me*? I seem to remember a long string of "whys" coming from your mouth a few years back.'

'You always have to make those clever remarks, don't you, Pol?' he said with a certain distaste.

'It's good for you, father,' I replied lightly. 'It keeps you on your toes, and that helps you to ward off senility – for a little while, anyway.'

'What did you mean by that, Aunt Pol?' Geran asked me.

'It's a game they play, Geran,' Beltira explained. 'It embarrasses them to admit that they actually like each other, so they play this game instead. It's their way of saying that they don't really hate each other.'

The twins have such sweet faces that I think we tend to forget just how wise they are. Beltira had seen right to the center of our silly game, and his explanation embarrassed both my father and me.

Fortunately, Brand stepped in to cover our confusion. 'It would seem that my prince is very gifted,' the Rivan Warder mused. 'We'll have to protect that mind.'

'That's my job, Brand,' I told him.

'*Polgara,*' mother's voice came to me at that point, '*listen very carefully. The Master has a question to ask you.*'

Then we all sensed the Master's presence. We couldn't see him, but we knew that he was there. 'Dost thou accept this responsibility freely, my daughter?' he asked me intently.

This was the task I'd accepted at Beldaran's wedding. I'd sworn to take it up then, and nothing had really happened in the past two thousand or so years to make me change my mind. A great many things fell into place at that point. In a sense, the two eons which had passed since I'd first pledged myself to take up this task had merely been preparation – an education, if you will. Now I was ready to be Geran's guardian and protector – no matter where EVENTS would take him or the line which would descend from him. I'd already pledged my word to accept this responsibility, but evidently the Master wanted confirmation. 'I accepted this task freely once before, Master,' I replied, laying my hand rather possessively on Geran's shoulder, 'and I accept it freely now. Truly, I shall guard and guide the Rivan line for so long as it be necessary. Yea, even unto the end of days, if need be.'

As I said it, I felt a peculiar sort of surge, and I seemed to hear a vast ringing sound echoing from the farthest star. Quite clearly my affirmation of my previous vow was an EVENT of the first magnitude. I'd done a few fairly important things before, but this was the first time that the stars had ever applauded me.

'Well then,' I said to my somewhat awed family, 'now that we've settled that, supper's almost ready, so why don't you gentlemen go wash your hands while I set the table?'

CHAPTER 26

If you choose to look at it in a certain light, my acceptance of the task was automatic, even instinctive. My little epiphany on board the ship that carried us from the Isle of the Winds as I'd comforted the grief-stricken Geran lay at the core of my willingness to devote the rest of my life to the descendants of my sister and Riva Iron-grip. The line was of my blood – my pack, if you will – and rearing and protecting each child in the line was an obligation I'd have accepted even had the Master not extracted that pledge from me.

But there was another, less wolfish, reason for my ready acceptance. I was fully convinced that the death of Ontrose had closed certain doors to me. I was certain that I'd never marry or have children of my own. The rearing of my sister's descendants would fill that aching emptiness.

The following morning I was seized with an almost overpowering urge to leave the Vale. It was as if my reaffirmation of my pledge had opened a whole new chapter in my life, and I wanted to get on with it. Looking back, however, I'll confess that my motives were a little less admirable. My pledge had made Geran mine, and I wanted to keep him all to myself.

Isn't it odd the way our minds work sometimes?

Anyway, my sandy-haired charge and I left the Vale after a few days, and the dependable, mottled Squire carried us back up into the Sendarian mountains. I was really in no great hurry to get home, so our pace was leisurely. I'm sure Squire approved of that. I've observed that horses lie a lot. A horse loves to run, but he always behaves as if it's a terrible imposition when you ask him to do that.

'What was it like, Aunt Pol?' Geran asked me one evening after supper when we'd spread our blankets on the ground, the camp-fire had burned down to embers, and the close and friendly darkness was enfolding us. 'I mean, what was it like to grow up in the Vale surrounded by magic and sorcerers the way you were?'

'My sister and I hadn't really known any other kind of life, Geran, so it didn't really seem particularly unusual to us.'

'She was my grandmother, wasn't she? – your sister, I mean.'

'Your ultimate grandmother, yes.' I stepped around some things rather carefully. Geran didn't really need to know about mother just yet. I lay back and looked up at the stars. 'Our father was off in Mallorea when we were born,' I told him. 'He and Bear-shoulders and the boys were stealing the Orb from Torak.'

'It wasn't really stealing, was it? I mean, the Orb belonged to us in the first place after all. Torak's the one who stole it.'

'Well, he stole it from the Master, but it amounts to the same thing, I guess. Anyway, my sister and I were raised by uncle Beldin.'

Geran giggled. 'I *like* him,' he said.

'Yes, I noticed.' Then I continued with a slightly sanitized version of my childhood in the Vale. Geran listened eagerly. If you want a little boy's undivided attention, tell him stories. After a while, however, he drifted off to sleep, and I fell silent. I watched the endless progression of the stars for a while, noting that a couple of the constellations had moved since I'd last taken a good look at them. And then I too slept.

When we reached my house I noticed something peculiar. I'd visited it any number of times since I'd buried it in roses, and it'd always seemed almost unbearably lonely. It was an empty place that hadn't been meant to be empty, but now that sense of loneliness wasn't there any more. Geran was there with me, and that was all I really needed. I decided that we could probably forego the housecleaning. Geran had learned to live with the loss of his family, and he now seemed to want to spend most of his time in my library with my copies of the Mrin and Darine. Eventually, he reacted to the Mrin with the same sense of frustration it stirred in all of us. 'It doesn't make sense, Aunt Pol!' he exclaimed one evening, banging his fist on the table.

'I know,' I replied. 'It isn't supposed to.'

'Why do we all waste so much time on it then?'

'Because it tells us what's going to happen in the future.'

'But if we can't make any sense out of it, how does that help us?'

'Oh, we can make *some* sense out of it if we work with it. It's all jumbled together that way to keep people who don't have any business knowing what's going to happen from finding out.'

'You mean it's written in code?'

'You could put it that way, yes.'

'I think I'll stick with the other one – the Darine. It's easier to read and it's not so splotched up with ink-smears.'

'Whatever suits you, Geran.'

I was more than a little surprised – and pleased – to discover that my young nephew had a surprisingly quick mind. He'd been raised as an Alorn, and you don't really expect to find brains in an Alorn – except for the Drasnians, of course. A Drasnian's intelligence, however, is devoted almost exclusively to swindling his neighbors, so he doesn't waste it on things philosophical.

Geran and I lived quietly in our secluded house for several years. He needed time to grow up, and I needed time to get used to my new occupation. He was about twelve or so, and his voice was beginning to change, when a notion came to him that was surprisingly acute. 'Do you know what I think, Aunt Pol?'

'What was that, dear?'

'I've been working on this for a while, and it sort of seems to me that you and grandfather and our uncles live outside of time and the world the rest of us live in. It's almost as if you lived someplace else – only it's right here at the same time.'

I laid my book aside. 'Go on, Geran,' I urged him.

'This other world you live in is all around the rest of us, but we can't see it. There are different rules there, too. You all have to live for thousands of years, and you have to learn how to use magic, and you have to spend a lot of time reading old books that none of us can understand. Then, every once in a while, you have to come out into our world to tell the kings what they're supposed to do, and they have to do it, whether they like it or not. Anyway, I've been sort of wondering why. Why do we need two worlds this way? Why not just one? Then it came to me. It's even more complicated than I thought, because there aren't just two worlds, but three. The Gods live in one world – out there among the stars – and ordinary people like me live right here on this one where nothing very unusual ever happens. You and grandfather and the uncles live in the third one – the one that's between the world of the Gods and the world of ordinary people. You live there because you're our connection to the Gods. The Gods tell you what's supposed to be done, and you pass the instructions on to us. You live forever, and you can do magic things and see the future and all that because

427

you were chosen to live in that special world between the Gods and the rest of us so that you can guide us in the right direction. Does that make any sense, Aunt Pol?'

'A great deal of sense, Geran.'

'There's more.'

'I rather thought there might be.'

'Torak's out there in the world of the Gods, too, and he's got people living in the in-between world the same as you and the others do.'

'Yes. We're called disciples. Torak's disciples are Urvon, Ctuchik, and Zedar.'

'Yes. I read about them. Anyway, Torak has the idea that *one* thing's going to happen, and our Gods believe that it's going to be something else.'

'That sums it up fairly well, yes.'

'Then the war of the Gods never really ended, did it?'

'No. It's still going on.'

'Who's going to win?'

'We don't know.'

'*Aunt Pol!*' He said it with a note of anguished protest in his voice. 'Your whole library's filled with all these prophecies and you *still* don't know who's going to win? *Some* book here *has* to come right out and tell us.'

I waved at the shelves. 'If there is, it's in there somewhere. Feel free to browse your way through. Let me know if you find it.'

'That's not fair!'

I laughed and gathered him in my arms impulsively. He was such a dear, serious boy!

'Well, it's not, is it?' he grumbled.

I laughed even more.

As Geran approached his sixteenth birthday, I realized that if the line of the Rivan King were to be continued, it was time for me to take him out into the world so that he could find himself a wife. I gave some thought to where we might want to live, and Sulturn seemed like a good place to me. Mother, however, had different ideas about that. 'No, Pol,' her voice came to me one night, '*not Sulturn, Muros.*'

'Why Muros?'

'*Because that's where the young lady he's going to marry lives.*'

'Who is she?'

'*Her name's Eldara.*'

'That's an Algar name.'

428

'That stands to reason, Pol, since her father's an Algar. His name's *Hattan*, and he's the second son of a clan chief. He married a Sendarian woman when his clan drove a herd of cattle to Muros. He settled down there and went into business as a cattle buyer. He has connections with all the Algar clans, so he's very prosperous. Take Geran to Muros, Pol. Let's get him married off.'

'Whatever you say, mother.'

I thought it over and decided that Geran and I would need a certain status. A prosperous merchant probably wouldn't be *too* excited about marrying his daughter off to some country bumpkin. Clearly, Geran and I would have to go to the city of Sendar. I was going to need some money.

Squire was an elderly horse by now, but he was still sound, even though he did puff a bit when he went uphill. I had Geran dust off and polish one of the small carriages in the barn while I packed some respectable clothes for us in a stout trunk, and in the late spring of the year 4012, my young charge and I set out across Sendaria to the capital city of Sendar. It was a nice time of year for a trip, and there was nothing pressing about our journey, so I let Squire set his own pace. We went southwesterly, and after a few days we reached the crossroads where the country lane we were following intersected with the imperial highway.

'Which way here, Aunt Pol?' Geran, who was driving our little carriage, asked me.

'South, Geran, toward Medalia. Then we'll take the high road to Sendar.'

'All right. Move along, Squire.'

Our ancient horse sighed and plodded on.

Medalia had changed a great deal during the centuries since I'd last been there. Sendaria was a peaceable kingdom now, so the defensive wall that'd surrounded Medalia when it'd been a part of my duchy had fallen into disrepair. I disapproved of that, but I decided not to make an issue of it.

It was a week or so later when we reached Sendar, and we took rooms in a substantial inn. After dinner, I went through our trunk and laid out assorted finery for us. 'Do we really have to dress up like that, aunt Pol?' Geran asked with a certain distaste. It was definitely time to get him out of the country and back to civilization.

'Yes,' I told him quite firmly. 'We're going to the palace tomorrow morning, and I'd rather not have to go in through one of the servants' entrances.'

429

'Are we going there to see the king?'

'No, not really. Our business is with the Royal Treasurer. We *might* have to talk with the king to get our business taken care of, though, depending on how thick-headed the Treasurer is.'

'I don't understand.'

'We need money, and I have plenty of that here. I have to persuade the Treasurer that I'm who I say I am and that the money belongs to me.'

'Isn't it a little dangerous to trust all your money to somebody else? He might try to cheat you.'

'Sendarians are very honest, Geran. I don't think the Treasurer would do that – and if he has, I have ways to persuade him that he's made a mistake.'

And so, early the next morning, Prince Geran and I went to the palace of King Falben of Sendaria and to the solidly built wing of that palace that was the repository of the royal treasury. There was the usual delay before we were admitted to the musty-smelling office of the Royal Treasurer. Over the years I've noticed that people who are preoccupied with money always seem to have that same odor about them. Money's almost always locked up somewhere, and nobody who takes care of it ever seems to think of opening the windows to air the place out.

Baron Stilnan, the Royal Treasurer, was a very serious man whose office walls were covered from floor to ceiling with bookcases filled to overflowing with leather-bound account books. There was an almost religious hush in the baron's office. That's appropriate, I guess, since money *is* a religion to the man who spends all his time counting it.

'I know you're busy, your Excellency,' I said after Geran and I had been escorted into his office and had seated ourselves, 'so I'll get right to the point. Quite some time ago my family placed certain funds in the care of the crown. I'm here to withdraw some of that money.'

'I'd need verification of that, Lady –?'

'We can get to names and other things later, your Excellency. The funds in question are recorded in Volume One of your account books – page 736, if I remember correctly.'

He looked dubious, but he went to his bookshelf and pulled down the last volume on the left of the top shelf.

'You'll find a sealed piece of parchment pinned to the page, Baron,' I advised him. 'There's a word written on that parchment. It's a sort of password that's there to identify me.' I pushed a scrap of paper with the name 'Ontrose' written on it across his desk. 'I think you'll find that this is the word.'

Baron Stilnan blew the dust off the heavy account book, leafed through, found the page, and unpinned the parchment. 'This is the royal seal of King Fundor the Magnificent!' he exclaimed.

'Yes,' I said, 'I know. Fundor was kind enough to take over the management of the account. The name I gave you matches the name on the parchment, doesn't it?'

'Yes, it does. The entry says that the original deposit was made by the Duchess of Erat. Are you her descendant, madame?'

'I *am* the duchess, Baron, and I haven't any descendants.'

'The entry's a hundred and eighty years old, my Lady.'

'Has it been that long? Where *does* the time go?'

'I'll have to consult with King Falben about this, my Lady. The account's under royal protection, so he's the only one who can release funds.'

I sighed. 'What a bother. Please keep this to yourself, Baron. I have reasons for not wanting my business here to become general knowledge.'

'Only the king shall know of it, my Lady.'

King Falben of Sendaria was a plain-looking man dressed in sober brown. He was about forty, and there was a bustling sort of air about him that you see in people who have a dozen or more things to do all at the same time. 'Now,' he said as he entered the office, 'what's this all about, my Lady? Stilnan here was babbling something about a very old account in the royal treasury.'

'The baron summed it up fairly well, then, your Majesty,' I replied with a formal curtsey. 'I placed the funds in the royal treasury some years back. I need some money right now, so I'm here to withdraw part of the account. Why don't you show his Majesty the entry in the account book, Baron Stilnan?' I suggested, 'and the attached document? It might save some time.'

Falben read the relevant material quickly. 'You claim to be the Lady Polgara?' he demanded of me, his tone suspicious.

'She doesn't claim to be, your Majesty,' Geran told him. 'She *is* Lady Polgara.'

'My nephew, Geran,' I introduced the young man.

'I'll need something more than just his word, my Lady,' Falben said. 'There are all sorts of swindlers running around these days.'

'Oh, very well,' I sighed. Then I elevated the King of Sendaria. I've found that to be the fastest way to prove my identity to sceptics. There's something about standing on empty air that almost immediately brings people around to my way of thinking. 'Satisfied?' I asked the startled monarch. He stood frozen in mid-air, his eyes wide with astonishment. He nodded violently, and I gently lowered him to the floor. 'I'm sorry, your Majesty,' I apologized. 'We're both busy, and that usually settles these tiresome arguments in the shortest possible time.'

'I can see why,' Falben said in a strained tone of voice. Then he went to Stilnan's desk and looked at the open account book. 'Did you want to withdraw the entire balance, Lady Polgara?' he asked, sounding slightly worried.

'How much is there? I haven't been keeping track of it.'

'The last entry shows something over a half million nobles, my Lady.'

'The noble's a one-ounce gold coin?'

He nodded.

'I don't think it'd be a good idea for me to leave here with fifteen tons of gold in my pocket, do you?'

He laughed weakly. 'You *could* do it if you wanted to, Lady Polgara. I've heard stories about you.'

'Exaggerations, your Majesty. I think five hundred nobles should cover my current expenses.'

'Fetch it, Stilnan,' the king commanded. 'I have a confession to make, Lady Polgara.'

'Honest confession is good for the soul, your Majesty.'

'I'm ashamed to admit that your account's a little encumbered. We've occasionally used it as security for temporary loans when our tax revenues fell a little short of our current needs.'

'That's a legitimate use for dormant money, your Majesty,' I forgave him.

'Might I ask the source of this fortune?'

'Rents, your Majesty. My duchy was extensive and I've been renting out farmsteads for quite a long time now. I don't really charge that much rent, but it *does* seem to be piling up, doesn't it? Maybe I'll buy something with it someday – Tol Honeth, perhaps.'

He laughed. 'It's probably for sale, Lady Polgara. Everything the Tolnedrans own is for sale.'

Baron Stilnan returned with two large canvas bags of jingling coins. He insisted that I count the money, and then he entered the transaction in the musty old account book.

'Oh, one last thing, your Majesty,' I said. 'I'd rather that word of this visit didn't get noised about.'

'Which visit was that, Lady Polgara? I have a terrible memory.'

I laughed, curtsied, and then Geran and I left the royal palace.

'He seemed like a nice enough fellow,' Geran noted, plodding along beside me through the streets of Sendar with those two jingling canvas bags.

'I rather liked him,' I agreed. Then I frowned. 'When gold coins rattle together, they make a very distinctive sound, don't they? I think I'd better devise some way to keep them quiet. We don't want to attract attention.'

'Are we going home now, Aunt Pol?'

'No, Geran. Actually, we're going to Muros.'

'Muros? Whatever for?'

'I haven't raised you to be a hermit, Geran. It's time for you to get out in the world and meet people.'

'Who do I need to meet?' he asked curiously.

'I thought it might be nice if you and your wife met each other before the wedding,' I replied. 'That's up to you, though. If you really like surprises, we can go back home and I'll just send for the lucky girl.'

He blushed furiously and let the matter drop.

Muros hasn't changed very much over the centuries. It is – and probably always will be – a dusty town permeated with the strong odor of the stockyards. For obvious reasons, there's a lot of money in Muros. The vast Algar cattle herds have been called 'gold on the hoof', and the town literally seethes with cattle-buyers from all the kingdoms of the west. Geran and I took lodgings in a sedate inn on a quiet street, and I went looking for a suitable house for us to occupy on a more permanent basis. I've spent a lot of time over the years shopping for real estate, and I've developed a kind of instinctive reaction that saves time in the long run. When I see the right house, I know immediately that it's the one I want. This time, the house was a well-built place on a quiet back street. It didn't come up to the standards of my town house in Vo Wacune nor my country house on Lake Erat, but I didn't really want it to. Geran and I would be posing as members of the minor nobility, and the house was suitable for a baroness who was well off, but not exactly rolling in money. It fit our fictional status quite well.

The house was owned by a wiry little Drasnian name Khalon, and he and I haggled a bit before we concluded the transaction. The poor fellow got himself soundly beaten when I reverted to the Drasnian Secret Language to conduct our negotiations. He was ashamed to admit that he was out of practice, so he accepted a ridiculously low offer without actually translating my gesture into a real number. Then his pride prevented him from confessing that he'd misunderstood. In short, I neatly skinned him and hung his hide on a fence.

'I think I've been had,' Khalon muttered after we'd sealed the transaction with a handshake.

'Yes,' I agreed, 'you have. Why didn't you ask for clarification?'

'I'd have sooner died. You won't noise this about, will you?'

'Wild horses couldn't drag it out of me. Now, might I ask a favor of you?'

'You want to swindle me out of my furniture, too?'

'No. I'll furnish my house in my own way. I need an introduction to a man named Hattan.'

'The Algar cattle-buyer?'

'That's him. Do you know him?'

'Oh, yes. He's well-known – and hated – here in Muros.'

'Hated?'

'The Tolnedrans absolutely despise him. He knows all the clan chiefs of Algaria by their first names, so he always gets the first pick out of the Algar herds. He skims the cream off the top of every herd that comes over the mountains. Are you thinking of going into the cattle business, Baroness?'

'No, Khalon, not really. It has to do with something else.'

'I'll be busy packing things – and selling off my furniture – for a few days. Then I'll take you on around to Hattan's place of business and introduce you.'

'Are you going back to Boktor, Khalan?'

'No, Baroness. I don't like Drasnian winters. I'm getting tired of cows. so I'm moving to Camaar. I've heard that there's profit to be made in the spice-trade, and spices smell much nicer than cows.'

About a week later, Khalon introduced me to Hattan. At my request, he presented me to the tall, lean man dressed in horse-hide as Baroness Pelera. I've used assorted pseudonyms over the years, since my real name's probably engraved on the mind of every Murgo who comes west. After a goodly number of cooperative mothers had named their daughters after the legendary 'Polgara the Sorceress', however, that cumbersome subterfuge became unnecessary, and the simplified 'Pol' was usually enough to conceal my identity.

Despite the fact that he'd lived in Sendaria for years, Hattan still wore horse-hide clothing and shaved his head except for the single flowing scalp-lock hanging down his back. His success as a cattle-buyer rested on his Algar heritage, so he made a point of dressing appropriately.

434

Hattan and I took to each other immediately. I've always liked Algars, since I grew up in their backyard. Hattan didn't talk a lot and then only in a very quiet voice. When you spend most of your life with cows, you learn not to startle them with loud noises – unless you enjoy rounding them up again.

Khalon had grossly understated the feelings other cattle-buyers in Muros had for Hattan. Hatred only began to describe it. His intimate contacts with the Algarian clan chiefs gave him an enormous advantage over the Tolnedrans in particular. Algars almost automatically dislike Tolnedrans anyway, so the Algarian clan chiefs made a habit of culling through their herds and reserving the finest cows for Hattan before they ever reached Muros. The sight of all that prime beef that wasn't available to them drove the Tolnedrans absolutely wild.

In time, Hattan invited Geran and me to meet his family. His wife, Layna, was a plump, giddy-seeming Sendarian lady who was far more shrewd than she appeared on the surface. Geran was polite to her, but most of his attention was locked onto Eldara, a tall, raven-haired beauty of his own age. Eldara seemed just as taken with him, and the two of them sat looking at each other without saying a word in much the same way as Beldaran and Riva had. I caught a very strong odor of 'tampering' in the wind. Destiny – or prophecy, call it what you will – was obviously taking a hand in this matter.

'They seem to be getting along fairly well,' Hattan noted after Geran and Eldara had silently gazed into each other's faces for an hour or so.

'But they aren't saying anything,' Layna protested.

'Oh, yes they are, Layna,' Hattan said to his wife. 'You just aren't listening. I suppose we'd better start making arrangements.'

'Arrangements for what?' Layna demanded.

'For the wedding, dear,' I told her.

'What wedding?'

'That one,' her husband said, pointing at the silent young couple.

'They're only sixteen, Hattan. They're too young to get married.'

'Not really,' her husband disagreed. 'Believe me, Layna, I've seen this sort of thing in the past. Let's run them through the marriage ceremony *before* they start getting creative. This *is* Sendaria, my love, and the proprieties *are* sort of important here. Just because you and I got an early start doesn't need to set a precedent for the children, does it?'

She blushed furiously.

'Yes, Baroness?' Hattan said to me with one raised eyebrow.

'Nothing,' I replied.

We postponed the wedding for a month or so for the sake for appearances, and Hattan, Layna, and I concentrated very hard on making sure that the children were never left alone together. As I recall, I caught Geran climbing out his bedroom window in the middle of the night five or six times during that interminable month. Hattan took a more direct approach. He simply installed iron bars on Eldara's window.

It was about noon on an overcast day when Hattan stopped by while Layna was keeping watch over our youthful enthusiasts. 'I think we need to talk,' he said.

'Of course. Was it about the dowry?'

'Did you want a herd of cows?'

'Hardly.'

'Then we can skip over that. Pelera's not your real name, is it, my Lady? You're actually Belgarath's daughter, Polgara, aren't you?'

I stared at him, stunned. 'How did you find that out, Hattan?'

'I've got eyes, Lady Polgara, and I use them. I'm an Alorn, so I know all the stories. They describe you very precisely. They don't really do you justice, though. You're probably the most beautiful woman in the world, but that's beside the point. Geran's not really your nephew, is he?'

'Sort of,' I replied. 'The relationship's more complicated, but we simplify it for the sake of convenience.'

'All right,' the lean Algar said, 'then I know who he is, too. Don't worry, Lady Polgara, I know how to keep things to myself. We're going to have to take some precautions, aren't we?'

'I can handle it, Hattan.'

'I'm sure you can, but I'd like to lend a hand anyway. Muros might not be the best place in Sendaria for the children to live, you know. There are too many foreigners here. Sulturn or Medalia would probably be safer.' He squinted at me. 'I think you're going to have to move around a lot, you know. If the stories I've heard about you are true, you aren't going to age the way other people do, so you probably shouldn't stay in one place for more than ten years, and I'd stay clear of the nobility, if I were you. People notice baronesses and other high-born ladies, and you don't want to be noticed.'

'You've thought your way completely through this, haven't you, Hattan?'

'My daughter's involved too, so I've brooded about it a bit. Would a suggestion offend you?'

'Not at all.'

'When you get on out into the future, you might think about apprenticing these nephews you're looking after to various craftsmen. A carpenter doesn't have to explain why he moves from town to town. Craftsmen move around, and nobody's really curious about why – as long as the craftsman's good at what he does. Every town's got a carpenter or two, a couple of brick-masons, an apothecary shop, and so on. A tradesman's a fixture, and he's invisible to strangers.'

'Hattan, you're a treasure!'

'I wouldn't go *that* far, Lady Polgara.'

'You've just solved a problem I've been beating myself over the head with for several years now. You've just told me how to keep a long line of young men invisible, and invisibility's very difficult. I've tried it, so I know.'

'I think your biggest problem's going to be with the young men themselves,' he said. 'It might be safer not to even tell them who they really are. The only trouble with that is that when the important one comes along, he's going to *have* to know, because there are things he's going to have to do – and he might just have to do some of them at short notice.' He smiled faintly. 'Interesting problem you've got there, Polgara, but I'll let you work it out.'

'Thanks, Hattan,' I replied sarcastically.

'No charge, my Lady.' Then he laughed.

The wedding took place in late summer that year. Hattan and I overrode Layna's urges in the direction of extravagance and ostentation. My Algar friend and I were positive that Geran and Eldara would probably have only vague sketchy memories of the ceremony anyway, and there were some obvious reasons for keeping the whole affair rather quiet. In our circumstances, hiring the town-crier to shout the news to the roof-tops of Muros wouldn't have been the course of prudence. Hattan had some difficulty persuading his wife that there was no real need for a wedding that'd go down in local history books, and I diverted her rather smoothly by raising the issue of Eldara's wedding gown. I drew rather heavily on the designs of my instructress in the healing arts for that gown. I didn't *exactly* copy Arell's design of Beldaran's wedding gown – at least not down to the last stitch – but I'll confess to a bit of constructive plagiarism in the business. The fact that Eldara had raven-black hair while Beldaran's hair had been pale blonde *did* dictate a few subtle variations, but all in all, the gown turned out rather well, I thought. Eldara was absolutely radiant when her father escorted her into the wedding chapel, and Geran's reaction was very much the same as his ultimate paternal grandfather's had been.

As I recall, I *did* choke just a bit when the priest who conducted the ceremony invoked the blessings of the Gods at the conclusion of the ceremony. Sendarian religion is tolerant to a fault, and ecumenicism lies at its very core. Religious tolerance is all well and good, I suppose, but when the kindly old priest asked Torak to bless a union that would ultimately produce the man destined to kill him, I quite nearly went into a seizure. Hattan, who was sitting between his weepy wife and me, took me firmly by the wrist. 'Steady,' he murmured.

'Do you know what that priest just did?' I whispered in a strangled tone.

He nodded. 'It *was* a little inappropriate, I suppose, but it's only a formality. I'm sure that Torak's too busy to really be paying attention.' He paused. 'You might want to keep an eye out for a dragon lurking around the outskirts of town for the next few weeks, though.'

'A dragon?'

'Don't the Murgos call Torak "the Dragon-God of Angarak"? I'm sure you could deal with him, Pol, but I'd really rather he didn't come to pay us a call. Cows are very skittish, and if Torak starts flying over Muros belching fire, it could be very bad for business.'

'Are you trying to be funny, Hattan?'

'Me? Why, whatever gave you *that* idea, Pol?'

CHAPTER 27

Geran and Eldara were deliriously happy, of course. I've noticed over the years that these pre-ordained marriages usually are. The Purpose of the Universe has ways of rewarding those who do what it wants them to do. In time – and it actually wasn't a very long time – Eldara started throwing up every morning, so I knew that things were proceeding normally.

I delivered her of a son in the early summer of 4013 with a certain satisfaction. Even though Geran and his new wife had done all the work, I took a certain pride in the fact that I'd made all the arrangements and that I was performing my task satisfactorily. The Rivan line was safe – for another generation, anyway.

Geran and Eldara had decided – after much discussion – to name their new son Davon, and I think that disappointed Hattan, who'd been holding out for an Algarian name for his grandson. Personally, I was just as happy that the baby had been given a more common-place name. Algarian names tend to be just a trifle over-dramatic, and under the circumstances I didn't really want anything about the little boy to stand out.

Eldara's delivery had been a fairly easy one, and she was soon back on her feet again. I debated with myself at some length before I sat my little family down to have a talk with them. Despite Hattan's reservations, I'd come to the conclusion that it would be best if the heirs to Iron-grip's throne, *and* their wives, should know just exactly who they were and what dangers were lurking around out there. So after supper one evening in the early autumn, I asked Geran and Eldara to come to my library 'for a little family conference'. I prudently 'encouraged' our servants to become very sleepy, and then I took Geran and his wife and baby to my library and closed the door behind us. 'How much have you told your wife about us, Geran?' I asked my nephew rather bluntly.

'Well, I didn't lie to her, Aunt Pol, but there *were* a few things I sort of glossed over.'

'You kept secrets from me?' Eldara asked accusingly. 'I didn't keep any from you, Geran.'

'He was obeying my orders, Eldara,' I assured her. 'We're talking about a family secret here, and Geran's been forbidden to reveal it to *anybody* without my explicit permission.'

'Didn't you trust me, Aunt Pol?' she asked, sounding a little hurt.

'I had to get to know you a little better, Eldara. I had to make sure that you knew how to keep things to yourself. Your father's very good at that, but now and then I've come across young ladies who just *have* to talk about things. I've noticed that you've got very good sense, though, and you don't blurt things out. You've probably noticed that your husband's not a Sendar.'

'He told me that he was born in one of the Alorn kingdoms,' she replied. 'We were sort of busy when he told me, so –' she stopped and blushed.

'I don't think we need to go into that, Eldara. Actually, Geran's a Rivan, and he's a descendant of a very important family on the Isle of the Winds.'

'How important?' she asked.

'You don't get much *more* important. It was about eleven years ago when Geran's family were all murdered by a group of Nyissans. My father and I managed to save Geran, but we were too late to save the others.'

Her eyes went very wide at that.

'Does it help at all to know that you'd be the Queen of Riva if certain things hadn't happened, love?' Geran asked her.

'You don't act all that much like a king.' She said it almost accusingly. 'Are kings supposed to snore the way you do?'

'My grandfather did,' he replied, shrugging.

'I'll let you two discuss the finer points of regal behavior when you're alone,' I told them. 'Let's stick to the point here. Geran has some very determined enemies who'd like nothing better than to kill him – *and* to kill your baby as well.'

She drew her sleeping infant closer to her breast. 'I'd like to see them try!' she said fiercely.

'Well, *I* wouldn't,' I said firmly. 'Geran's enemies are very powerful, and they can hire murderers by the dozen and spies by the hundred. I'm sure they're out there looking for us right now. The safest thing for us to do is to see to it that they don't find us. There are two ways to do that. We can go way out into the mountains and hide in a cave, or we can stay right here in the open and be so ordinary that when they look at us they don't even see us. We'll try that second one for right now. I've talked things over with your father, and the first thing tomorrow morning, Geran's going to start out on his new career.'

'What career is that, Aunt Pol?' Geran asked me.

'Your father-in-law's going to take you into the cattle business, Geran.'

'I don't know anything about cows.'

'You're going to learn, and you're going to pick it up very quickly. Your life depends on it, so you'll have lots of incentive.'

And so it was that the heir to the Rivan throne started getting up early so that he could go to work every morning. He was totally confused at first, but Hattan brought him along patiently, and, more importantly, introduced him to the Algar clan-chiefs. It wasn't too long before Geran was pulling his weight in the family business, and Hattan was quite proud of him.

'He's very good, Pol,' Eldara's father told me after Geran had struck a bargain with one of the Algar clans that involved driving a herd of cows north along the Tolnedran causeway that crossed the fens to Boktor instead of over the Sendarian Mountains to Muros. Everyone did well on that venture – except for the Tolnedrans. They provided the highway, of course, but that was the total extent of their involvement. I'm told that the screams in Tol Honeth echoed for ten miles in either direction along the Nedrane River, and the next year the causeway became a toll-road.

When Geran was at work, he was surrounded by Hattan's men, who were for the most part transplanted Algars, and so he was quite safe as he roamed around out in the cow-pens. This gave me the opportunity to get to know Eldara better – and to play with the baby, of course.

Young Davon was cut from the same cloth as his father, and his father was very much like my sister's own son, Daran. Certain characteristics have always bred true in the Rivan line. For the most part, they've all had that same sandy blond hair, for one thing. Iron-grip's black hair showed up only occasionally. Moreover, they've all been very serious, earnest little boys with a wide streak of good, solid common sense. Of course, that could be cultural rather than hereditary, since most of them have been born and raised in Sendaria.

The seasons turned and the years went by, and Davon grew like

441

a well-watered weed. By the time he was twelve, he was quite nearly as tall as his father. I've never really liked Muros all that much, given the perpetual dust and the smell of the stockyards, but we *were* happy there.

Then, a few days after Davon's twelfth birthday, Hattan stopped by, and he and I went into my library to have a long talk. 'Do you remember that chat we had before Geran and Eldara were married, Pol?' the tall Algar, whose scalp-lock was turning iron grey now, said to me.

'Very well, Hattan. We've been following the course you laid out for us quite well, haven't we?'

'All except for the fact that you're not visibly aging,' he said. 'Could you possibly use magic to make your hair turn grey? That should put a few years on you.'

I sighed. 'Someday we're going to have to have a talk about what you call magic, Hattan,' I said.

'Do you mean you can't?' He sounded startled.

'Oh, I *could*,' I told him, 'but grey hair isn't really grey, you know.'

'It *looks* grey.'

'Look a little closer, Hattan. Your scalp-lock looks grey because it's a mixture of black and white hairs. I'd have to turn half of my hair white – strand by strand.'

'That might take a while,' he conceded.

'*Quite* a while, actually. There are some chemicals I can cook out of certain common weeds that'll color my hair. It won't look *quite* the same as yours, but it should get me by. There are a few cosmetics I can use to make myself appear older, too.'

'Wouldn't it be easier to just move on? Go to Sulturn, maybe? – or Darine?'

'Are you trying to get rid of me, Hattan?'

'Of course not. We all love you, Pol, but we *do* have to put the safety of the children first.'

'There's an easier way to take care of it,' I told him. 'Since I'm so old now, I'll just become a recluse and stay in the house. We old people do that fairly often, you know.'

'I don't want to imprison you, Pol.'

'You aren't, Hattan. Actually, I rather like the idea. It'll give me a chance to catch up on my reading. I'll still be right here in the event of an emergency, and I won't have to endure all those endless hours of mindless gossiping.'

'Oh, one other thing – before I forget,' he added. 'How does the idea of apprenticing Davon to a tanner strike you?'

442

I wrinkled my nose. 'I have to live in the same house with him, Hattan, and tanners as a group tend to be a little fragrant.'

'Not if they bathe regularly – with good strong soap. Even a nobleman starts to get strong on the downwind side if he only takes one bath a year.'

'Why a tanner? Why not a barrel-maker?'

'It's a logical extension of my own business, Pol. I've got access to an almost unlimited supply of cow-hides, and I can get them for pennies. If Davon learns how to tan those hides, he can sell the leather at a handsome profit.'

'A little empire building there, Hattan?' I teased. 'You want to use the whole cow, don't you? What do you plan to do with the hooves and horns?'

'I could always build a glue factory, I suppose. Thanks for the idea, Pol. It hadn't occurred to me.'

'You're *serious*!'

'I'm just taking care of my family, Pol. I'm going to leave them a prosperous business when Belar calls me home.'

'I think you've been in Sendaria too long, Hattan. Why don't you take a year off and go back to Algaria – herd cows or breed horses or something?'

'I've already looked into that, Pol. I'm currently negotiating for several hundred acres of good pasture land. I know Sendars very well by now. Algars like horses that run fast, but Sendars prefer more sensible animals. It's a little hard to plow a field at a dead run.'

'Are you certain that there's not a strain of Tolnedran in your background, Hattan? Is profit the only thing you can think about?'

He shrugged. 'Actually, I get bored, Pol. Once everything connected with a business venture gets to be a habit, I start looking around for new challenges. I can't help it if they all end up making money. I know a tanner named Alnik who's getting along in years and whose son isn't really interested in the family business. I'll talk with him, and once Davon's learned the trade, we'll buy Alnik out and set our boy up in business for himself. Trust me, Pol. This is all going to work out just fine.'

'I thought our whole idea was to be inconspicuous, Hattan. I'd hardly call the richest family in southeastern Sendaria inconspicuous.'

'I think you're missing the point, Pol. The line you're protecting *will* be inconspicuous, because they'll *seem* to descend from *me*. After a few generations, nobody'll even think to ask about the other side of their heritage. They'll be a fixture – an institution – with no apparent connection to the Isle of the Winds. You can't *get* much more invisible than that, can you?'

Once again Hattan had startled me with his uncommon shrewd-ness. He'd reminded me that someone can be just as invisible by standing still as he can by running away and hiding. I learned a great deal about being ordinary from my Algarian friend. My own background had been anything *but* ordinary. I'd been 'Polgara the Sorceress' and 'The Duchess of Erat', and those positions had been *very* visible. Now I was going to learn how to be the great-aunt of the village tanner – even though Muros wasn't exactly a village. Little by little, I'd fade into the background, and that suited our purposes perfectly. Once we'd polished this deception, no Murgo – or Grolim – could *ever* find us.

Davon was a good boy, so he didn't object to his apprenticeship – at least not openly. By the time he was eighteen, he was a master tanner, and his employer's establishment was producing the finest leather in all of Sendaria.

Our extended family had a feast on Erastide that year, and I officiated in the kitchen, naturally. After we'd all eaten more than was really good for us, Davon leaned back in his chair. 'I've been thinking about something,' he told the rest of us. 'If we're going to buy Alnik's business, we'll be producing most of the leather in this part of Sendaria. What if we were to hire some young cobblers who were just getting started? We could attach a work-shop to the tan-nery and manufacture shoes.'

'You can't really expect to make money that way, Davon,' Geran objected. 'Shoes have to be fitted to the feet of the one who's going to wear them.'

'I've done a little measuring, father,' Davon disagreed. He laughed sheepishly. 'People think I'm crazy because I always want to measure their feet. I'm getting better at it, though. I can guess the length of a man's foot down to a quarter of an inch now. Your feet are eight and a half inches long, by the way. Children's feet – and women's – are smaller, but there are only so many lengths of feet in all of Muros. Nobody's got three-inch feet, and nobody's got nineteen-inch ones. If our cobblers turn out shoes in all the more common lengths, we'll find people who can wear them. I can almost guarantee that.'

'Go ahead and smirk, Hattan,' I said to my friend.

'About what, Pol?'

'You've succeeded in corrupting another generation, haven't you?'

444

'Would I do that, Pol?' he asked innocently.

'Yes, as a matter of fact, I think you would.'

Hattan and I pooled some of our money the following spring, we bought out Alnik the tanner, and then turned the tannery over to Davon, who immediately started manufacturing solid, sensible shoes that were very popular among farmers. People who wanted fancy shoes continued to have them made by traditional cobblers, but ordinary working people began to patronize the shop that was the end of a long line of processes. Raw hides went in one end of Davon's tannery, and work shoes came out the other. The people of Muros were beginning to notice this family. Such Angaraks as passed through, however, paid almost no attention to it – unless they wanted to buy cows or shoes.

It was in the year 4039 that we finally got Davon married off. He was twenty-three at the time, and I'd started to worry just a bit. Marriage is something that shouldn't be put off *too* long. Bachelorhood *can* be sort of habit forming after a while. Hattan, who was in his late fifties by then, told me that I worried too much about things like that. 'We're unusual people, Pol,' he said to me just before the wedding. 'If I were just another Algar, I'd be sitting on a horse near the River Aldur watching a herd of cows right now. I'd have an Algar wife and ten children, and we'd all be living in wagons. But I'm not just another Algar, so I'm married to Layna, and I'm living in Muros getting rich instead of keeping cows out of trouble on the plains of Algaria. I was older than Davon is right now when I married Layna. I needed some time to get my feet on the ground before I got married. Nobles and peasants marry early. Businessmen tend to wait.'

Davon's bride-to-be was a very pretty blonde girl named Alnana. She had a bright, sunny personality, and she was a joy to be around. Eldara and I considered her rather carefully and decided that she'd be acceptable. Young men always think that *they're* the ones who make these decisions, but they tend to overlook certain realities in these matters. The influence of the women of the house is *very* strong in the business of choosing suitable wives.

No. I won't pursue that. Women know about it already, and men don't really need to know.

The wedding of Davon and Alnana was the social event of the season that fall. Our family was quite prominent in Muros by now, and we had no real reason to keep the affair unostentatious as we had when Geran had come in out of nowhere to marry Eldara. Weddings are major events in the lives of the merchant class, so they tend to make them lavish.

After the wedding, Davon and Alnana took up residence in a new wing of my house. Things were a little crowded to suit my tastes, but we all got along quite well, so there was a minimum of friction.

Hattan, my dear, dear friend, lived long enough to see his great-grandson, Alten, born in 4041, and then one blustery spring morning out in the stockyards, Hattan was gored by a large belligerent Algar bull. Cows are such silly animals most of the time that we tend to forget that they always go about fully armed. Hattan died almost immediately, so there wasn't anything I could really have done, but that didn't prevent me from blaming myself. It sometimes seems that I've spent half of my life sunk to the eyebrows in self-recrimination. That's one of the major drawbacks of the study and practice of healing. Healers are always shocked and outraged when they discover something *else* that they can't heal. No one has yet come up with a way to heal death, however, so a physician has to learn to accept his losses and move on.

Layna was totally devastated, of course, and she didn't long survive her husband. Once again natural mortality was thinning the ranks of those I loved the most.

I consoled myself – as I've done so many times – by devoting a great amount of time to my new nephew. By the time he was six years old there was no question whatsoever that he was a member of the little family to which I was devoting my life. When the three of them, Geran, Davon, and Alten, were together, we could all see the almost mirror-image resemblances. Davon and Alten would never have to waste time wondering what they'd look like when they grew older. All they had to do was look at Geran.

Geran's sandy-colored hair began to be touched with grey at the temples after he turned fifty. It actually made him look rather distinguished. It was in 4051 when the grave sensibility greying hair seems to bestow upon even the silliest of men brought Geran and me to the closest thing I think we ever had to an argument. 'I've been asked to stand for election to the town council, Aunt Pol,' he told me one summer evening when we were alone together in my garden. 'I've been giving it some fairly serious consideration.'

'Are you out of your mind, Geran?' I asked sharply.

'I could do a lot better job than some of the incumbents,' he said defensively. 'Most of *them* are just using their offices to line their own pockets.'

'That's not your concern, Geran.'

'I live here too, Aunt Pol. The well-being of the city's as much my concern as it is everybody else's.'

'Who raised this idiotic notion?'

'The Earl of Muros himself.' He said it with a certain pride.

'Use your head, Geran!' I told him. 'You *can't* do something that'd attract so much attention to you.'

'People don't really pay all that much attention to the members of the council, Aunt Pol.'

'You're talking about the local people. Outsiders – including Murgos – pay a *lot* of attention to the people in power. All we'd need would be to have some Murgo asking around about your origins. When he found out that you came here in 4012 – just ten years after King Gorek's assassination – and that I'd come here with you, everything would fly out the window.'

'You worry too much,' he scoffed.

'*Somebody* has to. Too many things match up for a Murgo to just shrug them all off as coincidence – your age, your appearance, *my* presence, and the fact that I don't get old. He'd have suspicions, and he'd take them to Ctuchik. Ctuchik doesn't worry about niceties, Geran. If he has the faintest suspicion that you're the survivor of that massacre at Riva, he'll have you and your entire family butchered. Is getting elected to some silly office *that* important to you?'

'I can afford to hire guards. I can protect my family.'

'Why don't you just paint a sign saying 'King of Riva' and hang it around your neck? Guards, Geran? Why not hire trumpeters to blow fanfares, too?'

'I could do so much for the city and its people, Aunt Pol.'

'I'm sure you could, but Muros isn't your concern. Riva's the town you're interested in. Someday, one of your descendants is going to sit on the throne there. Concern yourself with *that*, not with street repair and garbage disposal in a dusty town on the Sendarian plain.'

'All right, Aunt Pol,' he said, clearly irritated. 'Don't beat me over the head with it. I'll give my apologies to Oldrik and tell him that I'm too busy right now to make speeches about corrupt officials.'

'Oldrik?'

'The Earl of Muros. He and I are rather close friends, actually. He asks my advice on certain things now and then.'

'Oh, dear,' I sighed.

'I can't live under a rock, Aunt Pol,' he said plaintively. 'The town of Muros has been good to me. I should do something to pay them back.'

'Build them a public park or open a hospital for the poor. *Don't get involved in their politics.'*

He sighed. 'Whatever you say, Aunt Pol,' he surrendered.

Despite my intervention that kept him out of office, Geran was becoming much too prominent in Muros for my comfort. I began to get an uneasy feeling that sooner or later one of Ctuchik's agents might just decide to have a look into the background of this 'first citizen', and so I began making some plans.

As it turned out, that wasn't premature. It was, in fact, just a little late.

Young Alten continued to grow, and by the time he was twelve, he was almost as tall as his father. Every so often, one of the heirs I've nurtured reverts to type, perhaps to remind me that the blood of Bear-shoulders still runs in their veins. Alten was going through one of those gangly stages all adolescent males have to endure. Sometimes it almost seemed that I could *see* him grow. He was about fourteen, I think, when he came home one afternoon with a puzzled look on his face. 'Are we important people, Aunt Pol?' he asked me.

'Your grandfather seemed to think so a few years back,' I replied. 'He wanted to stand for election to the town council.'

'I didn't know that.'

'I talked him out of it. Why this sudden interest in fame, Alten? You're an apprentice cobbler. You'll become famous if you make good shoes.'

'The cobbler I'm apprenticed to broke his favorite needle this morning,' he explained. 'He sent me out to buy him a new one. I was in the central market and there was this foreigner there asking questions about us.'

'What kind of foreigner?' I asked quickly. I was suddenly very alert.

'I'm not really sure, Aunt Pol. He wasn't a Tolnedran or a Drasnian. I'm sure of that.'

'What did he look like?'

'He was a big man with swarthy skin – darker than a Tolnedran or an Arend – and he had funny-shaped eyes.'

'Scars on his cheeks?' I pressed, my heart sinking.

'Now that you mention it, I think he did. He was wearing a black robe that looked sort of rusty. Anyway, he was really curious about us. He wanted to know when grandfather came here to Muros, and he *really* wanted to know about you. He described you very well, and I can't imagine when it was he ever saw you, since you almost never go out of the house.'

'Someone told him about me, Alten. Go back to the tannery and get your father and then go find your grandfather. He may be out in the cattle pens somewhere. Tell them both that this is very urgent. We all have to get together and talk. Oh, one other thing. Stay away from the foreigner with the scarred face.'

'Yes, ma'am,' he said, already moving toward the door.

I knew that there were going to be objections – rather violent ones – so I did something I hadn't really been obliged to do for quite a long time. I didn't try to reason with my growing family; I issued commands. 'There's a Murgo in town,' I told them when they'd all assembled. 'He's been asking questions about us. We'll have to leave town immediately.'

'This is a bad time, Aunt Pol,' Davon objected. 'My foreman at the shoe shop just quit his job. I've got to find a replacement for him before I can go anywhere.'

'Leave that to the new owner.'

'What new owner?'

'The fellow who buys your shop.'

'I'm not selling my shop!'

'Burn it down, then.'

'What are you talking about?'

'I'm talking about keeping this family alive, Davon. When Murgos start asking questions about us, we pack up and leave.'

'I've invested my whole life in that shop! It's very important to me!'

'Important enough to die for? Important enough to kill Alnana and Alten for?'

'What are you talking about?'

'Tell him about what happened on the beach at Riva in 4002, Geran.'

'She's right, Davon,' Geran told his son. 'When Ctuchik's people start getting close to us, we run – or die. The whole of Cthol Murgos wants to kill us.'

'But our lives are here!' Alnana objected, right on the verge of tears.

'And so are our graves – if we stay,' Geran said bluntly. 'If we don't move – and right now – none of us will be alive next week.' He stared at the ceiling. 'Oldrik, the Earl of Muros, is my friend. We'll turn the family business over to him. He'll sell it for us and send the money to the royal treasury in Sendar.'

'Surely you're not going to just give our life's work to the king, father!' Davon exploded.

'No, I'm not. I'm not *that* patriotic. Aunt Pol's got a fortune that the king takes care of. We'll just add our money to hers for now – until we find a new place to hide.'

'Why not just kill the Murgo?' Alten demanded.

'Interesting idea, Alten,' I said coolly. 'Are you any good at murdering people? Have you had lots of practice?'

'Well –' he faltered.

'I didn't think so. All right then, Geran. Go talk to Oldrik.'

'First thing in the morning, Aunt Pol.'

'No, Geran. Do it right now. I'll write a short note to the king with that password so he'll know what to do with your money. By tomorrow morning, we'll be miles away from Muros. Davon, you and Alten go back to the shoe-shop. Tell your cobblers that something's come up. Call it a family emergency, and don't get *too* specific. Tell them that we have to go to Camaar.'

'*Are* we going to Camaar, Aunt Pol?'

'Of course not, but I want that Murgo to think that's where we're going. Oh, by the way, Geran, have Oldrik sell this house, too. We won't need it any more.'

'Where *are* we going, Aunt Pol?' Alten asked me.

'To a place where there are roses,' I said, smiling.

Geran sighed.

'Look on the bright side, Geran,' I said. 'This time, you'll have help when you start cleaning the house.'

And that's exactly what we did. We left Muros about two hours before dawn, traveling westward on the imperial highway that led to Camaar, and when we were about three leagues out of town, we took the secondary road that branched off toward the western end of Lake Camaar. We reached the lake about noon, and then we doubled back along the north shore and took a back road toward Medalia.

We had two wagons and a couple of riding horses, and I'd browbeaten my family into wearing the clothes of common farmers. The wagons were actually more for show than convenience. The food and blankets were necessary, but the several pieces of nondescript furniture piled on top of them were there to make it appear that we were nothing more than an extended farm family on the move.

It took us a week and a half to reach Lake Erat, and the family hid out in the forest overnight while I went owl to meticulously investigate the area. I found no sign of any Angaraks, and so we

450

moved cautiously along a barely visible wood-cutter's track to the edge of my rose-thicket.

I made another quick survey at that point. There were three wood-cutters about a mile away, and just to be on the safe side, I murmured 'sleep' to them from the limb upon which I was perched. Then I went back to my family, asked the roses to make way for us, and we all went on to the manor house.

'What a magnificent home!' Geran's wife, Eldara, exclaimed.

'I'm glad you like it, dear,' I told her. 'Get used to it, because we'll probably be here for several years.'

'Long enough to get the place cleaned up, anyway,' Geran said with a tone of resignation.

'I don't understand,' Eldara said with a puzzled look.

'You will, dear,' Geran told her. 'Believe me, you will. Where did we leave the mops and brooms, Aunt Pol?'

'In that storage room just off the kitchen, Geran.'

'Well,' Geran said to his family, 'I guess we'd better go inside and get started.'

CHAPTER 28

My house on the shores of Lake Erat was our refuge of last resort during those early years – my version of 'a cave in the mountains'. I used it for that purpose several times until I grew more skilled at escape and evasion. Just the knowledge that it was there and that it was highly unlikely that any Murgo could find it gave me a profound sense of security.

That first time was slightly different from later ones, since there was a very good reason for us to make our stay an extended one. Geran had been born a prince, and his earliest memories and all his deeply ingrained instincts were based on that fact. Anonymity was just not a part of his nature. He'd been born to a royal family, and, since it was a good royal family, he'd been raised to take his responsibilities more seriously than his privileges. He tended to take charge of things and went out of his way to help his neighbors. That was probably what was behind his near-brush with elective office. It was highly admirable, but was also quite probably the worst thing he could have done. Cold logic told me that Geran was simply too good for the outside world. And so, though it withers my soul to admit it, our years among the roses had only one purpose – to give Geran and his wife time to grow old and die.

Does that seem cold-blooded? I loved Geran – as much as I would have had he been my own son. My first responsibility, however, was to the blood-line, not to individuals, and the safety of the line hinged on keeping those inheritors who were incapable of maintaining their anonymity completely isolated from public view. It happened several times during the centuries that followed, and it always pained me when I was obliged to take one of those earnest young men to my manor house and to keep him there until the years carried him off. I sometimes wonder if my centuries as Duchess of Erat hadn't just been to prepare me for the endless funeral I was forced to endure as a part of the task that'd been laid upon me. I'd lost Killane and Asrana and Malon and Ontrose, and there in that house by the lake I was patiently waiting to lose Geran and Eldara so that I could move on.

Prince Geran of Riva died in his sleep in 4066, not long after his seventieth birthday. His death wasn't really unexpected, since he'd been in decline for a number of years. We grieved his loss, and I'm happy to say that no member of our little family brightly announced that 'it's better this way'. That particular empty-headed platitude offends me to the verge of physical violence. I'm a physician, after all, death is my enemy, not my friend.

We buried Geran on the same hilltop where Killane rested, and we returned then to the now somehow empty house.

Two years later, Eldara joined her husband, and I began to make some subtle suggestions to the rest of the family that we might want to start thinking about going back out into the world.

I gave them a year to absorb the idea and then, one summer evening after supper when we were all sitting on the terrace, I brought it out into the open. 'Where do you think we should go?' I asked them.

'Back home, of course,' Alnana replied quickly.

'I don't think that'd be a good idea, dear,' I disagreed. 'Our enemies are probably waiting for us there.'

'But my sisters live in Muros,' she protested.

'All the more reason not to go there,' I told her. 'Murgo assassins tend to kill everyone in sight once they start murdering people. If we go back to Muros, we could very well be putting your sisters – and their families as well – in mortal danger.'

'You mean that I'm never going to see them again?' she cried.

'At least you'll know that they're alive, Alnana,' I told her.

'If we want to get as far away from Muros as possible, we should go to Camaar – or Darine,' Davon suggested.

'Not Camaar,' I said.

'Why not?'

'There are too many people of foreign birth there. We're trying to avoid Murgos, not to cuddle up to them.'

'Darine, then?' Alten said.

I pursed my lips. 'That might be the best. Darine's crawling with Alorns, and Alorns have certain hereditary prejudices.'

'Oh?'

'They instinctively hate Murgos. Racial prejudice is stupid and very unattractive, but it *can* be useful sometimes. I'm sure that there are nice Murgos – somewhere in the world – but the ones we'll encounter here in the west aren't likely to be among them. Any time you see a Murgo west of the Escarpment or north of Sthiss Tor, you can be fairly certain that he's here to kill you.'

'What about all the other Angaraks?' Alten asked.

'The Malloreans live on the other side of the Sea of the East, and they take their orders from Urvon, not Ctuchik. Thulls are too stupid to pose much of a threat, and the Nadraks are an enigma. Nobody can ever be really sure *whose* side a Nadrak is on. Ctuchik relies almost exclusively on the Murgos – the Dagashi in particular. They're the ones we have to watch out for. Let's give some serious thought to Darine. With so many Alorns living there, any Murgo in Darine's going to be more interested in staying alive than he'll be in killing us.'

And so it was that in the late fall of 4068 we packed some 'sensible' clothes, closed up the manor house, and went on up to the port city lying on the Gulf of Cherek, posing as relocating tradesmen. We took lodgings in a comfortable inn far enough back from the waterfront to avoid the characteristic odor of the harbor, and Davon and Alten went exploring almost before we were unpacked. I knew them well enough to know that it'd be useless to forbid their exploration, but I *did* manage to get them to wear nondescript clothing.

'It's awfully cramped, isn't it?' Alten observed when they returned. 'Are all these northern towns so jammed together?'

'No cows,' I explained.

'I didn't follow that, Aunt Pol,' he confessed.

'Muros has wide streets because Algars drive herds of cattle through town from time to time. The houses in northern towns are built next to each other in order to save money. When you build your house between two others, the side walls are already in place. All you have to build is the front and back – and a roof, of course.'

'Are you teasing me, Aunt Pol?' he accused.

'Would I do that, Alten?'

Davon was quite enthusiastic about having a house built for us, but I advised against it. 'We're fugitives on the run, dear,' I reminded him. 'Any time there's a danger of discovery, we have to take flight. When you build a house, you get attached to it, and that attachment can be fatal. When the time comes to run, you don't want anything holding you back. This inn will serve until we can find a suitable house that's already standing.'

'I'll nose around a bit, Aunt Pol. I'll be out and about anyway.'

'Oh?'

'I need to find something to do.'

'Another shoe factory?'

'I'm not sure. I suppose I can fall back on that if I have to, but it might not be a bad idea for me to try something new. That inquisitive Murgo back in Muros probably found out about the family business and passed the information on to Ctuchik.'

'I'm sure he did.'

'We'd probably better stay away from tanneries and shoe shops then. Wouldn't that be the first place a Murgo would look?'

'Almost certainly. You've learned your lessons very well, Davon.'

'You've spent enough time pounding them into us, Aunt Pol. We can live as other people do – up to a point. About the only difference is that we have to keep our eyes and ears open and not go out of our way to attract attention.'

'That sums it up fairly well, yes.'

'I probably shouldn't say this, but father wasn't really very good at that. Sometimes he seemed to forget that we didn't want to be noticed.' He held up his right hand and looked at the pale splotch on his palm. 'Should I hide this birthmark, Aunt Pol?' he asked. 'Does Ctuchik know about it?'

'I'm not certain. He might.'

'I'll hide it then. I'm a tanner, so I know all about dyes that change the color of skins.' He stood up. 'I think Alten and I'll take another turn around town. I'm getting fidgety.'

'Oh?'

'I need something to keep me busy, Aunt Pol. I haven't made any money for years now, so I'd better get at it before I forget how.'

'You sound like a Sendar, Davon.'

'I *am* a Sendar, Aunt Pol. Isn't that the idea?'

I think that of all the heirs to Iron-grip's throne, Davon had the clearest idea of just exactly what we were doing.

He and his son Alten wandered around Darine together for a week or so, but then Alten caught cold, and I made him stay home. Davon went out alone several times, and then one snowy day he came back to the inn with a small bundle under his arm. Alnana, Alten, and I were sitting by the fire when he came in, his cheeks ruddy from the cold. 'What do you think of this?' he asked us, unwrapping the fur he was carrying.

'Oh, Davon, it's lovely!' Alnana exclaimed, touching the jet-black fur. 'It's so soft! No cow ever had fur like that. What is it?'

'It's sable, dear,' Davon replied. 'It comes from a large weasel that's common in the mountains of Gar og Nadrak. I know quite a bit about animal skins, but I've never seen anything like this.'

'It was highly prized by the nobility in northern Arendia quite a long time ago,' I told him.

'It'd take a lot of these to make a coat,' he said.

'Sable coats were very rare, Davon. They were terribly expensive. Most ladies had one or two coats with sable collars and cuffs, though. Sable was more in the nature of an accessory rather than a garment itself.'

'I wonder if that custom might be revived,' he mused. 'I know where I can get my hands on these, but I'd need a market.' He handed the fur to his son. 'You've worked with leather, Alten,' he said. 'Would this be very hard to sew?'

Alten, who was about twenty-seven by then, pursed his lips, turning the pelt this way and that. 'It's thinner than cow-hide,' he noted, 'so it's not as strong, and I don't think we'd want to make shoes out of it. It'd take a very fine seam, though.'

I gave him a speculative look. Alten was a handsome young fellow, but the years of isolation in the manor house had made him bashful, and I thought I saw a way to get him past that. 'I know a bit about dressmaking,' I told them. 'Alnana and I can come up with some designs, and Alten can sew them up. There are rich merchants here in Darine, and rich men's wives love to spend money and show off. A furrier's shop in the better part of town might be profitable.' It was an innocuous enough proposal, but its real purpose was to put Alten in a situation where he'd be around women all day long every day. His bashfulness would soon go away, and then I could get him married off. Bachelorhood was not an option in this particular family.

Davon found us a house near the south gate of Darine. It was an old house, but it was still solid, and at least the roof didn't leak. We moved there from the inn, and the task of finding workmen to repair it fell to me, since Davon and Alten were concentrating their attention on our business venture. Before we could open a fur-shop, however, we were going to have to create a demand, so Alnana and I drifted around Darine that winter wearing coats with luxurious collars and cuffs, glorious turban-like fur hats, and rich-looking fur

456

muffs to keep our little hands warm. The fur-cuffed leather boots might have been a little excessive, but we *were* walking advertisements, after all.

Alten took a few orders that winter, and there appeared to be sufficient demand for us to open a shop. We were swamped with customers almost immediately, and competitors began to spring up.

I had a few qualms when Davon brought a lean, evil-looking, and half-drunk Nadrak to our shop the following spring. The Nadrak's name was Kablek. He was loud and boisterous, and he didn't smell any too nice. 'All right, Davon,' he was saying as the two of them entered the shop, 'show me what you were talking about. I still say that it's the fur that matters, not the hide it grows out of.'

'The fur isn't worth much if it falls out, Kablek,' Davon explained patiently. 'Your trappers don't take proper care of the pelts back there in the mountains. A green, half-rotten hide isn't worth bringing out of the woods.'

'An honest trapper doesn't have time to fool around with the pelts he takes.'

'What's he doing in his spare time? Getting drunk? It's up to you, Kablek, but you'll get a better price for your pelts if your trappers stay sober long enough to scrape the hides and soak them in tannin before they rot.'

'A trapper doesn't have room on his pack-horse for a pot that big,' Kablek scoffed.

'He's always got room for two kegs of beer, doesn't he?'

'Those are just staples, Davon – part of his food supply.'

'Tell him to drink water.'

'That's against our religion, I think.'

Davon shrugged. 'Suit yourself, Kablek. Sooner or later I'll find *some* Nadrak fur-trader who can see beyond the rim of his beer tankard. Whichever one of you figures it all out first is going to get my exclusive business.'

'All right, show me these pelts you don't like.'

'Back here,' Davon said, leading the weaving Nadrak back into the work-room. They were back there for about a half-hour, and Alnana, Alten, and I could hear Kablek quite clearly. His language was *very* colorful. Then the two of them came out again. 'I didn't realize they were quite that bad,' Kablek admitted glumly. 'Tell me exactly what the trapper ought to do to take care of that.'

Davon explained how the bark of certain trees preserved animal skins. 'If your trappers do that as soon as they take the pelt, I'll be able to finish the process here,' he concluded. 'Believe me, Kablek, it'll at least double the price you'll get when you bring them here to Darine.'

'I'll see what the trappers have to say about that.'

'If you refuse to buy rotten pelts, they'll get your point almost immediately.'

'I'll try it,' Kablek grunted. Then he squinted at me. 'Are you sure you won't sell this one to me?' he asked Davon. 'You've got two, and no sane man needs two of them.'

'I'm sorry, Kablek, but she's not for sale.'

Kablek gave him a sour look. 'I'm going back to that tavern,' he said. 'I'll see you next spring.' Then he reeled out of the shop.

'What was that all about?' I demanded.

'He didn't believe me when I told him that the pelts he was trying to sell me weren't very good.'

'That's not what I meant, Davon. *What* is it that's not for sale?'

'You, Aunt Pol,' Davon said innocently. 'His offer *was* very attractive, though. You should be flattered.'

'*What*?' Alnana almost screamed.

'It's a peculiarity of Nadrak culture, dear,' I explained. 'Women are considered property, and they can be bought and sold.'

'Slavery?'

'It's a little more complicated than that, Alnana. I'll explain it to you someday – when we're alone.'

A month or so later, a demure young woman with dark blonde hair came into the shop, ostensibly to look at sable muffs.

'*That's the one, Pol,*' mother's voice came to me.

'*I sort of noticed that myself,*' I sent the thought back. '*It's almost like a bell ringing, isn't it?*'

'*You're getting better at this, Pol. A few more generations and I'll be out of a job.*'

The blonde girl's name was Ellette, and she and Alten evidently also heard the bell mother and I'd been talking about.

They were married the following winter, and Alten didn't seem *too* unhappy about giving up bachelorhood.

We were all quite happy in Darine, but just between you and me, I had some reservations about the situation there. The family was still just a little too prosperous – and too much in the public eye – to suit me. There were also inevitable contacts with foreigners. Kablek was a friend of the family, and I more or less trusted him – as far as I've ever trusted any Angarak – but I'd have felt much better had we never met. The best-intentioned Angarak in the world will still tell any Grolim who comes by just about anything the Grolim wants to know. I decided during our stay in Darine that port cities should be avoided, and large interior cities as well. Villages would undoubtedly be safer. Townsmen are too busy and too self-important to pay all that much attention to strangers, but villagers don't really have that much to talk about, so every passing stranger is the main topic of conversation in the village tavern for a week or so. That in itself would give me plenty of warning, since there are ways for me to listen in on such discussions without being forced to endure the sour reek of stale beer. Village life can be boring, but the safety it'd provide would more than make up for the tedium.

The family prospered in Darine, and we lingered there for probably too many years. In 4071, Alten's wife Ellette gave birth to a son, whom Alten insisted on naming Geran in honor of his grandfather. I didn't really think that was a good idea, all things considered, but Alten was adamant. Davon continued to buy furs from Nadraks and occasional Drasnians, and Alten continued to convert those furs into garments that sold very well. Alnana died 4077, and Davon went into a steep decline after her death. That's more common than you might think. Sometimes grief will carry you off faster than any disease.

It was in the year 4080 that one of those itinerant pestilences which roamed the ancient world sprang up again in Darine, and it wiped out half the population, including Davon, Alten, and Ellette, who all died within a few hours of each other despite my best efforts to save them. That was one time when I didn't flee from some inquisitive Murgo. I fled that disease instead. Immediately after the funeral, I closed up the house and the shop, took whatever money was lying around, and young Geran and I left Darine, going to – where else – the safety of my house by the lake.

We stayed there for several years, and to pass the time – and provide for the future – I taught Geran the rudiments of the healing arts. He was an attentive, though hardly gifted, student, and I had some hopes for his future. When we came out of seclusion and I set him up in practice in Medalia, however, I soon realized that he'd never be a first-rate physician. He seemed to lack the ability to diagnose the illnesses his patients brought to him.

He married late – in his mid-thirties – and his wife bore him a son to continue the line, and four daughters as well.

Despite my disappointment in Geran professionally, I'll concede that his status as a mediocre physician served our ultimate purpose far better than might have been the case were he a world-renowned healer. He earned enough to get us all by, but that was about all,

459

and that helped to lower his son's expectations. The first Geran had been a prince, and Davon and Alten had been extremely prosperous tradesmen. The second Geran was a near-failure in his own profession, so his son didn't grow up in a splendid house surrounded by servants. He was good with his hands, though, so I apprenticed him to a carpenter when he was about twelve. Circumstances seemed to be cooperating with Hattan's grand scheme for submerging Iron-grip's heirs in obscurity.

Over the next couple of centuries, I sampled most of the trades and crafts in Sendaria. I raised coopers and weavers, stone-cutters and cabinet-makers, blacksmiths and masons. My young nephews were all serious, rather self-effacing craftsmen who took some pride in their work, and with rare exceptions, I didn't provide them with *too* many details about their heritage. Royal blood doesn't really mean very much to a young fellow who spills it every time a tool slips and he barks his knuckles.

We weren't exactly vagabonds, but we moved rather frequently, descending, in the view of some I'm sure, to smaller and smaller towns and villages with each move. The notion of all our neighbors serving as watch-dogs appealed to me, and it worked rather well. I received ample warning whenever a Murgo passed through whichever village we were living in, and if the Murgo lingered, I could come up with 'a family emergency' to get us out of town in a hurry.

I was living in the improbably named village of Remote Rundorun which lay some leagues off the main road that linked Sendar and Seline. My only family at that time was a descendant of Iron-grip and Beldaran whose name was Darion. When the gossip about a Murgo merchant passing through town reached me, I decided that a change of scene might be appropriate. This time, however, I decided to change tack and move to a large town rather than an even smaller village with an even more ridiculous name. Darion and I packed up our clothing, and I paid a passing wagoner to take us to the town of Sulturn in central Sendaria.

I've always rather liked Sulturn anyway. It's not as cramped as Medalia or Seline, and the breeze off the lake is refreshing during the hot summer months. Darion was about fourteen or so when we moved there, and I apprenticed him to a cabinet-maker. He was a strapping young man who gave some promise of being quite a bit larger than his immediate ancestors. He wouldn't be quite as big as Bull-neck had been, but that was all right with me. Hiding giants might have been very challenging. Darion spent the first year of his apprenticeship whittling wooden pegs. The craftsman to whom he was apprenticed was a traditionalist who absolutely despised nails, believing that good furniture must be pegged together, since nails work themselves loose, and wobbly cabinets are a sin against the Gods.

After his year of whittling, Darion was allowed to start building the backs and sides of wardrobes – those free-standing clothes-closets that were popular in Sendaria at the time. A wardrobe is an awkward piece of furniture, but it *does* allow you to rearrange your bedroom in ways that aren't possible when your clothes closets are built into the wall.

After a couple of years, Darion's employer – I won't use the traditional 'master', since it has a different meaning in my family – finally relented and allowed his apprentice to build the front of a cabinet. The gruff fellow inspected the result rather carefully, pointed out a slight flaw in a piece of molding, and then grudgingly admitted that my nephew wasn't a *total* incompetent.

Darion's next project was a china cabinet, and try though he might, the sour tempered master-builder couldn't find anything wrong with it.

By the time Darion was twenty, he was doing most of the work in the shop, and his teacher was puttering around building bird-houses and other frivolities. The people of Sulturn knew who was really producing the fine furniture that came out of the shop, and a number of them suggested to me that Darion might be wise to go into business for himself.

I had a simpler answer, however. I went to Darion's employer and bought him out, suggesting that it might be nice if he were to spend his twilight years with his son and his grandchildren on their farm at the south end of the lake.

'Where did you get the money, Aunt Pol?' Darion asked me curiously when I told him what I'd done.

'I have certain resources, dear,' I replied evasively. Money's always been a problem for me – not its lack, but its excess. Over those long centuries I almost always had several hundred Sendarian gold nobles tucked away somewhere. I didn't make an issue of the fact, largely because a craftsman works harder if he doesn't know about the treasure lying under the hearthstone or hidden inside a wall. I wanted those young men to be absolutely convinced that they were the family's sole support, and frugality's a virtue anyway, isn't it?

In 4413, when Darion was about 22, he began 'walking out' with a very pretty Sendarian girl named Selana. That silent bell mother and I had spoken of was still working, and it rang inside my head the first time I saw the tall blonde girl.

Darion and Selana were married in the early spring of 4414, and prior to the wedding Darion put aside his cabinetry and started work on converting the loft over his shop into living quarters for us. Our lease on the somewhat shabby house near the lake was running out anyway, and our incipient groom thought it appropriate to bring his new wife home to a place he actually owned. There are some drawbacks to living and working in the same building, but at least Darion didn't have to walk very far to work in the morning.

After the wedding of Darion and Selana, we settled down in a kind of blissful domesticity. Selana and I cooked and kept house upstairs, and Darion built and sold cabinetry down below. In many respects our circumstances were an ideal fulfillment of Hattan's design for the proper way for an heir to live. Darion was respected as a reliable craftsman, but he was not prominent. He made a comfortable living, but a man who lives upstairs over his shop could hardly be called a merchant prince.

And then in the late autumn of 4415, my father paid us a call. Over the years, I'd sensed his presence in my general vicinity any number of times, but this was the first time he'd actually thrust himself upon us. I'd expected him to keep an eye on me, and I'd probably have been disappointed in him if he hadn't. Though he was not as intimately involved with the family as I was, he was nonetheless interested in them.

Father's a little clumsy when he releases his Will, so I heard him enter the shop downstairs before he even came up to the second floor. When he burst in on us, I saw that he'd disguised himself by taking the form of a tall man with a dense black beard that seemed to start just under his lower eyelids. I'm sure the disguise worked on others, but I recognize my father's mind, not his outward appearance, so when he came in while we were eating supper, I recognized him immediately. 'What are you doing here, Old Man?' I demanded. 'I thought I told you to stay away from me.'

'We've got to get you and the children out of here, Pol,' he replied urgently, shifting back into his real form.

That *really* startled Darion and Selana. 'Who is this man, Aunt Pol?' Darion demanded in a half-strangled tone.

'My father,' I replied, making it sound deprecating.

'Holy Belgarath?' I hadn't really kept my background a secret, and father's got a sort of towering reputation – a reputation that tarnishes rather quickly once you get to know him.

'That "holy" might be open to some question,' I replied, not so much for Darion's benefit as for father's. I still enjoy tweaking his beard now and then.

'This is an emergency, Pol,' father said. 'We've got to leave Sulturn right now. If you're not going to learn how to use hair dye, you probably shouldn't unpack when you move into a new town. Every Grolim in the world knows about that lock in your hair.'

'What are you talking about, father?'

'There's a Murgo at an inn down by the waterfront west of here, and he's been asking after you. He's pouring beer into a very talkative Sendar, so he knows exactly where you are by now. Start packing.'

'Why didn't you just kill him, father? A dead Murgo doesn't pose much of a problem.'

'*Aunt Pol!*' Darion exclaimed in horror.

'How much does he know, Pol?' father asked, pointing at Darion.

'As much as he needs to know.'

'Does he know who he is?'

'In a general sort of way.'

'Oh, *Pol!*' father said disgustedly. 'Keeping a secret just for the sake of having a secret is childish. Start packing while I explain to him who he really is. Just take the necessities. We can buy what you need in Kotu.'

'*Kotu?*' I hadn't expected that, and I wasn't sure I liked the idea.

'Sendaria's getting too dangerous, Pol. You've had to cut and run a few too many times. The Murgos – and Grolims – are starting to concentrate their attention here. Let's get you and the children into one of the Alorn kingdoms for a while. Throw some things in a bag while I explain the situation to Darion and his wife.'

'I still think you should have run a knife into the Murgo.'

'That'd just be a waste of time, Pol. Word of a dead Murgo in an alley would get back to the Grolims, and they'd be crawling all over you in less than a week.'

He was going to buy horses, he said, but I brushed that idea aside. Selana was a healthy girl, but she was pregnant, and bouncing around in a saddle isn't good for pregnant ladies. I didn't pay much attention while father explained a few realities to Darion and Selana. I'd heard the story before – and lived through most of it. Darion looked slightly skeptical, but he *behaved* as if he believed my father. Then he suggested that we leave town in his somewhat wobbly delivery cart. Father liked the notion immediately, since it reminded him of the Master's favorite disguise. Then, though I hate to admit it, the Old Wolf had a stroke of genius. 'I think a fire here might be useful,' he mused.

That *really* upset Darion and Selana. Everything they owned was in this building, and they hadn't yet fully come to grips with the idea that they'd never be coming back to Sulturn to gather up the remnants of their previous life. That was a part of the value of father's plan. Not only would it get the immediate and undivided attention of everyone in town, but it'd also quench any yearnings Darion and Selana might have to come back to pick up mementos.

Father went back to the inn to pick up his horse, and that's when I conjured up the three skeletons that'd convince the townspeople – and the curious Murgo – that Darion, Selena and I'd all died in the fire. I wanted the trail that Murgo'd been following to come to a dead end here in Sulturn.

Father drove the cart out of Muros with Darion, Selena, and I all concealed under a sheet of canvas in the back, and some hours after midnight we were on the road north toward Medalia while Darion's shop burned merrily behind us.

We rode north through the tag-end of a blustery autumn for the next two weeks. If you really want to get from Sulturn to Darine in a hurry, you'll buy yourself a good horse and stay on the Tolnedran highways. If you push your horse, you can probably make it in five days. Pounding through towns and villages as if Torak himself were snapping at your heels attracts attention, though, so father took the back roads and country lanes instead, and he didn't crowd his horse. Autumn's a nice time to travel, though, so I didn't really mind. Trees tend to show off in the autumn, and a brisk wind fills the air around you with color.

We finally reached Darine, sold father's horse and Darion's cart, and took ship for the Drasnian port of Kotu.

I don't like Kotu. I never have – probably because of the perpetual reek of the fens that hangs over the town like a curse. Moreover, I find the intricate scheming of the Drasnian merchants of Kotu very tiresome. If a Drasnian owes you money, he'd rather die than pay you without devising *some* way to profit from the transaction.

I rather hate to admit it, but I'd missed my father over the years. He has all manner of character defects of which I soundly disapprove, but he *is* an entertaining old rascal, and there's an almost brutal practicality about him that I've never been able to duplicate. The idea of burning Darion's shop to the ground would never have occurred to me. Maybe I'm too much of a sentimentalist.

Father and Darion got on well together. Darion had the good

sense to listen to the Old Wolf's advice, and father approved of that. I'm quite sure that Darion had some reservations about changing trades in Kotu. For Darion, it was the furniture that was important, not the decorations on it, so becoming a wood-carver was a definite step down in his view of things. Father cut across the objections with characteristic directness. 'Wouldn't you say that staying alive is more important than some obscure sense of artistic integrity?' he asked.

That more or less stifled Darion's objections.

Father remained with us in Kotu until we got settled in. He dragooned us into changing our names and concocted a hair-dye – which, incidentally, didn't work – to hide the tell-tale lock in my hair, and then he left. My father's a walking legend, and no amount of disguising himself or assuming false names will ever hide his true identity for very long. It was safer for all of us after he moved on.

Selana gave birth to a son the following spring, and Darion – rather shrewdly, I thought – broke with tradition by giving his infant son a Drasnian name rather than a Rivan or Sendarian one. The child's name was Khelan, and that jarred my sense of the way things ought to be just a bit. Looking back over the centuries, I can only think of two other times when a local name was appended to one of Iron-grip's descendants. Anonymity's all very well and good, I suppose, but *really* –

It was not long after Khelan's birth that a voice came to me during the night, and this time it *wasn't* mother's voice.

'*Are you awake, Pol?*' father asked me.

'*I am now,*' I replied. '*What's afoot, father?*'

'*I'm at the Arendish Fair, and I've just had an absolutely fascinating discussion with Ctuchik.*'

'*What's he doing at the Arendish Fair?*'

'*Looking for you, actually. He yearns for your company.*'

'*And he's eavesdropping on you right now. Very clever, father.*'

'*Don't be ridiculous, Pol. I know how to keep him from hearing me when I do this. Don't get any ideas about moving back to Sendaria for a while. Sendaria's mine right now.*'

'*What are you talking about?*'

'*Ctuchik's got an underling named Chamdar. He's moderately gifted, and Ctuchik's nailed him to my backside.*'

'*That's gross, father.*'

'*I'm just a plain-spoken country boy, Pol. I say it the way it is. Chamdar's going to be as close to me as my shadow. Ctuchik's convinced that I know*' where you are and that I periodically drop in on you. Chamdar's following me in order to find you.'

'What's this got to do with where I choose to live?'

'You've been detected in Sendaria from time to time, Pol, so Ctuchik considers Sendaria to be your natural habitat. I'm going to play a little game with Chamdar for a while, and I don't want you cluttering up the playing field.'

'Why not just kill him and get him out of the way?'

'I know this Chamdar and what he looks like. I'd rather have a familiar face on my trail than a total stranger. I'll lead him around Sendaria until he gets to know every back lane and country crossroad in the whole silly kingdom – intimately. He'll be so sure that you're still there that the Alorn kingdoms won't ever cross his mind. Just give me some room, Pol. I'll keep Chamdar out of your hair.'

'Don't you have better things to do?'

'Not really. What you're doing is only slightly less important than the cracking of the world was. This is my little contribution to your task.' Then he gave vent to an evil-sounding chuckle.

'What's so humorous?'

'I'm going to have a lot of fun with this, Pol. I think that if you listen very carefully, you'll be able to hear Chamdar's howls of frustration many many times over the next several centuries. Just stay out of Sendaria, and I'll guarantee your safety.'

'Where are you going now?'

'I think I'll lead Chamdar to Tol Honeth for a while – give him a taste of luxury before he has to start living in gutters.' He laughed again. 'Ctuchik's been kind enough to provide me with a tail. Just to show him what I think of it, I think I'll drag it through the mud for a while. Sleep well, Pol.'

That's my father for you.

PART SIX

Vo Mimbre

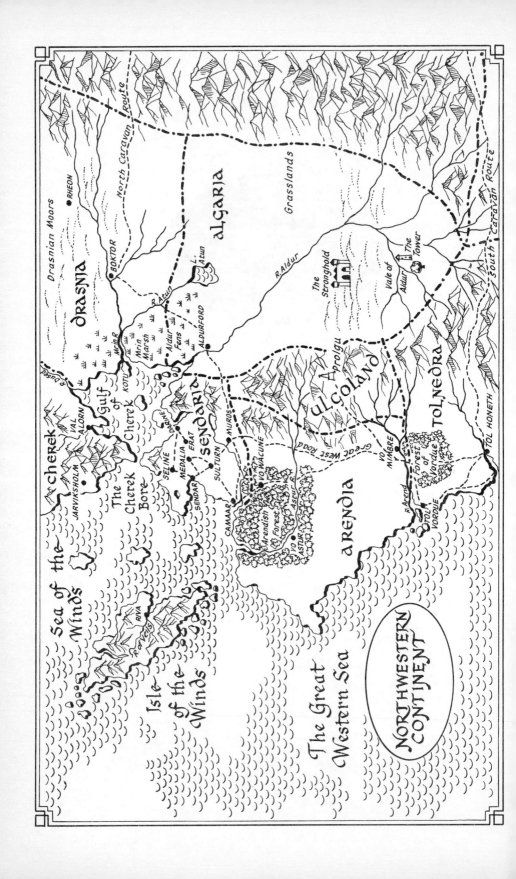

CHAPTER 29

Although father made light of Chamdar's arrival in the west, he obviously took Ctuchik's underling very seriously. Chamdar was no ordinary Grolim driven by fear and mindless obedience. He was shrewd, ambitious, and very clever. In some respects he was even more dangerous than Ctuchik himself.

Looking back on the early years of my task, I'm forced to concede that my preoccupation with Sendaria and its people had lured me into a grave error. I'd been unwilling to set aside my previous duty when I'd accepted my new one, so I'd always chosen to conceal Iron-grip's heirs inside Sendaria's borders. That had simplified things for Ctuchik's Grolims by narrowing their field of search. After a few years they knew that they didn't have to look for me in Arendia or Tolnedra, because I was always in Sendaria.

Father peremptorily corrected my mistake by banishing me from the place I loved. I looked upon the four and a half centuries I was forced to live in the Alorn kingdoms as a period of exile, but I *did* learn to ignore national boundaries during those interminable years. I still yearned to return to Sendaria, though. I'd invested a large part of my life in that land and even though I no longer ruled the nation which had grown out of my former duchy, I still liked to be in place to deal with anything that might possibly start to fall apart. Duties can sometimes be very much like a pair of comfortable old shoes. We're reluctant to put them aside even when we have new ones.

Although I wasn't really at ease in Kotu, Darion and Selana were young, and they soon adjusted to life there. Their newborn son had a Drasnian name, and their costume was now Drasnian. Fortunately, morality isn't like costume. You don't put it on and take it off. Deep down where it really counted, Darion and Selana were still Sendars. Darion didn't swindle his customers, and Selana didn't involve herself in the backbiting and scheming of the neighborhood ladies. Drasnians are obsessed with social status, I've noticed. The trait may even have its source in Dras himself. Bull-neck never let his brothers forget that he was the first-born of Bear-shoulders. Drasnian ladies frequently try to elevate their own social status by bringing down the current social lioness – usually by inventing clever lies about her. Selana chose not to participate, and she made that very clear. For some reason, not one neighbor lady ever tried to entertain *me* with gossip. Isn't that peculiar?

Oddly, considering the fact that this *was* Drasnia, the strict morality of Darion and Selana raised them in the eyes of their neighbors far more than any amount of scheming, swindling, or spiteful gossip possibly could have. Despite their behavior, it seems that Drasnians *do* respect decency.

That line of thought raises an interesting notion. Could it possibly be that our itinerant Prince Kheldar, the thief who always has a well-planned escape route out of every town in the world firmly in mind, is secretly ashamed of his outrageous behavior and that a hidden yearning for honesty and decency lurks somewhere deep down in his grubby little soul?

On second thought, though, probably not.

Got you that time, didn't I, Silk?

At any rate, Darion and Selana lived out their lives in Kotu, respected and secure in the good opinion of their neighbors. Khelan, their son, was raised as a Drasnian, but after our obligatory 'little talk' on his eighteenth birthday, he knew who he really was and why it was necessary for him to keep that information to himself. To his credit, Khelan didn't ask that almost inevitable question, 'Why didn't you tell me before, Aunt Pol?' Since he was culturally a Drasnian, he realized that I hadn't told him before because he hadn't needed to know before.

We apprenticed him to a ship-builder, and he did very well in that line. Drasnian vessels of the forty-fifth century were little more than coastal freighters that plied the trade-routes in the Gulf of Cherek. They were broad of beam so that they could carry more cargo, and they wallowed along like pregnant whales. They resembled Cherek war-boats only insofar as both kinds of vessels were propelled by sails and both floated. The Cherek war-boats almost flew before the wind, but anything beyond a healthy sneeze tended to capsize a Drasnian freighter. Khelan was intelligent enough to pinpoint the reason for this distressing tendency, and he promoted the idea that a deeper keel might help to keep Drasnian ships right-side up. I'm sure that Drasnian sea-captains understood what he was driving at, but they resisted all the same – probably because they were so fond of shallow, hidden coves in secluded spots along various coasts. Far be it from me to suggest that *all* Drasnian sea-captains are smugglers. There almost have to be at least a *few* law-abiding Drasnians, and just because I've never met one doesn't prove that there aren't any.

My line of protégés – if that's the proper term – lived and prospered in Kotu until the end of the forty-fifth century, and then I relocated them to Boktor. I usually avoided national capitals over those long centuries. Ctuchik was relying heavily on the Dagashi, and the Dagashi aren't visibly Murgo. They could move around in the west without being readily identifiable, and the logical place to start looking for something in any kingdom is the capital. The problem with Drasnia is the fact that there aren't really that many towns there. Oh, there are a few fishing villages in the fens to the west of Boktor, but I absolutely refused to live in that stinking swamp. Silk once referred to the western part of his homeland as 'dear old mucky Drasnia', and that more or less sums it up.

The moors of eastern Drasnia are almost as bad. The moors are a vast emptiness where winter comes early and stays late. It's a region suitable only for the raising of reindeer, the primary occupation of prehistoric Drasnians. It wasn't the weather that kept me out of eastern Drasnia, however. That region butts up against Gar og Nadrak, and I didn't think it prudent to live that close to an Angarak kingdom. Moreover, eastern Drasnia is the natural home of the Bear-Cult in that kingdom. The combination of isolation and miserable weather insulates the minds of eastern Drasnian Cultists from such dangerous outside innovations as fire and the wheel.

My little family lived in Boktor for about seventy years, and then I uprooted them and took them to Cherek, where we resided in a village some distance to the west of Val Alorn. The growing season is short that far to the north, and the local men-folk devoted their winters to logging. A sea-faring nation such as Cherek always needs more timber than even the most industrious peasantry can provide. One of Iron-grip's heirs, Dariel, turned out to be an inventor, and after looking rather closely at the local mill, where a water-wheel provided power to grind wheat into flour, he devised a way to make a water-wheel power a saw that converted raw logs into beams and planks. Dariel made a fortune with that idea, and his saw-mill was the family business for well over two centuries. I felt safe in Cherek because Chereks, the most elemental Alorns, automatically killed any Angarak they came across. There were plenty of taverns in Cherek, but there weren't any Murgos asking questions in any of them. Even the Dagashi avoided Cherek.

Eventually, however, mother suggested that it was time to move on, more to prevent the line from becoming so totally Cherek that it'd be impossible to erase certain inborn Cherekish traits. The ultimate product of the Rivan line was to be 'the Godslayer', and mother thought it might be best if he knew *which* God he was supposed to slay. The notion of a berserker wielding Iron-grip's sword and hacking his way through the entire pantheon didn't sit too well with mother.

Strangely, given my prejudices, I rather enjoyed our stay in Cherek. The long succession of busty, blonde Cherek ladies who married my assorted nephews all shared the legendary Cherek fertility, and I often found myself literally awash with blonde children. I *always* had babies to play with while we were in Cherek.

In the year 4750, however, mother grew insistent, and after a long talk with the boy's parents I took the most recent heir, Gariel, to Algaria. Back in the forty-first century, Prince Geran of Riva had married the daughter of Hattan, the younger brother of a clan-chief, and so Gariel was a hereditary member of Hattan's clan. I pointed this out to Hurtal, the then-current clan-chief, and Gariel and I were accepted into the extended family of the clan.

I don't enjoy the nomadic life of the Algar clans. It probably has to do with my upbringing. I like permanence and stability, and I find the notion of having a cow decide where I'm going to live slightly offensive. About the best thing you can say about the life of a nomad is the fact that he doesn't stay in one place long enough for his garbage pile to overwhelm him.

Gariel learned how to ride horses and herd cows, and I fell back on my sometime occupation as a physician. I delivered babies by the score and aided mares in difficult foaling. I wasn't really offended when I was called from my bed to help a pregnant horse. I noticed almost immediately that a mare in foal doesn't ask silly questions during the birth the way my human patients did.

Since Gariel had grown up in Cherek where almost everyone's blond, the only brunette he'd ever encountered had been me. Algars are darker than Chereks, and Gariel was absolutely fascinated by the dark-haired Algar girls. Since Gariel was new to the clan, the girls hadn't watched him go through all the awkward stages of growing up, so they found him to be equally fascinating. I was hard-pressed to keep my young charge and his new-found friends from exploring the outer reaches of those shared fascinations.

I'm sorry, but that's about as delicately as I can put it. Mother was much more blunt when she told me that Gariel's first son *would* be his heir – with or *without* benefit of clergy.

We finally got him safely married to a tall, beautiful Algar named Silar, and I was able to catch up on my sleep. When their son was born in 4756, I suggested that we might dust off one of the traditional names of the line, and they obliged me by naming the infant Daran. There were a dozen or so names we've used off and on down through the centuries, and I've found that these repetitions give us a sense of continuity and purpose that sustains a little family that's obliged to live in obscurity.

Young Daran quite literally grew up on horseback, and I think that when he was a boy he hovered on the very brink of becoming what the Algars call a Sha-Dar – even as Hettar currently is. The Sha-Darim are known as 'Horse-Lords', men whose affinity for horses somehow links their minds with the group minds of entire horse-herds. I moved decisively to head that off. The Sha-Darim are so obsessed with horses that they seldom marry, and that option simply wasn't open to Daran. The Sha-Darim also became irrational in some ways – as Hettar demonstrated in Ulgoland that time he tried to tame a Hrulga stallion. The Hrulgin *look* like horses, but they're carnivores, so Hettar didn't have much success – except that he managed to keep the Hrulga from having him for breakfast.

In time, Daran *did* marry a young Algar named Selara, and their son, Geran, was born in 4779. Note that repetition again. I was determined to keep the line of succession Rivan, and one of the ways I accomplished that was to make sure that they all had Rivan names. Like his father, Geran grew up to be a horse-herder, and I began to give some thought to relocation again. Algars are perfectly content with their nomadic life, but my task involved not merely hiding and protecting the heirs, but also nurturing and molding them. An Algar herder is quite probably the most independent and free of all men. Freedom's all very well, I suppose, but it has no place in the make-up of an incipient king. A king – and by extension

473

his heir – is the least free of all men. It's a commonplace to say that a king wears a crown; but in reality, it's the other way around.

My options in Algaria were severely limited. The only two places in the entire kingdom that didn't move around on wheels were the Stronghold, which isn't really a city but a baited trap set for any Murgos who come down the Eastern Escarpment to steal horses, and the village of Aldurford, Fleet-foot's first capital. After Geran married and his son, Darel, was born in 4801, I began a careful campaign of corrupting the newest heir, stressing the inconvenience of living in a moving village and being dragged along behind a herd of cows interested only in grass. I told Darel stories about town-life with its comfort and convenience and all the joys of civilization as opposed to the loneliness of the nomadic life. A helpful blizzard in the winter of 4821 convinced him that there might be something to what I'd been telling him. After he'd spent twenty-eight hours in the saddle with a screaming wind driving snow into his face, he began to get my drift. I encouraged him to strike up an acquaintance with the son of our resident blacksmith, and he picked up the rudiments of that useful trade. That's what probably turned the trick. There was no real need for two blacksmiths in the clan, so Darel would have to strike out on his own if he wanted to follow his trade.

As luck had it, he'd formed no permanent attachment to any of the girls in our clan, and so he had nothing to hold him back when he and I moved to Aldurford in 4825. The then current blacksmith in Aldurford was a bit too fond of strong drink, and he spent far more time in the local tavern than he did in his smithy. Thus, when I set Darel up in business on the outskirts of town, he soon had plenty of work to keep him out of mischief.

He was thirty when he finally married a local beauty, Adana, and they were very happy together. I shouldn't admit it, but I was probably even happier than they were. Nomads tend not to bathe often, and people who spend all their time with horses and cows grow fragrant after a while. After Darel and I set up housekeeping in Aldurford, I bathed twice a day for almost a solid year.

The marriage of Darel and Adana was a good one, and Adana and I got along well together. I'd bought us a small house on the outskirts of town, and Darel's new wife and I spent most of our time together in the kitchen. 'Aunt Pol?' she said to me one afternoon. I noticed that her face was troubled.

'Yes, Adana?'

'Is it possible that Darel and I are doing something wrong?' She blushed furiously. 'I mean, shouldn't I be pregnant by now? I *really* want to have babies, but –' she faltered.

'Sometimes it takes a while, dear,' I told her. 'It's not exactly the same as nailing pieces of wood together. There's always an element of luck involved, you know.'

'I *do* so want to give Darel a son, Aunt Pol.'

'Yes, dear,' I said, smiling, 'I know.' Of course I knew. Producing children is the ultimate expression of love for any woman, and Adana loved her blacksmith husband with a peculiarly fervent passion. 'Come here a moment, dear,' I said to her.

She obediently came to me, and I laid one hand on her lower abdomen. Then I sent a gently probing thought out through my fingers, and found the source of the problem almost immediately. Adana's problem was chemical in nature. There was an imbalance that interfered with normal procreation.

If you're that curious about it, you could read some medical texts, I suppose. I wouldn't want to rob you of the joy of discovery, so I won't get too specific here.

'I'll have to take a little trip down to the Vale, Adana,' I told her.

'Is it permanent, Aunt Pol?' she asked, her eyes filled with tears. 'Am I barren?'

'Don't be such a goose, Adana,' I laughed. 'You just need a little tonic, that's all. I need to look up the proper formula in one of the books in my father's tower, that's all.' The word 'tonic' is very useful for physicians. Everyone knows that a tonic is good for you – and that it doesn't taste very good. The patients always make faces at the taste, but they take it religiously.

The next morning I went a ways out of Aldurford, changed form and flew on down to the Vale to spend several days with father's medical library. The twins told me that father was off in Sendaria merrily leading Chamdar around by the nose. Subtlety's never been one of father's strong points, so his normal method of luring Chamdar to another village involved the murder of any Murgo who was handy. Chamdar, of course, assumed that the murder was an indication that the Murgo had been hot on my trail, so he'd immediately rush to the village in question to try to pick up that trail. Chamdar was no fool, so after about five or six of these casual murders, he knew exactly what father was doing, but he still couldn't ignore the chance that *this* murder was significant, so he had no choice but to follow up on it. I'm sure it entertained my father enormously, and it *did* keep him out of mischief – more or less – and the whole business kept Chamdar so preoccupied that the idea that I might *not* be in Sendaria apparently never occurred to him.

I finally tracked down the proper concoction of herbs to normalize Adana's chemical imbalance, and then I flew on back up to Aldurford and mixed up a large jar of the 'tonic'. Adana didn't much care for the taste of it, but she religiously drank three doses a day. It wasn't too long before Darel came out of their bedroom one morning with that silly look on his face that all young men display when they've just been told the happy news. 'Adana's going to have a baby, Aunt Pol!' he said excitedly. 'I'm going to be a father!'

'That's nice, dear,' I replied calmly. 'What would you like for breakfast?' I just *love* to do that to young men when they get too full of themselves. Parenthood in a male-dominated society is one of those profoundly unfair things. The woman does all the work, and the man takes all the credit.

'Could you fix something nice for Adana, Aunt Pol?' he almost begged me. 'I think she's entitled to breakfast in bed, don't you?'

'Oh, dear,' I sighed. It was going to be one of *those*. Every now and then I've come across a young man who's absolutely convinced that pregnancy's a form of invalidism, and he inevitably wants to chain his wife to the bed for nine months. It took me several days to clear away *that* idiocy.

It was in the year 4841 that Adana gave birth to a son, Garel – a good Rivan name – and I heaved a vast sigh of relief. This was the first time I'd encountered infertility in all the years of my stewardship, and the possibility that it might recur was a continuing nightmare that's haunted me for centuries.

It was in the year 4850 that the eclipse which has become so famous occurred. I'd seen eclipses of the sun before, but this one was somehow quite different. Primitive man – and that term encompasses most of humanity – looks upon an eclipse with superstitious awe. Astronomers know what causes them, and can even predict them with a fair degree of accuracy. The eclipse of 4850, however, was an EVENT of the first magnitude, and its sudden appearance had been totally unpredictable, but the simple fact that it was *necessary* hasn't yet occurred to them. All the prophecies speak of the eclipse, so it *had* to happen. It's entirely possible that Torak himself simply obscured the sun to fulfill the prophecy which announced his coming. He *could* have done that, you know.

*   *   *

476

Did you want me to run through the mathematics involved in predicting an eclipse for you? No? I didn't think so.

Anyway, while the world was still enveloped in that noon-time darkness, mother's voice startled me by its intensity. *'This is what we've been waiting for, Pol,'* she declared triumphantly. *'Start getting ready.'*

'Ready for what?'

'Torak's coming. He's left Ashaba, and he's on his way to Mal Zeth. He'll set aside the current king and assume total control of all of Mallorea. Then he'll come west to reclaim the Orb.'

'How much time have we got?'

'Probably not enough. You'll lose more than your share of battles, but that won't matter. This is one of those things that have to be settled by an EVENT. The Child of Light and the Child of Dark will meet in Arendia.'

'Is Darel the Child of Light?'

'No. The EVENT that involves Torak and the Rivan King's still quite a ways off.'

'Well, who is the Child of Light?'

'At the moment, I am.'

'You?'

'I won't be the one who meets Torak in Arendia, though, and neither will Darel. We're involved in a series of EVENTS that're preparing the way for the major one.'

'Must you be so cryptic, mother?' I asked with some asperity.

'Yes, actually I must. If you know too much, you'll do things differently from the way you're supposed to do them. Let's not tamper with this, Pol. This isn't a good place for unrestrained creativity.'

And then she was gone.

An eclipse, that unnatural night at high noon, is normally followed by an equally unnatural-seeming brightness when the sun returns. The eclipse of 4850 was different. It *didn't* get light again after the eclipse had passed because thick, heavy clouds had rolled in while the sun had been blotted out. Then it started to rain.

And it rained off and on for the next twenty-five years.

A day or so after 'Torak's Eclipse', I sent my thought down to the twins in their tower in the Vale. Perhaps I should note in passing that I'm far more proficient in this mode of communication than the rest of my family because I've had more practice. I *did*, as you'll recall, run my duchy from mother's cottage following the fall of Vo Wacune. I kept Malon Killaneson hopping during those years, so I'm almost as good at *thinking* to people as I am at talking to them.

477

'Uncles,' I said to get the twins' attention, 'where's my father?'

'We haven't heard from him, Pol,' Belkira replied.

'He's probably running around warning everybody,' Beltira added. 'Wasn't the eclipse spectacular?'

'So's the eruption of a volcano – or a tidal wave,' I replied drily. 'If the Old Wolf happens to check in with you, tell him that I need to talk with him – soon.'

'We'll pass it on, Pol,' Belkira promised.

'I'd appreciate it.'

The months rolled by, however, and there was still no word from my vagrant father. I started to grow irritated with him.

Then in the spring of 4851, Darel's heart stopped beating while he was hammering at a piece of white-hot steel in his smithy. I've always taken these sudden heart stoppages as some kind of personal insult. There aren't enough overt symptoms in advance to let you know that they're coming. If the victim survives the first attack, a physician can do things to prevent or delay the second. All too often, however, the first one is fatal. What appears to be a perfectly normal, healthy person simply dies in his tracks, and he's dead before he hits the floor. It's only then, in retrospect, that the physician realizes that there've been quite a number of subtle warnings that are so ordinary that they've been overlooked. I'd assumed that Darel had a red face because of the heat of his forge, and the fact that his left arm sometimes ached wasn't remarkable, because his right arm also ached. He was a blacksmith, after all, and you don't spend your days pounding on hot steel without earning a *few* aches and pains.

There was absolutely nothing I could do, and the frustration of that drove me almost wild.

Adana and Garel, who was ten at the time, were absolutely devastated by Darel's death. The only good thing about a lingering illness lies in the fact that it prepares the family for the inevitable. Part of the tragedy of the death of a craftsman in most societies lies in the fact that his widow and orphans are not only bereaved but also immediately cast into poverty. With no money coming in, they frequently descend to the status of beggars at the local church door. My secret hoard of inconvenient money suddenly stopped being inconvenient. We were able to keep our house on the outskirts of Aldurford, and we ate regularly.

I'm sure that I profoundly disappointed several budding entrepreneurs in Aldurford by laughing in their faces when they made offers to buy Darel's smithy. There are people in this world who are very much like vultures. They hover over death-beds drooling in anticipa-

478

tion. Then, when the new widow is virtually out of her mind with grief, they make ridiculously low offers for the family business. The vultures of Aldurford got a quick lesson in civil behavior when they came swooping in this time, however. I told them quite casually that I wasn't interested in selling the smithy and that I was seriously thinking about expanding the business. By now I was conversant with almost all useful trades and crafts, so I talked of furniture marts, clothing shops, bakeries, and butcher shops – all attached to the smithy. 'It'd be so much more convenient for the people of Aldurford, don't you think?' I suggested brightly. 'They wouldn't have to spend whole days wandering around town to buy what they needed. They could do all their shopping – and buying – in one place.'

The local tradesmen all turned pale at the thought of that kind of well-organized competition, so they formed a kind of consortium, pooled their cash reserves, and bought me out at about three times what the smithy was worth.

I *love* to do that to people who think they're more clever than I am. It's so much fun to watch that look of condescending superiority melt off their faces to be replaced by stark terror.

Finally, in the early summer of 4852, father spoke briefly with the twins and asked them to advise me that he was preparing to honor me with a visit. Between the time when he spoke with them and the time they finally passed the word to me, they evidently were permitted to make a breakthrough in one of the murkier passages of the Mrin. When they told me that Brand would be the Child of Light in the meeting in Arendia, I was just a bit put out with mother for being so cryptic about it during the eclipse. What had been the point? I was going to find out anyway, so why had she worked so hard to hide it from me? I suspected that her reasons may have been obscurely wolfish.

It took father about two weeks to finally get around to stopping by in Aldurford, and I was just a bit short with him when he finally arrived. It seemed that my whole family was getting some kind of vast entertainment out of keeping me in the dark.

The sky had temporarily cleared, and it was bright blue as father and I walked down to the river and on out past the last house in Aldurford. The sun was very bright, and a breeze rippled the surface of the water. 'I hope you've been enjoying yourself, father,' I said. I'll admit that I was just a bit spiteful about it.

'What's that supposed to mean?'

'It's been two years since the eclipse, Old Man,' I pointed out. 'I hadn't realized just how far down I was on your list of priorities.'

'Don't get your nose out of joint, Pol,' he told me. 'You know how to move at a moment's notice. Other people take quite a bit longer. I wanted to get *them* moving before I came here. I wasn't deliberately ignoring you.'

I turned that over a few times, trying to find something wrong with it. Then I gave up on that. 'The twins asked me to pass something on,' I told him.

'Oh?'

'Brand's the one who's going to met Torak when this all comes to a head in Arendia.'

'*Brand?*'

'That's what the Mrin says.' Then I quoted the obscure passage to him.

'That's ridiculous!' he fumed. 'Brand can't take up Riva's sword. The Orb won't permit it. Give me your hand, Pol. You and I need to talk with the twins. I want some clarifications, and I think you'd better hear it too.' Father absolutely refuses to admit that I'm much better at communicating with others over long distances than he is. He can be such a little boy sometimes.

The twins were having a great deal of difficulty with the Mrin, so about the best they could do was to give us a sketchy sort of outline of what we were supposed to do.

'*Absolutely out of the question!*' I responded when Beltira told me to take Garel and Adana to the Stronghold. '*It's directly in Torak's path if he's bound for Arendia.*'

'*I'm only passing on what the Mrin says, Pol,*' Beltira replied. '*The Stronghold won't fall to Torak. The Mrin's very clear about that. There'll be a siege, but it won't accomplish anything.*'

'*I don't like it.*'

'It'll be all right, Pol,' father told me, speaking aloud. 'You and I have things to do. We have to go to Riva, and we can't take Garel to the Isle of the Winds. If he gets that close to the Orb, it'll light up like a new-risen sun, and every star in this end of the universe will start to ring like a bell. Then that sword'll attach itself to his hand as if it's been glued there. He isn't the one who's going to use the sword, so we've got to keep him away from it.' Then he sent his thought back to the twins. '*Have you heard from Beldin?*' he asked them.

'*Just a few days ago,*' Belkira answered. '*Torak's still at Mal Zeth, and he's got Urvon and Zedar with him.*'

'We've still got some time, then. They aren't going to be able to march the whole of Mallorea this way overnight.'

'We'll see.' Belkira didn't sound nearly as optimistic as father did.

Father and I went back to our house and I instructed Adana to circulate one of those 'family emergency' stories around Aldurford, and then we left for the Stronghold.

It rained almost steadily as we rode on down across the sodden plains of Algaria to that man-made mountain rearing up above the grassland. I'm sure that all that rain was good for the grass, but I didn't care for it all that much.

The Algars have devoted eons to the construction of their stronghold, and it shows. The walls are incredibly thick and they're so high that the place resembles a mountain. People throw the word 'unassailable' around without actually giving much thought to what it means. If precision of language interests you, drop on down to southern Algaria and take a look at the Stronghold. After that, you'll know exactly what 'unassailable' involves. I rather imagine that even Torak quailed a bit when he first saw it.

When we arrived, father had a talk with Cho-Ram, the young Chief of the Clan-Chiefs of Algaria. That's a cumbersome way to say 'king', but it provides a certain insight into the Algar concept of government.

Cho-Ram's family immediately 'adopted' Garel and his mother. Adana knew just exactly who her son was, so becoming a member of the royal family of Algaria didn't seem all that peculiar to her. Garel was uncomfortable with his new-found status, however, and though he was really a bit young to know just who he really was, I decided to bend the rules a bit and have that obligatory 'little talk' with him right then rather than to wait.

Once they were settled in, father, Cho-Ram and I left for the Isle of the Winds.

I'll apologize in advance for what will probably be a depressing overuse of the word 'dreary' in forthcoming pages. There are limits to language, though, and twenty-five years of almost continual rain will exhaust almost anybody's vocabulary. I *could* fall back on some of uncle Beldin's more colorful adjectives, I suppose, but this document might fall into the hands of children, and children aren't supposed to know what those words really mean.

We rode north when we left the Stronghold, skirting the eastern frontier of Ulgoland, and we turned west when we reached the Sendarian mountains. Then we rode on down that long river valley to Camaar, took ship, and sailed across to the Isle of the Winds.

Since it's almost always raining in the City of Riva anyway, the climate change wasn't quite so noticeable there.

Brand, the Rivan Warder, met us on the stone wharf when we made port, and I looked rather closely at this man who was to be one of the more significant 'Children of Light'. He was a big man, broad in the shoulders and massive in the chest. In that regard he resembled a Cherek, but he didn't behave like a Cherek. Chereks are boisterous, but Brand was soft-spoken. Chereks tend to be profane, but Brand's speech was polished, urbane. Though there was very little in the way of physical resemblance, this particular Rivan Warder reminded me a great deal of the first one, my dear, dear friend, Kamion.

Uncle Beldin and my father have speculated endlessly about the peculiar repetitions which have cropped up over the eons, and they've come up with a theory to explain just why things keep happening over and over again. To boil it all down to its simplest terms, their theory holds that 'the accident' – that cataclysmic celestial explosion that disrupted the Purpose of the Universe – had stopped all progression, and we were doomed to unending repetition until somebody came along to set everything in motion again by correcting the mistake.

Brand appeared to be a repetition of Kamion – and also, in a peculiar sort of way, of Ontrose. I found that to be reassuring, since of all the men I'd known until then, either of those two was the most qualified to meet Torak in single combat.

Eldrig of Cherek and Rhodar of Drasnia hadn't yet arrived at Riva, so father, Brand, Cho-Ram and I spent many hours conferring in that blue-draped council chamber high in one of the towers of the citadel. Brand was so startled that his urbane manner slipped just a bit when I told him that *he* was the one who was going to face Torak in Arendia.

'*Me?*' he said in a choked voice.

Then father recited the passage from the Mrin, '"And let him who stands in the stead of the Guardian meet the Child of Dark in the domain of the Bull-God."' Father gave him one of those infuriating little smirks he's so fond of. 'You're standing in for the Rivan King at the moment, Brand,' he said, 'so I guess that means that you've been elected.'

'I didn't even know I was a candidate. What am I supposed to do?'

'We're not sure. *You* will be when the time comes, though. When you come face to face with One-eye, the Necessity's going to take over. It always does in these situations.'

'I'd be a lot more comfortable if I knew what was supposed to happen.'

'We all would, but it doesn't work that way. Don't worry, Brand. You'll do just fine.'

After Eldrig and Rhodar joined us, we got down to the business of mapping out our strategy, and after a few meetings, King Ormik of Sendaria joined us. Father uses the word 'strategy' as if it actually meant something, but the Alorns each knew what their traditional roles would be. The Chereks would be our navy, the Drasnians would be our infantry, and the Algars would be our cavalry. They already knew what to do, so all the bleak faces and ponderous talk were little more than a way to show off and to build morale.

After those grown-up children who ruled the northern part of the continent finished playing, the conference concluded, and I returned to the Stronghold. I lived quietly there despite the turmoil swirling around in the world. Turmoil or not, I still had my task. Garel was twenty-one years old when he married an Algar girl, Aravina, in the year 4860, and in 4861, I delivered Aravina of a son, Gelane.

As I almost always did after the delivery of one of the heirs, I held Gelane for a little while after he was born. Aravina might have been his mother, but *my* face was the first one he saw. It has something to do with our peculiar background, I think. Wolf-puppies are not exactly like ducklings, who automatically believe that the first moving thing they see is their mother, but there *are* some similarities. It might not really make any difference, but I always try to form that initial attachment – just to be on the safe side.

CHAPTER 30

It wasn't long after Gelane was born that father came by the Strong-hold with uncle Beldin, who'd made one of his periodic trips back from Mallorea to fill us in on what was happening on the other side of the Sea of the East. They visited briefly with Cho-Ram and with Garel, Aravina and the baby, and then the three of us adjourned to one of the squat, round towers atop the battlements of the Algars' overgrown Murgo-trap.

My uncle looked almost absently out of one of the narrow, slitted windows with the wind ruffling his hair. 'Nice view,' he noted, staring out at the endless ocean of grass lying far below.

'We aren't here for sightseeing, Beldin,' father said. 'Why don't you tell Pol what's going on in Mallorea?'

Uncle sprawled in a chair at the roughly made table of the guard-tower. 'Why don't we go back a bit?' he suggested. 'Burnt-face has changed a lot, but he's still not equipped to deal with a secular society. Back before the cracking of the world, he made *all* of the decisions for the Angaraks. A good Angarak wouldn't even scratch his own backside without permission from Torak. Then, after he'd cracked the world apart and the Master's Orb had dissolved half his face, Torak took all the old-style Angaraks to Cthol Mishrak and left the generals at Mal Zeth and the Grolims at Mal Yaska to run the rest of Angarak society. Over the centuries, the generals in particular grew more and more secular. Then the Melcenes and their bureau-crats joined the Angarak empire, and they buffed the raw edges off the basic barbarism of the Angarak character. Mal Zeth became a civilized city. It wasn't Tol Honeth by any stretch of the imagination, but it wasn't Korim either.'

'Was Korim really all that bad?' I asked him.

'Probably worse, Pol,' he replied. 'Independent thought was strictly prohibited. Torak did all the thinking, and the Grolims gutted anybody who even suggested that the sun might come up tomorrow morning. Anyway, Zedar had been with Torak at Ashaba for all those centuries while old One-eye was busy having religious experiences.' Uncle paused. 'I just had an interesting thought,' he mused. 'When the spirit of prophecy hits someone, it seems to erase his brain. Torak was probably on about the same mental level as that idiot on the banks of the Mrin for all those years.'

'What's that got to do with anything?' father demanded.

Beldin shrugged and scratched at his stomach. 'I just thought it was interesting. Anyway, One-eye finally snapped out of his brainless reverie and came out of Ashaba, darkening the sun in the process, and he had no idea of what'd happened to his Angaraks. He'd been isolated in his iron tower at Cthol Mishrak and even more isolated at Ashaba. He'd been completely out of touch for forty-eight centuries or so. He stopped by Mal Yaska on his way to the capital, and that gave Urvon the opportunity to present him with a long list of grievances. Right at the top of the list was the fact that the generals at Mal Zeth were ignoring him, and Urvon can't *bear* being ignored. He advised his Master that the generals were all unredeemed heretics. Since Urvon got to him first and talked very fast, Torak left Mal Yaska absolutely convinced that Mal Zeth was a hotbed of secular heresy, so he virtually depopulated the city when he got there. Then he turned Urvon and his Grolims loose on the rest of the continent, and the priesthood started settling old scores with their gutting knives. The altars of Torak ran red for years.'

I shuddered.

'It was probably Zedar who finally convinced Torak that butchering your own army isn't the best way to prepare for a foreign war, so Burnt-face finally reined Urvon in. By then the Angaraks, Melcenes, and Karands were all so terrified of the Grolims that they'd march into fire if Urvon ordered them to. It was probably the most amazing regression in history. A whole civilization collapsed back into the stone age in about ten years. Right now the average Mallorean's on a par with the Thulls. Urvon's even gone so far as to make reading a crime – except for his Grolims, of course – but even the Grolim libraries have been purged of all secular books. I'm waiting for him to outlaw the wheel.'

Father's expression grew horrified. 'They've been burning books?' he exclaimed.

'Don't tie your guts in a knot, Belgarath,' uncle told him. 'The scholars at the university of Melcene carted off all their libraries and hid them in places where the Grolims can't find them, and if nothing else, the Dals at Kell have probably got copies of every book that's ever been written, and the Grolims won't go anywhere near Kell.'

'I'm not sure that I would either,' father admitted. 'The Dals are a very unusual people.'

'"Unusual" only begins to cover it,' Beldin agreed. 'Anyway, the army that's going to come out of Mallorea is going to have numbers and not much else. Their brains have been erased.'

'Those are the best kind of enemies,' father almost gloated. 'Give me a stupid enemy every time.'

'I'll try to remember that.' Then uncle looked around. 'Is there anything to drink up here?'

'Maybe you can have something with supper,' I told him.

'Why not before supper?'

'I wouldn't want you to spoil your appetite, uncle dear.'

Since the entire purpose of the impending Angarak invasion was to regain the Orb, the Alorns were certain to bear the brunt of that assault, and father and I had provided them with far more information than we'd given the non-Alorn rulers. When the Murgos and Nadraks closed the caravan routes in the autumn of 4864, however, the Tolnedrans in particular began to get wind of the fact that something significant was afoot. To make matters even worse for the merchant princes of Tol Honeth, Brand closed the port of Riva that winter – ostensibly for renovations. At that point even a simpleton would have realized that the Alorns and Angaraks were clearing things away in preparation for something fairly earth-shaking, and Ran Borune IV was far from being a simpleton.

We all met again at Riva that winter to review our preparations, and I suggested to father that courtesy, if nothing else, demanded that we advise Ran Borune of the impending invasion. 'If this is all going to come to a climax in Arendia, father,' I said, 'we're probably going to need the Tolnedran legions, so let's stay on the good side of the emperor.'

Father grunted – he does that a lot – but he went on down to Tol Honeth to speak with the youthful Ran Borune. While they were talking, my sometimes bumbling father had a stroke of pure genius. Rather than waste time and effort hammering at the unassailable wall of Ran Borune's scepticism about just how we were getting all this information, father blandly lied to him, handing all the credit to the Drasnian intelligence service. That's been a very useful myth over the centuries.

It was still too early for the Tolnedrans – or anybody else, for that matter – to do anything definitive about the activities of the Angaraks, but at least father's warning gave Ran Borune time to start getting his legions into better physical condition. Once peace breaks out, professional soldiers tend to become flabby in a very short period of time. Regular exercise is time-consuming, and the soldiers are preoccupied with more important things – such as drinking, carousing, and chasing women who don't really mind getting caught.

Then in the early spring of the year 4865 – so early in fact that the ice hadn't yet broken up – the Malloreans began their westward trek across that string of rocky islets between Mallorea and the western continent. Some idiot who'd never actually seen those islands had designated them as 'the land bridge'. If I couldn't build a better bridge than that, I'd take up gardening instead.

I think we've all berated ourselves about our failure to reason out what Torak would do when his army reached the barren land of the Morindim lying to the north of Gar og Nadrak. The Mrin assured us that Torak had an appointment in Arendia, so we all assumed that he'd march down the Nadrak coast to Mishrak ac Thull and then turn west and cross Algaria to reach the lands of the Arends.

Torak himself was far too arrogant for subterfuge, so it was probably Zedar who sent several regiments of red-tuniced Malloreans to Thull Zelik with orders to wander about the streets to deceive the ever-present Drasnian spies. The presence of those Malloreans in Mishrak ac Thull reinforced our conviction that Torak would march directly to the Eastern Escarpment to invade Algaria.

But he didn't. He went through the forests of Gar og Nadrak instead and invaded Drasnia. To say that we were unprepared for that would be the grossest of understatements. We'd assembled a huge Alorn army on the eastern plains of Algaria to meet the expected invasion, so we'd stripped Drasnia of most of its defenders. We were badly out of position when Torak's army of Malloreans, Nadraks, Murgos, and Thulls swept out of the Nadrak forest onto the moors of eastern Drasnia. Torak immediately sent about half his army to Drasnia's southern frontier, effectively cutting off our efforts to rush north to defend our Drasnian friends, and then the Dragon-God's forces began to methodically slaughter every Drasnian they could lay their hands on.

The carnage was dreadful. Such Drasnians as were not killed on sight were turned over to the Grolims for the gruesome sacrificial rites so dear to the heart of their insane God.

487

By midsummer in the year 4866, Drasnia had been largely depopulated – except for the few refugees hiding out in the fens. One escape column trekked north into Morindland and eventually reached Cherek. Thousands of Drasnian refugees were taken by ship from Kotu to other lands lying to the north and west, and the crack regiments of the Drasnian army who'd been assigned the impossible task of defending their homeland were literally driven onto Cherek vessels and freighted to the mouth of the Aldur River and forced to march south to the Stronghold. King Rhodar had desperately wanted to mount a defense of Boktor, but father had dragged him to Kotu and forced him to board King Eldrig's war-boat. I don't think Rhodar ever trusted my father after that.

Once he had absolute control of Drasnia, Torak paused to regroup and to give the reinforcements still streaming across the land bridge time to catch up to him.

Let's clarify something here. Torak himself is no military genius. Back during the War of the Gods when he was actually making the decisions, he made so many mistakes that it's a wonder that his Angaraks didn't become extinct. The Dragon-God has an almost Arendish fondness for the mass frontal assault and the last stand. The overall Angarak strategy in the forty-ninth century came from Zedar, not Torak. Uncle Beldin has deduced – correctly, I believe – that when Torak sent Urvon to Mal Yaska and Ctuchik to Rak Cthol, he sent Zedar to Mal Zeth to work behind the scenes. Zedar was probably the shrewdest of Torak's disciples, and the generals at Mal Zeth gave him an excellent education in tactics and strategy. Torak's heavy-handedness was still much in evidence, but most of the subtlety of the Angarak invasion of the west can be attributed to my father's apostate brother.

After Drasnia had been crushed, the Alorn Council, joined by King Ormik of Sendaria, met at Riva for an emergency session. Before our meetings began, however, I went through the bleak hallways of the Citadel to have a word with the Rivan Warder. There were several things I wanted him to understand.

Most kings select towers for their place of study, probably because 'eminence' suggests elevation. Brand – all of the Brands – have been modest, self-effacing men who know that they're caretakers more than rulers. Brand's study was buried deep inside the Citadel, and there were several meeting-rooms nearby where he could conduct the actual day-to-day business of running the Isle. At least that way he didn't have to climb several flights of stairs to get to his desk.

488

'A word with you, Lord Brand?' I asked him, pausing in the doorway of his slightly cluttered, candle-lit work-room.

'Of course, Lady Polgara,' he replied, rising to his feet. He was very tall, and his shoulders were huge. He held a chair for me, and I sat down. Then he resumed his own seat. 'What can I do for you, my Lady?'

'You can start by dropping all the formality, Brand,' I replied. 'We're too busy for that.'

He smiled. 'Bad habits are hard to break, Pol,' he apologized.

'I've noticed. You're a very polite and civilized man, Brand, so all your instincts are going to command you to defer to Eldrig. He's older, and he's the king of the original Alorn nation. I know that it's always been the custom to let the King of Cherek take the lead in the meetings of the Alorn Council, but this time we're going to set that custom aside. In this particular situation, you outrank the King of Cherek.'

'I don't wear a crown, Pol,' he pointed out. 'Rhodar outranks me, and he doesn't even have a kingdom anymore.'

'You're going to be the Child of Light, Brand. That means that you outrank everybody. I'm not talking about bowing and sitting down first or any of that other nonsense. I'm talking about command. I know that you're diplomatic enough not to offend Eldrig, but let's get your position established right at the outset. The time's going to come when you'll be getting instructions from something far more significant than any earthly king. You're going to be the instrument of the Purpose of the Universe. You'll be issuing some orders that'll come from the Purpose, and we don't want Eldrig to start countermanding your orders. Let's get him into the habit of obedience right at the outset. I've been involved in enough wars to know that command has to come from one source. You can't run a military operation with a committee.'

'Just exactly what's involved in this "Child of Light" business? I'm not too well-versed in theology.'

'The Universe came into being with a Purpose, Brand.'

'Yes, I understand that part. The Gods created it.'

'No. You've got that part backwards. The Universe came first, and *then* the Gods.'

'The priests of Belar don't agree with that.'

'Naturally not. UL *might* have come into existence at the same time as the Universe, but nothing pre-dated it.' I paused. 'That's a *personal* belief of mine, Brand, so it's open to argument. It's beside the point, though.'

489

'Who's UL?'

'The God of the Ulgos. He's the father of the other Gods.'

Brand's eyes grew wide, and he swallowed hard.

'We're getting away from the subject here. The Universe came into being with a Purpose. Then there was a cosmic accident – a star exploded in a place where it wasn't supposed to – and the Purpose was divided. Those two Purposes have been fighting with each other ever since. That's an oversimplification, of course, but you get the point, I'm sure.'

'I've seen lots of family squabbles, Pol.'

'I guess it *is* sort of like a family squabble at that. Anyway, these two Purposes can't meet directly. The whole Universe would explode if they did, so they have to work through surrogates.'

'The Child of Light and the Child of Dark?'

'Exactly. Every now and then these two meet – usually for a very short period of time – about a half-second, actually.'

'You can't have much of a duel in a half-a-second, Pol.'

'Stop thinking of it as a duel, Brand. That's not what it is.'

'That's a relief. Torak's the Child of Dark, isn't he?'

'Usually, yes.'

'A man wouldn't have much chance in a duel with a God, would he?'

'That depends on the man. Since *this* meeting's going to take place during a war, there probably will be a duel – or at least the appearance of a duel. You and Torak will bang your swords off each other for a while, but the EVENT won't have anything to do with that.'

'EVENT?'

'A word we use to describe these meetings. It's sort of like an abbreviation. Don't get carried away with the fact that Torak's a God and you aren't. That has nothing to do with what's going to happen.'

'What *is* going to happen, Pol?'

'You're going to make a choice.'

'A choice? That's all? What are the options?'

'We don't know. *You* will when the time comes, though. Father was the Child of Light once – when he and Bear-shoulders were on the way to Cthol Mishrak. Zedar was the Child of Dark that time, and when they met, father chose *not* to kill Zedar. As it turned out, that was the right choice.'

'What if I choose wrong when the time comes?'

I shrugged. 'We'll lose.'

'*Pol!*' his protest was anguished.

I laid my hand on his. I liked this man. 'Don't worry, Brand. You won't be permitted to make the wrong choice.'

'Then we'll win?'

'That's not certain either. Torak also has to choose. His choice may be better than yours. The two Purposes are very evenly matched. Sometimes one wins, and sometimes the other does.'

'Then I'm not going to be anything but the voice of this Purpose? It makes the choice, and I announce it?'

'No dear one. *You* make the choice.'

'I wish I were dead,' he said glumly.

'That's not one of the choices available to you, Brand. At this point, I don't even think you could kill yourself. Like it or not, you *are* going to meet Torak in Arendia, and you *are* going to make a choice.'

'What if I refuse to make a choice?'

'That's also a choice, Brand. You can't get out of this. Now, stop worrying about the fact that Torak's a God and you aren't. That doesn't make the slightest bit of difference. You'll be equals when the two of you meet. That's all the rank you need. Father and I'll explain this to the others, so there won't be any arguments. You *will* be in command.' I paused. 'We'll put it to the other kings rather gently,' I continued, 'so I don't think you'll need to beat Eldrig over the head with it. A casual announcement that you're the Purpose of the Universe might make him start questioning your sanity.'

'I'm already questioning it, Pol,' he admitted. 'Is this conversation really happening, or am I just imagining it?'

I unfastened a brooch from the neck of my gown and quite deliberately stabbed him in the back of the hand with the pin.

He gave a startled exclamation and jerked his hand back. 'Why did you do that?' he demanded.

'Let it bleed, Brand,' I told him. Then I blotted the drop of blood from his hand with my handkerchief and handed the frilly little piece of cloth to him. 'Keep this tucked away somewhere, dear one,' I instructed. 'You must *never* question your own sanity in this. Any time you start to have doubts, take this out and look at the blood spot. This conversation is *really* happening, and you really *are* the Child of Light – or you will be when the time comes. I'm a physician, Brand, so you can believe me when I tell that you're not insane. Now, go wash that hand, and I'll bandage it for you.'

We held our meetings in the traditional conference room high in one of the towers of Iron-grip's Citadel. A lot of memories crowded in on me there, but I pushed them back to concentrate on the

491

business at hand. Most of our discussions involved a guessing game. Torak had surprised us once, and we couldn't really afford another surprise like that, so we argued at some length about his next probable move. King Rhodar of the lost nation of Drasnia didn't say very much, but he didn't have to. His face was careworn anyway, and his mournful, sorrowing presence was a constant rebuke to all of us and a constant reminder of the consequences of guessing wrong.

Since we couldn't really respond until Torak made his next move, the conference didn't produce anything very meaningful. My only real contribution was the suggestion that it might be the neighborly thing to do to advise the other western kingdoms that the end of the world was at hand.

Father and I left the Isle of the Winds by ship, and we were deposited on a rainy beach on the north side of the Hook of Arendia to begin our search for the elusive Asturians.

After the Mimbrates had destroyed Vo Astur, the Asturian nobility had taken to the woods to engage in centuries of guerrilla warfare. In the Asturian view of the world, shooting a lone Mimbrate traveler in the back with an arrow constituted a major victory to be celebrated around the campfires for weeks on end. The Mimbrates, quite naturally, disapproved of that practice, and so armored knights made periodic sweeps through the forest to locate and destroy those bands of enthusiasts. The Asturians grew quite adept at concealing their encampments, so father and I spent a delightful week and a half searching for the elusive Duke of Asturia, Eldallan. The almost perpetual rain seething down among the trees added whole new dimensions to the word 'uncomfortable'.

Unless driven by hunger, predators normally sit out rainstorms in some sheltered place, but there was one wolf and one owl in that soggy forest who were obliged to move around almost constantly.

Have you any idea at all of just how bad a wet wolf smells when he gets near a campfire? Just the thought of father's fragrance during our search turns my stomach.

As luck had it, a brief break in the weather dissipated the perpetual mist hanging in the forest, and I flew on up above the treetops and saw the smoke rising from a dozen or so campfires some distance off to the east. When we investigated, we found the encampment we'd been searching for.

Given their highly developed sense of romanticism, the costume of choice among the young Asturian 'patriots' consisted of green or brown tunics and hose and rakish caps decorated with long feathers. The Mimbrates had designated them as outlaws, and they were playing the part for all they were worth. Literature has its place, I suppose, but the ballads composed by third-rate poets extolling the exploits of this or that outlaw out to rob rich Mimbrates and to distribute the booty to the poor Asturian peasants set the imaginations of generations of brainless Asturian nobles afire, and they postured and posed in their green clothing and spent hours practicing with their bows, riddling whole battalions of straw dummies dressed in rusty Mimbrate armor with yard-long arrows.

All right, I'm prejudiced against Asturians. So what?

Duke Eldallan and his cohorts were less than cooperative when father and I entered their extensive encampment. We were not exactly taken prisoner, but there were a lot of arrows pointed in our general direction as we approached the rustic 'throne' where Eldallan sat with his eight-year-old daughter, Mayaserana, on his knee.

The Duke of Asturia was a thin man in his early thirties with long, carefully-combed blond hair. He wore forest green, his longbow was handy, and he obviously had a high opinion of himself. He received father's introduction of us with a look of scepticism. My father's customary shabby appearance obviously didn't match the picture of 'a mighty wizard' as laid down in assorted Arendish epics. He might not have believed father, but a short while later he definitely believed me.

He shrugged off the news of the destruction of Drasnia as 'an Alorn problem', and made much of his near-religious obligation to exterminate the Mimbrates. I finally grew tired of his posturing and stepped in. 'Why don't you let me talk with him, father?' I said. 'I know Arends a little better than you do.'

'Gladly,' the Old Wolf grunted.

'Please forgive my father, your Grace,' I said to Eldallan. 'Diplomacy's not one of his strong points.'

Then Eldallan made the mistake of mentioning my former association with the Wacite Arends as if it had been some kind of major moral failing. I decided that since he wanted to be nasty about this, I'd give him more nasty than he was equipped to accept.

'Very well, your Grace,' I said rather coldly, 'I'll *show* you what the Angaraks did to Drasnia, and then I'll leave it up to you to decide if you'd like to have the same thing happen here.'

'Illusions!' he snorted.

'No, your Grace. Not illusions, but reality. I speak as the Duchess of Erat, and no true gentlemen would question the word of a noble-woman – or have I erred in assuming that there *are* gentlemen in Asturia?'

He bridled at that. 'Are you questioning my honor?'

'Aren't you questioning mine?'

I don't think he'd expected that. He choked on it a bit, and then he gave in. 'Very well, your Grace,' he said. 'If you give me your word of honor that what you propose to show me really happened, I'll have no choice but to accept it.'

'Your Grace is too kind.' I gently probed at his mind and found there an unreasoning terror of the notion of being burned alive. That gave me all that I needed.

I set a series of disconnected images before him and compelled him to watch them unfold with the force of my Will. There was enough generalized butchery in those images to keep him from guessing that I was concentrating my efforts on the one thing he feared the most. The seas of blood and the incidental dismember-ments were in the nature of punctuation to the lovingly recreated scenes of screaming Drasnians trapped inside burning buildings or being bodily hurled into great bonfires by laughing Angaraks. I added the customary shrieks of agony and doused him with the sickening odor of burning flesh.

Eldallan began to scream and writhe in his chair, but I still went on and on until I was absolutely certain that he wouldn't argue with us any more. I might have held him there longer, but the presence of his little daughter, Mayaserana, forced me to relent. Mayaserana was a beautiful little girl with dark hair and huge eyes, and her involuntary little screams and sobs as her father twisted and groaned tore at my heart.

'What did you do to my father, bad Lady?' she demanded in an accusing voice when I released Eldallan.

'He'll be fine in just a little bit, dear,' I assured her. 'He just had a nightmare, that's all.'

'But it's daytime – and he isn't even asleep.'

I took her in my arms. 'That happens sometimes, Mayaserana,' I told her. 'He'll be all right.'

After the Duke of Asturia had recovered, father proposed a truce between Asturia and Mimbre, ' – a temporary truce, you understand, just during the present emergency. Of course, if you just happen to find peace with the Mimbrates entertaining, you and Aldorigen might want to consider extending it.'

494

'You're surely not proposing an actual meeting between me and that Mimbrate butcher, are you?'

'Only if you'll both agree to be chained to the walls at opposite ends of the room, Eldallan. I'll make arrangements with the Sendarian ambassador in Vo Mimbre. We'll have the Sendars serve as go-betweens – at least until the Angaraks actually invade Arendia. When that happens, we'll come up with a way to keep you and the Mimbrates at opposite ends of the battlefields.'

Then father and I went on down across the rain-soaked plain of southern Arendia to Vo Mimbre. Once again I was almost over-whelmed with memories. I don't think my father has ever fully understood just how great an attachment I have for Arendia. Arends are a child-like people, and in a very real sense I had been their universal mother for almost six hundred years.

The dark-haired Duke – or 'King' as he preferred it – Aldorigen was terrified of snakes, of all things, and that seriously strained my creativity, since there aren't very many snakes in Drasnia. I'll confess to a deliberate falsehood here. I created an Angarak 'custom' out of whole cloth, and Duke Aldorigen found my imaginary snake pits into which whole Drasnian villages were cast while shrieking in terror entertaining enough to bring him around to our way of thinking.

All right, it was dishonest. Did you want me to suspend the story while we discuss the ethical implications of 'ends justifying the means' for a week or two?

After father had rammed his truce down Aldorigen's throat and had more or less commanded the Sendarian ambassador to serve as liaison between Mimbre and Asturia, we prepared to leave the golden city. Before we left, however, I took a very long look at Aldorigen's sandy-haired son, Korodullin. He was eight or nine years old, as I recall. To be honest, the word 'coincidence' never even occurred to me. I was just a little surprised to discover that the 'bell' which has periodically rung inside my head isn't *always* set off by the descendants of Beldaran and Riva Iron-grip. Other destined arrangements also make it ring. I clearly remember listen-ing to it the first time Relg met Taiba. Oddly, though, I didn't hear any bells the first time I met Durnik.

Aldorigen provided us with horses, and so my father and I, bundled up to ward off that perpetual rain, forded the River Arend about ten leagues downstream from Vo Mimbre and plodded on down through northern Tolnedra to that gleaming island that is Tol Honeth.

When we reached the marble-clad imperial palace, we were taken directly to the emperor without the usual delay. Father's earlier visit had convinced Ran Borune that he was an emissary for the Alorn kings, which wasn't exactly true, though it did have some basis in fact, I suppose. The obliteration of Drasnia had brought the kingdoms of the north to the forefront of Ran Borune's attention, and he hungered for any information anyone could provide. 'Ah, there you are, Belgarath,' he said crisply when we were escorted into his somewhat overly ornate office. 'Dreadful about Drasnia. Please convey my deepest sympathy to Rhodar the next time you see him. Have the Alorns come up with any ideas about where Kal Torak might strike next?'

'Tentatively, your Imperial Majesty,' father replied. 'Oh, this is my daughter Polgara, by the way.'

'Charmed, I'm sure,' the young emperor said perfunctorily. Ran Borune and I were not getting off to a good start. 'I *really* need to know where Torak's going to go, Belgarath. Have you got any spies in his army?'

'I wouldn't exactly call them spies, Ran Borune,' father said a bit sourly. 'Kal Torak doesn't have any non-Angaraks in his army – at least not yet. We haven't seen Melcenes or Dals or Karands among his forces.'

'Have the Alorns made any sort of plans as yet?'

'Nothing very definitive. They're trying to keep defenses in place on all the likely fronts. Our major advantage lies in the mobility of the Alorns. Those Cherek war-boats can put an army down on any beach in the western world in a very short period of time. The defensive forces in Algaria, Cherek, and Sendaria should be sufficient to delay Torak until reinforcements arrive.'

'Are there any clues in those religious writings?'

'The prophecies, you mean?'

'I *hate* that word,' Ran Borune said just a bit absently. 'It absolutely reeks of superstition.'

'Possibly,' father admitted, 'but there are enough correspondences between the Alorn prophecies and the Angarak ones that they might give us some clues about what this fellow who calls himself Kal Torak will try next. A man who thinks he's a God usually tries to fulfill any prophecy that's handy in order to prove his divinity.'

*   *   *

Just a word here. Note that none of us ever came right out and told Ran Borune that the invader from the east was really Torak himself. We maintained the fiction that we were dealing with an Angarak madman instead. There wasn't much point in offending Tolnedran sensibilities by arguing theology with them when there were easier ways to get their cooperation.

'I guess I hadn't thought about that,' Ran Borune conceded. 'Will the Alorns need some of my legions in the north?'

'I don't think so. Thanks all the same.'

'Are you and Lady Polgara planning to stay here for long? Can I offer you the hospitality of the palace here?'

'We appreciate the thought, Ran Borune,' I told him, 'but it might cause you some problems. The Honethites and Vorduvians could make hay of the fact that you're consorting with "heathen sorcerers".'

'I'm the emperor here, Lady Polgara, and I'll consort with whomever I bloody-well please. If the Vorduvians and Honethites don't like it, that's just too bad.' He gave me an odd look. 'You seem quite conversant with our little peculiarities, my Lady.'

'A diversion of mine, your Majesty,' I replied. 'I find that reading Tolnedran political commentary puts me to sleep at night almost as fast as Arendish epics do.'

He winced. 'I think I had that coming, didn't I?' he said ruefully.

'Yes, your Majesty, you did. Look upon it as instructional. Father always tells me that it's our duty to teach up the young.'

'Please,' he said lightly, 'no more thrusts. I surrender.'

'Wise decision there, Ran Borune,' father said. 'People who fence with Pol usually come away leaking from all sorts of places. We'll be staying at the Cherek embassy, I think. I need to move around and contact several people, and an escort of palace spies trailing along behind me might be a little cumbersome. I'll also need to stay in contact with the Alorn kings, and the Cherek ambassador's got a war-boat available. Who's the current Nyissan ambassador?'

'A slithery sort of fellow named Podiss.'

'I'll talk with him. Let's keep Salmissra advised. She's got some resources I might need later on, so I don't want her to be sitting in a corner someplace pouting. We'll keep you advised, so don't waste time putting spies on my trail.'

Then father and I went to the Cherek embassy. Late that night, Beltira's voice reached father just as he was dropping off to sleep. He reported that Torak's forces had marched into Algaria, and then

497

he got down to the bad news. Uncle Beldin had advised the twins that a second Mallorean army under Urvon had massed at the Dalasian port of Dal Zerba and had already begun crossing the Sea of the East to southern Cthol Murgos. Quite clearly, the closing of the caravan routes in both the north *and* in the south had been ordered to keep troop movements a secret. Now we had two Angarak armies to worry about.

Father and I went back to the palace and bullied the emperor's servants into waking him. He wasn't *too* happy about the news we brought him. We suggested that he stay flexible and not commit his forces to either front, and then father and I left for Nyissa.

I'd never been in the land of the snake-people before nor met one of that interminable string of identical Salmissras. The Serpent-God, Issa, unlike the other gods, had not taken several disciples as Torak or our Master had, but had devoted all his love to one handmaiden, the original Salmissra. The notion of extending her life had evidently not occurred to the sluggish Issa, and so the Nyissans had simply replaced her when she'd died. The first qualification had been a physical resemblance to the original, and a lengthy education had imprinted the personality of the first Salmissra on all the candidates. They had good reason to study very hard, since nineteen of those candidates were put to death immediately after the selection of the new Serpent Queen. As a result, one Salmissra was virtually indistinguishable from her predecessors. As father put it, 'If you've met one Salmissra, you've met them all.' I had no real reason to be fond of those Salmissras, but father persuaded me that we might need the rather specialized talents of the Nyissans at some time during the course of the Angarak invasion, so I was civil – barely – when we entered that garish, snake-infested palace in Sthiss Tor.

Salmissra's throne room was a dimly-lighted hall that focused on the enormous statue of the Serpent-God. A dais stood in front of that statue, and Salmissra reclined on a throne that was more couch than chair upon that dais. Before her throne there knelt several dozen yellow-robed eunuchs who chanted slogans of adoration in unison. The Serpent Queen was very pale, almost chalk white. She had glossy black hair and peculiarly colorless eyes. I'll admit that she was beautiful, and her gauze-like gown left very little to the imagination. She received our information with a reptilian indifference, not even bothering to take her eyes from her mirror. 'Why should I involve myself in your war with the Angaraks?' she asked.

'It's not just our war, Salmissra,' I said. 'It concerns all of us.'

'Not me, it doesn't. One of my predecessors discovered the folly of becoming involved in this private feud between the Alorns and the Angaraks. I'm not going to make that same mistake. Nyissa will remain neutral.' Her pale eyes fixed themselves on my face, and I knew – without knowing how I knew – that one day the snake woman and I were going to have a confrontation, and Salmissra's eyes clearly told me that she also knew that it was coming.

My father totally missed that silent interchange. Women have always had ways to communicate with each other that men can't begin to comprehend. Father tried to persuade Salmissra that Urvon would obliterate Nyissa as he passed through on his way north. He was wasting his breath, of course. Salmissra didn't *care* about what happened to Nyissa. Her only concern was herself. That was one of the characteristics her education had hammered into her. Her personal survival – and her personal appetites – were all that mattered to her. I realized that, even if father didn't, so I cast my parting remarks to her on a personal level, suggesting that she might find being bent backward over a blood-soaked altar while several Grolims carved out her heart rather unpleasant.

That got her attention, even if nothing else did.

As father and I were leaving her musty-smelling palace, I asked him a question that'd been nagging at me just a bit. 'Have the Nyissans compiled any kind of reference-works on their pharmacology?'

'I don't know,' he replied with a shrug. 'Why?'

'They have some very interesting herbal compounds. Salmissra was absolutely awash with about six or eight that I could detect.'

'Really?' He seemed a bit surprised. 'I thought that was just her natural personality.'

'It is, but she's taking some things that enhance it. She has some *very* interesting appetites. When this is all over, I might just come down here and investigate. Some of those herbs might be very useful.'

'Most of them are poisonous, Pol.'

'Lots of things are poisonous, father. An overdose of most of the healing herbs can be fatal. Proper dosage is the key to herbal medicine.'

'Your reputation as a physician might start to deteriorate if you begin experimenting with poison, Pol.'

'Experimentation is the source of all medical advances, father. You lose a few patients along the way, but you save more in the long run.'

'Sometimes you're as cold-blooded as Salmissra is, Pol.'

'Are you only just beginning to realize that, father? I'm disappointed in you.'

Well of *course* I didn't mean it. Sometimes I wonder about you.

CHAPTER 31

'That wasn't particularly fruitful, was it, Pol?' father grumbled as he and I left Salmissra's gaudy palace and walked out into the rainy streets.

'Did you really expect her to welcome you with open arms, father?' I asked him. 'You've never been all that popular in Nyissa, you know.'

'Well,' he sighed, 'at least she's not going to welcome Urvon either. Maybe that's the best we can hope for. Let's go to Maragor and see if we can get Mara's attention.'

It was winter, the rainy season in Nyissa, but the climate change which had followed Torak's Eclipse made it a little hard to distinguish one rainy season from another. I absolutely *hate* flying in the rain, but we didn't really have much choice.

We followed the River of the Serpent up to the rapids near the headwaters and then veered north to cross the mountains to haunted Maragor's southern frontier. We saw several of the rude mining camps that lined Maragor's southern frontier. I clinically noted that there weren't any camps north of that border. The gold-hunters were obsessed men, but not *that* obsessed.

The seething rain made it difficult for us to see the rolling basin that had been Maragor, but father knew the way, so I simply followed him to Mar Amon. When we were just outside the ruins, he dipped his falcon wings a couple of times, and we descended to a grove of winter-stripped beech trees that overlooked the ruin and resumed our own forms. 'This isn't going to be pleasant, Pol,' father said glumly. 'Mara's even crazier than Torak, and he's filled Maragor from end to end with phantoms he's dredged up out of his own

501

insanity. You're going to see some fairly gruesome things, I'm afraid.'

'I've heard all the stories, father.'

'Stories are one thing, Pol. Actually seeing and hearing these apparitions is a little more hair-raising.'

'I can deal with it, Old Wolf.'

'Don't get over-confident, Pol. Crazy or not, Mara's still a God, and the sense of his presence is still overwhelming. The Master's presence is fairly gentle, but Mara tends to bowl people over just by putting in an appearance. Did you happen to come across Chaldan while you were in Arendia?'

'No. Chaldan only talks to his priests – at least that's what the priests say.'

He nodded. 'Priests are pretty much the same the world over. They seem to feel that their exclusive contact with God gives them a certain job security. If just any old peasant can talk with God, the priests are redundant, and they might have to go out and get honest work.'

'You're in a cynical humor today.'

'Blame it on the weather. Anyway, brace yourself. Our meeting with Mara's likely to be moderately unpleasant. Gods hold grudges for a long time, and Mara still blames all of us for not coming to the aid of the Marags when the Tolnedrans invaded Maragor. I've met him several times, and he knows who I am – unless he's forgotten me. I may have to lie to him just a bit here. We haven't been specifically ordered to come here, so we're sort of doing what we think the Master wants us to do. Just to be on the safe side, I'd better tell Mara that we're acting on instructions. Mara's not crazy enough to go up against the Master, so he won't automatically obliterate us. But be careful here, Pol. Don't drop your guard, and whatever you do, *don't* let any random chunks of gold lying about distract you. If you even so much as *think* about gold, Mara will erase your mind.'

'I'm not really that greedy, father.'

'Really? Where did you get all the money you keep pulling out of your sleeve when you want to buy something, then?'

'Prudent investments, father. If you cultivate money – prune it, water it, and fertilize it – it'll grow for you the same as roses or radishes will. Don't worry, Old Wolf. I'm not really interested in random gold.'

'Good. Let's go on into the city and see if I can talk some sense into Mara.'

502

Mar Amon is a very disturbing sort of place, not only because of the multitude of mutilated ghosts infesting it, but also because it's part reality and part illusion. Mara has in effect rebuilt the city, replacing destroyed buildings with images of what they were before the Tolnedrans came. The buildings are insubstantial, but you can't tell that by looking at them. As father and I followed that spiraling street that wound its way toward the central temple, we saw horrors enough to last a lifetime. The Tolnedran legionnaires are normally paid in brass coins, so they seldom see gold. The ground of Maragor was littered with it, and all semblance of discipline collapsed. The legions became nothing more than a greedy, mindless mob, and mobs commit atrocities. Mara almost lovingly recreated the victims of those atrocities and unleashed them to forever keep Maragor inviolate. I heartily approve of the chastisement Nedra imposed on his more rampantly greedy worshipers after the invasion of Maragor. A merchant prince from Tol Honeth can't help thinking about gold when it's lying all about him, and greed is an open door to insanity in Maragor. The monastery at Mar Terrin *sounds* like a very nice idea, but it is, in fact, the most hideous prison on the face of the earth. The inmates of that prison are condemned – not to death, but to perpetual insanity.

'BELGARATH!' Mara's howl was more than thunder. 'WHY HAST THOU INTRUDED THYSELF UPON MY GRIEF?' The weeping God was immense, and in his arms he held the body of a slaughtered child.

'It is in obedience to our Master's command that my daughter Polgara and I have sought thee out, Lord Mara,' father lied smoothly. 'Thy brother Torak hath mounted an invasion of the west, Lord. Aldur, our Master, hath instructed us to advise thee of the Dragon-God's coming.'

'LET HIM COME,' Mara replied, still weeping. 'HIS ANGARAKS ARE NO MORE IMMUNE TO MADNESS THAN ARE THE MUR-DERING CHILDREN OF NEDRA.'

Father bowed. 'As thou seest fit, Lord Mara,' he said. 'Thus my daughter and I have fulfilled the task lain upon us by our Master. Now will we depart and trouble thee no more.'

'That was quick,' I muttered to him as we retraced our steps through the illusion called Mar Amon.

Father shrugged. 'Actually, it turned out even better than I'd hoped.'

'I didn't exactly follow that,' I admitted.

'Maragor's sort of a back door to Tolnedra,' he explained. 'Urvon might be planning to come through northern Cthol Murgos and invade Tolnedra from this direction instead of coming up through Nyissa. Now Mara knows he's coming, so we've closed that door. Urvon's army might be sane when they come into Maragor, but they'll be raving madmen when they go out.' He looked rather pleased with himself. 'I might have hoped for a little more commitment from Mara, but he'll cover this front for us, and I'll settle for that. Let's go have a talk with the Gorim. We might as well advise everybody about what's happening at the same time. Then we won't have to make this trip again.'

'Are we going to enlist the Ulgos, then?'

'I don't think they'd care to attend, but let's not insult them by neglecting their invitation.'

'Busy-work.'

'That one missed me, Pol.'

'We're just running around telling people about a party they won't be interested in attending.'

'Call it diplomatic courtesy, Pol.'

'I'd rather call it a waste of time.'

'There's an element of that in all diplomacy. Let's go to Prolgu, shall we?'

The endless rain which had so bedeviled the low country during the years since Torak's Eclipse had fallen as snow in the mountains of holy Ulgo, but father and I didn't have to make the trip on foot, so we avoided that particular unpleasantness. Flying when it's snowing is tiresome, but not nearly as tiresome as wading through hip-deep snowbanks. It also avoided encounters with the frolicsome creatures who live in the mountains of Ulgoland.

Prolgu, of course, is a mountain more than a city. The Algars constructed that mountain they call the Stronghold, but the Ulgos integrated Prolgu with the mountain where the original Gorim met with UL and shamed the father of the Gods into accepting the outcasts of the world.

We came to earth in an abandoned city like none other in all the world. Most ancient cities were ruined as the result of war, and war leaves some fairly visible marks on the walls and buildings. Prolgu, however, had not been destroyed by any human agency. The Ulgos had simply moved down into the caves beneath the city, leaving their houses standing intact and vacant behind them. An abandoned city would normally attract looters, but I rather think it might have taken a very special kind of looter to trek to Prolgu to wander through those empty streets in search of valuables. The mountains

504

of Ulgo quite literally teem with creatures that look upon humans as something to eat. Even the mice are dangerous, or so the story goes.

I've rarely had occasion to go to Prolgu. My family's made a practice of dividing up our labors, and maintaining contact with the Ulgos has always been one of my father's tasks. We wandered, seemingly without purpose, through the snow-clogged streets with the blizzard swirling about us as evening approached and the light began to fade.

'Ah, there it is,' father said finally, pointing at a house that seemed no different from any of the others. 'This snow isn't making things any easier.'

'I don't think it's supposed to, father.'

'Was that meant to be funny?'

'No, not particularly.'

Like all the houses of Prolgu, the one we entered had long since lost its roof, and there was a dusting of snow on the floor when we entered. Father led me to a central room and scraped here and there with his foot for several minutes. 'Well, finally,' he muttered to himself when he found the flagstone he'd been looking for. He picked up a large rock from one corner of the room and banged on the flagstone three times.

Nothing happened.

He banged again, and the sound seemed somehow hollow.

Then there was a low grinding sound, and the very large, flat stone tilted upward to reveal a dimly lighted space beneath. '*Belgarath*,' a hollow sounding voice came from down there, '*Yad ho, groja UL.*'

'It's a formality,' father muttered to me. Then he said, '*Yad ho, groja UL. Yad mar ishum.*'

'*Veed mo, Belgarath. Mar ishum Ulgo.*'

'We've been invited to enter,' father said to me. 'Have you studied the Ulgo language at all?'

'Not intensively. The grammar's Dalish, isn't it?'

'Yes. It's more ancient than Morind or Karandese, though. The languages of isolated peoples tend to petrify – and you don't get much more isolated than the Ulgos. Let's go on down and talk to the Gorim.'

'You'll have to translate for me, father.'

'Not really. The Gorim speaks our language.'

'That's helpful.'

The light in the caverns of Ulgo is of chemical origin, and it's very dim. I couldn't see how big the caves were, but the echoes

505

strongly suggested that they were vast. I'm never entirely comfortable in the Ulgo caves. The image of moles keeps intruding on me. Theirs is an orderly society, though, and they live in neat apartments cut into the walls of long, dim galleries, and they go about their daily occupations in much the same way as they would if they lived above ground. I rather wryly conceded that there was at least one benefit to living underground. The weather was never a problem.

For the most part, the Ulgos ignored my father and me as we passed through their galleries. We skirted several enormous chasms and went along one edge of a dark lake as big as an underground sea. That sea was fed by waterfalls cascading down from the surface to whisper endlessly in the dimness. The echoes of those waterfalls joined with the echoes of the Hymn to UL sung at regular intervals by the devout, and those combined echoes turn all of Ulgo into one vast cathedral.

The house of the Gorim of Ulgo is constructed of a marble so fine that it puts the stately buildings of imperial Tol Honeth to shame. It sits on a small islet in the center of a shallow underground lake, and it's reached by a formal-looking causeway. The white-robed and white-bearded old Gorim, probably the holiest man in the world, stood waiting for us at the far end of that causeway. I hadn't been in the Ulgo caves in over a millennium, but this Gorim was very much like his predecessors.

'It's been a while, Belgarath,' the Gorim greeted my father when we reached the isle.

'I know, Gorim,' father apologized. 'I've been busy, so I've been sort of letting my social obligations slide. You haven't met my daughter, have you?'

'Sacred Polgara? I don't believe so.'

'Sacred? You might want to wait until you know her a little better before you start assigning descriptions to her, Gorim. Pol's a little on the prickly side.'

'That'll do, father,' I told him. Then I curtsied to the Gorim. '*Iad Hara, Gorim an Ulgo,*' I greeted him.

'Dalish?' He seemed startled. 'I haven't heard anyone speak the Dalish language in over a century. You're gifted, Polgara.'

'Probably not, Holy Gorim,' I replied. 'My studies have led me down some fairly obscure paths. I don't speak Ulgo as yet, though, so I fell back on Dalish. My accent probably isn't too good.'

'It's close. You might want to spend a month or two at Kell if you feel the need of polishing it.'

'*After* the current crisis, Pol,' father cautioned.

506

'Is there another crisis afoot?' the Gorim asked.

'Isn't there always?' father said sourly. 'This one's a bit more serious, though.'

'Let's go inside,' Gorim suggested. 'If the world's coming to an end, maybe I'd better be sitting down when you tell me about it.'

I took to the Gorim of Ulgo immediately. He was a kindly old man with an understated sense of humor. He didn't laugh very much when father told him that Torak had come out of Ashaba and led his Malloreans across the land-bridge, however. 'This is troubling, Belgarath,' he said with a frown.

'Truly,' father agreed. 'May I speak bluntly?'

'Of course.'

'The people of Ulgo aren't warriors, and they're not accustomed to the world above. If nothing else, sunlight would probably be blinding to them – if the sun ever comes out again.'

'I didn't exactly follow that, Belgarath.'

'There was a change in the weather after Torak's Eclipse,' father explained. 'It's been raining more or less continually for the past fifteen or so years.'

'Did we anticipate that?'

'We probably should have. Our prophecies mention the rain, but we thought they were talking about some passing rain squall, not a semi-permanent climate change. Sometimes I get a little cross about being tampered with. Everything's written down in the Darine and the Mrin, but I'm not permitted to understand what I'm reading until that overly-clever Necessity's jolly-well ready to have me understand it. I honestly believe he thinks he's funny.'

Gorim smiled faintly. 'Now, there's a concept we might want to investigate,' he said.

'I'd rather not,' father said in a grumpy voice. 'I don't want to come to grips with the idea that the Universe is some vast, obscure joke.' He shook his head. 'What happened in Drasnia's a fair indication that we're looking at a very messy war, Gorim. Your people are devout, and the violence that's staring us in the face isn't the kind of thing they're equipped to deal with. The Alorns, Tolnedrans, and Arends are built for this kind of thing, so why don't we just let them deal with it? We'll keep you advised, and when Torak starts moving his army across Ulgoland, we'll give you enough warning so that you can seal up the mouths of your caves and leave the Angaraks to the Algroths, Hrulgin, and Eldrakyn.'

'I shall consult with Holy UL,' Gorim said. 'The circumstances might prompt him to set aside his distaste for violence.'

507

'That's entirely up to him, Gorim,' father said. 'I've done many foolish things in my life, but trying to tell UL what to do isn't going to be one of them.'

Our conversation became general after that, and the Gorim's servants brought us supper. Ulgo cooking is slightly bland, but I kept my opinion about that to myself. I wasn't entirely certain whether or not the Ulgos might have religious objections to herbs and spices.

After we'd eaten, father and the Gorim talked for a while, and then the Old Wolf and I were provided with rooms where we could sleep. I was just drifting off when mother's voice came to me. 'Welcome to Ulgo, Pol,' she said.

'You sound like a resident, mother.'

'Naturally,' she said. 'Where else did you think I was?'

'I didn't really think about it. I suppose I thought you were everywhere.'

'These are caves, Pol, and a cave's very much like a den, wouldn't you say?'

'I hadn't thought of that, I guess.'

'Obviously. Holy UL wants to speak with us. Come along. I'll guide you.'

I rose and dressed, and then I quietly left the Gorim's house. Mother's voice led me through the labyrinthine maze of galleries out to the edge of that underground city. The passageways we entered there showed fewer and fewer signs of human modification, and after I'd squeezed my way through a narrow embrasure, the rubble littering the uneven floor was a fair indication that we were in unexplored territory.

Then, just as I rounded a sharp turn, the sense of mother's presence in my mind was suddenly gone – or more accurately, it had moved. Mother was just ahead of me, and now she was really there. The Ulgos light their subterranean world by mixing two chemicals that then give off a phosphorescent kind of glow. In this as yet unexplored gallery, the walls themselves glowed. That may have also been some chemical reaction, but I rather doubt it.

Tawny-haired and golden-eyed, mother sat quite calmly on a simple three-legged stool in a neat little room that contained a bed, a table and a small cooking stove. The walls were unfinished, and mother's cooking utensils and dishes were neatly stacked on a ledge behind the stove. To put it succinctly, this was not a room; it was a den.

Mother rose to her feet and held out her arms to me, and I literally flew to embrace her. We clung to each other for quite some time, and I'll admit that I cried. Then she gently sat me at her small, rough table and made tea for us.

'You said that UL wanted to speak with us, mother,' I reminded her as we sat facing each other with our hands intertwined on the table-top.

'He's giving us a bit of time to get used to each other, Pol. UL has an exquisite sense of propriety, so he's giving us this private time. How's *he* been?' Mother almost never used father's name when speaking of him.

'Father never changes, mother. You should know that.'

'We can always hope.' Then she laughed, and mother very seldom laughs. 'And Beldin and the twins?'

'They're still the same too. We're a very strange family, you know. We exist outside of time, so we don't change just because a few thousand years have passed.'

'*You're* going to change just a little rather soon.'

'Oh?'

'You and I are going to become *very* close.'

'You're being cryptic, mother.'

'It's the way of wolves to be cryptic.'

Then one of the walls of mother's den began to glow with a soft, filmy light, and the Father of the Gods stepped out of the solid rock. I'd see him before, of course – when Beldaran had died and he'd come for her – but I'd been so distraught that I'd never been positive that he'd really been there. His presence filled me with awe. He looked very much like our Master, old and white bearded, but he seemed more robust – even muscular.

'Ah,' mother said, rising calmly, 'there you are. Would you like a cup of tea?' Her almost domestic greeting startled me.

'An it please thee, Poledra,' the God responded, taking a seat at the table.

'You remember Polgara, of course,' mother said to him.

The ancient God inclined his head slightly to me, and then he fixed me with a penetrating gaze that probably saw everything. 'Thou art to be commended, Poledra,' he said to mother. 'Thou has wrought a masterpiece.'

'She *did* turn out rather well, didn't she?' mother replied modestly.

'She is equal – and more than equal – to her task.' Then he looked at me again. 'Well met, Polgara,' he greeted me. 'How fares thine ancient father?'

'He is well, most Holy,' I replied. 'The matter currently at hand

509

doesn't give him much leisure to pursue his bad habits, so he isn't destroying his health the way he usually does.'

He actually laughed at that, and I began to feel a bit more at ease.

'I have summoned thee for a reason, Polgara,' he said then. 'Much as I delight in exchanging pleasantries with thee, something will soon come to pass of which thou must be aware, lest the sudden surprise unseat thy reason.'

'That sounds ominous, most Holy.'

'Methinks it will not be so, Polgara. Thou hast ever been close to thy mother, but in this particular time thou wilt be even closer than thou and thy sister were whilst ye were both still enwombed.'

I gave him a puzzled look.

'It hath long been the practice of the members of thy family to assume forms other than thine own.'

'Yes,' I admitted.

'Necessity now requires that thou and thy mother assume the same form.'

'We've done that already, most Holy. We've spent many happy hours flying together as owls.'

'Thou has misperceived my meaning, Polgara. When I spake of "the same form", I was not speaking of two separate owls. There will be but one owl, and it shall encompass both of ye within its substance. In short, at the proper moment shall ye both in combination create the image of but a single owl, and all simultaneous shall ye both cause your separate beings to flow into that image.'

'Is that *possible*?' I exclaimed.

'My son Aldur asked that self-same question,' he said. 'Thy thought is much as his.'

'To what end, most Holy?' I asked, puzzled. 'What's the purpose of this experiment?'

'In this merging shalt thou and thy mother become so totally entwined and closed in that no hint of thy presence – either to the eye *or* to the mind – shall escape the enclosed sphere of your combined being. Thus, no man or God shall be aware of the fact that what he says or does is being heard and observed.'

'Truly? What an amazing thing! And who is to be honored by having mother and me spy on him?'

'Who else, Polgara? Thou and thy mother will seek out the rusting habitation of my son, Torak, which even now doth roll and rattle across the plains of Algaria. My son is very lonely, as he hath been since he raised Aldur's Orb and with its power did rend the earth asunder. Now is he outcast and despiséd, and he doth feel his isolation most keenly. Oft doth he talk at some length with his disciples – random talk with no purpose other than to fend off his aching sense of isolation. At this particular time, his most constant confidant is Zedar the apostate, and their conversations are wide ranging.'

I took it up from there. 'Then mother and I will perch in the rafters of his rusty tin palace and eavesdrop on all his plans, strategies, and goals?'

'The information thou must obtain doth have no bearing on military matters, Polgara. Torak knows of thee. Indeed, thou and thy father do fill his thoughts. He has a design of which thou *must* be aware. Thine awareness of that design shall be a preparation for a choice which thou wilt be obliged to make at some day in the future. I would not alarm thee for all this world, but the fate of the universe shall hinge upon thy choice.'

Holy UL may not have intended to alarm me, but he did nonetheless. 'Couldst thou not advise me of thy son's design, most Holy?' I asked. 'Coming face to face with Torak – even if he can't see me – isn't the sort of thing I look forward to.'

'Thou art braver than whole armies, Polgara,' he said, 'and we all have supreme confidence in thee.'

'I'll be with you, Pol,' mother assured me. 'I won't let Torak hurt you.'

'I'm not really worried about that, mother, I'd just rather not be compelled to look into that diseased mind.' I realized what I'd just said. 'Nothing personal intended there, most Holy,' I apologized to UL.

'Thou hast not offended me, Polgara.' Then he sighed. 'Torak hath not always been as he is now,' he said sadly. 'Through no fault of its own, the Orb hath brutalized and corrupted my son. He is lost to me and to his brothers, Polgara, and his loss doth sear our souls.' Then he rose to his feet. 'Thy mother – as always – shall instruct thee in this. Be guided by her, and steel thine heart for that which thou art doomed to discover.'

And then he was gone.

'He didn't even touch his tea,' mother complained.

Father and I left the caverns of Ulgo the following morning, and when we came out once more into the snow-clogged and empty city of Prolgu, he suggested that we might as well have a look at Torak's army before returning to Riva. I didn't come right out and say it, but his proposal startled me just a bit. In ordinary times father can best be described as a monument to indolence. Once I even heard uncle Beldin apologize to the twins for a temporary lapse in his own industriousness by saying, 'Sorry, brothers, I'm feeling sort of Belgarathy today.' The twins, of course, knew exactly what he meant by that. When a situation arises that requires his attention, though, father can go for weeks with little food and almost no sleep at all. His almost superhuman endurance in those situations never fails to astound me. As a physician, I know that 'storing up sleep' is a physically impossible absurdity. Father, however, has never made a study of medicine, so the term 'physical impossibility' doesn't have much meaning for him.

Now there's something for you to think about. If you don't know that you *can't* do something, isn't there a remote possibility that you'll go ahead and do it anyway in absolute defiance of physical law? That might be one of the drawbacks of education. If you don't *know* that you can't pick yourself up by the scruff of the neck and hold yourself at arm's length, maybe you can.

I wonder if I could get Mandorallen to try that.

When father and I flew on down out of the Ulgo mountains, we were both pleased to discover that the rain had temporarily let up, though the sky remained cloudy and threatening.

There's a kind of unreality about the world when it's viewed from a great height. Things which have enormous importance to those on the ground seem to shrink into insignificance. Men and their animals look like tiny creeping insects, and I've yet to see a national boundary etched across the face of the earth. I was startled nonetheless by the sheer size of the Angarak army crawling across the bland face of the Algarian plain. It's been estimated that Torak invaded Drasnia with a half-million soldiers, and his campaign there hadn't significantly reduced that number. As father and I drifted overhead, we saw the Algar cavalry units busily correcting that with their typical slash and run tactics. The folded – even wrinkled – surface of the plain provided many places of concealment for the small cavalry units, and they could – and did – come boiling out of those gullies and ravines at a dead run to amputate bits and pieces of the Angarak army as Torak doggedly lumbered southward toward the Stronghold. Taken individually, these little nicks and cuts weren't really significant, but viewed in the aggregate, they could best be described as a continuing hemorrhage. I doubt that Torak even realized it, but he was slowly bleeding to death as he plodded south. The Angarak attempts to pursue and chastise their attackers only made things worse, since the Angarak pursuers rarely returned. I saw cavalry tactics at their finest down there. The initial assault of the Algar horsemen was relatively meaningless – a slap in the face, so to speak. Its only purpose was to sting the crack units of Angarak cavalry into pursuit – a pursuit that drew them into ambushes laid for them in various shallow ravines out beyond the edge of the main body of the army. Cho-Ram's horsemen were methodically skimming the cream off Torak's army.

When that process started to become tedious, the Algars entertained themselves by stampeding oceans of cattle right over the top of the assembled Malloreans, Murgos, Nadraks and Thulls. From a strategic point of view, Algaria was nothing more than a vast trap, and the Dragon-God had sprung it on himself.

It went on and on and on, tedious repetitions of the same ghastly little play. After a day or so, I'd seen enough, but father lingered. He seems to revel in that sort of thing for some reason.

On the third evening we flew some distance out to the flank of the invading army, and after we'd settled to earth I rather tartly told my bloodthirsty parent that I'd seen enough.

'I suppose you're right, Pol,' he said almost regretfully. 'We'd probably better get on back to the Isle of the Winds to let the Alorns know what's afoot.' Then he laughed. 'You know, I think we all underestimated Algar Fleet-foot. This country of his is a stroke of pure genius. He deliberately turned his people into nomads so that there wouldn't be any towns. The whole of Algaria's nothing but a vast emptiness with grass growing on it. The Algars don't have towns to defend, so they can give up huge pieces of their country without a second thought. They know that after the Angaraks have moved on, they can return. The only place of any significance in the whole silly kingdom is the Stronghold, and that's not even a city. It's nothing but bait.'

'I always rather liked Algar,' I admitted. 'Under different circumstances, I might have set my cap for him. He could have made a very interesting husband.'

'*Polgara!*' Father actually sounded shocked, and I laughed about that for quite some time – long enough, anyway, to make him grouchy. I *love* to do that to him.

The weather went to pieces again that night, and father and I left Algaria the next morning in a drizzling rain. We crossed the Sendarian mountains and arrived at Riva on the Isle of the Winds two days later.

The Alorn Kings were most concerned about the second Angarak army commanded by Urvon. I guess that you can't really enjoy a war if you have to keep looking back over your shoulder for unexpected enemies. The Alorns were also a bit upset when father suggested that we pick up our headquarters and move it to Tol Honeth. Alorns can be such children sometimes. They had this splendid war going on, and they selfishly didn't want to share it.

I now knew Brand well enough to speak candidly with him. 'Aren't we being just a little blasé about this, my friend?' I suggested. 'You're going to meet a God in single combat, and you're shrugging it off as if it were some meaningless little chore – like fixing a fence or chopping wood for the evening fire.'

'There's not much point in getting excited about it, Pol,' he said in his deep, soft voice. 'It's going to happen whether I like it or not. I can't hide and I can't run away, so why should I lose any sleep over it?'

'For my sake, couldn't you *simulate* worrying about it?'

His face creased into an expression of anticipated terror that was absolutely grotesque. 'How's this?' he asked me.

I couldn't help but laugh. 'I give up,' I said. Brand didn't *look* very much like Kamion had, but there were some distinct similarities in their behavior, and some even greater similarities in their relationship with me.

'Good,' he said. 'My jaws are starting to lock up, so I don't think I can hold this expression for long.'

'Your wife's name is Aren, isn't it?'

'Yes. Why?'

'I think she and I'd better get acquainted. You and I are going to be spending quite a bit of time together for several years, so I'd like to make sure she doesn't break out in a bad case of jealousy.'

'Aren's a sensible woman. She knows I wouldn't do anything improper.'

'Brand,' I said quite firmly, 'I'm sure you're a good administrator and a fearsome warrior, but you don't know very much about women.'

'I've been married to Aren for almost twenty years, Pol,' he objected.

'That has absolutely nothing to do with it, Brand. She won't be nearly as attractive if she suddenly turns bright green, and you won't be nearly as robust if she starts feeding you boiled hay for the next twenty years.'

'She wouldn't do that – would she?'

'Let's play it safe, Brand.' I thought about it. 'When you introduce

514

me to Aren, introduce me as "Ancient Polgara". Let's make an issue of my age.'

'Be serious, Pol. You're not old.'

'Darlin' boy,' I said, fondly patting his cheek. 'In actuality, though, I just turned two thousand, eight hundred and sixty seven. Feel free to flaunt that number in Aren's face. No woman in her right mind is jealous of an old crone.'

'Anybody who calls you that will answer to me, Pol,' he said fiercely.

'We're getting along better and better, Brand.' I smiled at him. 'This is just a subterfuge to pull Aren's teeth before she bites you.'

'I think you're exaggerating the danger, Pol, but I'll be guided by you in this matter.'

'An' aren't y' the dearest boy-o in th' whole wide world t' say so?'

'I'm sorry, Pol, but I don't understand why you're speaking so oddly.'

'It's a long story, Brand – a *very* long story. Someday when we have lots of time, I'll tell it to you.'

After father and I'd bullied the Alorn kings into moving their headquarters to Tol Honeth, he and I went to the Stronghold to have a look at the defenses.

There was an unpleasant surprise waiting for me when we reached the Stronghold. My recent meetings with Gods had filled me with the sense of Destiny and Purpose that implies order. It does not, however, take pure accident into account. Garel, heir to Iron-grip's throne, had ridden out with some Algar friends to scout the surrounding grasslands for advance parties of the approaching invaders. Garel's horse had stumbled, and Garel had been thrown from his saddle. Everyone who rides a horse falls off now and then. It's embarrassing, but usually nothing more. This time, however, Garel landed wrong, and the fall broke his neck, killing him instantly.

His wife, Aravina, was nearly mad with grief, and her mother-in-law, Adana, seemed to be at her wits' end trying to deal with that. My approach was somewhat simpler. I drugged Aravina into near insensibility and kept her that way. My primary concern – as always – was the little boy, Gelane. I've had a lot of practice comforting little boys over the centuries, so I knew what had to be done. Someday, perhaps, I'll discover a way to deal with my own sorrow.

Torak's army was approaching the Stronghold, however, so I didn't really have the leisure to grieve. Gelane was almost six years

515

old now, but that really isn't very old. The current situation, however, dictated a break in tradition. I sat Gelane down and told him just exactly who he really was.

The childhood and early adolescence of an orphaned heir has always been the most dangerous time in my ongoing task. I'd taken an oath to defend and protect the Rivan line, and a five- or six-year-old boy whose father has died is the sole receptacle of that blood-line. Little girls are sensible. Their period of irrationality comes later. Little boys, on the other hand, become irrational almost as soon as they learn to walk. Garion, for example, took up rafting on a pond at Faldor's farm without bothering to learn how to swim first. If I sometimes seem a bit hysterical, you can probably lay the blame for that condition on about fourteen centuries of trying to keep little boys from killing themselves. It was in the hope of impressing Gelane with the importance of being at least a little bit careful that I told him of his heritage, stressing the fact that if he managed to get himself killed, the line would die with him. He seemed to understand, but with little boys, you never really know.

Then came that rainy evening when mother's voice pulled my attention from the passages of the Mrin Codex that seemed to concentrate on the current situation. 'Polgara,' she said in an oddly gentle tone, 'it's time. Come up to the northern battlements. I'll meet you there.'

I laid the scroll aside and left my room deep inside the thick walls of the Stronghold to climb the seemingly endless stairs up to the parapet atop the mountainous structure.

It was drizzling rain, and there was just enough wind blowing to make things decidedly unpleasant up there. Mother, garbed in that plain brown peasant dress, stood at the battlements looking out into the rainy night. She was actually there, and I wasn't as yet that accustomed to her real presence.

'I'm here, mother,' I said.

'Good,' she replied, her golden eyes a mystery. 'Just relax, Pol. UL told me exactly what to do, so follow my lead as we do this.'

'Of course.' I was apprehensive, nonetheless.

'It won't hurt, Pol,' she said, smiling faintly.

'I know, but doing something for the first time always makes me just a little nervous.'

'Look upon it as an adventure, Pol. Now, then, first we make the image of the owl, and the details have to match rather closely – down to the last feather, actually.'

It took us quite a while that first time. We were both familiar

516

with the generic owl, but we had to reconcile a number of minute differences to form the image of an individual bird.

'What do you think?' mother asked after we'd dealt with several inconsistencies.

'It looks owlish enough to me.'

'I rather thought so myself. Now then, we have to do this simultaneously, so don't hurry. The actual merger's going to start before we enter the image. It begins in the instant we become fluid, or so UL tells me, and the merger's almost complete *before* we go into the bird-shape.'

'I think I see why, yes.'

'This won't be easy for you, Pol. I've been inside your mind often enough to be very familiar with you, but you'll be encountering things you haven't experienced before. I wasn't born human, so there's a lot of wolf left in me. I have a few instincts you probably won't like.'

I smiled faintly. 'I'll try to remember that.'

'All right, then. Let's begin.'

I can't really describe it, so I won't even try. There's a moment during the process of changing form that I hadn't really paid much attention to. It's that very brief instant when your entire being is in transition from your own form to that other one. Mother's use of the term 'fluid' is really quite precise. In a sense, you're melting down so that you can flow from one form to the other. It was at that point that mother and I merged, and it was our combined awareness that flowed into our owl.

Mother's suggestion that I might find her a bit strange was a serious understatement, but I think she overlooked the fact that even though I'd never adopted the form of a wolf, I was, nonetheless, hereditarily part wolf myself at the deepest levels of my being.

I rather suspect that merging was easier for me than it'd been for mother. I still remembered that time before Beldaran and I'd been born, so close proximity – even union – was not totally alien to me. On second thoughts, though, mother had probably been born as one of a litter, so she'd been through that herself.

An idle thought came to me even as mother and I flowed into the owl, and the answer, naturally, was right there. I *did*, as a matter of fact, have aunts and uncles I'd never known, and now I *did* know them – and love them – even as mother had when they were all playful puppies.

We preened our feathers almost absently as we grew accustomed to our union, and then, our thoughts unified, we rose on snowy wings into the rain-swept darkness.

We flew out toward the north, and we soon saw the smouldering campfires of the Angarak army which had settled for the night not three leagues from the Stronghold. We continued on to the center of that huge encampment, and there we spied the iron pavilion of the Dragon-God. Silently we settled on the ornamental battlements. Of course, everything about the pavilion was ornamental. The whole thing was no more than a decoration stacked atop a very large wagon. Torak's ego was even more grotesquely expanded than we'd imagined.

We peered around with our large, golden eyes, and we spied an embrasured window near the top of one of the towers, and we found that detail not only amusing but convenient. A few wing beats lifted us to that embrasure, and our clawed feet caught its lower edge. Then we wormed our way inside, enclosing ourselves as we did so – enclosing so completely that we were turned all inward. It was that inward turning, of course, that made us invisible and permitted no stray thought to escape to warn Torak of our presence.

'I am ill at ease, Zedar.' The voice was hollow, echoing, and we immediately saw why. Torak lounged on his iron throne almost in a posture of repose, but his maimed face was still enclosed in that polished steel mask. The mask that hid his maiming had become a part of him.

'It is always thus before a battle, Master,' Zedar replied. 'I share thy disquiet.'

'Can the reports we have received of the nature of this Algar fortress indeed be true?' Torak asked in his harsh, hollow voice.

'The Alorns are a stupid people, Master,' Zedar sneered. 'Set any empty, meaningless task before them and they will mindlessly pursue it for generations. Like ants, the Algars have been piling rocks atop that absurd heap of stone for eons now.'

'It is an inconvenience, nothing more, Zedar. I will brush it aside and continue on toward my goal. Aldur's Orb *will* be mine again, and with it yet another prize.'

'Oh?'

'Long have I considered this, Zedar, and now is my mind set upon a goal. I *will* have lordship and dominion over all this world and a jewel will ornament my crown.'

'Aldur's Orb, Master?' Zedar guessed.

'Cthrag Yaska – my brother's Orb – is no ornament, Zedar. It is but a means to an end. Truly I tell thee, Zedar, I do hate that accursed jewel for what it hath done unto me. The jewel of which I spake is more fair. I will be the king of all the world, and it is fitting that a king should have a queen. Already have I chosen she who shall share my throne.' Then he laughed a hideous laugh. 'She is not fond of me, but, truly, I shall much enjoy bending her to my will. She *will* obey me – nay, even worship me.'

'And who is this fortunate woman who will be thy queen, Master?'

'Think, Zedar. Truly, it was thine own clever deception of my brother's handmaiden, Salmissra, which set me upon my present course.' He sighed. 'My brothers have cast me out, so now must I father a new race of Gods to assist me in my domination of the world. Who of all the women of this world is fit to share my throne – and my bed?'

'Polgara?' Zedar asked incredulously.

'Thou art quick, Zedar,' the One-eyed God said. 'Indeed, our pilgrimage upon the face of this continent hath two goals – two prizes. The first prize is Cthrag Yaska, my brother's Orb. The second, and no less important, is Polgara, daughter of Belgarath. She will be mine, Zedar. I *will* have Polgara to wife, and will she, nil she, Polgara *will* be mine!'

CHAPTER 32

I shrieked in the silence of mind and heart at this suddenly revealed horror, and it was only mother's iron control that kept my terror and revulsion from echoing from the Eastern Escarpment to the mountains of Ulgoland. All thought ceased as I realized that should a direct confrontation between Torak and me ever take place, his Will would crush mine and I'd inevitably succumb to his hideous blandishments. I would become his slave – and worse. I think that had mother not been so totally merged with me, I would have gone mad. Her method of preventing that was fairly direct. She simply suspended my awareness and took over. I have no memory of our owl wriggling back out of Torak's tin palace nor of taking wing as mother flew us up and up through the rainy darkness.

'All right, Polgara!' Her voice at the center of my stunned consciousness was crisp, 'Snap out of it!'

'Oh, mother!' I wailed.

'Stop that! You had to know about this, Pol, and you had to hear it from his own mouth. Now pull yourself together. We have things that have to be done.'

I looked around and saw that we were much higher than owls usually fly. Our wings were locked and we were making a long, shallow descent toward the mountainous Algarian Stronghold. 'As soon as we get back, you'd better wake your father and let him know that Torak's arrived, but he doesn't need to know about what we just heard. Go ahead and call him, Pol. It takes him a while to start moving when he first wakes up, so we'll be there before he climbs all those stairs.'

I grimly pushed my revulsion aside. *'I think you'd better come up here, father,'* I sent my thought out to my snoring parent.

'Where are you?' his thought was blurred with sleep.

'I can't understand you, father. Just come up the parapet on top of the north wall. There's something you'd better have a look at.'

'Keep a tight grip on yourself, Pol,' mother suggested. 'He'll ask questions, and you won't want to be too specific when you answer.'

'I do that most of the time anyway, mother.' I'd pushed my private horror aside enough to be rational.

We swooped in and settled on the parapet just before father came puffing up the steep stairs. He took one look at the form that enclosed me and immediately began to scold me. 'I've asked you not to do that, Pol.' He couldn't know, of course, that I wasn't alone in that assumed form, but I was, and I was awed by the depth of mother's love for this shabby and sometimes foolish old man.

Then mother and I flowed out of our assumed form and she wasn't there any more. Our separation was actually painful to me. 'I'm not trying to offend you, father,' I half-apologized, 'but I'm following instructions.' My choice of terms was quite deliberate. The word 'instructions' tends to cut off arguments in our family. I suppose that my omission of just *whose* instructions I was following might be considered an untruth – if you want to be picky about it. 'I think you'd better take a look at that,' I said then, pointing at the sea of Angaraks advancing through the mist like an incoming tide.

'I was sort of hoping that they'd get lost, or something,' father muttered. 'Are you sure Torak's with them?'

'Yes, father. I went out and looked. That iron pavilion of his is right in the center of the crowd.'

'You did *what*? Polgara, that's *Torak* out there! Now he know that you're here!'

I'd just *seen* Torak, so I didn't really need to listen to my father's introduction. 'Don't get excited, Old Man. I was *told* to do it. Torak had no way of even knowing I was there. He's inside his pavilion, and Zedar's with him.'

'How long has this been going on?'

I deliberately sidestepped his question. 'Since he left Mallorea, I'd imagine. Let's go alert the Algars, and then I think we'll have time for some breakfast. I've been up all night, and I'm positively ravenous.' He was obviously very curious about the means I'd used to hide my presence from Torak and Zedar, but the word 'breakfast' worked its usual miracle on my father. If you say 'food' or 'beer' to father, you'll have his immediate, undivided attention.

After breakfast, we went back up to the parapet to see how Torak and his henchmen planned to assault the Algarian mountain. They started out conventionally, catapulting rocks at the walls, but that had no more effect than a quarter century of rain had. I'd imagine that was very depressing for the catapult crews. Then the Angaraks rolled up huge battering rams, and that was also a waste of time and effort, since the gates weren't locked.

That must have made the Angarak generals suspicious, because the Thulls were given the honor of making the first assault. Any time an Angarak army encounters something dirty or dangerous, they always send in the Thulls. Several regiments of the thick-bodied, dull-eyed Thulls rushed through the gates. They wandered through the labyrinthine maze inside for a while, and then the Algars and Drasnians rose from their places of concealment atop the walls of the unroofed maze and annihilated the Thullish regiments to the last man. I'm sure that the massed troops outside heard all the screaming, but they chose not to come inside to find out what was happening. I thought that was moderately tacky, but I privately approved. Torak's brute-force attacks weren't likely to gain him entry, and if he planned to propose marriage to me, he was going to have to get inside first.

During the night after the failed assault, the Algars amused themselves by catapulting dead Thulls into the Angarak encampment, and then when murky dawn put in her appearance, the Algar horsemen who'd been savaging the flanks of Torak's army as he'd marched south arrived and very quietly encircled him. His foraging parties found out about that as soon as they rode out in search of food. Torak himself didn't need to eat, but his army did, and they were on very short rations for the next several years.

Things settled down after a week or so, and father and I concluded that the siege of the Stronghold would probably continue for a number of years and that our continued presence wouldn't really serve any purpose. We had things to do elsewhere, so we decided to go back to the Isle of the Winds. Before we left, though, I had one more talk with Gelane.

'This is very exciting, Aunt Pol,' the little boy said.

'The excitement wears a little thin after a while, Gelane.'

'How long do these siege things usually last?'

'Several years, usually.'

'That long? Don't the people outside get tired of it? Can't they see that they're not going to get inside?'

'They're soldiers, Gelane. Sometimes it takes soldiers a little longer to think their way through things than it does ordinary people.'

'You don't like soldiers, do you, Aunt Pol?'

'They're all right – as individuals. It's when you lump them together into an army that their brains desert them. I want you to be very careful here, Gelane. Stay out of sight, and don't stand in front of any open windows. One of the reasons Torak has for being here is that he wants to kill you.'

'*Me?* Why me? What'd I ever do to him?'

'It's not anything you've done, Gelane; it's what you *might* do sometime in the future.'

'Oh?'

'You – or your son, or your son's son, or somebody on down the line of sons that'll descend from you – is going to kill Torak. If he kills you now, he won't have to worry about that.'

His eyes grew very bright at that. 'Maybe I'd better get a sword and start practicing,' he said enthusiastically.

'Oh, dear,' I said, realizing my mistake when it was too late. You don't *ever* want to suggest heroism to a little boy. He shouldn't even know what the word *means* until he's at least twenty. 'Gelane,' I said patiently, 'you're only six years old. Right now, you couldn't even *lift* a sword, much less swing one. Here's what you should do. There's a pile of rocks in the southeast corner of the maze in the middle of the Stronghold.'

'Yes, I've seen them.'

'The best thing for you to do is to pick up one of those rocks and carry it up the stairs to the top of the Stronghold. Then you take it over to the battlements and drop it on the Angaraks outside the walls.'

'I'll bet they wouldn't like that at all, would they?'

'Not very much, no.'

'What do I do then, Aunt Pol?'

'Go get another rock.'

'Those rocks look awfully heavy.'

'Yes, they do, don't they? That's the idea, though, Gelane. Picking up heavy things is a good way to make your muscles bigger, and you're going to have to be very strong if you're going to get into a sword-fight with Torak.'

'How long will it take – to get big muscles, I mean?'

'Oh, I don't know – six or eight years, maybe. Possibly ten.'

'Maybe I'll learn how to shoot a bow and arrow instead.'

'That might be more interesting. Look after your mother, Gelane. I'll come by from time to time to see how you're coming along with your archery.'

'I'll practice a lot, Aunt Pol,' he promised.

*   *   *

I hope you took notes there. The secret word in dealing with little boys is 'diversion'. Don't forbid things. Make them sound unpleasant instead. Boyish enthusiasm diminishes in direct proportion to the amount of sweat involved.

Trust me. I've been doing this for a long time.

Father and I left the Stronghold at first light the next morning and flew west to Camaar. We spent the night in our usual inn and flew on to Riva to gather up the Alorn kings. Then we sailed south in a small fleet of Cherek war-boats.

Ran Borune himself met us on the wharves, and that was most unusual. The politics of the situation here were very murky, though, so Ran Borune went out of his way to avoid offending the sometimes prickly Alorn kings. I liked Ran Borune. He was a small man, like all members of the Borune family. Father's introduction of the Dryad strain into the Borune line had done some rather peculiar things. A pure Dryad for example, would never give birth to a male child, but their tiny size carried over into the men of the family, and you'll seldom see a male Borune who tops five feet.

To avoid offending Tolnedran sensibilities, father and I had hinted around the edges of an outright lie, leading our southern allies to believe that the names 'Belgarath' and 'Polgara' were in the nature of hereditary titles passed down through generations in order to impress gullible Alorn monarchs. I'm told that a whole sub-division of the history department at the University of Tol Honeth has devoted years to the study of us, and they've even gone so far as to devise a genealogy of this mysterious family that wields so much power in the kingdoms of the north. The Duchess of Erat, for example, was 'Polgara VII', and during the Angarak invasion, I was 'Polgara LXXXIII'.

I'm not certain if that sub-department's still functioning, but if they are I'm probably currently referred to as 'Polgara CXVII.'

Isn't that impressive?

The emperor was accompanied by his Chief of Staff, General Cerran. Cerran was an Anadile, a member of a southern Tolnedran family that's always been closely allied with the Borunes. We were lucky to have Cerran, since the man was a tactical genius. He was a blocky, no-nonsense sort of fellow with heavy shoulders and no sign of the paunch that almost all men develop in their fifties.

524

The Alorn kings had arrived in Tol Honeth some weeks ago, and they joined us and we all trooped up the hill to the imperial compound, and Ran Borune advised us that the Imperial War College was at our disposal for our strategy sessions. It was a pleasant building, but its most significant feature was the fact that all the maps were there. A nation that's spent well over a thousand years building roads is going to have a lot of maps, and I'd imagine that if someone were really curious, he could find a map somewhere in the War College that'd show the precise location of his own house.

Although we worked at the Imperial War College, we lived in the various Alorn embassies. It's not that we wanted to keep secrets, it was just that guests in the imperial palace seem to attract followers. I won't use the word 'spies', but I think you get my point.

Father's ploy of hinting that the Drasnian Intelligence Service, even as dislocated as it had been by the Angarak invasion, was providing the information we were actually getting from other sources gave the Tolnedrans a graceful way to avoid accepting things they weren't prepared to look straight in the face. A Tolnedran will go to absurd lengths to maintain his staunch belief that there's no such thing as magic. It's a little awkward sometimes, but we've always managed to work our way around it. Deep down, we all know that it's pure subterfuge, but as long as we all behave as if we believe it, relations with the Tolnedrans can go smoothly.

Thus, when uncle Beldin arrived in Tol Honeth to report what he'd seen in southern Cthol Murgos, we passed him off as a Drasnian spy. Beldin's had a lot of experience at spying anyway, so he was able to pull it off rather well. General Cerran found uncle's report of the friction between Ctuchik and Urvon particularly interesting. 'Evidently, Angarak society's not as monolithic as it seems,' he mused.

'Monolithic?' Beldin snorted. 'Far from it, general. If Torak didn't have his fist wrapped firmly around the heart of every one of his worshipers, they'd all be gleefully butchering each other – which is more or less what's happening in southern Cthol Murgos right now.'

'Maybe if we're lucky, both sides will win,' Cho-Ram suggested.

'In the light of this Murgo distaste for Malloreans, how long would you say that it's going to take Urvon to march his army across southern Cthol Murgos, Master Beldin?' Cerran asked.

'Half a year at least,' Beldin said with a shrug. 'I think we can count on the Murgos to make the march interesting.'

'That answers one question anyway.'

'I didn't follow that, general.'

'Your friend here – and his lovely daughter of course – have told us that this fellow who calls himself "Kal Torak" feels a powerful religious obligation to be in Arendia on a certain specific date.'

'It's a little more complicated than that, but let that slide – unless you'd like to hear an extended theological dissertation on the peculiarities of the Angarak religion.'

'Ah – no thanks, Master Beldin,' Cerran replied with a faint smile. 'We don't know exactly what that date is, but we can make a pretty good guess.'

'Oh?'

'Kal Torak's going to want Urvon in place near the southern border of Nyissa when that date gets closer. He'll want to give himself plenty of time because a two-pronged attack doesn't work very well if one of the prongs isn't in place yet. That means that Urvon's going to have to get an early start. Let's ignore that, though, and use your six-month figure. The battle's going to begin when Urvon marches out of Rak Hagga. We'll want to start moving into place then. We'll get confirmation when Torak abandons the siege of the Stronghold to come west. That'll be forty-five days before the fighting starts. As you suggested, there are bound to be delays, but let's use Kal Torak's calendar just to be on the safe side. We'll move when Urvon moves. We might get there early, but it's better to be early than late.'

' 'Tis a wonderful clever fellow th' man is, don't y' know,' Beldin said to my father.

'Will you stop that?' father said irritably. Then he dipped his head slightly to General Cerran. 'You're a very useful man to have around, General. Most of my military experience has been with Alorns, and they tend to make things up as they go along. Careful planning seems to bore them for some reason.'

'*Belgarath!*' the grey-bearded King Eldrig objected.

'It's just a difference in approach, your Majesty,' General Cerran smoothed things over. 'Experience has taught me that things go wrong during military operations, and I try to take those things into account. My estimates are very conservative, but even if Urvon and Kal Torak don't exactly follow my timetable, we'll still have our defenses in place in plenty of time. I hate being late for social engagements, don't you?'

'You look upon war as a social engagement, General?' father asked, sounding a bit startled.

'I'm a soldier, Belgarath. A good war's the closest thing a soldier has to a social life.'

'He's going to take some getting used to, isn't he?' Beldin chuckled. 'He's got a good mind, though.'

'You're too kind, Master Beldin,' the general murmured.

Our strategy sessions progressed in a much more orderly fashion than they had at Riva. Cerran was a methodical man who ticked off such things as 'when', 'where', and 'how' on his fingers. We'd already decided that 'when' would be determined by some fairly visible activity on the part of the two Angarak forces. Then we moved on to 'where'. The Mrin told us that the final battle would take place in Arendia, and our convenient fiction that our knowledge of that had come from Drasnian Intelligence had been accepted by the Tolnedrans as a verified fact. Arendia's a big place, though, and it wasn't until the sixth year of the siege of the Stronghold that the twins wrested the exact location out of the Mrin. After that, *we* knew that the battle would take place at Vo Mimbre. All we had to do then was convince the Tolnedrans that we knew what we were talking about.

After one of our sessions, I motioned to Brand, and the two of us took a stroll around the rain-drenched grounds of the imperial compound.

'You wanted to speak with me, Pol?' Brand asked me.

'We're going to have to lead General Cerran rather gently, Brand,' I replied. 'I think you're best qualified to do that. Cerran knows that the Alorn kings all defer to you, even though he doesn't know exactly why.'

'My overpowering presence, perhaps?' he suggested.

'The outcome of a dice-game might be more in keeping with the basic Alorn character, Brand,' I twitted him.

'Polgara!' he protested mildly.

'Whatever the reason, Cerran looks upon you as the leader of the Alorns, so he's going to listen to you rather carefully. Cerran likes to reason things out, so we're going to have to stress the disadvantages of all other possible battlefields and then let *him* decide that Vo Mimbre's the only possible place. If we don't, he'll feel obliged to have us spread our forces all over southern Arendia.'

'That'd be disastrous,' Brand exclaimed.

'Moderately disastrous, yes. Now, then, I spent a great deal of time in Arendia during the third millennium, so I'm familiar with all the cities. You're about to get an education in geography, dear boy. I want you to be very familiar with the terrain around every city in Mimbre. There are tactical disadvantages to almost any city on earth, and Mimbrate cities are no exception. Your job's to stress the disadvantages of every town and city – *except* Vo Mimbre. It has its own disadvantages, but we'll gloss over those. We don't want General Cerran to choose any battleground except Vo Mimbre, so we'll just close all the other doors to him so that he's only got that one choice.'

'You're very good at this, Pol,' he said admiringly.

'I've had lots of practice. Wars are the national pastime among the Arends. A healthy sneeze can start a war in Arendia. I spent six hundred or more years trying to keep the Arends from sneezing at the wrong time. I'll talk with Eldrig and the others, and they'll back you up in your assessments of the various towns and cities.'

'This would all be a lot easier if the Tolnedrans would just accept the fact that you and your father aren't like other people.'

'That goes against their religion, dear one,' I said with a slight smile.

'What *is* the basis of the Tolnedran religion, Pol?'

'Money. The Tolnedrans invented it, so they think it's holy. They're afraid of magic because a magician could conceivably *create* money instead of swindling it out of others.'

'Could *you* create money, Pol?' His eyes had come alight at the mere mention of the idea.

I shrugged. 'Probably, but why should I bother? I've already got more than I can spend. We're getting off the path here. This Tolnedran superstition's inconvenient, I'll grant you, but we can work our way around it.'

After General Cerran had reached the conclusion we wanted him to reach, my father's disposition started to go sour for some reason. I put up with his bad temper for about a week, and then I went to his room in the Cherek embassy to find out what his problem was.

'*This* is the problem, Pol!' he exploded, banging his fist down on the scroll of the Mrin. 'It doesn't make sense!'

'It's not supposed to, father. It's *supposed* to sound like pure gibberish. Tell me about your problem. Maybe I can help.'

Father's discontent with the passage in the Mrin lay in the seeming suggestion that Brand was going to be in two places at the same time. His tone was decidedly grouchy as he read it to me. "And the Child of Light shall take the jewel from its accustomed place and shall cause it to be delivered up to the Child of Light before the gates of the golden city." His frustration seemed right on the verge of driving him to destroy the scroll.

'Calm down, father,' I told him. 'Apoplexy's not going to solve anything.' I saw the answer immediately, of course, but how was I

528

going to explain it? 'How long would you say that one these EVENTS takes to run its course?' I asked.

'As long as it takes, I suppose.'

'Centuries? Oh, come now, father. As powerful as those two contending Necessities are, a confrontation like that would destroy the whole universe. A single instant's probably closer to the truth. Then, after the EVENT's taken place, that particular Child of Light doesn't really have any further need of the title, does he? He's done what he's supposed to do, and the title can be passed on. One Child of Light will take the sword down off the wall, another will carry it here from Riva, and it'll be handed over to Brand. They'll be passing the title along at the same time they pass the sword.'

'I think you're straining to make it all fit, Pol,' he said.

'Can you come up with anything else?'

'Not really. I guess I'd better go to the Isle.'

'Oh? What for?'

'To get the sword, of course. Brand's going to need it.' He'd obviously leapt to a conclusion that seemed to me to have several large holes in it. He seemed to believe that *he* was going to be the Child of Light who'd take the sword down off the wall in the Hall of the Rivan King. By the time he got to Riva, though, mother'd already taken care of that, and the sword played no part in it. All glowing with blue light, she'd entered the Hall, removed the Orb from the pommel of Iron-grip's sword, and embedded it in the center of a shield. I rather suspect that took some of the wind out of father's sails. I *also* suspect that he began to understand – dimly – that mother wasn't quite as dead as he'd believed. He seemed a bit crestfallen when he returned to Tol Honeth.

It was in the spring of 4874 that uncle Beldin returned again from southern Cthol Murgos to report that Urvon had left Rak Hagga to begin his trek across the continent. If General Cerran's timetable was correct, we had less than a year to complete our preparations. *One* of those was already in progress. Brand reported to father that he was 'hearing voices'. This isn't the sort of thing a physician really wants to hear. When someone announces that he 'hears voices', the physician normally reserves a room for the poor fellow in the nearest asylum, since it's a clear indication that the patient's brains have sprung a leak.

Brand, however, hadn't gone crazy. The voice he was hearing was that of the Necessity, and it was very carefully coaching him in exactly what he was going to have to do during his face-to-face confrontation with Torak. That confrontation was fast approaching, but for right now, our unseen friend was more concerned about the deployment of the Tolnedran forces. Quite obviously, General Cerran's legions would tip the balance at Vo Mimbre. The problem, of course, was that the legions were in the south preparing to keep Urvon from reaching Vo Mimbre in time for the battle. The Necessity assured Brand that Urvon wasn't going to be a problem, but convincing Cerran of that fact immediately raised yet another problem. 'God told me so' doesn't really carry much weight in any argument. And the declaration that 'I changed myself into a bird and flew on down there to have a look' carries even less. We decided not to do it that way.

Then, in the early spring of 4875, Torak gave up at the Stronghold and started marching west. If Cerran's timetable held true, the Angaraks would be at the gates of Vo Mimbre in about a month and a half – and the legions were still in the south. As I'd rather expected he would, UL took a hand in things at that point. The cat-eyed Ulgos came out of their caves by night and wreaked havoc in Torak's sleeping army. The Angaraks didn't move very fast after that.

It was while the Angaraks were cautiously inching their way across the mountains of Ulgo that Uncle Beldin gleefully advised my father that an unnatural snowstorm had buried Urvon and Ctuchik up to the ears in the great desert of Araga. And *that*, incidentally, explained the quarter-century-long rainstorm that'd plagued us all. The weather patterns had changed just in preparation for the blizzard that stopped Torak's second army dead in its tracks.

Father was chortling with glee when he conveyed Beldin's message to me, but he stopped chortling when I pointed out the fact that the blizzard wouldn't mean anything until General Cerran knew that it'd happened. 'I don't think he'll just take our word for it, father,' I predicted. 'He'll demand proof, and there's no way we can provide that proof – unless you'd like to pick him up and carry him down to that desert so that he can see for himself. He won't abandon that southern frontier just on our say-so – particularly since both he and Ran Borune know that we'd really like their company at Vo Mimbre.'

We presented our information as having come from our 'usual reliable sources', and, as I'd suspected he might, General Cerran received the news with profound scepticism.

Eventually, it was Ran Borune who suggested a compromise. Half of the southern legions would come north, and the other half would stay where they were. Cerran was a soldier, so even when he received orders that he didn't entirely agree with, he expanded them to make them work better. He added the eight ceremonial legions from Tol Honeth and nineteen training legions to make it appear that the Tolnedran presence at Vo Mimbre was larger than it really was. The ceremonial legions probably couldn't march more than a mile without collapsing, and the raw recruits in the training legions could probably walk, but marching in step was still beyond their capabilities. When Torak looked out the window of his rusty tin palace, though, he'd see about seventy-five thousand legionaries bearing down on him, and he'd have no way of knowing that better than a third of them wouldn't know which end of a sword was which. The Chereks would ferry the southern legions and the imaginary ones from around Tol Honeth and Tol Vordue to the River Arend. We could only hope that they'd get there in time.

Then the twins arrived, and they privately advised us that the battle would last for three days and that – as we'd expected – the whole issue would be decided by the meeting of Brand and Kal Torak. The chore facing my father and me was fairly simple. All we had to do was make sure that Torak didn't reach Vo Mimbre before all our forces were in place, and that probably wouldn't be much more difficult than reversing the tides or stopping the sun in its orbit.

The two of us left Tol Honeth as evening fell over the marble city, and we entered a grove of birch-trees a mile or so north of town.

'You'd better tell him that you'll be using our owl during all this, Pol,' Mother's voice suggested. 'He won't like it very much, but let's get him into the habit of seeing the owl from time to time.'

'I'll take care of it, mother,' I replied. 'I've come up with a way to head off all those tiresome arguments.'

'You have? Some day you'll have to share that with me.'

'Just listen, mother,' I suggested. 'Listen and learn.'

'That was tacky, Pol, very tacky.'

'I'm glad you liked it.'

Father was squinting off toward the west. 'We'll lose the light before long,' he noted. 'Oh, well, there aren't any mountain ranges between here and Vo Mimbre, so we're not likely to crash into anything in the dark.'

'You're not going to like this, father,' I warned him, 'but I've been instructed to use the form of that snowy owl between now and the EVENT, so you'll have to grit your teeth and accept it. I *am* going to follow my instructions, whether you like it or not.'

'Am I permitted to ask who's giving you those instructions?' he grated.

'Of course you can ask, father,' I said graciously. 'Don't hold your breath waiting for an answer, though.'

'I *hate* this,' he complained.

I patted his cheek. 'Be brave, Old Man,' I said.

Then I shimmered into that familiar form.

It was well past midnight when the two of us came to roost atop the battlements of Aldorigen's palace in the center of Vo Mimbre. The sentries pacing the battlements may have noticed a pair of birds soaring in, but they didn't pay much attention. They were on the lookout for men, not birds. We settled in some deep shadows near the head of a flight of stairs, and as soon as a plodding sentry had passed, we resumed our natural forms, went on down the stairs, and proceeded directly to the throne-room to wait for Aldorigen. 'Why don't you let me handle this, father?' I said. 'I'm more familiar with Arends than you are, so I won't offend them. Besides, Aldorigen's already afraid of me, so he'll pay closer attention if I'm the one who's talking.'

'Feel free, Pol. Trying to talk with Arends always makes me want to start screaming, for some reason.'

'Oh, *father*!' I said wearily. 'Here,' I said, then, willing a small scroll into existence and handing it to him. 'Just look wise and pretend to be reading this while I do all the talking.'

He looked at the scroll. 'This is blank, Pol,' he objected.

'So what? Were you expecting a bed-time story? You're the performer, father. Improvise. Simulate reading something of earth-shaking importance. Try to keep your exclamations of astonishment and wonder to a minimum, though. If you get *too* excited, Aldorigen might want to look at the scroll.'

'You're enjoying this, aren't you, Pol?'

'Yes, as a matter of fact, I am.' I gave him that smug little look, and he knew what *that* meant.

Dawn was turning the cloud-bank piled up on the eastern horizon a fiery red when Aldorigen and his now-grown son Korodullin entered the throne-room in the midst of an argument. 'He is a miscreant, sire,' Korodullin asserted, 'an outlaw. His presence here would profane the most sacred place in all Arendia.'

'I know that he is a scoundrel and a rogue, Korodullin,' Aldorigen replied, trying to placate his hot-headed son, 'but I have given mine oath. Thou shalt not speak disparagingly unto him, nor offer any impertinence whilst he is within the confines of Vo Mimbre. If thou canst not restrain thine ire, remain in thy chambers until he doth depart. I will have thy pledge to that effect, or I shall have thee confined.'

The archaic language immediately took me back to the third millennium, and when I spoke, it seemed almost that I was taking up a conversation that'd broken off two thousand or so years back. 'Good morrow, your Majesty,' I greeted Aldorigen with a curtsey. 'Mine agéd father and I have but recently arrived from Tol Honeth, and, though all bemused by the splendor of this most renowned of cities, have we come straightway hither to consult with thee and to divulge unto thee certain information concerning that which hath come to pass and which doth concern thee and thy realm most poignantly.'

Aldorigen responded with fairly typical Mimbrate long-windedness, and we exchanged pleasantries for the obligatory half hour or so, and then we got down to business. My message – instruction, if you'd prefer – was simple. I was there to prohibit a Mimbrate assault on the Angaraks who'd soon be camped outside Vo Mimbre until we were ready for them to come out of the city. That took a while. It's very hard to persuade someone who believes that he's invincible that a bit of prudence might be in order.

While I was pounding this into his head, he advised me that his Asturian counterpart, Eldallan of Asturia, was coming to Vo Mimbre for a council of war. I saw an enormous potential for disaster in that plan, given a thousand or so years of senseless slaughter in the Asturian forest. Putting a Mimbrate and an Asturian in the same room was very likely to be hard on the furniture, if not the entire building. Korodullin was already well on the way to a number of quaint forms of greeting, darkly hinting that the rascally Asturian duke would most probably seize the opportunity to defect to the Angarak side in the attack on Vo Mimbre to insure the city's destruction.

Father threw a quick thought at me, but I was already well ahead of him. I don't think father ever fully comprehended the significance of my title, 'Duchess of Erat', nor the persistence of old traditions in Arendia. I had been – and still was – the equal of Aldorigen and Eldallan. They both knew that, and they also knew that I could make them *very* uncomfortable if I chose.

I proceeded then to shame Aldorigen and his hot-headed son into a semblance of good manners. When you throw words such as 'timid' and 'womanish' into a Mimbrate's teeth, you'll definitely get his attention.

It was precisely at noon when Duke Eldallan and his very pretty daughter, Mayaserana, arrived and were rather coldly escorted into Aldorigen's throne-room.

Then I heard that internal bell again, and when I saw the looks of hereditary hatred Mayaserana and Korodullin were exchanging, I almost laughed aloud. This promised to be a very interesting – and noisy – courtship.

'You're getting more perceptive, Pol,' mother's voice complimented me.

'Perhaps so, but how am I going to keep them from killing each other before the ceremony?'

I'm sure you'll think of something.'

The air in the throne-room positively reeked of animosity, and I realized that this ill-advised conference hovered right on the edge of an absolute disaster, so I stepped in and threw my rank into their faces again. 'This will cease immediately!' I commanded Aldorigen and Eldallan. 'I cannot believe mine ears! I had thought that ye were serious men, but now I perceive mine error. Can it truly be that the rulers of Asturia and Mimbre have grown so childish? Are ye both so foolish as to cuddle animosity to your breasts as ye would some cherished toy from earliest childhood? The world about us is on fire, my Lords. Ye *must* set aside this petty bickering and join with the Alorns and Tolnedrans in quenching it. This absurd exchange of threat and insult doth weary me, and presently shall I be obliged to demonstrate the full extent of mine irritation. Thou, Eldallan, shalt join thine archers with the Sendars and Rivans and move against the Angarak rear. And thou, Aldorigen, shalt defend thy walls but make no move 'gainst thy besiegers until the third day of the battle, and shalt emerge only at the pre-arranged signal. Since it doth appear that ye have played at war for two eons and more and still have no better grasp of the art than the newest recruit in a Tolnedran legion, I must here assert mine authority. These are mine instructions, and ye *shall* obey, lest ye bring down my wrath upon your heads.' I sighed then, a bit theatrically, I'll admit. 'Clearly I was in error in the third millennium when I had hoped that my beloved child, Arendia, might someday reach maturity. That was obviously a vain hope. Arends might grow old and grey, but they will never mature. Mine alternative in those by-gone years was clear, but my love for Arendia had made it most repugnant. Now I see that I should have set that repugnance aside and performed my duty. Since all Arends are incapable of adulthood, I see now that I should have annexed both Mimbre and Asturia and ruled them by imperial decree. I am sure that it would not have overtaxed my abilities to teach ye how to kneel in the presence of thine empress and to obey her commands utterly.'

That jerked them both up short. I pretended to consider the idea further, looking them both up and down like sides of beef. 'Perchance it is not yet too late for that to come to pass. I shall consider it. Thou, Aldorigen, and thou, Eldallan, are presentable, and could be – with firm instruction – suitably well-spoken, so ye would make adequate vassals to mine imperial throne. I will think on it and advise ye of my decision anon. But first, we must deal with Kal Torak.'

Well, of *course* I didn't have imperial ambitions! Where are your brains? Still, 'Empress Polgara of Arendia' *does* sort of have a nice ring to it, wouldn't you say?

I think it was the notion of change of government that made Aldorigen and Eldallan suddenly very polite to each other, and Eldallan's suggestion that after the battle they might have a friendly little get-together – with swords – to discuss their differences at greater length sealed the whole bargain.

Aldorigen provided father and me with suitable quarters, and after we settled in, the Old Wolf stopped by. 'You weren't really serious about the "empress" business, were you, Pol?' he asked a bit nervously.

'Don't be absurd, father.'

'I wouldn't be too quick to throw away a good idea, though,' he mused. 'It'd be one way to put an end to this silly civil war.'

'Feel free to annex the notion, father. You'd make a splendid emperor.'

'Are you out of your mind?'

'I was just going to ask you the same question. Have you heard from uncle Beldin?'

'He and General Cerran are riding south to start the legions marching toward the coast. Eldrig's war-boats are already on their way down there to pick them up.'

'It's going to take time for them to get here, father,' I reminded him. Have you come up with a way to delay Torak as yet?'

'I'm still working on it.'

'Work a little faster. I've got some very personal reasons to want a lot of soldiers around me when Torak arrives.'

'Oh?'

'We can talk about it later. Get to work, father.'

'What are you going to do?'

'I thought I might spend an hour or so in my bathtub.'

'You're going to melt if you don't stop spending so much time bathing, Pol.'

'I rather doubt that, father. Run along now.'

He slammed the door behind him as he went out.

Father's strategy for delaying the Angarak army verged on genius, though I hate to admit that. Not only did it slow Torak's advance to a crawl, but it also locked a pair of Arends who'd previously hated each other into a lifelong friendship that boded well for the future of poor Arendia. The only fault I could find with it lay in the fact that *I* was the one who was to have the dubious pleasure of herding a group of Asturians around. I wasn't really very fond of Asturians for reasons that should be obvious.

Father's plan was not particularly complex. The River Arend had numerous tributaries, all running bank-full after a quarter century of steady rainfall. Those tributaries were all spanned by bridges. Father thought it might be useful to take a thousand Mimbrate knights to the foot of the Ulgo mountains and start tearing down those bridges. I was assigned the chore of taking a thousand Asturian bowmen to the same vicinity to hinder the Angarak attempts to rebuild those bridges.

The knight who led the Mimbrate bridge-wreckers was Baron Mandor, a descendant of Mandorin and Asrana and an ancestor of our own Mandorallen. The leader of the Asturian bowmen was the happy-go-lucky Baron Wildantor, an irrepressible red-head from whom Lelldorin was descended. Necessity was tampering again, obviously.

Despite my long-standing prejudice against Asturians, I found Wildantor almost impossible to dislike. His bright red hair was like a flame, and his sense of humor infectious. I think the only time he wasn't laughing, chuckling, or giggling was when he was drawing his bow. Then, of course, he was all business. Baron Mandor wasn't really equipped to deal with someone like Wildantor. Mandor was a very serious man with virtually no sense of humor at all, and once it finally dawned on him that almost everything Wildantor said was intended to be funny, he gradually began to discover just how much fun it could be to laugh. The joke that ultimately sealed their unnatural friendship, however, came from Mandor's lips, and I'm sure it was unintended. When Wildantor tossed off the suggestion, 'Why don't we agree not to kill each other when this is over?' Mandor pondered the implications of it for several moments and then gravely replied, 'Doth that not violate the precepts of our religion?' Wildantor collapsed, laughing uncontrollably. What really made it funny was the fact that Mandor was absolutely serious. He flushed slightly at the Asturian's laughter, and then, slowly realizing that his sincere question lay at the very center of the ongoing tragedy that was Arendia, he too began to laugh. It was rueful laughter at first, but then it grew more joyous. The two of them had finally realized that Arendia was really nothing more than a very bad joke.

Despite the growing friendship between the two, however, Father and I were obliged to concentrate quite a bit of effort to keep the other Mimbrates and Asturians separated.

Father was devious enough to let the Angaraks rebuild the bridges across the first three tributaries unmolested. On the fourth rushing stream, however, Murgo bridge-builders quite suddenly started sprouting Asturian arrows. After that, the Angaraks grew very cautious, and it took them a long time to cross each river. That was the whole idea, of course.

The final cementing of the growing friendship came when Wildantor was showing off. He stood alone on a trembling, undermined bridge, singlehandedly holding off the entire Angarak force. I've never seen anyone shoot arrows so fast. When an archer has four arrows in the air all at the same time, you know that he's really attending to business.

'Pol,' mother's voice said calmly, *'he's going to fall into the water. Don't interfere, and don't let your father get involved, either. Mandor will save him. It's supposed to happen that way.'*

And it did, of course. The bridge Wildantor stood on shuddered and collapsed, and the river swept the red-haired Asturian downstream. Mandor raced downriver to the next destroyed bridge, dashed out to the broken end, and reached down toward the seething water. 'Wildantor!' he bellowed. 'To me!'

And the half-drowning Asturian veered across the turbulent stream, reached up, and their hands crashed together. In a symbolic sense, neither of them ever let go again.

CHAPTER 33

We continued our slow withdrawal – I won't say retreat – for the next several days, and our little force became more adept as they gradually came to accept the fact that their alliance was holding firm. The Mimbrate knights and Asturian bowmen, reassured perhaps by the growing friendship between Mandor and Wildantor, began to lay aside their hereditary animosity to concentrate their efforts on the task at hand. The Mimbrates grew more skilled at bridge-wrecking with practice, and several impromptu alliances began to crop up. One little group of knights grew very adept at weakening bridges rather than destroying them outright, and the knight in charge spoke with his Asturian counterpart, suggesting that the archers might restrain their enthusiasm just enough to allow the span to become crowded with advancing Murgos. That was the point at which several knights concealed upstream started rolling logs into the swiftly flowing river. The weakened bridge collapsed when the logs smashed into the already shaky underpinnings, and several hundred Murgos went swimming – for a short while, anyway. A suit of steel chain-mail isn't the best swimming costume in the world, I noticed. The celebration involving those knights and archers that evening was rowdy, and I saw Mimbrates and Asturians linked arm in arm singing ancient drinking songs as if they'd known each other all their lives.

When we'd left Vo Mimbre, our major concern had been to keep the Mimbrates and Asturians separated. When we returned, nothing we could have done would have kept them apart. Mutual animosity had been replaced by comradeship. I'm fairly sure that hadn't been what Torak had in mind when he'd come west.

There was a heroes' welcome awaiting us upon our return. I'm sure that some of the citizens of Vo Mimbre choked a bit over cheers directed at Asturians, but that's not really important, is it?

Father's scheme had won us the requisite five days, and the twins, who'd arrived at Vo Mimbre during our absence, advised us that uncle Beldin and General Cerran had reached Tol Honeth with the southern legions. Father sent out his thought and spoke briefly with his twisted brother, and he assured us that the Tolnedrans and Chereks would reach Vo Mimbre on schedule. We were ready, and tomorrow the battle would begin.

Mother spoke with me briefly while father was out looking over the defenses of the city. *'Pol, she said, 'when he comes back, tell him that you're going out to keep an eye on the Angaraks. I think you and I should look in on Torak again.'*

'Oh?'

'I don't like surprises, so let's keep an eye on Torak and Zedar.'

'All right, mother.'

Father was a bit on edge when he came back, but that was to be expected, I suppose. Everybody's a little edgy on the night before a battle.

'I'm going out to have a look around, father,' I told him.

'I don't suppose you'd pay any attention to me if I said that I forbid it, would you?'

'Not really.'

'Then I won't waste my breath. Don't be out all night.'

I almost laughed out loud. The tone in which he said it was almost exactly the tone he'd used at Riva during the preparations for Beldaran's wedding when I'd spent my time breaking hearts and he'd spent his chewing on his fingernails. The irony of the situation might have escaped him, however. Back at Riva, he'd been worried about my hordes of suitors. I had a suitor here at Vo Mimbre as well, and this time *I* was the one who was worried.

Mother and I merged again, and all turned inward, we were once again totally undetectable. We located Torak's rusting black palace and went inside again through that convenient embrasure.

'I will punish them, Zedar,' Torak was saying in his dramatically resonant voice.

'Well do they deserve it, Master,' Zedar said obsequiously. 'In their petty squabbling, they have failed thee. Their lives are forfeit for their misdeeds.'

'Be not over-quick to condemn them, Zedar,' Torak replied ominously. 'Thou hast still not yet fully atoned for thine *own* failure in Morinland some several centuries back.'

'Prithee, Master, forgive me. Let not thy wrath fall upon me, though my punishment be richly deserved.'

'There are no punishments or rewards, Zedar,' Torak replied darkly, 'only consequences. Urvon and Ctuchik shall learn the meaning of consequences in the fullness of time – even as shalt thou. For now, however, I have need of thee and thy two brothers.'

I suspect that Zedar choked a bit at the notion of calling Urvon and Ctuchik 'brothers'.

Torak, his polished steel mask glowing in the lamplight, sat brooding morosely. Then he sighed. 'I am troubled, Zedar,' he confessed. 'A great discrepancy looms before me.'

'Reveal it, Master,' Zedar urged. 'Mayhap between us we might resolve it.'

'Thine o'erweening self-confidence doth amuse me, Zedar,' Torak responded. 'Hast thou perused the document which doth expound the ravings of that sub-human on the banks of the Mrin in far northern Drasnia?'

'At some length, Master.'

'And art thou also familiar with the truth which was revealed to me at Ashaba?'

'Yea, Master.'

'Didst thou not perceive that the two do not precisely coincide? Both spake of the battle which shall begin here before Vo Mimbre a few hours hence.'

'Yes, I did so understand.'

'But the account from Mrin doth not agree with that from Ashaba. Mrin doth hang the fate of the world on the third day of the forthcoming battle.'

'I did perceive as much, Master.'

'Ashaba, however, doth not. Ashaba's concentration doth lie upon the second day, or upon the fourth.'

'I had not fully recognized that, Master,' Zedar confessed. 'What thinkest thou might be the import of this discrepancy?'

'The import, methinks, doth rest upon him who shall confront me at the battle's height. Should the Godslayer and I meet on the second day – or upon the fourth, I shall easily overthrow him. Should we meet upon that fatal third day, then shall the spirit of the Purpose infuse him, and I shall surely perish.' He suddenly broke off, muttering incoherently, his voice distorted by the hollow echoes inside his steel mask. 'Accursed rain!' he burst out suddenly, 'and accursed be the rivers which have delayed mine advance! We have come hither too late, Zedar! Had we arrived but two days –

one day – earlier, the world would have been *mine*. Now is the outcome cast into the lap of chance, and I am unquiet about this, for chance hath never been my friend. I left Ashaba in the sure and certain knowledge that I should arrive here at the proper time, and gladly have I sacrificed Angarak lives uncounted to achieve that goal, and still have I reached this place but one single day too late. Will I or nil I, I must face the Overlord of the West on that fatal third day, should fickle chance so decree. I am mightily discontented, Zedar, discontented beyond measure!'

'*He thinks it's Gelane!*' I gasped inside our enclosed awareness.

'*What?*' Mother's thought was as stunned as mine.

'*He actually believes that it's Gelane who's going to challenge him!*'

'*How did you arrive at that?*'

'*The terms "Godslayer" and "Overlord of the West" refer to the Rivan King. Somehow, Torak thinks that Gelane's returned to Riva and taken up the sword. He doesn't even know that Brand's the one who's going to challenge him.*'

Mother considered that. '*You could be right, Pol,*' she agreed. '*Torak's information comes from Ctuchik and Ctuchik relies on Chamdar. Your father's been distracting Chamdar for several centuries with all those clever games in Sendaria. Torak doesn't really know anything at all about the heir to the throne of Riva. He could very well believe that it's the heir he'll be facing on that third day.*'

'*I'm sure of it, mother. That would explain why you were told to take the Orb off the pommel of Iron-grip's sword and put it in the shield instead. Brand's weapon isn't going to be a sword; it's going to be that shield.*'

Torak was still talking, so mother and I set our private discussion aside to listen.

'Thou *must* take the city on the morrow, Zedar,' Torak instructed. 'My meeting with the descendant of Iron-grip *must* take place on the following day. Sacrifice the whole of Angarak if need be, but Vo Mimbre *must* be mine ere the sun doth seek his bed.'

'It shall be as my Master commands,' Zedar promised. 'E'en now are mine engines of war being moved into place. I pledge to thee, Lord, that Vo Mimbre will fall on this day, for I shall hurl all of Angarak 'gainst those golden walls.' Clearly, Zedar's eight-year siege of the Algarian Stronghold hadn't taught him the folly of making rash promises.

Then Torak launched himself into a rambling monologue that didn't really make too much sense. History hadn't treated Torak very well, and his resentment towered like a mountain. So many things he'd believed should be his had been denied him that his sanity had slipped away. Under different circumstances, I might have pitied him.

'I think we've heard enough, Pol,' mother said at that point. 'We're not accomplishing anything by sitting here listening while he feels sorry for himself.'

'Whatever you say, mother,' I agreed.

Our owl squeezed its way back out through the embrasure and flew on silent wings back toward Vo Mimbre. The weather had cleared after that blizzard down in Ashaba, and the stars were out. I'd missed the stars. People with abnormally long life spans always seem to grow fond of the stars. There's a sense of permanence about them that's comforting when all else around us is falling away.

Although Torak hadn't done it entirely by himself, he *had* cracked the world apart back during the War of the Gods, so I'm sure he could have dismantled the walls of Vo Mimbre with a single thought. Clearly, however, he was not permitted to do that. The exquisitely convoluted rules of the eternal game between the two contending Destinies forbade the exercise of Divine Will during these EVENTS. The consequences of breaking those rules were quite severe – as Ctuchik was to discover at Rak Cthol. Torak could act only through *human* agency – right up until the moment when he faced Brand, and even that EVENT would be tightly controlled by rules.

'The rest of us are under similar constraints, Pol,' mother's voice replied to my unspoken thought. 'Warn your father. Tell him that this isn't a good time for experiments. Suggest that dropping a comet on the Angaraks at this point wouldn't be a good idea.'

'He wouldn't do that, mother.'

'Oh, really? You've never seen the kinds of silly things he does when he gets irritated, Pol. I saw him throw a hammer away after he'd smashed his thumb with it once.'

'Everybody does that once in a while, mother.'

'He threw it at the sky, Polgara. That was several thousand years ago, and as far as I know, it's still going – at least I hope it is. Sometimes it only takes a very small thing to explode a star in the wrong place at the wrong time. That happened once already. We don't want it to happen again, do we?'

'Not really,' I agreed. 'We've got enough to worry about as it is. Are we really sure that nobody's going to be able to use the Will and the Word during this battle?

'I don't think we can say for sure. Watch Zedar very closely. If he can *get away with doing something without dissolving on the spot, we should be able to do similar things. Let Zedar take the risks.'*

'I knew that he'd eventually be useful for something, mother. I'm not sure that taking all the risks will warm his heart very much, though.'

'What a shame.'

We settled onto the battlements of Aldorigen's palace shortly after midnight. *'Run along, Pol,'* mother suggested. *'I'll go back out and keep an eye on things while you report to your father.'*

'Run along'? Sometimes mother's use of language can be *very* deflating. That 'run along' had the strong odor of 'go out and play'.

I detached myself from our owl and resumed my own form even as mother swooped away.

My report to father and the twins was far from complete. I made no mention of Torak's mistaken conclusion that his opponent in the forthcoming duel was going to be Gelane. Father tends to make things up as he goes along, and that made me *very* nervous. Gelane was safe at the Stronghold, and I wanted him to *stay* safe. My father's a very gifted performer, but it's not a good idea to just push him out onto the stage and let him improvise. Overacting is second nature to him, and the notion of bringing Gelane to Vo Mimbre to display him atop the battlements for Torak's entertainment at the height of the battle might have been dramatic, but it would also put my youthful charge in great danger. As long as father didn't know what Torak believed, he'd have no reason to start getting creative. I learned a long time ago not to tell father any more than he absolutely needed to know.

I did, however, tell him that Torak hadn't once left his rusty tin bucket of a palace since he'd crossed the land bridge. Father probably didn't need to know that, but the fact that Torak was staying in isolation might help to stem his inventiveness.

'You might want to keep something in mind for future reference, father,' I added. 'Torak's disciples aren't at all like us. We're a family, but they aren't. Zedar, Urvon, and Ctuchik hate each other with a passion that's almost holy. Zedar was having a great deal of trouble keeping his gloating under control while he was talking with Torak. Urvon and Ctuchik are currently in disfavor, and that makes Zedar the cock of the walk. He's going to try to consolidate that by delivering Vo Mimbre to Torak in one day. He'll throw everything he's got at us tomorrow. Torak might abide by the prohibitions laid down by the Necessities, but I don't think we can be sure that Zedar won't break the rules.'

'That's the story of Zedar's life, Pol,' father grunted sourly. 'He's

543

made a career out of breaking the rules. What else were the two of them talking about?'

'Their instructions, for the most part. Evidently the Ashabine Oracles gave Torak far more in the way of details than the Mrin Codex gives us. The third day of this little confrontation's going to be *very* important, father. The legions absolutely *must* be here, because their presence will force Torak to accept Brand's challenge.'

His eyes brightened. 'Well, now,' he said. 'Isn't *that* interesting?'

'Don't start gloating, father. Torak's ordered Zedar to throw everything they've got at Vo Mimbre. If they can take the city, the advantage swings back to them. Once we go past that third day, we'll be looking at an entirely different EVENT, and we don't want that at all.'

'Are they going to try to delay Eldrig's war-boats?' Beltira asked.

'Zedar suggested it, but Torak said no. He doesn't want to split his forces. How long is it until morning?'

'Three or four hours,' father replied.

'I'll have time for a bath, then.'

Father rolled his eyes toward the ceiling.

Dawn stained the sky off to the west, but Zedar was obviously waiting for specific instructions before launching his attack. Then, as the rim of the sun peeped up over the Ulgo mountains, a horn-blast came from the iron pavilion, and Zedar's siege engines, all in unison, whipped forward to hurl a huge shower of rocks upon the city, and that began the battle of Vo Mimbre.

There was the usual adjusting of the catapults until the rocks were all hitting the walls instead of being scattered all over the city. Then things settled down into the tedious thudding of rocks smashing into the walls.

We could clearly see the Angarak troops massing at some distance behind the catapults. Still father waited. Then, about mid-morning, he ordered Wildantor to respond. The Asturian archers raised their bows and loosed their arrows in unison. The hail-storm of steel-tipped arrows fell onto the Thulls manning the siege-engines, and the bombardment of the walls stopped instantly. The surviving Thulls fled back into the teeth of the massed Angaraks, leaving their siege-engines unmanned and unprotected.

That was when Mandor signaled his mounted knights at the north gate. The gate opened, and the knights charged out, armed with battle axes rather than lances. When they returned, Zedar's siege-engines had all been reduced to kindling-wood.

I found the sound of Torak's screams of rage and disappointment rather charming, actually. Evidently the idea that we might retaliate against his attacks had never occurred to him – as his childish temper-tantrum clearly demonstrated. Had he actually thought that we'd just meekly hand the city over to him just because he wanted it? I rather imagine that Zedar's life hung by a thread at that point. Desperately, and obviously without thinking, he ordered a frontal assault on that north gate. The assault melted under a storm of arrows, and those few Angaraks who reached the walls were drenched with boiling pitch and then set on fire. The sun went down, and the first day was over. We were still safely inside the walls, and Zedar was obliged to return to Torak's palace to report his failure. Mother and I both wanted to eavesdrop on *that* particular conversation.

As smoky evening settled over Vo Mimbre, mother and I merged again and flew on silent wings over the wreckage of Angarak to the place where Torak's rusty palace stood.

'Methinks I have erred, Zedar,' Torak was saying ominously when we wriggled through our favorite little window. 'An Angarak disciple would not have failed me so miserably this day. Should I summon Ctuchik or Urvon to replace thee?'

Zedar choked a bit on that. 'Prithee, Master,' he begged. 'Permit me to redeem myself in thine eyes. I do now perceive mine error. Mine engines were not equal to the task I set them. I shall begin anew, and by first light shall engines invincible be at mine immediate disposal. Vo Mimbre is doomed, Master.'

'Or *thou* art, Zedar,' Torak replied in that dreadful, echoing voice of his. 'Do that which is necessary to place me inside those golden walls by nightfall.'

'Were it not for the restrictions which have been lain upon us, might I easily accomplish that task, Lord.'

'The restrictions have been lain upon *me*, Zedar. They need not be of concern to thee.'

Zedar's eyes brightened. 'Then I may proceed without fear of the chastisement of Necessity?'

'Thou art *commanded* to proceed, Zedar. Should that result in thy chastisement, it is no concern of mine. Take comfort in the fact that I shall always remember thee fondly when thou art gone, however. But this is war, Zedar, and wars do frequently carry off friends. It is regrettable, but the attainment of a goal doth always take precedence. Should it come to pass that thou must lay down thy life so that I may achieve mine ends, so be it.'

The casual indifference of the Dragon-God chilled Zedar's blood,

I'm sure, and it quite probably rearranged his thinking about just how important he was in Torak's view of the world.

Mother and I returned to the city, and once again she told me to 'go out and play' while she continued her surveillance of our enemies. She wasn't *quite* as cold-blooded about it as Torak had been, but still –

Then, even as I was going down the stairs to the throne-room, I realized that the battle had erased – or pushed into the background – Torak's unwholesome lust for me. I was terribly disappointed in him. A genuine suitor would *never* have let anything as petty as the fate of the world distract him from what was supposed to occupy his every waking thought. I sadly concluded that he probably didn't really love me as much as he'd claimed. Sometimes a girl just can't depend on *anybody* to do what's right.

Everyone was in the throne-room when I entered.

'What are they up to, Pol?' father asked. Father's protests when I'd told him that I was 'going out to have a look' had been vehement, but his objections hadn't been *quite* strong enough to prevent him from using every scrap of information I'd managed to pick up. I've noticed over the years that men frequently take strong positions that are mostly for show. Then, having established their towering nobility, they come back down to earth and take advantage of whatever turns up.

'Zedar seems to have fallen out of favor,' I answered my father's question. 'He was supposed to take Vo Mimbre yesterday, and Torak was seriously put out with him for his failure.'

'Torak's never been noted for his forgiving nature,' Beltira said.

'The years haven't mellowed him very much, uncle.'

'Were you able to pick up any hints about what we should expect tomorrow, Pol?' father pressed.

'Nothing very specific, Father. Torak himself is going to abide by the restrictions the Necessities have placed on him, but he as much as ordered Zedar to ignore them. He *did* say that he'd be just broken-hearted if the Necessities should obliterate Zedar for breaking the rules, but if that's the way it turns out – ah, well. Zedar seemed to be quite upset about Torak's willingness to feed him to the wolves.'

'I wonder if our brother's starting to have some regrets about changing sides yet,' Belkira said with an almost saintly smile.

'I rather think that Zedar's going to follow his Master's lead in this,' I told them. 'Zedar just *adores* his own skin, so he's not likely to risk it. More probably he'll order some Grolim priest – or several Grolim priests – to stick *their* necks out instead. Grolims are fanatics anyway, and the notion of dying for their God fills them with ecstasy.'

'We could speculate all night about that,' father said. 'Just to be on the safe side, though, we'd better assume that they'll try it and that it'll work. If it doesn't, fine; if it does, we'd better be ready. We might as well try to get some sleep now. I think we'll all need to be alert tomorrow.'

The conference broke up, but father caught me in the hall afterward. 'I think we'd better start repositioning our forces,' he said. 'I'll go tell Cho-Ram and Rhodar to start closing up the gap between them and Torak's east flank. Then I'll go talk with Brand and Ormik and have them ease down from the north. I want those armies to be in place and fresh when Beldin gets here the day after tomorrow. Keep an eye on things here, Pol. Zedar might decide to get an early start.'

'I'll see to it, father,' I replied.

It was well before dawn when Zedar's new engines began hurling rocks at Vo Mimbre. He'd constructed mangonels, over-sized catapults that could throw half-ton boulders at the walls. The thunderous crashing of those boulders shook every building in Vo Mimbre, and the sound was positively deafening. Worse yet, Zedar's new engines had enough range to put them back out of the reach of Asturian arrows.

When father returned, he suggested that the twins could plagiarize from Zedar and build mangonels for us as well. As is always the case when there's a parity of weaponry, the defenders of any fortified place have the advantage. Zedar was hurling rocks at our walls; we were throwing rocks – or fire – at people. Our walls stood; Torak's Angaraks didn't. Our showers of fist-sized rocks brained Angaraks by the score, and our rain-squalls of burning pitch created new comets right on the spot, since people who are on fire always seem to want to run somewhere.

Zedar became desperate at that point, and he uncharacteristically risked his *own* neck to summon a wind-storm to deflect the arrows of the Asturian archers when he mounted his next frontal assault. That was a mistake, of course. The twins knew Zedar very well, and they recognized the difference between *his* Will and that of some expendable Grolim's. All they had to do at that point was follow his lead. If Zedar didn't evaporate in a puff of smoke when he used the Will and the Word to do something, it was obviously safe to do something similar in the same way. Zedar *had* to take chances, but as long as we simply followed his lead, we weren't in any danger. Blazing the trail in a dangerous situation probably didn't make Zedar very happy, but Torak's ultimatum didn't give him much choice. The twins erected a barrier of pure force, and Zedar's wind-storm was neatly divided to flow around the dead calm which had been suddenly clapped over Vo Mimbre.

Then, driven to desperation, Zedar enlisted the Grolim priests to help him dry out the sea of mud surrounding the besieged city. It took father and the twins a while to realize what was afoot, but by the time Zedar mixed the now-dry mud with his wind-storm to send clouds of billowing dust toward our walls, I'd already arrived at a solution. The twins and I broke off a piece of Zedar's wind-storm, sent it swirling, tornado-like, several miles down the River Arend, and then brought it back in the form of a waterspout. Then we relaxed our grip on it. The resulting downpour laid the dust, and we saw a horde of Murgos who'd been tiptoeing through the obscuring dust-storm. The Asturian archers took it from there.

Father's contribution to the affair was a bit childish, but he seemed to enjoy it. Giving an enemy an abbreviated version of the seven-year itch doesn't really accomplish very much, but father was quite proud of it, for some reason.

And so we'd survived the second day of the battle. I knew just how significant that was, but I hadn't bothered to share the information – largely at mother's insistence. 'It would only confuse them, Pol,' she assured me. 'Men confuse easily anyway, so let's just keep the importance of the third day to ourselves. Let's not give your father an opportunity to wallow in excessive cleverness. He might upset the balance of things that are supposed to happen.'

I'm sorry to have let that out, mother, but father's been just a little too smug lately. Maybe it's time for him to find out what *really* happened at Vo Mimbre.

The Arendish poet, Davoul the Lame, a weedy-looking fellow with a bad limp and an exaggerated opinion of his own rather mediocre talent, perpetrated a literary monstrosity he called 'The Latter Days of the House of Mimbre,' during which he made much of Torak's refusal to emerge from his rusty resting place. Davoul didn't explain the Dragon-God's reluctance, but I think that those of you who've been paying attention have already guessed exactly what was behind it. To put it quite bluntly, Torak was afraid of that third day, since the Ashabine Oracles told him that if his duel with the Child of Light were to take place on that third day, he'd lose. Evidently, he'd been forbidden to come out on the second day, so he'd been forced to rely on Zedar to take the city. Zedar had failed, and now Torak faced that day he so feared. When you get right down to it, though, all he really had to do was stay home. If he'd done that, he'd have won.

Don't rush me. I'll get to *why* he came out in my own time.

The key to our entire campaign was the Tolnedran legions, of course, so just before dawn, I flew down the River Arend to make sure that Eldrig's war-boats were coming upstream with those vital reinforcements. I'll admit that I was enormously relieved to see that they were approximately where they were supposed to be. Then Beltira left the city to join the forces we had deployed to the east, Belkira went north to join the Sendars, Rivans and Asturians, and father and I simply flew out and settled in a tree to watch and to call out our commands. Father, of course, was totally unaware of the fact that I wasn't alone in that now-familiar owl. Fooling my father wasn't very difficult – or very important. What really mattered was the fact that *Torak* didn't know that mother was there either. Mother was the Master's hidden disciple, and Torak didn't even know that she existed. I'm absolutely convinced that it was *her* presence at Vo Mimbre that ultimately defeated the One-eyed God.

The business with all that horn-blowing had been father's idea. It didn't actually serve any purpose – except to satisfy father's need for high drama. Members of our family were spread around among our forces, and we had much more subtle ways to communicate than tootling at each other, but father stubbornly insisted upon those periodic horn-concertos. I'll admit that the Arends absolutely *loved* the idea of mysterious horn-blasts echoing from the nearby hills and also that those calls and responses made the Angaraks *very* nervous. The Nadraks in particular were edgy about the horn calls, and so Yar lek Thun sent scouts out into the woods to see what was happening. The Asturian archers with Brand's force were waiting for them, and Yar lek Thun didn't get the reports he yearned for.

Then Ad Rak Cthoros of the Murgos sent out scouts to the east, and the Algar cavalry disposed of them as well.

At the next call of the horns, we got the answer we'd been waiting for. Uncle Beldin and General Cerran responded with a chorus of Tolnedran trumpets. The Chereks and the Tolnedran legions had arrived on the battlefield.

That's when father, our resident field-marshal, soared up to his post high above to direct his forces. When everything on the ground was to his satisfaction, he ordered Brand to give the signal for our opening ploy. Brand sounded two horn blasts, and they were echoed by Cho-Ram. Mandor's answer was immediately followed by the banging open of the gates of Vo Mimbre and the thundering charge of the Mimbrate knights.

Zedar – who should have known better – took the form of a raven and flew out of the iron pavilion to see what we were doing.

Mother surprised me at that point. Without any warning at all, she launched our shared form from our perch and lifted us high above that flapping black raven. Since we were so totally merged, I shared her thoughts and feelings, and I was more than a little surprised to discover that mother's enmity for Zedar predated his apostasy. Mother, it appeared, had disliked Zedar the first time she'd laid eyes on him. I got the distinct impression that he'd said something to father about her that'd earned him a special place in her heart. Father's always believed that the owl that came plummeting out of the sky that morning was simply trying to frighten Zedar, but he was wrong. Mother was trying her very best to kill Zedar.

I wonder how things might have turned out if she'd succeeded.

The charge of the Mimbrate knights at the Battle of Vo Mimbre has spawned whole libraries of mediocre poetry, but from a strategic point of view, its only purpose was to pin the Malloreans in place, and it did exactly that. It was dramatic, noisy, noble, and very stirring, but it was really rather secondary. Torak's understanding of battle tactics was really quite limited, since he'd never really engaged in a battle between equally matched forces before. During the War of the Gods, he'd been outnumbered. During this war, it'd been the other way around. He'd assumed that the attacks on his armies would come from his flanks and his rear, and he'd placed his hordes of Malloreans in the center to reinforce the Murgos, Nadraks, and Thulls when necessary. The suicidal charge of the Mimbrates prevented the Malloreans from meeting other dangers, and it forced Torak, surrounded and outmaneuvered, to accept Brand's challenge, the one thing he really didn't want to do.

Then Zedar tried again, as a deer this time. I've always had some suspicions about that. Given Zedar's nature, isn't it possible that he was simply trying to run away? The form of a deer was a serious blunder, however, as I'm sure Zedar realized when father started biting chunks out of his haunches.

Our combined forces inexorably tightened around the Angaraks. Torak's army began to suffer dreadful casualties. Individual Angarak soldiers began to look longingly at the far banks of the River Arend. I now saw why Kal Torak had so feared this third day of battle.

I'll concede that father's generalship during the battles was masterly. He countered the enemy's every move almost before Zedar made it. The charge of the Mimbrate knights was decimating the Malloreans, but even before Zedar could issue orders to the Murgos, father unleashed Beltira and his combined force of Algars, Drasnians and Ulgo irregulars, effectively pinning down the most numerous of the Western Angaraks.

With the legions and Eldrig's Cherek berserkers marching up the Valley, Zedar didn't dare weaken his right flank by ordering the Nadraks and Thulls to come in and reinforce the Malloreans. The only available force Zedar had left were his reserves, and once he committed them to the battle raging before the city gates, Belkira was free to advance against the Angarak rear.

It was at that stage of the battle that mother and I, still merged in our assumed form, drifted across the bloody ground toward Torak's pavilion. Battlefield intelligence has always been sketchy at best. Many a battle has been lost simply because ordinary generals have to wait for couriers or scouts to report enemy movements before they can respond. Father didn't have that problem. The rest of us could – and did – communicate with him directly and almost instantaneously. Moreover, mother and I could eavesdrop on Torak and Zedar and pass along what we heard, so father could counter Zedar's moves before he even made them.

Zedar was pleading with Torak to arm himself and go out of the pavilion to strengthen Angarak resolve, but the Dragon-God adamantly refused, since *this* was the day he'd so long feared.

I've looked into the Ashabine Oracles recently, and I can't for the life of me see how Torak erred so profoundly in his interpretation of certain passages. He evidently assumed automatically that *he* was – and almost always would be – the Child of Dark. Then, by extension, he leapt to the conclusion that the Child of Light would always be the Rivan King, Iron-grip's heir. That combination *did* take place at Cthol Mishrak when Garion ultimately destroyed Torak, but that was a different EVENT, and it took place in a different war, some five hundred years later. Torak evidently confused the two, and that was the error that won the day for us at Vo Mimbre.

Despite Zedar's shrill importunings, Torak himself remained quite

551

calm. 'It is not yet time for me to go forth to confront mine enemies, Zedar,' he said. 'As I have told thee, this day is in the hands of pure chance. I do further assure thee, however, that one EVENT shall precede my meeting with the Child of Light, and in *that* EVENT shall I prevail, for it shall be a contest of Wills, and *my* Will doth far outstrip the Will of the one who shall contend with me. *That* is the contest which shall decide this day's outcome.'

Merged though we were, *some* of mother's thought still remained concealed from me, but I *did* catch a faint tightening of her resolve. Mother was obviously preparing herself for something, and she was deliberately keeping it from me.

'I *must* reinforce the Malloreans, Master,' Zedar was saying with a note of desperation. 'Have I thy permission to commit such forces as we are holding in reserve?'

'As it seemeth best to thee, Zedar,' Torak replied with that God-like indifference that must have driven his disciple wild.

Zedar went to the entrance of the pavilion and issued his commands to the couriers posted outside. A short while later, the Angarak reserves began their march toward the battle raging before the city gates – even as the Chereks and General Cerran's legions broke through the Nadrak lines to come to the aid of the Mimbrate knights.

Then, as the confusion on the battlefield increased, father added to it by telling uncle Belkira to unleash the Rivans, Sendars and Asturian archers who'd been concealed in the forest to the north. Bleak and silent, they emerged to occupy the positions Zedar's reserves had just vacated.

The messengers, all bearing bad news, almost had to line up outside the iron pavilion at that point.

'Lord Zedar!' the first exclaimed in a shrill voice, 'King Ad rak Cthoros is slain, and the Murgos are in confusion!'

'Lord Zedar!' the second courier interrupted, 'the Nadraks and Thulls are in disarray and do attempt to take flight!'

'Lord Zedar!' the third bearer of bad tidings broke in, 'the force to our north is vast! There are Asturian archers with them, and their longbows will obliterate our reserves! Our center is in deadly peril, and the reserves will be unable to come to their aid! We cannot attack the archers, because they are protected by Sendars and Rivans!

'*Rivans!*' Torak roared. 'The Rivans have come to this place to confront me?'

'Yea, most Holy,' the now terrified messenger replied. 'The grey-cloaks do march with the Sendars and Asturians upon our rear! Our fate is sealed!'

'Kill him,' Torak told one of the Grolims standing in attendance. 'It is not the place of a messenger to speculate.'

Two Grolims, their eyes alight with fanatic zeal, fell upon the unfortunate messenger, their knives flashing. He groaned, and then fell to the floor.

'Doth he who stands at the forefront of the Rivans bear a sword?' Torak demanded of the other messengers, who all stood ashen faced and staring at their fallen compatriot.

'Yea, oh my God,' one of them replied, his voice squeaky with terror.

'And doth that sword flame in his hands?'

'Nay, my God. It doth seem but an ordinary sword.'

'Now is my victory assured!' Torak exulted.

'My Lord?' Zedar sounded baffled.

'He who doth come against me is *not* the Rivan King, Zedar! It is *not* the Godslayer whom I must face this day! His sword is but common iron, and it is not infused by the might of Cthrag Yaska! Verily, upon this day I will prevail. Bid my servants arm me, Zedar, for now I *will* go forth from this place, and the world shall be mine!'

'*Father!*' I almost shouted the thought. *Torak's coming out!'*

'*Of course he is, Pol,*' father replied smugly. '*That's just the way I planned it.*' Trust father to take credit for almost anything that happens. '*Come out of there now. It's time for you and me to join Brand. Don't dawdle, Pol. We don't want to be late.*'

'*I do wish he'd grow up.*' Mother's thought was almost clinical as we wriggled back out of the narrow window. Things were moving very fast now, but I still had time to develop a strong suspicion that something was about to happen that I wouldn't like. That suspicion was powerfully reinforced by the fact that *this* time, mother remained merged with me when we discarded our owl. She'd never done that before, and she adamantly refused to explain it.

Brand was evidently in the grip of that powerful awareness that's characteristic of the Children of Light. He seemed almost inhumanly calm and completely detached from what was about to happen.

Immediately after father arrived, however, Brand's expression and manner abruptly changed. His face took on a look of inhuman resolve, and when he spoke it was in a voice of thunder or the deep subterranean roar of an earthquake. 'In the name of Belar I defy thee, Torak, maimed and accursed! In the name of Aldur also I cast my despite into thy teeth! Let the bloodshed be abated, and I will

553

meet thee – man against God – and I shall prevail against thee! Before thee I cast my gage! Take it up or stand exposed as craven before men and Gods!'

Torak, with Zedar close behind him, had come out of that ridiculous tin castle by now, and Brand's challenge didn't seem to sit too well with the God of Angarak. He roared out his rage and lashed out with his massive sword, shattering boulders and showering the area around him with sparks. That's when Zedar bolted.

'Who among mortal kind is so foolish as to thus defy the King of the World?' Torak bellowed. 'Who among ye would contend with a God?'

'I am Brand, Warder of Riva, and I defy thee, foul and misshapen Godling, and all thy putrid host! Bring forth thy might! Take up my gage or slink away and come no more against the kingdoms of the west!'

The entire purpose of the challenge, of course, had been to so enrage Torak that his mind would stop functioning. Had the God of Angarak been thinking clearly, he'd have smelled the trap being set for him. His rage, however, seems to have obliterated any suspicion or even any traces of sanity. 'BEHOLD!' he said in a mighty voice, 'I am Torak, King of Kings and Lord of Lords! I fear no man of mortal kind nor the dim shades of long-forgotten gods! I will go forth and destroy this loud-mouthed Rivan fool, and mine enemies shall fall away before my wrath, and Cthrag Yaska shall be mine again, and the world also!'

And that, of course, was what the entire battle, the whole war, had been all about. Everything we'd suffered had only had one goal – to get Torak close enough to the Master's Orb so that *it* could dispose of him.

The thunderous exchange had stunned both armies into immobility. The fighting broke off as Kal Torak strode north through his cringing troops and Brand, with my wolfish father trotting along beside him and mother and I in our combined owl hovering over his head, marched south to meet his enemy.

When they were about twenty paces apart, an EVENT occurred, an EVENT that father didn't even notice. Brand identified himself and added a few more insults just for good measure to keep Torak's brain on fire.

Torak, however, spoke to father. 'Begone, Belgarath,' he warned. 'Flee if thou wouldst save thy life.'

Father responded appropriately, snarling his defiance.

Then Torak fixed his single eye on me, but he did not threaten.

554

His tone was honeyed, and the force of his Will overpowering. 'Abjure thy father, Polgara, and come with me. I will wed thee and make thee Queen of all the world, and thy might and thy power shall be second only to mine.'

I've seen small, helpless creatures in the presence of a snake on occasion. The mouse or rabbit knows that the snake is there, and he knows that it's dangerous, but he seems frozen in place, unable to move as the reptile slowly approaches. I found myself in much the same condition. Torak's Will had simply overwhelmed me.

The histories of that brief encounter all state that I screamed my defiance of the One-eyed God, but I didn't. I was unable to utter even a single sound. Torak had met me, and he had conquered me. His single eye burned with triumph as he felt all of my defenses crumble.

What Torak didn't know, and could not know, was that he faced *three* of the Master's disciples in that moment rather than just two, and he didn't even know of the existence of the third. It was the third disciple who defeated him at Vo Mimbre, probably because the third disciple had ties not only to Aldur, but also to UL, Torak's own father.

Our owl, trembling in every feather, hovered indecisively over Brand's head, and then I felt the whole of my awareness shunted off into a very small corner of our shared form, and the third disciple, my mother, took over. I've been in the presence of Gods many times, but I've never felt anything as overpowering as mother's Will on that day. She drew that force about her and hurled it directly into Torak's teeth. Had he been human, that force would have exploded him into atoms. The vehicle of her Will was our shared voice, and had it not been so carefully directed, it probably would have shattered glass in all the kingdoms of the west. Because that voice was so tightly controlled and directed, I don't think anyone actually recognized just how enormous it really was. Birds squawk, warble, tweet, and scream all the time, and nobody really pays much attention. Torak *didn't* shrug it off, though. Mother's shriek of defiance carried overtones of the voice of Aldur, and it *also* was the voice of UL. Torak's Will, which he thought to be so overwhelming, had been directed at *me*, since he didn't even know that mother was there. The shriek of response, which he *thought* was coming from me, was so vast that it made the blow he'd aimed at me seem puny by comparison. The maimed God of Angarak was suddenly made uncertain and afraid. I think I may be the only one who saw him visibly flinch when it struck him or saw the burning of the Eye that

Was Not flicker with fear and indecision. It was at that point that Torak's supreme self-confidence shriveled within him, and he was filled with self-doubt when he faced the Rivan Warder. That doubt and fear made the outcome inevitable.

History reports that it was Brand who defeated Torak that day before the walls of Vo Mimbre, but history is wrong. It was *mother* who defeated him, and she used our combined voice to do it. In a peculiar way, my mother won the Battle of Vo Mimbre.

PART SEVEN

Annath

CHAPTER 34

'Prepare then to perish all!' Torak thundered, but the faint hint of doubt in his voice suggested that he was not as absolutely certain as his doomsday pronouncement seemed to indicate. The Ashabine Oracles had warned him about the third day of the battle, but so firm was his belief that he'd face the Rivan King and his star-born sword on that day that when it was *Brand* who offered the challenge, Torak exultantly believed that he'd won and that the warning about the third day was no longer valid. It was that and only that that persuaded him to come out of the iron pavilion on that fatal day. What he failed to realize was that Brand wasn't his opponent on that field, it was the Master's Orb.

He'd emerged from his pavilion sublimely convinced that he was going to get everything he wanted on this day, and it was that conviction that led him to hurl his Will at *me*; but mother had simply shunted me out of the way and had answered for me, disdainfully rejecting him. The appearance of Brand instead of the Rivan King suggested to Torak that he'd win; mother's scornful rejection suggested that he'd lose. Torak was a God, and he wasn't equipped to deal with uncertainty. Thus it was with doubt gnawing at his soul that he rushed at Brand, flailing at him with that huge sword. There almost seemed to be a kind of desperation in his charge. Brand, on the other hand, seemed calm, even abstracted. His responses were studied, one might almost say slightly bored.

The duel seemed to last forever, with Torak growing more frenzied and Brand growing progressively more indifferent. Finally, the Dragon-God hacked his way through Brand's defenses and cut a deep gash in Brand's shoulder, and that was the signal we'd been waiting for without even knowing that we were waiting for it. I strongly suspect that it was part of the agreement between the contending Purposes that Torak had to draw blood before Brand could overwhelm him. Brand's shoulder gushed blood and father howled even as I screamed.

Then Brand was unleashed. His studied, almost bored expression vanished, replaced with an intent alertness. He scraped his sword-edge down across the face of his shield, cutting away the soldier's cloak which had hidden what was embedded in the shield's center. The Master's Orb, all ablaze, struck the Dragon-God full in the face with its fire.

Of course that had been what the whole war had been about. We'd spent ten years and sacrificed thousands of lives with no other purpose than to bring Torak to a place where he'd be forced to face the Orb at a certain predetermined place and time.

I don't think any of us had fully understood just how painful the presence of the Orb would be for the God of Angarak. He screamed as its baleful fire struck him and seared his face again. Screaming still, he cast off his shield and threw away his sword, desperately trying to cover his face.

And that's when Brand struck him down. Swiftly seizing his sword-hilt in both hands, the Rivan Warder drove his blade directly into the maimed God's left eye-socket where the Eye that was Not still blazed as brightly as it had on that day almost fifty centuries before when the Orb had punished him for raising it to crack the world.

Torak shrieked again, staggering back. He jerked Brand's sword from his eye, and bright blood gushed forth. Weeping blood, the God of Angarak stood stock still for a moment. Then he toppled, and the very earth shuddered.

I don't believe that anyone on that vast battlefield moved or made a sound for the space of a hundred heartbeats after that thunderous fall. What had just happened was such a titanic EVENT that I was a bit surprised that the sun didn't falter and then stop in his inexorable course. I was probably the only one there who heard a single sound – the exulting sound of mother's howls of triumph. My mother's spent thousands of years in the form of the woman we know as Poledra, but down in the deepest levels of her being, she's still a wolf.

My own sense of triumph was heavily overlaid with relief. I'm usually very sure of myself, but my brief encounter with Torak's Will had shaken me to the core of my being. I'd discovered that when Torak commanded, I *had* to obey, and that discovery had filled me with uncertainty and terror.

What followed the fall of Torak wasn't pleasant. The Angaraks were surrounded and completely demoralized. To massacre them – and there's no other word for it – was excessive, to say the very least. Brand, however, was implacable. Finally, General Cerran firmly suggested that enough was enough, but Brand was an Alorn at the very bottom, and when it comes to killing Angaraks, no Alorn can ever get enough. The butchery went on through the night, and when the sun rose, there weren't any live Angaraks left on the battlefield.

Then, when there was no one left to kill, Brand, his wounded shoulder bandaged and his arm in a sling, ordered his Alorns to bring Torak's body to him so that he could 'look upon the face of the King of the World' – only Torak's body wasn't there anymore. That's when Brand rather peremptorily sent for my family and me. The twins, Beldin, father and I picked our way across the littered field to the hilltop where Brand stood surveying the wreckage of Angarak. 'Where is he?' he demanded of us in a tone I really didn't like much.

'Where's who?' Beldin replied.

'Torak, of course. Nobody seems to be able to find his body.'

'What an amazing thing,' Beldin said sardonically. 'You didn't actually think you'd find him, did you? Zedar carried him off just as soon as the sun went down.'

'He *what*?'

'Didn't you tell him?' Beldin said to father.

'He didn't need to know about it. If he had, he might have tried to stop it.'

'What's going on here?' Brand's regal tone was starting to irritate me.

'It was part of the agreement between the Necessities,' father explained. 'In exchange for your victory, you weren't to be allowed to keep Torak's body – not that it'd have done any good if you had. This wasn't the last EVENT, Brand, and we haven't seen the last of Torak.'

'But he's dead.'

'No, Brand,' I told him as gently as I could. 'You didn't *really* think that sword of yours could kill him, did you? The only sword that can do that is still hanging on the wall back at Riva.'

'Hang it all, Pol!' he exclaimed. '*Nobody* survives a sword-thrust through the head!'

'Except a God, Brand. He's comatose, but he *will* wake up again. The final duel's still out in the future, and that one's going to involve

561

Torak and the Rivan king. That'll be the one where they take out their *real* swords and where somebody *really* gets killed. You did very well here, dear one, but try to keep your perspective. What happened here was really nothing more than a skirmish.'

I could tell that he *really* didn't like that, but his distinctly imperial behavior was starting to run away with him, and I felt that he needed to be brought up short. 'Then all of this has been for nothing,' he said dejectedly.

'I wouldn't exactly call it nothing, Brand,' father said. 'If Torak had won here, he'd own the world. You stopped him. That counts for something, doesn't it?'

Brand sighed. 'I suppose so,' he said. Then he looked out over the bloody field. 'I guess we'd better clean this up. It's summer, and if we just leave all those bodies lying out there to rot, there'll be a pestilence in Vo Mimbre before the snow flies.'

The funeral pyres were vast, and it took every tree from the forest just to the north to consume all those dead Angaraks.

After we'd tidied up, we discovered that Aldorigen and Eldallan had gone off some distance to discuss their differences. The discussion was evidently quite spirited, since they were both dead when they were finally discovered. There was a rather profound object-lesson in that fact. If Mimbre and Asturia were to continue their centuries-old squabble, it was quite obvious that they'd soon go down that very same road.

There were hot-heads on both sides who'd have preferred to ignore the obvious, but Mandorin and Wildantor, the two Arendish heroes of the battle, stepped in to put an end to the bickering by the simple expedient of offering to fight any of their compatriots who were too fond of their antagonism to listen to reason. There's a certain direct charm to the assertion that 'If you don't do it my way, I'll kill you.'

Anyway, the two Arendish friends approached Brand with an absurd proposal. They offered him the crown of Arendia. As luck had it, I was close enough to Brand to dig my elbow sharply into his ribs to keep him from laughing in their faces. He managed to keep a straight face and diplomatically declined, pleading a prior commitment.

That bell that rings inside my head when two young people who are destined to marry meet for the first time had already given me the answer to Arendia's political problems, and I'd obliquely suggested it to Brand – quite some time before the battle, actually. When he raised the possibility to Mandorin and Wildantor, however, they both burst out laughing. The reason for their laughter became obvious when the proposal was presented to Korodullin and Maya-serana. Terms such as 'Mimbrate butcher' and 'outlaw wench' do not bode well for the prospects of a happy marriage.

That's when I stepped in. 'Why don't you children think this over before you make a final decision?' I suggested. 'You both need to calm down and talk it over between you – in private.' Then I ordered them to be locked up together in a little room at the top of the south tower of the palace.

'They'll kill each other, Pol,' father predicted when we were alone.

'No, actually they won't. Trust me, Old Man. I know exactly what I'm doing. I *have* arranged a lot of marriages, after all.'

'Not like this one – and if one of them kills the other, Arendia's going to explode in our faces.'

'Nobody's going to get killed, father, and nothing's going to explode. It may not look like it, but the notion of marrying each other is already planted, and it's starting to seep into their minds – slowly, I'll grant you. They're Arends after all, and nothing seeps through solid stone very fast.'

'I still think it's a mistake.'

'I don't suppose you'd care to make a wager on that, would you, father?' I offered.

He glared at me and then left, muttering to himself. Father and I have occasionally made wagers with each other, and as nearly as I can recall, he hasn't won any yet.

Then came the famous conference that resulted in what history calls 'the Accords of Vo Mimbre'. We didn't treat Tolnedra very well during that conference, I'm afraid. The presence of the legions at the battle had saved the world from Angarak enslavement, and then we turned right around and treated Tolnedra like a defeated enemy. First, however, we had to head off the enthusiastic Alorn Kings, who all wanted to offer Brand the crown of the King of the World. When Mergon, the Tolnedran ambassador, protested, the Alorns started flexing their muscles. Maybe someday, somewhere, there'll be an international conference where everyone behaves like a civilized adult, but when it finally rolls around it'll probably signal the end of the world.

My only real contribution to our impromptu get-together was so obscure that it didn't even make sense to me at the time. It does now, of course, but that's only in retrospect. I was adamant about it, and the others gave up and put it in the Accords just as I dictated it. 'From this day forward upon her sixteenth birthday shall each

Princess of Imperial Tolnedra present herself in the Hall of the Rivan King. In her wedding gown shall she be clad, and three days shall she abide there against the coming of the King. And if he comes not to claim her, shall she be free to go wheresoever her father, the Emperor, shall decree, for she shall not be the favored one.'

Mergon, the Tolnedran ambassador, objected violently, of course, but I had all these nice burly Alorns around me to flex their muscles and make dire predictions about what would happen if the Tolnedrans chose to ignore my simple little request.

That took care of the Tolnedran government, but it didn't really have much impact on Ce'Nedra, who turned out to be the lucky girl. She seems to have had certain objections. She didn't have a very high opinion of her pre-ordained husband in the first place, and when she discovered that he outranked her, she went up in flames. Rank and station were very important to Ce'Nedra, evidently. I'll grant you that our tiny princess can be absolutely adorable – when she wants something – but she aged me far more than several dozen centuries ever did. To give you some idea of just how stubborn she could be, it finally took a God – Eriond – to get her anywhere near the Hall of the Rivan King on the appointed day. It's entirely possible that Eriond will unify the world in peace and harmony, but that won't even come close to his victory over Ce'Nedra that day in the caverns of Ulgo.

That, of course, brings us to the question of just *who* it was who prompted mother to insist that I slip that ridiculous obligation into the Accords of Vo Mimbre. If we were out to elect the most probable perpetrator, my vote would go to UL. I'm sure that Gods have a sense of humor, and UL's would probably be the most obscure.

Note that I avoided the word 'perverted' there. Still, one *does* have to wonder about a God who turns his chosen people into moles, doesn't one?

Despite my reservations about the Father of the Gods and his probable involvement, I *will* credit the Gorim of Ulgo with keeping the entire conference from blowing up into a general war. The very presence of 'the holiest man in the world' kept everyone at least marginally civil, and when he read the Accords to us after it was all over, the document had a faint tinge of 'Holy Writ', and the various items it contained seemed to have almost the force of religious obligations. People are used to doing peculiar things for religious reasons, so the fact that many things in the Accords didn't make any sense was smoothed over as long as we all tacitly agreed to view them as religious.

It had taken us several weeks to hammer out the Accords, and that had given Korodullin and Mayaserana enough time to stop talking about politics and get down to more important things. When . Brand sent for them, they came hand in hand into the throne-room with that rather silly look on their faces that I recognized immediately. They'd *definitely* made peace with each other. I leaned over to whisper to my father almost as soon as the blushing pair entered. 'I think you just lost our wager, Old Man,' I said. 'I seem to forget. What was it you put on the line when we made the bet?'

He glared at me.

'I told you so, father,' I said sweetly. 'Try to get used to the sound of that. I'm going to tell you that I told you so quite often over the next several centuries. Look upon it as educational. Maybe the next time I tell you that I know what I'm doing, you'll believe me.'

'Do you mind, Polgara?'

'Not at all, father. I just wanted to be sure that you remembered, that's all.' I gave my head a little toss. 'I told you so,' I added.

Mandor and Wildantor went out and found a priest to perform the wedding ceremony. I didn't see any blood or visible bruises on the priest when they brought him in, but his slightly frightened eyes hinted that there'd been some threats. It was a start, I guess. Threats are a *little* more civilized than open violence.

We'd just come through a war, so there was a great deal of disordered confusion in Vo Mimbre. The wedding of Korodullin and Mayaserana, therefore, was not surrounded by all the pomp and ceremony – and parties – which would have taken place in peacetime. I don't think that really disappointed the bride and groom very much. Once Mandorin had patiently pounded the idea that the wedding technically unified Arendia – under a Mimbrate king – the priest of Chaldan became very cooperative, and his spur-of-the-moment wedding sermon wasn't really too bad. What escaped him – and most of the Mimbrate wedding guests – was the fact that the wedding produced a *joint* monarchy. The unification of my poor Arendia took place in the royal bedchamber.

Then it was time for us to point the Alorns in a generally northerly direction and to tell them to go home. The presence of a unified Aloria no more than two hundred leagues north of Tol Honeth was probably making Ran Borune *very* nervous. Moreover, there were inevitably members of the Bear-Cult in the ranks of the Alorn armies, and it wouldn't have been a good idea to give them time to start having religious experiences brought on by our proximity to Tol Honeth and all its wealth.

Father and I rode with Brand on up to the Arendish Fair. Then we said goodbye and rode east toward the border of Ulgoland, where we were met by several battalions of Algar horsemen. It was courteous of Cho-Ram to provide us with an escort, so father and I didn't make an issue of the fact that the Algars were more of an inconvenience than anything else. It was late summer anyway, and since there wasn't anything pressing for us to do, we didn't really mind a horseback ride through the mountains.

'I'm going on down to the Vale,' father said when we reached the Algarian plain. 'Are you going back to Aldurford?'

'I don't think so. There were a lot of Algar soldiers at Vo Mimbre, and I wouldn't want some neighbor who's a veteran to start making some connections. Gelane and I'd better start fresh somewhere.'

'Maybe you're right. Let's get you out of sight somewhere. Have you got anyplace particular in mind?'

'I think I'll take the boy to Sendaria. After Vo Mimbre, there aren't too many Murgos left in the world, and they aren't going to be welcome in Sendaria – or anyplace else, for that matter.'

He shrugged. 'That's your decision, Pol. Gelane's *your* responsibility, so whatever you decide is all right with me.'

'Thank you.' I wasn't really trying to be sarcastic, but it *did* sort of come out that way. 'Is there something pressing for you to attend to at the Vale?'

'I need a vacation, that's about all. I've been running a little light on sleep for the past several years.' He scratched at his bearded cheek. 'I'll give things a while to settle down, and then I want to look in on those families I've been watching for the last millennium or so. I want to make sure that they're all still intact.'

'What if they aren't?'

'I'll have to make some other arrangements.'

'Enjoy yourself, but stay out of my hair, father, and this time I mean it.'

'Whatever you say, Pol. Give my best to Gelane.' Then he rode off south toward the Vale while the Algars and I went on toward the Stronghold. It occurred to me as we rode that I sometimes underestimated my father. I'd devoted centuries to *one* family, but father had been manipulating several all at one time. That probably explained why he seemed so much like a vagabond most of the time.

Gelane was fourteen now, and that's probably the most troublesome age for a young man. He hovered between childhood and adulthood, and he bitterly resented the fact that he hadn't been permitted to share the fun at Vo Mimbre.

A part of the problem – the major part most likely – arose from Gelane's awareness of his identity. When I'd taken Garel, his father, to the Stronghold, he'd been placed under Cho-Ram's personal protection, and Cho-Ram hadn't fully understood why it was necessary to keep his ward's identity a secret. Algar society is closed to outsiders, so Algars all view each other as relatives. They don't bother keeping secrets because there's no one to keep them from. Thus, Gelane had grown up knowing who he was and in the company of those who *also* knew who he was. He didn't exactly put on airs, but he *was* accustomed to having people address him as 'your Highness'. He had a regal sort of air about him that started causing problems almost as soon as I reached the Stronghold.

'I don't think I want to go to Sendaria, Aunt Pol,' he responded when I broached the plan to him. 'I wouldn't like that very much.'

'You don't have to like it, Gelane,' I said firmly, 'but that's where we're going.'

'Why can't we stay here? All my friends are here.'

'You'll make new ones when we get to Sendaria.'

'I have *some* rights, Aunt Pol.' What *is* it about adolescents that makes them all start talking about their 'rights' in any argument?

'Of course you do, dear,' I said sweetly. 'You have the absolute right to have me make your decisions for you.'

'That's not fair!'

'It wasn't intended to be. Run along now. Tell all your friends goodbye and start packing. We're leaving tomorrow morning.'

'You can't order me around.'

'Actually, I can. I'm very good at ordering people around – and for some reason, they always end up doing exactly what I tell them to do. There's the door. Use it – or would you rather have me throw you through?'

I've seldom had to take that position with any of Iron-grip's heirs, but Gelane had somehow gotten out of control. As soon as he left, slamming the door behind him, I went through the echoing halls of the Stronghold to have a word with his mother, Aravina. It only took me a few minutes to discover the source of Gelane's unruliness. Aravina was a very pretty Algar lady, but the untimely death of Gelane's father had largely broken her spirit. She was so immersed in her own grief that she'd paid little or no attention to her son's behavior. It's a part of the nature of adolescents to test limits to see

567

just how far they can go. The wise parent doesn't permit that to get out of hand. Gentle firmness at the early stages of this testing is far kinder in the long run than the inevitable harshness that becomes necessary later on.

If you're contemplating parenthood, take notes. There'll be tests later on – and *I* won't be the one who'll grade those tests.

I chose to settle my family in Seline rather than Muros, Medalia, or Sulturn, largely because King Ormik had deployed the troops from the northern provinces of Sendaria along the coast to ward off any possible Angarak surprise attacks, and so there'd be few veterans of the Battle of Vo Mimbre living there. Father and I *had* been fairly visible at Vo Mimbre, after all, and I didn't think it'd be appropriate to have some former comrades-in-arms invite me to share a few tankards of strong ale in the local tavern while we exchanged war-stories.

Gelane didn't like Seline, and it showed. A more or less permanent sneer settled over his still beardless face as he walked about the rainy streets of his new home. Adolescent males tend to do that a lot. I'm sure they practice that expression of lofty disdain in front of a mirror every chance they get. I think that in a perfect society both strong drink and mirrors would be prohibited for adolescents. Gelane's sneer disappeared quite abruptly one morning when he approached the reflective altar of his self-adoration and discovered that a very large, shiny pimple had mysteriously appeared overnight on the very tip of his nose.

The pimple went away eventually – almost as soon as Gelane's expression became more sunny. I think it may have something to do with the body's chemistry. A sour expression probably sours the blood, and everybody knows that sour blood makes one's face break out.

I bought us a modest little house near the commercial district in Seline, and after a bit of constructive snooping among the local craftsmen, I located Osrig, a sober, sensible cooper of late middle age with no immediate heir. Osrig made good barrels, and his former apprentices were all successfully following the trade in nearby towns and villages, a clear indication that their former master was a good teacher. I spoke with Osrig one day, some money changed hands, and then I went home to advise my nephew that I'd made a decision about his life's work.

'Barrels?' he protested. 'I don't know anything about barrels, Aunt Pol.'

'I know, dear,' I replied. 'That's why you start out as an apprentice. You have to learn how to make them before you can go into business for yourself.'

'I don't want to be a barrel-maker.'

'It's a useful product, Gelane, and barrels aren't likely to go out of fashion, so you'll have a secure future.'

'But it's so *ordinary*, Aunt Pol.'

'Yes. That's the whole idea. You *want* to be ordinary.'

'No I don't. Can't we find something more interesting for me to do? Maybe I could be a sailor or something – or maybe go into the army. I think I'd like to be a soldier.'

'I've seen your bedroom, Gelane. You wouldn't make a very good soldier.'

'What's my bedroom got to do with it?'

'A soldier has to make his bed every morning – and pick up all his dirty clothes. You're a nice boy, but neatness isn't one of your strong points. A soldier with dented armor and a rusty sword doesn't impress his enemies very much.'

His expression grew mournful. 'Barrels?' He said it with a note of resignation.

'Barrels, Gelane.'

'That's not much of an occupation for a king, Aunt Pol.'

'Don't start polishing your crown until they put it on your head, dear. Stick to barrels instead.'

'Torak's dead, Aunt Pol. I don't have to hide from him any more.'

'No, dear. Torak's *not* dead. He's just asleep. Just as soon as you put on the crown of Riva and pick up the sword, he'll wake up and come looking for you. We don't want him to do that, so concentrate on barrels. Now, you'd better eat some supper and go to bed. You'll be getting up early tomorrow morning. Osrig's going to be expecting you at the shop as soon as it gets light.'

'Osrig?'

'Your master. He's the one who's going to teach you how to make barrels that don't leak.'

I hate to use the word 'chance' here, since I've learned over the years that when we're talking about *my* peculiar family, pure random chance seldom has much to do with how things turn out. This time, though, chance might have had a lot to do with it. I could have bought Gelane an apprenticeship to any one of a dozen or so craftsmen who followed entirely different trades. Osrig, however, fitted all my requirements. He was skilled, he was a good teacher, he was growing old, and he didn't have a son waiting to inherit the family business. As soon as Gelane learned the trade, I could buy Osrig out and set my reluctant nephew up in business for himself. That was my goal. The end product of that business was really secondary. The important thing was to merge him into the general population to the point that he'd be invisible in the event that Chamdar came looking for him. We could always hope that Chamdar hadn't survived the Battle of Vo Mimbre, but I've learned over the years not to depend too much on hope.

We settled in, and Gelane learned how to make barrels while I stayed home with Aravina doing everything I could to bring her out of the melancholia which came very close to incapacitating her. Melancholia's a difficult condition to deal with. The admonition, 'Oh, cheer up', doesn't really work, no matter how often you say it. There are some herbs and compounds of herbs that numb that overpowering sadness, but numb people don't function very well.

Osrig, as I mentioned, was a very good teacher, and Gelane was soon making barrels that didn't leak very much. His products moved down a definite descending scale. His first barrel gushed water from every seam. The second spurted. The third dribbled. The next three only oozed. After that, they were mostly watertight, and he actually began to take some pride in his work. When a craftsman reaches that point, the battle's largely over. Whether he liked the idea or not, Gelane was now a cooper.

Then, when our young barrel-maker was sixteen, he met a very pretty girl named Enalla, the daughter of a local carpenter, and the customary bell rang in the corridors of my mind. Gelane was absolutely smitten with her, and she with him, so they began 'walking out with each other.' That's a Sendarian euphemism for what a young pair does when they're looking for an opportunity to slip away together to explore the differences between boys and girls. Enalla's mother and I took turns preventing that, so about all Gelane and Enalla were able to manage were a few hastily stolen kisses.

After a month or so they were formally engaged, so the kisses were now acceptable – within certain rather tightly controlled limits. Then, shortly after Gelane's seventeenth birthday, he and his radiant Enalla were married. The entire courtship had been rather plodding and pedestrian, but this *was* Sendaria after all, and the local society of merchants and craftsmen was conservative. Conservative people don't like surprises – like the ritual kidnaping of the bride-to-be by her adoring bridegroom and several of his half-drunk friends that's common in some of the rowdier clans in Algaria.

After the wedding there was the ceremonial wedding supper –

the traditional lavish feast which insures the attendance of just about everybody in the neighborhood. After he'd eaten his fill – and then some – Gelane's grey-haired employer drew me aside for some serious discussion. I always rather liked Osrig. He was a Sendar to his fingertips, the kind of man who made me proud of the part I'd played in creating Sendaria. He was sober, practical, and eminently sensible. He paid his taxes, didn't cheat his customers, and abstained from some of the more colorful aspects of language so admired by Chereks and Drasnians. He was a solidly-built man in his mid-fifties, and he was probably the one who really raised Gelane. Sometimes that task *does* fall on the shoulders of a young man's first employer.

'Well, Mistress Pol,' he said to me with a slight smile, 'we seem to have gotten our boy married off.'

I looked across the crowded room filled with chattering guests at our bride and groom, who seemed oblivious of everything going on around them. 'Why, I do believe you're right, Master Osrig,' I replied.

'I just had an idea you might want to consider, Mistress Pol.'

'Oh?'

'Why don't we go ahead and give him a wedding present?'

'What did you have in mind, Master Osrig?'

'You didn't come right out and say it, Mistress Pol, but when we first spoke about my taking Gelane on as my apprentice, you sort of suggested that if things worked out, you might consider buying my shop and the business.'

'I wasn't exactly suggesting, Master Osrig. As I remember, I was fairly specific about it.'

'Why, so you were. Anyway, Gelane's quick, and he makes good barrels. Here lately, I've been giving him some instruction in getting along with customers, negotiating prices, and chasing down the ones who are slow to pay – you know, the business side of the craft.'

'Oh, yes, Osrig, I know all about dealing with customers.'

'Gelane does that very well, too. I've been watching him, and I'd say that he's ready. It seems to me that his wedding today gives us the perfect opportunity to change his status in the business world as well. He's a married man now, and that's fairly important to businessmen. Bachelors can be unreliable, but married men are solid and dependable. I know my customers, and that sort of thing is very important to them. To cut all this short, why don't we go ahead and complete our arrangements this very day? I like Gelane, and I'll make you a good price. I'll stay around for a few months to

571

guide him along, and then I'll start to slowly fade back out of sight.'

'You're very generous, Master Osrig. If we can agree on this, we'll make this day one that Gelane will never forget.'

He coughed, looking slightly embarrassed. 'I *have* got a slightly ulterior motive, Mistress Pol,' he confessed.

'Oh?'

'As a part of our arrangement, I want it clearly understood that I won't open the shop any more. It'll be his now, and it'll be *his* job to open for business every morning.'

'I'm not sure I understand, Master Osrig.'

'I'm ashamed to admit it, Mistress Pol, but I absolutely *hate* getting up early in the morning. If we can agree on all the other details, I want it firmly established that I won't be coming in to work until noon. I've hated getting up early for forty years now. When you buy my shop, you'll be setting me free, Pol. I'll still wake up just about dawn out of habit, but then I'll be able to roll over and go back to sleep again.'

'Why don't we go ahead and set you free, Osrig? We can draw up the papers right now, and then I'll go get your money for you. We should have it all taken care of in just a few days.'

'I'll accept your note for the time being, Pol. Then we can give Gelane the keys to his business this very afternoon, and when the sun comes knocking on my door tomorrow morning, I'll tell him that I'm not taking orders from him anymore.' He chuckled. 'I'm even going to make a special point of staying up late tonight, just to make going back to sleep that much more delicious.'

And so it was that Gelane became a husband and a shop-owner on the very same day. Osrig stayed up late that night, and Gelane didn't sleep very much, either. It was for entirely different reasons, however.

Despite his youth, Gelane gained a certain celebrity that day. Good fortune had positively rained down on him all at once, and that's a very rare occurrence. It was rare enough, at any rate, to arouse a great deal of envy among the other apprentices in Seline, and there was a fair amount of spiteful gossip among them on the fairly frequent occasions when they slipped away from work for those quick visits to the local taverns. Nobody pays much attention to the idle backbiting of assorted mediocre apprentices, but even the more substantial merchants and craftsman noticed what had happened. I heard one burger put it rather succinctly. 'The lucky dog married a beautiful girl *and* became the owner of his own business all on the same day. I'm going to keep my eye on that one. He's a comer, mark my words.'

Looking back, I think I might have been wiser to have deferred the transfer of the barrel-works to Gelane for a year or so. I'm sure Osrig would have agreed to such a delay had I given him my word that from that day forward Gelane *would* open the shop every morning. Maybe the chance to get everything all accomplished in one day seemed just to good to pass up. Sometimes my sense of economy gets ahead of me.

Gelane's celebrity wore off, of course, and after a year or so he was merely 'Gelane the cooper' instead of 'that lucky dog'. People bought barrels from him because he made good barrels, but other than that, no particular fame attached itself to him.

That brief time when he was 'special', however, reawakened Gelane's sense of his own importance, and that's very dangerous for someone whose major goal is supposed to be staying out of sight.

In retrospect, I'm sure that Brand's attempt to cleanse the world of Angaraks hadn't succeeded nearly as well as he'd hoped it would. There weren't any Murgo 'merchants' sitting in nearly every tavern in the west, but the Murgos weren't the only Angaraks on our side of the Sea of the East. Chamdar had access to the Dagashi, and they're a lot less visible than Murgos.

Anyway, after a year or so, Master Osrig had quietly faded out of our lives and Gelane converted the loft over his shop into living quarters. That's when Aravina suffered a recurrence of that deep, incapacitating melancholia, and I was forced to devote all my attention to her. After the initial crisis had passed, I noticed that our usually sunny Enalla was showing some signs of discontentment. 'What *is* your problem, Enalla?' I asked her pointedly one morning after Gelane had gone downstairs to open the shop for business.

'I don't think Gelane loves me any more, Aunt Pol,' she replied disconsolately.

'Don't be absurd. He adores you.'

'Why does he find excuses to go out every night then? If he isn't "looking into a new place to buy oak boards to use for barrel staves" – *after* all the lumber yards have closed, he's "trying to find a fellow who hasn't paid his bill". He's so obvious sometimes. Do you know what I think, Aunt Pol? I think some tavern wench – or worse – has taken his eye. He doesn't even seem interested in –' she suddenly blushed. 'Well, you know – *that*.'

I knew exactly what she meant by 'that'. 'I'll look into it, Enalla. How long's this been going on?'

'Almost two months now. You and I were both very concerned about mother Aravina, and something happened to Gelane while neither of us was watching.' She paused. 'Do we always have to do that, Aunt Pol? – keep an eye on them every minute of the day or night, I mean?'

'Usually, yes.'

'Don't they ever grow up?'

'Some do. Some don't. My father hasn't managed it yet, and he's much, much older than Gelane. Does our boy go out every single night?'

'He has been lately.'

'Good. I'll follow him tonight then. Let's find out where he's going and who's become the center of his attention.'

'He'll see you if you try to follow him, Aunt Pol.'

'He might, but he won't know that it's me. I'll give Aravina something to make her sleep this evening. You can watch over her while I go find out what Gelane's up to.'

As it turned out, what Gelane was 'up to' took me totally by surprise. I'd been periodically in contact with my father, so I knew that uncle Beldin had found the cave where Zedar was hiding his comatose Master, and I also knew that father was in Tolnedra, hot on the heels of a man who called himself 'Asharak the Murgo'.

I'm sure that name rings a few bells. It turned out to be Chamdar's favorite pseudonym.

Anyway, Chamdar was supposedly sprinkling most of Tolnedra with blood-red coins in his efforts to locate 'a dark-haired lady with a white streak in her hair'. Chamdar wasn't slow, by any means, and he'd neatly filched a page from father's book. Before the Angarak invasion, father'd spent centuries leading Chamdar a merry chase around Sendaria, and now Chamdar returned the favor by doing exactly the same thing to father in Tolnedra.

Father's response was absolutely brilliant. It didn't work, but it was brilliant all the same. The 'new hair style' that suddenly erupted in Tolnedra, Arendia, and Sendaria would have driven Chamdar to distraction, I sure. He'd spent centuries looking for me, and now he'd be coming across me every time he turned a corner in every town from Tol Borune to Darine. The only problem with that was that as it turned out, Chamdar already knew exactly where I was.

After supper that evening, Gelane mumbled a highly unconvincing story about an elusive debtor. Then he went downstairs, fetched something out of a cupboard that supposedly contained only some tools, and then left the shop. Once he was out in the street with a canvas bag over his shoulder, he looked around furtively for any signs of pursuit, but he didn't look up at the rooftops, so he didn't see the brown-spotted owl watching him intently.

I'm certain that had Silk been there, he'd have groaned at just how inept Gelane was in his efforts to be inconspicuous. Tiptoing isn't really the best way to escape notice. At any rate, he finally reached the edge of town where it bordered on Lake Seline, and he followed the lakeshore to a fairly extensive grove of trees lying about a mile to the east of town. It was a dark, moonless night, and Gelane was virtually invisible as he crept though the undergrowth. I was up among the branches of the trees above him, and it wasn't long until I began catching fleeting glimpses of the ruddy glow of a fire just a ways off. The fire was obviously Gelane's destination, so I drifted on ahead to have a look.

It was not exactly a bonfire, but it came close. It was big enough at any rate to illuminate a fair-sized clearing and the dozen or more men gathered there. I'd seen that sort of gathering before, and I started biting off a number of colorful phrases with my beak.

The fellow who seemed to be in charge of the little group had black hair, a dense black beard, and he wore the robe of a priest of Belar. It was fairly obvious that the other men were all of Alorn descent, since they were not only tall and blond, but they were also all wearing bearskin tunics. Somehow the Bear-Cult had found its way to Sendaria.

Then Gelane entered the clearing, and he wasn't carrying the canvas bag anymore, but he *was* wearing what had been inside. The heir to the Rivan throne was wearing a bearskin tunic.

That's when I started pillaging extinct languages for swear-words. How *could* Gelane have been so stupid?

The eyes of the black-haired priest of Belar came alight as Gelane, shaggy but regal, entered the clearing. 'All hail!' the ecclesiast declaimed, gesturing toward my nephew. 'All hail the Rivan King, Godslayer and overlord of the west! Hail him who will lead us against the infidels of the south – against Arendia, against Tolnedra, against snake-infested Nyissa! There shall he covert the heathens of the south with his mighty sword to the worship of the one true God, Belar of Aloria!'

CHAPTER 35

I considered what I'd just seen and heard as I flew back to Seline, leaving Gelane to bask in the adoration of his worshipers. Rational Bear-Cultists – if that's not a contradiction in terms – had always maintained the superficial fiction that their hunger to 'convert' the southern kingdoms grew out of a desire to unify the armies which would move against the Angaraks. Belar, of course, had never said anything about a conversion of his allies prior to any war. Stealing the worshipers of his brother Gods would have been the worst form of bad manners. Belar has his faults, but discourtesy isn't one of them. The notion of conversion had been added by radical clergymen with their eyes far more firmly fixed on the treasure-houses of Tol Honeth than upon heaven. The black-bearded priest back at the campfire was obviously a revisionist of the first order. Very few in the west knew that Torak wasn't really dead, and his apparent demise had neatly removed the cult's reason for existence. The pious pronouncement that the goal of the cult was the destruction of Torak rather than the looting of southern treasuries had evaporated at Vo Mimbre. The priest of the newly-formed cult of Gelane was fast on his feet, I'll give him that much.

'*Father, I need you.*' I sent the thought out even as I was changing back *into* my own form in the street outside the barrel-works.

'*What's the matter?*' his thought came back.

'*We've got a problem. You'd better get here as soon as you can.*'

'*What is it?*'

'*I'll tell you when you get here. Somebody might be eavesdropping. Wear a different face.*' It was a logical precaution, but my real purpose had been to spur my indolent father into moving instead of talking. My life would be so much easier if father'd just do what he's told to do instead of wasting time arguing with me.

It was just getting light when I felt him as he altered his form on the outskirts of Seline. Gelane, who'd crept back into the house long after midnight, was still asleep, so I took a broom and went outside. I was sweeping off the steps when a bald-headed fat man came up the street. I naturally knew who he was. Sometimes my father's so enthralled by appearances that he forgets how unimportant they really are. People are who they *are*. How they look has very little to do with it. 'Where have you been?' I demanded. I'll admit that my tone was a little waspish. Then I led him into the shaving-littered shop and showed him Gelane's bearskin tunic.

'How long's this been going on?' he demanded, speaking quietly in the dim light of the barrel-works.

'I'm not positive, father. Gelane's been evasive for about the last six months, and he's been going out every night. Enalla thinks he's being unfaithful.'

'His wife?'

I nodded and put the tunic back into the cupboard. 'Let's go outside,' I suggested. 'We need to talk.'

We went on down the street a ways, and I filled him in on recent events. Then I endured his scolding for allowing this to happen, and we finally got around to what we were going to do about it.

My father's extended – and extended and extended – 'History of the World' will tell those of you patient enough to plow through it that he followed Gelane the following evening and witnessed the ceremonial adulation of the local cult when my errant nephew reached the bonfire in the woods. Then, once he'd gotten his emotions under control, the Old Wolf called me, suggesting that I join him. I thought that was nice of him.

A lot of things fell into place when father identified the bearded priest as Chamdar. There are ways father could have conjured up Chamdar's image for me, but for some reason, neither of us had thought of using one of them. We never did really find out how Chamdar'd tracked me down, but I can make a fairly educated guess. Somewhere in some tavern an idle wayfarer had mentioned 'that lucky dog', and there'd been a Dagashi present. Then Chamdar had come to Seline to have a look for himself – Ah, well, it was too late to start looking for that 'cave in the mountains' now. Clearly, Ctuchik's underling had leeched Gelane's identity from the young man's thoughts – as well as Gelane's yearning for celebrity – and the rest been easy. The local chapter of the Bear-Cult was clearly specious, but the members weren't intelligent enough to recognize rampant revisionism when they saw it. Gelane received the recognition – and adulation – he so yearned for, and Chamdar got his hands on a Rivan King.

We absolutely *had* to sever that connection. I knew of a way to do that, and it was far less drastic than father's notion of erasing Gelane's mind would have been. There were dangers involved in making Chamdar's rambling thoughts audible. If he were to become aware of what I was doing, he quite probably would have killed Gelane on the spot – or at least tried to. To prevent that, I had to overlay his awareness with a kind of reflective reverie. His mind had to wander sufficiently to dull his alertness. It wasn't easy, which is why I chose to do it myself rather than just hand it over to father. My father tends in the direction of blunt force when he does something. Subtlety's never been one of his strong points.

Aside from the more obvious physical differences, that may be the one thing that most distinguishes men from women. We think differently, and so we do things differently. Many people – men mostly – get very upset by these differences, but can you imagine how boring life would be if we all thought and acted in exactly the same way? Actually, gentlemen, it's much more fun this way.

Anyway, Gelane was making a fairly windy speech about how important he was when Chamdar's now-audible ruminations brought my boastful nephew up short. The announcement, 'Ctuchik will reward me if I kill this dolt', definitely got Gelane's attention – as well as the attention of the other Cultists. Father advised me later that two of the shaggily-dressed fanatics were very upset by what Chamdar revealed. Evidently Chamdar had prudently decided to bring a pair of bodyguards along.

The rambling of Ctuchik's less than loyal underling went on and on – long enough at any rate for Gelane to regain his senses and realize just how much his swollen ego had been used to dupe him. When Chamdar's day-dream reached its culmination and in his mind's eye he was being exalted to first disciplehood, Gelane gave im a quick demonstration of unrestrained Alornishness by punching him square in the face.

Chamdar reeled and fell, and his now-scrambled wits lost all control of his puppet, my nephew. With the evaporation of Chamdar's hold on him, the full force of Gelane's own foolishness struck him very nearly as hard as he'd just struck Chamdar. That wasn't a good time for extended soul-searching, since Chamdar's pair of disguised bodyguards whipped out some very ugly knives to rush to their employer's defense. Fortunately, the other Cultists took the defense of Gelane to be a religious obligation, and their piety along those lines was commendable, to say the very least.

After Chamdar had fled and his bodyguards had been swarmed under, Gelane got hold of himself. 'We've been tricked!' he exclaimed. 'That was no priest of Belar!'

'What shall we do, Godslayer?' one hulking Alorn demanded. 'Should we chase him down and kill him?'

'Don't ever call me that again!' Gelane commanded. 'I'm not the Godslayer! I've dishonored my name!' He ripped off his bear-skin and violently hurled it into the fire. 'The Bear-Cult is a lie and a deception!'

'I don't know about the rest of you,' the first Alorn declared, 'but I'm going to go find that priest and rip him up the middle!' And they all dashed out to flounder around in the bushes.

'That was very slick, Pol,' father complimented me after he'd discarded his feathers. 'Where did you learn how to do that?'

'In Vo Wacune,' I replied. 'I had to force a confession out of an Asturian spy, and I didn't much care for the conventional ways to do that. It's fairly simple, actually. Someday when we've got some time, I'll show you how to do it.' I cocked my head to listen to the Alorns crashing through the brush. 'Let's wait until Gelane's playmates go home before we collar him and drag him back to the barrel-works. I don't know that we need to let the other Cultists know that we've been around.'

'Truly,' he agreed.

The heretic Cult members floundered around in the undergrowth for quite some time, but by then Chamdar was probably half-way to Camaar. 'What do we do now, your Majesty?' one of them asked Gelane as they trooped back to the fire.

'Let's just forget about that "your Majesty" business,' Gelane told him. 'That was nothing but a Grolim trick. I think we should all swear to keep this whole thing secret. Our neighbors are Sendars, so we'll look like idiots if we start talking about the Bear-Cult as if it really meant something.'

The all agreed readily. Nobody really likes to look foolish. They swore on their mother's graves, their swords – though they didn't actually have swords – and their somewhat questionable honor that no word of their temporary amusement would ever pass their lips. Then Gelane sent them all home.

When he was alone, Gelane started to weep, and that's when father and I came out of the woods.

'Not too smooth there, was it, Gelane?' father said dryly. 'It's very noble to believe that everybody always speaks the truth, but didn't it occur to you that it might be just a trifle on the gullible side?'

Gelane didn't seem surprised to see us. In spite of his display of poor judgement, he was still a fairly clever young man. 'Who really was that fellow who called himself a priest, grandfather?'

'His name's Chamdar, and you've already guessed that he's a Grolim. Was your head turned off, Gelane? Couldn't you tell by the color of his skin and the shape of his eyes that he's an Angarak?'

'That wouldn't make any difference here, father,' I explained. 'This is Sendaria, and I spent several centuries erasing any outward awareness of racial differences.'

'Brotherhood's a very nice thing, Pol,' he said, 'but if somebody who happens to be green is out to kill you, color blindness isn't really a very useful trait. Let's go back to town. We've got packing to do.'

'Where are we going, grandfather?' Gelane asked him.

'I haven't decided yet. We *do* have to get out of Sendaria, though.'

My heart sank. I knew what that meant.

'Why don't you buy yourself some new clothes, father?' I asked him as we entered the city.

'These *are* new, Pol.'

'Oh? Which garbage heap did you find them on?'

'Look a little closer, Pol,' he replied. 'I paid a Tol Honeth tailor a lot of money for these. The patches and frayed cuffs are just for show. The clothes are very well-made and they'll last me for centuries.'

'Couldn't you afford shoes that matched?'

'I didn't want them to match. I want to look like an out-at-the-heels vagabond.'

'I think you've succeeded far beyond your wildest dreams. It's a costume, then?'

'Of course it is. People don't pay much attention to wandering tramps. When I wear these, I can go through a town or village and nobody'll remember that I've been there after a day or two.'

'Don't you *ever* come off stage?'

'I'm more interesting this way.' He tossed that off with his usual flamboyance. 'My real character's rather boring. I could be a duke if you'd prefer, your Grace.'

'Spare me.'

'Why did you call her that, grandfather?' Gelane asked. '"Your Grace," I mean?'

'Secrets again, Pol?' father sighed. 'You and your secrets.' Then he looked appraisingly at Gelane, obviously remembering the young man's self-adulatory speech at the bonfire. 'Your Majesty,' he said with orotund formality, 'may I present her Grace, the Duchess of Erat?'

Gelane blinked and then stared at me. 'You're *not!*' he exclaimed.

'Well, I was, dear. That was a long time ago, though.'

'You're the most famous person in Sendarian history!'

'It's nice to be noticed.'

'Why didn't you tell me? My manners were terrible, Aunt Pol. You should have told me.'

'So you could bow and scrape to me in public? You've got a long way to go, Gelane. We don't *want* to be special, remember? That's why you're a cooper instead of a magistrate or a country squire.' I saw an opening there, so I jumped on it. 'There are two sides to nobility, Gelane. Most people only see the fine houses, the fancy clothes, and all the bowing and scraping by lesser nobles. The other side's more important, though, and much simpler. Duty, Gelane, duty. Keep that in front of your eyes every waking moment. You are – or could be – the Rivan King. That'd involve some very complicated duties, but the way things stand right now, your only duty is to the line of succession. You perform that duty by staying alive, and there are a large number of people in the world who want to kill you before you have a son.'

'I guess I lost sight of that, Aunt Pol,' he confessed. 'When that Chamdar fellow called me the Rivan King, it went to my head. I thought I was important.'

'You *are* important, Gelane,' I told him very firmly. 'You and your wife are probably the most important people in the world right now. That means that you've got the heaviest burden of duty in the world, and it can all be boiled down to one word. "Hide." Wherever you go, hide. Stay out of sight. The best way to do that is to be ordinary.'

'You'd better listen to her, Gelane,' father said. 'Oh, and one word of advice from a professional – and I *am*, you know, – a professional, I mean. Don't let that "I've got a secret" look start getting the best of you. Pretend to be stupid, if you have to.' Then the old fraud gave me a sly look. 'Would you like to have me give him some acting lessons, Pol?'

'Now that you mention it, I think you should, father.'

The look of consternation that crossed his face was the high point of my entire evening.

Father came up with all sorts of lame justifications for what was probably his spur-of-the-moment decision to move us all to Cherek. That's another indication of the difference between men and women. A man always feels the need to justify his decisions with logic, and logic, in a formal sense, usually has nothing to do with an important decision. Our minds are far too complex to make choices that way. Women know that, but men appear to have skipped school on the day the subject was discussed.

Enalla and I circulated the usual 'family emergency' fiction, identifying our ancestral home as Muros this time. Then Gelane sold his shop, gathered up his tools, and bought a wagon and a team of horses.

We traveled southeasterly for about ten leagues to further the ruse that we were bound for Muros, but then we turned off the imperial highway and followed a back road to the capital at Sendar. While father was down at the harbor looking for a Cherek sea-captain who was bound for Val Alorn, I went to King Ormik's palace to visit my money. I was a little startled by how much my hoard had grown since the last time I'd made a withdrawal. If you leave money alone, it reproduces itself almost as fast as rabbits do. Anyway, I took some thirty-five pounds or so of gold coins out of my 'contingency fund' and then rejoined Gelane, Enalla, and Aravina at the sedate inn where we'd taken rooms. I didn't make an issue of what I'd been doing. The presence of money does strange things to people sometimes.

Father had located a burly, bearded, and probably unreliable Cherek sea-captain, and the next morning we sailed for Val Alorn.

The key to the prosperity of Cherek and Drasnia has always been the existence of the Cherek Bore, that intimidating tidal maelstrom that blocks the narrow strait between the northern tip of Sendaria and the southern tip of the Cherek peninsula. Chereks find a passage through the Bore exhilarating. I don't. Why don't we leave it at that?

It was autumn by the time we reached the harbor at Val Alorn, and father put us up in a substantial inn far enough back from the harbor to avoid the rowdier parts of the city along the waterfront. After we'd settled in, he drew me off to one side. 'I'll go talk to Eldrig,' he told me. 'Let's keep Gelane away from the palace this time. He seems to be settling down now, but just to be on the safe side, let's not expose him to throne-rooms and other regal trappings.'

'Well put,' I murmured.

Father never told me what sort of threats he used to brow-beat King Eldrig into permitting his royal visitor to leave Val Alorn for the back country without making his presence in Cherek a matter of public record. Eldrig himself needed to know that we were here, but nobody else did.

We left Val Alorn the following morning and followed a poorly maintained road up into the foothills of the Cherek mountains to the village of Emgaard several leagues to the west of the capital.

'Have you ever done much fishing, Gelane?' father asked casually once we were underway.

'A few times, grandfather,' Gelane replied. 'Seline's right on the lakeshore, after all, but I never saw much point to it, personally. If I want fish for supper, I can buy some at the market. Sitting in the rain in a leaky boat waiting for some fish to get hungry isn't very exciting, and I *did* have a business to run, after all.'

'There's a world of difference between lake-fishing and stream fishing, Gelane,' father told him. 'You're right about how boring lake fishing can be. Fishing a mountain stream's altogether different. When we get to Emgaard, we'll have a try at it. I think you might like it.' What was father up to now?

The village of Emgaard was one of those picturesque mountain towns with houses that looked as if they'd come straight out of a cookie-cutter. It had steep roofs, ornamentally scrolled eaves, and neatly kept yards, each closely cropped by the resident goat. Goats make excellent pets in a land where garbage disposal is rudimentary at best.

As we approached the little town, father told us that King Eldrig had assured him that no veterans of the Battle of Vo Mimbre lived here, so we weren't likely to come across any former comrades-in-arms. We took rooms in the local inn, and even before we were settled in, my father sent Gelane out to cut a couple of fishing poles.

'Fishing, father?' I asked. 'Is this some new pastime? You've never taken much interest in it before.'

'Oh, fishing's not so bad, Pol. You don't have to work at it very hard. Eldrig tells me that most of the locals here are enthusiastic about it, though, and this is a way for Gelane to gain access to the town and its people. The region's supposed to be famous for the trout fishing, and a true fanatic would move anywhere to pursue his hobby. That should explain why he left Sendaria. Nobody really expects rational behavior from a fanatic.'

I was just a little dubious about it. 'You heard him back on the road, father. He's not really *that* interested in fishing.'

Father grinned at me. 'I can fix that, Pol,' he assured me. 'Gelane's not interested because he's never caught a big one. I'll see to it that he takes a large trout in fast water this very afternoon, and that'll hook him as neatly as he hooks the fish. After today, he'll be so addicted to trout fishing that it'll be all he talks – or thinks – about. He won't even remember the Bear-Cult or his hereditary throne. Have you got plenty of money?'

'Enough.' I've learned that it's not a good idea to be very specific about numbers when you're discussing money with my father.

'You can go ahead and buy him a shop – and you'll need a house to live in, but don't expect him to pay much attention to business.'

'One fish isn't going to change him overnight, father.'

'There'll be *two* fish, Pol – the big one he catches, and the much, much bigger one that gets away from him. I can almost guarantee that he'll spend the rest of his life chasing that one. I'd imagine that a year from now he'll have forgotten all about what happened in Seline.'

'You're more clever than you look, father.'

'I know,' he said with a wicked grin. 'That's one of my many gifts, Pol.'

I gathered from the look of disappointed yearning on Gelane's face that evening that 'the one that got away' had been of monumental proportions. It must have been, since the one he *did* catch and deprecatingly referred to as 'this minnow' fed everybody at the inn for two nights running.

'Hooked him,' father murmured smugly to me while Gelane was showing off his prize in the common room of the inn.

'I noticed that,' I replied. 'Was the other fish really so big? '

'He was the biggest one I could find in that part of the creek. I didn't submerge myself in his awareness, but I got the impression that he sort of owns a large pool at the foot of a waterfall. Fish have very strange minds. They don't eat because they're hungry; they eat to keep other fish from getting all the food. That's why that big one struck Gelane's lure.'

'Did you break Gelane's fish-line?'

'No. The fish took care of that all by himself. He's a clever old fish, and he's been hooked many times before, so he knows exactly what do to. He jumped just once, and he's longer than Gelane's leg. Brace yourself, Pol. You're going to hear a lot about that fish.'

'You *do* realize that what you're doing is terribly dishonest, don't you, father?'

'When has that ever got in my way, Pol? Honesty's a nice enough thing, I suppose, but I've never let it interfere when I was doing something important. That heavy thud on the other end of Gelane's line and the sight of that monster blasting up out of the depths of that pool is going to keep Gelane out of mischief for the rest of his life, and that's all I was really after. I'll stay around here for a few months, but I don't think it'll really be necessary. Go ahead and set him up in business, Pol, but don't expect much work out of him when the fish are biting.'

I had my doubts about father's little scheme, but the years proved that he was right. Oddly enough, I married a man who's almost as much a fanatic about fishing as Gelane was. I'm fairly sure, however, that 'the big one' wouldn't have gotten away from my Durnik.

A cabinet-maker in Emgaard had died the week before our arrival, and I was quick enough to get to his bereaved widow before the vultures swooped in. I bought the shop and the attached residence from her before they had the chance to cheat her, and the price I paid her was not only fair, it was generous. Owls, after all, *are* nicer than vultures. The cabinet shop wasn't large, but it was big enough for a barrel-maker who hung a 'gone fishing' sign on his door quite regularly.

Then winter arrived, and father said his farewells and went off to see if he could locate Chamdar. Gelane made barrels during the day and manufactured fishing lures in the evening. Enalla wasn't *too* happy about her husband's new obsession, but she brightened up when I pointed out that a husband who thinks about fish all the time isn't likely to become involved with other women.

Aravina died in her sleep one night the following spring, and I couldn't really pinpoint the cause of her death. I could be melodramatic and say that she'd died of a broken heart, but from a purely physiological point of view, that's an absurdity. Absurd or not, though, I had a strong suspicion that her periodic bouts of melancholia *had* in fact contributed to her death.

Gelane and Enalla mourned her loss, of course, but their lives went on. Gelane was a good enough cooper that his local customers were patient with him when the fish were biting. Emgaard is fairly remote, and its nearby streams aren't heavily fished, so Gelane wasn't the *only* businessman in town whose 'gone fishing' sign was always handy. They'd gather in the local tavern after the sun went down and talk for hours about their sport. The dry-goods store was attached to the tavern, and I happened to be in that part of the establishment one night while Gelane was over in the tavern picking up tips on how to outsmart trout. The local fishermen were gathered in a semi-circle around the fireplace with their feet up on the hearth-stone telling lies for all they were worth. 'I saw old Crooked Jaw walking on his tail across that pond of his this morning,' one of them announced. 'He seems to have come through the winter fairly well.'

'He always does,' another fisherman noted. 'There's a lot of feed in that beaver pond of his. There's not much current to wash it away.'

'Who's Crooked Jaw?' Gelane asked, just a little timidly. He sat in a chair away from the fireplace, obviously not wanting to push himself in on the veterans.

'He's a big old trout who made a stupid mistake when he was hardly more than a minnow,' the first angler replied. 'He took the hook of some earl or something who didn't know very much about fishing. Anyway, as close as we can tell, the earl yanked a whole lot too hard, and he broke that young fish's jaw. That's how the fish got his name. His lower jaw's all twisted off to one side. As far as we know, Crooked Jaw spent all the time while his jaw was healing up thinking about the mistake he'd made. Believe you me, young feller, it takes a *real* clever lure to get Crooked Jaw to even look at it. He don't hardly *ever* make no mistakes.'

'Have all the fish around here got names?' Gelane asked.

'Naw,' another fisherman laughed, 'just the big ones as is too smart t' get therselves caught.'

'I hooked a fairly large one in the pool below that waterfall just outside of town the first day I was here,' Gelane said modestly. 'He wasn't on the end of my line very long, though – and there wasn't much of my line left after he broke free. I think he took about half of it with him.'

'Oh, that was Old Twister,' another grizzled angler immediately identified the fish. 'That pool there's his private property, and he collects fishing line.'

Gelane gave him a puzzled look.

'All the big ones hereabouts have their own favorite pools,' another old fisherman explained. 'Crooked Jaw lives in that beaver pond, Twister lives in that pool under the falls, Dancer lives near the deep bend a mile or so above the falls, and the High Jumper lives in the riffle on the downstream side.' He looked around at the other anglers with an unspoken question in his eyes, and they all nodded. 'Why don't you pull your chair closer to the fire, young feller?' the old man suggested. 'I get a crick in my neck when I try to talk to somebody back over my shoulder.'

And that was when Gelane joined the local fraternity. He pulled

586

his chair up into the place the other fishermen made for him, and then he spoke, politely, of course. 'I didn't quite follow what you meant when you said that Twister collects fishing line,' he said to the grizzled man who'd identified the fish in question.

'It's a trick he's got,' the angler explained. 'I think Twister's got delicate lips, and he don't like the way a fishhook bites in. So what he does is roll over and over in the water, wrappin' the fish-line around him. Then, after he's got your line all snarled up, he swims on downstream at about a mile a minute. Now, Twister's a big, heavy rascal, an' when he hits the end of your line, he snaps it like a cobweb. Happens all the time.'

'That was Twister I hooked then,' Gelane said excitedly. 'That's exactly what he did to me.' His eyes grew dreamy. 'I'll get him, though,' he predicted. 'Someday I'll get him.'

'I wish you all the luck in the world, friend,' a balding angler said. 'Old Twister's almost pushed me into poverty just buying new fishing line every time I walk by that pool of his.'

The 'fishing club' was comprised for the most part of local businessmen, and when Gelane modestly admitted that he'd just set up his barrel-works, he was immediately accepted as a kindred spirit – which is to say that everybody realized that barrels took second place in his view of the world. My father's a sly one, I'll give him that. Nothing Gelane could have done in Emgaard would have gained him acceptance quite as quickly as picking up his fishing pole had.

When autumn finally rolled around and the fishing season more or less ended, Gelane went back to making barrels and attending to various other domestic duties. He hadn't as yet caught Old Twister, but he *did* catch Enalla at an appropriate time, so by Erastide she was quite obviously pregnant.

It's a peculiarity of village life that nothing cements a family's position in the community quite so much as the wife's first pregnancy. In a peculiar sort of way, the incipient infant becomes the property of the entire village. The ladies all stop by to give the new mother-to-be advice – most of it bad – and the men-folk spend hours congratulating the father-to-be. We'd only lived in Emgaard for about a year and a half, but in the eyes of our fellow villagers were now 'old-timers'. We'd merged with the rest of the village, and there's no better way to become invisible.

In the early summer of 4899 Enalla went into labor, and it was an easy delivery. Enalla didn't think so, but it was. The infant was a boy, naturally. It almost always is in the Rivan line for a number of very good reasons, heredity being only one of them.

Gelane insisted that his son be named Garel, in honor of his own father, and I really had no objection to that. It wasn't a Cherek name, but it was Alorn enough not to be considered unusual. On the evening of the eventful day, when Enalla was sleeping and Gelane and I sat by the small fire, he with his infant son and I with my sewing, he looked reflectively into the fire. 'You know something, Aunt Pol?' he said quietly.

'What's that, dear?'

'I'm really happy about the way things have turned out. I didn't really like it in Sendaria.'

'Oh?'

'When I lived at the Stronghold back during the war, I got all puffed up. I lived with King Cho-Ram's family, and everybody went around calling me "Your Highness". Then after Vo Mimbre, you took us to Seline and made me learn how to make wooden barrels. I didn't really like that, you know. I thought it was beneath me. That's how Chamdar got his hook in my jaw. That "Rivan King" business was like an angle-worm waved in Old Twister's face. If I did that, Twister wouldn't be able to help himself; he'd have to bite my bait. Does Chamdar ever do any fishing, Aunt Pol? If he does, he's probably very good. He certainly hooked me easily enough.' He laughed then, just a bit ruefully. 'Of course, I'm not nearly as clever as Old Twister is.'

'We broke Chamdar's line, though,' I told him.

'You mean *you* did. If you hadn't made it possible for me to hear what he was thinking, he'd have had me on a platter for supper. Anyway, I'm glad we moved here to Cherek. The people here in Emgaard aren't quite as serious as the Sendars in Seline were. Is it against the law to laugh in Sendaria? Sendars never seem to enjoy life. If I'd have hung my "gone fishing" sign on the door of the barrel-works in Seline, everybody in town would have talked about it for a year. Here in Emgaard, they just shrug and let it go at that. You know, I go for whole weeks without even thinking about crowns and thrones and all that foolishness. I've got good friends here, and now I've got a new son. I love it here, Aunt Pol, I really do. Everything I want in the whole wide world is here.'

'Including Old Twister,' I added, smiling fondly at him.

'Oh, yes,' he agreed. 'Old Twister and I have this little appointment. I *will* catch him one day, Aunt Pol, but don't start polishing your roasting pan, because after I catch him, I'm going to let him go again.'

Now, *that* startled me. 'You're going to do what?'

'I'm going to unhook him, unwrap my line from around him and then slip him back into the stream.'

'If you're just going to turn him loose, why catch him?'

He grinned broadly. 'For the fun of catching him, Aunt Pol. And, of course, if I turn him loose, I can catch him again.'

Men!

It was during Enalla's pregnancy that my wandering father went to Gar og Nadrak to follow up on one of those deliberately vague hints in the Darine Codex, and while he was there, he teamed up with a Nadrak gold-hunter named Rablek – and would you believe that they actually stumbled across a sizeable deposit of gold? I've seen my father's stack of gold bars, and though he's not quite as rich as I am, at least I don't have to worry about his picking my pocket every time he needs a few pennies for beer.

I sent word to him about Garel's birth, and he stopped by that autumn to have a look at his new grandson. Then he and I had a chance to talk. 'How did the fishing business work out?' he asked me.

'Probably better than you imagined it would,' I replied. 'Every man in Emgaard drops everything he's doing when the fish start biting, and they accepted Gelane as a brother just as soon as he told them about Old Twister.'

'Who's Old Twister?'

'That big fish that got away from Gelane the first day we got here.'

'The local fish have names?'

'A quaint custom here in Emgaard. Any word about Chamdar?'

'Not a peep. I think he's gone down a hole some place.'

'I believe I can live without his company.'

'Don't worry, Pol. I'll get him someday.'

'Now you sound just like Gelane. He says the same thing about Old Twister. There's a difference though. Gelane wants to catch Old Twister, but then he wants to let him go again.'

'What for?'

'So he can catch him again.'

'That's absolutely absurd.'

'I know. It's what he wants to do, though. Give my best to the twins. Will you be staying for supper?'

'What are we having?'

'Fish. What else?'

'I think I'll pass, Pol. I'm in the mood for baked ham this evening.'

'This particular fish didn't have a name, father. It's not like we'll be eating an old friend.'

'Thanks all the same, Pol. Stay in touch.' And then he left.

Our lives passed quietly and uneventfully in Emgaard. As he grew more proficient at his hobby, Gelane reached the point where he caught Old Twister at least once a year, and during the winter months he'd take food out to that secluded little pool in the swiftly-running mountain stream and feed his friend. I'm certain that Twister appreciated that, and he probably reached the point that he actually recognized his benefactor – by his smell certainly, if not by his appearance.

Enalla had two more children in rapid succession, both girls, so I had lots of babies to play with.

Old Twister died, of natural causes probably, in the winter of 4801, and given the number of predators and scavengers along the banks of any mountain stream it's really rather remarkable that Gelane actually found him. My nephew's face was sorrowful, and there were even tears in his eyes when he brought the huge trout home. He leaned his fish-pole against the side of the house, and I don't believe he ever touched it again. Then he sadly buried his friend near the stone wall in my garden, and he transplanted a pair of rose-bushes to mark the spot. You would not *believe* how big those bushes grew or how beautiful the roses were. Maybe in some strange sort of way that was Twister's thanks for all the times Gelane had fed him in the winter.

Late that summer – 4902, I think – something got into the stream that supplied water to our village. I don't think it was a dead animal, because the illness that swept through Emgaard didn't have that kind of symptoms. Despite my best efforts, many people in Emgaard died, and among them was Gelane. My time for grieving came only later, since there were still those among the sick who could be saved. Then, after the illness had run its course, I devoted much of my time trying to locate the source of the infection, but it eluded me.

Enalla and the children had not fallen ill, but the impact of my nephew's death was probably even more devastating than a personal illness ever could have been. There was at that particular time only one real vulture in Emsat, and he approached Enalla filled with false sympathy and an insultingly small offer for Gelane's shop. 'Why don't you let me handle it, dear?' I suggested.

'Oh, would you, Aunt Pol? I can't decide what to do.'

'I can, dear,' I told her, and I did. I visited the tavern that very evening and advised the local fishermen's group of the offer and let them know that I found the fellow who'd made it *very* offensive. They took care of the matter for me, and our local entrepreneur left town the very next morning – right after I'd treated a number of cuts and abrasions and set the broken bone in his right arm. Evidently, he'd fallen down a flight of stairs – repeatedly. Small town justice in Cherek is very direct, I noticed.

We might have left the village after that, but Enalla was reluctant to leave Gelane's grave behind, and by now she had many friends in the village. Garel and his sisters grew up there, and when Garel was sixteen, the bell rang in my head again. The girl who rang it was a bubbly blonde Cherek girl named Merel, and we got the pair of them married on fairly short notice. There weren't any bars for windows in Emgaard, and the village was immersed in a deep forest where there was far too much underbrush for my comfort, given the inevitable adolescent urge for exploration. Merel was one of those incredibly fertile Cherek girls who seem to be almost constantly pregnant. Every couple of years, Garel, who was now the village carpenter, added more rooms to our house, but he could still barely keep up. His eldest son, Darion, ended up with thirteen brothers and sisters.

I kept the family in Emgaard for probably longer than I'd stayed in one place since I'd left Arendia. There weren't any Angaraks in Cherek, after all, and the people in Emgaard shrugged off my longevity with the fairly simple, but wildly inaccurate explanation, 'She's a physician, after all, and everybody knows that physicians all know how to live for hundreds of years. They do it with all them secret herbs, you know.' I always choked just a little when I heard one of them say that, largely because he pronounced the 'h' in 'herbs'. It was their misconception, not their mispronunciation, that made it possible for me to remain in Emgaard with the descendants of Gelane and Enalla. I knew that I was breaking one of the primary rules, but it's safe to do that in Cherek, because just about everybody in Cherek breaks the rules every time he gets the chance.

We were all very happy there, and the centuries moved by at their stately pace almost unnoticed. I even lost track of the years, and I'm usually careful about that. I think it was in 5250 – or maybe it was '51 – when father stopped by for one of his infrequent visits. This time it wasn't a purely social call, though. 'The twins are starting to dig some hints out of the Mrin that we're getting close to the Godslayer, Pol,' he said gravely.

'Is it soon, father?'

'Well, no, not too soon, but definitely within the next century or so.'

'If we're getting that close, I'd better start thinking about relocating to Sendaria, hadn't I?'

He gave me a quizzical look.

'I can read the Darine and the Mrin as well as you can, father,' I told him pointedly. 'I know where the Godslayer's supposed to be born.'

'Don't jump just yet, Pol. The twins might be able to dig out a more specific time for us to work with, and I don't want you wandering around in Sendaria when I don't have Chamdar's location pinpointed. Who's the current heir?'

'His name's Geran, father. I like to keep that name well-polished for some very personal reasons. He just got married, so I don't think his son's going to be the one we've been waiting for.'

'Oh? Why not?'

'His bride's a Cherek, father, and a friendly glance is enough to make a Cherek girl pregnant. She'll probably go into labor before I can get packed and move us to Sendaria.'

'Are Chereks really *that* fertile?'

'Why do you think they all have such large families?'

'I thought it might have something to do with the climate.'

'What could the climate have to do with it?'

'Well, there are all those long, cold winter nights with nothing to do but –' He broke off abruptly.

'Yes, father?' I said sweetly. 'Do go on. I find your scientific speculation absolutely *fascinating*.'

He actually blushed.

CHAPTER 36

It wasn't too long after father's visit that mother also paid me a call – figuratively speaking, of course. *'Pol,'* her voice came to me.

'Yes, mother?' I replied, setting aside the pot I'd been scrubbing.

'You're going to have to go to Nyissa. Ctuchik's trying to subvert Salmissra. Somebody's going to have to set her straight.'

'Why me?' I didn't mean it, of course.

There was a long pause, and then my mother laughed. *'Because I said so, Pol. Whatever possessed you to ask such a foolish question?'*

'It's a family trait, mother. I've been listening to young boys ask that same question for twelve centuries or so now. Isn't it infuriating?'

'How do you usually answer?'

'About the same way you just did. I'll speak with the twins and ask them to fill in for me here. Then I'll go talk with the snake woman. Is Ctuchik corrupting her personally?'

'No. Ctuchik almost never leaves Rak Cthol. He's got Chamdar handling it.'

'Ah, that'd explain why father hasn't been able to find him.'

'How is he?'

I shrugged. *'About the same – unfortunately. You know father.'*

'Be nice.' And then she was gone.

I sent out my thought to the twins, and they came winging in about two days later.

'I think I'd rather that father didn't know where I'm going,' I said just before I left. 'He always seems to muddy things up when he sticks his nose into things I'm already taking care of.'

'You shouldn't talk that way about your father, Pol,' Beltira chided gently.

'Well, doesn't he?'

'I suppose he does, but it's not nice to come right out and say it like that, is it?'

I laughed and then introduced them to my little family. I wasn't too specific about the reason for my business trip, however. Then I went out into the surrounding forest and took my favorite alternative form of the falcon. I could have used the eagle, I suppose, but eagles are just a little too impressed by their own overwhelming nobility for my taste. In a peculiar way, eagles are the Arends of the bird world. Falcons are far more sensible, and they have an obsessive love of flying fast. Any time two falcons get together, there's almost always an impromptu race, which does sort of interrupt things during the mating season.

I winged my way down over the Cherek Bore and that patchwork quilt of greens and browns that's called Sendaria. From my vantage point several thousand feet above I was able to see just how neat and orderly Sendaria really was, and I heartily approved of that. Neatness is not perhaps one of the major virtues, but it *does* count.

I settled down for the night in a tree in the Asturian forest just south of the Camaar River, and I took wing again at first light the next day. I passed on down across Mimbre and on into Tolnedra before I stopped again.

Go ahead and say it. Yes, as a matter of fact, it *is* over a thousand miles from Val Alorn to Sthiss Tor, and no bird alive could possibly cover that much distance in three days, so I cheated. Does that answer your question?

It was humid in Sthiss Tor, and I hate places where the air's chewy. I came to rest in a tree outside the garishly colored walls of the city of the snake people and considered my options. I immediately discarded the notion of my favorite alternative form. The snowy owl isn't indigenous to Nyissa, and white birds *do* tend to stick out at night. The answer was fairly simple, of course, but I didn't care for it very much. I'm sure that bats are hard-working, industrious, and nice to their mothers, but I've always had an unreasoning sort of prejudice against them for some reason. They have such *ugly* faces! I gritted my beak and changed form.

It took some getting used to, I'll admit that. The flight of a bat is not at all like the flight of a bird. Feathers are sometimes inconvenient, but they make it much easier to fly. A bat has to literally claw his way through the air. I managed *that* part after a while, but it took me even longer to get used to the business of steering by

594

echoes. Did you know that bats do that? They aren't squeaking just for the fun of it, you know. A bat can fly in total darkness without ever running into anything. You would not *believe* how sharp their ears are. Once I'd assumed that form, I could hear the whine of a mosquito from a hundred yards away.

I flapped my way up into the air, passed over the nauseatingly colored wall of the city, and then zig-zagged my way through the stinking alleys toward the grotesque palace that was the center of Sthiss Tor. Then I flew over the wall of the compound and perched – upside down – under a hideous statue of something that'd obviously grown out of the imagination of some drug-crazed sculptor. I watched as assorted functionaries passed in and out through a very large doorway. They were almost all a bit plump, and there wasn't so much as a single whisker among them. I'd never fully understood the reasoning behind the Nyissan custom of obliging all of the Serpent Queen's servants to be eunuchs. Given the appetites of that long line of Salmissras, the idea seems uneconomical, to say the very least. It was at that point that I began to reconsider my previous aversion to bats. The bat's face may be ugly and his jointed wings ungainly, but his ears more than make up for those drawbacks. I could hear every word the palace eunuchs were saying. I could even hear the dry slither of all the snakes creeping around in dark corners. *That* made me a bit uncomfortable. The bat *is* a rodent, after all, and rodents are a staple in the diet of most reptiles.

'It's absolutely ridiculous, Rissus,' one shaved-headed eunuch was saying to his companion. 'Can't she even *read*?' He spoke in a rich contralto voice.

'I'm sure she can, Salas,' Rissus replied, 'but she's got her mind – or what's left of it – on other things.'

'You'd think her teachers would have warned her that the Angaraks have tried this before. How can she possibly be so gullible as to believe that a God would want to marry her?'

'She's been brought up to believe that Issa wants to marry her, Salas. If one God yearns for her company, why not another?'

'Everybody knows what happened the last time one of our queens fell into that Angarak trap,' Salas fretted. 'This Asharak fellow's leading her down that very same path, and the very same thing will happen. We'll have Alorns swinging through the rafters like apes if this goes any further.'

'Did *you* want to volunteer to tell her that?'

'Not me, Rissus. Her pet snake's molting right now, and he's *very* short tempered. That's *not* the way I want to die.'

Rissus shrugged. 'The answer's all around us, Salas. Asharak's going to have to eat or drink sometime – eventually.' He shook his head. 'That's what's got me so baffled. I've laced every meal and every flagon of wine that's presented to him with enough sarka to kill a legion, but he absolutely refuses to eat or drink.'

'What about odek?' Salas suggested. 'He'd absorb that right through his skin.'

'He never takes his gloves off! How can I kill somebody if he won't cooperate?'

'Why not just run a knife into him?'

'He's a Murgo, Salas. I'm not going to get into a knife-fight with a Murgo. I think we're going to have to hire a professional assassin.'

'They're awfully expensive, Rissus.'

'Look upon it as a patriotic duty, old boy. I can juggle the numbers in my account books enough so that we can get our money back. Let's go to the throne-room. Asharak usually visits the queen at midnight – between her other social engagements.'

Then the two of them went on inside the palace.

Even though I'd been hanging upside down, I'd found the conversation to be absolutely fascinating. I gathered that the current Salmissra wasn't held in very high regard by her servants. She evidently had very limited intellectual gifts, and even those had been clouded by whichever of the dozens of narcotics available to her was her favorite. I was really disappointed in Chamdar, though. Couldn't the Angaraks come up with something a bit more original than Zedar's tired old ploy? The remark Rissus had made as the two of them were entering the palace seemed to present an opportunity just too good to pass up, though. If Chamdar was still posing as Asharak the Murgo, *and* if he had a more or less standing appointment with Salmissra at midnight, I could confront the both of them at the same time and take care of everything all at once. Thrift is another virtue like neatness. It *does* count, but not for very much.

I remembered that when father and I'd visited Sthiss Tor before the Battle of Vo Mimbre, Salmissra's palace wasn't very well lighted, and so I kept my disguise and flew in through that wide doorway. The ceilings were high and buried in deep shadows, and I wasn't the only bat up there among the rafters. I flitted along the vaulted corridor leading to the throne-room, and when Salas and his friend entered, I was able to dart through high above them before they closed the door. Then I circled upward and came to roost – which is awkward for a bat – on the shoulder of the gigantic statue of the

Serpent-God, Issa, which rose behind the dais upon which Salmissra's throne stood.

The Serpent Queen wasn't there, and the eunuchs lounged around on the polished floor talking idly. Several of them, I noticed, were semi-comatose, and I wondered which was really worse, beer or the assorted narcotics the Nyissans found so entertaining. I suspect that my major objection to beer, wine, and more potent beverages springs from the noise – and the smell. A drunken man tends to bellow like a bull, and he smells terrible. A drugged man just goes to sleep, and he doesn't usually stink. I think it may be a question of aesthetics more than anything else. I pondered the question of exactly how I was going to approach Chamdar. The notion of assuming the form of an eagle the size of a barn briefly crossed my mind. I could seize him in my talons and soar up with him to a height of four or five miles and drop him.

'No, Pol,' mother's voice said quite firmly. 'We're going to need him later.'

'Spoilsport!' I accused in my high-pitched bat-voice. 'Can't you knock or something, mother? I never know for sure whether you're there or not.'

'Just assume that I'm always here, Pol. You'll be fairly close. Do you remember Countess Asrana?'

'How could I ever forget her?'

'You might want to think over just how she might deal with Chamdar.'

I did that for a moment, and then I quite nearly burst out laughing. 'Oh, mother!' I said gaily. 'That's a terrible thing to suggest.'

'Good, though,' she added.

The more I thought about it, the more I appreciated mother's suggestion. The gay, light-hearted Asrana would have driven the humorless Grolim absolutely wild, and wild Grolims tend to make mistakes, mistakes so obvious that even a drugged Salmissra would see them immediately.

Then the Serpent Queen languidly entered her throne-room, and the assembled eunuchs all assumed their customary groveling posture. The queen, of course, might as well have been the same one father and I had spoken with prior to the Battle of Vo Mimbre. There's nothing remarkable about that, since a close physical resemblance to the original Salmissra was the prime requirement for each of her successors. She undulated her way across the polished floor to her reclining throne, sat and began adoring herself in her mirror. I rather carefully probed at her mind, and what a chaos I found there! She was literally awash with several conflicting narcotics that combined to elevate her to a state of chemical ecstasy. When she was in that condition, she'd have probably believed that the sky was falling should anyone choose to tell her so. That most likely explained Chamdar's lack of any originality. He didn't have to come up with anything new or different. Zedar's tired old fiction was good enough,

Then, almost before Salmissra had settled in, the door to the throne-room opened again and Chamdar himself was escorted in. He'd shaved off the shaggy beard he'd worn in Seline, and now I was able to see his scarred Murgo face.

The doorkeeper rapped the butt of his staff of office on the floor and announced, 'The emissary of Ctuchik of Rak Cthol craves audience with her Divine Majesty!' His tone was slightly bored.

'The emissary approaches Divine Salmissra,' the eunuchs intoned in unison, and they didn't seem too excited either.

'Ah,' Salmissra almost drawled, 'so good of you to drop by, Asharak.'

'I am ever at your Divine Majesty's service,' he responded in his harshly accented voice. I gathered that the accent was a part of Chamdar's disguise, because he certainly hadn't spoken that way back at Seline.

I dropped off the back side of the statue and fluttered as quietly as I could to the floor behind the image of the Serpent-God. Then, carefully muffling the sound of what I was doing, I resumed my own form.

'Have you come to remind me how much the Dragon-God adores me, Asharak?' Salmissra asked in a decidedly kittenish manner.

Asharak responded even as I started to saunter around the massive statue. 'The whole world is stunned by your exquisite beauty, your Majesty. My poor words cannot possibly convey the depth of my God's longing for –' He broke off suddenly, staring at me in astonishment. 'What are –' he half-choked.

'Why, Chammy, dear,' I said in a fair imitation of Asrana's voice and manner, 'fancy meeting you here! What a delightful surprise!' Then I looked directly at the Serpent Queen. 'Ah, there you are, Sally. Where the deuce have you been? I've been looking all over for you.' The whole speech had been classic Asrana.

'What are *you* doing here?' Chamdar demanded.

'I just stopped by to say hello to Sally here,' I replied. 'It's not at all polite to pass through without paying one's respects, you know. Where have you been keeping yourself, dear boy? My father's been looking all over for you. Have you been hiding from him again?

Naughty, naughty, Chammy. He'll be *terribly* put out with you, you know. Father can be such an old stick in the mud sometimes.'

'Who is she?' Salmissra demanded, 'and why is she calling you by that name?'

'Have you been riding that tired old horse again, Chammy? What a bore. "Asharak the Murgo?" *Really* Chammy, I'm disappointed in you.' I looked at the confused-looking Queen of Nyissa. 'Has he been lying to you, Sally? You didn't *really* believe him, did you? "Asharak the Murgo" indeed! He's worn the spots off that one in most of the civilized world. Everybody knows that his name's really Chamdar, and that he's Ctuchik's favorite boot-licker. Chammy here's been living on a steady diet of boot-polish for over a thousand years now.'

'Who *are* you?' Salmissra demanded. 'And how *dare* you call me by that absurd name?'

'My name's Polgara, Sally, and I'll call you whatever I jolly-well choose to call you.' I dropped the light-hearted tone and delivered *that* announcement with a definite hint of steel in it.

I could almost feel the narcotics draining out of her blood. *'Polgara?'* she exclaimed.

'She lies!' Chamdar declared, his own voice slightly shrill and his eyes going wild.

'Oh, Chammy, how on earth would *you* know? You've been searching for me for a thousand and more years, and you've never once even seen me. If you're the best Ctuchik can come up with, my father's been overstating the peril. I could delete you without even working up an appetite.' I knew that it was melodramatic to the point of absurdity, but I leveled my forefinger slightly off to one side of him and disintegrated a polished flagstone with a sizzling thunderbolt. I've seldom done that, so perhaps I over-did it just a bit. The fragments, all jagged and red-hot, sprayed the groveling eunuchs, and they all immediately stopped being bored. They scrambled away, squealing like terrified mice.

'Oops,' I said apologetically. 'A little excessive, maybe. Sorry about the floor tiles, Sally. Now, where was I? Oh yes, now I remember.' And I exploded several more flagstones in the general vicinity of Chamdar's feet.

He began hopping around wildly. 'There you are, Sally,' I drawled. 'Murgos *do* know how to dance. All you have to do is give them a bit of encouragement.'

'Have you come here to kill me?' Salmissra quavered.

'Kill you? Good heavens no, Sally dear. You and I both know that isn't what I'm going to do to you.' I made only the slightest move with just one finger as I released my Will. What I was doing was only an illusion, after all, so I didn't have to wave both arms when I did it. 'Look in your mirror, Sally. *That's* what I'm going to do to whichever Salmissra is unlucky enough to make me cross with her.'

Telling Salmissra – any Salmissra – to look in her mirror is almost like telling water to run downhill. She took one look at the large mirror beside her throne and screamed in absolute horror. Staring back at her with unblinking eyes and a flickering tongue was a very large, mottled snake. 'No!' the Serpent Queen shrieked, desperately feeling her face, her hair, and her body with violently trembling hands to assure herself that the hideous reflection wasn't really what she looked like. 'Make it go away!' she squealed.

'Not just yet, Sally, dear,' I said in my best frigid tone. 'I want you to remember that image. Now then, has Chammy here been trying to foist his tired old promise off on you? You didn't *really* believe that Torak was going to marry you, did you?'

'He told me so!' Salmissra said, pointing an accusing finger at the now shaken Grolim.

'Oh, Chammy, Chammy, Chammy!' I chided. 'Whatever am I going to do with you? You *know* that was a lie. You know perfectly well that Torak's heart belongs to another.' I was gambling there of course. I wasn't entirely sure that Chamdar had been at Vo Mimbre.

'Who is it that Torak loves?' Salmissra demanded in a slightly stricken voice. In spite of everything, I guess she still harbored some hopes.

'Who?' I said. 'Why me of course, Sally. I thought everybody knew that. He even proposed to me once, and it absolutely broke his heart when I turned him down. Actually, that's why he lost the duel with Brand at Vo Mimbre. The poor dear only has one eye, you know, and it was so full of tears of disappointment that he didn't even see Brand's sword coming. Don't you just *love* it when your admirers fight duels with each other to prove their love? It's so romantic to see all that blood spurting. I just quivered all over to see Torak standing there with that sword stuck right through his head like that.'

I heard a broken sob, and I glanced quickly at Chamdar. The Murgo was actually weeping! Of course Torak *was* his God.

'Now, then, Sally, I think you'd better ask the fellow called Salas what happened to the Salmissra who ordered the murder of the Rivan King. If you believe Chammy's lies you'll be walking down the same path. If the Alorns catch up with you, they'll burn you at the stake. Think about that and then take another look in your mirror. It's the stake or the snake, Sally, and that's not really very much of a choice, is it?' Then I leveled that well-known 'steely gaze' at the still red-eyed Chamdar. 'Chammy, you naughty, naughty boy! Now you march right out of here and go back to Rak Cthol. Tell Ctuchik that he'd better come up with something new, because this one's all worn out now. Oh, and give him my regards, will you? Tell him that I yearn for the day of our meeting.'

'But –' he started to protest.

'You heard her, Chamdar!' Salmissra snapped. 'Get out of my sight. And you'd better hurry. Your diplomatic immunity expires in about a half an hour, and after that, there'll be a sizeable price on your head. Now get out!'

Chamdar fled.

'Nice touch, there,' I complimented Salmissra.

'Can I really do that, Pol?' she asked.

'It's your kingdom, dear,' I assured her. 'You can do anything you want to do.'

'Is it possible for you and me to be friends?' she asked.

'I think we already are,' I said, smiling.

'Then would you *please* get that awful snake out of my mirror?'

I spent several months in Sthiss Tor gradually leeching the assorted narcotics out of Salmissra's blood until she reached the point of being able to think coherently. She was no mental giant, but once she came out of that drug-induced fog, she began to function rationally. The eunuchs who actually ran the government were more than a little upset by my intervention, so one evening after Salmissra had drifted off to sleep, I sent for Rissus, who probably wielded more power than most of his cohorts – enough at any rate that he had to take the usual precautions to keep them from poisoning him. He seemed a bit apprehensive when he entered the garish sitting-room of the Serpent Queen's private apartment. 'You wanted to see me, Lady Polgara?' he said in his eunuch's contralto.

'Yes, Rissus,' I said. 'I thought that you and I ought to have a little chat.'

'Of course, Lady Polgara.'

'I'm sure you've noticed the change that's come over your queen.'

'How could I miss it? You've got her completely under your control. How *did* you manage to pull that off so quickly?'

'I offered her friendship, Rissus. She's a very lonely person, you know.'

'How could she possibly be lonely? She's got a whole stable of pretty boys to entertain her.'

'Salmissra needs friendship, Rissus, and there's none of that involved in her frolics with her pretty boys. She's not brilliant by any stretch of the imagination, but she's clever enough to rule here if you and Salas and some of the others advise her. Are you feeling up to statesmanship, Rissus? Could you set aside your petty scheming and the incidental poisonings of your rivals and concentrate on actually making the government work?'

'What an unnatural thing to suggest,' he murmured.

'Shocking, isn't it?' I agreed. 'Here's the way we'll do it. I've had a fair amount of experience in positions of power at times, and I'm going to start reminiscing – telling Salmissra stories about how I managed this or that crisis, the tedious business of coddling powerful nobles, arranging the tax-code so that it didn't generate an immediate rebellion, and all the other tricks of running a government. The whole idea will be to get Salmissra interested in the field of politics. Then, when she starts asking questions, I'll pretend to be unfamiliar with Nyissan customs and suggest that she send for you. The whole idea is to rather gently educate her to the point that she's an adequate ruler. From there, we'll move on to letting her make decisions.'

He gave me a shrewd look. 'Where's the catch, Lady Polgara?' he asked. 'What's in this for you?'

'I want stability here in Nyissa, Rissus. There are things afoot that you aren't aware of, and they're going to be fairly titanic. I don't want Ctuchik dictating Nyissan policy.'

'You won't get any arguments from me there, Polgara.'

'Good. Now, then, I've weaned her off some of the more incapacitating narcotics, but let's reduce her intake of the others as well. I know there are certain compounds she has to take regularly to keep her from visibly aging, but let's cut her dosage to an absolute minimum. Who's her apothecary?'

'Speaking,' he said with a faint smile.

'Really? It's very unusual for a pharmacologist to be in a position of power in government.'

'Not in Nyissa it isn't, Polgara. Here in Sthiss Tor, the key to the queen's drug cabinet is the key to power. It may sound immodest, but I'm the most skilled pharmacologist in all of Nyissa. In a land of addicts, the apothecary rules, but it's all sort of under the table. It might be nice to be official.'

'Shall we take our Salmissra in hand and make a real queen of her then, Rissus?'

'That might be nice. A real queen would be sort of a novelty. We could achieve that stability you want – set up strict procedures for poisoning opponents, limitations on the use of professional assassins, and all that.' He leaned back reflectively. 'Things have been chaotic here in Nyissa for the last century or so,' he noted. 'Maybe it's time for us to set up some rules, and around here, nobody's going to pay attention to rules unless they're handed down from the throne. Yes, I'll agree to your proposal. Let's go ahead and make a real queen out of Salmissra.'

And so we did that. From earliest childhood, Salmissra had never had a real friend. At the first sign of her affection for any of those around her, the sound of the tops coming off all the poison bottles rattled the windows. She was desperately lonely and more than a little afraid. I assured her that nobody in his right mind would try to poison *me*, and she opened her heart to me with an almost child-like trust. Actually, it was rather touching. I discovered a simple uncomplicated little girl under all the trappings of her royalty, and I became genuinely fond of her.

That's happened to me on occasion. The most impossible friend-ship I've developed is the one I have for Zakath. *That* one should have stopped the sun. My affection for Salmissra didn't even come close to that one.

I had a professional interest in Nyissan pharmacology, so between us, Salmissra and I ran poor Rissus ragged. When he wasn't giving *her* lessons in practical politics – Nyissan style – he was introducing me to the exotic world of Nyissan herbs. Oddly, there were even some roots, berries, leaves, and twigs in the jungles of Nyissa that were actually beneficial – under tightly controlled circumstances, of course.

After I'd been in Nyissa for a half-year or so, the twins advised me that father had stopped by Emgaard and that he wanted to see me. Salmissra wept when I told her that I was going to have to leave soon, but I'd carefully insinuated Rissus and Salas into her affection, so I was sure that they could fill in the gap in their queen's life. To insure that they'd never betray her childlike trust, I told them that if they did, I'd come back to Nyissa and feed them to the leeches that infested the River of the Serpent. You wouldn't *believe* how fervently they promised to be good after *that* little exchange.

Then I went to the throne-room and said goodbye to the Serpent Queen. She wept and clung to me, but I gently untangled her arms from about my neck, kissed her cheek, and handed her over to Rissus and Salas. Then I left.

It was early in the winter when I reached the Vale, and the snow was piled deeply around father's tower. I swooped in, resumed my own form, and braced myself.

'Well, Pol,' he said as I came up the stairs. 'I was sort of wondering if you'd decided to stay the winter in Nyissa.'

'That's the rainy season down there, father,' I reminded him. 'Sthiss Tor's bad enough already without adding a steady downpour. You wanted to see me?'

'I always want to see you, Pol. I yearn for your company all the time.'

'Please,' I said, 'spare me. What's bothering you now?'

'Did it occur to you to let me know what you were doing?'

'Not really, no. It wasn't anything I couldn't handle, father.'

'I sort of like to stay abreast of things, Pol.'

'There wouldn't be any problem if that's *all* you did, father, but you're nosey.'

'Pol!' he protested.

'But you are, father, and you know it. Oh, I met Chamdar down there. I don't think he enjoyed our meeting very much, but *I* certainly did.'

'Was he breathing the last time you saw him?'

'I think he was breathing fire, father. I spiked his scheme by exposing him to Salmissra, and she put a price on his head.'

'Slick,' he complimented me.

'I rather liked it. Have you got anything to eat around here? I'm positively famished.'

'There's something in that pot over there. I forget exactly what it is.'

I went to his fireplace and lifted the lid. 'Was it pea-soup, perhaps?'

'I don't think so.'

'Maybe we'd better throw it out, then.'

'Why?'

'Because it's green, father. I think you might have let it age a little too long. Go down to the pantry and bring up a ham. I'll fix us something to eat and tell you all about what Salmissra and I did to poor old Chammy.'

Father laughed uproariously when I gave him a slightly embellished account of my adventure in the land of the Snake People.

'You did very well, Pol,' he approved when I'd finished. 'Were you *really* that fond of Salmissra, though?'

'She wasn't at all like most of the others, father,' I told him a bit sadly. 'I believe she was quite a bit like the one who had Gorek assassinated. I think I felt much the same about this one as you did about the other one. She's very vulnerable, and once I showed her that I was her friend, she was very affectionate. She even cried when I left.'

'I didn't think anybody named Salmissra even knew how to cry.'

'You're wrong, father. They all do. They've learned not to let it show is all. Oh, I saw movement on the south caravan route on my way here.'

'Yes. The Murgos have reopened trade with Tolnedra. That's a polite way of saying that we're going to go back to seeing spies every time we turn around again. You'd better go on to Cherek and let the twins come back home and start digging into the Mrin again. If anybody's going to make sense out of it, it'll be them.'

'First thing in the morning, father,' I told him. 'Oh, that whatever-it-was you had growing in your cooking pot is in that bucket by the head of the stairs. I'd take it out and bury it, if I were you. I think it's getting very close to coming alive, and I don't believe you'd want it crawling into bed with you.'

And so I went on back to Emgaard to take up my task again, and the twins went back to the Vale to take up theirs. My sojourn in Nyissa had been something of the order of a vacation, but every vacation comes to an end eventually, and it was good to get back to work again.

Then, in 5300, the twins made another breakthrough, and they confidently announced that this was the century of the Godslayer. I spoke at some length with Geran, who was by now quite elderly, and with his son, Darion, a stone-cutter. Geran, as I said, was quite old, and he was just a little vague. I don't think he really understood when I told him that we were going to have to move to Sendaria.

'I think it'd be kinder if we left him here, Aunt Pol,' Darion told me. 'He won't leave mother's grave anyway, and I don't think he'd understand why it's necessary. Why don't we just say that we're going on a trip and let it go at that? After a month or so, he probably won't even remember us. I'll get someone to stay with him here, and he'll be all right.'

I didn't like it, but Darion was probably right. Geran was doddering on the edge of senility right now, and I knew of no quicker way to kill him than to uproot him at his age.

Darion, his wife Esena, and their ten-year-old son, Darral, went with me to Val Alorn, and we took ship for Darine and traveled on down to Medalia, where I bought us a house and set Darion up in business as a stone-cutter. The products that came out of his shop were tombstones, for the most part, and that's a gloomy sort of business. Darral learned his father's trade, and when he was sixteen or so, he married Alara, the daughter of a local dry goods merchant.

Father pestered us almost continually until, in 5329, Alara finally gave birth to a baby boy. Father's face fell the first time he looked at the baby, Geran. 'He's not the one, Pol,' he reported.

'That's not my fault, father,' I told him. 'Oh, by the way, in just a few years, I'm going to be moving Darral and his family.'

'Oh?'

'Medalia's right on the main road between Darine and Muros, and there are just a few too many strangers passing through town for my comfort. I want a place that's just a little more remote.'

'Oh? Where have you decided to settle?'

'It's a little village up in the mountains.'

'What's the name of the place?'

'Annath, father. It's right next to the Algarian border, and there's a big stone-quarry there, so Darral should be able to find work that doesn't involve tombstones.'

CHAPTER 37

Did you perhaps notice that my explanation of the decision to move my little family to Annath was slightly less than candid? I thought you might have noticed that. I've found over the years that it's not really a good idea to give my father *too* much information. Father has an overpowering urge to dabble in things, and his dabbling frequently ends up being disastrous. I suspect that my father thinks of himself as an artist, but his definition of art and mine are worlds apart.

Actually, I'd never even seen Annath, and my decision to move there was based entirely on its proximity to the Algarian border. Mother had told me that Geran was destined to marry an Algarian girl named Ildera, and I thought it might be a good idea if the two of them were to grow up in the same general vicinity.

As it turned out, though, our move was delayed by old Darion's final illness, which was unfortunately quite protracted. I dislike lingering illnesses even more than I hate those sudden heart stoppages. A decent illness would run its course in a week or ten days, and the patient would then recover or die. Death has little dignity if it's either too quick or too slow. Anyway, Darion hung on until 5334, and after his funeral, a change of scene was definitely in order. Everything in Medalia reminded us of our loss.

Darral sold his stoneworks and our house, and we packed up such possessions as we wanted to keep in a pair of wagons and left Medalia early on a summer morning with Darrel driving one wagon and me driving the other.

*   *   *

Yes, as a matter of fact, I *do* know how to drive a team of horses. Why do you keep asking these silly questions? We'll never reach the end of this if you keep interrupting me like that.

It was summer, as I recall, and summer's a nice time to travel in the mountains. There was no real hurry, so we took our time. At one point, Darral reined in his team, looking speculatively at a mountain stream that was gurgling over smooth round stones and joyously plunging into deep quiet pools. 'What do you think, Aunt Pol?' he called back to me. 'This might be a good place to camp for the night, and we really ought to rest the horses.'

'It's only noon, Darral,' Alara pointed out.

'Well, this is a good place, and we *have* pushed the horses pretty hard. It's all been uphill, you know.' He sounded sincerely concerned about the horses, and he seemed to be making a special point of not looking at the stream. I knew the signs, of course. I'd seen them often enough back in Emgaard. I looped the reins of my team around the brake handle of my wagon and climbed down. 'Over there,' I said, pointing at a mossy little area under some low-hanging cedar trees. 'Before you get started, unhitch the horses, water them, and stake them out in that meadow. Then build a fire-pit and gather enough firewood for supper *and* for breakfast.'

'I sort of thought –'

'I'm sure you did, dear. Get the work done first, and *then* you can go play.'

He gave me a sort of sheepish look and then absolutely flew into his chores.

'What did you mean by that, Aunt Pol?' Alara asked me. 'Darral's a grown man now. He doesn't play any more.'

'Oh, *really*? You have a lot to learn, Alara. Take a look at your husband's face. He hasn't worn that expression since he was about nine years old.'

'What's he going to do?'

'He's going to offer to provide supper, dear.'

'We've got dried beef and flour and peas and all in the back of your wagon.'

'Yes, I know. He'll say that he's tired of the same old thing every night, though.'

'Why would he do that?'

'He wants to go fishing, Alara. That little steam's seducing him for all it's worth, and he's not resisting very hard.'

'He can't catch enough fish to feed us all in one afternoon.'

'Well, he might, and there's always tomorrow.'

'Tomorrow?' Her face grew indignant. 'That's absurd! We'll never get to Annath if he stops every time we come to some little brook.'

'You'd probably better get used to it, Alara. I think it runs in the family. Tomorrow morning, one of the horses will be lame, or a wagon wheel will have to be greased – and of course it'll be too late to start out by the time he's finished.'

'How long will this last?'

'That probably depends entirely on how the fish are biting. I'd give it about three days – unless Old Twister has some relatives here in these mountains.'

'Who's Old Twister?'

So, while Darral was furiously chopping firewood, I told her about Gelane's years-long campaign to catch that wily old trout in the stream outside Emgaard. It passed the time, and it put Alara in a much better humor. Alara was a serious young lady, and laughing was good for her. Darral finished with his firewood, cut himself and his son some willow saplings to use for poles and went off to entertain the fish. 'Oh, one thing, dear,' I said to Alara. 'Don't, whatever you do, reach for a knife if they happen to bring home some fish.'

'Why would I reach for a knife, Aunt Pol?'

'Exactly. That's the fundamental rule you've always got to keep out in plain sight. You've got to establish it right from the start.'

'I don't understand.'

'Look him right in the face, cross your arms, and say, "You caught them, so you clean them." Never deviate from that, even if he's managed to fall and break his arm. *He* cleans the fish. You don't. He may pout about it, but don't weaken. If you relent even once, you'll betray all of womankind.'

She laughed. 'You're joking, aren't you, Aunt Pol?'

'Not even one little bit. Don't *ever* clean a fish. Tell him that it's against your religion or something. Believe me, dear, if you ever clean so much as *one* fish, you'll be doing it for the rest of your life.'

Darral and his little son Geran actually caught fish in that small stream – enough at any rate to still the yearning almost all men fall prey to when they happen across fast water. It took them two days to do it, though, which is a fairly standard period of time for it. Then we moved on, plodding through the mountains toward our destination.

The mountain gorge where Annath lay ran from north to south, and we reached it about mid-afternoon on a glorious summer day.

I was struck by the similarity of the village to Emgaard. Mountain towns are almost always strung out along the banks of a stream, and that puts them at the bottom of a gorge. I suppose you *could* build a village on a hilltop, but you won't be popular with the women of the town if you do, since the chore of carrying water inevitably falls to the women. Women like to be close to a stream, and most women would be happier if the stream ran *through* the kitchen.

I liked what I saw about the village, but I *did* feel an apprehensive chill the first time it came into view. Something rather dreadful was going to happen here in Annath.

Virtually everyone in town turned out when our wagons rolled down the single street. People in small towns do that, you know.

'Where wuz it y' wuz a-goin', stranger?' a grizzled old codger with a woodsy dialect asked Darral.

'Right here, friend,' Darral replied, 'and I think we can drop that "stranger". My family and I've come here to settle permanently, so I'm sure we'll all get to know each other.'

'An' whut might yer name be?'

Darral grinned at him. 'Well, it *might* be "Belgarath" or maybe "Kal Torak". Would you be inclined to believe me if I offered you one of those?'

'Not hordly,' the old fellow chuckled.

'Oh, well,' Darral sighed. 'It was worth a try, I guess. Actually, my name's Darral, and this is my wife Alara. The lady driving the other wagon's my Aunt Pol, and the little boy sleeping beside her is my son, Geran.'

'I'm proud t' make yer acquaintance, Darral,' the old fellow said. 'My name's Farnstal, an' I'm usual th' one as greets strangers – mostly on accounta I'm a nosey old coot. Th' inn's on down th' street a piece, an' y' kin settle in thar till y' makes more permanent arrangements. What might be yer trade, Darral?'

'I'm a stone-cutter – from over near Sulturn. I used to spend all my time chiseling tombstones, but that's gloomy work, so I decided to find something more cheerful to do.'

'If y' knows yer way around a hammer an' chisel, y've come t' th' right place, Darral. Th' menfolk hereabouts bin choppin' stone blocks outta that mounting over thar since about three weeks afore th' earth wuz made, an' we'll prob'ly keep on achoppin' until a couple months after it comes to an end. Why don't we drift on down t' th' inn an' git you folks settled in? Then we kin all git acquainted.'

Darral was very smooth, you'll note. His easy manner slipped us into the society of Annath with scarcely a ripple. You'll also note that he was just a little imprecise about our point of origin. It wasn't exactly an out and out lie. Medalia and Sulturn aren't really *too* far apart – ninety miles or so is about all – so you might say that Darral was only ninety miles from the truth.

We went on down to the tiny inn with most of the townspeople following along behind us. Small towns are almost always like that. We took rooms, and several of the townsmen helped Darral unhitch the horses. The women of the town, of course, homed in on Alara and me, and the children immediately absconded with Geran. By the time the sun went down, we weren't strangers any more.

Nobody owned the mountain where the local stone-quarry was, so the villagers had formed a 'share and share alike' cooperative venture to gouge granite blocks from its side. Farnstal told Darral that 'a stone-mason feller from Muros comes by in th' fall t' take 'em off our hands every year – which sorta keeps 'em from pilin' up an' gittin' underfoot. That way we don't hafta build no wagons er feed no oxen t' haul 'em all down t' civilization an' git rid of 'em. I ain't never bin real close friends with no ox, personal.'

'You know, I feel much the same way,' Darral agreed. 'To my way of looking at it, the proper place for an ox is on the supper-table.'

'I'll float my stick alongside yers on that score.'

Darral took his tools to the quarry the next morning and started cutting stone blocks almost as if he'd always lived there, and the women of the town took Alara and me to the upper end of the single street and pointed out a vacant, seriously run-down house.

'Who does it belong to?' I asked a plump lady named Elna.

'Why probably to whoever moves in and fixes the roof,' Elna replied. 'The family that owned it all died of the pox about ten years ago, and it's been standing empty ever since.'

'It doesn't really belong to anybody, Pol,' another matron assured me. 'I live two houses down, and the place is an awful eyesore the way it is. We've all asked our menfolk to tear it down, but you know how men are. The best we've been able to get out of them is, "we'll get around to it – someday". I haven't been holding my breath.'

'We can't just move in,' Alara objected.

'Why not?' Elna asked her. 'You need a house, and we need neighbors. The answer's sitting right there growing moss.' She looked around at the other ladies. I got the distinct impression that she was the local social lioness. 'Why don't we all talk with our husbands this evening, ladies? If Alara here wants formal permission to move into the place, we'll just tell our menfolk to take a vote on the matter – and we'll let them all know that they'll get a steady diet of boiled tripe if they vote wrong.'

They all laughed knowingly at that. Never underestimate the power of the woman who runs the kitchen.

Since it was summer and the evenings were quite long, it only took Darral – and the rest of the men in town – about a week to repair the roof and the doors and windows. Then the town ladies joined Alara and me in a day of furious house-cleaning, and it was all done. We were home, and that's always very nice.

I don't know that I've ever known a town as friendly as Annath. Everyone there went out of his way to help us get settled in, and they were always dropping by 'just to visit'. A goodly part of that was due to the isolation of the place, of course, and the hunger for news – any news – of the outside world. Then, when Darral chanced to mention the fact that I was a physician, our place in the community was secure. There'd never been a physician in town before, so now the villagers could go ahead and get sick without the danger of having home remedies rammed down their throats. A lot of home remedies actually *do* work, but the one thing they all have in common, whether they work or not, is their universally foul taste. I've never quite understood where that notion, 'if it tastes bad, it's good for you' came from. Some of *my* remedies are actually quite delicious.

I didn't care much for the stone-mason from Muros who came to town that fall followed by a long string of empty wagons. He behaved as if he were doing us a favor by hauling away our stone blocks. I've known a lot of businessmen over the years, and businessmen don't do *anything* unless it's profitable. He arrived looking bored, and he sneeringly appraised the neat stacks of stone blocks at the mouth of the quarry. Then he made his offer with a note of finality.

Darral, who knew quite a bit about business himself, was wise enough to hold his tongue until the fellow had left with his plunder. 'Was that about what he usually offers?' he asked the other townsmen.

'It's purty much what he alluz pays, Darral,' old Farnstal replied. 'It seemed a little light t' us, fust time he come here, but he wint on an' on 'bout th' expense o' freightin' all that stone back t' Muros an' sich, an' then he ups an' sez "take 'er or leave 'er", an' thar warn't no other buyers handy, so we tuk 'er. It's gotten t' be sorta like a habit, I guess. I'm a-ketchin' a hint that y' might think we jist got ourselves stung.'

'I've bought granite blocks before, Farnstal, and that wasn't the price *I* had to pay.' Darral squinted at the ceiling. 'Do we cut stone in the wintertime?' he asked.

''Tain't hordly a good idee, Darral,' Farnstal replied. 'Th' snow piles up fearful deep up thar on th' top edge of the quarry, an' a good sneeze is all she'd take t' bust 'er loose. A feller whut's roped t' that stone face could wind up apickin' a avalanche outten his teeth if somebody happens t' git hisself a itchy nose at th' wrong time.'

'Well then,' Darral said, 'when winter comes, I think I'll take a little trip on down to the low country and ask a few questions about the going price of granite. We're cutting very fine stone here, gentlemen. Are the other faces all of the same quality?'

'There's a layer of slate up near the top of the east face,' a hulking stone-cutter named Wilg rumbled in his deep voice. 'We don't waste our time with that, but the man from Muros is good enough to haul it away for us.'

'Oh, I'm *sure* he is,' Darral said sardonically. 'And he doesn't even charge us for the hauling, does he?'

'Not a penny,' Wilg replied.

'How charitable of him. I believe I'll take a small block of our granite and a few slabs of that slate with me when I go. I think I'd like to shop around for some prices. It might just be that next year there'll be two or three other bidders for our stone. A little competition might teach the man from Muros the value of being truthful and honest with people.'

'You think he's been cheating us on the price of our granite?' Wilg rumbled ominously.

'It's not just the granite, Wilg,' Darral said. 'Have you ever been in a town of any size?'

'Medalia once.'

'What were the roofs of most of the houses made of?'

'Slate, I think it was.' Wilg stopped abruptly, his eyes first widening and then narrowing dangerously. 'We've been giving him that slate for nothing, and when he gets it back to Muros, he sells it, right?'

'It certainly looks that way to me,' Darral replied.

'I wonder if I could still catch up to him,' Wilg muttered grimly, clenching and unclenching his huge fists.

'Don't be a-worryin' yerself none about it, Wilg,' Farnstal advised. 'He's bin skinnin' us fer years now, so I kin practical guarantee that he'll come back next fall with his skinnin' knife all sharp th' way he alluz does. Then we'll *all* be able t' git in a lick er two at 'im. He'll be a-bleedin' outta places he didn't even know he *had* 'fore he leaves.' He cocked an eye at my nephew. 'Yer a real handy feller t' have around, Darral,' he said. 'We bin stuck back here in th' mountings fer s' long, we clean fergot how sivilized people acts.' He shook his head mournfully. 'Seems ez how bein' honest jist ain't in style no more back in sivilization. But I'll tell y' one thing fer certain sure.'

'Oh? What's that?'

'Come next summer, there's one feller from Muros ez is gonna git hisself a quick lesson in honest. After Wilg here holds him down an' I jump up and down on his belly fer a hour er so, he'll be s' honest it'll jist make y' sick t' look at 'im.'

'I can hardly wait,' Darral said with a broad grin.

Darral *did* make a quick tour of the towns and cities of northern Sendaria that winter, and the local inn was filled to overflowing with eager buyers the next summer. Over his objections, my nephew was appointed by acclamation to handle the negotiations, and the village of Annath was suddenly ankle deep in money. Our local granite, as it turned out, was of the very highest quality, and the slate, which the villagers had literally thrown away, was even better. Darral took the simplest approach to our new would-be buyers. He held an auction – 'How much am I bid for this stack of blocks?' and so on. Every buyer went away happy and with his wagons groaning.

The man from Muros was late that year, so he missed all the excitement, *and* the view of the back end of all those wagons rolling out of town. 'Where's the granite?' he demanded. 'You don't expect me and my teamsters to load it on the wagons ourselves, do you?'

'I'm afraid we don't have anything for you this year, friend,' Darral told him in a pleasant tone.

'What do you *mean*, you don't have anything?' The mason's voice was shrill. 'Did every man in the whole town turn lazy? Why didn't you let me know you didn't have any stone for me? I've made this trip for nothing. This is going to cost you next year, you know. Maybe I won't even bother next year.'

'We'll miss you,' Darral murmured. 'Not too much, but we *will* miss you. There's a new procedure here in Annath, friend. We hold an auction here now.'

'Who'd come this far for third-rate stone?'

'There were about a dozen or so, weren't there?' Darral asked the other stone-cutters. 'I sort of lost count during the bidding.'

'You can't do this to me!' the Muros mason screamed. 'We've got a contract. I'll have the law on you for this!'

'What contract?'

'It's a verbal contract.'

'Oh? Who was it with?'

'It was with Merlo, that's who.'

The stone-cutters of Annath all burst out laughing. 'Merlo's been dead for five years now,' one of them said, 'and he was ninety-four when he died. Merlo would say anything anybody wanted him to say, if that somebody happened to be willing to buy him a tankard of beer. He was the town drunk, and his word wasn't worth any more than the price of the last tankard of beer. If you want to take that to a lawyer, go right ahead. All you'll get out of it is a quick lesson in *real* swindling. You won't get anything from us, but that lawyer will probably get everything you own out of you.'

The stone-mason's eyes grew desperate. 'What about all that worthless slate I've been hauling away for you?' he said. 'I'll take that, if you haven't got anything else.' His eyes narrowed shrewdly. 'I'll have to charge you for taking it away, though. Always before, I was only doing it out of friendship.'

'Funny thing about that slate,' Darral said. 'A man from Darine looked at it, and he outbid everybody else for it. We got as much for the slate as we did for the granite. Isn't that strange? Oh, by the way, a couple of my neighbors would like to have a little chat with you.' He looked over his shoulder at the others. 'Has anybody seen Wilg and old Farnstal?' he asked mildly.

'I think they're waiting on the road just north of town, Darral,' one of the quarry workers replied with a sly smirk. 'I think they want to speak privately with our friend here.'

We didn't hear either Wilg or Farnstal when they spoke to the man from Muros, but we *did* hear him. They probably heard him back in Muros.

'Is he honest now?' Darral asked the wickedly grinning pair when they returned to town much later.

'Jist ez honest ez a newborn lamb,' Farnstal replied. 'I think it might be on accounta he got hisself religion 'bout half-way thoo our little discussion.'

'Religion?'

'He wuz a-doin' a whole lotta prayin' there along tords th' end, warn't he, Wilg?'

'It sounded a lot like praying to me,' Wilg agreed.

615

The celebration in Annath that night was longer and more boisterous than the one after the auction had been. Money's all very nice, but sometimes getting even is even nicer.

Darral was the hero of Annath after that, and now we were firmly established. I don't think in all those years that I've ever felt more secure. Figuratively speaking, I'd finally found my 'cave in the mountains'.

In 5338, after we'd been in Annath for about four years, mother paid me another of those visits. *'You're going to have to go back to Nyissa, Pol,'* she told me.

'Now what?' I grumbled. *'I thought I had that all settled.'*

'There's a new Salmissra on the throne, Pol, and the Angaraks are taking another run at her.'

'I think I'll fly on down to Rak Cthol and turn Ctuchik into a toad,' I muttered darkly.

'It isn't Ctuchik. This time it's Zedar again. I think Ctuchik and Zedar are playing some obscure game with each other, and whichever one of them subverts Salmissra wins.'

'What a bore. I'll send for father and have him fill in for me here. Then I'll run on down to Nyissa and settle this once and for all. This is starting to make me tired.'

I wasn't really very polite to my father when he arrived. I overrode his objections, refused to answer his questions, and flatly told him what to do. It was probably a little blunt. I think there were faint overtones of 'Sit! Stay!' involved in it.

When I reached Sthiss Tor, I didn't bother with bats or anything like that. I simply marched up to the palace door, announced who I was, and told them that I *would* see Salmissra. Several eunuchs tried to block my way, but that stopped when I started translocating them in all directions. Some found themselves clinging to rafters high overhead and others were suddenly out in the surrounding jungle with no memory of how they got there. Then I transposed myself into the form of that ogress that'd been so useful back on that forest road in southern Sendaria a few eons ago, and I was suddenly all alone in the corridor leading to Salmissra's throne-room. I changed back and went on in.

Zedar was with the current Salmissra when I entered, and he really looked terrible. He was shabby and run down, and there was a haunted look in his eyes. The five centuries he'd spent in that cave watching his Master mildewing hadn't really been very good to him. He stared at me as I entered, and the light of recognition dawned in his eyes. *'Polgara?'* he exclaimed in startled voice. Someone had evidently described me to him. 'Is that really you?'

'Marvelous to see you again, old boy,' I lied. 'Who's watching over Torak's carcass? Ctuchik, perhaps?'

'Don't be absurd.' He frowned and raised a quizzical eyebrow. 'You seem to know me,' he said, 'but I don't seem to recall that we've ever met before.'

'We weren't formally introduced, dear boy, but I had the privilege – if that's the right word – of being present during your conversations with One-eye back at Vo Mimbre.'

'That's impossible! I'd have sensed your presence.'

'No, as a matter of fact, you wouldn't have. Don't tell me that you don't know how to do that. Your Master's left a huge gap in your education, old boy. Shall we get down to business here? I'm much too busy to have to come down to this stinking swamp every generation or so to straighten things out.' Then I looked directly at the Serpent Queen. She closely resembled Sally, of course, but there were some differences. She had no trace of Sally's endearing vulnerability, for one thing. *This* Salmissra was made of steel. 'I won't waste any time here, Salmissra. You *do* know what I'll do to you if you interfere with the Godslayer, don't you? You have your own ways to see into the future, so you know exactly what's going to happen.'

Her eyes narrowed. 'Threats, Polgara? You're threatening me in my own throne-room?'

'It's not a threat, Salmissra. It's just a statement of fact. The next time you see me, it *will* happen.'

'Issa will protect me.'

'If he happens to be awake. I wouldn't count on that very much, though. You have yearnings for immortality, Salmissra. I can arrange that. You won't like it very much, but I'll see to it that you'll live forever. You probably won't want to look at your mirror afterward, though. Zedar and Ctuchik – and maybe even Urvon – are going to keep waving Torak in front of you until you're old and tired, but I wouldn't believe them, dear. Torak only loves himself. There's no room in his heart for anybody else – except me, of course. And when you get down to the bottom of it, he doesn't even love me. All he wants is to dominate me and make me worship him. That's why he lost at Vo Mimbre.' I gave Zedar a thin smile. 'Isn't that about the way it went, Zedar? Torak absolutely *knew* he wasn't supposed to take the field on that third day, didn't he? But he went ahead and did it anyway. That's why he's lying in that cave down in Cthol Murgos growing moldier by the hour. You've attached

617

yourself to a defective, Zedar, and eventually, you'll have to live with the consequences.'

Then, quite suddenly, I had a horrible premonition, and I knew exactly what the fate of my father's brother was going to be, and it was too horrible to even contemplate. And in that same moment I knew that it would be Zedar who would ultimately find and deliver the one who would replace Torak to all of mankind. At last I understood the absolute necessity of Zedar's existence. He would give humanity the greatest gift it would ever receive, and all he'd get in return would be living entombment.

I think Zedar himself may have caught a hint of that premonition as well, because his face turned very pale.

I looked back at the serpent queen. 'Take my advice, Salmissra,' I told her. 'Don't get involved in this diseased game Ctuchik and Zedar are playing with you. No matter how much they promise, neither of them can deliver up Torak's affection. They don't control Torak. It's the other way around, and when you get right down to the bottom of it, Torak doesn't even particularly like his disciples. Zedar found out about that at Vo Mimbre, didn't you, Zedar? The possibility that you'd vanish in a puff of smoke if you broke the rules didn't particularly bother Torak, did it? You gave up the love of one God for the indifference of another. Very poor choice there, old boy.'

A look of almost overwhelming regret came over his face, accompanied by absolute hopelessness. It was so naked that I was almost ashamed of myself.

'I'm so happy that the three of us had the chance for this little chat,' I told them. 'I hope that it's cleared the air. Now you both fully understand what I'm going to do to you if you keep on interfering in something that's really none of your business. Be guided by me in this, gentles all, for, should ye persist, our next meeting shall be *most* unpleasant.'

I just threw that in. I thought it had a nice archaic ring to it. Evidently something of my father's nature has filtered down to me, because every so often I get this overpowering urge to be melodramatic. Hereditary character defect there, perhaps.

Then I left Sthiss Tor, but I didn't immediately return to Annath. I spent several weeks high in the Tolnedran mountains pondering that sudden insight that had come to me in Salmissra's throne-room. I knew that Zedar *would* be the one to find Eriond, though I didn't even know Eriond's name at that point. The more I thought about it, the more I began to catch a strong odor of 'tampering'. There was a difference, though. I'd encountered that kind of thing before, and there's a different feel – 'odor', if you will – to mother's tampering, or UL's, or that of the Purpose. This time it was quite different. I didn't recognize it at all, and that made me a little edgy. A new player had evidently taken a seat in the game. I recognize it now, of course. I should, after all, since I raised this new player from a little boy here in this very cottage.

One of these days I think I'll have a talk with Eriond about that. I think I'd like to get to the bottom of these little visitations. If there's a reason for them, I suppose they're all right, but if they're just for fun, somebody's going to get a piece of my mind.

I was also *very* unhappy about what it was becoming increasingly obvious that I was going to have to do to Salmissra. She and I both knew it was going to happen, but she was evidently going to be persuaded by someone that I wouldn't really be able to do it. My only solace now lies in the fact that since she's become adjusted to it, she's not really too unhappy that it happened, and Nyissa's much better off with her on the throne in her present form.

No matter how I twisted and turned it around, there was nothing I could really do to prevent what was already destined to happen. Finally, I gave up and went back to Annath.

Father scolded me when I returned, of course, but I didn't really pay too much attention to him, since I already knew most of what he was trying to tell me anyway.

After the winter had passed, father's wanderlust bit him again, and he went back out to have a look at the world. I could have told him that it was still there, but he had to see for himself, I guess.

I went on over into Algaria and made contact with the clan which had already produced Ildera, the girl who was destined to marry Geran. I had a private talk with her father, the clan-chief, and along about midsummer, the clan moved its herds and set up a more or less permanent encampment just across the border from Annath. The word 'border' doesn't mean much around there, though. If you look around and see trees, you're in Sendaria; if it's grass, you're in Algaria. There were visits back and forth across that vague line of demarcation, of course, and eventually, Geran, who was nine, met the seven-year-old Ildera. I wasn't even there, but I heard that bell nonetheless. Everything was right on schedule.

When Geran was about twelve, his father started taking him to the stone-quarry to begin his education. He developed the usual aches, pains and blisters right at first, but in time his muscles hardened and he grew more skilled at the family profession.

Life moved along quietly in Annath. Back in the remote mountain villages of Sendaria it's fairly common for the citizens to be unaware of the current king's name and for the death of a cow to be the major topic of discussion for a year or so.

Then in 5345, father and the twins came to Annath. 'There are some people you need to meet, Pol,' father told me. 'Beltira and Belkira can fill in for you here while I take you around to introduce you to some of the people you've been reading about in the Mrin for the last three thousand years.'

I didn't really object. I'd more or less had enough of rural isolation for a while.

We crossed the border into Algaria, and I met the grim-faced little boy named Hettar. 'I think that one's going to be a problem, father,' I predicted as we rode away from King Cho-Ram's encampment.

'It's possible, Pol,' he agreed.

'We'll probably have to chain him to a post when he grows up. I'm not really all that fond of Murgos myself, but Hettar's right on the verge of turning it into a religion.'

'The Murgos *did* kill his parents, Pol.'

'Yes. He told me about that. But he'll be the King of the Algars one day, and that seething hatred of his is likely to cause us some problems.'

'I can handle him, Pol,' father said confidently.

'Of *course* you can,' I replied. 'Where do we go next?'

'Boktor. Brace yourself, Pol. Prince Kheldar's a very slippery young man.'

'He's only ten years old, father.'

'I know, but he's already as slippery as an eel.'

Kheldar turned out to be even slipperier than that. He was charming, exquisitely polite, and totally without scruples. Oddly enough, I rather liked him.

Then father and I went to Trellheim in Cherek to meet Barak and his cousin, Crown Prince Anheg. I had one of those peculiar feelings that come over us from time to time when I first met them. It seemed almost that Anrak, Iron-grip's cousin, was coming back to haunt me. Barak and Anheg were both Chereks down to their toenails, and you know what that means. They were both, however, extremely intelligent. They managed to hide it well, though.

620

It was late autumn by then, and father took me back to Annath. 'We can go talk with the others next summer, Pol,' he said. 'I wanted you to meet the Alorns first. They're the ones most likely to cause problems.'

'I thought you liked Alorns, father.'

'Whatever gave you that idea?'

'You spend a lot of time with them.'

'I *have* to spend time with them, Pol. Every Alorn's a disaster just waiting to happen. The Master told me to keep an eye on the Alorns about five thousand years ago, and it's turned into a full-time job. He told me to do it, and I'll do it. I won't like it, though.'

'You're such a good boy, father.'

The following spring, mother's voice came to me. *'It's time for you to go back to school, Pol,'* she announced.

'Oh?'

'There are a couple of things you're going to need to know how to do fairly soon.'

'Such as what?'

'You're going to need to know how to play with people's memories.'

'Would you define "play with", mother?'

'I want you to practice making people forget some things that have happened the way you did when we first started your training, and then you'll learn how to replace those memories with the image of things that didn't happen.'

'Can we actually do that?'

'Yes, we can. People do it to themselves all the time. It's a way of altering reality. The fish that got away always gets bigger as time goes by.'

'You know, I've noticed that myself. How do I go about doing it?'

Her explanation was fairly obscure, dealing as it did with the peculiar nature of human memory. When you get down to the bottom of it, only about half of what we remember really happened. We tend to modify things to make ourselves look better in our own eyes and in the eyes of others. Then, if what we did wasn't really very admirable, we tend to forget that it ever happened. A normal human being's grasp on reality is very tenuous at best. Our imaginary lives are usually much nicer.

To practice, I tampered – marginally – with the memories of some of the people in Annath, and it was actually quite easy.

'Why am I learning how to do this, mother?' I asked her after a few weeks.

'There are a couple of people who are mentioned – sort of around the

621

edges – in the Mrin. I think we'd better look in on them to make sure that they'll really be on our side.'

'Everybody in the western kingdoms will be on our side, mother.'

'That's the whole point, Pol. These people aren't from the west. They're living over in Gar og Nadrak.'

CHAPTER 38

'I can't wear these clothes in public, mother!'

'You look very nice, Pol. The clothes show off your figure.'

'I can do that by not wearing anything at all! I'm not going out in public wearing something that fits me like a second skin!'

'There does seem to be something missing, though.'

'You noticed. How observant of you.'

'Be nice. Oh, I know. We forgot the daggers.'

'Daggers?'

'Four of them usually – two at your belt and one tucked in the top of each of your boots.'

'Why do I need so many?'

'It's a Nadrak custom, Pol. It's a Nadrak woman's way of telling men that it's all right to look at her, but touching will get them in trouble.'

The twins were filling in for me in Annath until father arrived, and mother had taken me a ways back into the forest to instruct me in the peculiarities of Nadrak custom and costume. The clothes in which she'd garbed me consisted of black leather boots, tight-fitting black leather trousers, and an even tighter-fitting black leather vest. A simple inventory might sound masculine, but when I put the clothes on I saw that no one who saw me was likely to be confused about my gender. I immediately saw why Nadrak women might need daggers – lots of daggers. 'Do Nadrak men understand what the daggers mean?' I asked.

'Usually – if they're sober. Every so often they get playful and need to be reminded to keep their hands to themselves. A few nicks and cuts usually gets the point across.'

'Are you trying to be funny?'

'Would I do that?'

I willed four Ulgo knives into existence. If you want to intimidate someone, show him an Ulgo knife. The sight of something with a hooked point and saw-toothed edges tends to make people a bit queasy.

'Those are horrible, Pol!'

'Isn't that the idea? I want to be sure that nobody gets drunk enough to start taking chances.'

'You do realize that they'll lower your price, don't you?'

'Price?'

'Nadrak women are property, Pol. Everybody knows that.'

'Oh, yes. I'd forgotten about that. Is there anything else you've neglected to tell me?'

'You'll have to wear a collar – tastefully ornamented with jewels if you were expensive. Don't worry about the chain. Nadrak women don't attach the chain to the collar except on formal occasions. We'll stop somewhere on our way to Yar Nadrak so that you can watch a Nadrak woman dance. You'll need to know how to do that.'

'I already know how to dance, mother.'

'Not the way they do it in Gar og Nadrak. When a Nadrak woman dances, she challenges every man in the room. That's the main reason she needs the daggers.'

'Why dance that way if it causes that kind of problem?'

'Probably for the fun of it, Pol. It drives Nadrak men absolutely crazy.'

I realized that Nadrak women took the sport of 'breaking hearts' all the way out to the extreme edge. This little trip *might* just be more interesting than I'd expected.

Then mother and I merged into the form of a falcon and winged our way northeasterly to the land of the Nadraks. The two men we were looking for were in the capital at Yar Nadrak, but mother suggested that we stop at a nameless hamlet in the endless forests of Gar og Nadrak to witness the performance of a Nadrak dancer named Ayalla.

The hamlet had that slap-dash, 'Oh, that's good enough' quality about it that seems to be endemic in Gar og Nadrak. The buildings were made of logs and canvas, and none of them even approached being square or plumb. They sagged and leaned off in all directions, but that didn't seem to bother the fur trappers and gold hunters who came out of the forest from time to time when they grew hungry for civilization. Mother and I flew in over the town and perched on the sill of an unglazed window high up in the back wall of the local tavern.

'Ayalla's owner's named Kablek, Pol,' mother told me. 'He owns this tavern, and Ayalla's something in the nature of a business asset. She dances here every night, and that's what brings in all the customers. Kablek's getting rich here because of her. He waters down his beer to the point that it doesn't even foam any more, and he charges outrageous prices for it.'

'He sounds like a Tolnedran.'

'Yes, he does rather – but without the polish.'

The crowd in Kablek's tavern was rowdy, but there were a number of burly fellows with stout cudgels roaming around to keep order. They broke up the knife-fights, but largely ignored the fist-fights – unless the participants started splintering the furniture.

Kablek and his serving-men sold beer at a furious rate until about mid-evening, and then the patrons began to chant, 'Ayalla, Ayalla, Ayalla!' stamping their feet and pounding on the rough tables with their fists. Kablek let that go on for several minutes, still pouring beer for all he was worth, and then he climbed up on the long counter along the back wall of his establishment and bellowed, 'Last call, gentlemen! Get your beer now. We don't sell none while Ayalla's dancing!'

That precipitated a rush to the counter. Then, when he saw that everybody's tankard was full, Kablek held up his hand for silence. 'This is the beat!' he announced, and he began to clap his callused hands together – three measured beats followed by four staccato ones. 'Don't lose that beat, men. Ayalla don't like that, and she's real quick with her knives.'

Their answering laughter was a little nervous. A performer always wants to hold her audience – but with a knife?

Then, with a professionally dramatic flair, Ayalla appeared in a well-lighted doorway. I was forced to admit that she was stunningly beautiful, with blue-black hair, sparkling black eyes, and a sensual mouth. Technically, she was a slave, a piece of property, but no Tolnedran emperor could ever have matched her imperial bearing. Slave or not, Ayalla literally owned everything – and everyone – she laid her eyes on. Her dress, if you could call something that flimsy a dress, was of pale, gauzy, Mallorean silk, and it whispered as she moved. It left her arms bare to the shoulders and stopped just above her soft leather boots where her jeweled dagger-hilts peeped coyly at the onlookers.

The audience cheered, but Ayalla looked slightly bored. Her expression changed, however, when the onlookers began that compelling beat. Her face became intent and the sheer force of her overwhelming presence struck her audience and captured them. Her dance began slowly, almost indolently, and then her pace quickened. Her feet seemed almost to flicker as she whirled about the room to that compelling beat.

'Breathe, Pol!' mother's voice cracked. 'I'm starting to see spots in front of our eyes.'

I explosively let out the breath I'd been unconsciously holding. Ayalla's performance had even captured me. 'Gifted, isn't she?' I suggested mildly.

Ayalla slowed her dance and concluded with an outrageously sensual strut that challenged every man in the room. The placement of her hands on her dagger hilts as she seemed to be offering herself announced quite clearly what she'd do to anyone foolish enough to accept her offer.

Dear Gods! That looked like fun!

'Well, Pol?' mother asked. 'Do you think you could do that?'

'It might take some practice,' I admitted, 'but not too much. I know exactly what she's doing. She's very proud of being a woman, isn't she?'

'Oh, yes. That she is.'

'That's what her dancing's all about, and I can definitely handle that part. The steps aren't really important. It's her attitude that matters, and I have an attitude of my own. Give me a week, mother, and I'll be a better dancer than she is.'

'My, aren't we confident.'

'Trust me. Where to now?'

'Yar Nadrak, the capital. You'll need to select an owner and then we'll get started.'

Most of you are probably unfamiliar with the peculiar nature of Nadrak society. Women are property among the Nadraks, but they're not property in the same sense that horses, boots, or wagons are property. Nadrak women *select* their owners, and if the chosen one doesn't live up to her expectations, she can always fall back on her daggers to persuade him to sell her to somebody she likes better – and she gets half of her sale price every time. A Nadrak woman who pays close attention to business can die wealthy, if she wants to.

Yar Nadrak is a mosquito-infested, tar-smeared city built on a marshy point where the surrounding forest has been cleared by setting it on fire – and those are its good points.

There was no reason to avoid it any longer, so when I resumed my own form, I wore the leather clothing mother had provided for me. I strutted through the city gate, noting the polished steel mask of Torak gazing down at me as I did. The presence of that dreadful reminder may have had something to do with what happened next.

'Don't be in such a rush, Dearie,' one of the half-drunk gate-guards said, leering at me suggestively and taking hold of my arm. I decided to establish some ground-rules right then and there. I swept one leg against the sides of his knees and he buckled and fell. Then I dropped on top of him, one of my knees driving into the pit of his stomach. I drew my Ulgo daggers from my belt and crossed their saw-toothed edges against his throat. 'Any last words?' I asked him.

'What are you *doing*?' he wheezed.

'I'm getting ready to cut your throat,' I explained patiently. 'You touched me, and nobody touches Polanna and lives. Everybody knows that. Brace yourself. This'll be over before you know it.'

'It was an accident!' he squealed. 'I didn't mean to touch you!'

'I'm sorry. I didn't realize that. You should have been more careful.'

'You'll forgive me then?'

'Of course I'll forgive you, silly boy. I'll still have to cut your throat, but I'll really regret it. Just lie still. This won't take but a minute.'

Now what was I going to do? I'm sure everybody around me was terribly impressed, but how was I going to extricate myself without actually killing this idiot?

'Polanna! Let him go!' The voice was deep and masculine, and it seemed to be coming from somewhere behind me. It was *not* behind me, though, and the speaker wasn't a man. Mother had come to my rescue.

'But he touched me!' I protested.

'It was a mistake. Let him up.'

'I've been insulted. I can't just let that slide.'

'We don't have time for this, Polanna. Nick him once and let it go at that. A little blood will wash away the insult. You don't have to fill the gutter with it over an accident.'

'Oh, all right.' I gave in. I gave my terrified victim a little slice on the point of his chin, got up, and jammed my daggers into their sheaths. Then I marched on into the city. I don't think anybody even noticed that I appeared to be alone.

'*A little excessive there, Pol.*' Mother's tone was acid.

'*It got out of hand, I guess.*'

'*Polanna? Where did you come up with "Polanna"?*'

'*It just popped into my head. I thought it sounded sort of Nadraky.*'

'*Nadraky?*'

627

'Let it pass, mother. Let's shop around and find me an owner.'

I'd never shopped for an owner before, and it's not quite the same as shopping for a pair of shoes or a side of beef. We finally settled on a rich fur trader named Gallak. He was prosperous enough to have the necessary contacts *and* not to live in a hovel. Like most Nadraks, he was a lean man with shrewd eyes. The only real problem we had with him was that he was much more interested in money than he was in the finer things in life – including women. It took a bit more effort to insert some memories into his mind as a result of that peculiarity, but mother and I got around that by playing on his greed. We waved the notion of the profit he'd make when he re-sold me in front of him, and that was all it took.

I slipped into his house late one night while he was sleeping, scattered some of my possessions around and fixed up one of his spare rooms to make it look like my personal bed chamber. Then, just as it was starting to get light, I built a fire in his kitchen and started cooking. When everything was ready, I went to his bedroom and shook him awake. 'Your breakfast's ready, Gallak,' I told him. 'Get up.'

He stretched and yawned. 'Good morning, Polanna,' he said calmly. 'Did you sleep well?' He clearly remembered buying me in a back-country tavern about six weeks ago, and in his mind I'd been around long enough for him to get to know me.

He ate his breakfast and complimented me on my cooking – which in his own mind he did every time I cooked for him. Then he checked my collar to make sure it was still locked, told me to have a nice day, and went off to work. So far as he knew, I was now a fixture in his life, and he had no way of knowing that he'd never seen me before that very morning.

'Now then,' mother said after he'd left, *'we want to find a man named Yarblek. He's going to be fairly important later on, so we'd better get to know him.'*

'I don't exactly have total freedom of movement, mother,' I reminded her.

'Whatever gave you that idea?'

'I'm a slave, mother. I can't just wander the streets as I please, can I?'

'You're missing the point, Pol. Gallak's your owner, not your master. You're property, not a slave.'

'Is there a difference?'

'There's a world of difference, Pol. Your collar gives you absolute free-dom, and it tells everybody that if anyone interferes with you, Gallak will have him killed. You've got more freedom here than you had as the Duchess

of Erat. You can go anywhere you want to go, and you don't have to do anything you don't want to do. Nadrak women have more freedom than any other females in the whole world – except for wolves, of course.'

'What a fascinating concept.'

Despite the fact that he was only fifteen or so at the time, Yarblek was already well-known in Yar Nadrak. Well-known or not, Yarblek was a little hard to find, and my search for him led me into the seedier parts of town. Evidently, word of the incident at the city gate had gotten around, because all manner of evil-looking scoundrels went out of their way to stay out of mine. Obviously, my description had accompanied those stories, so the rascals of Yar Nadrak knew me on sight. It's hard to get information when nobody wants to talk to you, though, so I picked one scruffy fellow and pointed my finger at him. 'You,' I said peremptorily, 'come here.'

'I didn't do anything,' he protested.

'I didn't say you had. Come here.'

'Do I have to?'

'Yes.' I pointed at the street in front of me. 'Here,' I instructed. 'Now.'

'Yes, Polanna. At once.' He almost ran across the street, and when he stopped where I'd indicated, he carefully put his hands behind his back to avoid any mistakes.

'I'm looking for a young fellow named Yarblek. Do you know him?'

'Everybody knows Yablek, Polanna.'

'Good. Where can I find him?'

'He usually spends his time in the Rat's Nest – that's a tavern over near the east gate. If he's not there, the tavern-keeper should know where you can find him.'

'Thank you. See? That didn't hurt at all, did it?'

'I don't seem to be bleeding from anyplace – yet.' Then his eyes grew curious. 'Did you *really* cut that gate-guard's head off with those saws you carry instead of knives?'

'Of course not. All I did was nick him a little.'

'I sort of thought it might have been an exaggeration. You don't seem all that blood-thirsty to me.' Then he winked at me. 'I won't tell anybody, though. You've got the whole thieves' quarter terrorized, and I just *love* to see all those rascals quaking in their boots.'

'You're a nice boy,' I told him, patting his cheek. Then I went on down the muddy street toward the east gate of the city.

The Rat's Nest tavern was aptly named. It was draped with

cobwebs and the floor needed shoveling more than sweeping. I marched up to the wobbly, scarred counter. 'Which one of these drunken sots is Yarblek?' I demanded of the fellow on the other side of the counter.

'That's him over there in the corner – the young fellow who's still trying to sleep off what he drank last night. Are you going to kill him?'

'Whatever gave you that idea?'

'You're the one they call Polanna, aren't you? The word's out that you kill people just for looking at you.'

'Nonsense. I haven't killed a single person yet today – so far. Now if you'll excuse me, I think I'll go over and have a few words with Yarblek.'

It didn't take much to wake Yarblek – a single creaky board, actually. His hand flashed to his dagger-hilt before he even got his eyes open. Then he looked at me boldly. 'Have a seat, Dearie,' he invited, pushing out a stool with one foot. 'You're new here, aren't you? I don't think I've seen you here before. Would you like to have me buy you something to drink?'

'Aren't you a little young to be frequenting taverns, Master Yarblek?' I asked, sitting down on the stool he'd offered.

'I've never been young, Dearie,' he boasted. 'I was all grown up the day I was born. 'I was weaned on strong beer, and I killed my first man when I was seven.' And he went on – and on and on – boasting about how much he could drink, how many men he'd killed, and how no woman could resist his charms. His expression and his quick, easy laughter suggested that he didn't really expect me to believe all his lies, but rather that he was simply trying to entertain me. All in all, I found him to be a shabby, boastful adolescent, but I picked up a few hints that he was much shrewder than he appeared to be on the surface, and I felt fairly confident that if he didn't make any serious blunders, he might actually live long enough to reach adulthood, and that if he did, he'd be up to whatever it was that he was supposed to do.

I'll admit that the possibility that he'd eventually go into business with Prince Kheldar and become one of the richest men in the world never even occurred to me.

After a while, I grew tired of all his bragging. 'You look tired, Yarblek,' I suggested.

'Never too tired to talk with a beautiful woman,' he said. Then his eyes drooped shut and he started to snore.

It probably wasn't necessary, given his condition, but just to be

630

on the safe side, I erased his memory of our meeting – *and* that of the man behind the counter as well.

'Mother,' I sent out my thought as I left the Rat's Nest.

'Yes, Pol?'

'I found Yarblek. He's quite young, but he shows a lot of promise – if he lives.'

'I have it on very good authority that he will, Pol. Can we trust him?'

'We probably shouldn't, but I get the feeling that we can.'

'We'll be here for quite a while. You can look in on him from time to time and see how he's coming along.'

'Who's the other one I have to meet?'

'The new king, Drosta lek Thun.'

'How new?'

'He was crowned in 5342. He's about twenty or so now.'

'We're expecting help from the king of an Angarak nation?'

'I'm not the one who's making the decisions, Pol. You're supposed to talk with him and see if you can find out why he might decide to change sides.'

'Getting into his palace might be a little tricky.'

'I think Gallak might be able to help us with that.'

'Maybe. I'll talk with him this evening and sound him out.'

My adjustment to the living arrangements in Gallak's house was probably more difficult than Gallak's was. I was forced to keep reminding myself that he believed that I'd been living under his roof for six weeks and that he was used to having me around. 'How did your day go, Polanna?' he asked pleasantly after supper.

'About the same as usual,' I replied. 'I went down to the bazaar to have a look at some of the shops I haven't visited yet. I didn't buy anything, though.'

'Do you need some money?'

'No. I'm fine. Have you ever met King Drosta?'

'A couple of times, why?'

'Just curious. What kind of man is he?'

'Young. He might grow up some day – hopefully before he's eighty.'

'I didn't quite follow that.'

'His Majesty's very fond of women.' Gallak's tone was disapproving.

'I don't find anything wrong with that.'

'I do – if it's the only thing a man can think about. Our king can't seem to think of anything else. I doubt that he even knows the names of most of his advisors.'

631

'How stupid.'

'He's not really stupid, Polanna. Actually, he's very clever – in an erratic sort of way – but his brains shut down entirely when a woman starts to dance. Don't get me wrong. I enjoy the performance of a good dancer as much as the next man, but Drosta starts drooling before the dancer even gets started – and I mean he actually drools. He's an ugly young fellow to begin with, and the slobbering doesn't improve him very much. There's going to be a new king on the throne in Drasnia soon, and Drosta should be concentrating on some new trade agreements, but his advisors can't drag him out of the brothels long enough to even meet with the Drasnian trade envoys.'

'Shocking,' I murmured.

'My feelings exactly. Can we talk about something else? Just the thought of that lecher makes my skin crawl.'

That gave me something to think about, and the next morning after Gallak had gone off to swindle some people, I started to practice my dancing. I didn't need a roomful of men to clap out the beat for me, since I could keep that in my head. I cleared some furniture out of the way and mirrored one wall of the room with a single thought. Then I got down to business. As I'd noticed when I'd watched Ayalla dance, the key to a truly outstanding performance is attitude, not the steps. By mid-afternoon, it was beginning to come to me.

I practiced faithfully for two weeks. The major obstacle I encountered had to do with flaunting. Some of the movements in Nadrak dancing embarrassed me, and I knew that I was going to have to overcome that if I hoped to give the kind of performance I had in mind. Oddly, I found that dancing with my daggers clenched in my fists helped enormously. When I held those Ulgo knives, I could flaunt myself in ways Ayalla had never dreamt of. All I had to do then was to come up with a way to suppress the blushing. My dancing even shocked me, which was probably the whole idea.

Winter came and went, and Gallak and I settled into a Nadrakish sort of domesticity. He spent his days swindling customers, and I spent mine practicing my dancing.

No, I wasn't dancing just for the fun of it. Gallak's assessment of King Drosta's personality had suggested to me the perfect way to get close enough to the Nadrak king to evaluate him. By spring, I knew that if my dancing were only half as good as I thought it was,

Drosta would be drooling bucketfuls before I was even half-way through my performance.

As the snow in the streets of Yar Nadrak started to melt, I began to feign a restlessness. Gallak and I *had* been sort of housebound during the winter, and he readily agreed that a bit of social life might be in order.

Social life in Gar og Nadrak is rather rudimentary, since about all that's involved is a visit to the local tavern. I don't care much for taverns myself, but this was business. Before we left the house, I changed clothes. I suppose I *could* have given a performance dressed in leather, but I don't think it'd have had the same impact.

I sat with Gallak at a table in the tavern called the Wild Boar. I even drank a couple of tankards of the fruity-tasting Nadrak ale. I was just a little nervous, actually. The other people in the tavern all grew slightly tipsy, and along about mid-evening a young woman who was the property of one of Gallak's competitors in the fur trade was urged by her owner to favor us with a dance. The tavern patrons took up the clapping in unison, and the young woman began to dance. She was no match for Ayalla, but she wasn't really all that bad. The applause at the conclusion of her dance was thunderous.

Silently, without even looking at him, I nudged my owner's ego just a bit. 'My Polanna can dance better than that,' he asserted loudly.

'That's Gallak for you,' the dancer's owner snorted. 'He always has to be better than everybody else.'

'Offer him a wager,' I whispered to Gallak.

'Do you really know how to dance?' he whispered back just a little apprehensively.

'I'll turn your bones to water,' I assured him.

'We'll try it, I guess.' He didn't sound too sure. 'All right, Rasak,' he said to his competitor, 'would you like to lay a wager on it?' He reached for his money-pouch. 'I've got ten gold pieces that says that Polanna's a better dancer than your Eyana. We'll let our friends here decide which is best.'

'Ten? You sound awfully sure of yourself, Gallak.'

'Sure enough to back it with money. Are we having some second thoughts, Rasak?'

'All right. Ten it is.'

The crowd cheered and stamped their feet. Then they began that rhythmic beat.

I took a deep breath, rose to my feet and removed my outer dress. My dancing costume was closely modeled on the one Ayalla had

633

worn in the tavern back in the forest. I briefly noticed that Rasak's expression was just a little sick when he saw me in that flimsy blue costume.

All right, let's not make an issue of it. I'd long since outgrown knobby knees and adolescent gangliness. Moreover, the fact that I'd been dancing for hours every day for six months or more had put me in fighting trim – figuratively speaking, of course.

Sorry about the pun. It was inadvertent.

And so I danced for them. I'd been a little nervous about dancing in public – I think it's called 'stage-fright' by professional performers – but once I began to dance, the nervousness translated itself into a heightened excitement, and I danced far better than I had during those long hours of practice. There's nothing like an audience to encourage one to do one's best. I may not have turned their bones to water, but I'm sure I softened a few.

There was a stunned silence when I concluded my performance with that outrageous strut. I *owned* this crowd! The applause and cheering were absolutely deafening, and Rasak didn't even bother to put the question to a vote. He paid up without so much as a whimper.

I danced frequently after that. Gallak, who always kept his eye on the main chance, saw a way to use my gifts during his business dealings. 'Why don't we have Polanna dance for us while you mull over my offer?' began cropping up rather frequently during assorted negotiations.

It was probably inevitable, given the fact that most of my performances took place in taverns, that sooner or later I'd have to demonstrate my willingness to actually use my knives to remind some spectator that he was supposed to keep his hands to himself. Gallak had been negotiating with a wall-eyed fellow named Kreblar, and their haggling had reached an impasse. That's when Gallak drew his weapon of choice – me. He'd grown very skilled at inserting me into his business negotiations by then, so his suggestion that I dance for them and the other patrons of the tavern where they'd been negotiating was smoothly slipped into the conversation. Kreblar had drunk a few too many tankards of the fruity Nadrak ale by then, and he seemed to assume that I was dancing for him alone.

It was at the conclusion of my dance when I was strutting back to the table where the three of us were seated that he stepped across the line. His off-center eye was gleaming in the general direction of the far wall, and he roughly seized my arm. 'There's a good girl!' he half-bellowed. 'Come on now, give us a kiss!' and he began to paw at me.

My training as a surgeon was very helpful at that point. I brought my knee up sharply and caught him on the point of the chin with it even as I drew my knife out of my boot-top. His head snapped back, but I ignored his exposed throat and neatly sliced him across the chest instead, reasoning that his ribs would keep my knife edge from going too deep.

His squeal was piercing, and he gaped down in horror at the blood gushing through the neat gash I'd just sliced through his shirt. 'You mustn't do that, you know,' I chided him, not even bothering to raise my voice. I wiped my knife clean on his shirt collar, slipped it back into its sheath, and then I looked around at the other tavern patrons. 'Does anybody here happen to have a needle and thread?' I asked them. 'We'll all be wading in blood if I don't sew poor Kreblar here back together.'

A cobbler provided what I needed, and I had Gallak and three or four others stretch Kreblar back over the table and hold him down. Then, humming softly to myself, I neatly stitched up the gash that ran from armpit to armpit across Kreblar's chest, ignoring his squeals.

I'm not sure exactly why, but I think the sewing chilled the blood of the onlookers far more than the gashing had. People are funny sometimes.

In time, my fame spread in Yar Nadrak, and as I'd more or less anticipated, Gallak finally received an invitation to 'stop by the palace, and bring Polanna with you'. My hours of practice and those public performances had finally paid off.

King Drosta's palace was in the center of Yar Nadrak, and as closely as I was able to determine, it was the only stone building in the entire city. Nadraks, however, aren't very good at working with stone, so the palace was as lopsided as were all the other buildings in town. When Gallak and I entered the throne-room, I saw there the only Grolim I encountered during my entire stay. I warily sent an inquiring thought toward his mind and discovered that he didn't really have one. He was a Grolim, right enough, but he was only marginally talented, and as nearly as I could determine, he hadn't drawn a sober breath in the past ten years. Torak's hold on the Nadraks was tenuous, to say the very least.

King Drosta was rather young to be occupying a throne, and he appeared to feel that his major responsibility was to enjoy himself.

He was thin to the point of emaciation, and his face was splotched with angry purple eruptions and deeply indented scars. His hair was coarse, black, and rather sparse, and his obviously expensive yellow clothing was none too clean.

Since being presented at court is a formal occasion, I was wearing my chain, and Gallak led me around by it in the socially approved manner. I wore my dancing costume, which was more or less concealed beneath a blue outer dress. Gallak led me up to the foot of the throne, and when we got there, he bowed to his king. 'My name's Gallak, your Majesty,' he said. 'You sent for me?'

'Ah, there you are, Gallak,' Drosta replied in a shrill, almost hysterical voice. 'We've been waiting for you.' Then he eyed me up and down, and his look was insultingly obvious. 'So this is the famous Polanna,' he said. 'She's a looker, isn't she?' He giggled nervously. 'Would you like to sell her, Gallak?'

'Ah – no, your Majesty,' Gallak replied. 'I don't think so.' I thought that was a wise decision, since Gallak was only a chain's length away from my daggers.

'Maybe you might want to rent her to me then.' Drosta seemed to think that was funny because he laughed uproariously.

'That would be *my* decision, Drosta,' I told him coldly, 'and I doubt that you've got enough money.'

'Proud of yourself, aren't you?' he said.

'I know how much I'm worth,' I said, shrugging.

'They tell me you're a dancer.'

'They weren't wrong.'

'Are you a good dancer?'

'The best you'll ever see.' Modesty's not a Nadrak virtue, but that remark probably even exceeded ordinary Nadrak boastfulness.

'You'll have to prove that to me, Polanna.'

'Whenever you wish, Drosta. Before we start, though, maybe you should look at these.' I reached inside my dress, drew out my daggers, and showed them to him.

'Are you threatening me?' he demanded, his eyes bulging out even further.

'It wasn't intended as a threat, Drosta – just a statement of fact. This is what'll happen to you if your appreciation gets the better of you.'

'I don't think I've ever seen a knife with a hook on its point before. What's the purpose of that?'

'The hooks pull things out – things that most people prefer to keep inside.' I looked at the implements admiringly. 'Aren't they

636

lovely?' I said. 'They're designed to hurt more coming out than they do going in.'

His face turned slightly green, and he shuddered. 'This is a terrible woman, Gallak,' he said to my owner. 'How can you stand being around her?'

'She's good for me, your Majesty,' Gallak replied. 'She teaches me good manners. Not only that, she's the best cook in Gar og Nadrak.'

'In the world, actually, Gallak,' I corrected him. 'Well, Drosta,' I said then, 'what's it to be? Did you want me to dance for you, or would you like supper?'

'Dance first, Polanna,' he leered. 'Let's see if your dancing whets my appetite.' Then he looked around his crowded throne-room. 'Clear the floor!' he commanded. 'Give this girl some room! Let's find out if she's as good as she seems to think she is!'

I took that to be a challenge, so I cast aside my customary restraint and added some elements I'd never tried in public before.

No, I won't describe them here – the children, you understand.

King Drosta was trembling violently as I strutted back to reclaim my outer garment, and there was a somewhat awed look on his face. 'Torak's teeth!' he swore. 'I've never *seen* anything like that before!'

'I told you I was the best, Drosta,' I reminded him.

'Are you positive you don't want to sell her, Gallak?' Drosta pleaded.

'I think it's my patriotic duty not to, your Majesty,' my owner told him. 'You have a reputation for excitability, and you might get carried away some day. I couldn't in good conscience sell Polanna to you, since there's no heir to the throne to succeed you.'

'You wouldn't *really* kill me, would you, Polanna?' Drosta asked hopefully.

'I'd regret it terribly, Drosta, but rules *are* rules, you understand. I'd try to make it as painless as possible, of course, but I'm sure there'd be some discomfort involved. My daggers aren't designed for quickness – or neatness, for that matter. The process is usually *very* messy.'

'You're a cruel woman, Polanna. You flaunt something irresistible in front of me and then you tell me that you'll yank out about twenty yards of my guts if I reach for it.'

637

'That fairly well sums it up, yes. What would you like for supper, your Majesty?'

Gallak, Drosta, and I adjourned to the kitchens then, and I cooked supper for them.

'We've got trouble, Gallak,' Drosta said reflectively as he sprawled in a chair at the long table.

'Oh?' Gallak said.

'How extensive are your contacts over in Drasnia?'

'I've never been across the border personally, but I've got some people in Boktor.'

'There'll be a new king over there before long, won't there?'

Gallak nodded. 'The old one's sinking fast. The Crown Prince's name's Rhodar. He's fat, but he's got a quick mind.'

'I think I'd like to make some contacts with him. I've got a problem he might be able to help me with.'

'Oh? Which problem is that?'

'Its name is Taur Urgas, and it's sitting on the throne in Rak Goska.'

'The Murgos, you mean?'

'It's always the Murgos, Gallak. The world would be a much nicer place without the Murgos. Taur Urgas is crazy. Of course, that's not too noticeable in Cthol Murgos. The whole race is crazy, but Taur Urgas raises it to an art form. I'm trying to establish some contacts with Zakath over in Mallorea. He's the crown prince there, and he's fairly civilized. I'm hoping that he'll see the advantage of having an ally here on the western continent. Sooner or later, Taur Urgas is going to try to unify the western Angaraks, and I'd rather not be forced to bow down to a crazy Murgo.'

'Wouldn't it offend Taur Urgas if you made an alliance with Zakath?'

'I don't care if it offends him. If I've got Mallorea on my side, there won't be much he can do about it. I've got a lot of territory, Gallak, but I don't have very many people. If the Murgos march north, they'll swallow us up. I *have* to form an alliance with *somebody*!' He banged his fist down on the table.'

'Is that why you want to get in touch with Rhodar?' I broke in.

'Of course. I'd ally myself with the Morindim if I thought it'd do any good. Have you got *anybody* we can trust to carry messages to Rhodar for me, Gallak?'

'None that I'd trust *that* much, your Majesty.'

I had a flash of inspiration at that point, and I have quite a few suspicions about its origin. 'There's a young man I've heard of here in town, and from what I've heard, he's very shrewd – even though he doesn't shave regularly yet. He's got some rough edges, so you might have to train him a bit, but he's quick, so he'll pick it up in no time. He hasn't had time to build up much of a reputation as yet, so with a little training, he'd probably make the perfect emissary. He's quick, intelligent, and relatively anonymous.'

'What's his name?' Drosta asked.

'Yarblek.'

'Oh, that one,' Gallak said. 'I've heard of him myself. He brags a lot, but I don't think he really expects people to believe his boasting.' He considered it. 'You know, he might just work out pretty well – if we can train him – and I can get him to Boktor more or less unobserved. I send caravans there a couple of times a year, and I could hide Yarblek among my ox-drivers.' Then he snapped his fingers. 'Here's a thought,' he added. 'I know a fellow named Javelin at the Drasnian embassy. He's supposed to be a clerk of some kind, but I'm fairly sure he's a spy. I could talk with him, and he could pass the word back to Boktor that Yarblek's carrying a message from you to Rhodar. That should get Yarblek into the palace.'

Drosta chewed on one of his fingernails. 'I'll need to see him,' he said. 'If he's as good as you both think he is, he might be the answer to my problem. Where do I find him?'

'He frequents a tavern called the Rat's Nest, your Majesty,' I supplied. 'It's in the thieves' quarter near the east gate.'

'I'll send for him.' He looked at me. 'How old did you say he is, Polanna?'

'I didn't say,' I replied. 'About fifteen or so, from what I've heard.'

'That's awfully young.'

'That depends on the individual, Drosta,' I disagreed. 'And you *will* have time to train him. Taur Urgas hasn't started to march yet, so you've got some time to play with.'

'There's something in that,' Drosta conceded, 'and young ones are easier to mold than the ones already set in their ways.'

'And they usually work cheap,' Gallak added. 'If you give him a title of some kind – "special Emissary", or something like that – he might even work for nothing.'

'What a wonderful idea,' Drosta said enthusiastically.

I'd assumed that mother'd sent me to Gar og Nadrak just to assess the characters of Yarblek and Drosta, but it'd gone a little further than that, obviously. Not only had I met them, but I'd brought them together, and that had been the real purpose of my visit. Drosta was enthusiastic about Yarblek right at first, but I understand that his enthusiasm wore off after Yarblek found out what his services to his king were really worth. I wouldn't swear to it, but I suspect Yarblek's price started going up shortly after he met Silk.

'This has been quite an evening,' Drosta said expansively. 'I got to watch the best dancer in my whole kingdom, and then she helps me to solve a problem that's been nagging at me ever since I took the throne. Yes, quite an evening indeed.'

'And you haven't even tasted your supper yet,' I added.

'Will it be as good as the rest of the evening's been?'

'Better, probably,' I promised.

CHAPTER 39

'Was that more or less what you had in mind, mother?' I sent the thought out after Gallak and I got home.

'Approximately, yes. You're quick on your feet, Pol. Bringing the two of them together like that was a stroke of genius.'

'I rather liked it myself. If we're going to be using them somewhere out there in the future, I thought it might be more convenient if they were already hooked together. Am I more or less finished here?'

'I think that covers just about everything.'

'The next question is just exactly how I'm going to get out of town so that we can fly on back to Annath. Erasing the memory of everyone who's seen me here in Yar Nadrak might be just a bit challenging.'

'Why not just send word to your father? He's not doing anything useful right now, and he's got that stack of gold bars gathering dust in his tower. Tell him to come here and buy you from Gallak. He needs some exercise anyway, and he's just a little too attached to that gold of his, wouldn't you say?'

'That's terrible, mother!' It was all I could do to keep from laughing out loud.

'I'm glad you approve,' she replied placidly.

I waited for a couple of weeks, observing the progress of my 'Yarblek scheme', and then, when things seemed to be moving in the proper direction, I went across town to the Drasnian embassy to speak with Margrave Khendon, the man known as Javelin. A clerk carried my name into his office, and I was immediately admitted.

'Polanna,' he greeted me with a polite nod of his head, 'I'm honored by this visit. Is there something I can do for you?'

'I think you may know my father, Margrave,' I said, looking

around a bit cautiously for any peep-holes or listening posts. Spying *is* the national industry of Drasnia, after all.

'I wouldn't really think so, Polanna. I haven't been in Yar Nadrak all that long, so I don't know all that many Nadraks.'

'My father's not a Nadrak, Margrave. We haven't as yet pin-pointed his racial origins. Anyway, he's in a Sendarian mountain village called Annath right at the moment, and I need to get word to him. It's a matter of some delicacy, so I immediately thought of you. The Drasnian intelligence service is famous for its ability to keep secrets.'

'And for finding them out,' he added, looking rather directly at me. 'I get the feeling that you're not an ordinary Nadrak dancer, Polanna,'

'No, I'm not. I'm better than all the others.'

'That's not exactly what I meant. You're not a Nadrak, for one thing. Your eyes are the wrong shape.'

'I'll speak with them about that. Anyway, I'd like to have you get word to my father in Annath. Let him know that I've done what I was supposed to do here in Yar Nadrak and that I'd like to have him come here and buy me back from my owner – a fur-trader named Gallak.'

'Ah – it might be helpful if I knew your father's name, Polanna. I'm sure I could run him down eventually, but having his name might speed things up.'

'How silly of me. I'm sorry, Khendon.' Then I gave him a sly sidelong glance. 'Maybe you should go back to the academy for a quick refresher course, though. I'm a bit hurt that you didn't recognize me the moment I came through the door.'

Then he looked more closely at me, ignoring the leather clothing and the daggers. Then he blinked and rose quickly to his feet. 'Your Grace,' he said with an exquisite bow. 'The very building trembles in your august presence.'

'Your embassy was built by Nadrak laborers, Khendon. A good sneeze would make it tremble.'

'Nadrak construction *is* a bit slap-dash, isn't it,' he agreed. His eyes narrowed, and one of his cheeks started to twitch. 'Some things are starting to fit together now,' he noted. 'This business with Yar-blek was all your idea, wasn't it?'

'How perceptive of you, Margrave. It all has to do with something that's going to happen on out in the future. I needed to establish a connection between Yarblek and King Drosta – *and* between Drosta and Prince Rhodar. It's going to have a serious impact on something fairly significant. Don't ask questions, Javelin, because you're not going to get any answers. I'm having enough trouble keeping my father from tampering with the future, so I don't need *you* muddying up the waters as well.' I pushed the note I'd written and sealed that morning across his desk. 'Just see to it that my father gets this. It explains everything to him. Don't bother prying it open. It just tells him to come here and to buy me from Gallak. The Purpose of the Universe will be ever so grateful to you for this service.'

'You're taking a lot of the fun out of this, you know,' he accused.

'Just do as you're told, and don't ask questions, Javelin. All shall be revealed unto thee in the fullness of time.' I just threw that in.

Javelin picked up on it immediately. 'I shall be guided by thee in this, your Grace,' he replied extravagantly. 'I will, however, will thee or nil thee, make a few guesses.'

'Guess all you want, dear boy, but don't start dipping your fingers into it just yet.' I rose from my chair. 'Absolutely splendid talking with you, old chap,' I added lightly. 'Oh, incidentally, remind my father to bring *lots* of money with him when he comes to Yar Nadrak. I think he may be a bit surprised to discover how much I'm really worth.'

Javelin set aside his normal business and made the trip to Annath in person. I *was* a sort of living legend, after all. That can be tiresome now and then, but there *are* a few advantages to it, I suppose.

Father took his time getting to Yar Nadrak, naturally. Father takes his time about almost everything. After you've lived for seven thousand or so years, time doesn't really mean all that much to you, I guess. Then again, it's altogether possible that he had some trouble making a decision about buying me. He was extemely fond of that gold he and Yarblek's ancestor had extracted from that stream-bed up near the lands of the Morindim, and parting with some of it may have been causing him a few problems.

Eventually, however, he passed the test – and make no mistake about it, it *was* a test – and he showed up in Yar Nadrak with a saddle-bag filled with gold. Apparently I *was* worth something to him, after all.

I sensed his presence when he was a couple of miles out of town, and I accompanied Gallak to his place of business that morning. Gallak had a warehouse, of course, but he did most of his business in a tavern. Where else?

I waited until the old vagabond was about three doors away from the tavern, and then I told Gallak that I felt like dancing. I thought that might be a nice way to welcome father to Yar Nadrak – *and* let him know that he was getting his money's worth.

He entered the front door unobtrusively. Father's very good at unobtrusiveness. He seemed just a trifle surprised when he saw what I was doing. I definitely got his attention. Then, to entertain him, I exaggerated the performance just a bit. The tavern patrons started cheering, and father's eyes hardened into a kind of possessive belligerence. What a dear man he was! He still cared for me, even as he had before Beldaran's wedding. Three thousand years slipped away, and we were right back at the same place we'd been when I was only sixteen. My grip on him hadn't slipped a bit.

I concluded my dance to deafening cheers and then strutted back to Gallak's table. Father pushed his way through the crowd trying his best to conceal his pugnaciousness. 'That's quite a woman you've got there, friend,' he observed. 'Would you care to sell her?'

They exchanged a few wary pleasantries, and then we got down to some serious haggling about my price.

Father started out with an insultingly low bid, and I stepped in and countered with an absurdly high one. Then father raised his offer, and Gallak reduced his price. I started to get irritated when father stubbornly refused to go higher than ten bars of gold. What *is* this thing men have with the number ten? There's nothing magic about it, is there?

Along toward the end, I once again added my own voice to Gallak's. The ultimate price wasn't really all that important. I just wanted to push my father off that ten. Eleven would have satisfied me, but Gallak surprised me by holding out, and he and father eventually settled on twelve. That's a fairly respectable price, I suppose. Father's gold bars weigh ten ounces apiece, and a hundred and twenty ounces of gold – sixty of which would be mine – isn't bad, I guess.

It was late summer by the time father and I left Yar Nadrak, and we traveled west at father's usual pace, which ranges from a slow walk to a dead stop, and so it was autumn by the time we reached the range of high mountains which forms the spine of the continent. Father took a look at the turning leaves and the mountains lying ahead of us, and he picked up the pace a bit. By then, of course, it was too late. Winter's been catching up with my father for eons now, and he always seems surprised and slightly offended when it does.

The blizzard which caught us on the eastern slopes of the mountains was fairly savage, and it howled around our makeshift shelter for three days. I'm rather proud of the fact that I didn't once use the word 'dawdling' or the expression 'poking along' during our conversations in those three days.

Then we set out again, but it was obviously not getting us anywhere. The snow on level ground was about four feet deep, and the drifts were much deeper. 'There's no help for it, father,' I said finally. 'We're going to have to change form and fly out of here.'

His refusal surprised me just a bit, and his excuse, 'There might be Grolims around,' was really very flimsy. If we went falcon, we could be over Drasnia long before any Grolim got to within five miles of our present location. We plodded on through the snow, and we must have covered almost an entire mile before that first blizzard's second cousin swept in, forcing us to put up another rude shelter.

The wind howled all night, and about the middle of the next morning, we heard someone hail our makeshift little hut. 'Hello, the camp,' a voice called to us. 'I'm coming in. Don't get excited.'

He was old. My father's old, but father seems to ignore it. This fur-garbed fellow in some peculiar way seemed to have outgrown it. His hair and beard were of that rare silvery-white, almost luminous color, and his eyes were of a deep blue. I got the strange feeling that he saw everything. His face almost nestled in the deep fur of his collar, and his lushly-furred hat was nearly rakish. 'Looks like you two got yourselves in trouble, didn't you?' he suggested humorously as he trudged up to our shelter.

'We thought we could outrun it,' father replied with some resignation.

'Not much chance of that. These mountains are the natural home of snow. This is where it lives. Which way were you bound?'

'Drasnia,' father said.

'I'd say you got a late start – too late. You won't make Drasnia this winter.' He sighed. 'Well, there's no help for it, I guess. You'd better winter with me. I've got a cave about a mile from here. Gather up your belongings and bring your horses. I guess I can put up with some company for one winter.'

Father accepted the invitation a bit too quickly. 'We don't really have much choice, Pol,' he muttered to me as we packed our things in bundles to tie to our saddles.

I decided not make an issue of it, but we *did* in fact have a choice – the same choice we'd had since we left Yar Nadrak. Either my father was choosing to ignore it, or he was being encouraged to forget it. I spent the winter trying to figure out which.

The old fellow never did tell us what his name was. For all I could tell, he'd forgotten it. He told us that he'd spent his life up in these mountains looking for gold, but he didn't seem particularly obsessed by it. He just liked the mountains.

His cave was really fairly comfortable. It was quite large, and he kept it neat and orderly. When we entered through the narrow opening, he stirred up his fire and then showed us where to put our horses. His donkey was there, and after a little while, the donkey and our horses became friends. The donkey, however, seemed more like a dog than a beast of burden. The old gold-hunter allowed – or encouraged – him to roam at will through the cave. That caused me a number of problems that winter. The donkey was a curious little beast, and he was forever getting in my way. He absolutely *had* to see what I was doing. I think he liked me, because he was continually nuzzling me or gently butting me with his head. He loved to have his ears rubbed. I rather liked him, but I *didn't* like being awakened every morning by his snuffling at my neck. What bothered me the most, however, was his stubborn insistence on watching me while I bathed. I knew it was absurd, but his watching always made me blush for some reason.

Father and the old man spent the winter talking without really saying anything. They obviously liked each other, though they really didn't have much in common. After a while, I began to get a strong odor of tampering here. I don't think it was anything particularly earth-shaking, but for some obscure reason father and I were *supposed* to spend some time with this old fellow. The thing that struck me the most about him was the fact that there was quite probably nobody in the entire world more free than this solitary old man in the mountains.

Every now and then when my life has become hectic, I'll think back to that snowy winter, and a great peace seems to descend on me. Maybe that was the reason for our stay. It *has* helped me retain my sanity any number of times.

Spring finally came to the mountains, and father and I resumed our journey. 'Did that make any sense to you, father?' I asked when we were a few miles up the trail.

'What was that, Pol?' he asked, his face aglow with pleasant incomprehension.

I gave up. Quite obviously he hadn't the faintest idea of what I was talking about. 'Never mind,' I sighed.

We reached Boktor about a week later, and the city still had a frightened, wary air about it. A pestilence had swept the country

646

the preceding summer – one of those virulent diseases that strikes without warning, kills off about a third of the population, and then disappears as quickly as it had come. Had I not been so intent on returning to Annath, I might have investigated the disease in hopes of finding some remedy. The majority of humanity is carried off by one disease or another, and as a physician I find that offensive. Philosophically, however, I'm forced to admit its practicality. In the light of human fertility, there almost has to be *some* means of controlling the population; and in the long run, disease is more humane than war or starvation.

My, isn't *that* gloomy?

Anyway, this particular plague had carried off large numbers of Drasnians, and among them had been the king. Father and I stayed long enough to attend the coronation of Crown Prince Rhodar. I questioned the chubby king-to-be rather obliquely and was pleased to discover that he *had*, in fact, been visited by a scruffy-looking young Nadrak named Yarblek.

After Rhodar's coronation, father made an independent decision that I really didn't like. He sold our horses and bought a rowboat. 'We'll go on down through the fens,' he said in that irritatingly imperial tone he sometimes assumes.

'We'll do what?'

I think my tone might have conveyed my feelings about *that* decision. 'There are a lot of people traveling the Great North Road this time of year, Pol,' he explained defensively, 'and there might be some unfriendly eyes concealed in that crowd.' He *still* refused to even consider that most logical alternative. Even though it was spring and the waterfowl were migrating, the sky wasn't really all *that* crowded.

And so he poled us down into that reeking swamp. The mosquitoes were very happy to see us, I'm sure, and they *also* butted their heads against us in greeting. My disposition turned sour after the first mile.

The mosquitoes weren't the only creatures inhabiting the swamps, though. The turtles watched us glide by with dull-eyed reptilian indifference, but the fenlings, those small aquatic animals distantly related to otters, frolicked and played around our boat, and their squeaky chittering was almost like giggling. Evidently, the fenlings found the idea of humans stupid enough to deliberately come into the fens vastly amusing.

647

It was raining when father poled us around a bend in the slow-moving, meandering stream we were following through the reeds, and we caught sight of the neat, thatch-roofed cottage that was the home of Vordai, the witch of the fens.

Stories about Vordai had been surfacing in all manner of places for about three centuries, wild exaggerations as it turned out. Witches deal with spirits – and with the weather, of course. We don't do things like that. Perhaps the best way to put it is to say that witches deal with specifics, and we deal with generalities. That's an oversimplification, of course, but isn't almost everything?

The fenlings had alerted Vordai to our approach, and she was waiting in her doorway as father drove the nose of our boat up onto the muddy shore of her tree-covered little island. Her greeting wasn't exactly cordial. 'You might as well come inside,' she said without much emotion – 'at least until the rain lets up.'

Father and I got out of our boat and went up the path to her door. 'So you're Vordai,' I said to the aged but still beautiful woman in the doorway.

'And you would be Polgara,' she replied.

'You two know each other?' Father sounded surprised.

'By reputation, Old Wolf,' I told him. 'Vordai here is the one they call "the witch of the fens". She's been outcast, and this is the only place in Drasnia where she's really safe.'

'Probably because all the wood here is soggy enough to make burning people at the stake very difficult,' she added. 'Come in out of the rain.'

The interior of her cottage was scrupulously neat, her fireplace was well-banked, and there was a vase of wildflowers sitting on her table. The brown dress she wore reminded me of the dress my mother had been wearing that time I'd actually met her in the caves of Ulgo. Vordai, however, limped, and mother didn't.

She wordlessly took our wet clothing, hung it near the fire to dry and gave us blankets in which to wrap ourselves. 'Seat yourselves,' she told us then, pointing at the table. 'There should be enough in the pot for all of us.' The odor coming from her pot identified the meal she'd prepared as a delicately seasoned fish soup. Vordai was clearly an outstanding cook.

'You knew we were coming, didn't you?' I asked her.

'Naturally. I *am* a witch, after all.'

Then one of the fenlings came loping in and reported something in that excited chittering sound.

'Yes,' Vordai answered the sleek little beast, 'I know.'

'It's true then,' I said. I'd heard some wild stories about Vordai's ability to communicate with swamp creatures. 'You shouldn't really have tampered with them, you know.'

'It didn't hurt them,' she said with a shrug, 'and I find them to be much nicer to talk with than humans.'

There was an injured quality about this beautiful old woman that I couldn't quite put my finger on. Life hadn't treated her well, granted, but there was something else I couldn't quite fathom. She intrigued me more than I can say, and she also challenged the physician in me. Physicians fix things that have gone wrong, but my problem here was that I wasn't exactly sure what was really wrong. And so I decided to find out. I'm not one to pass up a challenge – or had you noticed that?

After we'd eaten, I sent a silent, not so subtle message to my father. *'Go away,'* I told him.

'What?'

'Go outside. I need to be alone with Vordai. Go. Now.'

His face grew slightly sullen. 'I'm going out to turn the boat over,' he said aloud. 'There's no point in letting the rain fill it up with water.' Then he got up and left, looking slightly ridiculous in that blanket.

'I'll help you with the dishes,' I told our hostess. The little domestic chores we share bring women closer together, but Vordai stubbornly refused to open her heart to me – so I did it the other way. I reached out with a tenuous thought, and once I was past her defensive barrier, I found the source of her life-long bitterness. It was a man, naturally. The origin of women's problems almost always is. It was a pedestrian thing, actually. When Vordai had been about fifteen, she'd fallen deeply – and silently – in love. The man had been quite a bit older than she was, and to put it bluntly, he was as stupid as a stump. They'd lived in a soggy little village on the edge of the fens, and Vordai's efforts to attract and capture the heart of the lumpish fellow had been unconventional. She used her gifts to help her neighbors. Unfortunately, her quarry was religious – in the worst possible way. He yearned in the depths of his grubby soul to 'stamp out the abomination of witchcraft', and it had been *he* who had led the mob which had been out to burn her at the stake. She'd been forced to flee into the fens, leaving behind her all hope of love, marriage and children. And that was why – even after three hundred years – she was out here in the fens devoting all her boundless love to the fenlings. Hers was a silly little story of a deep, but misplaced, affection that still burned in her heart.

649

'Oh, dear,' I said, my eyes suddenly filling with tears.

She gave me a startled look, and she suddenly realized that I'd subtly invaded her mind. At first her reaction was one of outrage at my unwelcome invasion, but then she realized that I'd done it out of compassion. I was a sorceress after all, so I had no real objection to witchcraft. Her defensive wall crumbled, and she wailed, 'Oh, Polgara!' She began to weep, and I took her in my arms and held her gently for quite some time, stroking her hair and murmuring comfort to her. There wasn't really anything else I could do. I knew what was wrong now, but there was no way that I could fix it.

The rain let up, and father and I put our now-dry clothes back on and resumed our journey. I spent a lot of time pondering those two meetings while father poled us on though the swamp. Both in the Nadrak mountains and again in Boktor, father had come up with very lame excuses for us not to simply fly back to Annath. Father could come up with all kinds of excuses to *avoid* work, but on these occasions, his excuses put him directly in its path, and that was so unusual as to get my attention immediately. For some reason, we'd *had* to meet that old man in the Nadrak mountains and Vordai in the fens. I finally gave up. Father and I *weren't* the center of the universe, after all, and perhaps those meetings were for someone *else's* benefit.

Well, of *course* I know who they were for – *now*. Vordai and the gold-hunter were to be part of *Garion's* education, and father and I were little more than bystanders. It's so obvious that I'm surprised you missed it.

We reached Aldurford and made our way along the eastern foothills of the Sendarian Mountains until we struck the little-used track leading up a long valley to Annath. It was mid-afternoon when we reached the stone quarry, and Geran, the newest heir, was waiting for us. Geran had been a gangling adolescent when I'd left for Gar og Nadrak, but he was a young man now. That happens frequently, you know. Sometimes it happens overnight. Unlike most of the young men I've raised, Geran had dark, almost black hair, and his eyes were a deep, deep blue. He wasn't as tall, but he looked a great deal like Riva Iron-grip himself. 'Aunt Pol!' he exclaimed with some relief. 'I was afraid you wouldn't make it back in time for the wedding.'

'Which wedding was that, dear?' I'm not sure why I said that. I *knew* which wedding he was talking about.

650

'Mine, of course,' he replied. 'Ildera and I are getting married next week.'

'My, my,' I said. 'Imagine that.'

Village weddings normally involve village people – the bride and groom in particular. Not infrequently, they're neighbors, and they've usually grown up together. This time, however, they not only came from different places, but were of different nationalities. The problems that arose out of those differences didn't involve the happy couple this time, though. The problems arose from their mothers, Geran's mother, Alara, and Ildera's mother, Olane. They detested each other. Ildera's father, Grettan, was the Chief of his clan, and that seems to have gone to Olane's head. She made no secret of the fact that to her way of looking at it, Ildera was marrying beneath herself. In Alara's eyes, her son was the Crown Prince of Riva, and Olane's condescension *really* grated on her nerves. I had to virtually ride herd on her constantly to keep her from proudly announcing her son's eminence. It was a very harrowing time for me.

Perhaps if I hadn't been away during the final stages of the courtship, I might have been able to head things off, but now it was too late. It had reached the point where the bride and groom were secondary. The personal animosity between Alara and Olane had spread, and the local Sendars and the clansmen from Algaria were unspoken antagonists.

'All right, gentlemen,' I said to father and Darral one evening, 'we've got a problem. I'll keep Alara and Olane from each other's throats, but *you* two are going to have to keep order in the streets – and in the local tavern. I don't want any bloodshed before the ceremony. If these idiots want to beat each other into a large communal pulp, it's your job to make sure that they do it *after* the wedding.'

'I could talk with Knapp, the tavern owner,' Darral said dubiously. 'Maybe I could persuade him to close for renovations or something. He might agree. A general brawl would probably wreck his place of business.'

Father shook his head. 'They're bad-tempered enough already,' he said. 'Closing the tavern would just make it worse.'

'Close the border, maybe?' Darral was reaching for straws there. 'Grettan might agree to that. Or maybe we could stampede their cows. That might keep the Algars busy for a while.'

'I don't really care how you do it, gentlemen,' I told them, 'but keep the peace. That's an order, in case you hadn't noticed.'

Geran and Ildera seemed oblivious to the undeclared war between their mothers. They'd reached that happy stage of mindless obliviousness to everything going on around them that's the usual prelude to a happy marriage. I'd seen it before, of course. That afternoon in Camaar sort of leaps to mind. It always does, since that was the day I lost my sister. Geran and Ildera didn't go *quite* as far as Beldaran and Riva had gone, but they came close.

The antagonism between Alara and Olane didn't find its outlet in open violence, but rather in competition. They tried to outdo each other in every single detail of the upcoming occasion. They bickered with false smiles frozen in place on their faces about which of them was going to provide the flowers. I headed *that* off by announcing that *I'd* take care of it, 'since you ladies have so many other things to attend to. Besides, I can do it much less expensively than either of you can.' I even fell back on thrift to fend off an incipient clash of arms.

Then Olane smugly showed off Ildera's wedding gown, and Alara began to chew on her own liver over that. She tore Annath apart and finally found an out of date and ill fitting doublet for Geran to wear at the ceremony. The doublet was of a faded purple, and it really didn't look all that nice, but she crammed her reluctant son into it and then paraded him in front of Olane with a spiteful little smile on her face. I assessed the impact of the dress and the doublet and silently ruled that clash to be a draw. Draws didn't set too well with the competitors, though. The wedding supper, jointly prepared, was a clear win for Olane. She *did* have access to unlimited beef, after all. Alara took the one about the officiating priest, however. Olane's champion was the clan's priest of Belar, but Alara's was the local Sendarian priest. Sendars are ecumenical to a fault, so Alara's priest could invoke the blessing of all seven Gods. I kept my mouth shut about UL, fearing that Alara might postpone the wedding until she could make contact with the Gorim of Ulgo. Alara and Olane bickered back and forth, their faces both locked in those icy smiles that absolutely reeked of false politeness and were meant to conceal their real feelings but didn't even come close to succeeding. Spurious reasoning about the two priests flowed back and forth until we were all knee-deep in logical fallacies. 'Both of them!' I decided finally, just to put an end to it.

'I didn't quite follow that, Pol,' Alara said sweetly.

'Both priests will officiate.'

'But –'

'No buts. Both priests, ladies, and that's the end of this.' I had to do that fairly often during that undeclared war.

When the wedding day finally arrived, I was exhausted. If I could just survive this one day, I was definitely going to give myself a vacation. I felt that if I heard, 'But, Olane, dear –' or 'But, Alara, sweetie –' one more time, I'd just scream.

The ceremony, since there were two priests in contention, dragged on for two hours, and the wedding guests, who were *really* looking forward to the post-ceremonial festivities, grew restive.

Ildera was stunningly beautiful, and Geran so handsome that the village girls of Annath were almost audibly gnashing their teeth over the fact that they'd let him get away.

I largely ignored the wedding sermons, but I *did* choke just a bit when the Sendarian priest invoked the blessing of Torak on the marriage. This was most definitely the wrong wedding for that.

Then the ceremony was finally over, and Geran and Ildera were man and wife. They endured the wedding supper, obviously impatient to go to the neat stone cottage Geran and his father had built at the south end of Annath's single street. They definitely had plans for the evening. Father, Darral, and Grettan kept the peace during the supper, but that was about as far as the pacification went. We all trooped down that long street, accompanying the happy couple home, and then I went back to Darral's house and fell into bed. I was absolutely exhausted.

The citizens of Annath and the Algar clansmen were all very civilized, of course, so the fights didn't start until after the sun went down.

CHAPTER 40

I spoke with father the next morning, and he entertained me with a humorous description of the post-wedding festivities. I always take father's accounts of such events with a large grain of salt, since father has a deep-seated need for artful embellishment.

'Broke the priest's *jaw*?' I exclaimed at one point.

'As neatly as you'd snap a twig,' father smirked. 'Caught him right on the point of the chin with his fist. Of course, the priest wasn't expecting it. Over in Algaria, people don't hit the priests of Belar. He won't be giving any of those long-winded sermons of his for a while – at least not until his jaw heals. Then, just after that, Knapp the tavern keeper was trying to get everybody to take the fight outside, and some rascal bonked him on top of the head with a stool.'

'Bonked?'

'That's the sound it made, Pol – "Bonk!" Just like that. Knapp went down like a poled ox, and the revelers continued to break up his tavern.'

I sighed.

'What's wrong?'

'I was looking forward to a day of rest. I guess I'd better go tend the injured.'

'They'll heal, Pol. It was a friendly fight. Nobody even thought about drawing a dagger.'

'Broken bones need to be set, father.'

'You can't fix everything, Pol.'

'Who came up with *that* rule? What are your plans?'

'I think I'll go back to the Vale. Chamdar's in Tolnedra right now, but I'm sure he's got Grolims and Dagashi snooping around in

Sendaria. I don't want to attract attention to this place, and I *am* fairly recognizable.'

'Wise decision. Give my best to the twins.'

'I'll do that.'

I spent the rest of the morning tending to the assorted cuts, bruises, abrasions, and broken bones, and then I went on down to visit the newly-weds. They were polite, of course, but I got the distinct impression that they had plans for the rest of the day so I trudged on home and went back to bed.

In the days that followed Alara rearranged the events of the wedding day in her own mind so that it became a day of absolute triumph for her. Oh, well, it didn't hurt anything, and if it made her happy –

The location of Geran's cottage down at the south end of town was slightly inconvenient, but that might have had something to do with his selection of the site. His mother was a bit possessive about him and more than just a bit domineering. We all loved her, of course, but she had a tendency to be just a bit erratic. I probably should have paid closer attention to that.

There was a world out there beyond the last house in Annath, however, and it kept moving along, whether we noticed it or not.

It was at about the same time as the wedding that Taur Urgas came up with his insane scheme to assassinate emperor Zakath of Mallorea. The scheme involved Zakath's beloved, and she was among the casualties when everything fell apart. After that, Zakath became obsessed with the idea of exterminating the Murgo race – a commendable goal, I suppose, but it *did* sort of get in the way when more important things were going on. Taur Urgas was every bit as crazy as Drosta had said he was, and Zakath wasn't much better. Cho-Ram of Algaria later cured the insanity of Taur Urgas, and Cyradis, the Seeress of Kell, cured Zakath's. They used entirely different methods, however.

I don't think I'd fully realized just how much my isolation in Annath had kept me out of touch with current affairs until father stopped by in the spring of 5349 and told me of the dissension among the Angaraks. There's a kind of charm about rustic life, but the entire world could end, and it'd take several years for the news to reach a place like Annath.

Then, in the autumn of that same year, tragedy struck my little family. It was an ordinary autumn day with a chill in the air and with the leaves of birch and aspen a riot of bright colors. As usual,

Darral and Geran went to work in the stone quarry. Then, just before lunch, the south face of the quarry quite suddenly broke away and fell to the floor of the pit, crushing my nephew, Darral.

Accidents happen all the time, and a stone quarry's not the safest place in the world to work, but as it turned out, the death of Darral was no accident. It was the first hint we had that Chamdar – or Asharak the Murgo, whichever you prefer – had found us at last.

My grief at Darral's death almost incapacitated me. Father made it to Annath in time for the funeral, but I almost completely ignored him. I was in no mood for platitudes. I stayed in my room for two weeks, and when I finally came out, father was gone. Alara moved woodenly about her kitchen, but I didn't really pay much attention. I started taking my meals in my room, since I didn't want to talk to *anybody*, much less those who shared my grief.

When I finally *did* come out, I discovered that Alara had gone strange on me. I was confident that I could take care of it, but that was a mistake. No physician should *ever* treat the illnesses of her own family, since objectivity is essential in the practice of medicine, and who can be objective about her own family? I delayed, and by the time I got around to my diagnosis, it was too late. Of course, it may have been too late right at the outset, since Alara's madness had an outside source.

'Whatever is the matter, Pol?' she asked me one afternoon a week or so after I'd come out of my seclusion. She'd found me with tears in my eyes and her tone was concerned. 'Did you hurt yourself?' She sounded only mildly interested and a little vague.

I looked at her sharply. Her face was placid, and that should have alerted me right then and there.

'Come along now, dear,' she said in a comforting sort of way. 'Pull yourself together. It's time for us to start fixing supper. Darral will be coming home from work soon, and he'll be hungry.'

That jerked me back to reality almost immediately. I'd seen this delusion in others after a death in the family. Sometimes the human mind does strange things to protect itself. If something's just too horrible to contemplate, the mind will refuse to contemplate it. In Alara's mind, Darral was still alive, and he'd be coming home for supper before long.

There are two ways to deal with this not uncommon condition. My own emotional turmoil caused me to choose the wrong one. 'Have you forgotten, Alara?' I said mildly. 'Darral had to go on a business trip. He wants to see if he can find more bidders for our yearly production of stone block.'

'Why didn't he tell me?' She sounded a little hurt.

I reverted to subterfuge at that point. I smacked my forehead with my palm. 'It's my fault, Alara,' I lied. 'He came home this morning – while you were visiting with Ildera. He told me that there were some builders in Erat he wanted to talk with and that he'd be gone for a few weeks. There were some wagoners who were going in that direction, and one of them had offered him a ride. He had to leave immediately. One of our neighbor ladies fell ill, and I was so busy with her that I forgot to tell you that Darral was away on business. I'm very sorry, Alara.'

'Oh, that's all right, Pol,' she forgave me. Then her face brightened. 'Here's a thought. Now that Darral won't be underfoot for a while, we'll be able to concentrate on our autumn housecleaning. We'll have everything all bright and shiny when he comes home.'

I knew right then that I'd made a mistake, but it was too late now to correct it. The 'business trip' would only reinforce Alara's delusion and make it that much harder to cure in the long run. 'Why don't you fix us a light supper, dear?' I suggested. 'I have to go tell Ildera something.'

'All right, Pol. Don't be too long now.'

I hurried on down to the far end of Annath to the somewhat blocky cottage Geran had built for him and his bride. Geran was a conscientious builder who wanted the things he constructed to last, so there were hints of 'fortress' about his cottage. I knocked at the stout door.

Ildera, blonde and lovely, opened it. 'Aunt Pol,' she greeted me. I glanced around quickly to make sure she was alone. 'Is there something the matter?' she asked.

'We've got a problem, Ildera,' I told her.

'Oh?'

'Alara's mind has slipped.'

'Dear Gods!'

'It's not dangerous – yet. She's not raving or anything, but she's erased the memory of Darral's death from her mind. This afternoon she told me that she was expecting him home for supper.'

'Oh, Aunt Pol!' Ildera's eyes had gone wide. 'What can we do?'

'We lie to her, Ildera. I conjured up a story about a business trip on the spur of the moment – just to get her past suppertime – and now we're stuck with it, I'm afraid. Tell Geran about it when he comes home. We'll all have to tell Alara the same story. I said that

657

Darral caught a ride with some wagoners and that he's going to Erat to drum up some more business. I came here to make sure that we'd all be telling her the same story.'

'We're going to *have* to tell her the truth eventually, Aunt Pol.'

'I'm not so sure about that, Ildera. Darral's business trip might have to be protracted.'

'Can't you – ? ' Ildera made a vaguely mysterious gesture intended to suggest sorcery. The knowledge that I was 'talented' had been a part of Ildera's indoctrination in our little family, and as is usually the case, she grossly overestimated the kinds of things I could do with that talent.

'I don't think so, Ildera. The mind's a very complicated piece of machinery. If you fix one part of it, you might damage another part beyond repair. I love Alara too much to start experimenting on her. There are some combinations of herbs that'll keep her calm and happy. I'll rely on those until I can come up with a safe alternative.'

'Whatever you think best, Aunt Pol.' Ildera laughed a bit ruefully. 'The Gods know that *I* wouldn't be very good at it. I can't even dig a splinter out of my own finger.' Then her expression grew serious. 'You *do* realize that this means that we'll have to isolate her from the rest of the village, don't you? One wrong word could destroy her sanity for good.'

'I'll work on that,' I promised her. 'Tell Geran about this, and tell him that *I'll* take care of it. I don't want him sticking his nose into it. That wrong word you mentioned could come from him just as easily as from some village gossip.'

'I don't think he'll cause you any problems there, Aunt Pol. He's so busy examining every inch of the south face of the quarry for the flaw that caused that rock-slide that he can't even think about anything else.'

'As long as it keeps him out of the way. Oh, my father sent word that he'll be visiting us again soon. If he stops here before he comes on up to our house, tell him about Alara's condition and how we're dealing with it. Warn him that I'll rip out his beard if he interferes.'

'*Aunt Pol!*'

'Well, part of it, anyway. I'd better get on back home. One of us is going to have to stay with Alara almost constantly from now on.'

Father arrived two days later, but I didn't want to talk with him in front of Alara. 'Get out of here, father!' I ordered. 'I'm busy. Go talk with Geran and Ildera. They'll tell you what's happening.' I pointed at the door. 'Out!' I commanded.

Father, of course, totally misunderstood. He assumed that my outburst was the result of my ongoing grief, and he was wrong. I had something much more important to deal with.

Later that day I sent for Ildera, and she sat with her mother-in-law while I took father out to the edge·of the forest so that we could talk.

'She's completely insane?' Father sighed when I told him about Alara's condition.

'I didn't say that, Old Wolf. All I said was that she's blocked out the fact that she's a widow.'

'That sounds fairly insane to me, Pol.'

'You really don't know what you're talking about, father. Insanity's rarely total. Alara's illness is limited to one fact. Aside from that, she's perfectly all right.'

'Your definition of "all right" is worlds apart from mine, Pol. How long do you plan to let this go on?'

'As long as it takes, father. I *won't* destroy Alara just to satisfy some picky little concept of reality. She's a bit lonesome for her husband, but that's as far as her misery goes. I'll keep her happy for the rest of her life, if I have to.'

He shrugged. 'You're the expert, Pol.'

'I'm glad you noticed that. What are you up to at the moment?'

'I'm marking time, Pol, just like everybody else. The whole universe is holding its breath waiting for Ildera to start to bulge.'

'That's a crude way to put it.'

'I'm a crude sort of fellow.'

'You know, I've noticed that myself.'

After father went back to the Vale, Ildera and I let it be generally known in Annath that Alara was 'under the weather' and needed absolute peace and quiet – 'her recent bereavement, you understand'. The ladies of Annath all nodded sagely, pretending to understand, and so there weren't any visitors to our house on the north end of town. We made sure that Alara never left the house unaccompanied, and Geran's new wife demonstrated a surprising agility at changing the subject whenever someone encountered her and her mother-in-law in the village streets. She could cut off the word 'condolences' almost before it left anyone's lips. Protecting Alara's tenuous grip on sanity became our major occupation, and we grew better and better at it. Ildera, however, had another job to see to, and I occasionally fretted about her failure to get on with it. She continued to aid me in caring for Alara, and her waistline stayed trim and girlish.

In 5351, Javelin paid father a visit in the Vale to report that

Asharak the Murgo had vanished, despite the best efforts of Drasnian intelligence to keep him under surveillance. As it turned out, of course, Asharak had evaded those who'd been assigned the job of following him at least once already. He'd come to the vicinity of Annath not too long after the wedding of Geran and Ildera to tamper with the geology of the south face of the stone quarry.

Father immediately went to Tol Honeth and virtually disassembled the city trying to find traces of Chamdar, and when that failed, he expanded his search to the rest of Tolnedra. That futile search kept him very busy for the next couple of years.

Meanwhile, back in Annath, Ildera and I took turns keeping watch over Alara, calling on Geran to fill in for us when we were both exhausted. The 'tonic' Alara took twice a day kept her just a little vague about the passage of time, and my recently found skill at implanting some memories and erasing others made it all the easier for us to control her perception of time. That was the key to keeping Alara tranquil. As long as she didn't know how long Darral's 'business trip' was really taking, she stayed happy. I even went so far as to 'dusty-up' the house a few times – usually while she was asleep or down at the other end of town visiting Ildera – so that we could spend a week cleaning house. We cleaned house four times during the autumn of 5353, but Alara only remembered the last time. House-cleaning is tedious and repetitious anyway, so the memory of having done it isn't the sort of memory one clings to very hard.

I'm sure that there are some self-righteous people who'll read this and be outraged by my ongoing deception of Alara. These are the sort of people who secretly delight in causing pain 'for her own good'. It wouldn't really pay people like that to take me to task for my way of dealing with Alara's insanity. I might just decide that it'd be good for *them* if their heads were on backward.

Another Erastide came and went, and Annath, as usual, was cut off from the rest of the world by the heavy winter snows. Our little family celebration of the holiday was subdued. By now, the villagers all knew that Alara was 'a little strange', and they good-heartedly respected our need to keep her more or less in seclusion. They weren't indifferent, though, and any time Ildera or I were out and about, they'd ask how our Alara was doing. The best we could give them was, 'about the same', and they'd sigh and nod mournfully. Villagers the world over can be nosey, but their curiosity grows out of a genuine concern for their neighbors.

It was obvious to me by now that Alara would never really get better. Her condition was permanent. There wasn't any cure, but my combination of herbs and 'tampering' kept her moderately serene and sometimes even a little happy. Under the circumstances, it was the best I could manage.

Then, when the spring thaw of 5354 was melting off the snow and the local streams were all running bank full, Ildera came up the muddy street of Annath early one morning with a radiant smile on her face. 'I think I'm pregnant, Aunt Pol,' she announced.

'It's about time,' I noted.

She looked just a little hurt, but then I laughed and threw my arms about her. 'I'm only teasing, Ildera,' I told her, holding her very close. 'I'm *so* happy for you.'

'I'm sort of pleased about it myself,' she said. 'Now, what should I do to put a stop to all the throwing up every morning?'

'Eat something, dear.'

'You said what?'

'Put something to eat on the table beside the bed before you go to sleep. When you wake up in the morning, eat it before you get out of bed.'

'Would that work?'

'It always has. Trust me, Ildera. This is one aspect of medicine that I'm very good at. I've had *lots* of practice.' I looked appraisingly at her tummy. 'You don't show yet.'

She made a rueful little face. 'There goes my girlish figure, I guess. None of my dresses are going to fit, though.'

'I'll sew you up some nice smocks, Ildera.'

'Should we tell Alara?' she asked, glancing at her mother-in-law's bedroom door.

'Let me think about that a bit first.' Then I laid my hand on her still-girlish belly and sent a gently probing thought into her. 'Three weeks,' I said.

'Three weeks what? Please, Aunt Pol, don't be cryptic.'

'You've been pregnant for three weeks.'

'Oh. It must have been that last blizzard then.'

'I didn't exactly follow that, dear.'

'Well it was snowing very hard outside, and there wasn't really anything else to do that afternoon.' She gave me an arch little smile. 'Should I go on, Aunt Pol?' she asked me.

This time, I was the one who blushed. 'No, Ildera,' I said. 'I sort of get the picture.'

'I thought that maybe you might be curious – from a professional point of view. Are you absolutely *sure* you don't want all the details, Aunt Pol?'

'Ildera! You stop that immediately!' My face was actually flaming by now.

Her laughter was silvery. 'Got you that time, didn't I, Aunt Pol?' she said. What an adorable girl she was! I absolutely *loved* her.

That night I sent my thought out to the twins down in the Vale. *'Have you any idea at all of where my father is?'* I asked them.

'He was in Tolnedra the last time we talked with him, Pol,' Belkira replied. *'He's moving around a lot, so he's a little hard to keep track of.'*

'I need to get a message to him,' I told them. *'There are some unfriendly ears out there, though, so I don't want to get too specific.'*

'If it's urgent, we'll come up there, and then you can go looking for him,' Beltira offered.

'No, it's not that urgent – not yet, anyway. It's just that something's going on here that takes a certain fairly predictable amount of time.' I thought that was nice and cryptic. *'Have you found anything new and exciting in the Mrin lately?'*

'Nothing recently,' Belkira replied. *'Everything seems to be frozen.'*

'It's springtime now, Uncle,' I told him. *'Have you ever noticed how spring always seems to thaw things out?'* I was fairly sure that the twins would catch the meaning I'd hidden in that seemingly casual observation.

'Why yes,' Beltira agreed, *'now that you mention it, we've noticed the same thing ourselves. How far along is spring where you are?'*

'About three weeks, uncle. The snow's starting to melt, and the wildflowers should come peeping through before too long.'

I was fairly sure that if some Grolim happened to be listening, he'd be just fascinated by my weather report.

'I've always rather liked wildflowers,' Belkira added.

'I'm fond of them myself. If you hear from my father, give him my regards, would you?'

'Of course, Pol.'

I was rather smug about the way I'd managed to tell them about Ildera's condition without actually coming right out and saying anything about it. As it turned out, however, I seem to have underestimated Chamdar by more than a little.

In the years following what happened at Annath, father, my uncles and I have pieced together Chamdar's movements during the fourth decade of the fifty-fourth century. Father in particular became almost obsessed with the project and he was the one who finally verified

662

Chamdar's involvement in what happened to Darral. He happened across a talkative old fellow in one of those rowdy taverns in Muros who, after some prodding, dredged up an incident out of a nearly dormant memory. He recalled that a Murgo matching Chamdar's description had been asking for directions to Annath in 5349 – 'On accounta that wuz th' same year my old ox, Butter, died. Calt him Butter 'cuz he wuz alluz buttin' his head aginst me.'

At some point in his shady past my father had developed the knack of winnowing not only thoughts, but also images, out of other men's minds, and so when the somewhat tipsy old fellow remembered the incident, father was able to recognize Chamdar from his informant's rather blurred recollection. Chamdar *had* passed through Muros in 5349, and he *had* been looking for Annath just before Darral had been killed. I wouldn't want to have to pursue our case against Chamdar in a court of law, but it had never been our intention to take him before a magistrate. We had quicker, more certain ways to obtain justice.

Anyway, after I'd confirmed Ildera's pregnancy, we talked things over with Geran, and we decided not to try to keep it a secret from Alara. As it turned out, the news that she was about to become a grandmother made Alara very happy, and if things had turned out differently, it might even have restored her to sanity.

It was quiet in Annath that spring and summer. The menfolk went to work in the quarry every morning, and the women cooked, cleaned, washed clothes, and gossiped. Ildera bloomed – slowly of course – and she frequently gave vent to the pregnant woman's universal complaint, 'Why does this have to take so long?' All in all, it was a fairly normal pregnancy.

I thought things over frequently during the late spring and early summer, and I decided that after the baby was born, our family should probably move again. We'd been in Annath for twenty years now, and even though Annath was isolated, I felt that it wouldn't be a good idea for us to remain there much longer. I ran through my mental catalogue of all the towns and villages in Sendaria, crossing out all the places where I'd previously lived, since local folklore will cling to incidents that took place generations ago. I definitely didn't want to run across someone who might be able to dredge certain memories out of the long gone past. All it takes sometimes is for some idler to say to his friends, 'Have you noticed how much she looks like that lady they say lived over on Shadylane about three hundred years ago?' and my secret's out. Ultimately, I settled on the town of Wala, some miles to the south of the main road between Muros and Camaar. I hadn't lived in southern Sendaria for centuries, and Wala was a fairly new town, founded less than two hundred years ago.

To avoid any possible discovery, the twins and I relied rather heavily on the members of Ildera's clan to carry messages back and forth to each other. When there are unfriendly ears about, it's not a good idea to shout – figuratively speaking – back and forth. It was late summer when a horsehide clad Algar brought me a letter from them advising me that they'd finally located my father. Actually, I believe it was Mandorallen who tracked him down and gave him the message that 'a certain kinswoman of thine is with child'. Mandorallen's the perfect one to carry a message like that, since he wouldn't even *think* of trying to puzzle out what it meant.

Father immediately returned to the Vale, but – wisely, I thought – decided *not* to come to Annath. We didn't know where Chamdar was, and father didn't want to lead him right to me and my family. Instead, father went off to central Sendaria and started thrashing around in order to attract Chamdar's attention.

It was late autumn when Alara's condition took a turn for the worse. All during the spring and summer, she'd been so caught up in the progress of Ildera's pregnancy that she'd seemed at times almost normal. Then as the leaves began to turn, she quite suddenly developed a fixation that Darral was lost somewhere in the surrounding mountains. I know now who it was who'd implanted that fixation, but at the time it totally baffled me. I simply couldn't let her out of my sight for a moment. The minute I turned my back, she was gone. I frequently – after hours of searching – found her wandering aimlessly in the surrounding forest, plaintively calling out her husband's name. Those pitiful cries tore at my heart, and I couldn't bring myself to scold her.

In retrospect, I'll concede that Chamdar was no ordinary Grolim. He was extraordinarily skilled at concealing himself. I never once caught any sense of his presence nor any hint of what he was doing to Alara's mind. Moreover, he knew me far better than I was prepared to admit. He knew, for example, that all it took to send me off into the surrounding forest was Alara's absence. Most Grolims wouldn't have had any conception of my love for the members of my family, since love's an alien concept to the Grolims. Chamdar not only understood it, but he also used it to skillfully pull me out of Annath at the critical moment.

Winter came early that year. The first heavy snowfall swept across the mountains before the aspen trees had even finished shedding their leaves, and that combination always makes for a very cluttered forest. When a thick, wet snow piles up on unshed leaves, its weight breaks branches, and it's very difficult to wade your way through the resulting brush-pile. After Alara had escaped me a few times, I gave some thought to throwing caution to the winds and conducting my searches for her from the air. I firmly set that idea aside, however. There was no point in announcing my location to Chamdar just to keep my feet dry.

I'm sure the irony of that didn't escape you. In essence, I was trying to hide from somebody who already knew exactly where I was. Chamdar was playing me like a lute. Every time I think of it, my blood starts to boil. If I knew how to do it, I'd resurrect him so that Garion could set fire to him again.

Then about sunset on Erastide eve, Ildera went into false labor. I'm certain now that Chamdar arranged that as well. A village lady brought Geran's urgent summons to me, and I quickly looked in on Alara. She appeared to be sound asleep, so I carefully reached into her dozing mind and reinforced that sleep. Then I gathered up my instruments and went on down to the other end of town to deliver the newest member of my family.

Ildera's false labor continued for several hours, and then her contractions and labor pains diminished.

'What's wrong, Aunt Pol?' Geran demanded, his voice a little shrill.

'Nothing's wrong, Geran,' I assured him. 'This happens all the time. Ildera's just not quite ready yet, that's all.'

'You mean she's *practicing*?'

I'd never heard it put quite that way before, and it struck me as enormously funny.

Geran was a bit offended by my laughter, however.

'She's just fine, Geran,' I assured him. 'This is what midwives call "false labor". It happens so often that there's even a name for it. The real thing will come along in the next day or so. She'll sleep now, and you might as well do the same thing. Nothing's going to happen for a while.'

Then I closed up my bag and trudged back up through the snow to my own house.

And Alara wasn't there when I returned.

I should have realized at that point that Chamdar had broken my grip on Alara's mind. *Nobody* wakes up after I tell him to sleep until I'm ready for him to wake up.

It had been quite cold for a week or more, but there hadn't been any fresh snow, so the village itself and all the surrounding area was criss-crossed with footprints that went off in all directions. I concentrated my search to the north, the direction Alara had usually taken on those futile quests of hers, but once again, Chamdar was ahead of me. This time, she went south. Although it was dangerous, I sent out brief spurts of searching thought, but I still couldn't find her. That seemed very odd to me. I kept ranging back and forth in wide arcs, and eventually reached an open meadow back in the forest. There were deer tracks, rabbit tracks, and lots of bird tracks out in that meadow, but no human footprints. Alara had not gone north.

I judged that it was very close to midnight by now, and it was bitterly cold out there in that dark forest. I'd already covered the north, the northeast and the northwest in my methodical search. Since Annath lay at the bottom of a gorge, sheer cliffs blocked off the east and west. That left the southern quarter, and I was at least five miles away from that.

At that point, I threw caution to the winds and changed form. If that happened to alert Chamdar, that was just too bad. As cold as it had become, Alara's main danger now lay in the distinct possibility that she'd freeze to death before dawn. I absolutely *had* to find her.

I had no way of knowing that not long after I'd left Ildera's bedside, her false labor became genuine. Geran tried desperately to find me, but of course he couldn't. The local midwife attended Ildera during the birth, and Garion was born shortly after midnight.

I was nowhere near, but fortunately, the delivery wasn't too difficult. Ildera was an Alorn, after all, and Alorn women are all designed for childbirth.

It took me all night to find Alara. Her body lay at the foot of a fairly high cliff six or eight miles south of the stone quarry. That explained why I'd been unable to find her with my mind when I'd first discovered that she was missing. The frozen condition of her body was a clear indication that she'd died before I'd even become aware of the fact that she'd wandered off.

I was absolutely devastated when I found her, and I wept and tore at my hair, blaming myself again and again.

Then I suddenly stopped, staring in horror at the thick column of smoke rising from Annath in that first faint light of the dawn of

Erastide. Something was burning in a village made entirely of stone!

I swallowed my grief, and as it subsided, I sensed my father's presence. He was much closer to the fire than I was. *'Father!'* It was almost a silent scream.

'You'd better get back here, Pol!' he replied bleakly. *'Now!'*

I have no idea whatsoever of how I traveled those miles from Alara's frozen body to Geran's burning house. For all I knew, I translocated myself, and that's very dangerous out there in the mountains. If there happens to be a peak in your way, you'll go *through* it, not around, and that's not the sort of thing I'd care to experiment with.

Father was kneeling over a small, blanket-wrapped bundle in the door yard, and Geran's solid stone house was totally engulfed in flames. 'What happened here, father?' I almost shrieked at him.

'It was Chamdar!' he roared back at me, his eyes filled with vengeful fury. 'What were you thinking of, Pol? Why did you run off like that?'

The question cut into me like a knife, and now, even after all these years, I can still feel it twisting inside me.

CHAPTER 41

I looked at Geran's familiar stone cottage now engulfed in impossible flame, and tears were streaming from my eyes. 'Is there any hope at all?' I asked father, though I knew there wasn't.

'None,' he answered shortly, wiping his own eyes with a deliberately rough hand. 'They're both already dead.'

My entire family had been destroyed in a single night, and no matter how I squirmed and tried to evade it, I knew that it was my fault. 'I've failed, father!' I cried out in anguish. 'I've failed!'

'There's no time for that now, Pol!' he snapped. 'We've got to get the baby out of here. Chamdar got away from me, and he could be anywhere.' Father's reddened eyes grew hard as he looked at the fire erupting from the very stones of the cottage. He was quite obviously considering some unpleasant things to do to Chamdar.

'Why did you let him escape?' I asked, realizing that I hadn't been the only one who'd failed that night.

'I didn't have any choice,' father explained. 'That idiot threw the baby at me. There's nothing we can do here, Pol. Let's move!'

I reached down and tenderly lifted the baby. I turned back the blanket and looked for the first time into the face of the Godslayer. It was a very ordinary face, but the whole world seemed to reel as I looked into those drowsy blue eyes. Someday he might indeed slay a God, but right now, he was just a sleepy, orphaned baby. I held him very close against my heart. Chamdar'd have to go through me to get this one.

'I suppose we'd better come up with a name for him,' father said. 'People might talk if we just call him "Godslayer".'

'His name's Garion, father. Ildera and I decided on that months ago.'

'Garion? Not bad, I guess. Where did you come up with it?'

'Ildera had a dream. I think there might have been some tampering involved. She told me that his real name would be "Belgarion", but that we should call him "Garion" until he grows up.' I steeled my heart. 'Chamdar's got a lot to answer for, doesn't he?'

'Indeed he does,' father replied in a flinty kind of voice, 'and I'm personally going to see to it that it takes him at least a week to do all his answering. What happened to Alara?'

'She's dead too, father. She fell off a cliff. We'll have to bury her on our way out of town.'

'Make that *two* weeks!' he grated. 'I'm sure I can come up with a way to keep Chamdar alive for at least that long.'

'Good!' I said. 'I'll take Garion to safety. You go after Chamdar. Take notes, father. I want *lots* of details when you tell me about it.' I was feeling at least as savage as father was at that point.

'Not a chance, Pol.' Father said it regretfully. 'I've got to get the two of you to safety first. Our main responsibility's wrapped up in that blanket. I'll deal with Chamdar after I know you're safe.'

We left the now collapsing house and followed the snow-covered road on down past the quarry, and then we set off through the trees to the base of the cliff that had claimed Alara. About all we could really do was to pile rocks over her, and we couldn't even mark her grave. Her gravestone's in my heart, though, and I'm sure it'll always be there.

Father stole a she-goat from an isolated farmstead, and I devised a nursing bottle. The little nanny-goat seemed actually fond of Garion, and probably wouldn't have objected to nursing him. I didn't really think that'd be appropriate, though. The goat probably thought I was being silly, but over the centuries, goats have learned to expect humans to be silly, I suppose. Father and I stuck to the woods on our journey down to the low country, and he was very careful to erase our tracks in the snow as we went. If it'd been up to me, I'd have left those tracks where they were and set off signal fires to attract Chamdar or any of his Grolim underlings. I was feeling vengeful, and I *really* wanted to kill Angaraks about then.

We avoided all roads and camped out in caves or under fallen trees. It took us several days to reach the foothills, and we came out onto a fairly well-traveled road near the village of Outer Gralt. We didn't go into the town, but continued on, making our way toward my house on the shores of Lake Erat, the place I always go when things fall apart.

As it always is when I've been away for a long time, the interior of the house was chill and dusty. I built a fire in the kitchen stove while father went on out beyond the rose-thicket to have a word with the twins.

He came back shivering. He dutifully stamped the snow off his feet at the door, looking longingly at my roaring stove.

'Don't bother,' I told him. 'You have to milk the goat. She's in the stable. You'd better feed her as well.'

'Couldn't I just –? '

'No, father. You're up and moving now, and I know how hard it is to get you started again once you've settled down. Get your chores done first, *then* you can sit down by the stove.'

He sighed and went back out. There were some things I needed back in the house, so I deposited Garion in a drawer so that I could search unimpeded. An open drawer's a very good place to stow a newborn infant, did you know that?

I found a cradle and some baby clothes back in the house. Over the years, quite a few babies had been born there, and I seldom throw anything away that I might need later. By the time father returned with a pail of warm goat's milk, Garion was dressed, lying in an eight-hundred year old cradle, and holding a little rattle that had been made generations ago.

'I think it's colder down here than it is up in the mountains,' father noted, holding his hands out over the stove.

'It just seems that way, father. Were you able to contact the twins?'

'Oh, I got them, all right. I just hope they understood what I was saying to them when I said we needed them in the rose-garden.'

'I'm sure they did.'

'I'm still going to stay here until they arrive. *Then* I'm going to track down Chamdar and settle this once and for all. I should have killed him a long time ago.'

'You're starting to sound like uncle Beldin.'

'Beldin's approach to problems might be simplistic, Pol, but it *does* have the charm of being permanent.' Then he looked at me gravely. 'Have you decided where you're going to take the baby yet? I probably ought to know the name of the town.'

'I don't think I'll go to a town, father – not this time. Towns have a tendency to leak information. I don't like being at the mercy of the gabbiest old drunkard in town. I think I'll try an isolated farm instead, and I'm going to do something differently this time.'

'Oh? What's that ?'

'I've always made a point of telling the young man in question

670

who he really is so that he understands the necessity for ordinariness.'

'What's wrong with that?'

'Some of them haven't been very good actors. Sometimes they get carried away – probably because they're related to you.'

'What's that supposed to mean?'

'You over-act, father. I'm sorry, but you do. You go to extremes. I'll fix it so that Garion doesn't *have* to act.'

'How do you plan to manage that ?'

'It's simple, father. I just won't tell him who he is. I'll let him find it out for himself. I'll raise him as an ordinary farm boy, and he'll *believe* that he's an ordinary farm boy. Acting won't be necessary. All he'll have to do is just be himself.'

'I think that might be a little dangerous, Pol. He's bound to find out eventually who *you* are. You give that away a dozen times a day.'

'Then I'll have to learn to control myself, won't I?'

He shook his head stubbornly. 'It won't work. There are dozens of books out there that describe you all the way down to your toenails.'

'They won't mean very much to him if he can't read, will they?'

'Pol! He's going to be a king! You can't put an illiterate on a throne!'

'Dras Bull-neck worked out fairly well, as I recall.'

'That was three thousand years ago, Pol. The world was different then.'

'Not all that much different, father. If it bothers you so much, you can teach him how to read after he's been crowned.'

'*Me*? Why me?'

I gave him a smug little smirk that spoke volumes, and then let it drop.

The twins arrived the following morning to take over father's guard-duty, and my vengeful parent went off in search of Asharak the Murgo.

I spent the rest of that winter in the kitchen with Garion – and with whichever of the twins wasn't on guard duty at the moment. I planned to leave just as soon as the weather broke, and I didn't see much sense in heating the whole house, so I kept the kitchen doors closed. The kitchen had a large iron stove, and that suited me right down to the ground. The other rooms had fireplaces, which are pretty, but not very efficient.

Garion and I grew very close during those interminable months.

671

He was a loveable baby, and I owed him a great deal because of my ghastly failure at Annath. His mind was barely awakened, but a bit of gentle probing gave me a few hints about what he'd become, and a few more hints about how much trouble I'd have raising him without losing my mind. This boy was going to be a challenge.

Spring eventually arrived, and after the mud had dried on the local country lanes, I selected a few of my most nondescript dresses, some odds and ends of clothing for Garion, and bundled them all up in a slightly threadbare blanket. Then I bade the twins goodbye and set out with my bundle slung over one shoulder and Garion in my arms and my goat trailing along behind me.

I reached the village of Upper Gralt, which wasn't at all like Outer Gralt, by late afternoon. I went to a seedy-looking inn and haggled down the price of a single room for the night. I wanted to give the impression of teetering perilously on the brink of poverty. After I'd fed Garion and put him down for the night, I went on back downstairs to have a word with the innkeeper. 'I'm looking for work,' I told him.

'Sorry, but I'm not hiring right now.'

'That wasn't what I had in mind,' I told him. 'Do you know of any local farmers who might need a good cook or housekeeper?'

He frowned, scratching at one cheek. 'You might try Faldor,' he suggested. 'Some of his farmhands were by last week, and they said that Faldor's cook's starting to slip quite a bit. She's getting old, and she's slowing down. Faldor's men were complaining about the meals always being late and only about half-cooked. It's coming on toward planting time, and if a farm kitchen's falling apart at planting time or harvest time, the farm hands start looking for new jobs. Faldor's got a big farm, and he can't plant it all by himself. If there's not an opening for a cook right now, there probably will be in just a few weeks.'

'Where's his farm?'

'About a day's walk off toward the west. Faldor's a good-hearted fellow, and even if he can't hire you right away, he'll make sure that you and your baby don't go hungry. Just follow that road that leads west out of here toward the Medalia highway. Faldor's place is the only one on the south side of the road, so you can't miss it.'

'I'll find it,' I assured him. 'Thank you for the information.' Then I checked on my goat out in the stables, climbed back up the stairs, and went to bed, nestling Garion close in my arms.

The next morning dawned clear and bright. I fed Garion and we were on the road leading off toward the west soon after the sun had peeped above the horizon. I knew exactly where I was going and I now had a sense of purpose, so my goat and I stepped right along.

It was about mid-afternoon when we topped a rise and saw a large neat farmstead lying about a half mile south of the road in the next valley. It looked almost as if it were walled in, but that wasn't actually the case. The farm buildings were laid out in a square, with the barns, stables, and work-shops on the ground floor and the sleeping rooms for the farm hands lining a second floor gallery. All the buildings faced inward onto a large open compound, and everything was all in one place. The largest building stood at the back of the compound opposite that main gate. It was neat, well-organized, and convenient.

I definitely approved of what I saw, though it all may have been arranged so that I would well in advance. I went on down the hill and entered the compound, a little puzzled at what sounded very much like a bell singing out in measured tones.

As soon as I entered, I saw that what I'd been hearing hadn't been a bell, but the sound of a smith hammering on a glowing horseshoe in his open-fronted smithy.

That, of course, explains how I missed the sound of that secret personal bell of mine. It was artfully concealed in the sound of that hammer on the steel anvil.

The smith's hammering had a steady, no-nonsense rhythm to it, announcing that here was a fellow who was serious about his work. He was a rather plain-looking young man, about twenty-five and of medium height and deceptively medium build. The heavy sound of his hammer spoke volumes about just how strong he really was. He wore an ordinary tunic and a burn-spotted leather apron. That made a lot of sense. When you work with white-hot metal, you should really have something sturdy between your skin and the work.

I waited until the smith turned and quenched the horseshoe in the water barrel beside his anvil, sending up a cloud of steam. 'Excuse me, Master smith,' I said politely, shifting Garion in my arms, 'have you any idea of where I might find farmer Faldor?'

Then he turned to look at me. I rather liked his open, honest face. 'He's probably in his counting-room at this time of day, Mistress,' he replied politely in a pleasant voice.

'Thank you,' I said, inclining my head. 'Now we come to the more technical questions. Exactly where *is* farmer Faldor's counting-room?'

He laughed, and I noticed that he had very even, white teeth. His laugh was open and honest. I was taking to this man right away. I knew instinctively that he could be a very good friend. 'Why don't I just show you the way, Mistress?' he offered, laying down his hammer. 'My name's Durnik, by the way.'

'And mine's Pol.' I curtsied slightly. 'I'm happy to make your acquaintance, Goodman Durnik.'

'And I yours, Mistress Pol,' he replied, ducking his head slightly in a sort of bow. 'I'll take you up to meet Faldor. We can hope that his column of figures all added up today.'

'Does he have trouble making them come out?'

'All the time, Mistress Pol. All the time. Faldor's a very good farmer and the best master in this part of Sendaria, but arithmetic's not his strong point. He gets grouchy when his numbers don't add up.' Durnik pointed at the main house. 'His quarters are upstairs over the kitchen and dining-room. I don't envy him that. The smells coming out of the kitchen lately haven't been too appetizing.'

'That's sort of what I'm here to talk with him about, Goodman Durnik.'

'Are you a cook, perhaps?' His brown eyes grew hopeful.

'I can boil water without burning the bottom of it, if that's what you mean.'

'Praise the Gods,' he said fervently. 'Poor Nala can't even manage that any more. Can you imagine what burning water smells like?'

We both laughed as we crossed the compound to the large kitchen door. 'Wait here,' I told my goat. I knew that it was probably a waste of breath. She'd go exploring as soon as I was out of sight, but I was sure that I could find her again.

The kitchen was well-designed, I saw, with work-tables and cutting boards in the center, stoves and ovens lining the walls, and the storage bins and pantries at the back. It was very cluttered, however, with knives and pans littering the work-tables rather than being hung back up where they belonged. There was definitely a problem here, and its source was snoring in a chair by the stove. It was fairly late in the afternoon, but supper hadn't even been started yet. The kitchen was disorganized, and the kitchen helpers were wandering around aimlessly while the head cook snored. It was clear that Mistress Nala wasn't taking her job seriously any more.

Farmer Faldor was a tall, lean, horse-faced man with a long nose and an even longer chin. As I was to discover, he was a devoutly religious man who felt it to be his duty to look after the well-being of his employees, physical as well as spiritual. When I first saw him, he was struggling with a column of figures. One glance told me where he was making his mistake, but I didn't think I should point it out to him until I got to know him better.

'This is Mistress Pol, Faldor,' Durnik introduced me. 'She wanted to speak with you about the possibility of employment in the kitchen.'

'Mistress Pol,' Faldor greeted me, politely rising to his feet.

'Farmer Faldor,' I replied with a little curtsey.

'Have you had much experience working in kitchens?'

'Oh, yes,' I replied, 'a great deal of experience.'

'Our kitchen certainly needs help right now,' he said mournfully. 'Nala used to be very good, but she's older now and putting on a lot of weight. It's slowing her down. She just can't seem to get started any more.'

'It's an occupational hazard, Master Faldor. It has to do with tasting.'

'I didn't exactly follow that, Mistress Pol.'

'A good cook has to check the quality of what she's preparing. The only way I know of to do that is to taste it. If a cook isn't careful about that, every sip or nibble goes straight to her hips. How many are you feeding currently?'

'Fifty-three right now,' he replied. 'There'll be more when we get into the planting. Do you think you could handle that big a kitchen?'

'Easily, Master Faldor, but why don't we wait until after supper before we make any permanent decisions? You might not like my cooking, and it's good business to examine the product before you buy it.'

'That makes sense, Mistress Pol,' he agreed.

Just then Garion started to fuss a bit. I put him over my shoulder and patted his back to make him burp.

'Your baby, Mistress Pol?' Faldor asked.

'My nephew,' I replied sadly. 'His parents died.'

Faldor sighed. 'Tragic,' he murmured.

'Yes. I'll step around Mistress Nala rather carefully, Master Faldor,' I promised. 'From what I gather, she's served well and faithfully here, and it wouldn't be proper to just push her aside.'

'I'm glad you understand that, Mistress Pol,' he said gravely.

'That's assuming that my cooking doesn't make everyone sick,' I amended with a slight smile. 'How many kitchen helpers are there?'

'Six – counting Nala herself. Would that be enough?'

675

'More than enough, Master Faldor. Is there someplace where I could put my belongings? It's a little late, and I'd better get to fixing supper if we want to eat before midnight.'

'Why don't you show her to that vacant room up on the west side, Durnik?' Faldor suggested. Then he sighed with some resignation. 'And I guess I'd better get back to my addition here. This thing refuses to come out even.'

'Would it help at all if I told you that twelve and nine makes twenty-one and not twenty-two?' I asked him mildly.

He stared down at his figures and then carefully counted it out on his fingers. 'Why, I *do* believe you're right, Mistress Pol,' he said. 'It *does*, doesn't it?'

'It always has before.' Then Durnik and I left.

'Is he usually that pliable?' I asked Durnik as we went on downstairs.

'I didn't quite follow that, Mistress Pol.'

'He didn't ask where I'd worked before, he didn't really ask if I knew anything at all about cooking, and he didn't even ask where I'd come from.'

'Mistress Pol,' Durnik said, 'the kitchen here is sort of a continuing disaster – like a fire in the barn or an epidemic of cow-pox. Faldor's not pliable so much as he's desperate. If Torak himself showed up claiming to be a cook, Faldor'd hire him without a second thought.'

'I see. Well, I guess I'll have to fix that.'

I dropped off my bundle in the small room Durnik showed me, asked him to round up my goat and put her in the stables, and then I went back to the kitchen. Nala was still sleeping, and the other kitchen helpers were sort of aimlessly going through the motions of getting ready to start on the evening meal. 'I'm the new kitchen-helper, ladies,' I told them. 'My name's Pol, and I think we'd better get started on supper, don't you?'

'We can't really do that until Nala wakes up, Mistress Pol,' a thin, pale girl with a runny nose told me, sniffing. 'She might get offended.'

'We won't actually be doing anything but just getting things ready,' I lied, ' – you know, peeling carrots, cutting up vegetables, putting water to boil – that sort of thing.'

'Oh,' she said, wiping her nose on her sleeve. 'That might be all right, I guess.' I saw immediately that I had a long way to go here. Nala's semi-comatose state had encouraged a great deal of laxity in the kitchen.

I decided that stew would probably have to do for this evening.

There wasn't really enough time for anything else. I took an oblique approach to the other kitchen helpers. After I'd stowed Garion in an out-of-the way vegetable bin, I started making 'suggestions', usually prefaced with 'would you like to –' or 'Don't you think that –' or 'shouldn't we perhaps –'. Then, when I'd managed to put them all to work, I went into the spice pantry to inventory the condiments. I was muttering darkly even before I was finished. The spice jars were all there, of course, but half of them were empty. I threw a furtive look back over my shoulder to make sure I wasn't being observed, and then I cheated.

Nala awoke when we started braising the stew meat. 'What's going on here?' she demanded.

'We were just getting things ready to start fixing supper, Nala,' the girl with the runny nose reported. 'Mistress Pol here thought it might be a good idea. You know how Faldor is when supper's late.'

'Mistress Pol?' Nala asked, eyeing me suspiciously.

'I just came to work here this afternoon, Mistress Nala,' I said to her with a polite little curtsey. 'Enna here said you were feeling a little under the weather.' I put one arm familiarly around the shoulder of the red-nosed girl. 'I didn't think we should disturb you. What do you think? Would stew be all right for this evening?'

Nala pretended to consider it. 'Whatever you decide, Mistress Pol,' she consented with a little shrug. What else could she say? Everything was ready to go into the stew-pot.

I looked at her rather closely. 'You don't look at all well, Mistress Nala,' I said with mock concern. Then I laid the back of my hand to her forehead. 'You've got a fever,' I told her. 'We'd better do something about that just as soon as we get the stew to simmering and the biscuits in the oven.'

'I *do* feel a little feverish, Pol,' she admitted.

Of *course* she felt feverish. I'd just elevated her temperature with the back of my hand. I *really* wanted this job.

The vegetables and braised stew meat cascaded into the large bubbling stew-pots, and then I compounded a mixture of ordinary cooking spices to counteract Nala's 'fever'. After that, I hovered over the stew-pots with my collection of seasonings.

The stew we served that evening was barely adequate in my opinion, but Faldor and his farm hands went at it like starving men, some of them even going so far as to pour the last dribblings of gravy over biscuits.

'Oh, my,' Faldor said, groaning and putting his hands on his belly. 'I think I ate too much.'

'You're not the only one, Faldor,' Durnik agreed, also groaning. Then he gestured toward me as I stood in the doorway with Garion in my arms. 'I think we should keep her, don't you?'

'Um,' Faldor replied. 'I'll tell you what, Durnik. As soon as you're able to walk, why don't you just nip across the compound and close and lock the gate? We wouldn't want to let her get away, now would we?'

And that was how I cooked my way into a permanent place at Faldor's farm. As I mentioned, the stew wasn't really all that spectacular, but it was several cuts above what Nala had been offering.

As soon as supper was over, I beckoned to Enna, the pale blonde girl with the red nose. 'Yes, Mistress Pol?' she said, coming obediently.

I reached out and touched her nose. 'How long have you had the sniffles?' I asked her.

'Weeks,' she said, rolling her eyes upward.

'I rather thought you might have.'

'It's not a cold, Mistress Pol,' she said. 'I don't feel achy or feverish.'

'No, it's not a cold. It's spring, Enna, and there are some things in bloom right now that don't agree with you. Let's fix that right now.'

'Are you a physician, Mistress Pol?'

'I wouldn't go all that far, Enna,' I replied. 'I know a few home remedies is about all. Let's dry up that nose of yours. We *do* work around food, after all, and – well, I'm sure you get my point.'

She giggled and then she sniffed.

Though we all still deferred to Nala, her instructions became increasingly vague. By the end of the week, I was the one who was really running the kitchen, but I'd still periodically carry a spoonful of whatever we were preparing to her for approval. It didn't really inconvenience me that much, so I spoon-fed her.

Within a month, the goat, Garion and I were all settled in, and I'm sure that in the minds of Faldor, Durnik and the other farm workers we'd always been there. I cleaned and straightened up our little sleeping room, but Garion spent most of his time in that vegetable bin. I always knew just exactly where he was, even when my back was turned to him.

I was very comfortable at Faldor's farm. These people were Sendars all the way down to the bone, and in a very real sense, I'd created the Sendars, so coming here was much like coming home.

It was midsummer when uncle Beltira stopped by, ostensibly to ask directions to Upper Gralt. I took him just outside the gate and pretended to be pointing out the way while we talked.

'We've been tearing this end of Sendaria apart looking for you, Pol,' he said. 'I'd have walked right by if I hadn't caught sight of your goat. Why didn't you get in touch with us?'

'I'm trying to stay out of sight until father tracks down Chamdar. Is he having any luck with that?'

'He hasn't told us so yet. He's in Tolnedra right now. The last time he talked with us, he and that young Prince Kheldar were hot on the trail of Asharak the Murgo. We've been out of touch for a few weeks, so we can't be sure if they've succeeded yet or not.'

'Well, I'd better stay under cover until they find him and start shipping pieces of him back to Ctuchik. Get word to father about where I am, but you'd probably better have Drasnian intelligence carry the message. As long as Chamdar's still all in one piece, I'd rather not have my location echoing off every hilltop.'

He nodded. 'You seem almost happy here, Pol,' he observed.

'I like what I'm doing, and I like the people here on this farm. I wouldn't exactly say that I'm happy, though. That might change after father and Silk dispose of Chamdar.'

'Who's Silk?'

'Prince Kheldar. It was his nickname at the academy. I'd better get back to the kitchen. My helpers all mean well, but they need a lot of supervision. Give my best to uncle Belkira.'

'I will, Pol. We love you, you know.'

'Yes, as a matter of fact I do – and I love you too. Now scoot.'

'Yes, ma'am.' And then we both laughed.

Garion started crawling shortly after Beltira's visit, and my life suddenly became much more interesting. He *was* in a kitchen, after all, and a crawling baby underfoot in a place where there are knives, cleavers, pots of boiling water, and scurrying kitchen workers added a certain amount of excitement to my life. I could never be exactly sure of where he was. Dear Gods, that little boy could move fast! I soon became adept at herding him around with my feet. I'm sure I frequently looked like an acrobat – pinching a pie-crust with one hand, seasoning a bowl of dressing with the other and scooping a very active little boy out of harm's way with my foot. Garion thought that was lots of fun, but it didn't entertain *me* all that much. I really wasn't looking forward to the day when he started walking, and I began to give some serious consideration to putting him on a leash or something.

Harvest time on a farm is the busiest part of the year for the people who grow food for a living, and my kitchen was no exception. Notice that I could call it *my* kitchen now. Mistress Nala's legs finally went bad on her, and so she went off to live with her youngest daughter on the northern end of Lake Medalia. Anyway, Faldor's farm hands had to be fed four times a day during the harvest, and that kept my helpers and me busy from well before dawn until several hours past sunset. I think everybody on the farm was very happy to see the last wagonload of turnips come in out of the fields.

And then after the harvest was done and all the leaves had fallen from the trees, an itinerant storyteller stopped by to cadge a few meals out of Faldor. He was a shabbily-dressed old rascal with mis-matched shoes and a piece of rope for a belt. His hair and beard were white and close-cropped, and he had glue on his fingers. He must have had, since everything he touched stuck to them. I knew that he was coming of course, since I'd sensed his familiar presence when he was still five miles beyond the gate.

No, I didn't even consider locking the gate before he arrived. Well, not very seriously, anyway.

My goat recognized him, of course, and she smoothly jumped the gate of her stall and ran out to greet him, her tail wagging furiously. He smiled and scratched her ears, and then he asked Durnik the smith where he might find 'the owner of this fine establishment'.

He introduced himself to Faldor, pretending to be 'the greatest story-teller in all of Sendaria', which might even have been true, now that I think of it, and then he gravitated to my kitchen where all the food and drink was. He turned on his not inconsiderable charm and entertained my helpers while we prepared supper. He made it look as if he were trying to ingratiate himself with me when he took some time out from his random pilferage to play with Garion. I was being careful not to watch him *too* obviously, but I *did* happen to catch a glimpse of the tears that filled his eyes once or twice while he and Garion were playing a little game of 'tickle-tickle, giggle-giggle'. My feelings for the Old Wolf softened noticeably at that point. Though he tries to hide it, father *does* have his sentimental side.

He paid for his supper that evening by telling stories after we'd all eaten. The one that got the most applause was the one he called

'How Belgarath and four companions stole back the Orb of Aldur from the One-Eyed God of Angarak'. The farm hands went absolutely wild over that one. 'My friend,' Faldor said at the end of the story, 'that was absolutely amazing! You told that story almost as if you'd actually been there in person!'

I had a little trouble keeping a straight face along about then. I'll admit, however, that if he really sets his mind to it, my father can hold an audience spellbound for hours on end, and he never seems to tire of the sound of his own voice.

Then, after Faldor and his farmhands had all retired for the night and I'd shooed my helpers off to their beds, father, Garion and I had the kitchen to ourselves. I blew out most of the lamps, leaving only one still burning to dimly light my kitchen. I laid out a few things in preparation for tomorrow's breakfast, and father was sitting off in a corner holding the sleeping little boy on his lap.

I caught a faint flicker of movement at the kitchen door, and I turned quickly. It was my little nanny goat, and her golden eyes glowed in the dim light. 'You,' I commanded her, 'go back to the stables where you belong.'

'Oh, leave her be, Pol,' father said tolerantly. 'She's a member of the family too, you know.'

'Peculiar notion,' I murmured. Then I looked him squarely in the face. 'Well, Old Wolf,' I said quietly, 'did you finally run Chamdar down?'

'We didn't even get close to him, Pol,' he admitted, dropping his characterization and speaking very seriously. 'I'm giving some thought to taking a run down to Rak Cthol and jerking out Ctuchik's liver.'

'Interesting notion. What's he done lately that you don't like?'

'He's sending counterfeit Chamdars into the west.'

'Would you like to clarify that?'

'He's modified some ordinary Murgos – or Grolims, for all I know – to make them look exactly like Asharak the Murgo. That makes Drasnian intelligence absolutely worthless. Silk was terribly upset when I told him that he'd been following the wrong man. That was the only good thing to come out of the whole affair.'

'That one went by a little fast, father.'

'Our Prince Kheldar's terribly impressed with himself, Pol. He was in dire need of a large dose of humility. His face almost fell off when I told him that he'd been wasting his time on a forgery.'

'Then you haven't really got any idea at all of where the real Chamdar might be?'

'Not a clue, Pol. Not a clue. About the best I can do to distract him is to go up into the Alorn kingdoms and thrash around, making a lot of noise and spreading rumors. Chamdar's got access to a lot of gold, so he can hire spies in addition to the Dagashi who're probably standing at every crossroads from Val Alorn to Sthiss Tor. The best way I know of to distract his Dagashi and his home-grown spies is to flop around waving my arms to make sure that a lot of Alorns are talking about "that funny old man who tells stories". That'll be the easy part. All it takes to get an Alorn to start talking is a couple of tankards of ale, and all it takes to make him stop is about two dozen more.' He looked at me gravely. 'It isn't much, Pol, but it's about the best I can come up with for the moment. You're awfully exposed here, you know. Maybe you'd better go back to your house on Lake Erat.'

'No, father, I'll stay right here. My manor house is just a little too isolated, and it's very important for Garion to have people around him while he's growing up. A hermit wouldn't make a very good king.'

'And you actually like it here, don't you Pol?' he asked shrewdly.

'It's as good a place as any, father. I'm doing something that I like to do, and very few people stop by here. I like these people, and they like me. I'm as happy here as I'd be anyplace, I guess. Besides, if Garion grows up here, he'll be honest, anyway, and honesty's a rare commodity on thrones lately, I've noticed.'

'Do you really want to submerge yourself in this rustic setting, Pol?'

'I think that maybe I do, father. I'm still bleeding from what happened in Annath, and steady work and quiet surroundings help to heal that sort of thing.'

'It *is* a step down the social scale, Pol. You started out as the Duchess of Erat, ruling over this entire kingdom, and now you're only the head cook on a remote farm. Are you sure you wouldn't prefer to take Garion to Sulturn or Muros and buy him an apprenticeship the way you've done with the others?'

'No, father. Garion's not like the others. He's going to be the Child of Light – if he isn't already – and I don't want to clutter his mind with cabinetry, tombstones, or shoemaking. I want him to have a good mind, but one that's uncluttered and undeveloped. That's the best way I know of to prepare him for some of the surprises that'll pop up as he goes along.'

'I don't see how keeping him stupid is going to prepare him for what's in store for him.'

682

'How old were you when you stumbled across the Master's tower that snowy night seven thousand years ago?'

'Not very. Fifteen or sixteen at the most, I think.'

'You turned out all right – except for a few bad habits – and you were probably much stupider than Garion's going to be. I'll see to that personally.'

'You're going to stay here, then?'

'I think I should, father. I'm having one of those feelings. This is the place where Garion's supposed to grow up. It's not fancy, and he won't be important here, but this is the place. I knew that when I first saw it. It's a little isolated and awfully provincial, but there are people here who Garion absolutely has to get to know, and I'll do what's right for him, no matter what it costs me.'

Father lifted the drowsing baby and stroked his bushy face across the little boy's nose. Garion giggled, and father laughed. 'Garion, my boy,' he said expansively, 'you may just be the luckiest fellow in the world to have your Aunt Pol to look after you.' Then the old fraud gave me a sly look and winked. 'That's except for me, of course. She's been looking after *me* for longer than I care to remember. I guess that makes us both lucky, wouldn't you say?'

Garion giggled again.

I looked fondly at this shabby old man and the giggling baby, and I remembered something uncle Beltira had said a long time ago. He'd been explaining the unspoken game father and I have been playing with each other for centuries. He'd told the young prince that our sometimes spiteful-seeming remarks were not what they really appeared on the surface. The gentle twin had smiled and had said, 'It's just their way to avoid coming right out and admitting that they're genuinely fond of each other, Geran. They'd be too embarrassed to admit that they love each other, so they play this little game instead. It's their own private and peculiar way to keep saying "I love you" over and over again. They might not even know it themselves, but they say it to each other almost every time they meet.'

I was ruefully forced to admit that the twins and Beldin had seen through our little subterfuge all the time – even if father and I hadn't. I'd spent three thousand and more years trying to avoid that simple admission, but finally it was so obvious to me that I wondered why I'd gone to all the trouble. I loved my father. It was as simple as that. I loved him in spite of his many flaws and bad habits. That stunning realization brought tears of happiness to my eyes as that love filled my heart.

'*There, now,*' mother's voice echoed a little smugly in my mind. '*That wasn't really all that hard, was it?*' There was a slight difference to that usually sourceless voice this time, however. It seemed to be coming from the kitchen doorway. I turned sharply and stared unbelievingly at the little nanny-goat standing there looking intently at me with her mischievous golden eyes.

'*Somebody had to feed the baby, Pol,*' mother's voice explained. '*I thought it might be best to keep it in the family.*'

I gave up entirely at that point and burst out in a sort of rueful laughter.

'What's so funny, Pol?' father asked me in a puzzled voice.

'Nothing, father,' I replied. 'Nothing at all.'

EPILOGUE

IT WAS A GREY, THREATENING sort of winter day on the Isle of the Winds. His Royal Highness, Crown Prince Geran of Riva spent the day up on the battlements of the Hall of the Rivan King making snowmen – or snow-soldiers, to be more precise. Wolf was with him, as always. Wolf didn't really contribute very much to the project, but watched quizzically with his chin resting on his crossed paws instead. There were a lot of things that went on in the Hall of the Rivan King that Wolf didn't understand, but he was polite enough not to make an issue of them.

It was about noon when one of mother's ladies in waiting brought Geran's four-year-old sister, Princess Beldaran, up to the battlements. 'Her Majesty says that the little one needs some fresh air, your Highness,' the countess – or whatever she was – told Geran. 'You're supposed to watch her.'

Prince Geran sighed. It wasn't that he didn't love his baby sister, but he was currently involved in a work of art, and no artist likes to be disturbed when he's afire with creativity. Princess Beldaran was bundled up in furs to the point that she could barely move her short little arms. Beldaran didn't contribute much to her brother's masterpiece either, but made snowballs instead, gravely inspecting each one as it was completed, brushing off a few protruding lumps with one mittened hand, and then throwing it at her brother without so much as a change of expression. She didn't hit him very often, but it was just often enough to distract him. He ground his teeth together and ignored her. He loved her, but he did ignore her a lot. He'd discovered that it was quieter that way. Beldaran's voice was very much like mother's. 'Expressive' was father's word for it. Geran had some other words he used to describe his sister's penetrating voice, but he was very careful not to use those words around mother.

He was much relieved when the Countess – or whatever – came back up about a hour later to retrieve Beldaran. He was getting into putting the final touches to his art-work, and he really wanted to concentrate. After much consideration, he decided that the carrots he'd used for noses were just *too* comic-looking, so he replaced them with turnips. That was *much* better, he decided. He'd been working on these snow-sculptures for a week now, and they seemed to be coming along splendidly. Seven fierce, though bulbous, white soldiers already lined the battlements to glare down at the harbor, and Prince Geran was confident that if winter just lasted long enough, he'd have a whole regiment to command.

'Isn't that one bully, Wolf?' Geran asked his companion after he'd put the finishing touches on the seventh sentinel.

'One does not see the purpose of this,' Wolf noted politely. Geran thought he detected a note of criticism in his friend's observation. Wolf was so practical sometimes.

Prince Geran fell back on his grandfather's suggestion at that point. 'It is a custom,' he explained.

'Oh,' Wolf said. 'That is all right, then. Customs do not need a purpose.'

Grandfather had taught Geran the language of wolves during the summer the boy had spent in the Vale. It had really been necessary at that time, since grandfather and grandmother spoke exclusively in wolvish. Geran was rather proud of his command of the language, though Wolf sometimes gave him peculiar looks. Quite a bit of wolvish is conveyed by movements of the ears, and Geran couldn't wiggle his ears, so he moved them with his fingers instead. Wolf seemed to think that was just a bit odd.

Geran was very proud of Wolf. Other boys on the Isle of the Winds had dogs, and they called them pets. Wolf, however, was Geran's companion, and they talked together all the time. Wolf, Geran had noted, had some strange attitudes, and it was sometimes necessary to step around him carefully to avoid giving offense. Geran knew that wolves *do* play, but wolvish play is a kind of affectionate romping. Wolf couldn't really understand the complexity of human play, so Geran frequently fell back on the word 'custom'.

Geran seldom thought about Wolf's origins. Grandmother had found Wolf as an orphaned puppy in the forest near Kell over in Mallorea, and Geran concentrated very hard on erasing all his own memories of what had happened in Mallorea. He *did* have occasional nightmares about Zandramas, though – mostly involving the tiny points of light that glowed beneath her skin. Those nightmares were becoming less and less frequent, though, and Geran was confident that if he refused to think about them, they'd eventually go away entirely. He firmly pushed those fleeting thoughts out of his mind and concentrated instead on his snow-sentries.

Evening was settling over the battlements high above the city of Riva when father came up to fetch his son and Wolf. Geran knew that father was the Rivan King and 'Overlord of the West', but in Geran's eyes those were simply job-titles. Father was just 'father', no matter what others chose to call him. Father's face was sort of ordinary – unless some kind of emergency came along. When that happened, father's face became the *least* ordinary face in the whole world. Those rare emergencies sometimes obliged father to go get his sword, and when *that* happened, most sensible people ran for cover.

Father gravely surveyed his son's work in the gathering twilight. 'Nice soldiers,' he observed.

'They'd look a lot better if you'd let me borrow some of the things from the armory,' Geran said hopefully.

'That might not be a very good idea, Geran,' father replied. 'Not unless you want to spend the whole summer polishing the rust off them.'

'I guess I hadn't thought of that,' Geran admitted.

'One is curious to know how your day has gone,' father said politely to Wolf.

'It has been satisfactory,' Wolf replied.

'One is pleased that you have found it so.'

Father and Geran made a special point of not speaking in Wolvish around mother. Mother didn't like 'secret languages'. She always seemed to think that people who spoke in languages she didn't understand were speaking about *her*. Geran was forced to admit that quite frequently she was right about that. People *did* talk about mother a lot, and secret languages, be they Wolvish or the finger-wiggling Drasnian variety, tended to keep the noise level down on the Isle of the Winds. Geran loved mother, but she *was* excitable.

'Did you have a nice day, dear?' mother asked when Geran and father entered the royal apartment after dutifully stamping the snow off their feet in the corridor outside. Wolf, of course, didn't stamp his paws, but he'd already chewed the ice out from between his toes, so he didn't really track in very much water.

'It was just bully, mother,' Geran replied. All the boys Prince Geran knew used the word 'bully' every chance they got, and Geran was very fashion-conscious, so he also sprinkled his speech with 'bullies'. It was the stylish thing to do, after all.

'Your bath's ready, Geran,' mother told him.

'I'm not really all that dirty, mother,' he said without thinking. Then he bit his tongue. Whey did he *always* start talking before he considered the consequences?

'I don't care if you don't think you're dirty!' mother said, her voice going up several octaves. 'I told you to go bathe! Now move!'

'Yes, mother.'

Father flickered a quick 'you'd better do as she says' at Geran with a few barely perceptible moves of his fingers. 'You'll get in trouble if you don't.'

Geran sighed and nodded. He was very nearly as tall as mother by now, but she still loomed large in his awareness. Prince Geran was seven years old, and Wolf considered him to be an adult. Geran felt that his maturity entitled him to a little respect, but he didn't get very much of that from mother. He didn't really think that was very fair.

Living in the same house with mother was a constant adventure, and Geran had long since discovered that the best way to hold down the level of excitement was to do exactly as mother told him to do. Prince Geran had noticed that he was not alone in making that discovery. The unspoken motto of the entire castle – the entire Isle of the Winds, most likely – was 'don't cross the Queen'. the Rivans all adored their tiny queen anyway, and it wasn't really all that much trouble to do exactly as she told them to do. Keeping Queen Ce'Nedra happy was a national pastime, and making sure that everybody understood its importance was one of the major parts of the job of Kail, the Rivan Warder.

After Prince Geran had taken a rather rudimentary bath, he joined the rest of the family in the dining-room of the royal apartment. He *had*, however, made sure that the insides of his ears were slightly damp. Mother had this thing about clean ears. Prince Geran felt that as long as he could still hear, his ears were clean enough, but he always ducked his head under the water at the end of his bath just to keep mother happy.

He joined his family at the table, and the serving maid brought in dinner. They were having ham that evening, and Geran liked ham. There was, however, one major drawback to a ham dinner, and that was the traditional inclusion of spinach. For the life of him, Prince Geran could not understand why mother felt that ham and spinach went together. Geran privately felt that spinach didn't really go with anything. To make matters even worse, Wolf didn't care for spinach either, so Geran couldn't furtively slip forkfuls of the awful stuff under the table to his friend the way he could with chunks of the roast goat the kitchen periodically delivered to the royal table. Geran didn't care much for goat, but it ranked way above spinach in his opinion.

'How's your dinner, dear?' mother asked him.

'Bully, mother,' he replied quickly. 'Real bully.'

She rolled her eyes upward at his choice of language. Geran felt that mother didn't really have a very well-developed sense of style.

'What did Captain Greldik have to say?' mother asked father.

Geran knew Captain Greldik, the vagrant Cherek sea-captain, and he rather liked him. Mother, however, didn't approve of Captain Greldik. So far as Geran knew, no woman approved of Captain Greldik. They all seemed to feel that Greldik had a few too many bad habits. Worse yet, he didn't even care.

'Oh,' father said, 'I'm glad you reminded me. He says that Velvet's expecting a baby.'

'Silk's going to be a *father*?' mother exclaimed.

'That's what Greldik says.'

'I think the whole institution of parenthood's going to have to be redefined,' mother laughed.

'With Silk and Velvet for parents, we *know* what the baby's profession's going to be,' father added.

Geran didn't quite understand that part, since he was pondering a strategic dilemma just then. He'd put on a robe after his bath, and the robe had pockets – nice deep ones that were certainly large enough to hold and conceal the spinach on his plate until he could find an opportunity to dispose of the awful stuff. The problem with that lay in mother's unfortunate habit of conducting impromptu searches of his pockets without any warning. Geran had lost a whole pocketful of perfectly good fishing worms that way one day last summer. He was fairly sure that the echoes of the scream she'd emitted when she'd reached into his pocket and encountered the worms was still bouncing around in the rafters somewhere. Deciding that concealing the spinach in the pocket of his robe was just too risky, Geran reluctantly choked it down, vowing once again that his first act when he ascended the throne would be to issue a royal decree banishing spinach forever from his realm.

Prince Geran might have tried to outlast mother on the spinach business, sitting stubbornly in his chair without touching it until dawn or later, but it was rapidly coming up on the high point of his day. For the past several months, mother had been reading to him after she'd settled him down in his bed, and it was no ordinary book she was reading. This book had been written by his very own Aunt Pol, and he knew most of the people who appeared in the later pages. He knew Barak and Silk, Lelldorin and Mandorallen, Durnik and Queen Porenn, and Hettar and Adara. Aunt Pol's book was almost like a family reunion.

'Have you finished?' mother asked him after he'd laid his fork down.

'Yes, mother.'

'Have you been a good boy today?' Geran wondered what mother might do if he said, 'No.'

He prudently decided not to try it. 'Very good, mother,' he said instead. 'I didn't break a single thing.'

'Amazing,' she said. 'Now I suppose you'd like to have me read to you?'

'If it's not too much trouble, mother.' Geran knew the value of the polite approach when he wanted something.

'Very well,' mother said. 'You go pop into bed, and I'll be along just as soon as I get Beldaran settled in for the night.'

Geran got up, kissed his father good night, and went to his bedroom. He set his candle down on the little table beside his bed and looked around quickly, giving his room a quick pre-emptive survey. It wasn't *too* bad, but just to be on the safe side, he kicked the worst of the clutter under his bed.

'One is curious to know why you do that each night,' Wolf said.

'It is a new custom,' Geran replied, moving his ears with his fingers. 'One believes that if one's mother does not see what is lying on the floor of one's den, one's mother will not talk about it.'

Wolf's tongue lolled out in wolfish laughter. 'One notices that you are quick to learn,' he said. Then he hopped effortlessly up onto the bed, yawned and curled himself up into a furry ball the way he always did.

Prince Geran looked around and decided that the room was probably neat enough. Sometimes Geran's 'things' got ahead of him, and the only real disadvantage of having mother read to him every evening was the opportunity it gave her for a daily inspection. It seemed to Geran that mother had an unwholesome obsession with neatness. He'd frequently tried to explain to her that when he had his 'things' spread out on the floor, he could find exactly what he wanted almost immediately, but that when he put them all away as she wanted him to, it took hours to find what he wanted and that the search immediately returned everything right back to the floor where it had been in the first place. She'd listen patiently each time, and then she'd repeat the rather worn-out command, 'clean this pig-pen up'. He had once – and only once – suggested that the chore was beneath his dignity and that one of the servants should do it. He still shuddered at the memory of her reaction to *that* particular suggestion. He was positive that had there been a good following wind that day, mother's speech would have been clearly audible on the Sendarian coast.

He climbed up into his bed and placed several pillows on the side nearest the candle so that mother could prop herself up while reading. He reasoned that if she were comfortable, she might read longer. Then he snuggled down under the bolster, wriggling his feet down underneath Wolf. The really keen thing about having Wolf sleep with him was how warm Wolf was. Geran's feet never got cold.

After a little while mother came into the room with Aunt Pol's book under her arm. She absently scratched Wolf's ears, and Wolf's golden eyes opened briefly, and he wagged his tail a couple of times in appreciation. Then his eyes closed again. Wolf had told Geran that he was quite fond of mother, but Wolf wasn't very demonstrative, since he felt that it wasn't dignified.

Mother climbed into bed, plumped up the pillows Geran had placed there for her use, and then tucked her feet under one corner of his down-filled bolster. 'Are you warm enough?' she asked him.

'Yes, mother. Everything's just bully.'

She opened the book on her lap. 'Where were we?' she asked.

'Aunt Pol was looking for the crazy lady out in the snow,' Geran replied. 'At least that was what was happening when I fell asleep.' Then a momentary apprehension came over him. 'You didn't go on without me, did you?' he asked.

She laughed, 'Geran dear, this is a book. It doesn't run off or disappear once it's been read. Oh, speaking of that, how are your lessons coming?'

He sighed. 'All right – I guess. The book my tutor's got me reading isn't very interesting. It's a history book. Why do I have to have a Tolnedran tutor, mother? Why can't I have an Alorn one instead?'

'Because Tolnedrans are better teachers than Alorns, dear.' Mother *did* have opinions, Geran had noticed.

She leafed her way through the last third of Aunt Pol's book. 'Ah,' she said, 'here we are.'

'Before you start, mother, could I ask a question?'

'Of course.'

'Aunt Pol can do magic, can't she?'

'She doesn't really like that term, Geran, and neither does your grandfather.'

'I won't use it in front of them, then. If she can do magic things, why didn't she just wiggle her fingers and make the crazy lady not crazy any more?'

693

'I guess there are some things that magic can't do.'

That was a terrible let-down for Prince Geran. He'd long felt that some training in magic might be very useful when he became king. The people in father's government always seemed to be worrying about money, and if the king could just wave his hand and fill the room with it, they could all take the rest of the day off and go fishing, or something.

Mother took up the story of Aunt Pol's search for the madwoman, Alara, and it seemed to Geran that he could almost see the frigid mountains and dark forests around the village of Annath as Aunt Pol continued her desperate search. He almost held his breath, hoping that the gloomy part he was sure was coming might be averted. It wasn't, though.

'I hate it when a story does that,' he said.

'This isn't exactly a story, Geran,' mother explained. 'This really happened exactly the way Aunt Pol says it did.'

'Are we going to get to any happy parts soon?'

'Why don't you stop asking questions and find out?'

That seemed totally uncalled for to Geran.

Mother continued to read, and after a few minutes, Geran raised his hand slightly, even as he would have in his class-room. 'Could I ask just one question, mother?'

'If you wish.'

'How did grandfather *know* that Chamdar was burning down that house?'

'Your grandfather knows all kinds of things, Geran – even things he's not supposed to know. This time, though, I think that voice he carries around in his head told him about it.'

'I wish I had a voice inside *my* head to tell me things. That might keep me out of a lot of trouble.'

'*Amen!*' mother agreed fervently. Then she went on with the story.

When she got to the part about Aunt Pol's house on the shores of Lake Erat, Geran interrupted again without even thinking about it. 'Have you ever been there, mother? – Aunt Pol's house, I mean.'

'A couple of times,' mother replied.

'Is it really as big as she says it is?'

'Bigger, probably. Someday she might take you there and you'll be able to see it for yourself.'

'That'd be just bully, mother!' he said excitedly.

'What is it with this "bully" business?'

'All the boys my age say that a lot. It sort of means "very, very nice". It's a real good word. Everybody uses it all the time.'

'Oh, one of those. It'll pass – eventually.'

'What?'

'Never mind.' Then mother went back to her reading.

Prince Geran's eyelids began to droop when the story got as far as Faldor's farm. That part wasn't really very exciting, and somewhere during that endless discussion of how to make a pot of stew, the Crown Prince of Riva drifted off to sleep.

The little boy's regular breathing told Queen Ce'Nedra that she'd lost her audience. She slipped a scrap of paper between the pages of the book, and then she leaned back reflectively.

Aunt Pol's book had filled in all the gaps Ce'Nedra had noticed in Belgarath's book – and then some. The wealth of characters, many of them the towering figures of legend, quite nearly filled the Rivan Queen with awe. Riva Iron-grip was here, and Brand, the man who'd struck down a God. Beldaran, the most beautiful woman in history, was here. Asrana and Ontrose had nearly broken Ce'Nedra's heart. Aunt Pol's book had virtually erased the entire library of the History Department of the University of Tol Honeth and replaced it with what had *really* happened.

The staggering march of history was right *here* on the Rivan Queen's lap. She opened it again and read the part she loved the most, that quiet little scene in the kitchen at Faldor's farm when Polgara was no longer the Duchess of Erat, but merely the cook on a remote Sendarian farm. Rank meant absolutely nothing there, however. What *really* mattered was Polgara's gentle, unspoken realization that in spite of all his flaws and his seeming desertion of her mother before she and Beldaran were born, Polgara really loved her vagabond father. The animosity she'd clung to for all those centuries had been rather gently evaporated.

That subterranean little game Aunt Pol and her father had played with each other for centuries had produced a surprise winner, a winner they hadn't even realized was taking part in their game. They'd spent three thousand years nipping at each other in half-serious play, and for all that time, the wolf Poledra had watched them play, patiently waiting for them to squirm around into the exact position where she wanted them to be, and then she had pounced.

'You'd understand that, wouldn't you, Wolf?' she murmured to her son's companion.

Wolf opened his golden eyes and thumped his tail briefly in acknowledgment on the bed.

That startled Ce'Nedra just a bit. Wolf seemed to know exactly what she was thinking. Who *was* this Wolf, anyhow? She quickly pushed *that* thought into the back of her mind. The possibility that Wolf might not be who – or what – he seemed was something Ce'Nedra wasn't prepared to deal with just now. For now, the discovery that Poledra had won that game was enough for one evening.

Reluctant or not, though, there was *one* realization that crashed in on the Rivan Queen. Her husband's family pre-dated the cracking of the world, and there was no getting around the fact that it was the most important family in human history. When Ce'Nedra had first met Garion, she'd rather scornfully dismissed him as an illiterate, orphaned scullery boy from Sendaria, and she'd been wrong on all points. She herself had taught Garion how to read, but she was forced to admit that all she'd really done had been to open the book for him. She'd almost had to run to keep up with him once he'd learned the alphabet. He'd washed a few pots and pans in Faldor's kitchen, but he was a king, not a scullery boy. Garion wasn't a Sendarian, either, and as for his being an orphan, he was the farthest thing in the world from *being* an orphan. His family stretched back to the dawn of time. Ce'Nedra had fretted about the possibility that her husband might outrank her, but he didn't just outrank her, he *transcended* her. That *really* went down hard for the Rivan Queen.

She sighed. A whole group of unpleasant realizations were crowding in on Ce'Nedra. She glanced at her own reflection in her son's smeary mirror, and she lightly touched her deep red hair with her fingers. 'Well,' she sniffed, 'at least I'm prettier than he is.'

Then she realized just how ridiculous that final defense was, and she laughed in spite of herself. She threw up her arms in surrender. 'I give up,' she said, still laughing.

Then she slipped out of bed, tucked the bolster up under Geran's chin and lightly kissed him. 'Sleep well, my dear little Prince,' she murmured.

Then, not knowing exactly why, she stroked Wolf's head. 'You too, dear friend,' she said to him. 'Watch over our little boy.'

The Wolf looked at her gravely with those calm golden eyes, and then he did something totally unexpected. He gave the side of her face a quick, wet lick with his long tongue.

Ce'Nedra giggled in spite of herself, trying to wipe her cheek. She threw her arms around Wolf's massive head and hugged him.

Then the Rivan Queen blew out the candle, tiptoed out of the room, and quietly closed the door behind her.

*   *   *

Wolf lay there on the foot of Geran's bed looking at the dying fire in the fireplace with those golden eyes of his for quite a long time. Everything seemed to be as it was supposed to be, so Wolf sighed contentedly, stretched his muzzle out on his front paws, and went back to sleep.